Cobblestone Heroes

Ken McCoy

PIATKUS

Copyright © 1999 by Ken McCoy

First published in Great Britain in 1999 by
Judy Piatkus (Publishers) Ltd of
5 Windmill Street, London W1P 1HF

The moral right of the author has been asserted

A catalogue record for this book is available from the British Library

ISBN 0 7499 0504 2

Set in Times by
Phoenix Photosetting, Chatham, Kent
Printed and bound in Great Britain by
Mackays of Chatham PLC, Chatham, Kent

To my father and mother, Wilf and Olive.

To Judith Murdoch. For pointing me in the right direction.

Chapter One

Lily Bairstow sat on the top step crooning softly to baby William. On the step below sat eight-year-old Jimmy, the birthday boy. He was trying to read the *Beano* by the light of a flickering candle, laughing at the antics of the Bash Street Kids. Lily had left the cellar door slightly open to take the benefit of the heat coming from the fire smouldering wastefully in the recently black-leaded kitchen range. She jumped as a glowing ember spat out, its progress onto the hearth rug denied by the wire fireguard, one of the items on her check list. Doors unlocked [for quick getaway], lights out, fireguard up, wireless on [for any news], bottles of water for the kids. Baby William wouldn't need anything extra than her own built-in supplies. At strategic points down the cellar steps odd bits of candles were placed, all held in position by their own wax, and Lily prayed that the light wouldn't be seen through the broken coal grate. She couldn't afford another ten shilling blackout fine.

'Mam, will yer tell our Jimmy ter stop kicking me!' complained Susan, sitting one step further down, unhappy that her two-and-a-half-year seniority wasn't reflected in her position on the cellar steps. Jimmy had always been Mam's favourite, just because it was his birthday and he'd been poorly, it wasn't fair. She jabbed an elbow into her younger brother's thigh producing a loud howl of anguish totally disproportionate to the mild pain it caused.

'Ow! Mam, our Susan's just hit me. Will yer tell her ter stop!'

Lily shifted her position in an effort to free the limb required to exact her retribution, but her flailing arm was easily avoided by the much experienced Jimmy.

1

'I'll give yer both a good hiding if yer don't behave. Get down them steps into bed.'

'Aw, Mam!' moaned Susan. 'Do we have ter sleep on that mattress? It's all prickly!'

'Can't we stay here and listen to t' bombs?' asked Jimmy. 'I've never heard no bombs.'

'There won't be any bombs, it'll be a false alarm like it always is,' snapped his mother. 'Now, do as yer told and get into that damn bed!'

The word 'damn' was enough to spur the two children into action. It could well precede violent action from their mam if they didn't do as they were told. They both climbed reluctantly onto the horsehair mattress on the bottom bunk and pulled a heavy overcoat over the top of them. Everyone knew that the Luftwaffe never bombed Leeds, it was known as the Holy City – just out of range. It took them all their time to get to Sheffield. Still, there was no harm in taking precautions.

A man's first duty was to protect his family so the ceiling joists above them had been propped and reinforced by their joiner dad before he'd been mobilised to go and fight Hitler. Although up to now Adolf had little to fear from Fred Bairstow, who was still at Becketts Park Barracks about three miles away doing his square bashing.

It was January 1941 and up to then Fred had been held back doing reserve work. Joiners who could put right bomb damage were far more in demand than soldiers. A couple of weeks before he got his call up papers he'd gone back to his digs in bomb-blasted Sheffield, only to find they weren't there any more, thanks to a German incendiary. A month before that he'd been working on a bomb-damaged warehouse in Hull, only to arrive one morning to find all his good work laid to waste by the Luftwaffe.

So displeased was he with his working conditions that he'd caught a train back from Sheffield to Leeds and told his employers where they could stick their job. Ignoring their threats to report him to the authorities, he took a job with another firm working on an underground ordnance factory near Wetherby. Shortly afterwards he was called up. Fred reassured his worried wife that at least being in the army was a damn sight safer than being a wartime joiner.

Contrary to army regulations, Fred had spent many

unauthorised nights back in his wife's bed at number six Gorston Mount. A secreted bicycle had transported him there and back and he was in line for breaking the barracks' record for the number of times a new recruit had been put on report during basic training. Fred Bairstow thought the threats of dire punishment from his sergeant well worth it; after all, what were they going to do, give him the sack? The two bunk beds were homemade but serviceable if you only wanted to lie on them for a couple of hours. According to Fred's brother, Tommy, any longer and you'd be picking horsehairs out of your arse for a week.

This was the sixth time in a fortnight that the air raid warning siren had sent them scuttling into the cellar and they'd yet to hear a single enemy plane.

'The minute you hear that siren,' Fred had instructed, 'you get yourselves straight down them cellar steps and you don't move till you hear the All Clear, understand?'

They'd all nodded obediently and saluted. Fred had grinned and saluted back saying, 'At ease men.' Then he picked them up one by one and gave them all a smacking kiss. Susan and Jimmy pretended to hide their faces in embarrassment when it came to Mam's turn.

'I bet we never rotten well get bombed,' grumbled Jimmy, yanking the overcoat away from his sister, provoking another complaint to Lily.

'Mam, will yer tell our Jimmy ter stop pulling t' overcoat off me.'

'I'll tell yer dad what you've been up ter when he gets home this weekend!' snapped Lily.

A hollow threat if ever there was one. Fred Bairstow was the only father in the street who didn't smack his kids. Not that Lily would have minded if he did. A bit of back-up from her husband wouldn't have gone amiss. Jimmy had been a worry, a bout of rheumatic fever had left him with a weak heart. It had been touch and go for a while but it hadn't affected his spirit. His pals at St Joseph's Roman Catholic Primary called him Sparky, which pretty much described him. Susan watched over him like a mother hen. When it was thought he might not make it, she prayed continuously to the blue and white statue of the Virgin Mary in Mam and Dad's bedroom. She knew it was her who had brought him back from the dead like Lazarus and not the doctors, upon whom her mam and dad had heaped lavish, but misplaced thanks.

3

She mustn't tell anyone though, or she wouldn't get her reward in heaven.

Lily was getting really fed up with these air raid warnings. She'd planned on going to the pictures that night with her sister-in-law, Dorothy, whose husband Tommy was Fred's older brother. Tommy would be called up himself before much longer. Dorothy was all the better for knowing. No children as yet, her and Tommy never said why – maybe they liked the good life too much to be saddled with kids. Or maybe there was another reason. If there was, they'd never opened up about it.

Hilda Braddock, from number thirteen, was coming with them. Her daughter Glenys, the one with the bad leg from polio, said she'd babysit for a couple of sweet coupons. They were going to the Bughutch, or the Western Cinema, to give its rightful but less apt name, to see Errol Flynn in *The Sea Hawk*. It would have been Lily's first night out in weeks. She craned her head round the door to look at the clock on the mantelpiece. It said ten-past-eight which meant it was ten-to. The Bairstow family clock was always twenty minutes fast for some obscure reason. Susan and Jimmy had found it a bit confusing when they were learning to tell the time. Ten-to-eight, the second house was due to start in ten minutes. If the All Clear went any time during the next half hour they'd still make it, the manager, Lame Larry Gutteridge, wouldn't lose a house for the sake of half an hour, there was a permanent notice on the cinema door to that effect. She might still get to see Errol Flynn.

'Can't we have a blanket, Mam?' pleaded Susan. 'This coat won't cover both of us.'

Lily was still sitting on the top step with William, vainly trying to catch a bit of warmth from the back room fire.

'Am I to get no peace from you two?' she grumbled. 'What do you want me ter do? Go upstairs and get some blankets off my bed? Is that what yer want?'

Susan and Jimmy grinned smugly at each other from behind adjacent lapels. They knew their mam was going to do just that. No way would she let her kids ever be cold in bed.

'Look after William – and don't have him crying or I'll give you two summat ter cry about as well.'

Two faces nodded obediently as Lily placed baby William gently between them. Jimmy's ears pricked up.

'Did yer hear that?'

'Did I hear what?' asked an impatient Lily.

'I thought I heard a plane.'

The three of them listened intently, but silence reigned.

'It means yer going daft when yer hearing things, doesn't it, Mam?' gloated Susan.

'Just try and behave for two minutes,' sighed their mother, 'I'll fetch a couple of blankets.'

Oberleutnant Kurt Weidling nudged his Dornier 17 through the night sky. The eastern coast of England was on his left. The Luftwaffe were really stretching it to the limits sending him this far north. Three of them had set off, but the other two had taken hits from a lone Hurricane, itself limping back across the channel with smoke trailing from its engine. The British pilot must have had a bad day to have taken on the three of them. The lunatic had hurled his damaged aircraft straight at them from underneath, taking them completely by surprise. Weidling had caught a glimpse of a wild-eyed, blood-streaked young face as the Hurricane roared up from below, cannons blazing as he blasted the complete tailplane away from Kesselring's Dornier. Weidling's nose gunner had returned the compliment and both the Dornier and the Hurricane ended up in the sea. Three parachutes opened from the German aircraft but none from the Hurricane. The third Dornier had taken a raking hit all along the underside and radioed to Weidling that it was turning back.

'The fool Englishman should have ignored us and gone straight home,' Weidling grumbled to his navigator. 'Such waste, no one will thank him for such foolhardy behaviour.'

He swung left well before they reached the batteries guarding the Port of Hull and headed for his target. The grim January night sky gave away no clues to their whereabouts. He knew that finding the Royal Ordnance factory to the north east of Leeds would be well nigh impossible and they'd have insufficient fuel to come round again. Still, his was not to reason why. Drop the bombs somewhere in the vicinity and head for home, that's what Kurt planned to do. He wasn't one for heroics like the British Hurricane pilot. His wife and daughter back in Magdeburg wouldn't thank him for coming home a dead hero.

The clouds were now down to five hundred feet and as it made

5

little sense to fly below them with all the danger that entailed, Weidling took his aircraft up to fifteen thousand feet where the view was much more pleasant. Let the navigator do the hard work, he thought, I'll just fly the plane and look at the stars. No point making this war any more unpleasant than it already is. Such philosophy preserved many a life on both sides during the war.

'We're over Leeds now, sir,' reported his navigator eventually.

'Tell me when we're precisely over the Royal Ordnance factory,' ordered Kurt, lighting up a cigarette and smiling to himself, knowing the impossibility of such an order. Leutnant Hans Eberbach, the new navigator, was a keen but nervous young man. He wouldn't know what to do if he couldn't locate their target precisely, which of course he wouldn't be able to. Most navigators would hazard a guess, the bomb aimer would thankfully release his load and the captain would turn for home, mission accomplished. If they were to drop the bombs ten kilometres off target why not let Eberbach take the blame?

'We are all ready when you are, Hans, and we don't have the fuel for a second try,' said Weidling. Eberbach was sweating, this was his first bombing mission. According to his calculations they could be right over the target, more or less.

'Now!' he blurted.

'Now? Are you sure?'

'No! Wait!'

But the bombs had gone.

Fred's chickens had come home to roost. His comeuppance had arrived in the shape of a sergeant-major who told Fred he must be joking if he thought he was going home on leave that weekend after all his bleedin' antics.

'The army needs you 'ere, son. We 'ave a pile of coal what needs whitewashing and as yer in the buildin' trade, you're the only man for the job.'

The escape bicycle beckoned. This was his last chance of freedom and conjugal bliss before his posting. It was a chance well worth taking and Fred took it. His indoctrination into army life was very much incomplete. Free thinkers like Fred were much in abundance in the British Army in those days, a quality sadly overlooked by those in authority.

It was little more than a fifteen minute ride home if he got some speed up. He was scarcely two minutes into his journey when the sirens went.

'Good,' he thought to himself. 'That'll clear the streets if nothing else.'

The blackout was particularly effective that night. The clouds were heavy and low. A recent purge, resulting in many ill-afforded fines had had the desired effect and scarcely a chink of light emerged into the grimy black night, from any of the buildings he cycled past. A pair of dim, shuttered headlamps meandered noisily towards him, missing him by inches. The car driver happily oblivious to almost depriving His Majesty of one of his finest fighting men. Fred stopped and took his beret off. He'd asked for a six-and-seven-eighths and they'd given him a seven-and-a-half saying he'd probably grow into it. Still, it kept his ears warm. But tonight he wanted to look dashing for Lily. He jammed it into his epaulette and took out a packet of Senior Service.

'Put that light out!'

The harsh order came from the other side of the street. Fred peered into the blackness and just made out a helmeted figure, standing on the opposite pavement. Probably an A.R.P. warden. He blew out the match.

'It's a Swan Vestas, not a bloody searchlight,' he called out cheerfully.

'They got binoculars up there, they can probably see your fag.'

Fred pedalled off before he was ordered to douse his cigarette. He was standing on the pedals for the short, final push up Paradine Hill when he thought he heard a drone. Then again it could have been his bike. Fred knew that the Germans wouldn't choose a night like tonight to start bombing Leeds.

Turning into Back Gorton Mount, he swung off the bike and allowed the front wheel to bump open the gate of number six. He knew the latch was broken, he'd broken it himself by doing just this, time and time again, much to Lily's annoyance. He could hear the droning quite clearly now. It wasn't an aircraft noise he recognised, but that didn't mean much to Fred. To him they pretty much all sounded alike. A distant ack-ack gun fired off a few lively rounds, which made him wonder. The back door into the scullery wasn't locked. Fred opened it quietly, planning to surprise his family who would be in the cellar as per instructions or he would want to know why.

He caught a glimpse of Lily's back as she turned out of the back room to go up the stairs. Fred grinned to himself and tiptoed up behind her. He stood in the bedroom doorway watching her admire herself in the bedroom mirror, then she picked up their wedding photo from the dressing table and kissed it before placing it carefully back down, saluting and saying, 'At ease, soldier.' Fred undid his belt, dropped his trousers and saluted.

Lily had only been gone a few seconds when Jimmy heard the sound again. It was very faint, the plane must have been very high.

'Listen!' he said excitedly to Susan.

'It's not very loud.'

'It's high up that's why.'

'I bet it's not even German.'

Lily swung open the wardrobe door and looked at herself in the long mirror. She'd put on a few pounds since she'd married Fred twelve years ago but she didn't look bad for thirty-two. Eileen Garside was supposed to be coming round tomorrow night to give her a home perm. Lily wanted to look good for Fred. He'd be home at the weekend on proper official leave before he got his posting. Knowing the army, it'd be somewhere like Aldershot and she wouldn't see him till the war was over and at this rate that could be couple of years. Catterick would be good. She might still see him at weekends if he got sent to Catterick. There was a photo of them both on the dressing table. A proper studio photo done at Hilton Studios for their tenth wedding anniversary. Tommy had paid the seven-and-six it had cost as his anniversary present to them. Jammed into the frame of the mirror was a photo of Fred and Tommy, with their arms around her and Dorothy. She remembered the first time the four of them had been out together to the pictures – well, there were six of them actually because Fred and Tommy had each brought a ferret along to liven up what promised to be a boring film. It livened it up alright – the four of them got thrown out. Still, it hadn't put Dorothy off Tommy, for all her snooty ways.

Fred smiled up at her from their studio photograph, causing her to pick him up and kiss him. Placing the photo carefully down she saluted smartly and said, 'At ease, soldier.'

'Yes, ma'am,' said Fred.

Lily swung round in shock, which turned to immediate delight

8

at the sight of her grinning husband, standing to attention in the doorway in his ill-fitting khaki uniform, trousers round his ankles and saluting smartly, with his oversize beret pulled down over his ears. He'd decided against the 'dashing' look.

'Private 564896 Bairstow F. reporting for duty, ma'am!'

The first stick of bombs landed in the middle of Paradine Hill. The noise was deafening. Lily was blasted right across the bedroom into Fred. The windows came shattering in, cutting her on the cheek. She looked up into her husband's shocked face.

'What are you doing here?' was all she could think to say.

Fred was about to explain when a bomb dropped in the back yard, reducing numbers four, six and eight Gorton Mount, to a pile of rubble.

The first explosion had terrified the children who screamed and clung to each other. The second explosion numbed them into unconsciousness. They were the only survivors.

Thanks to Fred's reinforced cellar ceiling.

Chapter Two

For some inexplicable reason, kids' games were always seasonal. The conker season was the obvious one. This ran from September, pretty much up until Christmas. Cigarette cards followed in the New Year, whip and top and hopscotch at Easter then throughout spring and summer, skipping for the girls and marbles, or taws, for the boys. Football, cricket and rounders were all played in the back streets, their traditional seasons strictly adhered to. The first newly chalked wicket never appearing on any self-respecting wall until after Easter.

One of the great ignominies of youth was in the selection of teams. A circle would form and two natural captains would automatically emerge from the ranks and make a selection, each taking turn in choosing players of reducing talent from the dwindling circle. The final ones to be chosen would be embarrassingly aware of their lowly status within the team.

Jimmy was always picked last. No one had more enthusiasm or courage than him, but no one had less skill either. His rheumatic fever had left him with a dodgy heart, as he called it, not wishing to be thought in any way an invalid. Jimmy's greatest attribute was that he was a 'good laugh'.

It was late summer, 1944. Three and a half years since his mam and dad had been killed. They'd been famous for a while. The *Yorkshire Post* called them the 'Miracle Children'. Found alive after being buried for twelve hours. Fred and Lily had been found in the next street, still clinging to each other, Fred's trousers missing. Such was the black humour in those days that the word was that Fred and Lily had died 'on the job', and what a way to go!

It took three-and-a-half years and Leon Murgatroyd before this rumour reached Jimmy's ears. The wicket had been chalked on the wall which turned Broughton Terrace into a cul-de-sac, which was altogether too posh a word for the street where Jimmy and Susan now lived, with Auntie Dorothy and Uncle Tommy. It was just a couple of streets up Paradine Hill from the waste ground on which once stood their old house. The ten-feet-high wall separated the street from the local destructor, where rubbish was taken to be incinerated. The street's inhabitants took a certain pride in the fact that their destructor chimney was the highest in Leeds. There was something homely about the permanent mild pungency that descended on Broughton Terrace from its towering, smoke belching neighbour, but the residents scarcely noticed. It was a small price to pay for living in such well appointed dwellings.

Twenty terraced houses defiantly faced each other, ten either side, or backed on to each other in this case, as the cricket match was taking place in the back street. Each house had a back yard into which extended a single-storey lean-to, containing a scullery and an outside lavatory. The steps to the scullery would be regularly scoured with a donkey stone and inside would be a deep rectangular Belfast sink, a twin gas ring and a cast iron bath which would be covered up by a well-scrubbed pine board when not in use. This obviated the need for the tin bath, which people in inferior dwellings often hung on their outside walls. The owner-ship of a personal, practically en-suite outside lavatory set the tenants of Broughton Terrace a cut above such as them up the road in Walton Street, who had neither back yard nor personal lavvie. Just a shared convenience to which some had to walk half the length of the street, which was a bit awkward at two o'clock of a winter's morning, hence the proliferation in such areas of the much maligned po.

The streets were paved with cobbles and many a Yorkshire batsman had learned his craft in these streets, having to pick out, at the last split second, the curious deflections the ball would take when pitched on to them.

Leon Murgatroyd hadn't been invited to play cricket that day. Murgy, as he was unaffectionately known, was never invited to play or do anything, and with good reason. He just turned up and decided he was going to bat. He'd been clean bowled several times and refused to budge from the crease. Protests fell on deaf ears. Murgy was a bully.

It was Jimmy's turn to display his unique bowling action. His arm completing three revolutions before releasing the balding tennis ball, which invariably set off more vertical than horizontal. Fortunately he lacked the strength to send it any distance and the batsman frequently did more running before hitting the ball than after.

Murgy ran a few paces to where the ball was completing its descent before giving it an unnecessary swipe into Old Mrs McGinty's yard at number sixteen, thus ending the match, unless another ball could be found. Such was the terror in which Mrs McGinty, of the foul tongue and glass eye, was held.

'Get it, Bairstow!' demanded Murgy.

'Why me?' protested Jimmy. 'It were you what knocked it in there!'

'That's only 'cos you're rubbish at bowling. What's up, scared?' The last word was delivered with a sneer that got Jimmy's back up.

'Why don't *you* get it?' challenged Jimmy. 'You're scared as well.'

Murgy took exception to this.

'Who yer callin' scared, yer bloody cripple?'

'You, yer yitney!' proclaimed Jimmy, stoutly.

Murgy took an angry step towards Jimmy. He wasn't too sure about him. Jimmy was small but volatile and Murgy, like all bullies, didn't want to risk hitting someone who might hit back. He chose another strategy.

'At least me mam and dad didn't die shaggin' each other. At least my dad weren't a deserter like your dad.'

The other children went quiet. Susan was sitting on a nearby wall. Her sex didn't preclude her from playing, only the fact that she didn't much like cricket. If she had she would no doubt have been one of the captains. Susan excelled at all sports, much to Jimmy's annoyance. She slid down from the wall and walked over to stand beside Jimmy. Her question delivered with a quiet anger.

'What was that yer said, Murgy?'

'You heard. Yer dad were a deserter, everybody round here knows it. He deserted to come 'ome and shag yer mam.'

'My dad were never a deserter,' said Susan. 'Any road, your dad's in jail.'

'He's not, he's a prisoner of war is me dad.'

'He's a prisoner alright, he's in Armley jail. He's a thief is your dad.'

Some of the spectators sniggered. This angered Murgy, who was fifteen and the only kid there in long trousers. He was a year older than Susan and a good deal bigger. She was no match for him, or so he thought. He spat at her petulantly, and was much taken aback when she flew at him with a ferocity that initially counterbalanced their difference in size. The shame of being beaten by a mere girl forced Murgy to stand his ground, but not before he'd taken a couple of hefty blows to the nose causing it to bleed profusely. He made a grab at Susan, forcing her into a head-lock. The blood from his nose dripping liberally onto her fair hair.

'How about me an' you 'aving a shag?' he grinned up at the spectators, hoping for their approval. One or two grinned back uncertainly, but most felt uncomfortable at the course things were taking. Susan was choking from a combination of fury and the tight grip Murgy had on her.

Jimmy didn't say anything. He picked up the discarded bat and swung it with a strength born of rage at Murgy's sneering face. The onlookers winced at the sound of the bat breaking Murgy's nose and teeth. He let go of Susan, a grunting sound coming from his mouth. He was just spitting out a tooth when Jimmy gave him another whack for good measure, this time across the side of his head, knocking Murgy to the ground.

The spectators moved slowly forward to view the damage as Jimmy and Susan moved cautiously back from the circle. Little Jackie Crombie knelt down and made a cursory diagnosis of the fallen combatant.

'He's dead,' he pronounced. 'Dead as a nit!'

'Dead?' The word went from mouth to mouth round the circle, finally passed on to Jimmy and Susan.

'He's dead!'

'Hey! That's murder, isn't it?'

'Jimmy Bairstow's murdered Murgy!' Murdered Murgy, a satisfying phrase that tripped nicely off the tongue. Someone tried another variation with unseemly relish.

'Murgy's been murdered!'

Jimmy and Susan backed away from the crowd in horror, before turning and running home as fast as they could. Once inside Susan locked the door and they sat side by side on the settee, faces white, eyes streaming tears.

'Do you think I'll get hung?' sobbed Jimmy.

'I don't know.'

Auntie Dorothy was out at the shops. After their parents were killed she'd reluctantly agreed to take in the three children. Then Uncle Tommy got called up and not long after that William was sent away to a home. They weren't sure why, something to do with it being the best place for him under the circumstances. 'It'll be like a holiday for him,' Auntie Dorothy had said at the time. Jimmy and Susan were a bit put out at first that William should go on holiday and not them, then when he didn't come back they began to miss him. They'd been to visit him a couple of times and it didn't seem much like a holiday place to them. William always cried and asked to come home which upset the two of them, especially Susan. It was because he got so upset that the visits stopped, according to Auntie Dorothy. It didn't stop Jimmy and Susan nagging her though. Every day they asked when he'd be coming home. Auntie Dorothy always got annoyed – but it never stopped them asking. Then came that awful day last July when Auntie Dorothy broke the news that William had died. She'd been shouting at them as she'd been doing a lot since Uncle Tommy went to war and she came right out with it.

'William's dead!' she'd screamed at them. Then she'd added, 'There, are you satisfied now?' as if it was their fault he'd died.

It took them a while to get over his death. What they couldn't understand was why they hadn't gone to his funeral.

Tommy was brilliant, the next best thing to their own dad, but Auntie Dorothy was a poor substitute for their mam and not just because of William either.

Susan made up her mind.

'We'll have ter run away,' she decided. 'Somewhere where they'll never find us.'

Jimmy nodded glumly. Running away was better than being hung.

'We'll take the rent money and leave Auntie Dorothy an I.O.U. Then it's not stealing.'

Jimmy nodded again. He didn't want theft to be added to his crime sheet.

'When we find somewhere we like,' went on Susan, 'we'll write and let her know we're okay.'

Behind the clock was a ten shilling note and some change which Susan exchanged for a neatly written I.O.U. and a note thanking Auntie Dorothy for looking after them and sorry for the times we were naughty but now they were leaving and please give our fondest love to Uncle Tommy when he comes home from the war.

They left by the front door, which was the one least used. It was early afternoon and the sun warmed their frightened faces as they made their furtive way from shop doorway to shop doorway, finally boarding a tram to town with a last backward look to check they weren't being followed.

Jimmy and Susan stood on the concourse of Leeds Central Station looking blankly up at the destination boards. It was crowded. Mainly with servicemen coming home on, or going back from leave. The expression on their faces told which was which. There were tearful farewells and happy hellos, weepers and greeters. Everywhere there was a great bustling clamour. Talking, laughing, shouting, crying – and a muffled voice over the loud-speaker telling them that the train now standing on platform six was for Scarborough, calling at York, Malton and Seamer. No one took any notice of the two desperate fugitives. Susan bought a couple of penny platform tickets from a machine.

'Where we goin'?' asked Jimmy.

'I don't know, I haven't decided yet. We'll have a look at the trains first.'

Hand in nervous hand they walked past a huge, intimidating locomotive. Steam hissing from somewhere behind its mountainous oily wheels. The equally oily driver leaned out and winked down at them, then pulled a lever that released a deafening blast of steam, making them both jump and run out of range. They found themselves on platform six where a guard was walking the length of the train slamming doors shut and urging dawdling passengers to get on board.

'Off on yer holidays?' A grizzled old porter stood behind them, with a case in each hand and benevolent smile on his face.

'Yes, we're just, er – we're waiting for me mam, she went for a ...' Susan couldn't think of what her mam might have gone for.

'She's gone for a pee,' chipped in Jimmy.

15

'Well, she'll have to be quick, it's off in a minute.'

'Oh, there she is,' lied Susan, looking back up the platform over the porter's shoulder. Then, as he turned round to follow her gaze, she exclaimed quickly, 'Oh, 'eck! she's got on up there, she must think we're already on.'

'Right then, quick as you can, jump on here and walk back up the train to meet her.' The porter put down his cases, opened a door and helped the two of them on, waving goodbye through the window as the train moved off.

'Where we goin'?' enquired Jimmy.

'I think we're off on our holidays,' said Susan.

The train clattered happily through the sunny East Yorkshire countryside. Two young excited faces pressed against the window. Susan, her imagination running riot, pointing out the various points of interest like the seasoned traveller she wasn't.

Jimmy soon grew bored with his sister's travelogue and concentrated his attention on a faded photograph of the Yorkshire Coast above the seats opposite. Then he grew bored with that and decided to try and open a window.

The carriage window was held in position by a stout leather strap which could be loosened to let the window down. Jimmy attempted this and jumped back as the the strap flew violently out of his hand, causing the window to drop with a bang. The only other occupant of the carriage, a young man in ill-fitting khaki, sat opposite, amused by his travelling companions. He took a bar of Cadbury's chocolate from his pocket and, without looking up, knew only too well that there were two pairs of eyes watching him unwrap it. He broke off a couple of pieces and offered one each to the children.

'No, thank you very much,' declined a cautious Susan, but she was too late. Jimmy was already wolfing his piece down with great relish. Susan jabbed him with her elbow.

'Greedy glutton!'

'Go on,' urged the young soldier, still holding a piece out to her. 'I've got plenty more.'

'Thank you very much,' said Susan, kicking her brother into remembering his manners.

'Yes, thank you very much,' said Jimmy, through a mouthful of chocolate.

'My name's Freddie,' said the man. 'I'm in the army'

'I'm Susan and this is our Jimmy. I'm fourteen and he's eleven.'

'Eleven-an'-three-quarters,' corrected Jimmy.

'Pleased to meet you, Susan and Jimmy, are you on your own?'

The children lapsed into a suspicious silence. Maybe he was a secret policeman in disguise. Susan looked at Freddie's tanned, open face and decided he could be trusted. Freddie broke the silence.

'I'm going to Scarborough. I'm doing a signalling course. Do you know what that is?'

'No,' said Susan after some thought.

'I don't neither,' added Jimmy.

'I'm learning Morse Code and Semaphore.'

'Oh, right,' said Susan.

'Our dad was in the army,' said Jimmy. 'He were called Fred as well, but he's dead now.'

'We're running away,' confided Susan. 'Can't tell you why.'

'Won't your mother be worried?'

'We haven't got a mother,' explained Susan simply. 'Our mam and dad were killed by a German bomb. Nearly got us too, we were in the cellar.'

'We're The Miracle Children,' boasted Jimmy. 'I bet you've heard of us.'

'You're right, I have,' lied Freddie. 'But I'd like to hear the story from you.'

Susan told the story, with Jimmy butting in now and then to fill in any missing details. Neither mentioned the part where their mam went upstairs because *they'd* asked for extra blankets. They hadn't discussed it even with each other. The guilt was fading now.

But it would always be there.

She told how they'd gone to live with Uncle Tommy and Auntie Dorothy, but Uncle Tommy had been called up and Auntie Dorothy didn't like them very much – and she'd put their William in a home and he'd died.

The latter part of this information took Freddie aback but he thought it kinder not to ask them too much about it.

'So that's why you ran away, because you didn't get on with

your Auntie Dorothy.' The soldier spoke a lot posher than their dad.

'Yes,' said Susan.

'No,' said Jimmy, simultaneously.

Freddie looked at them both and smiled, then his eyes grew distant.

'I ran away when I was your age,' he said. 'I was away for nearly a week. Thought I could live off the countryside, but I ran away in March and nothing had started growing so I practically starved.'

'How did you get back home?' asked a curious Susan.

'Walked into a police station, easy as that. That's all you have to do if you want to go home. You might even get taken home in a police car.'

'I bet you had a mam and dad.' Susan was growing to like Freddie.

'Yes I have.'

'Are they posh like you?' asked Jimmy.

'Oh, much posher than me.'

'Blimey!' breathed Jimmy. 'I bet you can't understand nowt they say.'

Freddie laughed. 'They didn't understand anything I said, or anything I wanted to do. They wanted me to be an officer, at least my father did, but I don't like being in the army so why make a career out of something you don't like?'

Susan nodded her agreement to this philosophy. 'I want to be a comptometer operator,' she said sagely. She wasn't entirely certain what a comptometer did, but it was a word she'd recently learnt to get her tongue round and it sounded very grand.

'Really!' said Freddie, obviously impressed.

The train was pulling into Malton Station and an echoing loud-speaker was announcing that the train would be there for fifteen minutes if anyone wanted to get off for any reason. Freddie stretched and rose from his seat. 'Fancy a cuppa?' he asked.

Susan was still cautious. 'Do you promise not to give us away?'

'Promise.'

Susan sat in the sunshine on a weather-beaten wooden bench seat at the end of the platform. Her eyes watching Freddie as he and Jimmy went off to the station café for refreshments. She was only fourteen years old but Freddie was causing a strange, but not unpleasant fluttering in her stomach. The bench was beside the station garden. A mass of roses and fuchsias, the scent of which mingled with the smoke and steam coming from the train. Most of the passengers had alighted and were walking up and down the short concrete platform to enjoy the fresh air, to explore the limited amenities or simply to 'stretch their legs'.

When they came back, Freddie was laughing at something Jimmy had said.

'Hey! Susan!' shouted Jimmy. 'What did Hitler say when he fell through the bed?'

Dismayed, Susan looked round at the other disembarked passengers, who all seemed curious to know what Hitler had said. Knowing Jimmy it would be lavatorial and she didn't want Freddie to think she laughed at such things. She wanted him to think of her as a sophisticated future comptometer operator.

'Poland at last!' yelled Jimmy, loud enough for everyone to hear. 'Get it? Poland – po – under t' bed.'

One or two of the other passengers smiled, more at Jimmy's enthusiasm than his wit. Susan cringed as she accepted a mug of tea from Freddie.

'Excuse my brother,' she gave Freddie her most dazzling smile. 'He can be vulgar at times.'

'Oh, I don't know,' grinned Freddie. 'He's been making me laugh. He's a bit of a card is your brother.'

Susan blushed and went quiet, she didn't know how to deal with such situations. She'd never been in love before. Freddie took his tea across to a wooden fence and leaned over it, staring into the distance.

'I used to spend my summers not far from here. Mum and Dad had a country cottage . . .' He pointed above the adjacent houses towards a distant hill. 'Just beyond that hill. I used to walk it from this station for school hols. Takes about an hour, lovely walk. It must be, I don't know, three years since I last went there. Wonder what it's like?'

'Why don't we go and have a look?' asked Jimmy, simply.

'Because I'm due at the Grand Hotel in Scarborough at eight o'clock in the morning – and the army get very cross when you're late.'

'I know, they used ter get cross with me dad,' agreed Jimmy. 'He used to sneak out of the barracks and ride home on his bike to see us.'

'I think I'd have got on well with your dad,' smiled Freddie. 'We might have had a lot in common.'

'Maybe there's another train,' suggested Susan. A country walk with the man of her dreams seemed like such a good idea to her.

'I'll go and ask,' said Jimmy impetuously and before Freddie could give him an argument he was gone. With an amused smile, the young soldier watched Jimmy run off, his short grey trousers flapping loosely around his skinny legs. Freddie turned his attention to Susan, not noticing the adoration in her eyes.

'There's more to it than you've told me, isn't there?'

'More to what?'

'More to your running away. It'd take more than any old Auntie Dorothy to scare you two.'

'I can't tell you.'

'Okay, but if you need any help you'd better be quick and ask.'

'We'll be alright, thank you.'

No way was she going to involve Freddie in a murder charge. What sort of impression would that give?

Jimmy came hurtling back, skidding to a halt at the last minute as he almost ran straight past them.

'There's one at seven-twenty-three in the morning. Gets into Scarborough at seven-forty-two – or was it fifty-two?'

Freddie smiled and shook his head. 'That gives me either eight or eighteen minutes to get from the station to the Grand Hotel, and that's if the train's on time, which it never is. It'd be irresponsible of me to leave it so late.'

The disappointment on the children's faces was too much for him. 'So?' he added. 'What are we waiting for?'

Freddie lifted them over the fence one by one before vaulting over himself. Susan could have done the same with ease, but she much preferred this way.

It was early evening now and the late summer sun was warming their backs as the three of them headed towards the cottage. Freddie led the way, kitbag over his shoulder, whistling 'Pack Up Your Troubles In Your Old Kitbag And Smile, Smile, Smile.' Jimmy walked beside him singing lustily. Susan walked just a few steps behind, her eyes firmly fixed on the man of her dreams. He was tall, taller than their dad, maybe six feet, but a lot skinnier. His hair was thick and shiny black and needed a good comb. The thing she liked most about him was his smile. It was one of those smiles that lit up all his face and made you want to smile back. A smile like the sun coming out, that's what Mam would have said. She used to say that a lot about Dad when he was away. Maybe that's why she liked Freddie so much, he reminded her of Dad, only a bit younger. Susan couldn't remember a happier time, shame about the murder they had hanging over them. Still, you can't have everything.

This was an alien world to Jimmy and Susan. Fields and hedgerows and cows and sheep and barns and farms were all the stuff of books. The gritty West Riding of Yorkshire was their world, which, in its own way was as attractive a playground to kids as any old green field. But they couldn't help but marvel at the beauty all around them.

'Ugh!' groaned a disgusted Jimmy, as his foot squelched into a cow pat. Susan laughed as her brother scraped his shoe clean on the grass. Jimmy remembered a joke he'd heard at school, which until now had meant nothing to him.

'Hey, Freddie! Did yer hear about that feller what lost his flat cap in a cow field? He tried two dozen on before he found his own!' Jimmy howled with delight at the newly revealed significance of this latest addition to his repertoire. Freddie laughed, more at Jimmy than at the joke.

The path Freddie led them along took them temptingly close to an apple orchard. The heavily laden branches of one tree practically overhung the fence which ran crookedly beside the path. Freddie hoisted Jimmy up onto his shoulders.

'Right, Jimmy lad, it's apples for tea.'

Jimmy was oddly reluctant.

'Don't tell me a tyke like you has never been apple scrumping.'

'No,' said Jimmy truthfully. There weren't many orchards in Leeds. Not that he was above the odd bit of larceny. Many an illicit apple had found its way into Jimmy's pocket from the display outside Mallinson's greengrocers as Jimmy passed by on his way to school.

'He's wanted by the coppers,' explained Susan, who understood her brother's reluctance to be a party to further crime.

Jimmy gave her a look of horror at betraying their secret. He tried to repair the damage by changing the subject. 'It's alright,' he said, 'I'll get some.'

He reached out and plucked a dozen or so of the choice russet fruit and dropped them down to Susan, who caught them expertly, the late evening sun glinting off her long blonde hair as she darted laughingly about, catching the falling fruit.

'Oy!' The angry voice came from the other side of the orchard.

'Now there's a voice I haven't heard for a long time,' warned Freddie, with some urgency. 'Quick, kids, best be off!'

The three of them beat an urgent retreat up the path as the orchard's ancient owner arrived at the scene of the crime hurling loud and obscene abuse at the fleeing miscreants.

'An' don't think I don't know who yer are, yer thievin' young bugger. I'll be telling yer dad when next I see him!'

The three of them ran pell mell up the path, the odd contraband apple falling from their pockets, until they came to a stile where they stopped to catch their breath. Freddie sat down on the wooden step and smiled a nostalgic smile. 'It's like I've never been away. He threatened to tell my father every time I nicked his apples.'

'And did he?' asked Susan.

'No, he was frightened to death of Dad. Dad was a magistrate and old Dan Braithwaite back there was the local poacher. Mind you, if old Dan had had the sense to tell Dad, I'd have been for it.' Freddie looked up at Jimmy, who had climbed onto the drystone wall above him. 'Right, young James. It's about time you spilled the beans. What's all this about the coppers after you?'

'Oh that, it weren't nowt.'

'Well, if it weren't nowt,' said Freddie, gently mimmicking Jimmy's broad accent, 'you won't mind telling me.'

Jimmy looked at Susan for guidance. She just shrugged and bent down to pick a nearby buttercup. 'He did a murder!' she said suddenly.

Freddie did a double take of Susan's face to check for any signs of leg pulling. The look she returned was all too genuine, she wasn't kidding. He looked hard at Jimmy. These kids were serious.

'Murder? Who did you murder?'

Jimmy's face crumpled under even such sympathetic questioning. His sister answered for him.

'Leon Murgatroyd. He were beatin' me up and our Jimmy brayed him with a cricket bat.' She turned to her tearful brother. 'There's no need ter cry. Freddie won't tell nobody.' Then to Freddie, 'Will yer?'

22

'No,' said Freddie, standing up and placing a comforting hand on Jimmy's thin shoulder. 'No, of course not. It sounds to me that this Leon Murgatroyd got what he deserved.'

'Well, I don't suppose he deserved to die – actually,' admitted Susan.

'And who says he's dead?'

'Jackie Crombie, he had a right good look at Murgy and said he were dead alright.'

'Jackie Crombie eh? I suppose you mean *Doctor* Jacky Crombie?'

Freddie inclined his head and gave Susan the same look that her dad used to give her when she'd said something daft. She began to see what Freddie was getting at.

'And how old is this – *Doctor* Crombie?'

'Eleven,' she answered, almost embarrassed.

'Well now, perhaps you're not quite the wicked desperadoes you think you are,' smiled Freddie. He stood up. 'Come on,' he ordered. 'Onwards and upwards. Tomorrow we'll pick up a paper from Malton Station and see if there's any news of murder most foul in Leeds. If not, you're in the clear.'

Most of this conversation went on above Jimmy's head. As he trudged along beside Susan he whispered, 'What's he on about?'

'He thinks Murgy might not be dead.'

Jimmy visibly brightened at this news and took a noisy run at a herd of cows, scattering them with his whoops, treading into another cow pat and hopping around in disgust. Jimmy would never be a country boy.

The cottage, when they arrived, was something of a disappointment to Jimmy, who expected a thatched roof at the very least. It was nice enough as cottages go, but the years of neglect had taken a savage toll. Set in a large, untended garden, it was built of weathered, pale red brick with a stone slate roof in need of urgent repair and tiny leaded windows, also in need of some repair. Part of the wooden guttering had broken away, taking with it a rusting downspout, which leaned away from from the wall at an impossible angle. The paintwork was cracked and peeling and the stone window ledges spattered with bird droppings. A rustic bower was attached to the front of the house, around which grew a mass of roses, strangulated and untended for many years. There presumably, to provide a scented welcome to anyone wishing to enter the doorway beyond, but defeating this object with a thorny vengeance.

Freddie absent-mindedly fingered the cracked wooden sign on the gate which read 'Fiddler's Cottage' as he viewed his childhood holiday home with a measure of disappointment.

'Does it still belong to your dad?' enquired Susan.

Freddie nodded. 'For what it's worth. I thought someone was supposed to be looking after it. You should have seen it when I was a kid, it was beautiful.'

'I still think it's beautiful,' said Susan. 'It's sorta – natural. Miss Formby who takes us for nature study said Mother Nature was the best gardener – and she never had a lawn mower.'

Freddie smiled in surprise at the poetry in Susan's urban soul. 'Then this is Miss Formby's type of garden alright. Come on, let's see if we can get in. I don't fancy getting scratched to death on those rose thorns, so maybe we should try round the back. We used to keep a couple of spare keys in the shed ... that's if the shed's still there.'

The shed was very much worse for wear, but it was still there, so were the keys. However, it seemed they were unnecessary, the back door was already open. The lock violently smashed.

'Hello,' muttered Freddie. 'I think we've had visitors.'

'We never locked our doors at home,' said Jimmy.

'We never had owt to nick,' said Susan as they walked tentatively into the dark interior.

A loud flutter of wings brought a yell of fright from the children as a couple of frightened starlings made their getaway. Another bird, not quite so lucky, lay dead in front of the fireplace.

'They come down the chimney and can't find their way out,' explained Freddie.

He opened a couple of sets of curtains to let in some scattered light and the three of them surveyed the room. The sunlight illuminated the disturbed dust rising in clouds from everywhere they trod, and glinted off cobwebs galore. There was a three piece suite in cracked brown leather. An oak dining table with four ill-matching chairs and a tiled fireplace that had burned logs in its heyday. A brass oil lamp stood on the table and another lay cracked and useless on the floor, the oil from it had long since soaked into the threadbare Axminster, leaving a large black stain.

Other dark brownish stains spattered the carpet, some leading to a small hallway.

'What's through there?' asked Susan, pointing towards the hallway.

'Kitchen, and – my old bedroom,' said Freddie. He smiled to himself. 'I bet it's still in a tip.'

Jimmy was already through there. Freddie and Susan made to follow him, when he appeared at the hall doorway, breathing in small gasps, his face chalk-white.

Chapter Three

Kurt Weidling sat at the controls of his Dornier. He was alone. It was August 1944 and the war was going badly. Especially for Kurt. His wife and daughter had been killed during the fire bombing of Magdeburg some months ago. He hated his job, he hated the war, he hated the Führer and today he hated the SS, especially Colonel Otto von Manstein, for whom he was impatiently waiting on the tarmac of this God-forsaken hole. It was a secret mission, he'd been told. This was the third 'secret mission' he'd flown for the Colonel in as many weeks. Little fat Otto was feathering his own nest and the only person taking the risk was Kurt. His lone aircraft stood on an airfield just outside Brussels. Deserted now in the face of the Allied advance. His destination, Berlin.

Von Manstein had already been on board to bark out his instructions. He would be back in about half an hour. 'Guard this with your life!' he'd ordered, passing Kurt a small leather case. Kurt placed it on the empty navigator's seat and waited for the SS officer to return with the men carrying the rest of the booty. Kurt had a good idea what he was carrying, but it wouldn't be prudent to ask von Manstein for precise details. Mainly paintings and *objets d'art*, looted from houses all across France and Belgium. He'd been placed at von Manstein's disposal by his own commanding officer, Colonel Fischer, who, to Kurt's mind, was obviously in league with the SS man.

Kurt looked his watch, 10.15. p.m., von Manstein and his men should be back in ten minutes. How much longer must this stupid war go on? When could he go home? He gave an hollow laugh. Home, to what? The so-called Third Reich had taken too much away from him. His wife, his daughter, his house – and for what? Still Oberleutnant after four years of combat missions. His promotion held back because of his general attitude. Mind anywhere but on the job etcetera. What did they expect? If they wanted him to take an interest in the war they shouldn't put idiots in charge of him. And now these idiots were losing a war which, at the beginning, was theirs for the taking.

He picked up the leather case and weighed it speculatively in his hand. What was in it? Money? – probably not. Documents? – maybe. It was fastened with two buckled straps. Von Manstein had said nothing about not looking inside, only to guard it with his life. The least he could do was to find out what was worth more than his life. He scanned the perimeter of the airfield with his field binoculars to confirm to himself that he wouldn't be disturbed, then undid the two buckles and opened the case.

Inside was a large, black velvet bag, tied with a silk cord. Kurt undid the cord and emptied the contents onto the navigator's seat beneath him. Even in the dim cabin light the jewels shone with a brilliance that took Kurt's breath away. There were all kinds of stones, mostly diamonds though. Necklaces, bracelets, rings, two tiaras and many loose stones, too many to count. He stared at them for a while, not daring to touch anything. In the distance he saw the glow of hooded headlights approaching. Sweeping up the jewels, he put them back in the bag and the bag in the case. He'd buckled it up when he noticed the three rings still lying there on the navigator's seat. The headlights had entered the airfield now. He put the three rings in his pocket, telling himself, 'He'll never notice three rings out of all that lot – but what if he does? That'll be the end of Kurt Weidling's Luftwaffe career – what am I talking about? That'll be the end of Kurt Weidling.' With surprising clarity of thought, he started up the engines and taxied to the end of the runway. He could see the lorry clearly now, heading across the grass towards him. Von Manstein would wonder what he was doing. Kurt smiled to himself as he imagined the panic on little fat Otto's face when eventually he realised what was happening. He took off the brakes and sent the pencil-slim bomber rolling down the runway. The lorry turned awkwardly and tried to follow him, but Kurt was airborne. He thought he heard shots from ground but he was free and clear – and rich. A

27

manic grin lit up his face. As far as Oberleutnant Kurt Weidling was concerned, the war had ended early.

He headed north towards England, a plan slowly formulating in his racing brain. There was enough fuel for a long one-way trip. He would follow the route he took that time they'd sent him to bomb Leeds. Over the North Sea, far enough away from land to avoid the low level coastal radar. He couldn't guarantee landing it though, he'd have to parachute. No, forget parachuting, the very thought of that sent a chill up his spine. He'd parachuted out of his previous Dornier and spent three hours swinging from a tree until a French farmer, at the point of Kurt's Luger, had climbed up and freed him. Still, it could have been worse, at least he'd made it out alive, which was more than could be said for young Eberbach, who'd just been promoted to Oberleutant that week. A hundred and eighty miles he'd travelled, on one engine. The damn thing packed in just ten minutes from base. Eberbach was already dead. Feldwebel Blomberg, the gunner, had cradled his head in his lap all the way back, unable to stem the flow of blood sloshing all over the cabin floor. He'd coughed his last breath just as the second engine packed in, weird that. Eberbach would have been twenty-one the following day. What a stupid waste of life! What a stupid war!

Once Kurt cleared the Channel he felt reasonably safe. All the action was going on behind him now. He found a deep bank of cloud and flew into it, maintaining this stategy like a thief in the night, dodging from door to door, or in Kurt's case, cloud to cloud. Eventually, far below on his left he saw the Humber Estuary and altered his course to 280 degrees. The North Yorkshire moors.

On his map there looked to be many possibilities of landing sites, anything to avoid another night up a tree – or worse. His final plan was to ditch the plane, bury the jewels somewhere where he could find them later, then give himself up. The English were notoriously decent captors, so that part of it should be alright. All in all it was a good plan – not foolproof, but good enough for a spur of the moment effort. Then the starboard engine began to splutter.

Landing on rough moorland with one engine was suicidal even for a pilot of Kurt's ability; so his options had narrowed. Setting the controls at straight and level, Kurt pulled on a parachute and opened the door. He stood for a while looking out at the night sky, thinking about his beautiful wife and daughter, and how he wished they could be with him to share this new found wealth. Why did they have to die? What sort of animals could callously drop bombs on such innocent people?

The few seconds it took for the parachute to open seemed like an eternity. Kurt released his pent up breath and looked at darkness of the ground below him. He could well have qualified as the most useless parachutist in the Luftwaffe. Kurt had no control whatsoever over where he landed, otherwise he wouldn't have chosen to land on Freddie's cottage. He hit the roof with some considerable force, breaking several slates and his left leg. In great pain, he managed to release his parachute, which was swept away on the stiff breeze. Then he slid backwards off the roof and head first down the side of the cottage, ripping his side open on a sharp metal spike protruding from the wall, which in normal times was there to tie an innocent washing line to.

Kurt hit the ground in grave distress. The wound in his side pumping out blood. If he could only get inside the cottage, perhaps the people who lived there might help. He'd fallen right beside the back door. Raising himself on his good knee he banged as loud as he could, but there was no reply. He tried to open the door, but it was locked.

Taking out his pistol, Kurt emptied the chamber into the lock. Not caring who heard. As it happened the only person who did hear was Mrs Braithwaite, who woke her husband up with harsh instructions for him to investigate. Dan, who hadn't heard the shots, assured her it must be a fellow poacher about his clandestine business and good luck to him. He dropped back off to sleep with a stream of vitriol from his ever loving wife ringing in his uncaring ears.

The door swung open under the onslaught and Kurt dragged himself inside. Perhaps if he could find a bed to lie on he would be alright. Don't die now, Kurt, not now you've come this far. He dragged himself into the hallway and spotted Freddie's bedroom and the welcoming bed. A grim smile flickered across his lips, he'd be alright now. A good long rest and I'll be good as new. If only my side didn't hurt so much. His eyes suddenly slammed open in horror. The case! He'd forgotten the case! You stupid bastard, Weidling! No wonder you never got promotion, they were right, you're an idiot. He cursed himself soundly until he realised the truth of the situation. Then he smiled to himself, 'What the hell! I'm dying anyway. Better to be with my beautiful wife and daughter than hang around in this ugly world.' With a monumental effort he reached into his pocket and took out the three rings and held them up, one by one in the moonlight, the pale diamond light reflecting on his face as he died.

Freddie looked down at Kurt and shuddered. Susan and Jimmy stood in the doorway behind him, not daring to come any closer.

'Looks as though he's been dead a week or two,' guessed Freddie. 'Phew! He doesn't smell too good, does he? Bled to death by the look of it. He's German – Luftwaffe officer, a Flying Officer, I think. What the hell's he doing in my cottage?' He took a step back. 'Better not touch him, don't want to be accused of anything.'

'We're going to have to tell someone, aren't we?' said Susan, who could see this spoiling their romantic evening.

'Tomorrow maybe, not tonight,' said Freddie. 'We're not on the phone here. Besides,' he nodded at Kurt, 'he's not going anywhere.'

'I'm not spending no night with no dead German,' protested Jimmy.

'You don't have to,' said Freddie. 'There should be a tent in the hall cupboard. You two can sleep in the garden.'

'What about you?' asked a disappointed Susan, too young for any carnal inclinations towards Freddie, just an innocent childhood crush.

'I'll sleep upstairs.'

Susan's fear of sleeping in the same house as a dead German easily outweighed her infatuation with Freddie, so she elected to join Jimmy in the tent.

The sun had gone down over the distant hill by the time they'd got the tent erected. Or to be more precise, by the time Freddie had got it erected. Stolen apples, biscuits and chocolate from Freddie's kitbag and water from the kitchen tap went some way to satisfying their hunger. The three of them sat in the overgrown, moonlit garden beneath a vastness of stars, brighter and more majestic than anything the kids had ever seen before in the sooty skies above Leeds. They sat and talked for a while. Freddie told of his childhood in India and then in London. And how his ex-soldier father had moved them all to Yorkshire at the outbreak of the war. Apart from the cottage they had a large house in Harrogate where his father and mother lived. Freddie was twenty-one and after the war intended to study medicine, which his mother thought was a marvellous idea but his dad, Brigadier Harry Fforbes-Fiddler, wasn't too keen.

'Fiddler?' Susan and Jimmy howled with laughing. 'You're called Freddie Fiddler?'

'Alright, alright, have your fun, I've heard it all before,' said Freddie. 'I must say, there was a time when I would have preferred to have been christened George or Jack or anything but Frederick. But it was my mother's father's name – I don't think anyone stopped to think how funny it would sound with Fiddler stuck on the end. Oddly enough, I've grown to like it – it has a sort of ring to it, don't you think?'

'I think it's a lovely name,' lied Susan, after she'd calmed down.

'Freddie Fiddler, Freddie – Fiddler' repeated Jimmy, trying to work out what sort of a ring it had to it. Then his face creased with a laugh he tried hard to control, but failed miserably, setting his sister off.

Freddie shook his head and grinned ruefully. 'It's actually Fforbes-Fiddler, if you really want to rub it in, with Fforbes spelt with two Fs.'

'You mean like Freddie F-Forbes Fiddler?' said Susan.

'That's a lot of effing Fs,' chortled Jimmy.

'Too many for me,' agreed Freddie. 'No, I answer to plain old Freddie Fiddler. The old man doesn't like it, says I'm letting the side down, he's a terrible old snob, bit of a bully too if he can get away with it. Typical army type.'

Presently Jimmy fell asleep. Freddie picked him up, laid him on a groundsheet inside the tent and covered him with a blanket.

'Right then,' he said to Susan. 'Better get some kip ourselves, early start in the morning.'

Susan nodded, disappointed the night ever had to end, then lay down beside her sleeping brother, to plan her life with Freddie. There'd be just the two of them living in Fiddler's cottage. No dead Germans of course, or even lavatorial brothers. Just the two of them. Mr and Mrs Freddie Fiddler – it had a ring to it. It was around four in the morning when an owl hooted, waking Jimmy up with a start. He shook Susan awake.

'What was that?'

The owl obliged with another hoot.

'It's a flipping owl,' grumbed his sleepy sister. 'Have you woken me up just to listen to a rotten old owl?'

'How was I to know it was a flipping owl? I've never heard an owl before.'

'Well you have now, so go to sleep.'

Dorothy sat at the old upright piano in the back room. Not exactly an accomplished pianist, she played more for relaxation than for entertainment. It was Tommy's piano and Tommy could set the thing on fire with his vibrant ragtime style. The occasional bum note was of little concern to Tommy who played with his soul rather than his fingers. She smiled at the thought of him as she tinkled out her own simplified vesion of 'Morning' from Grieg's *Peer Gynt*. On the top of the piano in front of her were two photographs of her and Tommy, taken on Blackpool front. Tommy had managed to get the Tower growing out of her 'Kiss Me Quick' hat, and he was standing outside Gypsy Rose Lee's fortune telling booth with a look of despair on his face and a water pistol to his head.

The clock on the mantelpiece made a half-hearted attempt at chiming midnight but gave up after four-and-a-half pathetic bongs. They'd been gone over ten hours now. A disappointed Jackie Crombie had been round with the news that Leon Murgatroyd wasn't dead after all, only concussed with a broken nose and broken teeth. Dorothy wasn't absolutely clear why they'd run away, it had never occurred to her that Jackie's fatal diagnosis of Murgy's condition might have had something to do with it. At first she'd been annoyed at them for stealing the rent money, but now the anger had subsided, maybe she didn't blame them for running away, they knew she'd be no comfort to them, no matter what the problem was. Too wrapped up in her own problems, that was her trouble.

Dorothy had reported their disappearance to the police, who only became interested when they found an assault had taken place. Their interest waning dramatically when they realised who the victim was.

'It'll take more than a cricket bat to knock some sense into young Murgatroyd's thick head,' commented a sergeant drily, when the details of the incident were revealed. 'Bring your lad in when they turn up, I'll put the frighteners on him.'

'*If* they turn up,' complained Dorothy, annoyed at their lack of enthusiasm.

'They'll turn up, they always do.'

'Always?' Dorothy fixed the sergeant with a stern glare. He coughed with discomfort and dropped his gaze from this beautiful but angry face.

'I'll, er, I'll put the word out for my men to be on the, er, the lookout.'

'Thank you, sergeant.' She swirled round and flounced out of Paradine Hill Police Station followed by many admiring glances and a few lascivious comments, most of which she'd heard before. She stormed back up Paradine Hill consumed with anger and then with guilt at her treatment of Jimmy and Susan – and especially William.

William had been nagging at Dorothy's conscience for some time now. When Fred and Lily had been killed, the three children had been automatically brought to Dorothy and Tommy's house. It wasn't the ideal situation but what option did they have? They'd had a good time, her and Tommy. Neither wanted to be saddled with kids straight away, plenty of time for that, then the war broke out so they decided to start a family as soon as hostilities ended, even if it took a couple of years.

Tommy had been called up not long after and the whole business was a shock to Dorothy's system. Bringing up two boisterous children and a baby was difficult enough when they were your own, but to have to bring up someone else's and without a husband to help was above and beyond the call of duty. Each day she grew worse. She could see it in her own face – she'd burst into tears for no reason. Having a baby in the house meant she couldn't even get a part-time job to pick up a bit of much needed money. That's why she decided to send William into care. It would be only for a while to see how it went. That's what she told herself. That's what she told Tommy in her letter explaining what she'd done. She told Jimmy and Susan that he'd gone on holiday for a while.

She coped after that. A part-time job in Bretheridges Jam

Factory helped supplement the money Tommy sent home and things went a little better. It was heart-rending to see William's face every time they went to visit. Susan would tell him she'd be coming to get him soon. So she'd stopped going. She convinced herself it was better all round not to keep upsetting the lad. Besides, her nerves were getting worse even with just the two of them to look after. The constant nagging by the children about when their baby brother would be coming home was driving her mad. Then Tommy went off to France and the uncertainty of everything got too much for her. Every day she heard of someone's husband or son or brother being killed or going missing. People she knew. The D Day landings had taken a heavy toll, as had the fighting in the immediate aftermath. She hadn't heard from him for two months, not a letter, not even one of those cryptic crossed-out messages to tell her he was alive and well. The neighbours came round to tell her that no news was good news and still the children asked about William. Then Lord Haw Haw had announced over the wireless that the Polar Bear Regiment had been completely wiped out.

'Isn't Uncle Tommy a Polar Bear? asked Jimmy, as the evil propagandist delivered his crackling gloating message across the airwaves.

Mrs Crombie, who was listening with them, laughed. 'Ee, yer've not ter take no notice of owt he says, love. He's just saying it ter put the wind up yer. It's all lies.'

And it was lies, but no one knew for sure. Lord Haw Haw was cunning enough to sprinkle enough truth among his lies to sow seeds of worry amongst the listening population. They'd all been advised to switch off as soon as he broke into their programme. But many didn't.

As the ensuing days went by, Dorothy sank into a deep depression. Sitting at the window, watching and waiting for the postman to come with good news. News that didn't arrive – not in time anyway. And every day without fail, either Jimmy or Susan would ask about William. It was Susan who asked that day. The postman had been with an official looking letter which Dorothy had feverishly ripped open. It was from the Children's Home. William had had measles but he was okay now and was looking forward to a visit.

Riddled with despair and guilt she let the letter drop to the floor, the heading on the letter plain to be seen. '*Oxford House Children's Home*' Susan turned her head around to read it.

'It's about William, isn't it?' she cried. 'Is he coming home, Auntie?' As Susan bent down to pick up the letter, something inside Dorothy cracked. Before her niece could pick it up she stamped her foot on it.

'Leave it!' she commanded.

Susan jumped back. Startled by the sharpness of her auntie's voice.

'What is it, Auntie?' Susan looked first at Dorothy, then at Jimmy, who'd just come into the room.

Dorothy was breathing heavily now. Unable to understand what was happening to her. She'd been convinced the letter would contain good news about Tommy.

Why she said what she did shocked her.

'He's dead!' she screamed. 'Your brother's dead! Are you satisfied now!' Then she picked up the letter and ran upstairs where she dissolved, sobbing on the bed.

Jimmy and Susan looked at each other. Unable to take in the gravity of what they'd just been told. Then they put their arms around each other as they'd done all those years ago when the bomb dropped on their house. It was all they could think of.

Dorothy lay on the bed all day, undisturbed by Jimmy and Susan, who were coping with the news in their own way.

They'll get over it, she thought. As soon as I hear Tommy's okay, I'll tell them the truth. Pretend there's been some terrible mix up at the children's home.

Thus justifying her actions she went about her daily business. They'd missed the funeral, she explained to them, because the stupid bureaucrats in charge of things had told her too late. When in doubt always blame the stupid bureaucrats, that's what they're there for.

Jimmy and Susan, especially Susan, had cried on and off for days and then, with the resilience of the young, had accepted their baby brother's death. Susan prayed every night for the repose of his soul as well as Mam and Dad's and knew that they'd be looking after him. Jimmy felt better when Susan explained this to him.

A week after Dorothy had delivered the fateful news, she heard from Tommy – he was okay. That's all the letter said, but it was enough for Dorothy.

But she never told the kids the truth. They'd never mentioned William from that day and she was amazed at the burden this lifted from her. When Tommy gets home, that's the time to tell them, she thought. I can cope till then.

Gently closing the piano lid, Dorothy kissed the photograph of her husband and sat in the comfy chair. She didn't want the kids to find her in bed when they came home.

Jimmy couldn't sleep. He lay there thinking about the dead German.

'Betcha daren't sneak in an' look at him,' he challenged.

'You what? Look at who?'

'The dead German.'

'Look at him yerself!'

'I've looked at him. It were me what found him!'

'Well, I've looked at him as well! And I'd like to go to sleep now.'

'You didn't look at him properly like I did. He looked a lot deader than Leon Murgatroyd.'

'That's 'cause Leon Murgatroyd wasn't dead. You didn't hit him hard enough.'

'I hit him as hard as I could – betcha daren't go right up to him an' touch him.'

Susan hated being outdared by Jimmy. The trouble was, for a skinny kid, he was so flipping fearless. She decided to call his bluff. 'I'll go if you will!'

'Right,' said Jimmy, who now wished he hadn't started this.

'Come on then,' challenged Susan, convinced he'd back down.

'Right, you come on then.' Jimmy stood up with a look of determination that told Susan she wasn't going to get out of this one.

The two of them trod carefully and fearfully across the kitchen. A loud snoring came from upstairs, which destroyed many of Susan's romantic illusions about Freddie. A three-quarter moon shone through the bedroom window, bathing the dead German in an eerie light they could have done without. The children froze in the doorway, Jimmy moved in first and stood beside the bed, staring down at Kurt's face, which was very much worse for wear.

'I've never seen a dead person before,' he whispered to Susan who had nervously joined him.

'No, nor me. He whiffs a bit, doesn't he?'

'Phew!' agreed Jimmy.

Susan's eyes fell on Kurt's left hand, something was gleaming beneath his fingers.

'He's got something in his hand!' she whispered, as though not wanting to wake him up.

'Get it then!' urged Jimmy.

'You get it.'

'Why should I? You're the oldest!'

She knew he'd say that. Gently lifting Kurt's lifeless hand, she made a quick grab for what was underneath then ran out of the bedroom with Jimmy close on her heels. Neither of them stopping until they'd dived into the tent.

Susan opened her hand to reveal three rings. One, a large diamond solitaire, the second, a diamond cluster set round a larger central stone, and the third, a slightly smaller stone set in a heavy gold band and giving off a brilliant pale blue iridescence in the moonlight

'Bugger me!' breathed Jimmy, who normally never swore in front of his sister.

'It's jewels!' exclaimed Susan.

'We're rich,' said Jimmy.

'No, we're not, they're not ours,' argued Susan, to whom dishonesty was the most mortal of sins. There were other, more interesting sins she found out about later in life, most of which she would commit with enthusiastic regularity.

'Well, they can't be the German's, he's dead,' countered Jimmy. 'Anyway, he's our enemy so we wouldn't have to give things back even if he wasn't dead – which he is.' He added the last bit to give conclusive weight to his argument. Jimmy had his own sense of logic which always seemed to work to his advantage.

'We'd better ask Freddie, he'll know,' said Susan.

This disappointed Jimmy, who had a deep suspicion of all adults, even Freddie. 'Oh, alright,' he conceded. 'Have we to go wake him now, then?'

'Might as well.'

37

Their fear of the dead German forgotten as they rushed upstairs to where Freddie lay snoring away, happily oblivious to the twist this night would make to all their lives.

Freddie, being a sound sleeper, took some waking up. His tiredness was soon forgotten at the sight of the three rings. 'They belong to the German,' said Susan simply.

'He's dead, so they can't belong to him,' pointed out Jimmy, who thought he'd settled this argument already.

Freddie shook his head. 'Blessed if I know what to think. They were in his hand, you say?'

The children nodded. Their eyes fixed on Freddie as they awaited his decision as to ownership.

'My guess,' he said, 'is that they didn't belong to him either. I reckon that if we look round in the morning we'll find evidence of a parachute or some plane wreckage or something.'

'You've got to be in Scarborough,' Susan reminded him.

'I think finding a dead German's quite a good excuse for being late, even for the army. Anyway, I'm not going till I find out a bit more about our dead benefactor.'

Jimmy didn't know what a benefactor was, but it sounded encouraging. He walked to the window and looked out at the brightening landscape outside.

'It's morning now,' he announced, 'and I'm hungry.' Jimmy always had his priorities in order.

'Pass me my kitbag and we'll finish off the last of my provisions,' said Freddie. 'Then we'll see what we can find.'

It took them until lunchtime to find the parachute, which had blown into a nearby copse. They returned to the cottage to discuss what to do next.

'I'm convinced the jewels are stolen,' said Freddie to his two young companions. 'The proper owners may well be dead and if not would be almost impossible to track down. We could hand them over to the authorities, that would be the right thing to do. We might even get a reward – the odds are we wouldn't get anything.'

'What do you think he was doing with them?' asked Susan.

'Who knows?' replied Freddie. 'I've got a feeling they're not his though.'

'They're not much use to him now,' observed Jimmy. 'How much do yer think they're worth?' He wasn't the least bit interested in where the jewels came from.

'Quite a lot,' said Freddie, 'This big solitaire must be worth a few hundred at least, that's if it's genuine.' He picked up the shimmering two-carat solitaire and scratched it across the window, leaving a deep groove. He then held it up to the light allowing the facets to reflect their brilliance into the children's eyes.

'It's a beauty, they can't make paste diamonds like this.'

'I think we should keep 'em,' decided Jimmy.

'It'd be nice if we could get away with it,' said Freddie, who seemed to be on Jimmy's side. 'No one would miss them, let's face it, no one knows about them, except us.'

'Let's take a vote on it,' suggested Jimmy, who wanted to act before Freddie changed his mind. 'Hands up who wants to keep 'em.'

His own hand went up as he said it, Freddie looked at Susan, then slowly put his own hand up.

'That's it!' laughed Jimmy, triumphantly. Two out of three.'

'No,' cautioned Freddie. 'It has to be unanimous.'

Jimmy wasn't sure what unanimous meant but it sounded bad and his face dropped. Freddie looked at Susan and said gently, 'All three of us have to agree or it won't work.'

Susan's conscience disappeared under the onslaught of the young soldier's dark brown eyes. She raised her hand in the air.

'Right, spuds up,' declared Jimmy.

Freddie, whose public school education had sadly failed to teach him the time honoured way of deciding 'who goes first', looked bemused. Susan and Jimmy already held out their two clenched fists at the ready. Freddie did the same but didn't have a clue why. Jimmy took it upon himself to do the honours. He went round the small circle of fists, banging each one with his own right fist, one at a time.

'One potatie, two potatie, three potatie, four,' he sang, at a rate of one potatie per fist banged. 'Five potatie, six potatie, seven potatie, more.' The word 'more' came as he banged down on Susan's right fist. With a small scowl she tucked it away behind her, if it happened again she was out. The last one in got to choose first. Not surprisingly it was Jimmy, who had long since figured out how to work this method of dipping to his favour, no matter how many were in the circle. Unfortunately his 'spuds up' expertise wasn't matched by his knowledge of jewellery. He chose the diamond cluster. Susan, who was next, had already fallen in love with the blue stone, leaving the large solitaire to Freddie, who felt guilty at being left with what looked to be the pick of the crop so to speak.

'You do realise you've probably left me the best one,' he warned.

Jimmy held his ring up to the light. 'Rubbish!' he chortled. 'You can't fiddle us, Freddie Fiddler!' He and Susan laughed, but Freddie shook his head and slipped the ring into his pocket.

As the midday sun forced its way through the unwashed windows, the three of them sat round the kitchen table. Freddie examined their faces one by one, inducing in the children a feeling of mild apprehension.

'What's up?' queried Jimmy, nervously.

'What's up,' answered Freddie, 'is you two, that's what's up. Both sitting there, each with a valuable diamond ring in your pocket, but what do you think you're going to do with them?'

'Flog 'em,' answered Jimmy, surprised at such a question.

'And what would a scruffy little tyke like you be doing with a very expensive diamond ring?' asked Freddie.

Jimmy wasn't sure what Freddie was on about, but Susan understood. 'We can't sell them, can we?' she said.

'Not straight away you can't. You'll have to hide them somewhere safe until you're much older – and what's more important,' he reached across the table and held both their hands to emphasise his point, 'you must not tell anyone – and I mean no one. Not even Auntie Dorothy or Uncle Tommy.'

'Especially not Auntie Dorothy,' said Jimmy.

'No one!' said Freddie. There was an uncharacteristic gravity in his voice which took the children by surprise. He made them both swear a solemn oath of secrecy.

'What's the most sacred thing you can swear by?'

'Our Lady of Lourdes,' said Susan.

'Me mam and dad,' said Jimmy.

'Okay. Do you swear by Our Lady of Lourdes and your mam and dad that you'll never breathe a word of this to anyone so help you God and strike you down dead if you do?'

'I do,' said Jimmy and Susan together, although they weren't happy with the bit about God striking them down dead.

'Right then,' said Freddie. 'What you must do is keep them safe until the war's finished, then we'll meet up again and I'll see what I can work out.'

'But what if – you know?' asked Jimmy, uncertainly.

'You mean what if I don't come back?' He held up a hand to stop Susan's admonition of her younger brother. 'No, it's a fair question, there's a chance I might not.'

He didn't notice the look of panic on Susan's face. She made up her mind there and then to pray for Freddie's safe return every spare minute she had – and nobody prayed better then she did. Her panic subsided at this reassuring idea. Freddie rubbed his unshaven chin, his brows creased in thought. He held Susan in his gaze, unconsciously melting her beneath his thoughtful brown eyes.

'It'd be up to you, Susan,' he decided. 'When you're a young lady, say eighteen or so, you should take them, one at a time, to two different jewellers. But you'll need to dress the part and talk the part, not to arouse suspicion. We're talking about quite a lot of money. Enough to give you both a nice start in life, and God knows, you deserve it. I'm sure the previous owners of the stuff wouldn't begrudge you that.'

'*Dress the part and talk the part,*' odd words, but fortunately they stuck in Susan's mind.

The walk back to the station took much longer than the reverse journey the day before. Neither of the children wanted this magic time together to end. Not Jimmy, who still had a possible murder charge to face; and not Susan, because she was desperately in love with Freddie and just wanted this time to go on for ever.

Freddie solemnly shook hands with Jimmy and kissed Susan lightly on the forehead through the open train window.

'When do you think we'll see you again?' asked Susan, fighting to hold back the tears.

'I've got your address. As soon as the war's over, I'll come and see you.'

'Promise?'

'Promise,' smiled Freddie.

He stood and waved to them until their train was out of sight, before sitting disconsolately down on a platform seat to await his own train and whatever the army had to say about his absence.

Freddie notified the authorities about the dead German who was taken away and buried with whatever ceremony was due to an enemy soldier, which wasn't a lot. His aircraft had already been found, crashed on the Yorkshire moors, forty miles north of Freddie's cottage. A local search had been carried out for the crew and it was thought that at least three of them could still be at large.

But why did they leave behind a case containing a fortune in jewellery?

On their way from the tram stop to Auntie Dorothy's, they passed Bramham Street cemetery where their mam and dad lay buried beneath a single, economically lettered, granite slab. Climbing over the low wall to spare themselves the walk to the gate, they made their sacrilegious way across various overgrown graves to where Lily and Fred lay buried. They waited quite a while until an old lady, visiting her last two husbands, buried in nearby adjacent plots said her tearful goodbyes, seemingly favouring the earlier of the two. The children wondered what was wrong with the second incumbent, who, according to the inscription, had certainly stayed at his post a lot longer than his predecessor. But who knows about such things?

Between the two of them they managed to lift up the slab until it was standing on end, then, with Jimmy holding it balanced in position, Susan using a sharp stone, scraped out a shallow hole, just big enough to take the tiny potted meat jar they'd placed their diamond rings in. Then Jimmy let it go with a thud, prompting the two of them to apologise to their mam and dad for all this noise and inconvenience.

With their arms around each other they gritted their teeth and made their way way to number thirteen Broughton Terrace and whatever retribution lay in store.

Dorothy woke up with a jolt in the chair in which she'd spent the last few hours trying to catch up on the previous sleepless night. The clock was attempting to stike 6 p.m. but stopped after four-and-a-half bongs, it always stopped after four-and-a-half bongs, even at an hour when four-and-a-half were more bongs than necessary.

Pushing herself up from the chair with the resigned effort of a woman twice her age, she turned wearily towards the scullery to put the kettle on. She was just lighting the larger of the two gas rings when something through the window caught her eye. Her heart gave a great surge of joy at the sight of two familiar blond heads loitering beyond the wall. Dorothy rushed to the door, yanked it open and dashed out into the back yard, her eyes streaming with tears of intense relief. Without a word of welcome or admonition she took the two dumbstruck children in her arms and hugged them. The three of them bursting into tears.

It was the first time anyone had hugged them like this since their mam and dad had died and they stayed there until Dorothy eventually stepped back, blinking away her tears. Jimmy looked up at her with a worried expression on his face.

'Auntie Dorothy – Leon Murgatroyd – he's not dead or owt is he?' he paused, terrified what the answer might be. Dorothy smiled and ruffled his hair.

'Dead?' she smiled, a glimmer of realisation setting in. 'I'm afraid not, he's alive and kicking, worse luck.' Then she forced her face into a stern expression and added. 'But what you did was wrong. He's got a broken nose and broken teeth. The worst part about it all, was the worry you've caused me.'

The children looked bemused.

'Running away,' explained Dorothy. 'Didn't you think I'd worry?'

The children shrugged, in truth they didn't. Dorothy's face softened. 'Maybe I'm being unfair, maybe you'd no reason to think I'd worry – but I did – and I'm sorry I wasn't there for you when you needed me.'

'We weren't running away from you, Auntie Dorothy,' said Susan. 'We thought Murgy was dead. Jimmy thought he'd murdered him.'

'Ah! So you were running from the hangman's noose,' laughed their auntie. 'By the way, young Jackie Crombie filled me in chapter and verse about why you gave Murgy a crack with the cricket bat.'

The children looked embarrassed at what Jackie might have said. He just didn't care didn't Jackie. Dorothy turned her back on them to hide the grin of approval on her face and walked into the scullery. Thugs like Leon Murgatroyd deserved a good crack with a cricket bat now and again, and if it was a Bairstow that did it, then all the better. Suddenly she turned round, the grin still intact.

'I don't suppose he'll be saying things like that about your mam and dad again in a hurry.'

Over Dorothy's shoulder the kettle was beginning to show signs of boiling. 'Right,' she said, 'I'll make us some tea while you tell me all about what you've been up to.'

Jimmy's appearance at the police station caused many a raised eyebrow. Leon Murgatroyd was known to the constabulary as a local tearaway who needed a good clip from a dad. But his dad being in jail, wasn't there to give him a good clip. The sight of the waif-like Jimmy owning up to being young Leon Murgatroyd's chastiser caused a certain amount of hilarity among the policemen and Jimmy got the promised ticking off from the sergeant who did well to keep his face straight. As a chastened Jimmy turned to go, the sergeant gave Dorothy what he hoped was a conspiratorial smile. She gave him a withering look that wiped it straight off his face.

'We're leaving now,' she said frostily, 'so do you think it's possible, sergeant, for your men to keep their crude remarks to themselves, at least until I'm out of earshot?'

As Jimmy galloped off in front of her up Paradine Hill, happy at no longer being a wanted criminal and eager to enjoy the freedom this entailed, Dorothy's thoughts inevitably drifted to her beloved Tommy. It was three months since she'd last seen him and she hadn't much of a clue where he was. Somewhere in France probably – avid reading of the papers kept her roughly informed. In her pocket she fingered a censored communication she'd received from him just over a week ago. It used to be letters but now it was just a piece of printed paper with lines through all the bits of inappropriate information. At least he was still alive – or he had been two weeks ago when it had been sent. How would she would cope if anything ever happened to him? She shuddered and dismissed the possibility from her mind – mustn't think like that. It was bad enough when Jimmy and Susan had gone missing. How odd she should take it as badly as that, she'd just spent twenty-four hours with what seemed like a lump of lead in her stomach. And how guilty she was beginning to feel about the rotten way she'd treated them, then she thought about William and the guilt got just too much. Dorothy stopped and looked in Freeman's window, forcing such thoughts out of her head. Replacing them with thoughts of her lovely Tommy. If only he could come home, all their problems would be solved in a flash. She scanned the array of freshly baked confectionery on display and allowing herself to be drawn inside by the only tempting aroma on Paradine Hill.

Chapter Four

Gunner Bairstow T. sat down on a twenty-five pound shell, resting in its wooden cradle and lit up a Capstan Full Strength, almost immediately coughing out a lungful of smoke. He'd only been smoking a week and he still hadn't quite got the hang of it. His Battery had just arrived, after an arduous overnight march, at the new gun position. It was mid-January 1945. He was cold, he was fed up and his feet were wet. He hadn't seen his wife for nine months, nor his nephew and niece – and he was still unhappy about what had happened to his youngest nephew, William. Sending him off to a home wasn't his idea of looking after his dead brother's child.

Despite all his weeks of training and months of preparation for the big push across Europe, the most invaluable piece of advice had been given to him by his comrade-in-arms, Gunner Nobby Clarke. 'All yer need, Tommy me old son, is ter keep yer bowels open and yer socks dry – all the rest is bollocks.'

This turned out to be sound advice and dry socks had become almost an obsession with Tommy, who spent much of his spare time finding new ways of drying them. The other part of Nobby's advice was adequately taken care of by spasmodic German shells. He pulled a dry pair of socks on and revelled in the comfort as he slid his size-nine feet back into the size-ten boots.

After moving up to join their bit of Montgomery's 21st Army back in early November, this was the first progress they'd made, if you could call half a mile progress. Word had it that Monty and Eisenhower had been otherwise engaged further south in the Ardennes region of Belgium, where the Germans had broken through the Allied front, in what came to be known as the Battle of the Bulge. Now that that piece of nonsense had been taken care of, mainly by the American tank divisions, it was back to the business of winning the war.

They were in a muddy Dutch field just north of Nijmegen, facing General Gustav von Zangen's 15th Army spread out around Arnhem, just a few miles to the north across the Rhine. Back in September, the British First Airborne Division had been all but wiped out trying to take the bridges at Arnhem. Information such as this did little to fire Tommy with much enthusiasm for a prolonged military career.

His sensibilities had become somewhat brutalised over the last few weeks at the sudden loss of many new friends. So much so that he'd made up his mind not to become friendly with anyone else. Lance-Bombardier Nobby Clarke's annoyingly cheery Cockney manner made that difficult. He was also a difficult man to say 'no' to. As many French, Belgian and now Dutch girls found out to their cost. Tommy, as part of the war effort, had remained faithful to Dorothy. And it *had* been an effort.

'Gizza fag, Tommy.'

'No, smoke yer own fags,' said Tommy, determined not to give in this time.

'That's nice, innit? An' who taught you how ter smoke in the first place? If it weren't for me yer'd know nuffink about the pleasures of nicotine. That's bleedin' nice, that is. Yer do a mate a favour an' . . .'

Tommy threw Nobby a cigarette just to shut him up. 'That's yer last one, then it's your turn.'

'Say no more, Tommy me old son, you're a scholar an' a bleedin' gentleman,' grinned Nobby, leaning happily against a field gun and lighting up his cigarette.

To Nobby, O.P. meant 'other people's' – a brand of cigarette so much more satisfying than smoking your own. Whereas to Captain Hetherington, approaching them from the Command Post, it meant Observation Post, which is what he had in mind that morning for Tommy and Nobby.

He pointed at a shell-damaged farm building on top of a piece of higher ground a couple of hundred yards ahead. 'Run a wire up to the farm and set up an O.P. There's a German gun emplacement up ahead. We need to knock it out before we go any further.'

47

Tommy and Nobby saluted more smartly than was necessary. 'Yes, sir, very good, sir.' said Tommy.

The captain hesitated a second, alarmed at Tommy's uncharacteristic alacrity and wondered if he should emphasise the urgency of his request, but foolishly decided it wasn't necessary. He returned their salutes before hurrying back, ducking as a German shell whistled overhead. As soon as the officer was out of sight, the two men resumed their previous positions. Nobby took a deep, satisfying drag on his cigarette.

'Didn't say "when", did he?'

'He didn't, did he?' agreed Tommy. 'Mind you, I think he meant today.'

'In that case, we'd best give him the benefit of the bleedin' doubt,' said Nobby. 'Teach him a bleedin' lesson if we didn't though. Coming here with half an order, must think we're bleedin' mindreaders.'

Half an hour later, after leisurely finishing their cigarettes and a warming mug of hot tea, the two conscientious young soldiers made their way towards the farmhouse. Between them was a drum of telephone wire through which they'd stuck a brush handle for it to turn on, unravelling the wire as they went. At the tops of their voices they sang the latest rude version of Colonel Bogey.

'Hitler, has only got one ball.
Goering, has two but very small,
Himmler is very similar,
but poor old Goebbels has no balls at all . . .'

They both heard it coming, but thought it would travel over their heads like all the others had done. In any case there was no cover to run to, so they just kept on walking, unravelling and singing. The shell exploded about twenty yards away. Nobby was partially shielded by Tommy who took the full force of the blast which carried the two of them through the air, across a road and into the next field. Miraculously Nobby was still alive, seriously wounded but not expected to last long.

Bits of Tommy were spread far and wide, making him just another statistic – and Dorothy just another war widow.

Chapter Five

The children had had no contact from Freddie since he'd waved them off at Malton Station the previous year. The war in Europe had ended over a month ago. Susan had half-expected him to turn up at the street party held after V.E. day. After all, he had promised to come and see them as soon as the war was over.

Rarities such as real eggs had been produced, and chopped up with tomatoes to make the most delicious sandwiches. Jelly shivered on the street's long trestle tables, the first time most children had seen it. Bananas and other exotic fruit were still many years away from a regular spot on the greengrocer's shelves, but Jackie Crombie's grandad, who had something to do with the army stores in Catterick, managed to smuggle a huge box of such fruit and other delicacies through to the street, where they were shared out with a generosity of spirit peculiar to that happy time.

Mrs Bateson got drunk on apple cider and tried it on with Reg Byrne who'd avoided the armed services due to his feet. Mrs Byrne, who'd spent the war defending her stay-at-home husband from the caustic comments of service wives, took exception to this and threw a well-aimed custard tart at Mrs Bateson, who retaliated with a bowl of trifle which splattered Mrs Crombie's new cardigan. This was the start of the great food fight of Broughton Terrace, talked about for many years with little need for exaggeration. As the happy combatants retired to their kitchen sinks to clean up, Susan stood at the end of the street, looking in vain up and down Paradine Hill and wondering if she'd ever see Freddie again.

Dorothy, who hadn't even begun to get over Tommy, had given the festivities a miss. She'd walked up quietly behind her niece

49

and placed a friendly arm around her shoulder. It didn't take a genius to work out Susan's problem, Dorothy had been in love herself at fifteen. An unrequited bout of passion with David Ableson, a handsome young Jewish tailor who made all her father's suits.

'If it's any consolation I don't think he was killed,' she murmured the words gently, so as not to startle her niece.

Susan turned and attempted a smile.

'They were all listed in the *Yorkshire Post*, Freddie wasn't among them,' continued Dorothy. She'd never met Freddie but she'd heard so much about him from both Jimmy and Susan. The way Susan talked about him spoke volumes and she knew no unwanted advice from her would be heeded.

'He said he'd come as soon as the war's over,' said Susan, trying to keep her emotions in check.

'Most men won't be home for months yet, some of them maybe not until next year.'

This thought didn't seem to have occurred to Susan who perked up visibly and gave her aunt a hug. Dorothy wanted to tell her that Freddie had probably forgotten all about her, that he was much too old for her; but these thoughts she wisely kept to herself. She remembered her own reaction when she'd been given the same advice.

It was now late June with no word from Freddie. Why hadn't he been in touch? Was he okay? Susan was beginning to fear the worst, then she saw his picture in the *Yorkshire Evening Post*. 'War hero's son comes home,' it said. She viewed the photograph with mixed emotions. Initial shock at seeing the love of her life in such a state, then relief at knowing at least he was still alive, then annoyance that the paper had neglected to mention that Freddie must be a hero. It was him that was swathed in bandages, not his dad. Brigadier Harry F-Forbes-Fiddler M.C. J.P. who was beaming into the camera as he wheeled his heavily bandaged son out of an ambulance, into the house. She devoured the tiny article, memorising every precious word. He'd been blown up by a grenade in Belgium, that's where Uncle Tommy had been killed. Doctors had given up all hope at first but he'd made a miraculous recovery and was now well enough to convalesce at home.

She showed Dorothy the article and her aunt decided on the only possible course of action.

'You must go and see him, both you and Jimmy. He'd like that.'

Dorothy wasn't entirely sure why she'd suggested it. Perhaps she thought that Susan might see Freddie in a new, less glamorous light – or perhaps Freddie might put Susan straight about the impossibility of any romance. Susan certainly thought it was a great idea – and so did Jimmy, who'd never been to Harrogate.

A quick scrutiny of the telephone book in Paradine Hill post office turned up Freddie's address and the following Saturday they arrived at Freddie's gate with a bar of Cadbury's Fruit and Nut for Freddie, and an air of youthful exuberance, although youth was not a word one would readily associate with such a place. It was a large, old, grey-stone house in a long street of similar large, old, grey-stone houses. There were old grey trees neatly lining the street planted in neatly tended verges. No children played in the street, or in the gardens for that matter. This was a most unusual state of affairs for a Saturday morning. They'd left Broughton Terrace a couple of hours earlier, amid the clamour of a fiercely contested rounders match, several noisy games of taws, and a bitter argument between young Mrs Harrison at number seven and big Mrs Veitch at number eight, about hanging out washing on a Saturday morning. Apparently Mrs Veitch was defending the rights of her children to play in the street on a Saturday, unhindered by washing lines. The children themselves didn't actually mind. It was quite good fun playing rounders in and out of Mrs Harrison's interesting underwear.

Jimmy looked around disapprovingly at his surroundings as they walked up the driveway of Freddie's house. 'There's more life in Murgy's vest,' he muttered.

They walked past a gleaming black Wolseley and a statue of a naked nymph which took Jimmy's admiring eye. Susan grabbed her loitering brother by his arm and dragged him away. She gave the door a confident knock. It was opened by Freddie's father, the Brigadier.

'Yes?' He demanded, as if one word was all that the situation merited.

'We've come to see Freddie,' smiled Susan. 'He knows us, see,

51

and we've come to, er, to see him.' Her confidence faltered under the Brigadier's exasperated glare.

'Go away,' was all he said, and shut the door.

The children stood there, gobsmacked at such rudeness. They'd expect it from old Mrs McGinty at number sixteen, but she had an excuse, she wasn't all there. She used to sit on the outside lav with the door wide open and an umbrella up. But rudeness such as this was well beyond their scope of understanding.

'You rude man!' Susan addressed her angry remark to the door.

'What shall we do now?' asked Jimmy, as they walked back down the garden path.

'Well, we've come all this way to see him so I think we should!' said a determined Susan. 'We'll wait till old Bulldog Features goes out, then sneak round the back.'

'What if he doesn't go out?'

'Everybody goes out some time on a Saturday morning,' scoffed his sister, amazed at her brother's dimness.

Half an hour later, they were sitting on a low wall at the end of the street, wondering whether to break into the bar of chocolate, when the Wolseley came purring past them, with the Brigadier at the wheel.

'See, I told you he'd go out,' said Susan, getting up and walking off down the street, causing Jimmy to run to catch her up.

'What's the plan?' he asked excitedly. 'Shall we break in?'

'Don't be silly. First we'll go round the back and look through the windows – and see what we can see.'

This seemed an incomplete sort of plan to Jimmy, but he decided not to argue and followed his determined sister around the back of the house. A large window had been left open to allow in the gentle breeze, sighing through the poplar trees bordering the neat lawn. The children walked stealthily towards it, Susan in the lead. Cautiously she looked through the window, then turned round excitedly to her brother.

'It's him!' she exclaimed. 'It's Freddie, he's in here!'

She stood on her tiptoes and leaned in at the window. Freddie was lying in a bed just inside the room, his eyes closed, an open book lying on his chest beneath his sleeping fingers, its pages rippling over in the breeze.

'Freddie!' whispered Susan, as loudly as she dared.

Freddie's eyes flickered open and looked around the room's interior.

'We're here! Over here, in the window!'

With a painful effort, Freddie turned his head in her direction, his eyes opening in surprise at the sight of two excited children grinning at him through the window.

'Hiya, Freddie,' yelled Jimmy, then clasped his hand to his mouth as his sister shushed him.

'Hello, Freddie,' smiled Susan, as demurely as she knew how. 'Remember us?'

Freddie stared at them, his mouth opened – then closed, as if he'd changed his mind about saying anything.

'He doesn't remember anything!'

The voice came from behind them. The children cringed, not daring to turn round. But there was no menace in this voice, it was a woman's voice. Susan risked a look round, her brother slowly following suit. On the path stood a nice-looking, middle-aged lady, with greying hair and a vaguely amused smile playing on her lips.

'I suppose you're the children my husband was so rude to earlier?'

'Yes,' admitted Susan. 'Er no, well he wasn't really ru ...'

'Yes he was,' insisted the lady. 'I scolded him for it afterwards.' She laughed gently to herself. 'He's gone off to his golf club in a bit of a huff, I'm afraid. Probably ruin his game and he'll blame me for it when he gets home. Still, I can handle him. His bark's a lot worse than his bite – and he's very protective of Freddie. He threatened one newspaper reporter with his shotgun, so you two got off rather lightly. Anyway, I think we'd better introduce ourselves, I'm Mrs Fiddler.' She spoke with the controlled confidence found only in ladies of quality and elderly Roman Catholic nuns.

'Not Mrs *Fforbes*-Fiddler, like your husband?' inquired a curious Susan.

'No, that's *his* name. I used to be called Fforbes, but when we were married, Harry decided to hyphenate us. Better for his army image and all that. I don't think he was ever happy with plain old Harry Fiddler. But I can't be doing with all that.'

'Too many effing Fs,' grinned Jimmy, as if he'd just thought of it.

'Precisely,' laughed Mrs Fiddler.

'I'm Susan, and this is my brother Jimmy,' said Susan quickly, wishing her brother didn't have to make a joke out of everything.

'Pleased to meet you Susan and Jimmy,' smiled Mrs Fiddler. 'Look, come inside, where you can talk to your friend properly. I must say, I'm rather curious to learn how you know him so well.'

She led them through the back door, into a cool, spacious kitchen, fitted with gadgets completely foreign to the children. Gas cooker, fridge, electric kettle, washing machine, automatic mangle and two sinks and a picture of the King and Queen on the wall.

Pausing at the kitchen door while the two of them looked round, she smiled to herself, wondering what Harry would say if he knew she'd invited two tykes, obviously from what he would call the 'lower orders', into their house.

'Through here,' she directed, pointing towards what Harry called the 'drawing room' and she and Freddie rebelliously called the 'parlour'.

She herself had apparently married above her station, if Harry's parents were to be believed. Daughter of a village butcher, she'd been serving behind the bar in the Bell and Monkey when young Harry had fallen hopelessly in love with her, and she, surprisingly, with him.

Freddie was leaning up on one elbow, awaiting the arrival of his unexpected visitors. To Susan, his welcoming smile was just as warm and heart-melting as ever, but it was accompanied by a slight questioning of his eyebrows.

'Hello, Freddie,' she smiled, totally confident he would remember her – and how foolish poor Mrs Fiddler would feel when he did.

Freddie stared at them for what seemed an age then he gave an apologetic smile and said, 'I'm sorry, I know I should recognise you but I'm afraid I don't.'

'Perhaps if you reminded Freddie of where you know him from, it might jog his memory,' prompted his mother.

'Oh, right,' said Susan, and between them they launched into a breathless story about them running away because Jimmy thought he'd killed Leon Murgatroyd, but he hadn't actually, and the train journey and Dan Braithwaite's apples and the cottage and the dead German. Complete with interruptions and constant

54

reminders from whoever wasn't telling the story at the time. But neither mentioned the rings, not while Mrs Fiddler was there. The oath Freddie had made them swear that day was the most sacred thing either of them had ever done.

They finished the story simultaneously and stood with bated breath for Freddie to smile and say how could he forget such a day. But he didn't.

'Oh, I wish I could remember a day like that,' he said, shaking his head sadly. 'How many marvellous memories such as that must I have locked up in here,' he tapped the side of his head, then lay back resignedly on the pillows. His eyes closed and he fell into a sudden sleep.

'He's on quite strong medication,' explained Freddie's mother, 'You musn't think him rude.'

The visit was over. Mrs Fiddler walked quietly out of the room, Jimmy followed, but Susan hung back, gazing sadly down on Freddie's sleeping face.

'Freddie Fiddler,' she whispered. 'Maybe you don't remember me, and maybe you'll never love me, and maybe you think fifteen's too young for a person to say they're in love with someone. I happen to know that's what most grown-ups like to think. But if I'm not in love with you, then I don't want to be in love with anyone else, thank you very much, because this is bad enough for me – and if I'm not making sense it's your fault for confusing me.'

She moved her head away as a tear dropped on to his cheek. 'My mam and dad left me, and I loved them. Then Uncle Tommy and our William – and I loved them. And now you. And I love you, Freddie Fiddler, and I don't care if I am only fifteen.'

Susan picked up a corner of his bedsheet and wiped away her tears, then she backed away and took several deep breaths before turning to leave the room.

Chapter Six

Dorothy looked in the mirror and wondered how she could still be pretty after what had happened in the past months. Perhaps she wasn't pretty any more, perhaps it was wishful thinking. Her hand still shook as she put her lipstick on. Many's the time she'd gone out without make-up rather than go round looking like Coco the Clown. Not this morning though. This was the start of a new week. A new job. A new life. At least that was what she kept trying to tell herself. It was five months and thirteen days since she'd received the impersonal buff letter saying her Tommy was 'Missing in Action'.

To all intents and purposes he was still missing, insofar as he'd never been found, not much of him anyway, but the army had sufficient sensitivity not to mention that. He'd since graduated to 'Killed in Action' and Dorothy was now a proud war widow, complete with derisory widow's pension. A man from the War Ministry came and said he'd been killed in Holland and gave her some combat medals. He'd simply been in the wrong place at the wrong time, said the man. Dorothy had tearfully pointed out that being in Holland in 1945 was the wrong place at the wrong time and the man from the War Ministry chose not to tell her that he'd spent 1945 behind a desk in Huddersfield. He muttered a few words of embarrassed sympathy before leaving her to her grief and riding away on his motorbike, enshrouded in non-combatant's guilt.

In the aftermath of the war, four million service personnel descended on a Civvy Street that wasn't quite ready for them. Servicemen, who'd been looking forward to the day for years, arrived home only to be met by strangers. The young wives they'd left behind had become hard and old and independent, many having spent years on a factory floor. The men came home in their demob suits to children who didn't know them from Adam and resented this stranger who ousted them from their mother's bed.

Bright young men who'd gone off to war had returned damaged. Physically or mentally or both. For every happy rehabilitation there was an equally sad one. In many ways the post-war years were as difficult as the ones that had gone on before. Ex-Servicemen who were all treated like heroes during the conflict had now become something of an embarrassment.

Vera Bateson from number twelve had been notified that her husband Len had been posted 'Missing Presumed Killed'. Her grief was cushioned due to her not having seen him for over a year, so she took in a lodger who was employed in a reserved occupation at the same Royal Ordance Factory that Weidling had failed to bomb, dropping his bombs instead on Fred and Lily Bairstow. At the end of the war Len Bateson turned up in a Polish P.O.W. camp.

Driven by that same love for Vera that had kept him going during his long hard time of internment, he walked halfway across Europe into France. Eventually returning to Broughton Terrace in something less than triumph, only to find his beloved Vera in bed with the lodger.

The charge against him was attempted murder, but the judge let Len go free, having much sympathy for him and little for the lodger. Stories like this abounded after the war.

This morning Dorothy was due to start a full-time job in the Thrift Stores on Connington Road. Not much of a job, but she'd promised Tommy she'd do everything in her power to make sure the kids got a proper schooling. When she made the promise she didn't know what she was letting herself in for. She did now though. Susan needed to stay on that extra year to take her School Certificate if she was to get a decent job. Dorothy could really do with the money Susan could bring in. But she had promised Tommy. Just the thought of him brought the inevitable tears to her eyes. The day she married him had been the happiest and proudest day of her life. The fact that her own family had boycotted the wedding cast a cloud over the proceedings, but marrying Tommy Bairstow made up for all that.

The Bairstow brothers, Fred and Tommy, had been legends down at the Hippodrome Ballroom. Where there was a Bairstow brother there was fun to be had. No one could dance the Jitterbug like them, or the Waltz, the Foxtrot, the Quickstep, the Palais Glide and so on and so on. Tommy was the singer. He'd be invited up on to the bandstand and the audience would shout out their requests. And Tommy could sing alright – he had a voice like an angel – only he never took himself seriously and neither did Fred. Fred would get up and stand behind his brother, doing his hilarious comic dance, pulling faces, anything to make the audience laugh – and every time Tommy turned round, Fred would be standing there innocent as you like and the audience would howl with laughter. They'd talked about going on the clubs as a double act after the war – after they'd done their bit for king and country. Ironically, the one thing you never saw a Bairstow brother do was fight. Not that they were cowards, it's just that they could talk their way into a fight and joke their way out with a practised ease. The Bairstows were not fighting men. Pity no one told the army that. The Bairstows never raised a fist in anger to anyone. They raised many a laugh though. Dorothy smiled through her tears at the memory. Now they were both gone – Lily as well. She'd always got on well with Lily, although they were different types. Lily had been quite a bubbly girl until the arrival of three kids, which had quietened her down a lot. Quieten anybody down, having three kids. It had only taken two of them to quieten Dorothy down. Oh dear, there was that guilt again.

Dorothy had been a little more sophisticated. She came from a wealthy family in Alwoodley which was a damn sight posher than Paradine Hill. But she wouldn't take their charity if they came to her on bended knee. Which they hadn't. Her life had been already mapped out for her by her builder father, Sidney Allerdyce, chairman and managing director of Allerdyce Builders Ltd. Even to the extent of finding a suitable husband in the form of Eric Westerbrook, the doctor son of an ear nose and throat surgeon at Leeds Infirmary. Sid Allerdyce had dragged himself up from being a bricklayer to chairman of his own house building company and he insisted on his children turning their backs on the class of person he'd worked so hard to leave behind. He'd married the daughter of a wealthy publican, a boringly beautiful woman. Dull as she was she could surely have done better than Sid, who was no great catch in the beauty or personality stakes; but each seemed to know where they stood in the relationship. She was an unaffectionate woman, who looked on with a cold dispassion whenever her husband disciplined their daughter with regular heavy beatings.

The Allerdyce family had reckoned without the irresistible charms of Tommy Bairstow who swept their sophisticated daughter off her feet, with his outrageous sense of fun and not inconsiderable good looks. To look at they made a fine-looking couple. Dorothy was a real beauty. Well-educated, well-spoken and with a deep-rooted hatred of her brutish father.

A heavy knock on the front door made her jump. She looked at her watch, 7.45. Oh God! Who on earth could it be at this time on a morning? Front door as well, so it could be official.

Her heart quickened anxiously as she looked through the back window and saw her father, standing with his back to the door, surveying his lowly surroundings with obvious contempt. An expensive-looking, black Homburg was jammed unceremoniously down over his workman's head, his hair closely cropped right back to the folds of his thick, crimson neck. A shiny blue suit stretched across his fat back, pulling at his armpits and sitting uncomfortably on a body designed for overalls.

Pulling a small table away from behind the rarely used door, Dorothy took a deep, controlling breath and opened it. Her father turned round, his hand going to his hat by way of greeting, then changing its mind and returning to his side. Dorothy looked at the father she hadn't seen for years and opened with a line she'd rehearsed in her head for most of that time.

'By heck, Dad! Look at you – just goes to show, you can't buy class, can you?'

He gave a frown which meant he didn't understand what she was talking about, then beckoned to the Rover parked behind him. The only car in the street. His voice was harsh and uncompromising.

'Right, girl, yer've stuck it out long enough. I reckon yer've had yer come uppance and yer've paid yer dues. Get yer stuff together, yer comin' home with me.'

'Just like that, eh?'

'They'll be nowt said about this bloody mess yer got yerself into, but I reckon yer've only got God to thank for getting you out of it so smartly.'

'So that's what God's been up to is it? Getting me out of it. I was wondering where he was when I needed him.' She felt a surge of anger rising within her that she knew she'd have to control if she wanted to say all she had to say.

'Eric Westerbrook never got married, you know,' said her father, his unpleasant piggy eyes boring into his daughter. 'He never got over it when you wed that brainless pillock Bairstow. Got what were coming to him, if you ask me. Anyway, if yer play yer cards right yer could get back in with young Westerbrook.'

It was all Dorothy could do to stop herself from lashing out at her father, but that would spoil the moment.

'And what about Jimmy and Susan?' she said icily. 'Do you think *Young Westerbrook* will want a ready-made family?'

'Who's Jimmy and Susan? Look stop pissing me about, I'm due on site in half an hour, I haven't got time for all this bloody chit chat.'

'You know very well who Jimmy and Susan are – or at least you should. They're part of my family now.'

Sid scowled. It wasn't going as well as he thought. He figured she'd be overjoyed to be welcomed back after what she'd been through.

'Fred's brats,' he acknowledged grudgingly.

'My niece and nephew,' she corrected. 'Your great-niece and nephew,' she added, to rub salt in the wound.

'Hey! they're nowt ter do with me,' protested Sid, angrily. 'They're not even flesh and blood. No, he can't be expected to tek in anybody's brats. They'll have ter go into a home. That's what homes are there for. He'll want to father his own will Westerbrook's lad. Proper breeding, that's what counts.'

'*Westerbrook's Lad*? Breeding? You make him sound like a race horse. Mind you he's got the face for it and it'll take more than a couple of generations to breed an arsehole like you out,' retorted Dorothy scornfully, but still holding her anger in check. 'Anyway Jimmy and Susan already have a home. A better home than I ever had. They're decent kids – and that's a word you never learned from your posh pals.'

Her father's mounting fury had him struggling for words with which to retaliate, so Dorothy, being on a roll, jumped back in first.

'Tell me, Dad, do these posh pals of yours still laugh at you behind your back? Have you worked out why you're not a member of that precious golf club yet? Do you still use your fork like a shovel? Do you still fart like Flamborough foghorn? Are you still the big, loud-mouthed shithouse you always were?'

Dorothy had imagined this confrontation many times, so much so that she was surprisingly well rehearsed in what she had to say to him. There were many more insults in her repertoire but her father had heard enough. He exploded and took a violent step forward, his arm drawing back. Dorothy was ready, she slammed the door on him and had the bolt in place just before his heavy fist battered into it with frustrated rage. He pushed open the letterbox, through which he spat his parting message to his only daughter.

'You ungrateful little whoring bitch. Don't come grovelling ter my door from whatever gutter yer find yerself in. And remember this – if it's the last thing I do I'll make you regret them words! I'll say no more to yer!'

He turned to face the inevitable onlookers who'd all chosen that very moment to come casually out of a front door they hadn't used for months.

'She's no daughter of mine any more!' he roared, spraying spit all over his shiny black car. 'Do yer hear me? I don't know why I bloody bothered!'

Susan and Jimmy joined their auntie at the window to see what all the commotion was about. Dorothy looked down at them and smiled.

'That's your Great Uncle Sid. Wave bye-bye to Uncle Sid, children.'

Jimmy and Susan happily obliged as an enraged Sid screeched over the cobbles and out of Broughton Terrace for the first and last time: and for the first time since Tommy had died Dorothy felt good about herself.

'Thanks for that, Dad,' she said to herself, loud enough for Jimmy and Susan to hear. They of course, thought she was going potty.

Dorothy returned to the mirror to finish her lipstick. Her hands were steady now. She smiled back at Susan's reflection as she

61

watched her aunt's technique with lipstick and powder.

'You want to try this, don't you? I know the feeling. I couldn't wait when I was your age. Maybe tonight when I get home from work.'

Susan blushed a little then said, 'I'd like that, thanks, Auntie Dorothy – and thanks for, you know . . .'

'What?' Dorothy ran her bottom lip over her top lip to smooth out her handiwork.

'You know, for letting me stop on at school to take my School Certificate.' Susan was referring to a recent visit from her form teacher at St Winifred's College where Susan was a scholarship pupil.

'Susan's one of our brightest girls,' Miss Briers had said. I know things must be difficult for you, but that extra year would make all the difference in the world to Susan's career.'

Dorothy pulled a mock stern face at her niece's reflection. 'Just you make sure it's worthwhile.'

'I will.'

'Auntie Dorothy,' chirped Jimmy.

'Yes, Jimmy?'

'It's alright if you want me to leave when I'm fifteen, I won't mind, honest.'

Dorothy laughed. 'I'll bear it in mind. Oh, by the way, you didn't tell me much about your visit to Freddie the other day. How is he?'

'He's a lot better,' said Susan, who didn't really want to talk about him. To her the visit had been something of a disappointment. 'But he can't remember anything,' she added.

'He didn't know who we were,' added Jimmy.

'Good Lord! He must have it bad if he doesn't remember you two, still at least he's alive, that's the main thing.'

'It is, isn't it?' agreed Susan optimistically.

Dorothy's relationship with the children had improved dramatically since Tommy had died. They'd been a tower of strength – and Jimmy was showing signs of becoming every bit as entertaining as his dad and uncle. This was where she belonged. Her father's false world was a million miles from where she wanted to be. She returned her gaze to the mirror to check on the finished product and gave herself a nod of approval. Thirty-three years old now and yes, she was definitely still a good-looking woman. A shadow passed through her thoughts and brought an unconscious frown to her brow as it had done increasingly over the past few weeks.

How on earth could she have told them their brother was dead? And when was she going to tell the children the truth? Not today that's for sure. The shock of Tommy's death had pushed it to the back of her mind, but gradually, as she came round to accepting life without her lovely Tommy, the spectre of William began to emerge. She couldn't put it off much longer. Maybe next week. One step at a time, that's what they said, wasn't it?

Chapter Seven

Dorothy picked up the packet of butter she'd left behind the counter and dropped it casually into her overall pocket. The past four months had been hard, but she was managing, just. She'd settled into a routine. The wage she earned from the Thrift Stores wasn't a fortune, but together with her widow's pension they just scraped by. Not much left over for luxuries, such as clothes. Susan needed a new blazer desperately, and both the kids' shoes needed cobbling. Larry Gill, next door but one would do that if she got him the leather. He fancied her did Larry. Better not let Mrs Gill find out or there'd be no more free cobbling from Larry. She smiled to herself at what sounded like a crude innuendo. If there was ever to be anything like that again in her life, it wouldn't be with the likes of Larry Gill. She wouldn't mind it with somebody though. It had been a long time now since her last night with Tommy. She'd had another letter from Oxford House Children's Home in Cleckheaton informing her that William was now formally in the care of the Local Authority and would shortly be transferred to somewhere more suitable, but they didn't say where. This should have set warning bells ringing but Dorothy kept telling herself that she still hadn't come to terms with losing Tommy and she owed it to herself to give herself time. Deep down of course, she knew this was just an excuse. There just didn't seem to be any way to tell them without making her seem like the Wicked Witch of the West. Perhaps she was living in hope of providence turning up an opportunity. Whatever happened, she was determined to tell them before Christmas and bring their brother home.

Harry Evans would never notice the butter. Besides what was

he going to do, sack her? Well, hardly. He couldn't run the shop without her, anyway he was only the manager, it wasn't as if she was stealing from him. Not that that would worry her, the miserable old sod. Never a good word to say for anybody, never a word of praise for her and she knew she was good, all the customers told her. A lot better than Ethel, thick as two short planks was Ethel. He'd be retiring in a couple of years and they'd need someone to take his place. She quite fancied that, manageress. Nice title, more money. In the meantime she just had to supplement her wages as best she could. Wages! Slave labour more like. Two and a penny an hour less stoppages. She hadn't been so much as to the pictures in a year. No, the odd packet of butter here, the odd loaf there, and why not? She was entitled to it.

'I'm just nipping out for my dinner, Harry,' she called out to her boss who was in the storeroom round the back. 'So can you come through and serve? Ethel's late back – as usual.'

'Gimme a minute,' came the muffled reply.

Presently Harry came through, red faced from heaving boxes of sugar around. 'Before yer go,' he panted. 'There's just something I need to check.'

Dorothy looked at her watch, twelve-thirty-five. 'Hurry up, I'm five minutes into my dinner half hour.'

Harry was a small man, in his late fifties. He looked like a grocer, grocery had been his life; apart from four years in France in the Great War, where he'd been one of the very few who managed to stay clear of the fighting. The store had been his life. He'd once owned it but had sold out to the Thrift Stores Group and had regretted it ever since. Constantly looking over his shoulder, as he fully expected a younger man to push him into forced retirement, after which his life would have no meaning.

He gave Dorothy a funny look and without saying anything delved into her overall pocket and brought out the butter. 'What's this?' he demanded.

Dorothy tried to dismiss it. 'Oh heck! I stuck it there when I was tidying the shelves this morning. I must have forgotten it.'

'Like you forgot that loaf you took yesterday – and that bag of sugar on Monday.'

'Look, Harry, you'd better let me explain . . .'

Harry shook his head, 'It's been going on too long. I reckon you've been at it for weeks. It was Ethel who first saw you taking stuff.'

'Ethel? Good God, Harry – she's worse than me! If you suspected, why didn't you say something. At least it would have stopped me doing it.'

'Why did you do it?'

'For God's sake, that's a stupid question to ask a widow trying to bring up two children.'

Harry went to the till, took out three pound notes and some loose change. He grimly handed the money to Dorothy. 'I'm being more than fair to you. I could dock your wages to make up for what you've taken or I could report you to the police. But I'm not doing that, I'm paying you up to tonight.'

Dorothy looked disbelievingly at the money in her hand, then back up at Harry. 'So this is it then? I'm fired?'

Harry nodded and handed her the packet of butter. 'Here, you might as well have it.'

Dorothy took it dumbly. As she went out of the door she turned and said, 'You didn't answer my question. Why didn't you give me some sort of warning? That would have stopped me. You know I was good, you'll have a job getting anyone as good as me.'

'I don't want anyone as good as you. They were going to retire me early and give you my job. They'll have to keep me on now.'

'You're a bastard, you know that, don't you, Harry?'

Harry shrugged. 'But I'm a bastard who's still got a job.'

Raymond Donoghue came into Susan's life on the top deck of the number forty-two bus on her way back from school. It was October 1945 and she'd just started in the fifth form at St Winifred's. Her school blazer was a source of amusement to a group of girls returning from the afternoon shift at Penny Hill Dyeworks, whose circumstances, by virtue of them being in work, weren't quite as straitened as Susan's. She still wore the blazer she'd been bought second-hand for the start of the fourth year. The cuffs had been turned down to the limit, as had the hem. But Susan was a tall girl and the sleeves ended a good three inches from her wrist. Her boisterous existence had occasioned many a not-so-invisible mend by Auntie Dorothy, whose skills as a seamstress were less than legendary.

'Thought she were the Queen of the bleeding' May when she

passed her scholarship. Look at her now. Hey, Bairstow! Where'd yer get yer blazer? Off a bleeding' rag an' bone man?'

Susan's tormentor was Greta Birchall, who'd been in the same class as Susan at St Joseph's Junior School. Named after Greta Garbo and there the resemblance ended, for good looks could not be numbered amongst Greta's limited attributes. She had an older brother called Rudolph, who was no Valentino either. Only four girls out of a class of forty-six had managed a place at St Winifred's and Greta, being in what was euphemistically called the 'Transition Group', had not been one of them, she wouldn't have been one of them had forty-five managed places. Susan ignored them and gazed out of the window at the passing street below. A smoking paper boy stood beside a *Yorkshire Evening News* placard saying: SMOKING THOUGHT TO CAUSE CANCER. On the next corner a *Yorkshire Evening Post* paper boy sold his papers beside the rival headline HERTFORDSHIRE TRAIN CRASH – MANY DEAD. Their bus driver hooted impatiently as he veered out to pass a slow-moving, pony-drawn Rington's Tea van, the pony evacuated its bowel in what appeared to be retaliation, causing all the kids on the lower deck to howl with amusement, as kids do at such things. A copper coin hit Susan on the forehead and it began to bleed slightly.

'Here y'are – "penny for the guy"', cackled one of the other girls, eager to crack the best joke at Susan's expense.

Individually, Susan was more than a match for any of them and as courage was never something she was lacking, she foolishly spun round and grabbed Greta Birchall by the lapel of her blouse, dragging her up from her seat.

'You're a big brave girl, Birchall, when you've got your pals with you. How about just me and you?'

Greta's sneer turned to shock at the ease with which Susan dragged her out of her seat. Then she glanced over Susan's shoulder and sniggered. An arm came around Susan's neck and dragged her down the aisle of the bus onto the long back seat, where Greta and her three friends laid into her. Susan fought back like a tigress but was held down by sheer weight of numbers as Greta stood over her, gloating.

'Right, Miss Snotty Nose Susan Bairstow, let's see how stuck up you are without any clothes on.'

Pulling Susan's shoes off, she threw them out of the bus

window. She then dragged her blazer off, stuck her finger in a recent small tear and then, to a chorus of laughter from her friends, ripped it right across the back before throwing that out as well. As she made a grab for her skirt, Susan kicked out violently with a shoeless foot and caught Greta in the throat, sending her choking to her knees. The other three girls, seeing the acute distress their crony was in, momentarily let Susan go; long enough for her to push her way past them and vault over the rail on to the stairs. Almost immediately she heard a scuffle behind her.

'She's getting away, get her!'

'Leave her alone, she's had enough.'

'What's it ter do with you? Mind yer own bleeding business and get outa the way!'

Susan looked round at Raymond Donoghue who'd positioned himself stubbornly between the three remaining tormentors and Susan. He was a tall, broad lad who had little difficulty halting their progress. The girls were screaming atrocious obscenities over his shoulder, causing the conductor to tell them to watch their language or get off the bus. Violence, it seemed was okay but bad language was not.

'Sorry I didn't step in earlier,' apologised Raymond, as they stepped off the bus together. 'But with it being lasses – you know – it were a bit awkward. Here, I got your satchel for you, you left it on the seat when you . . .'

'When I made an idiot of myself and grabbed Birchall. Thanks anyway.' She took the satchel gratefully, it was real leather, she wouldn't want to lose that. A jubilant Uncle Tommy had bought her it when she passed her scholarship exam.

'A brainy Bairstow!' he'd laughed. 'That's a new one!' She'd turned up for school that first day wearing a brand new uniform, proud as a peacock. Greta Birchall had been right, she had been the Queen of the May back then. And now?

They were retracing the bus route in an effort to retrieve Susan's coat and shoes, their pace quickening as it dawned on Susan that someone might take a fancy to them. Even a torn school blazer would be of value to someone in those days.

Raymond picked up the blazer from a puddle in the gutter. Susan thanked him then looked at the badge on Raymond's dark blue blazer.

'My brother's at St Tommy's, he's in the second form.'

68

Raymond nodded. He knew he couldn't be expected to know a second former. 'I'm in the fifth,' he said. 'Same as you, I imagine.'

Susan nodded. 'That's right, I'm at St Winnie's. Not that you could tell, looking at this blazer.'

'I hope your mam's good at mending,' he said awkwardly.

'I haven't got a mam. It's my Auntie Dorothy. She'll not be so pleased when she sees this. She's only just finished mending it.'

'There's one of your shoes,' called out Raymond as he ran into the road and picked up a scuffed black shoe with a hole about to appear in the sole.

'Thanks,' replied Susan. 'The other one's over here.'

With her shoes back on, the pair of them turned and headed for home once again.

Raymond introduced himself. 'I'm Ray – and I reckon I know your name, Snotty Nose Susan Bairstow, isn't it?'

'Just Susan, thanks very much. By the way, I do know who you are, your sister was in the year above me at St Winifred's. I've seen you with her. She was supposed to be clever, why didn't she stay on to do her A levels?'

Her new friend kicked a tin can noisily along the footpath and replied. 'Same reason as I reckon you won't be doing yours – we're a bit skint. Me dad says there's no point doing your A levels unless you're going on to university and we can't afford to send her there.'

This was the first time Susan realised the limitations that lack of finance could place on her future and the idea of retrieving the jewels crossed her mind, as it had several times recently. She held up her blazer and groaned.

'I think it's beyond all hope – what do you think?'

'I think you're right,' agreed Ray stopping at the corner of Crawley Grove. 'I live up here.' He pointed up the street, similar to Susan's, festooned with washing lines under which three small boys kicked a tennis ball around.

'Oh, right,' Susan felt oddly disappointed that he had to leave her. 'See you, bye!'

Ray walked up the street a few steps then hesitated. 'Hang on!' he shouted. Susan stopped and turned to him. 'Our Eileen's got an old blazer. Shall I ask me mam if yer can borrow it till yer get yours mended?'

Susan shrugged, 'Yes, if you like. It's alright if she doesn't want to go though.' She followed Ray to a small terrace house and waited at the door as he went inside and shouted up the stairs.

'Mam, do you know where our Eileen's old blazer is?'

'Under t' stairs, what do you want it for?'

Susan took a step back as she realised the voice was coming from above her. Mrs Donoghue was sitting on the bedroom window sill, with her feet inside and her well upholstered bottom protruding above the street as she busily cleaned the windowpane. She looked down at Susan and gave a toothless smile. Ray stepped out and looked up at his mother.

'Can Susan borrow our Eileen's blazer? Some lasses on t' bus tore hers.'

'Hang on, I'll come down.'

Mrs Donoghue disappeared inside and clattered noisily down the uncarpeted stairs. She appeared at the door, teeth back in and wiping soapsuds onto her pinny.

'Hello, love, I'm Raymond's mam. Now then, what's all this about your blazer?'

Susan handed over her blazer for Mrs Donoghue to examine. She shook her head. 'I think it's beyond mending, love.' She looked closely at Susan. 'Aren't you Lily Bairstow's girl?'

Susan nodded, 'Yes, she was killed in the war. Me dad as well.'

'Yes, I know all about that, love. I remember that night myself. By heck! It were a beggar of night were that. Sounds to me like your troubles are still not over.'

Susan nodded her rueful agreement. Mrs Donoghue smiled at her. 'I remember your dad. Went out with him once. Mind you, so did most of the lasses round here. By heck! He were a beggar were yer dad – and that brother of his, Tommy – they made some sparks fly when they got together them two.'

'My Uncle Tommy got killed as well.'

'I know, love, I heard about that as well.' She shook her head sadly, then smiled at some fond memory she'd no intention of revealing to the children.

'Tell yer what, come inside and I'll get our Eileen's blazer for yer. She's no use for it and it's only gathering dust. You might as well have it.'

Susan knew only too well what a sacrifice this was. Although the blazer was old, she could easily have got seven and six for it

70

by selling it at the school. Second-hand blazers were at a premium.

'Thanks, Mrs Donoghue, I'll tell my Auntie Dorothy to give you something for it.'

'You'll tell her no such thing. I'm giving it to you, so let that be an end to it.'

Susan tried on the blazer, which was much nearer her size and a vast improvement on the one Maggie had ripped. Mrs Donoghue cocked her head to one side in appreciation. 'Very nice, mind you, I reckon you'll end up with the sort of figure that'll look good in owt. By the way, yer can tell them lasses on that bus if they rip that one they've me to answer to.'

Auntie Dorothy seemed pre-occupied as Susan told the story of the girls on the bus and the ripped blazer and how Mrs Donoghue had given her their Eileen's blazer which was a good fit and didn't have a single mend in it.

'I'm sorry, Susan, what were you saying? it's just that I've got a lot on my mind at the moment, what with one thing and another.' Dorothy was sitting on the settee, staring blankly at the *Yorkshire Evening Post*, miles away.

Susan chose not to repeat the story but went up to her bedroom to give her new blazer a good brush. She'd moved up into the attic when it was decided that a young lady should sleep in a separate room from her curious younger brother. As she passed Jimmy's room he poked his head round the door.

'She's been crying,' he said simply.

'Why?'

'No idea – she were crying when I came in from school. She didn't see me at first then she tried to let on she had summat in her eye.'

'I wonder if I should go see what's up?' asked Susan.

'I think it's private.'

Susan nodded her agreement to this assessment and sat down on the bottom attic step. She didn't want Auntie Dorothy to be upset. She'd grown to like her quite a lot and she certainly did her best for her and Jimmy. Maybe it was time to get the rings. Every time she thought along these lines she remembered the oath they'd sworn and shuddered at the very thought of breaking such a sacred vow. No way could she sell the rings without the help of an adult, besides, hers was to be her engagement ring. Jimmy, on the other hand, would have no such compunction and had tried to persuade her on numerous occasions to 'dig 'em up and flog 'em.'

Jimmy was in the second year at St Thomas's College, having amazed everybody, not least himself, by winning a scholarship place there, in the face of fierce competition.

'Shouldn't she still be at work?' Susan said suddenly.

'No idea,' answered Jimmy, sitting down on the step beside the sister he hated and loved with equal passion. 'Is that a new blazer?'

'Nearly. Raymond Donoghue's mam gave it to me. It's alright, isn't it?'

'Raymond Donoghue? Who's he then? Is he yer new boyfriend, then?'

'Don't be so soft,' protested Susan, rather too loudly. There was only one man in her life. Unfortunately he couldn't remember who she was. She carried a mental picture of Freddie, lying in bed, with one of her tears on his cheek.

'I think she's crying again,' said Jimmy. 'Listen! ...Told yer. She's crying again.'

Dorothy felt Susan's arm around her shoulder and straightened up as her niece sat beside her on the settee.

'Is it something very bad, Auntie Dorothy?'

'Oh, no. It's just me being silly.'

'Is it Uncle Tommy?'

Dorothy nodded. It wasn't such a lie. Tommy was always in her thoughts, maybe not at the forefront at the moment. But he was in there somewhere.

'I still cry about Mam and Dad,' said Susan comfortingly. 'So does Jimmy. Not so much as we did though. I try and remember what she looked like. She was very pretty, wasn't she?'

'She was beautiful was your mam.'

'My dad was funny, wasn't he?'

'They both were, him and your Uncle Tommy.' She smiled to herself at some distant memory. 'Did your mam ever tell you about the time they took a couple of ferrets into the pictures? I still laugh about that, even today.'

Jimmy, who'd been listening from the stairs, came across and sat on the floor in front of them. An expectant grin on his face at the prospect of another story about his dad and Uncle Tommy. Dorothy smiled down at him and continued:

'Your mam was just married to your dad at the time and I'd gone along to make up a foursome.' She looked at Susan and winked. 'Actually, you came with us. Just a big bump in your mam's tummy, but she carried you with some pride, I can tell you.'

Susan smiled back, she'd already worked out the date of her conception and figured she must have gone to Mam and Dad's wedding as well.

'God knows where they got the ferrets from,' continued Dorothy. 'They must have had them hidden in their jackets when we met them outside the pictures. We'd gone to see Al Jolson in *The Jazz Singer*.'

'Seen it,' interrupted Jimmy. 'Made in nineteen-twenty-seven starring Al Jolson and May McAvoy, first ever talking picture.'

'I wish you'd stop talking,' scolded Susan, before her brother launched himself into his version of 'Mammy'. Jimmy was an avid Al Jolson fan.

'It was on at the Crescent Picture Palace as it was then, on Atherton Street,' went on Dorothy.

'They call it "The Vogue" now,' interrupted Jimmy once again. Susan gave him a dig this time.

'Anyway,' said Dorothy, patiently. 'It was first house on a Saturday night and the place was absolutely packed. I knew they were up to something by the way they were wriggling about in their seats. Then all of a sudden these two big furry animals appeared. I've never seen a ferret before, nor since come to think of it – and I don't think too many people at the Crescent knew what they were either. They let them go under the seats and I tell you what, they were fast. One minute there was a commotion in the back stalls and two seconds later there were screams coming from the front stalls, then the side, then back to the middle – honestly, you've never known such pandemonium. Your dad and Uncle Tommy thought it was hilarious – so did your mother, I thought she was going to have you there and then!'

'What about you, Auntie, did you think it was funny?' laughed Susan.

'Well, I did and I didn't. You have to remember, this was my first date with your Uncle Tommy. What would you think if your boyfriend did a thing like that on your first date?'

This point of view had the children laughing even louder. 'What happened then?' asked Jimmy.

'I'll tell you what flipping well happened then,' went on Dorothy. 'The house lights went up and the manager came round. Some of the younger lads were rushing round trying to catch these ferrets, a woman in front of us was having hysterics, Al Jolson was singing, "Toot Toot Tootsie Goodbye" and some people had just had enough and were asking for their money back from this poor manager. Then as soon as he clapped eyes on your dad and Uncle Tommy he went absolutely potty. He knew it had to be them. They were so well-known for playing daft pranks like that. Anyway, we were kicked out, all four of us – banned from ever going back there as well. As far as I know I still am banned. Funny sort of first date when you come to think of it.'

Jimmy and Susan rocked with laughter at their auntie's story.

'Hey! Our Susan must be banned as well then,' deduced Jimmy. 'She were with yer!'

Even Dorothy laughed at this, her problems momentarily lifted.

'Everybody says they were funny,' said Susan proudly. 'I was talking to Mrs Donoghue today and she said that.' Susan paused then added, 'She said she used to go out with my dad.'

'There's lots of girls can say that, they could say the same about your Uncle Tommy as well.'

'But he picked me mam, didn't he?' Jimmy chipped in, 'And Uncle Tommy picked you – so you two must have been the best then.'

Dorothy smiled and ruffled Jimmy's hair. The Bairstow charm was safely in the hands of the next generation.

Chapter Eight

Dorothy sat down in the chair opposite Frank Sackfield the builder. She'd heard that Molly Butterworth, who'd been doing Frank's books was due to pack it in owing to a bout of pregnancy and Dorothy was hoping to step in before the job was advertised.

'I worked for Sid Allerdyce for five years as book-keeper cum secretary,' she chose not to mention that Sid was her father, as she feared it might not help. Sid was not a popular man. 'I know pretty much all there is to know about the business.'

Frank sat back in his chair and gave Dorothy an appreciative smile. She was a vast improvement on Molly Butterworth, in looks anyway – and if she'd held down a job with Sid Allerdyce she'd need to be a good worker. He'd asked her one or two questions but he knew more about setting on bricklayers than employing secretarial staff.

'I really need the job, Mr Sackfield,' she decided to pull out all the stops now. 'My husband was killed during the war and I'm bringing up his dead brother's children.'

'Your husband? Bairstow? Not Tommy Bairstow? Tommy and Fred Bairstow!'

'You knew him then?' It was probably a silly question, everyone in a mile radius of Paradine Hill had heard of Tommy and Fred Bairstow.

Frank chuckled to himself as everyone did when Tommy and Fred's names came into the conversation. 'Look, Mrs Bairstow,' he said. 'Right now there isn't a job. Work's a bit thin on the ground and to be honest with you, Molly getting pregnant's a blessing in disguise – but,' he added, seeing Dorothy's face drop.

'In the new year, things might be different. If there's a job going you'll get first refusal, before I even advertise.'

They stood up together and she took his proffered hand, 'Thanks, Mr Sackfield,' she said. 'I'd appreciate that.'

He watched her leave and knew there and then he was going to employ her before much longer – whether he needed to or not.

The first indication of a downturn in the Bairstow family fortunes was the non-appearance of pocket money. It was over a week since Dorothy had been sacked and all she'd managed to find herself was a cleaning job, two hours a day, three days a week and she didn't know if she could stick that. On her second day she'd heard the woman she worked for refer to her as a servant, which took Dorothy aback. She seriously toyed with the idea of telling Mrs High and Mighty Oldfield where she could stick her mop, and which end to put in first, in fact she might just stick it there for her. Dorothy did not have the mentality of a domestic.

Mrs Veitch opened the scullery door to Jimmy's businesslike knock. 'Have yer any empty jam jars ter take back, Mrs Veitch?' he asked politely.

'Mebbe one. I'll have a look.' She reappeared with an empty jar of Bretheridges Stawberry Preserve. 'You'll need to wash it out a bit before you take it back, you know.'

'I know, thanks, Mrs Veitch.'

Susan was working the other side of the street, which was a bit demeaning for a fifteen-year-old young lady, but if she wanted to see the Saturday matinée that afternoon, then needs must when the devil drives, as Auntie Dorothy had said earlier. In truth she was probably growing too old for the Saturday matinée, but she just wanted to see if Flash Gordon managed to escape from the Emperor Ming. She had a bit of a crush on Buster Crabbe. Nothing like her love for Freddie, of course.

Between them they collected just eight jam jars, which, at a penny each, would realise just eightpence. Fourpence short of their target. It cost sixpence each to get into the Bughutch. Normally they'd be given ninepence each every Saturday morning. Threepence for two ounces of sweets from Mrs Barrett's corner sweet shop and a tanner into the pictures. But not today.

'Sorry, kids,' Auntie Dorothy said sadly. 'I just can't manage it today. Maybe next week, eh?'

Susan and Jimmy accepted the situation with equanimity. They weren't the first kids in their street to go without pocket money. And there were other ways of doing things. Jam jars, for instance. There were strict territorial rules about the collecting of jam jars. Stick to your own street, pretty much outlined it in a nutshell. So, eightpence it was then, fourpence each, better than nothing.

Off they went to Bretheridges Jam Factory with eight glistening jam jars clinking away in a shopping basket. As they approached the front entrance, they passed the gate to the factory yard. A high iron gate with vicious looking spikes on the top, interlinked with barbed wire and locked with a massive padlock; the type of padlock that said 'don't even think about it' to any would-be lock picker.

'Somebody's left the key in the lock,' observed Susan in passing. 'Anybody could walk in there.'

'Oh yeah! And who'd want ter nick a load of empty jam jars?' scoffed Jimmy.

They both stopped in their tracks. Just inside the gate were dozens of crates, all stacked with empty jam jars. The children retraced their steps, the yard was deserted. In the padlock were two keys, one in the lock and one dangling on a chrome ring. With Jimmy acting as lookout, Susan took the key from the lock and tried the other one. It fitted, they were identical.

Susan unlocked the gate as Jimmy went inside and filled up the shopping bag with jam jars. The whole operation took just a few seconds. He was out and whistling his nonchalant way down the street as Susan clicked the padlock back into place. Leaving one key in the lock and slipping the spare key into her pocket.

Jimmy heaved his bag of jam jars onto the scarred wooden counter, as he had many times before, to supplement his pocket money. Susan leaned forward and shouted into the office at the back where a jovial looking man in overalls and a surgical boot sat engrossed in the *Daily Mirror* crossword.

'We've brought some jam jars back, mister!'

'That's what I like ter see,' said the jovial man, folding his paper and clumping towards them. 'Properly washed jars. You should see the state o' some of 'em. I refuse ter take 'em. "Take the buggers back and give 'em a wash," that's what I tell 'em –

one came in last week half full o' bloody fungus.' He leaned forward and added confidentially, 'Mind you, yer'd expect no better – they came in from Camp Road.'

Susan curled up her nose in disapproval at the state of Camp Road jam jars. Jimmy thought a joke might be appropriate.

'Me Uncle Tommy used ter be a window frame cleaner up Camp Road,' he said it with a deadpan face which creased into an appreciative grin as the man laughed uproariously at this juvenile comedian.

'Right then,' he said at last. 'Twenty-two jars at a penny each – that's one and eightpence.'

'One and tenpence,' corrected Jimmy and Susan.

The man laughed. 'Just testing, there'll never be no fooling you two, will there? I can see I shall have to watch me step with you two. Right, one and tenpence it is then.' The man counted out the coins onto the counter under the close scrutiny of the youngsters, who knew not to trust jovial men with surgical boots.

'Thanks mister,' called out Jimmy over his shoulder. 'See you next week.'

As they walked out into the grimy street Susan said, 'He tried to diddle us, didn't he?'

'I know,' agreed Jimmy. 'Diddling a couple of hard working kids, disgusting that!' They both burst into gales of laughter as they ran to Mrs Barrett's sweetshop and thence to follow the fortunes of Flash Gordon, Hopalong Cassidy, and the Three Stooges.

Dorothy watched guiltily through the bedroom window at Jimmy knocking on Vera Bateson's door and willed her to give him an empty jar. When Mrs Bateson shook her head and closed the door on a disappointed Jimmy, she burst into absurd tears.

She was letting them down. No matter how hard she tried. That business at the Thrift Stores was typical of her. All she had to do was keep her nose clean and she'd have been made manager. If she had, Ethel Styren would have gone, that's for sure. She'd a good mind to write to the Thrift Stores Head Office and tell them it was a put up job just so Harry and Ethel could keep their jobs. It probably wouldn't do any good though. Her word against theirs. She'd have to lie through her teeth to get away with it and she was no good at lying. Honesty is the best policy, that's what they say.

From now on she'd be honest Dorothy Bairstow – and she'd make damn sure the kids followed suit. The thought of having to clean for Mrs Oldfield again next week, and whatever other jobs she could pick up, depressed her even more. Jimmy and Susan came noisily into the house rattling jam jars. Dorothy daren't go down because she knew she'd weaken and give them their pocket money out of the rent tin. Not that it'd make any difference. The fifteen shillings in the tin wouldn't make it till Thursday anyway. God knows what was going to happen if she didn't get some more money coming in.

When Jimmy and Susan came in late that afternoon they didn't tell Auntie Dorothy precisely how they'd made the money to go to the pictures. They knew she wouldn't approve. She'd already told them all about what happened at the Thrift Stores, including the little plan that Harry and Ethel had cooked up between them. In a way, confessing the truth to them did her no harm at all, as the kids embellished the story very much in her favour and spread it all around the neighbourhood, prompting many sympathisers to boycott the Thrift Stores in favour of the newly opened Co-op.

'You managed it then,' she smiled, giving them both an embarrassingly long hug.

'Yes, we er, we went to another street,' explained Susan.

'Oh dear, I thought that wasn't allowed. I hope you won't get into any trouble.'

'We won't, Auntie,' Jimmy assured her. 'What's for tea?'

'I thought we'd have beans and spam.'

Jimmy nearly said, *what again*? But was stopped by a glare from Susan. The menu was becoming very limited lately and consisted largely of potatoes done in a variety of ways. Bread, untoasted or toasted on a fork by the fire. Tinned soup, tinned beans, spam and the very occasional egg.

'It's daft, is this,' complained Jimmy, later that evening, as they sat on the attic steps. 'We'll have ter tell her about our diamond rings.'

'You know what she said about not being honest. It cost her her job at the Thrift. That's why we're in the state we're in. If we tell her about the rings she'll most probably tell us to hand them in.'

Jimmy nodded, she was right.

'Tell you what,' went on his sister. 'If things don't get better between now and Christmas I'll try and sell one myself.'

'You? You heard what Freddie said. They'll be suspicious if a scruffy kid goes into a shop with an expensive diamond ring and tries to flog it.'

'Maybe, maybe not,' smiled Susan mysteriously. She wasn't happy at selling her engagement ring – still, maybe it wouldn't be necessary, there were *two* rings after all.

The rent didn't get paid that Thursday. At the usual rent collecting time the lights were turned out and everyone sat in the dark, waiting for Mr Simpson's very individual knock, one loud, two soft, three loud. Jimmy and Susan saw the funny side of this and Dorothy was constantly shushing them lest they were heard. She held her hand across Jimmy's mouth when the knock came. When he got no response Mr Simpson knocked again in reverse order. Three loud, two soft, one loud. Dorothy kept her hand firmly in place until she heard Simpson's footsteps leave the back yard and the gate slam angrily behind him.

On being released Jimmy exploded into muffled hysterics setting his sister and auntie off as well. They left it another half an hour until the landlord had collected his other rents in the street, then switched the lights back on. Dorothy smiled at the two giggling youngsters – but she knew it couldn't go on.

Neville Simpson knew she was in. He could have called back later and doubtless found the lights on, but he had other plans for Dorothy Bairstow. Neville was due to get married next year and his bride-to-be, Maggie Newton, of the 'Newton's the Butcher' family, was determined to be a virgin on her wedding night. This was causing Neville no end of frustration and he needed a spot of occasional relief to see him safely through to his wedding day. Vera Bateson was currently performing this service for him, but she was looking a bit haggard nowadays and Neville had his eye on someone far more attractive. The following week he called early and gave a different knock. Dorothy's face when she opened the door told him all he wanted to know.

'Good evening, Mrs Bairstow, I seemed to have missed you last week, so that'll be two weeks . . .' He said all this without looking up, his face studying his rent account book. Dorothy stood there, not knowing what to say. Neville looked up and smiled innocently.

'Is there a problem, Mrs Bairstow?'

Dorothy looked nervously at him. He was an unhealthy-looking man with a pale complexion and bushy ginger hair, and a nose that had been broken and badly set. She often wondered why he'd never been called up. He was the right age, probably not much older than her. His dad owned the business, but old Mr Simpson, who was much more of a gentleman than his son, never came round any more.

'I er, I was wondering if I could give you double next week,' said Dorothy nervously.

'That'd be treble actually – forty-five shillings. Are you sure you'll be able to manage that next week?' He was still smiling, but his teeth were yellow and crooked and his breath wasn't exactly fragrant. 'Look, may I come in?' he asked. 'We might be able to sort this out another way.'

Dorothy stood back from the door to let him pass. He put his account book down on the table and turned to face her. She was even better looking close up, in a tired sort of way. A lot better looking than Maggie Newton; still, he wasn't marrying Maggie Newton for her looks. He glanced around.

'Are the children in?'

'No, they're out playing.'

'Good – look, I'll get straight to the point, Dorothy.' He hesitated, 'Can I call you Dorothy?'

She nodded, at a loss to know what was happening.

'The truth of the matter is,' he went on, 'that you can't pay the rent. Nor will you be able to in the near future – not until you get another job. Am I making sense so far?'

Dorothy shrugged her agreement, she hadn't a clue what he was on about.

'You're a fine-looking woman, Dorothy, and many women in your position would take desperate steps in order to take care of their family.' Neville paused, needing to choose his words carefully. 'Some women would even sink to going on the streets.' He held up his hand as he saw Dorothy was about to intervene. 'Now – I wouldn't dream of suggesting that you'd sink so low – but if someone came along with, say, a private arrangement. Once a week say, in lieu of rent – something like that. How would you feel about it?'

His face was flushed with an almost orgasmic excitement at having made such a proposition. Dorothy was flushed with anger.

'You dirty-minded bastard! You want me to have it off with you to pay the rent? I'd beg on the bloody streets first. Get out of this bloody house, you filthy pervert! Good God! If your father knew what you were up to he'd have a heart attack!' She picked up his accounts book and threw it at him.

Neville backed out of the house, aghast at her reaction. As he went out of the door he turned and shouted nastily, 'Forty-five shillings next week, or notice to quit!'

Kicking the door shut behind him, she continued to vent her anger and despair on it until a crack appeared in the bottom panel. Then she sat down at the kitchen table and dissolved into floods of tears.

Dorothy had deliberately removed all her make-up and tied back the shining auburn hair which usually cascaded down over her slim shoulders. She'd taken Mrs Crombie up on a long-standing invitation to have Jimmy and Susan round for tea. So Dorothy was alone when the knock came on the door the following Thursday. Neville stood there, uncertain of his reception. Dorothy said nothing.

'Well?' he asked. 'Have you got it?'

She shook her head.

He took a piece of paper from his pocket and handed it to her. 'Notice to quit,' he said without emotion. 'You've got a week.'

Dorothy took a deep breath. 'You'd better come in,' she said dully.

A half-smile of elation crossed his face. Things seemed to be going his way. Without saying another word to him, she led the way to the stairs, pausing to make sure he was following her. He needed no further hints. Hers was the front bedroom. The one she'd shared with Tommy, whose photograph was turned face down on the dressing table. The curtains were already drawn, to prevent neighbours putting two and two together. She didn't turn the light on for the same reason, but it was early evening and the thin curtains let in sufficient light for them to see by. There were no bedclothes on the bed, just two large bath towels covering the mattress. Dorothy had thought about nothing else all week. Trying to come up with an alternative. But there was no alternative. If she lost the house the kids would be taken into care and she'd end up in lodgings.

Neville sat on the only chair in the room and stared at her, making her feel uncomfortable.

'What would you like me to do?' she asked uncertainly, trying to detach herself from the reality of the situation.

'Well, I, er – I'd like you to get undressed, please,' he replied hoarsely. Not quite believing she would actually do as he requested.

She kicked off her shoes then turned her back to him and slipped out of her blouse and skirt before sitting on the bed to unhook the stockings from her suspender belt. He made no move to start undressing himself, his breathing was quite audible now, tiny beads of sweat appearing on his forehead. Dorothy looked at him.

'What about you?' she asked. 'Are you just going to sit there?'

'Oh! R-right, y-yes,' he stammered. 'I er, I thought I'd let you go first.'

Having no make-up and severely tied back hair did little to hide the beauty underneath it all that had once turned Tommy Bairstow's head. Her figure was slightly fuller now, but still elegantly proportioned, statuesque even. Neville took a grimy handkerchief from his pocket and wiped his brow as Dorothy took a deep breath and stood up to finish what she had started. She turned her back to him once again.

'No, no,' he demanded. A desperate urgency creeping into his voice. 'Turn to face me. I want to see . . .'

She steeled herself and turned as he instructed, wishing for the first time in her life that she had an ugly body. Dorothy desperately wanted Simpson to be disappointed in what he saw. But she knew he wouldn't be. Reaching behind her back she nervously fumbled her brassière fastener, unhooking it at last. Then fixing her gaze at a point over his head, she very slowly, and with a tantalising reluctance, dropped her brassière, until her breasts were exposed to his lecherous gaze. She stood there for what seemed an age, trying to summon up the courage to take off her panties and knowing this awful man was drinking in every inch of her. Hooking her thumbs into the waistband, she inched them down with painful slowness, dreading the point at which she finally revealed herself to him. She lowered her gaze onto his sweating face as she finally let them drop to the floor. His eyes were transfixed between her legs as though he'd never seen a naked woman before.

And he'd certainly never seen one this beautiful.

Dorothy stood there facing him for a moment, hands on hips, almost defiantly, then lay down on one side of the bed and stared blankly up at the ceiling.

She heard him stand up, fumbling with his buttons. His breathing becoming increasingly heavy now. Dorothy expected him to get on the other side of the bed and was mildly surprised to see him standing over her. His naked body was unusually pale and without the vaguest hint of muscular definition. His was the body of a man who'd never done a hard day's work in his life. She turned her head away from the stink of his perspiration as he placed a damp hand on her breast, causing her to cringe with revulsion. His other hand went on to her stomach, then moved slowly down between her thighs. She instinctively brought her legs together and trapped his hand there, preventing any move-ment. Then she looked up into the sweating face of this foulest of men.

'Mr Simpson,' she asked quietly, but with barely concealed disgust. Deliberately using his surname to maintain some sort of incongruous formality. 'After, after this, I won't owe you anything – will I?'

He nodded vigorously. 'Oh no!' he gasped. 'Nothing at all – we're definitely quits after this.'

She relaxed her grip and prepared herself for the worst, closing her eyes and trying to imagine what the kids would be having for tea at Mrs Crombie's. He climbed onto the bed and knelt between her legs, forcing her thighs apart with his knees until she was concealing nothing from him. Suddenly he let out a loud moan and she felt a warm spattering on her breasts and stomach. She opened her eyes and saw that Neville was finished – no longer a threat to her.

He looked embarrassed, he even apologised. 'Sorry about that, I'll, er – well, yer know.' He got off the bed and turned his bony backside to her. Picking up his underpants and hopping comically on one leg as tried to get them on. Dorothy took the towel from the other side of the bed and quickly wiped him off her, then covered herself up until Neville was dressed. He left her there, saying something about same time next week but Dorothy didn't hear him, she was already crying quietly. Consumed with self-loathing. She couldn't do it again.

But she knew she must.

As soon as she heard the door close behind him she hurried downstairs, still naked, and slammed on the bolt, cursing loudly at this disgusting man she was locking out. She yanked off the wooden board covering the bath and threw it tearfully on the scullery floor; then turned on the taps and sat weeping in the bath as it filled up around her.

She was still there an hour later when Jimmy and Susan banged on the door asking to come in.

Chapter Nine

The jam jar scam was paying dividends for Jimmy and Susan, who'd taken another two dozen back the following Saturday and once again the jovial jam jar man had complimented them on their spotless product. He held one up to the light.

'Just look at that! Hardly need put 'em through our washers, keep 'em coming, I wish we had more kids like you.'

Jimmy and Susan took this compliment with a modesty and good grace that further impressed the man. Sunday morning was the best time to acquire the jars. The factory closed on a Sunday and an early morning expedition before ten o'clock mass was all too easy. Susan had already mentioned stealing jam jars in confession, but Father O'Flaherty had dismissed it as a third-rate venial sin, worthy of only two Hail Marys. Perhaps if she'd filled him in with details of the whole scam, her penance might have been more severe. She made up her mind to make her next confession to Father Proctor, no point boring Father O'Flaherty with the same old sin every time. She hadn't mentioned the ring yet, as she hadn't actually stolen it.

If Dorothy was pleased at them providing their own pocket money, she didn't seem to show it. Since losing her job at the Thrift Stores, she'd become more and more withdrawn. Snapping at them like she used to in the early days. Even raising her hand to Jimmy on one occasion, before withdrawing it and running out of the room and up the stairs. They'd been for tea at Jackie and Maureen Crombie's and had had to wait outside for ten minutes while she got out of the bath. Jimmy hadn't grumbled much, not enough to merit her nearly hitting him. They didn't need to listen at the bottom of the stairs to know she was crying. They looked at each other and shrugged helplessly.

'Wish we had a grandma and grandad like Jackie Crombie,' said Jimmy wistfully. 'I bet it's great having a grandma and grandad.'

'We might have for all we know,' said Susan. 'Dad's mam and dad are both dead, but me mam never knew who her mam and dad were. They might be still alive for all we know.'

'I hope they are. Did me mam ever tell you what happened?'

'Just that she were put in a home when she was a baby.'

'That's rotten that is,' muttered Jimmy. 'They can't be very nice people then – to do that, can they?'

'Maybe, maybe not. We don't know what the circumstances were. That's what me mam said.'

'Oh, yeah, that's right, we don't, do we?' accepted Jimmy, who knew what Mam said was always right.

'Do you know what we ought to do to cheer Auntie Dorothy up?' decided Susan, before going on to answer her own question. 'Pay next week's rent, that'd cheer her up no end.'

'That's fifteen bob! Where we goin' ter ger fifteen bob from?'

'Where'd you think?' grinned his sister.

'We can't take fifteen bob's worth of jam jars back – that's,' he began a mental calculation that Susan beat him to by a split second.

'A hundred and eighty,' she said triumphantly. 'If we really fill up our shopping bag, we can probably get thirty in – that's er,' she stopped to think for another couple of seconds, 'six trips. Easy.'

'They're bound ter get suspicious if we take all them back at once.'

Susan considered this then said brightly, 'Ah! – but we don't take 'em back at once, do we? What we do, next Sunday we get a hundred and eighty jam jars, we'll take a shopping bag each and make three trips. Then we'll hide them in the cellar like we have been doing and take them back next week, one bag each a night. First you go, then I go. We've only got to do it for three nights and we've got our fifteen bob.'

So the plot was hatched there and then. The fact that a variety of different personnel manned the empties counter during the week helped allay any suspicion and by Wednesday evening they had a bagful of change adding up to the magic figure of fifteen shillings. Mrs Crombie changed it into a ten shilling note and two half crowns, so the presentation could be made properly.

Dorothy came in from doing for Mrs Oldfield the following afternoon and sank gratefully into a chair. It was Thursday and Simpson would be round again. She intended telling him it was the wrong time of the month and could he come back next week. No man ever argued with that. Jimmy and Susan were already home, having both made a special effort to get back quickly. A steaming cup of tea appeared and their auntie accepted it suspiciously.

'Come on,' she demanded, 'what have you been up to?'

'Nowt,' protested an affronted Jimmy. 'We haven't been up ter nowt, have we, Susan?'

'We have actually,' admitted his sister.

'I thought so, come on, what is it?'

'Well,' said Susan, smirking at her grinning brother. 'You know we've been collecting jam jars?'

Dorothy's eyes narrowed. 'Yeess, I know you've been collecting jam jars – what's the problem?'

Jimmy couldn't contain himself any longer, 'We've got yer rent money!' he blurted, much to Susan's annoyance; he was always doing this.

'What?' exclaimed Dorothy.

'We've got this week's rent money,' repeated Susan, handing her auntie the fifteen shillings. Dorothy looked down at the money in shocked surprise.

'But how? How did you? Good grief!' She sank her head between her hands and stayed like that for a long time.

'Are you alright, Auntie?' asked a concerned Jimmy, who swore he would never understand grown-ups.

Dorothy nodded from where she was, not wanting the children to see her tears. They approached her from either side and, very tentatively, each put an arm around her shoulder.

'I'm sorry,' she sobbed. 'Don't think I'm not grateful. You must have gone to an enormous amount of trouble to do this for me. It's just that – well, I don't seem to be able to do much for you.'

'You look after us,' argued Susan kindly.

'After a fashion I do,' she lifted her head and wiped away her tears on her sleeve. 'I sometimes think you deserve a lot better than me.'

'Would yer like us to go out an' play?' asked Jimmy, who was not without tact at times like this.

Dorothy nodded. A knock came at the door and she looked up with a worried start. Susan ran to answer it, as though she knew who it would be. Ray stood there awkwardly, it was the first time he'd called on Susan. It was actually the first time he'd called on any girl.

'Oh, hiya, Ray,' she greeted. 'Auntie, I'm going out with Ray, I'll be back about si ...' She grimaced at Ray as her aunt interrupted her.

'Bring him in then, let's have a look at him.'

An embarrassed Ray entered the kitchen and presented himself for inspection. He was tall and pleasant-looking with dark, tousled hair and the beginnings of acne. Dorothy nodded her approval.

'If only I was a couple of years younger,' she smiled. Then to Susan. 'Back about six then, have a nice time and ...' Susan looked back at her auntie who looked on the verge of tears again. 'Thanks.'

Jimmy followed his sister out, leaving Dorothy to her confused thoughts. She looked at the clock, ten to five. He'd be here in twenty minutes. At least she wouldn't have to go through *that* again. Just pay him the rent and use the time of the month excuse next week and maybe even the week after. And then? Well, half an hour's unpleasantness for forty-five shillings. It seemed daft *not* to do it when she put it like that to herself. But it wasn't as easy as that, and she knew it.

He was late. It was nearly half-past. She wouldn't have been able to accommodate him anyway, with the kids coming in for their tea in half an hour. The knock came. Same stupid knock. She opened the door and he stood there grinning and holding out a pathetic bunch of chrysanthemums.

'Here,' he said. 'Gotcha some flow ... errs.'

'Oh, God,' she thought. 'The pig's drunk, just what I need.' She stood back to let him through and took the rent money out of her pocket.

'I've got the rent,' she said. He looked down at the money, stupidly.

'What? W-hat yer taking about? I haven't come for the rent.' He made to grab her but she took a quick backward step, positioning a dining chair between her and him.

'I don't want to do it, just take the rent and go, please.'

He didn't seem to hear her. 'I've had a little drink,' he explained, 'to make me last longer. Don't want a repeat of last week, do we?' He sniggered to himself as he took off his coat and threw it on the settee.

Dorothy thrust the money at him angrily. 'There won't be a repeat of last week because I'm not doing it,' she shouted. 'Just take your bloody rent and go!'

Her anger had a sobering effect on him. Realisation sinking in. 'Wotcha talking' about, yer stupid cow? Course we're doin' it again. That's what we agreed last week. Anyway I didn't get me money's worth last week. Shot me load before I got it in.' He grabbed hold of the chair Dorothy was using for protection and snatched it away from her, flinging it across the room, his drink-sodden eyes fixed excitedly on hers, advancing on her until she was backed up against the wall. She tried to push him away but he grabbed at her blouse, tearing it open, then pulled viciously at her brassière, exposing one of her breasts, his fingernails leaving livid scratches. Dorothy was frightened.

'Come here, yer whore!' snarled Neville.' I want me money's worth. Three pounds you owe and I want it out of your body, here and now!'

'But – but how can I owe three pounds after last week? You said we were quits, you got what you wanted. Please leave me alone,' begged Dorothy, crying now.

'Quits, my arse!' he roared. 'I want me three quid or I want you!'

The door opened and Susan stood there horrified at the sight of her Auntie Dorothy, blouse ripped open, being attacked by the landlord. Neville turned and leered at her. He released his grip on Dorothy and advanced on Susan.

'Your auntie doesn't want to play today – but why should I settle for mutton when there's a nice bit of lamb on offer?'

He made a drunken grab for Susan, who was taken completely by surprise and failed to get out of the way in time. She fell to the floor, taking Neville with her. He laughed at their predicament, belched loudly and tried to force himself on the terrified girl, kneeling over her as he attempted to unbuckle his belt. Dorothy felt a crimson rage envelop her. She picked up the piano stool and smashed him across the back with it, weeping with fear and fury.

He half stood up and turned, as if to see who was hitting him. The pure hatred on Dorothy's face provoking fear on his. He staggered to his feet, backed out of the door and ran into the street, chased by an hysterical Dorothy, desperately trying to land just one telling blow with the stool.

'You filthy perverted bastard, I'll kill you for that,' she screamed.

Constable Greenough couldn't have chosen a more opportune moment to be passing the end of the street. Or *in*opportune, depending upon your point of view. The sudden violent screaming giving him quite a start. He looked down the street and saw a terrified man emerge from a back yard, closely followed by screaming woman. He couldn't believe what he was seeing. It was Tommy's widow, Dorothy Bairstow, unless he was very much mistaken. Alan Greenough had been a good friend of Fred and Tommy and he always thought Dorothy was a sophisticated sort of woman. A bit too classy for Tommy in a way. But she looked far from classy now, her blouse ripped open, and even from this distance he could see her naked breasts.

'I'll kill you, I'll kill you!' she was screaming.

The terrified man stumbled, his arm coming up a fraction too late to ward off the stool, arching vengefully down onto his head and smashing into it with a sickening thud. P.C. Greenough winced. The man collapsed, blood pouring from a gash in his skull. Dorothy dropped the stool from her trembling hands, mortified at what she had done. Susan came running out and flung her arms around her auntie as they both looked down, horror-stricken at the lifeless-looking form of Neville Simpson.

Chapter Ten

Jimmy was just rounding the corner into the street when he was almost knocked down by Jackie Crombie, desperate to herald the news of Simpson's demise to the neighbourhood.

'Yer auntie's just murdered Simmo,' he gasped happily. 'She brayed him with a stool – yer should've seen it. She didn't half fetch him a bleedin' clout! There's blood all over t' street!'

Jackie had no time to elaborate further, he dashed down Paradine Hill, pausing here and there to breathlessly deliver his increasingly gory news. A crowd had gathered by the time the ambulance came. P.C. Greenough was bending over the still figure of Neville Simpson and a second constable was standing by a pale and dazed looking Dorothy, with a firm grip on her arm. Susan stood nearby, crying and being comforted by Mrs Veitch. No one could make any sense out of what had happened.

Jimmy watched horrified as his Auntie Dorothy was led away and taken the short distance to Paradine Hill Police Station, watched by many a curious eye, and with wild speculation hurrying from mouth to mouth. The ambulance came and went, with lights flashing and bell ringing, followed by Jackie Crombie, a dozen other whooping children and two barking dogs. Simpson was still alive but he didn't look too good and in the opinion of most onlookers in the know, 'It's only a question of time.' Constable Greenough took Susan back into the house to take a statement and Jimmy followed them in. The policeman looked up at the shocked boy standing quietly in the doorway.

'Do you think you could make us all a cup of tea, son?' he asked kindly.

Jimmy nodded. Things couldn't be too bad if the police could still think about mundane things like tea. He busied himself in the scullery, listening carefully to what his sister had to say.

It was hard to make her out through the sobs. But what he did hear made him angry beyond his years. Susan and P.C. Greenough sat opposite each other at the table, the policeman licking a thumb to open a stubborn page of his notebook. 'What exactly did you see when you came in?' he asked gently.

'He was shouting and swearing and pulling at Auntie Dorothy's clothes – and Auntie Dorothy was crying, and I think he was drunk, and then—' Susan stopped to regain her composure.

'Take your time, Susan, there's no rush. I just want to get it all down while it's still fresh in your memory.'

The policeman turned to Jimmy who was pouring out the cups of tea, unsure why his hand was shaking so much.

'Thanks Jimmy,' he said, taking two cups and giving one to Susan. 'Right, love, in your own time, what happened after that?'

Susan took a deep breath and continued. 'He came after me! He knocked me down. I was struggling, I couldn't move and he was laughing at me and . . .' She paused and looked across at Jimmy, wishing he wasn't listening to this. 'And he was trying to get his trousers off – and Auntie Dorothy hit him with a stool and he got up and ran out and . . .' Susan's words flooded out in a tearful torrent, halted only by the sound of Jimmy dropping his cup in anger, causing the other two to turn round. Susan was the person closest to him in the whole world although he would be loath to admit it.

'Auntie Dorothy did right,' he blurted. 'I hope the bloody bastard's dead!'

He ran past them and sat on the stairs to plan his vengeance on Simpson, who he hoped would survive in order to suffer whatever Jimmy had in store for him.

There was a knock on the back door and he heard P.C. Greenough talking to a man called Sackfield. He was asking after Auntie Dorothy and would she pop in see him as soon as she'd got the time.

'Do you mind if I ask what it's about?' asked the constable.

'Er – yes. I came to offer her a job – if she's still interested.'

As he left he was passed in the yard by Mrs Veitch who was promising to keep an eye on the children until Dorothy came home from the police station.

'It might not be tonight,' warned the constable.

'That's alright, we'll manage,' Mrs Veitch assured him.

P.C. Greenough went off with a feeling of dread inside him. He'd have to tell the story as he saw it, and what he saw was Simpson running away from Dorothy and her attacking him. He firmly believed Susan's side of the story, but facts were facts, and it was Simpson who was lying in hospital not Dorothy.

Dorothy didn't hear the cell door slam shut behind her. She didn't hear the custody sergeant ask her name and address. The accompanying constable had to help out on that one.

The mattress on the cell bed was hard but it suited her just fine. She didn't want to be comfortable. Her mind was swimming with a mixture of different awful images. Of *him* watching her get undressed, of *him* kneeling over her naked body. Then kneeling over Susan, then lying in the street with blood gushing from his head. But what she'd done hadn't purged her hatred of him. She needed to know he was dead. Or was it herself she hated for taking this loathsome creature into her bed? The bed she'd shared with her lovely Tommy. She was little more than a common prostitute. She sobbed well into the night before falling into a disturbed sleep.

The cell door clanged open early the next morning and an unpleasant-looking policewoman came in. Or rather she wobbled in with the knock-kneed gait of the unathletic obese. An outsize woman with two chins, a wispy moustache and a cup of tea which she placed sloppily on the floor beside the bed. Any fleeing villain would have little difficulty escaping this officer's pursuit. Dorothy awoke suddenly, completely disorientated. Then she remembered where she was and why, and a cloud of despondency enveloped her. The policewoman, who had seen this happen before, found it oh so amusing.

'Forgot where you were, dear?' she smirked. 'Thought you were at home in your nice warm bed snuggled up to your husband?'

She turned to leave then had another thought. 'Oh, by the way. Simpson's still alive but not expected to live, so with a bit of luck we've got a murderess on our hands. Don't think we've ever had a murderess down at Paradine before.'

Dorothy hurled her tea at the grinning policewoman, the cup

smashing on the cell door. 'Get out, you stupid bloody woman,' she screamed. 'Just, just get out!'

She wanted to think of something clever to say to wipe the silly smile off that woman's face. But she couldn't. The policewoman left, silly smile intact, locking the cell door on a tearful Dorothy. She opened the hatch in the cell door to fire in one final shot.

'By the way, if you're hoping to get bail this morning, keep hoping, but it won't do you any good. Magistrates never let mad women like you loose on the streets!'

'Why don't you get a shave, you fat freak!' was all Dorothy could manage in return. It had the desired effect, although Dorothy couldn't tell from where she was.

Mrs Veitch knocked on the door early. Jimmy and Susan were already up, debating whether or not to go to school.

'Best place for you,' insisted Mrs Veitch. 'Your auntie's up in court this morning, most likely she'll get bail. Probably be home by the time you get back.'

The children nodded at the logic of this. With a bit of luck the news wouldn't have reached school so at least they'd be out of the way of idle gossip.

They couldn't have been more wrong. St Winifred's was rife with rumour. The story of a rent man being beaten up by a mere woman went down well at a girls' school and by lunchtime Dorothy was being hailed as a heroine of the working classes, much the predominant class at St Winifred's.

Jimmy didn't fare quite so well. Scoggy Andrews and his pals from 2A had always looked down on the inferior beings from 2B, Jimmy included. The taunting began at morning break.

'Hey! Bairstow! Can yer get us tickets to yer auntie's hanging?'

Jimmy knew if he reacted he'd finish off second best. He walked away followed by the baying mob. Scoggy ran in front of him and pretended to have a noose around his neck, choking and lolling his tongue out. Jimmy wished he were bigger and stronger. Scoggy Andrews' nose was just waiting to be hit. If he could just get one clean blow in, then run, he might just get away with it. Running was something he was good at.

Then Scoggy overstepped the mark. 'Hey, Bairstow! When yer auntie kicks the bucket there'll be nobody left in your family. D'yer think God's trying ter tell yer summat?'

Jimmy's fist exploded on the end of his tormentor's nose. Every ounce of strength in his puny body went into that one venomous blow and Jimmy was a lot stronger than he looked. Scoggy yelped in pain as blood poured from his nose and obscenities from his mouth. Jimmy was already much too far away to hear any of this but unfortunately for Scoggy, Father Leitrim on one of his playground profanity patrols, did.

Dragging the shocked Scoggy by the scruff of his neck, the hard-faced priest took him away for the appropriate punishment. Bad language at St Thomas's was the language of the devil and must be mercilessly beaten out of any boy using it. And Jimmy knew that for once, justice was being done.

But today, the fortunes of the Bairstow family were mixed.

An ashen-faced Dorothy ascended the steps leading to the dock of Court Number Three in Leeds Town hall. She looked across the courtroom and recognised the sympathetic faces of Valerie Veitch and Mrs Crombie. She found herself racking her brains to remember Mrs Crombie's first name and her confused mind was still running through the alphabet when a clerk appeared with a Bible for her to swear on.

Alan Greenough was nowhere to be seen. He'd told her in the Black Maria on the way that he didn't think the police would be opposing bail. 'Most of the lads down at Paradine are on your side,' he'd assured her out of the side of his mouth lest the other travelling felons heard.

The charge was read out by a short, bilious-looking man in a black gown with a huge tear in it. The magistrate in the middle of the bench stared across at her as though she were some unpleasant kind of life form.

'Dorothy Anne Bairstow. You are charged with Attempted Murder, how do you plead?'

It sounded so much more than it was, she'd only clonked Simpson over the head with a stool. They made it sound as though she'd hacked him up with a machete.

'Not guilty, sir,' her voice was barely audible.

'Could you speak up, Mrs Bairstow?'

'Not guilty, sir,' she almost shouted this time.

'Mr Mitchell?' The magistrate in the centre looked over his glasses at the prosecuting solicitor. 'Do we have a case to answer?'

'Yes, sir, I wish to call P.C. Greenough to the stand.'

Alan Greenough walked briskly into the court, scarcely looking at Dorothy, and took the oath.

'Constable Greenough,' inquired Mitchell. 'Where were you at five-thirty on the evening of Thursday the fourteenth of November nineteen-forty-five?'

Alan Greenough took a notebook from the top pocket of his uniform. 'I was on foot patrol up Paradine Hill, sir.'

'Did you pass the end of Broughton Terrace?'

'Yes, sir.'

'And did you see anything unusual going on?'

'Yes, sir. I saw Dorothy,' he grimaced to himself at this unprofessional slip up, 'I mean Mrs Bairstow – chasing a man out into the street.' He stopped and looked across at Dorothy, then lowered his eyes to his notebook.

'Carry on, Constable Greenough,' insisted Mitchell.

'She looked very distressed, her blouse was torn and her . . .' he gave a dry, embarrassed cough. 'And her breasts were exposed!'

'Was she carrying anything?'

'Yes, sir, she had a piano stool in her hands.'

'Piano stool! That would be quite a heavy stool, would it not?'

'I imagine so, sir.'

'Go on, what happened then?'

'The man tripped and fell to the ground.'

'This man – was he acting in any way aggressively towards Mrs Bairstow?'

'Er, well, no, sir.'

'Did he look frightened?'

'Yes, sir.'

'Tell me what happened then, Constable Greenough.'

'Well, sir, she raised the stool in the air and struck him with it.'

'How many times?'

'Oh, only the once, sir,' Alan assured him earnestly, this being the only thing he'd said which went in Dorothy's favour.

'Was it a violent blow?'

Alan took a deep breath before saying, 'Yes, sir, quite violent.'

'Enough to kill a man?'

'Depends, sir.'

Mitchell ignored Alan's fudging, sensing he was on Dorothy's side. 'And was she shouting anything as she struck him?'

Alan's face dropped again. 'Yes, sir.' He looked across at Dorothy again and shrugged apologetically. 'She said she'd kill him!'

'Thank you, constable, that's all we need to know.' Mitchell sat down, well pleased with himself.

The magistrate looked down at Dorothy's solicitor. 'Do you have anything to ask this witness, Mr er . . .'

'Baldwin, sir, No, sir, I've nothing to ask the witness but I would like to explain to the court as to why my client acted in a manner totally out of character.'

'You may proceed, Mr Baldwin.'

'The reason my client's breasts were exposed was because the alleged victim had been attempting to rape not only her but also her niece who chanced to walk in on the incident.'

Mitchell sprang to his feet. 'It is the view of the prosecution that no rape was intended. The accused, having been caught in an act of promiscuity with my client by her niece, decided to recover her reputation by accusing him of rape.'

'And is this niece in court?'

'No, sir, she is not.'

'Pity.'

Dorothy had been adamant that Susan didn't become involved at this stage. She could say her piece when the matter came to trial.

The magistrates withdrew and reappeared ten minutes later to announce that the case was to be referred to the Assizes, to be heard in the new year at a date to be decided. This was of little concern to Dorothy who had a naïve faith in the British legal system and was convinced that when they heard her side of things she'd be found innocent.

Her solicitor stepped forward to apply for bail. He looked across at her and gave a reassuring smile that told her all was well, for the time being at least. The magistrate looked across at the prosecuting solicitor who was whispering to a uniformed police inspector who had just walked in the court.

'Is there a problem with bail, Mr Mitchell?' asked the magistrate.

'Yes, sir,' replied the prosecuting solicitor. 'We've just heard from the hospital that the victim has taken a turn for the worse and may not recover. The implication being that a more serious charge may be brought against Mrs Bairstow and in view of this we wish to oppose bail.'

'Do you really, Mr Mitchell?' mused the magistrate.

Dorothy's heart stopped. Surely there'd been some mistake. She looked pleadingly across at her solicitor who gave a helpless shrug. It was for the magistrates to decide, not him. He made one final plea.

'In view of the fact that it is my client who is the victim in all this, might I suggest that she is scarcely a danger to the public and hardly likely to run away from being tried for a crime she did not commit.'

The magistrate accepted his plea with a curt nod and leaned over in turn to his colleagues for their contribution. A series of nods followed as they coldly discussed Dorothy's immediate destiny. Her eyes were glued ferociously on them for any clues as to the outcome. Their eyes in turn looked studiously away from her as they came to their decision.

'In view of the potential seriousness of the crime, the court refuses bail. Take her away.'

The silence was replaced by a steady murmur as the court callously prepared itself for the next case.

Take her away. The finality of it staggered Dorothy. How could three ridiculous old duffers just have her *taken away*. Where to, for God's sake? It hadn't even been discussed. In desperation she ripped open her blouse and thrust her breasts towards the bench. The livid scratch marks that Simpson had left could be seen clearly across the court. The murmuring halted abruptly as every eye in the court was fixed on Dorothy's magnificent chest.

'Look at this!' she screamed defiantly. 'This isn't promiscuity, you idiots! This is rape!'

'You tell 'em, Dorothy love!' shouted Mrs Crombie.

'Nice tits, missis!' shouted a grinning, unkempt spectator from the back of the court, shortly before Alan Greenough led him unceremoniously out of the door.

The two policemen on either side of Dorothy stepped forward in unison and pinned her arms to her sides, spinning her round, and hurried her back down the steps to the cell that, only a few minutes ago, she'd thankfully vacated for what she thought was the last time.

Mrs Veitch and Mrs Crombie were still sitting at the back as the crowded court emptied. The clerk was reading out the next case. Drunk and disorderly. 'How do you plead?' – 'Guilty, yer Honour' – 'Fined five pounds and bound over to keep the peace.' It all seemed so insignificant compared to what had happened to their friend who didn't even belong amongst the riff-raff passing through this place. And what would happen to the children? No one had mentioned that. It was as if the court didn't know about them.

'Don't worry about the kids,' Mrs Crombie had yelled as they took her away. 'We'll keep an eye on 'em!'

Dorothy had looked across at her and seemed to nod her thanks before disappearing downwards.

'I should button your blouse up, Mrs Bairstow.'

The voice was Alan Greenough's who'd followed down to the cells. Still in a tearful daze, she took his advice.

'What are they going to do to me?' she said quietly, as she fumbled with the buttons. She sounded so helpless, like a small schoolgirl. 'What's happening to me?'

Alan Greenough turned sadly away. Nothing he could do or say would help. She was in for a hard time and how she survived it was up to her. Not for the first time in his life he was disillusioned with the justice system he had sworn to uphold.

There were six of them in the Black Maria bound for Ashinghurst Women's prison just outside Wakefield. Four convicted criminals and two prison officers, one male, one female. Dorothy was handcuffed to a brazen-looking young woman who spat on the floor as she entered the vehicle, narrowly missing the boots of another prisoner already seated.

'Watch it, yer slag,' snarled the seated prisoner. A mountainous woman with close-cropped hair and startling white teeth which seemed at odds with the rest of her.

Dorothy's handcuffed companion grinned at the woman. 'As I live an' bleedin' breathe, it's Dildo Delma the Drighlington Dyke. Who'd nick yer new gnashers off, Delma? Trigger the fucking Wonder 'orse?'

Dorothy's short time in captivity was beginning to inure her to such language and she made a mental resolution not to allow these words to creep into her own vocabulary.

'That's enough of that, you two,' grunted one of the female warders. 'I'm not at me best today so we'll have a nice restful journey. I'm sure neither of you want to pick up a black mark before we get there.'

An innocent sounding threat, but enough to shut these two aggressive women up – for the time being at least. After a while, her handcuffed companion gave Dorothy a double take.

'First time?'

'Is it that obvious?'

'You could say that, darlin'. I'm Rita, Rita Doidge. Part-time prossie and failed fraudster.'

'Hello, Rita, I'm Dorothy Bairstow,' she returned politely, wondering if she should add her own criminal qualifications, but Attempted Murder had a certain incongruity to it when associated with her.

'I'll call you Dolly then.'

'Watcher in for, Dolly darlin'?' sneered Delma. 'Fartin' in church?' She laughed at her own joke and earned a second admonition from the warder.

'I hit a man over the head with a piano stool, he was trying to rape me and my niece. They think he might die.'

The last sentence earned Dorothy a certain kudos from two of her fellow prisoners.

'Serve the bastard right – I hope the bastard dies,' announced a small woman sitting at the other side of Rita. Her thin, tinny voice tailing off under the warder's glare.

'Don't talk so bloody stupid,' admonished Rita. 'If he dies, they could top our Dolly. An' we don't want our Dolly topped, do we, girls? – we've only just met her.'

Rita turned her attention to Delma. 'Did yer hear that, yer fat faggot? Did yer hear what our Dolly does ter them what tries it on with her? Better watch yer step with our Dolly, yer fat fu . . .'

'Quiet!' roared the warder.

'Sorry, Miss,' apologised Rita, who didn't sound sorry at all.

101

Chapter Eleven

Jackie Crombie was waiting at the end of the street as Jimmy and Susan walked up Paradine Hill together. His skinny, short-trousered white legs shivered inside a pair of Wellingtons, recently handed down from sister Maureen. Having two children of different sexes made a difference to the economy of the Crombie household insofar as they were limited as to what could be handed down from sister to brother. Although they didn't always let this stand in their way, as Maureen's old knickers were currently doubling as Jackie's underpants, adding to Jacky's dread of ever getting knocked down by a car. His eyes constantly blinked from behind a pair of circular glasses, one of the lenses having been covered up with elastoplast in order to bully his other 'lazy' eye into doing a bit more work. Jackie's dad had cut his hair the night before and Jimmy was eternally thankful that Auntie Dorothy hadn't taken Mr Crombie up on his kind offer to cut Jimmy's hair for nowt.

'There's only a week between a good hair cut and a bad 'un,' were the words which rang in Jackie's ears every time his father sent him out to brave the world with mutilated locks. In Jackie's case a month was nearer the mark, by which time his dad was at it again.

Jackie's mother had told him to keep his big mouth shut about their Auntie Dorothy, and just ask them to pop in and see her. But news such as this was just too much for Jackie to keep to himself.

'Hey! Yer auntie's bin sent ter prison!' he yelled, as though having an auntie sent to prison was something to be proud of.

'Jackie Crombie, if this is one of your stupid lies I'll . . .' Susan didn't finish her threat. She saw Mrs Crombie appear at her gate with an expression that told her Jackie was telling the truth for once. A beckoning arm ordered Jackie to come in.

'Jackie! What did I just tell you? Come in here, NOW!'

As her son ran past she gave him a well-timed clip behind his ear then looked up at Jimmy and Susan.

'You'd best come in.'

They followed her in to her house knowing full well what she had to tell them. Auntie Dorothy wasn't coming home.

'What's going to happen to us, Mrs Crombie?' asked Susan with an air of resigned practicality.

'I'm not going into one o' them homes,' announced Jimmy. Jackie agreed with him wholeheartedly.

'They lock yer up in cupboards and don't give yer nowt to eat for a week, just for giving 'em a bit of cheek,' declared this happy harbinger of doom and gloom.

His mother aimed another blow to his head, which he rode with practised ease.

'Next time!' she warned. 'And it's up ter bed, my lad, and no tea nor supper.'

Jackie sat back, not quite realising what he was doing wrong, but kept his mouth shut all the same. Mrs Crombie turned her attention back to Jimmy and Susan.

'Right, you can have a bit of tea with us tonight. Mrs Veitch is going to help out as well – and it's Saturday tomorrow, so we've all got the weekend to sort out what to do for the best.'

'Thanks Mrs Crombie,' said Susan.

'Yes, thanks, Mrs Crombie,' echoed Jimmy as he dashed out of the door with Jackie.

Mrs Crombie bustled about in the scullery as she shouted through to Susan. 'We'd have you to stay with us but it'd be a bit crowded.' She didn't see the look of relief on Susan's face. 'You see, you'd have to share with our Maureen but she's only got a single bed, same with our Jackie.'

'It's alright,' assured Susan. 'We'll not come to any harm in our house – and I am nearly sixteen.' She was hoping Mrs Crombie didn't know when her birthday was. 'You're old enough when you're sixteen, aren't you?'

She didn't explain what you were old enough for at sixteen, but Mrs Crombie nodded all the same. She glanced approvingly at the assured young lady sitting in her kitchen and fatuously hoped that her Maureen, a year Susan's junior, would turn out as well.

'Mrs Crombie,' said Susan quietly, 'you do know why Auntie Dorothy hit him, don't you?'

'I don't know the full story, love, but I could see from the state of your auntie what he'd been up to. He was drunk, wasn't he?'

'Yes ... he tried to attack me. That's what made Auntie Dorothy so mad.'

Mrs Crombie put a comforting arm around Susan. 'I know, lass. He's tried it on with a few round here that's been behind with their rents. I'm naming no names, but there's them what's let him get away with it as well. Vera Bateson for one. If her Len ever found out, he'd have finished him for sure!'

When it all comes out in court, do you think they'll let her come home?'

'Course they will,' consoled Mrs Crombie, who didn't believe it for a minute.

That evening Jimmy and Susan sat on the attic stairs. An overcoat around both their shoulders to ward out the biting November cold.

'You know what we've got to do, don't you?' said Susan. Jimmy nodded. 'Run away. Do you think Freddie will help?' Susan gave a faraway smile. The idea of Freddie helping appealed to her. A knight in shining armour would come in handy right now. But this was the real world. 'No, not run away,' she said. 'We've got to sell one of the rings to pay the rent. Whatever we do, we mustn't let ourselves be kicked out. There's got to be a house for Auntie Dorothy to come home to.'

'And for us to live in.' added Jimmy.

'That too. So we'll do it tomorrow.'

'Right ... g' night.'

'Where do you think you're going?'

'I'm off ter bed, where d'yer think I'm going?' asked a puzzled Jimmy.

'I think you're going to the cemetery with me. I can't get the rings on my own! If we're going to sell the things tomorrow, we'll have to get them tonight. There'll be too many people about in the morning.'

'Blimey! Sounds a bit creepy!'

'Course if you're too scared!' Susan knew she'd got him there.

'I never said I was scared!'

'Right then, let's get our coats on.'

Dorothy sat on the bottom bunk and viewed her surroundings with horror. A decorator might have had the temerity to call the colour of the painted brick walls Eau de Nil, the residents called it puke green which was nearer the mark. It was littered with pencilled graffiti, an indication of the intellect of previous inmates who'd passed through. It ranged from the chillingly obscene to the pathetic cry for help, to the witty, and to the illiterate – mostly the latter. During the day the cell was illuminated by a high window, small enough to merit just a single bar down the middle. In the evenings they would be lit by a dismal forty-watt light bulb diffused behind a rectangle of reinforced glass and controlled by some outside hand that threw them into darkness at two-minutes-to-eight each night, provoking complaints that they'd been switched off early. Every second of light being precious. The cell measured perhaps ten feet by seven and was home to two people. The door, which was mercifully left open during waking hours, was painted dysentery brown, presumably to complement the walls. It was made of steel with a small sliding hatch controlled only from the outside. The floors were tiled and hosed down daily and woe betide any inmate who left anything not waterproof on the floor.

Dorothy's eyes were constantly drawn to the seatless w.c. in the corner. No amount of bleach would ever remove the ingrained stains that caused the water to look permanently discoloured. A lever on the wall controlled the desultory flush which would only rarely completely remove the waste. Two consecutive flushes took several minutes.

'Rule number one,' announced Rita from the bunk above. 'No crappin' in the lavvie. Save yer solids for the bog block during the day.'

Unknown to Dorothy, the warders had deliberately placed her with Rita simply because they didn't want another suicide on their hands. All remand prisoners were taken back to court once a week and it was embarrassing to have to explain to a magistrate that another of their charges had committed suicide. As they viewed Dorothy as one such potential embarrassment, they thought it a good idea to stick her with someone who'd keep her mind occupied. And there was no one better than Rita Doidge for that job.

Dorothy didn't answer. She didn't appreciate being lumbered with the loud-mouthed Rita. She eased herself onto the bunk and stared up at the bulge formed by her cellmate.

'There's worse places than this, yer know,' persisted the voice from above. 'Holloway – that's an arsehole of a place. Like a posh hotel this, compared to Holloway. Mind you, that's where you'll end up if yer get done fer murder.'

'They hang you for murder, you cretin!' snapped Dorothy.

Rita's head suddenly appeared, upside down. 'It's got ter be pre-meditated for 'em ter hang yer. Nobody pre-meditates a murder wiv a bleedin' pianna stool!'

Having delivered this piece of legal logic, Rita disappeared. This was of no comfort to Dorothy who at that moment didn't care whether they hung her or not. She just wanted to go home, away from this nightmare of stained toilets and strip searches and locked doors and fat dykes and loud-mouthed cellmates. Her determination to keep a stiff upper lip was finally deserting her. She felt the tears rising to the surface.

The hatch in the cell door slid noisily open and a face inspected the two occupants before slamming the hatch shut and moving on with a cheerful whistle. A simple act which infuriated Dorothy. She ran to the door and hammered on it.

'Stop whistling, you callous bastard,' she screamed hysterically.

The whistling stopped as the warder listened to what she was shouting. Returning to the hatch she looked back in, but this time couldn't see Dorothy who had slumped to the floor, blubbing like a baby.

'Everything alright in there?'

'Yes, Miss,' said Rita. 'First night nerves that's all.'

'Right, lights go out in five minutes.'

The hatch slammed shut again and the whistling recommenced. Dorothy had managed to get back to her bunk just as the lights went out. Just another inconvenience forced on her by this inhumane place. Try as she might she couldn't stop weeping.

'Christ Almighty, I hope I ain't been lumbered with a bloody screamer,' moaned Rita. 'Pull yerself tergevver, Dolly lass. It's bad enough bein' locked up wivout bein' locked up wiv a bloody screamer.'

It was two hours before the late winter dawn when Dorothy finally dropped off, eyes reddened with tears and her throat hoarse with sobbing. Her plight not helped by the contented snoring from the bunk above.

Chapter Twelve

'Bugger me! It's freezing.'

'Jimmy Bairstow, just watch your language,' snapped Susan. 'Just because there's no one looking after us doesn't mean to say you can start swearing.'

'It is cold though, isn't it?' shivered Jimmy.

'Yes – bloody cold!'

Jimmy opened his mouth to caution his sister, then saw the grin on her face. He returned the grin as he pulled his Uncle Tommy's flat cap right down over his ears, then turned up his collar against the biting wind as they headed down Paradine Hill towards Bramham Street Cemetery. A policeman, thankfully ending his lonely beat, glanced up the road at this huddled couple advancing on him. He might well have asked what a pair of youngsters was doing out and about at this late hour. An awkward question for which they didn't have a ready answer.

'Keep walking,' whispered Susan.

A wise strategy as it turned out, the policeman called out a cheery 'Goodnight' to them as he stamped his feet and disappeared into the warmth of the police station. They were both tall for their age and from a distance could well have been adults.

'He thought we were grown-ups,' chirped a delighted Jimmy.

'I hope the jeweller thinks the same tomorrow,' said Susan.

'Have you figured out how you're going ter get away with it?' asked Jimmy.

Susan smiled to herself. 'Just you wait till tomorrow, you'll see.'

Jimmy shrugged his shoulders in mild frustration. He hated mysteries, but he knew there was no point in trying to get anything more out of her. Best to pretend he wasn't bothered. At least it didn't give her the satisfaction of knowing how curious he was.

The cemetery gates were locked, which was a bit pointless, as the iron railings which had once enclosed it were long gone. Dismantled at the beginning of the war and sent away for re-cycling as tanks, bullets, ships and suchlike. The wall on which they had once stood was only three feet high and provided the cemetery's only protection. Any corpse wishing to escape would have no problem.

It was a clear night. The cold wind sending what clouds there were scudding across the wintry moon and casting eerie moving shadows over the graves. A brave, flickering gas lamp illuminated the grave of Sidney Tobin and his wife Florence April Rose, a fragrant name until you worked out her initials. Jimmy walked behind Susan and shuddered half with cold, half with apprehension.

'It's a bit spooky, isn't it?'

Susan nodded, she felt it as well. A yellow-eyed cat glared at them from an overhanging tree branch, hissing and leaping down as Jimmy lobbed a twig at it.

For the hundredth time they read their mam and dad's names etched into the moonlit gravestone.

FREDERICK WILLIAM BAIRSTOW 1909–1941
AND HIS BELOVED WIFE LILIAN 1908–1941
GOD BLESS.

The children stood there reverently for a while, hands clasped in silent prayer, before Susan spoke.

'I hope you don't mind, but we're going to have to disturb you again, aren't we, Jimmy?' She looked to her brother for support.

'We won't be a minute though,' said Jimmy.

They crossed themselves, perhaps hoping for some sort of advance absolution, then dug their hands under the slab and heaved it upright. Susan held it in position as Jimmy retrieved the jar. Then with a final apology she let it go with a thump that cracked it right across the middle.

'Bugger me!' blasphemed Jimmy, then clasped his hand to his mouth at such sacrilege. Susan burst into tears and knelt beside the broken slab which had cracked right between their dad's name and their mam's name.

'Oh heck! I'm ever so sorry.'

'She is, she's ever so sorry,' confirmed Jimmy.

Susan glared at her brother. 'It wasn't entirely *my* fault, you know. You dropped it last time, I was only doing what you did.' She returned her attention to the grave.

'What we'll do,' she explained to her parents, 'is when we sell the rings, we'll get you a proper headstone, all nicely engraved and all that, with all our names on, including our William's – won't we, Jimmy?'

'Yeah, we will,' said Jimmy. 'And a big crucifix on top with angels and stuff . . .'

'Alright, alright,' interrupted Susan, who didn't want her brother making promises they couldn't keep. 'Anyway, Mam and Dad, we'll have to go because it's late. So, sorry again and see you later.'

The two of them walked contritely away from the grave, Susan a pace in front. After a while she stopped and held her hand up, silently signalling Jimmy to do the same. Ahead of them was a marble tombstone, watched over by a weeping angel who had much to weep about insofar as both her arms were missing. One amputation obviously had occurred quite recently, as the broken limb lay on the ground beside her. Below the angel were a pair of shadowy figures locked in a feverish embrace. Susan pulled Jimmy behind a tree from where they both had a concealed view of the proceedings.

'What's happening?' whispered Jimmy, who wasn't nearly as naïve as he pretended.

'I think they're, you know, having it off.'

'Having what off?' whispered Jimmy, enjoying this.

'They're having . . .' she hesitated, stuck for a genteel word.

'Having a shag?' suggested Jimmy, who didn't know any genteel words. 'I've never seen anyone having a shag before.'

Susan blushed in the moonlight at having to witness such things in the company of her younger brother. The woman was writhing about in a most unladylike manner and pulling the man's trousers down with unbecoming urgency; her own underwear was already around her ankles in preparation for the big moment. It became apparent that the man was having difficulties, due mainly to drink.

Words of passion from the woman turned from words of encouragement, to words of exasperation and then to coarse criticism, which Susan and Jimmy couldn't quite understand.

'I've heard o' Brewer's Droop,' grumbled the woman, 'but this is ridiculous. Bloody hell! It's like trying to push a marshmallow into a money box.'

She giggled at her own coarse wit. Jimmy made a mental note to use it himself once he found out what it meant. The woman's cackling grew louder and coarser and her criticism of his manhood, harsher. The man lost his temper, drunkenly slurring his speech. The woman stepped back, still laughing at him. He just stood there swaying uncertainly. A ridulous figure, trousers round his ankles, thin white legs shining in the moonlight, recklessly exposed to the bitter elements and cursing intemperately at this cackling woman who was now bent over, pulling her knickers up. Suddenly the man bent down as if to pull up his trousers. As he straightened up, he had the weeping angel's broken arm in his hand. Time and time again he brought it crashing down on the woman's head, weeping with anger and frustration and battering her at last into a bloody and deathly silence.

He stood over her for what seemed like an age. The angel's arm dropping from his nerveless fingers. Jimmy and Susan were frozen with shock, scarcely daring to breathe. A twig broke beneath Jimmy's foot causing the man to look up. They both dodged back behind the broad trunk of the tree. Surely he'd be able to hear their hearts pounding with terror. The man started weeping and moaning to himself.

'What have I done? What have I done? Oh, my God, I didn't mean ter kill yer. Yer shouldn't have laughed at me, yer silly bitch. Oh, may God forgive me.'

He was still pulling up his trousers and moaning to himself when he ran past them, stumbling through the darkness, tripping up and crying with pain as he fell on something hard, then picking himself up and hurrying on. They waited until he was long gone, then set off running in the opposite direction. Not stopping to look at the woman he'd just battered to death. They didn't stop or speak to each other until they were back in the house and breathlessly huddled together in Jimmy's bedroom.

Susan was finding it very hard to take in. First Auntie Dorothy hitting Mr Simpson and then this, and both to do with the same thing – sex. She secretly renewed her vow of celibacy, until such time as her marriage to Freddie was consummated.

'Jimmy,' she said eventually. 'Did you recognise that man's voice?'

Jimmy thought for a minute. 'It sounded like Mr Bateson.'

'That's what I thought.'

There a long silence, broken by Jimmy.

'We ought ter tell the police,'

'I know,' agreed Susan reluctantly. 'But if we do, they'll ask us what we were doing in the cemetery at that time of night. We'll get put in a home for sure.'

'We'll most likely get put into a home, any road. Most likely an orphanage or summat,' grumbled Jimmy.

'Not if I can help it!' declared Susan with some determination. 'Tell you what, let's ring them up – *anonymously.*'

Jimmy very much liked the sound of this.

St Stephen's clock was just striking midnight as they ventured out once again to the telephone box on Glossop Steet. The one on Paradine Hill being too close to the Police Station.

Susan nervously dialled 999.

'Emergency, which service please?'

'There's been a murder in Bramham Cemetery,' she announced, with surprising calmness, holding a handkerchief over the receiver to disguise her voice. A ruse she'd seen so many times on the pictures.

'That'll be the police, I'm putting you through now.'

But Susan had already put the phone down. It was enough. As they turned into the top of Paradine Hill they saw policemen dashing out of the Police Station at the bottom, heading with some urgency towards the cemetery.

'Blast,' cursed Susan, as they got back in the house.

'What's up?'

'I forgot to tell the police it was Mr Bateson that did it.'

'Mebbe it wasn't him. Mebbe it was just somebody what sounded like him.'

'Maybe,' acknowledged Susan. But she wasn't convinced.

Jimmy woke to a loud hammering on the back door. He cautiously peeped through the bedrooms curtains and looked down into the back yard at Jackie Crombie, jumping up and down in excitement and looking up at Jimmy's window.

'There's been a murder!' shouted Jackie. 'Come on or we'll miss it!'

Jimmy couldn't work out what there was to miss, but he dressed hurriedly and shouted up to the attic to Susan who was already moving around.

'Jackie's at the door, he knows about the murder.'

'I know, I heard him.' Susan appeared at the top of the stairs already fully dressed. 'Pretend we don't know anything,' she said with a note of caution. 'I don't think we can afford to get involved in this.'

'Okay,' agreed Jimmy, with a certain reluctance. He would have loved to have gloated over Jackie Crombie just once, but he knew she was talking sense. He opened the door, and Jackie burst in like a tornado.

'This woman's been murdered in t' cemetery. I think she were a prossie. She had her throat cut from here to here!' He dramatically demonstrated the length of the cut with a sweeping finger. 'Oh! Me mam said I've to ask yer if yer want any breakfast at our house, but yer won't, will yer? 'Cos yer'll miss it if yer do!'

'We'd love some breakfast,' said Susan, stepping into the back room. 'Wouldn't we, Jimmy?'

Jackie's face dropped as Jimmy nodded. Then he turned and shot out of the house as fast as he'd come in.

There was not much to see when Jimmy and Susan walked tentatively past the cemetery an hour or so later. In the distance, at the scene of the murder, they could just make out uniformed figures moving around. At the gate an irritated-looking policeman was fending off Jackie's persistent questions.

'Look! Clear off, you flaming nuisance, before I tan yer little arse for yer!'

Jackie looked away hurt but his face brightened when he saw his friends.

'We're not allowed in,' he explained. 'I told him I only wanted to visit me dear old mother's grave.' He turned his back to the policeman and gave them a huge conspiratorial wink.

Susan was mildly shocked at such tempting of providence, but Jimmy couldn't help but admire such an enterprising lie.

'If he carries on telling stories like that, his mam'll be coming to visit *his* grave,' grumbled the policeman.

'I think he knows who you are,' said Jimmy.

113

'Just take him away,' beseeched the policeman, 'before we have a double murder on our hands!'

The three of them trudged back up Paradine Hill, leaving a relieved constable guarding the gate.

'Are you off to t' Bughutch this afternoon?' inquired Jackie. 'There's Hopalong Cassidy on.'

'No, we, er . . .' started Jimmy.

'We've got something else to do do,' cut in Susan.

'Yer mean yer've got no money,' commiserated Jackie genuinely. 'Me mam said you wouldn't have no money. She says yer'll most likely get kicked out of yer house. Specially with yer auntie braying Simmo like that.' He stopped and kicked a stone across the road. 'I wish I had an auntie like that,' he added admiringly.

This stark assessment of the situation, albeit from Jackie Crombie, gave Susan an added determination to go through with the selling of the ring that day. Leaving Jimmy and Jackie at the end of the street, she returned to the house, making Jimmy promise faithfully to meet her back there in an hour.

Rita swung down from her bunk as the wake-up buzzer sounded. There was no slopping out in this wing of the prison, thank God. She looked down at Dorothy.

'Just wait till yer doin' proper time, madam. Yer'll know what it's all about then.'

Hard as she'd become over this past couple of years, she still felt a pang of sympathy for Dorothy, but dismissed it from her mind as a weakness she couldn't afford in this place. It was Rita's third stay courtesy of His Majesty, and prison held few fears for her. A warder appeared at the door and looked down at her sleeping cellmate.

'Leave her,' she decided. 'She was still blubbering at two o'clock this morning. Been at it all night by all accounts. She'll not mind missing breakfast.'

'You're all heart, Miss Netherton,' said Rita, who'd met this warder before.

'It's her first day. We'll not make such a fuss of her again.'

'I'll tell her what you said, she'll really appreciate it.'

'You do that.'

Dorothy woke to the clamour of the wing. It took her a few

114

seconds to come round. The little sleep she'd had in the last two nights wasn't nearly enough. Rita walked in with a tin mug full of lukewarm tea which she handed to Dorothy.

'You looked so peaceful lying there that me an' Miss Netherton decided ter let yer have a lie in.'

'Who's Miss Netherton?' asked Dorothy dully, taking the tea without a word of thanks.

'She's our hostess. Caters to our every whim does Miss Netherton. I thought we'd have a game of tennis before elevenses, would you like to make up a foursome? I know a delightful couple on the bottom landing.'

'Piss off!'

'Aha! You've been swotting up on prison lingo, good for you,' exclaimed Rita cheerfully.

As both she and Rita were remand prisoners they weren't required to do any work. Unfortunately the same applied to Delma Albright who appeared at their cell door accompanied by a marginally smaller woman who, as it turned out, had similar sexual proclivities to Delma. She leered at Dorothy.

'I'll have you fer Christmas, Dolly darlin' – that's a promise.'

Dorothy felt a shiver of revulsion as she looked up at the fat slavering face ogling at her. She opened her mouth to speak but the words wouldn't come. Rita spoke on her behalf.

'She'd like yer to bugger off, yer big ugly mess, but she's too polite ter say it, aren't yer, Dolly?'

Delma took a menacing step towards Rita but stopped in her tracks when Miss Netherton appeared behind her.

'Back in your own cell, Albright,' commanded the stern-faced warder, 'NOW!'

Delma was the only one who didn't jump at the last shouted word. She merely turned and gave the warder a smile that displayed every one of her stolen teeth.

'Just bein' friendly, Miss. There's no law against bein' friendly.'

'There is if you try and get too friendly.'

'No such thing as too friendly where I come from.'

The warder regarded Delma coolly. 'You're confined to your cell for twenty-four hours, Albright.' She looked at her watch, 'Starting in thirty seconds. If you're not back by then it's forty-eight hours and so on until I'm spared your obnoxious company altogether!'

Delma opened and shut her mouth, then spun round and hurried back to her cell with the warder close on her heels.

'I don't wish to appear naïve but what did she mean when she said, *I'll have you for Christmas*?' asked Dorothy, still trembling.

'Not quite sure, Dolly love, but she's a mean bastard is Delma. Best keep out of her road.'

'I mean, how can one woman have another? I mean, it's not as if they've got anything to – you know – stick in you or anything. She can't do anything to me – can she?' Dorothy was rambling, seeking some sort of reassurance from Rita.

'Look, Dolly love, Delma's a bleedin' headcase. The way she upsets the screws she'll spend most of her time banged up. The rest of the time, just don't go near her.'

When Jimmy returned at the appointed time, there was a young woman in the front room, standing with her back to him. When she turned round, he gasped in amazement.

'Flippin' heck, our Susan! What have yer done to yerself?'

She was wearing Auntie Dorothy's best frock, suspiciously full at the bustline, a pair of high heels, nylon stockings, and long black gloves, all from the best end of Auntie's sparse wardrobe. Her long blonde hair was topped with a neat little pill box hat and around her neck was a delicate gold necklace, a birthday present from Uncle Tommy to Auntie Dorothy. She'd copied her auntie's stylish make-up right down to the slash of crimson lipstick showing off her dazzling white teeth. Jimmy was more than impressed.

'Yer look brilliant, our lass.' This was probably the first compliment he'd ever paid his sister.

'Thanks,' she said graciously, adopting the aloof air she hoped would see her through the job in hand. Her auntie had been an unwitting tutor. Dorothy's pseudo-middle-class upbringing had imprinted a certain style upon her that life in Broughton Terrace hadn't quite rubbed out. Susan had watched with occasional admiration, the way she dressed, the way she spoke and the assured way she dealt with people. There were exceptions to this of course, or she wouldn't be locked up in Ashinghurst Prison, but in general there was a lot to be admired about Auntie Dorothy.

116

Jimmy pointed curiously to the new, curvacious bustline. 'That's not all you, is it?'

Susan grinned and reached inside. She pulled out two pairs of knickers, one from each side, leaving the bustline empty and sagging.

'I needed a bit of padding,' she admitted ruefully.

Jimmy laughed out loud. 'Blimey,' he chortled. 'They were barrage balloons!'

'Do you think they're too much?' she asked worriedly, turning to the mirror look at herself after she completed the re-padding.

Jimmy cast a critical eye over her. 'No,' he said reassuringly. 'They're not as big as Jane Russell's.'

Susan picked up her auntie's best dark blue coat and slipped it on, then looked loftily down at her brother.

'Come along, young man,' she said elegantly. 'You and I have business to attend to.'

There were three jewellers on Briggate. The smallest, but most exclusive and respectable being Blackstone's [of London and Leeds].

Leaving Jimmy looking through the window, Susan swept through the door as she imagined Auntie Dorothy would, and with her heart in her mouth, walked up to the oldest of the three assistants, a middle-aged man with odd strands of hair carefully arranged across his marble-white bald head. His eyes lit up at the sight of this beautiful, elegant young lady.

Susan stood there, soulfully. She'd rehearsed this moment time and time again. Freddie's words still fresh in her mind. 'Dress the part and walk the part.' How much more confident she'd have felt with Freddie beside her.

'Can I help you, madam?' asked the man, expansively. Displaying an array of dazzling white tombstone teeth that looked to have been made for a mouth much bigger than his.

'I, I don't know,' replied Susan, hesitantly. 'I have a ring I wish to sell . . . I don't know whether I've come to the right place.'

'You most certainly have, madam. Providing the ring is of a certain, shall we say, quality.'

Susan took the ring out of her auntie's purse and placed it lovingly on the glass counter. The man screwed a glass into his eye and picked it up. His examination took longer than he expected. He put it back on the counter and looked at Susan with added respect.

'My word, a blue diamond,' he said. 'I don't think I'm personally qualified to assess its value. However, our managing director, Mr Blackstone, who is an expert in such things, is in this morning so if you'd allow me to take it to him?'

'I'd rather it didn't go out of my sight,' said Susan, not quite knowing why. 'I mean no offence, but I am aware of its value.'

'Quite,' said the man, somewhat unctuously. 'Perhaps if madam would like to follow me?'

He led her down a flight of stairs to a dingy basement, completely at odds with the elegant shop they'd just left. On either side were two long benches littered with parts of watches and clocks and various items of jewellery. An old man sat on a stool at the far end, hunched over an expensive-looking antique clock, whistling to himself as he worked. He had a skeletal face, a shock of the purest white hair and a magnifying glass screwed into his eye as though it belonged there. He was the oldest-looking man she'd ever seen.

'This is Mr Blackstone,' said the assistant awkwardly. 'Our, er, our managing director.' The old man removed the glass from a luminescent blue eye and held out a long bony hand.

'Delighted to meet you Miss er . . .?'

'Bairstow, Susan Bairstow,' said Susan, lightly holding the ends of his fingers, perhaps afraid she might snap something off.

'Delighted to meet you, Miss Bairstow. I must say you're the most decorative thing we've had down here in a long time.'

Susan smiled at the old man's charm.

'And how can I help?' he asked.

The assistant handed him the ring. 'Miss Bairstow has brought this ring in to sell and I explained that you'd be better qualified than me to assess its value.'

Mr Blackstone re-positioned his eye glass and held the ring in the light of a bright lamp. He whistled once again, this time tunelessly, more an expression of admiration. He looked up at Susan, his eyes twinkling.

'Would I be right in thinking that this is an engagement ring?'

Susan summoned up the tear which gave the old man his answer.

'He must have loved you very much.'

'He was killed in the war. He was a pilot.'

Up to now she hadn't told a lie. It helped her act along, but she was prepared for anything.

There was genuine sympathy on the old man's face. 'My grandson died too,' he said. 'It's hard to bear.'

Susan nodded. She knew as much as anyone about family grief.

'And now you wish to sell the ring?' Was he admonishing her? She looked at him searchingly.

'I need to get on with my life,' she said firmly. 'And I need the money.' Her heart was pounding all the time, but the two men interpreted her nervousness as sorrow at what she was having to do.

'Of course, please don't think I'm criticising. It's just that we both know what you have here. It's a very old, very rare jewel. I've never seen a blue diamond of such quality.'

'I am aware of its value.'

'I'm sure you are,' smiled Mr Blackstone. 'But we can't give you its full retail value. We're in business to make money ourselves.'

'I'm aware of that too – and I'm also aware that there are other jewellers in this town to whom I can take it.' It could have been Auntie Dorothy talking. Susan was beginning to enjoy herself.

The old man picked up the ring once again. 'Would you mind if I removed the stone?' he asked.

'Please do.' She'd no idea why he needed to do this.

He deftly removed the diamond and placed it on a small pair of scales.

'Point eight of a carat,' he announced. 'But as we both know the real value is in its colour and quality. Were it an ordinary diamond I'd value it at maybe a hundred. But if we were to sell this ring we'd be asking, oh – a thousand pounds for it.'

Susan suppressed a gasp. She was hoping for fifty quid at the most.

'But of course I can't offer you that,' he looked at her and rubbed his chin speculatively. 'Seven hundred,' he said suddenly.

'I was hoping for a little more than that,' responded Susan, mainly to disguise her elation at such an offer. 'Would you go up to eight hundred?'

'Seven-fifty.'

Susan smiled and shook his hand. 'I would like it in cash please.'

'What else?' said Mr Blackstone, who'd really taken to this young lady and he wished he was sixty years younger. 'However, we'll have to send out to the bank for such a sum. Perhaps you'll have a cup of tea or coffee whilst you wait?'

'Coffee would be lovely, thank you,' said Susan, who thought a young lady of her standing wouldn't be caught dead drinking anything as common as tea.

Susan was in something of a daze as she walked out of the shop, nervously clutching the one-hundred-and-fifty five-pound notes in her auntie's deep coat pocket. Jimmy was waiting outside expectantly.

'Did yer sell it?'

'Yes, I sold it.'

'Great! Did yer get enough ter pay the rent for a bit?'

Susan looked around at the bustling street to check that no one was paying any attention to this odd pair. An unmanned tram was waiting beside the underground toilet in the middle of the road, the exit of which was the focus of all the passenger's eyes, some of whom cheered sarcastically when the unconcerned driver emerged, looking at his pocket watch as if to say it was just about time he was setting off.

'Just put your hand in my pocket,' she said surreptitiously. 'Don't take anything out, I don't want everybody knowing.' Jimmy did as she asked.

'Blimey!' he exclaimed. 'Are these all pound notes?'

'No, they're all fivers. I got seven-hundred-and-fifty quid!'

'SEVEN HUNDRED AND FIF . . .!'

'Quiet!' Susan scolded. 'We don't want everybody knowing I'm walking round with a fortune in my pocket.'

'We're rich, aren't we?'

'I think so, and we've still got your ring to sell.'

They walked along in excited silence towards the tram stop. Then Jimmy said.

'Does this mean we can stop nicking jam jars?'

Susan pondered the question for a while. 'Why should we? It was good fun nicking jam jars. Tell you what though, I've got no change for the tram and I daren't give him a fiver. Let's go get you a new blazer, you scruffy little arab.'

120

'Well, it's one way of getting change,' grinned a happy Jimmy.

Susan considered buying a new blazer for herself, but decided that such ostentation would draw unwanted attention and settled for new shoes and a new school shirt each. They arrived home as they'd left, through the rarely used front door. It was Saturday afternoon and the streets were empty apart from Mrs Harrison scouring her front step, obviously expecting company. Everyone who was anyone would be safely ensconced in the Bughutch, cheering on Hopalong Cassidy.

They sat in the front room and opened a celebratory bottle of dandelion and burdock. Inside them that distinct glow of confidence which comes from knowing you're the richest people on the street.

Delma's friend appeared at Dorothy's cell door after first ensuring she was alone. Rita was down below playing table tennis, a game she'd grown quite expert at during her time in prison.

'Message from Delma,' she sneered, approaching Dorothy with beads of sweat glistening on her smirking face.

Dorothy backed away until the woman had her cornered. She made a grab for her and Dorothy froze with fear, just like she had when Simpson had attacked her less than forty-eight hours ago.

'Please leave me alone,' she pleaded fearfully.

'Them weren't my instructions. Delma wants to know what yer taste like!'

She felt the woman's tongue licking the side of her face, then her slobbering lips pressing hard against hers.

'Very nice, darlin' – but Delma wants ter know what yer feel like as well!'

She forced her hands up Dorothy's skirt and inside her pants causing her to weep with fear and disgust as the woman ran her lips and tongue all over Dorothy's tearful face. Instinctively she pulled her head away from her vile attacker, then with all her strength she smashed her forehead into the woman's face, again and again until she felt the hands drop away from her and saw the woman staggering backwards with blood pouring from her nose and yelping with pain. Dorothy couldn't speak, her heart was thumping, her breath was coming in short bursts. Rita rushed in, alerted by another inmate, and stepped to one side in amazement as the fat woman staggered out, weeping in pain with blood all down the front of her shirt. A crowd had gathered at the door.

'Bloody hell, Dolly,' gasped Rita. 'Yer don't like people messin' wiv yer, do yer?'

Seeing the distress Dorothy was in, Rita turned and shielded her from the women at the door.

'Show's over, folks. Lesson number one – don't mess around wiv my mate Dolly, she gets ever so bleedin' cross if yer do.'

Rita sat for a long time with her arm around Dorothy, not speaking, just waiting for the sobbing to subside. Eventually Dorothy braced herself and sat up straight, then turned to Rita.

'I don't know, Rita,' she sighed. 'Sex isn't what it used to be.'

Rita began to laugh and banged her new friend on the back. 'Good girl, Dolly, you'll survive this shithole yet!'

Chapter Thirteen

Almost a week had gone by and no one had been to take them away. No one at their respective schools had asked any questions. Everyone, it seemed, thought that someone else must be looking after their welfare. The police had Dorothy listed as having no children and up to now, Dorothy had made them no wiser. As far as she was concerned, the longer the children could be kept out of the clutches of authority the better. She'd already consigned one child to a home, she couldn't be a willing party to sending the other two.

Inevitable though it might be.

Susan, with the great optimism of youth, wrote regular letters to Freddie, keeping him informed of events, so that when his memory returned he'd be fully up to date. There was no doubt in her mind that Freddie's memory loss was anything more than a temporary state of affairs.

Mrs Crombie had made it her business to check on the welfare of Neville Simpson who had regained consciousness and would make a full recovery. 'So, at least they won't be hanging your auntie,' she said comfortingly.

An official knock at the door startled Jimmy and Susan, who looked at each other with some concern. Susan looked through the window into the yard where two large men stood beside a stern-faced woman. It was raining heavily, bouncing noisily off the dustbin and causing obvious discomfort to the visitors. Jimmy and Susan went to the door together, standing side by side to face the intruders.

The two large men wore matching black overcoats, trilby hats and gloves, dwarfing the woman standing between them, who wore a belted raincoat and a strange brown hat. Her nose was long and narrow and her little mean eyes very close together, topped by just the one long, bushy, caterpillar eyebrow. The rain had collected in the brims of all three hats and was overflowing steadily.

'Good evening,' said the woman, patronisingly, 'and you are?'

'Never mind who we are, who are you?' retorted Susan. Her experience at the jewellers had given her a depth of self-confidence she didn't know she had. That and the money hidden away upstairs. The woman made to come in out of the rain but Susan barred her way.

'May we come in?' asked the woman sharply.

'No,' said Susan with matching sharpness.

'Oh, my name is Miss Newton. I'm here to represent Mr Neville Simpson, who as you probably know is in hospital,' snapped the woman, unhappy at being kept out in the rain by this cocky schoolgirl.

Susan looked at the two men. 'And who are these gentlemen?'

Miss Newton was clearly annoyed. 'These are court bailiffs, here to enforce a notice to quit given to Mrs Bairstow a week ago for non-payment of rent.'

'My auntie Dorothy tried to pay the rent last week, but she was put off a bit when Mr Simpson tried to rape her.' Susan held the woman in a cold gaze and continued, 'Then he tried to rape me so Auntie Dorothy hit him with a stool.'

Miss Newton was flustered at Susan's icy calmness and Susan knew it. Jimmy was highly impressed with his sister. The rainwater gutter above Miss Newton was blocked and over-flowing, causing the uncomfortable trio to take evasive action every time a gust of wind blew the dripping water towards them.

'Don't talk ridiculous, child. Mr Simpson's not only a respectable businessman but he's also my fiancé. He and your aunt had an argument about rent which got totally out of control.'

'I was there, Miss Newton. You weren't,' said Susan. 'Besides, why should my aunt need to argue about rent? She has lots of money.'

'Now *that* I find very hard to believe, you and I know that aunt was flat broke,' snapped Miss Newton, regaining some of her composure then losing it as a sudden squall left the three of them soaked. Jimmy stepped out of sight so they wouldn't see him laughing.

'Really?' countered Susan. 'She was so flat broke she left us well provided for until she sorts out this nonsense with our rapist landlord. Just how much was she supposed to owe?'

Miss Newton shook the water from her hat and squinted through the rain at the two bailiffs. One of them shrugged and said, 'By law you must give the debtor an opportunity to pay.'

Taking a book out of her raincoat pocket, Miss Newton examined a set of figures with a sigh of exasperation as the rain immediately obliterated the ink.

'Three pounds fifteen shillings, including this week's rent,' she smiled damply, 'payable *now*!'

'And if we pay this money, do you promise these men won't try to rape me, like your nice fiancé tried to do last week?' asked Susan sweetly.

The two bailiffs shuffled uncomfortably. They didn't like being in this situation one bit. It certainly wasn't what they'd been told to expect. Susan took a five-pound note from her pocket and handed it to one of the men.

'Here, take for next week as well. I believe it comes to four pounds ten shillings.'

Miss Newton was completely taken aback by this unexpected turn of events. She snatched the money from the bailiff and fumbled in her bag for the ten shillings change.

'Keep the change, dear,' gloated Susan, loftily. 'Buy yourself a decent hat.'

Susan allowed the bailiffs inside to make out a receipt. As they left they politely tipped their hats to her; and Susan detected a smile of admiration on the face of at least one of them as they escorted the damp and defeated Miss Newton away.

For the first time in his life Jimmy gave his sister a kiss. Not much of a kiss, but coming from him it meant a lot.

'Susan Bairstow, you were bloody brilliant!'

'Jimmy Bairstow, watch your language. I was though, wasn't I?'

'Did you see her face when you told her to buy a decent hat?'

'Did you see her face when I said her fiancé was a rapist?'

'What about when they all got soaked?'

The two of them were still laughing when Mrs Crombie knocked and dashed in out of the rain.

'Are you two okay?' She looked puzzled. 'I know a bailiff when I see one. Who were that woman?'

'That was Simmo's lady friend,' explained Jimmy. 'Our Susan put her straight on a few things, didn't you, Susan?'

'I just told her the truth that's all,' said Susan. 'She's entitled to know the truth about the man she's marrying, isn't she, Mrs Crombie?'

'So, they didn't kick you out then? What about the rent?' asked Mrs Crombie.

'We paid it.' Susan gave her a challenging look that told her not to question how.

'Oh, I see,' said Mrs Crombie, who didn't see at all.

Chapter Fourteen

A flurry of snow sent most of the inmates scurrying back inside, but Dorothy merely turned up the collar of her coat and wrapped it around her neck. This daily freedom was far too precious to lose because of a few harmless snowflakes. Rita was sitting beside her on the wooden seat behind the canteen block, donated, according to the carved inscription, by the Friends of Ashinghurst Prison 1936.

'Soft sods,' commented Rita, Dorothy nodded her agreement. Most of the inmates were nowhere near as hard as she'd imagined they'd be. Many were sad recidivists, locked up by frustrated judges who'd been left with no option. There were cheats, liars, thieves, habitual prostitutes, but very few violent criminals. Dorothy was very much on her own in that respect – she and Delma Albright.

Delma was a psycopathic thug who should have been locked up somewhere a lot more secure than Ashinghurst. Accused of beating up a young prostitute who didn't want Delma as a client. Delma's fat friend was just an incompetent thief who looked upon Delma as some sort of soulmate. In truth they had much in common, unpleasant, revolting to behold, and not a bit jolly as most fat people are supposed to be. Delma glowered at the pair of them as she trudged past.

'Soon be Christmas, Dolly lass!' she sniggered, sending a shiver of revulsion through Dorothy.

It was two weeks before Christmas and Dorothy's fourth week inside. She'd viewed Simpson's recovery with mixed feelings. She would have felt no remorse at his death, although she was relieved to be spared the threat of the hangman's noose. The memories of his attack on her were still fresh in her mind, although confused somewhat by the subsequent attack by Delma's fat friend. The fact that she'd given as good as she got on both occasions somehow diluted the aftershock of the attacks. The damage she'd inflicted on Delma's friend kept away many an unwanted advance by sexually frustrated inmates who would otherwise have looked upon the demure Dorothy as an easy victim.

Delma Albright excepted.

Rita was in for theft and fraud. As a part-time prostitute she'd stolen a client's chequebook and written herself a cheque for fifty pounds. It had worked as well, but she didn't leave it there. With incredible stupidity, which she still couldn't believe herself, she walked back into the same branch a week later and tried to draw out another fifty. The client, who was married and prepared to accept his initial loss in order to keep his marriage intact, had stopped all the cheques, and the bank security man had stopped the empty-handed Rita on her way out.

'Rita – what made you become a prostitute?' Dorothy blurted out the question she'd been dying to ask Rita since they'd first met. 'Sorry,' she added immediately. 'Stupid question, tell me to mind my own business.'

Rita huddled herself up against the cold and brushed a few snowflakes out of her hair. It was a while before she decided to answer.

'Me old man left me,' she said. 'High an' bloody dry, went off ter war an' never came back.'

Dorothy nodded, ready to accept this as the full and final answer to what probably was an impertinent question.

'He ended up in Malaya,' Rita went on. 'Three bleedin' years I'd been on me own. We never had no kids, thank God. Do yer know, he never sent me a soddin' penny. He used ter write ter me and tell me he were savin' it all up so we could buy an 'ouse of us own when he got back. The lyin' bastard!' She spat out the last remark malevolently.

'I wouldn't care, but I'd been faithful to him. I'd gone three bleedin' years without. Not that I couldn't have – there were plenty what fancied me.'

She brushed more snow from her hair, it was coming down harder now and Dorothy wondered at the wisdom of staying out in it. But Rita was oblivious to any discomfort and continued with her story.

'Anyway, just after V.E. day I got this letter saying he met this slant-eyed bint – only he didn't put it that way – an' he were setting up home with her an' he weren't comin' back. He sent me a five-pound note an' d'yer know what I did? I burnt the bastard. I could have done with it an' all.'

Rita went quiet then, it seemed to Dorothy that she was fighting back the tears so she put her arm round her.

'Did you love him?' she asked gently.

'Aye,' admitted Rita. 'I bleedin' well did!'

She laid her head on Dorothy's shoulder as the snow came down ever faster. Neither bothered to brush it away, it had a purity alien to the world in which they found themselves. Rita sat up after a while and continued.

'So that were it, really. I had no money – an' I'd been buying stuff on tally, thinking my Tony'd settle up when he got back. It were t' tally man what started me off. I let him shag me a few times an' finished up wi' a clean slate.' Dorothy felt herself shudder at this, and not because of the cold. 'Seemed easy,' continued Rita, 'he weren't a bad lookin' bloke neither. Anyway, word seemed ter get round and I were at it every week. Not anybody mind. I were a bit picky an' I worked from home.'

'There, but for the Grace of God go many of us,' remarked Dorothy with feeling.

Rita didn't understand what her friend was talking about, and went on. 'Got done a few times for keeping a brothel, couple o' stretches, four weeks and six weeks. This is different though, could get two years for this when they take me previous into account.' She stopped and looked round at Dorothy. 'Bet yer think I'm a bad bastard, don't yer?'

'I think your language leaves a lot to be desired but on the whole you're okay.'

'Language? Oh aye, that's prison for yer. If yer can't beat 'em join 'em. I'm not as bad when I'm on the outside.' She grinned at Dorothy who was sitting there like a snowman, then shook some of the snow off herself. 'We're a couple o' barmy buggers when yer come ter think of it.'

Dorothy blew a snowflake off her nose and grinned back. 'This is the best time I've had since I came in here. I think we should stay here until they come and dig us out.'

There was another long period of snowy silence, broken by Rita. 'Yer'd never guess,' she challenged.

'Never guess what?'

'I'm in t' Sally Army!'

Dorothy turned to her snow-covered cellmate. 'You're right – I'd never have guessed.'

'They taught me to play t' cornet – I'm pretty good an' all. They know all about me, but they reckon I can be saved.'

'You mean you're in the band?'

'Yeah – we play every Sunday morning – one of 'em came ter see me last week. She told me there'd be a place waiting for me when I get out. She brought me cornet thinking I might want to keep it up while I'm inside.'

'I think you should,' encouraged Dorothy.

'What? Yer mean you wouldn't mind?'

'Why should I? Maybe you could teach me.'

Rita smiled, then said suddenly, 'I bet you've never done nowt really bad, have yer? I'm not talking about braying that pillock wiv a pianna stool, sounds ter me like he got what he deserved.'

Dorothy went quiet for a long time. A silence undisturbed by Rita, who sensed Dorothy had something to get off her mind. The snow fell gently and silently, the flakes had increased in size now and had completely covered the prison garden. A robin hopped around by the bins, burying its head in the snow and pulling out a crust of bread much too big for it to fly off with. Rita pursed her lips and attempted a bird whistle which only succeeded in scaring the bird onto the top of a hut from where it looked longingly down at the crust.

'I told my step-children their baby brother was dead!'

It sounded awful the way she said it, but she wanted it to sound awful, so she left it at that until Rita made a comment.

'I didn't know you had any step-children,' was all Rita could offer by way of reply. She didn't feel qualified to condemn something she didn't understand.

'I've got two,' said Dorothy, 'Jimmy and Susan. I sent their brother to a home because I was too useless to look after him.'

Such self-flagellation was not uncommon inside jails and Rita

130

just shrugged. 'I think yer a bleedin' saint takin' two of 'em on. Why did yer tell 'em he'd snuffed it?'

'They were forever nagging me to bring him home. I just cracked in the end.'

'What're they like – the two yer've got?' asked Rita, who figured this would have some bearing on the matter, especially if the two she'd got were a couple of toerags.

'They're great. I wouldn't want them any different – I love them!' Dorothy added the last bit in a tiny voice, spitting away a snowflake that had landed on her lower lip. 'I suppose I'd love William as well – if I had him.'

There was a long silence as Rita considered her advice. She hadn't been asked for advice but felt it incumbent upon her to at least make an effort.

'I reckon yer should tell 'em as soon as yer can. At least that bit'll be off yer mind. Tell 'em their kid's still alive – make up some excuse if yer want – but yer've got ter tell 'em.'

Dorothy could see the truth in this, she'd always known she'd have to tell them, but tomorrow always seemed to be the best time.

'I'll tell them when they come to visit me,' she determined. 'And when I get out of here, which I will, I won't rest until I've got him back.'

Officer Netherton watched them from the warmth of the canteen window and shook her head at the two animated snow-covered lumps sitting on the bench. From the window above, Delma Albright looked down on them with an ugly sneer on her face; she turned to her fat friend. 'You can have Randy Rita fer Christmas – I'm gonna give her stuck-up pal a Christmas she'll never bleedin' forget!'

Dorothy scarcely recognised the two young people, sitting apprehensively at the table, awaiting her arrival. Betty Crombie and Valerie Veitch had already been, and to be honest they'd been little comfort. But the sight of Jimmy and Susan, looking so well-dressed, lifted her spirits no end. She'd half-expected they'd be taken into care and was more than curious to know how they'd managed to avoid this. No doubt the neighbours had been rallying round, they did at times like this. Up to now she'd refused all visits from them, feeling they'd have enough to put up with without worrying about her. But now she had something to tell them.

They looked so out of place in this room. Two innocents sitting uncomfortably at a table surrounded by thieves, prostitutes, women of violence – *and these are just the visitors*, she joked to herself. It was this grim humour that had enabled her to survive this place.

'Hello, you two,' she smiled and held both their hands. Of all the people in the world, these were the two she was closest to. 'I've been terribly worried about you. How have you been managing?' She scarcely dare ask them about the unpaid rent.

Susan gave her a comforting smile. The prison seemed to have robbed Auntie Dorothy of all her glow.

'Actually we're managing very well indeed, aren't we, Jimmy?'

'We're brilliant,' agreed Jimmy.

'You've not ter worry about us,' reassured Susan. 'We've got everything organised. We're paying the rent and we've got enough money for live on till you get out. We've bought some new clothes as well.'

Dorothy looked at them in amazement. 'I daren't ask,' she said.

'Best not,' grinned Susan. 'But we're not doing anything illegal.' They'd agreed not to mention anything about the money for the ring, as they didn't know how she'd react.

'Is it anything to do with milk bottles?' Dorothy knew it couldn't be, but it was all she could think of.

Jimmy and Susan laughed heartily at this and for the first time in weeks, Dorothy laughed as well. Jimmy looked around, surveying the roomful of chattering felons, then leaned over to his aunt. 'Are there any murderers in here?'

Dorothy laughed at his natural curiosity. 'I've no idea, Jimmy. Anyway, this is the Remand Wing. Everyone here is technically innocent, like me.'

'We're going ter get you off when you go ter court. Our Susan's got this plan,' confided her nephew.

'Oh, right,' whispered Dorothy. 'I hope it's a good one,' Dorothy was only half-humouring Jimmy as she wouldn't put anything past these two.

'It is a good one, isn't it, Susan?'

Susan nodded. 'We don't want to get your hopes up too high, Auntie, but I think it might work.'

Dorothy couldn't imagine what the plan was, any more than she could figure out where they were getting their money from. All she knew was there were two special young people waiting for her as and when she did get out. Or would they be? She held them both in her gaze, knowing she couldn't keep her dreadful secret from them any longer.

'Look, kids,' she said almost hoarsely. 'There's something I've got to tell you – and you may not like me after I've told you, and to be honest I wouldn't blame you.'

Jimmy and Susan sat there quietly, not knowing what to expect. Dorothy took several deep breaths.

'William's not dead!' she said in little more than a whisper, averting her gaze, not knowing how they'd react.

It took a while for what she'd said to sink in. Susan spoke first.

'But – of course he is! He died two years ago – didn't he?'

Dorothy shook her head, guiltily.

Jimmy's face broke into a slow smile. 'Yer mean our brother's still alive? Honest?'

'Honest.'

Jimmy and Susan looked at each other then back at Dorothy.

'When did you find out?' asked Susan.

Dorothy examined her hands nervously. 'I've always known,' she admitted.

Susan was incredulous. '*Always* known, how do you mean? always known, I don't understand. You told us he was dead! You must have lied to us, Auntie. Why did you do that?'

'Why *did* you do that?' echoed Jimmy, who was confused now, not knowing whether to be happy or sad.

Dorothy sank her head between her hands, as they'd seen her do so often. 'I don't know if I can explain,' she said, tearfully. 'Not in a way to make you understand. I'm not sure if I understand myself.'

'I think we'd like you to try,' demanded Susan, who, like Jimmy, was totally confused.

'I was ill,' said Dorothy. 'Sad, depressed – call it what you like. If I hadn't been so useless, William wouldn't have gone away in the first place. I couldn't even cope with you two, much less a baby. It was at *my* insistence that he was sent away.'

133

'Uncle Tommy told us it was for his own good,' said Susan. 'I never understood that.'

'Uncle Tommy told you that to cover for my uselessness. The whole business of the war and your Uncle Tommy having to go away – and I just couldn't handle bringing up someone else's baby.'

Susan nodded, trying her best to understand. Jimmy copied her. 'But why did you tell us he was dead?' she asked.

Dorothy took a deep breath and continued, avoiding their eyes now. 'You just kept going on about him. When's he coming home, Auntie? When can we go to see him? Where's he living? Will they be looking after him? Not a day went by without you asking endless questions about him. You were driving me mad – so I . . .' her voice tailed off.

'So you thought you'd put a stop to all this by telling us he was dead?' Susan's face was colouring up. 'That's it, isn't it?'

Dorothy didn't reply.

'Isn't it?' repeated Susan, shouting now. 'Where is he, Auntie Dorothy? Where's our baby brother?'

People at the other tables broke off their conversations and looked at Susan, who was standing up, shouting at her auntie. A prison officer looked hard at them, wondering whether to intervene. Jimmy was still sitting, but looking most uncomfortable. Tears streamed down Dorothy's face as she looked back at her angry niece.

'I don't know,' she sobbed. 'I'm sorry, Susan, but I honestly don't know where he is. Please don't be angry with me.' She stood to walk round the table towards Susan. The officer moved swiftly over to restrain her, but Susan had already taken a pace backwards.

'We cried for days after you told us. How could you do that to us?'

'I'm so sorry,' wept Dorothy. 'I thought it was for the best. Tommy was in the army, I was just trying to cope as well as I could. I would have told you the truth when Tommy came home. We were going to get William back. I just – I just wanted you to stop going on about him.'

She struggled to free herself of the officer's grip, but Susan moved further away from her.

'Don't come anywhere near me,' she said tearfully, then turned

134

and went, leaving Jimmy sitting there, not knowing what to do.

'You'd better go after her,' said Dorothy.

Jimmy shrugged and opened his mouth to apologise on Susan's behalf then thought better of it.

'See you,' he said simply, then left.

Dorothy sat on her bunk pretty much at the end of her tether. Another mess. She should be used to it by now. But beneath all the self pity she felt a morsel of relief that the kids were alright. The news she'd given them was good news after all. They'd got their brother back, or they would one day. It seemed they were alright financially, God knows how, but they were. The only thing they had to worry about was having an idiot for their closest living adult relative. In an odd sort of way she felt relieved. Ah well, it'd soon be Christmas.

She gave a smile of resignation, picked up Rita's cornet and gave a blast into her dozing cellmate's ear. 'Right,' she said, 'I'm ready for my trumpet lesson now.'

Susan didn't speak to Jimmy all the way to Leeds on the bus. She couldn't believe anyone could be so cruel as to tell someone that their brother was dead just to stop them nagging.

They were waiting for their tram to Paradine Hill when Jimmy broke the silence.

'We did nag her a lot,' he muttered.

'You what?' snapped Susan.

'I know she shouldn't have done what she did, but we did nag her a lot. 'Specially me – I went on a lot when you weren't there.'

'Doesn't excuse what she did.'

'No, I don't s'pose it does,' accepted Jimmy. 'Still, it's great that our William's alive.'

It was as though Susan had forgotten this aspect of things. 'We'll find out where he is,' she said determinedly. 'We'll get him a brilliant Christmas present.'

'Yeah, we'll send him a cake with a file in it,' chortled Jimmy.

'We'll ring up that last place he was at,' decided Susan. 'That place in Cleckheaton, can you remember what they called it?'

'Oxford House.'

'Oxford House, that's it. We'll ring up Oxford House and try and track him down from there.'

135

Thus decided, the two of them climbed onto the tram and headed for home. One with more forgiveness in his heart than the other.

'Susan?'

'What?'

'Yer know that plan you were talking about.'

'What plan?'

'That plan you said might get Auntie Dorothy off.'

'What about it?'

'You never told me what it was.'

'I know.'

She was so infuriating at times. If he thought he could get away with it, Jimmy could have cheerfully thumped her. It was four days since they'd visited Auntie Dorothy, since when, Susan had scarcely spoken about her. They'd drawn a blank when they rang up Oxford House, apparently the person who dealt with such things wasn't there that week, so could they ring back next week. Jimmy poured more milk onto his cornflakes and turned over another page of his *Adventure*.

'Are you not going ter bother then?' he asked.

'Bother about what?' asked Susan, idly looking through Dorothy's ration book.

'You know what – your plan ter get Auntie Dorothy off.'

'I haven't made up my mind yet.'

'In a way she's locked up because of you. It was Simmo starting on you that made her go potty.'

Susan ignored this observation and stopped at the sweet coupon page.

'Have you been buying sweets without telling me?'

'Why?'

'There's some coupons missing, that's why.' She put the ration book in her school satchel. 'How can you afford extra sweets out of your pocket money?'

Jimmy grimaced. She was worse than Auntie Dorothy. 'There was threepence in the bottom of the rent tin,' he explained sheepishly.

'You're not supposed to do that,' insisted Susan. 'I thought I explained it to you. We mustn't let people suspect we've got a lot of money in the house.'

'It was only flipping threepence.'

'I don't care.'

Jimmy wasn't going to win this one so he returned to the previous discussion.

'Anyway, you're supposed to forgive people.'

'Go on then, I forgive you,' said Susan graciously.

'I'm not talking about me, I'm talking about me Auntie Dorothy.'

'Oh.' Susan was finding it hard to have any charitable thoughts about Auntie Dorothy. How can you forgive the unforgivable?

Jimmy decided to give it one last try before he went back to his comic.

'If Simmo had died me Auntie Dorothy might have been hung – and she was doing it to protect you.'

'I don't think she was thinking that far ahead at the time,' retorted Susan.

'I think you should write to her and forgive her, 'specially with it being Christmas. You should send her a Christmas card.'

'Look, we'd best be off,' she said, neatly changing the subject. 'No point being late on the last day of term.'

What Susan didn't know was that Jimmy had already sent their auntie a Christmas card from both of them. Dorothy cried tears of misplaced joy when she read it.

Chapter Fifteen

Neville Simpson came out of hospital a week before Christmas. The fifteen stitches holding his head wound together had been painfully removed. His fiancée, Maggie Newton, drove him home and was once again more withdrawn than usual, as she had been for the past couple of weeks. Neville scarcely noticed this. Maggie's moods were of little concern to him. The only thing of interest about Maggie was that she was her wealthy father's only daughter, otherwise Neville wouldn't have looked twice at her.

Maggie, for her part, knew her limitations. Cosmetically she was very much third division and although Neville was no Clark Gable, he was a lot better looking than her. But Susan's version of events had been worrying her, and as much as she didn't want to believe it, she knew the girl could well have been telling the truth.

She stopped the car outside Neville's father's house and switched off the engine, just staring contemplatively through the windscreen, making no move to get out. Neville's mother came to the door of the ugly Victorian edifice, the ground floor of which was occupied by the three Simpsons. The other two floors being divided up into six flats, the occupants of two of these had come to their windows to watch Neville's homecoming, more out of curiosity than affection.

'What's up?' asked Neville. His head was still swathed in bandages, completely obscuring his carroty hair.

'She's going to say you tried to rape her, isn't she?' Maggie's eyes were still firmly fixed on the street in front of her.

Neville shifted uncomfortably in his seat. 'How the hell do I know what the mad cow's going ter say?' he argued irritably. 'Do you mind getting the door for me, please, or am I supposed ter try and manage meself?'

'What exactly happened, Neville?'

Neville was becoming agitated. That bloody policeman hadn't seemed too happy with his explanation, but he could have done without Maggie becoming suspicious as well. If that bitch Bairstow had jeopardised his marriage he'd make sure they threw the bloody key away.

'I've already told yer,' he complained. 'She couldn't pay the rent and when I threatened her with eviction, she went barmy. She picked up this stool and chased me out into the street!'

Maggie swung round in her seat and gave him a challenging glare. 'Couldn't pay the rent? How come she left the kids so well provided for, then? They came up with the rent without any trouble when you sent me round. Made me look a right idiot in front of the bailiffs.'

Neville began to lose his temper. How dare this ugly bitch question him? Didn't she know how much of a favour he was doing her in offering to marry her?

'How do I know?' he snarled. 'She certainly didn't have any money when I went round there – besides, whatever I did ter her was in self-defence. There's a big difference between raping someone and just scratching their tits a bit.'

'You did what?'

Neville sat back, chastened by his own big mouth.

'Are you trying to say you scratched her tits in self-defence?'

'I didn't say that!'

'That's what it sounded like to me.'

A wave of revulsion grew inside her as she looked at him, seeing for the first time what a vile little man he was. 'You bastard! You did it, didn't you? You tried to rape her, and her niece.'

Neville's head was beginning to ache. 'No, no, it wasn't like that,' he protested. 'You've got it all wrong. Look, all this aggravation is giving me a headache.'

'Get out of the car, Neville!'

Neville looked at her and knew the engagement was off. He couldn't resist delivering a parting shot.

'It'll be a pleasure. I've been dreading waking up opposite your ugly mush, so I'll just have me ring back, please.' Maggie had already hurled it through the car door, which she pulled shut behind him, before driving off with a roar, leaving him scrabbling around looking for it, to the consternation of his mother and the amusement of two of his tenants.

Delma caught Dorothy's eye in the canteen during dinner and gave a slavering leer that almost made Dorothy throw up. Prising her enormous girth from her steel chair she waddled across to Dorothy's table.

'Make the most of your last week!' She spat out the words and sent a cold shiver of dread down Dorothy's spine.

'Take no notice,' advised Rita, without much conviction.

Delma waddled off, smirking. Her plan was foolproof. Doing it was all that mattered – she hadn't planned on getting away with it, just doing it. That's why it was so foolproof.

Needless to say, Jackie Crombie saw it first. He'd watched the man from the estate agents putting it up, bombarding him with a million questions until the man told him to piss off. He was waiting at the end of the street for them, jabbing an excited forefinger towards the sign fixed to the wall beside their front door:

FOR SALE
WITH VACANT POSSESSION
Simpson's Properties
Leeds 36428

'Yer house is up fer sale. This feller came round an' put this sign up. He told me ter piss off,' announced Jackie cheerfully. 'An this other feller's been looking for yer, so I told him you were at school and he said he'd come back in half an hour.'

Susan and Jimmy looked in consternation at each other. What was going on? They walked to the house in silence, punctuated only by persistent questioning by Jackie.

'Will yer get kicked out? Where you gonna live? Will yer have ter go in an 'ome?'

'Look, Jackie,' said an exasperated Susan. 'You know that man asked you to do?'

Jackie nodded uncertainly.

'Well, why don't you do it!' she yelled.

Jackie shrugged and mooched away to see if his tea was ready.

Jimmy and Susan were just going in through the back door when they heard a knock at the front. Susan looked through the curtains, then back at Jimmy with a huge smile on her face.

'It's Freddie,' she said excitedly. 'He can walk!'

He stood there on the pavement, beaming up at them, supported by two walking sticks. His father's car parked behind him.

'Freddie!' breathed Susan. 'You're better!'

'Well, I wouldn't exactly say that,' grinned Freddie. 'But I reckon I can manage these two steps if you invite me in.'

Susan blushed. 'Oh, sorry, yes, come in.'

Freddie mounted the steps slowly and with much grunting, until he stood in their front room with a look of triumph on his face. Susan offered him an easy chair but he chose a dining chair instead.

'I need to plan ahead,' he explained. 'It'd take me ten minutes to get up out of that chair. Still, mustn't grumble. The old pins are coming along nicely.'

Jimmy and Susan hovered in front of him, forcing him to smile at their awkwardness.

'Right, kids,' he said. 'First of all, thanks for your letters. Plenty of people wrote to me whilst I was laid up, but none of their letters matched yours for excitement.' He directed his comment at Susan, his smile was making her heart race. 'At first, I thought they were a product of an over active imagination,' he went on. 'Fortunately, the old brainbox has made a bit of a break through and I remember enough to believe every word you wrote ... I also remember something about the rings, but for the life of me I can't remember what I did with mine.'

'You can have a share of ours,' said Susan impetuously. An offer that Jimmy felt he should have been consulted about.

'No, no, no wouldn't dream of it,' laughed Freddie. 'But thanks for the offer anyway.' His face became serious. 'It occurs to me that you need all the help you can get.'

'It's occurred to me as well,' said Jimmy, forcing another smile out of Freddie. 'Simmo's put our house up for sale.'

Freddie nodded. 'Yes, I saw the man putting the sign up. By the way, who's the kid that never stops talking? I thought the sign man was going to throttle him.'

141

'That's Jackie Crombie,' said Jimmy. 'He's alright.'

'In small doses,' added Susan, sitting down beside Freddie at the table.

'Anyway, first things first,' continued Freddie. 'Regarding your recently resurrected brother. I rang Oxford House to see if I could begin to track him down.'

'So did we,' said Susan. 'They said the person we needed was away this week.'

'Yes, that's what they told us,' said Freddie, 'at first. Then Dad took it upon himself to do a bit of red tape slashing. He rang the woman back and gave her an almighty ear bashing. Threatened her with God knows what, and demanded to speak to her superior.'

'Your dad did this for us?' queried Susan. 'I got the impression that he didn't approve of us.'

Freddie laughed at her bluntness. 'He read about you in the papers and seeing as you've got some connection with me, he decided to take up the cudgels on your behalf. And believe me, he's a mean man with a cudgel.'

Susan's eyes were glued to him as he went on with his story.

'Apparently he was moved to an orphanage in Huddersfield a few months ago. They couldn't tell me much over the phone, but reading between the lines it occurs to me that young William's having a hard time of it.'

'Hey! It'd be great if we could get him back for Christmas,' exclaimed Jimmy.

'It's not as simple as that,' cautioned Freddie. 'He'd need to have a stable home to come to. You'd have to wait at least until your aunt got out of— came home. Even then the authorities might question her suitability, if she wasn't completely acquitted.'

Susan nodded, still not taking her eyes off Freddie. 'It's important that Auntie Dorothy's found not guilty then?' she concluded.

'Very important,' said Freddie. 'But from what you tell me she *isn't* guilty.'

'Well, she did clobber him,' admitted Susan.

'I should think she *did*,' said Freddie. 'I'd have clobbered him myself under the circumstances.'

'Would you?' breathed Susan dreamily, just for a second

picturing Freddie as her knight in shining armour springing bravely to her defence.

'Yes, I damn well would,' said Freddie, cutting through her thoughts, unaware of the effect he was having on her. 'By the way,' he asked, 'tell me it's none of my business if you like, but where are you keeping the money?'

'In the attic,' replied Susan.

Freddie shook his head. 'I was worried about that. It's time you opened a bank account.'

'I think I'll need your help for that,' smiled Susan. Freddie smiled back and saw, for the first time, a lovely young lady instead of the pretty tomboy he'd been so taken with, back at Fiddler's cottage. Susan lowered her eyes under his gaze and wished they were alone.

'Oh, before I forget,' remembered Freddie, 'You're both invited to Harrogate for Christmas lunch.'

The phone rang in Neville Simpson's office. He'd promoted himself into his father's chair when the old man had been taken ill. He picked it up and answered in his flat, West Riding vowels.

'Hello, Simpson's Properties – yes, that's correct. Three bedrooms including the attic. The price is four hundred and fifty for a quick sale.'

The caller was a solicitor, ringing on behalf of a client. 'My client is a businessman like yourself, Mr Simpson, and he's prepared to make a cash offer for a quick sale. But your price would have to be much lower.'

Neville's hatred of Dorothy Bairstow festered inside him like a cancer. She'd wrecked his intended marriage and robbed him of the woman of his dreams, the sole heiress to sixteen butcher's shops and a mansion in Pudsey. On taking over the reins of his father's business it had become obvious that Simpson Properties was practically insolvent. All the properties were mortgaged up to the hilt, many in a state of disrepair. Thousands of pounds' worth of rent arrears, incurred during the war, had been written off by his father as bad debts. In short, the business needed an injection of cash to keep it afloat, hence his engagement to the homely, but wealthy, Maggie Newton. Now that bitch Bairstow had ruined it. She needed teaching a lesson. He had no reason to sell her house, other than to cause problems for her and her brood; and if they insisted on paying the rent, then he'd sell the house from under them.

'Would your client continue to rent it out or would he want it with vacant possession?' asked Neville. The answer to this was of paramount importance to him.

'My client would require vacant possession on completion. Why, is this a problem?'

'No, no problem whatsoever,' oozed Simpson. 'The tenants will have moved out before you take possession.' Kicked out more like, with my own size tens, he sniggered to himself. 'I'm prepared to drop to four hundred for a quick completion.'

'My client won't go higher than three hundred and fifty.'

Three-fifty? Jesus Christ! He'd only put it in at four-fifty to get rid quick. His hatred of Dorothy got the better of him. 'Okay,' he conceded. 'I'm giving it away. Three-fifty it is then. Can I expect a signed contract tomorrow?'

'I'll have one sent round to your solicitor, subject to the usual searches of course.'

'Of course.'

Simpson gave details of his solicitor, then put the phone down and rubbed his hands gleefully. 'Got them, the bastards,' he said, to no one in particular.

It was the morning of Christmas Eve when he rang his solicitor for confirmation of exchange of contracts.

'That's correct, Mr Simpson, we exchanged about an hour ago. The purchaser had personal searches done to expedite matters. We've set the completion for the first of January, if that's alright by you. Give your tenants time to move into another of your properties, I expect.'

Neville put the phone down and reached for his coat. He looked in the mirror and fingered the livid scar on his head to remind him how much he hated that Bairstow bitch. A brown-toothed smirk flickered across his face.

'Here comes old Ebenezer bleedin' Scrooge,' he sniggered, then howled with laughter at his clever analogy.

Jimmy and Susan had bought each other modest Christmas presents in keeping with their frugal budget. Both presents were wrapped up and sitting on the kitchen table inviting guesses from their curious recipients.

'It's a book,' decided Susan, it had to be a book.

'Aw, no, did yer want a book? I was gonna buy you a book, but I didn't know you could read.'

Susan slapped his arm playfully. Another present sat on the dresser in the front room, cuff links for Freddie. William's train set and Auntie Dorothy's cardigan had already been posted, William's being the most expensive present of the four.

The knock was one they'd heard a hundred times before. Susan winked at Jimmy. 'It's him, I'll get it, you go upstairs.'

She opened the door and gave Simpson a smile he didn't expect. 'Hello, Mr Simpson, how nice to see you. Won't you come in?'

He stepped through the scullery into the back room and handed Susan a piece of paper. There was whisky on his breath.

'Whew! Your breath smells, Mr Simpson!' she gasped, taking a step back. Then looking at the paper she added, 'What's this?'

'Notice to quit,' he snapped. 'By law I don't have to give you notice as you're not the legal tenants. That would be your aunt, who's hardly likely to be a tenant of anyone other than His Majesty for some time to come.' He sniggered to himself at this. 'You have one week from today to remove yourselves and your belongings, such as they are.'

'But, but it's Christmas, Mr Simpson!'

'I know,' smirked Neville. 'Good, isn't it?'

'And, will you be wanting to rape me? Like last time?'

Neville didn't know what to make of this, although the prospect was quite exciting. Susan gave him a look of disappointment.

'No? That's a shame. Still, from what I hear you're all talk. All mouth and trousers, that's what I've heard.'

This touched a raw nerve with Neville. He reached out and grabbed her by her blouse.

'Listen, you little bitch!' he snarled. 'If your whore of an aunt hadn't hit me with that bloody stool I'd have given you a screwing you wouldn't have forgotten in a hurry. And I'd have done a lot more to your precious auntie than pull her tits out!' He released his grip and pushed her away contemptuously, then followed as she backed away. He was shouting now, out of control. 'I'd have screwed her arse off if you hadn't disturbed us! It's your fault she's in jail, another five minutes and I'd have finished the job and nobody would have been any wiser. She'd have kept her mouth shut or she'd have been out in the streets, and you lot with her!'

There was a hint of of madness in his malevolent eyes. Every word was accompanied by a spray of spit, which Susan struggled to avoid. She backed away from him, her face ashen. She'd gone a little too far with her taunting.

'It's okay, Susan, we've heard enough,' said P.C. Greenough stepping out of the small hallway at the bottom of the stairs. Behind him was Maggie Newton and Jimmy who hurled himself at Neville, kicking and gouging until Alan Greenough pulled him off.

'Jimmy, Jimmy, calm down, it's over!' said the policeman pulling the boy off the cowering Neville. With a restraining hand on Jimmy, P.C. Greenough read a shocked Neville his rights.

'Neville Simpson, I'm arresting you for indecent assault. You do not have to say anything, but anything you do say may be taken down and used in evidence.'

Neville's mouth opened and shut like a goldfish. He flopped down on a chair, totally defeated. Alan Greenough yanked him roughly back to his feet. 'Come on, you,' he growled. 'We've a nice little room for you to spend Christmas in!'

Neville glared at Susan, his eyes full of wild hatred. Then he gave her a twisted sneer. 'It doesn't alter things for you, you smug little bitch. A week today and you're out on the streets. This house is sold!'

'I know,' gloated Susan. 'I'm the one who bought it!' She took the contract out of a drawer and waved it under his nose. 'And I'd like to thank you for selling it to me at a knock-down price. I was told I'd have to pay five hundred for it.'

Neville howled with frustrated rage and tried in vain to stuggle free of the policeman's grip.

Jimmy, Susan and Maggie Newton listened as his hysterical screams disappeared down Paradine Hill.

'You're well rid of him, I suppose,' observed Susan.

'You suppose correctly,' agreed Maggie. 'I'll speak against him in court and hopefully never have anything to do with him again.'

'Oh, and sorry about being rotten to you before, you know,' apologised Susan.

'Apology accepted. You did me a favour in the long run.'

146

'When do you suppose Auntie Dorothy will come home?' asked Jimmy.

'Well,' cautioned Maggie, 'I'm afraid with it being Christmas Eve there's not much we can do to get her home for tomorrow. But I think with this new evidence she should be let out on bail until her trial comes up. That's if there is a trial now.'

'Thanks, Maggie,' said Jimmy.

'Any time,' smiled Maggie. 'Oh, and by the way.' She pulled a hat out of her pocket that was equally as atrocious as the brown affair they'd first seen her in. 'I bought this with the ten bob you gave me.'

'It's lovely,' lied Susan.

'You should have given her more,' said Jimmy, through smiling teeth as they waved Maggie goodbye. They sat down at the table and grinned at one another.

'What do you think of my plan then?'

'Quite good,' conceded Jimmy grudgingly, who'd been scared stiff for his sister when Simpson had lost his rag with her.

Chapter Sixteen

Hark the Herald Angels sing!
Beecham's Pills are just the thing.
Move ye gently move ye mild,
Two for an adult one for a child.
Regular administration,
Just the thing for constipation ...

Dorothy had never heard this version before that Christmas
morning. She was, it seemed, the only person in the canteen who
was singing the traditional words. Rita was playing her cornet,
accompanied by a spoon-playing shop-lifter and a warder playing
the mouth organ.

All in all it was a happy morning. Delma's threats had come to
nothing and there was to be turkey for Christmas dinner. A far
better meal than most of them would have got on the outside. She
saw Delma's fat friend approaching out of the corner of her eye
and decided to ignore her. The fat friend had kept her distance
from Dorothy since coming out of the hospital wing with a
misshapen nose and a reputation as a loser.

'Netherton wants ter see yer in her office,' she grunted in
passing. 'Says it's important.'

Dorothy watched her waddle away, wondering what on earth
Netherton could possibly want her for on Christmas morning.
Maybe she had some good news – why not? It was about time she
had some good news. With an optimism brought on by the spirit
of Christmas, she climbed the iron stairs to Netherton's office. It
was in the corner of the first floor landing where Dorothy and Rita
lived. Little more than a converted cell, the main difference being

that Netherton's door locked from the inside. The door was partially open when Dorothy arrived so she knocked and walked straight in. Netherton was lying on the floor, her eyes closed and a pool of blood around her head. Dorothy froze for a second, long enough for a truncheon to come flailing out from behind the door and smash across her right shin, breaking both tibia and fibula in one vicious blow. Her shriek of pain was drowned by Rita hitting the high notes and the canteen choir singing the last two scatalogical lines of the hymn,

> *How to art can man aspire?*
> *When his arsehole's not on fire.*

Dorothy went down as if poleaxed, the pain in her leg almost unbearable. She looked down and could see the smashed bones sticking out at a sickening angle. A large shadow fell over her and she knew without looking up who it was.

'Not so full o' yer bleedin' self now, are yer? Yer stuck up cow.'

Dorothy had never felt less full of herself than she did at that moment. The intense pain had vanished, replaced by intense terror. Miss Netherton was lying beside her, frighteningly still, her blood beginning to soak into Dorothy's blouse. Delma was standing astride her, like an obscene colossus. A gigantic mess of a woman, smiling contemptuously down on Dorothy with those gleaming horse teeth of hers. Swirling the black truncheon in her fat hand.

'Now then, where would yer like me ter stick this, Dolly darlin'?'

She lowered herself astride Dorothy. Heaving with one leg to push aside the body of the warder.

'I think we'll have rid of her. Don't want dead screws cramping our style, do we, Dolly darlin? No need ter say goodbye, yer'll soon be joinin' her!'

She heaved Netherton over her shoulder like a small child and walked out onto the landing, waving at the inmates gathered below, stunning them all into silence as they looked back at the horrific sight above them. With a great flashing equine grin, she raised the body above her head and with a shout of, 'Merry Christmas, girls!' hurled the mortal remains of Miss Netherton

149

down on top of them, before calmly strolling back into the dead warder's office and turning the key in the lock.

Freddie's car arrived at eleven o'clock on Christmas morning. Jimmy and Susan were already waiting at the open door, both dressed in their school blazers and latest finery. Susan locked the door and walked casually down the steps, secretly annoyed at Jimmy, who was already on the front seat where she wanted to sit, chattering excitedly to Freddie. Although Susan would never admit it, this was was the first time in her life she'd ever been in a car. Of course there was no need for Freddie to know that. She opened the back door and slid demurely onto the back seat as though it was an everyday occurrence.

'We've never been in a car before, have we, Susan?' chirped an excited Jimmy.

Not for the first time, Susan could have throttled him. '*You* might not have,' she argued.

'Oh yeah! And when have you been in a car before?' challenged Jimmy.

Freddie butted in to save Susan's obvious embarrassment. He looked in the mirror at Susan's blushing face.

'Yes, madam,' he said with mock servility, 'and where would madam wish to go this morning?'

Susan smiled back and quickly regained her composure. 'Take us to Harrogate, my good man,' she instructed, loftily. 'And don't spare the horses!'

'Very good, madam,' replied Freddie, touching a forelock.

The journey to Harrogate was an interesting one. The morning bright and frosty. For reasons best known to themselves, someone had chosen Christmas morning to transport a wagon load of cows from Harewood towards Harrogate. Behind the cattle truck was a bowler-hatted man hunched over the wheel of his Austin Seven and behind him drove Freddie and his Christmas guests. A young man in an open-topped M.G. drove up behind Freddie and hooted impatiently. Freddie politely cursed him, but in the spirit of the season, signalled him to pass and as he did so the Austin Seven took it upon himself to put his foot down and slowly overtake the cattle truck, pulling out in front of the M.G. who'd had ambitions to roar past all three of them.

The hooter started again, urging the Austin Seven to get a move on, because by now both cars were on the wrong side of the road. At this point, one of the cows decided to relieve itself, sending a steaming spray out between the slatted sides of the truck to disperse itself in the cold slipstream all over the M.G. driver. Freddie, spotting the M.G.'s predicament, drove up close behind him, trapping him in position, so that he might receive the full benefit of the cow's Christmas present. A classic manoeuvre which filled Jimmy with unbounded admiration for Freddie.

They were all agreed that this was possibly the funniest thing they'd ever seen in their lives and they were still laughing when they pulled up outside Freddie's house. Christmas was off to a good start.

'Welcome,' boomed the Brigadier, as they walked through the front door.

'Merry Christmas,' said Jimmy.

'Nice to see you again,' said Susan, who still hadn't forgotten his rudeness, but was prepared to forgive and forget in the spirit of Christmas. Freddie's father gave her a smile, half of admiration for a pretty girl, half of puzzlement, wondering where he'd seen her before.

Freddie led the way through to the 'parlour', pointing out various items of interest with his walking stick. 'That's my paternal grandfather,' he said, pointing to a painting of a rather stern military man, glowering down at them from the staircase wall. 'And that's my *maternal* grandfather,' he jabbed his stick at a faded sepia photograph of a young man in shirt sleeves and collarless shirt, leaning against a farm cart with a tankard in his hand. 'Guess whose side of the family I take after?' he grinned. 'Right, I'd like you to meet our Christmas dinner guests.'

The parlour was a large warm room with a fireplace as big as the Bairstows' scullery. Heavy gold satin curtains hung from ceiling to the thick, patterned carpet on which stood a variety of easy chairs, a settee as long as a small car and two low coffee tables covered with bowls of nuts, fruit and sweets. In the corner stood the biggest Christmas tree they'd ever seen. The fairy on top was just touching the ceiling some twelve feet above them and from the branches hung small parcels and lights and bright decorations.

A group of guests broke off their conversations and turned to greet the new arrivals with welcoming smiles. Jimmy and Susan tried to contain their embarrassment as Freddie introduced them as the 'Miracle Kids of Leeds and very good friends of mine.'

'I believe you've already met Mother.' Mary Fiddler smiled and gave them a warm handshake.

'And this is my Uncle Ben, Auntie Maude, my cousin Beatrice, my old schoolfriend Tricky Dicky Dodsworth and last but by no means least . . . my lady friend, Elizabeth.'

Susan was still smiling hellos to her fellow guests when she heard the last introduction. As soon as she looked down at the sophistated beauty smiling back at her, Susan's young heart was pierced with a pain she'd never known before.

'Hello, Susan,' said Elizabeth, patting the seat at the side of her. 'Freddie's told me so much about you. You must sit next to me and tell me more. My life seems ever so dull compared with yours.'

'Everyone's life's dull compared to Susan's, with the possible exception of young Jimmy over there,' laughed Freddie.

Jimmy had been taken under the wing of Tricky Dicky Dodsworth, an unconventionally dressed young man, who was already laughing at Jimmy's story of the cow and the M.G., brilliantly told as usual, in his unselfconscious Leeds accent.

Susan was fighting back the tears whilst trying to be polite to Elizabeth, whom she found to be infuriatingly nice. Who had she been fooling? How on earth could a schoolgirl like her hope to win the heart of a wonderful man like Freddie?

'I understand you're doing your School Certificate this year?' asked Elizabeth, deciding to keep the conversation on a light note and avoid some of the more controversial aspects of Susan's complicated life.

'Yes,' she answered politely.

'She'll walk it,' cut in Freddie. 'Bright girl, our Susan. Not like me, got through by the skin of my teeth.'

'Well, you're not an academic, darling,' smiled Elizabeth, taking his hand. 'But I suppose I'll just have to love you as you are.'

'What you see is what you get, Lizzie my love,' laughed Freddie.

Lizzie? Oh God, he's got a pet name for her. Susan was having one of the worst times of her life. She smiled grimly throughout this badinage. Her end of the conversation was little more than monosyllabic, which Elizabeth took to be shyness in the face of a roomful of adults, and understandably so.

'Perhaps you'd like to chat to Beatrice?' suggested Elizabeth, patronisingly, Susan thought. 'She's more your age. You don't want to be sitting round talking to old fogeys like us.'

'Old fogey – you?' bellowed the Brigadier, listening in on their conversation. 'What does that make me then?'

'An ancient old fart!' called out his brother Ben from the other side of the room. The laughter this produced was too much for Susan to bear. She stood up and rushed out in floods of tears. A concerned Mary followed her as the rest of them fell into an embarrassed silence.

'You should watch your language in front of young gels,' admonished the Brigadier.

'Perhaps I should go and apologise,' said a chastened Ben. 'I didn't mean to offend.'

'I don't think it was you, Uncle Ben,' consoled Freddie. 'I think it may be more to do with her aunt having to spend Christmas in prison simply for trying to protect her from this rapist chap.'

'Quite,' agreed the Brigadier. 'Sensitive young soul like that, seeing us all enjoying ourselves, while her poor aunt's incarcerated. She's bound to feel guilty, stands to reason.'

'Annoying thing is,' said Freddie, 'that the man she clobbered was arrested yesterday for assaulting her, but with it being Christmas we can't get her out on bail.'

'Really?' growled the Brigadier. 'You don't think so, eh?'

'You're a magistrate, Harry me boy,' said Ben, relieved to be absolved of blame for Susan's tearful exit. 'Don't you have any influence in such things?'

'I'll make a phone call,' decided the Brigadier. 'See if I can stir things up a bit.'

As the Brigadier went from the room with Freddie, Jimmy gave a puzzled frown. He didn't know what was wrong with Susan, but he knew it was nothing to do with Auntie Dorothy. He shrugged his bafflement at the behaviour of women in general and resumed his conversation with his new-found friend, Tricky Dicky Dodsworth.

Mary Fiddler found Susan sitting in the kitchen, weeping quietly. She stood behind her and placed her hands on Susan's shaking shoulders.

'I suspect you and I have something in common,' said Mary gently. She took a handkerchief from her pocket and gave it to Susan.

'What's that?' asked Susan, wiping her eyes fiercely, as though annoyed at her silly weakness.

'Perhaps I should have said some*one* in common.'

'Oh dear,' sighed Susan, 'is it that obvious?'

'Only to me.' Mary sat on the chair beside Susan. 'You see, I heard you talking to Freddie when you came last year – you know, when he fell asleep and you thought you were alone with him.'

Susan blushed. 'It's alright, Mrs Fiddler,' she said. 'I won't embarrass Freddie. I'm happy for him, honestly I am. Elizabeth seems very nice.'

'Yes, she does *seem* very nice, doesn't she?' agreed Freddie's mother. '—Still, you never know,' she added mysteriously.

Susan gave a rueful grin as she stood up and walked back to the dining room with Mary.

Dorothy opened her eyes then closed them quickly, as she couldn't believe what she'd seen the first time. She vaguely remembered Delma standing over her in Netherton's office, then seeing her heave the warder over her shoulder and carrying her to the landing rail. With her broken leg trailing behind her, Dorothy had pulled herself out of that room of horror, hard on Delma's unsuspecting heels. As Delma was shouting her Christmas greetings to the inmates below and tossing the dead warder down on them, Dorothy, with tears of pain and terror streaming down her face, was hauling herself into the cell next door, out of Delma's sight. She'd heard the shouts from below as Netherton's body went crashing down, then the slam and locking of the office door and then the rush of feet up the stairs.

Rita was in the lead. She'd seen Dorothy crawling out behind Delma and needed to get to her friend before Delma did.

A roar of rage came from behind the office door. Delma burst back out into the throng of inmates and warders, lashing out at everyone with great ham-like fists. Dorothy kept well out of sight as the battle raged; she saw Delma stagger past the cell door with one warder clinging to her back with her arms around her neck and another retreating backwards, belabouring Delma with a truncheon as she went, causing her gleaming teeth to fall out and bounce by the side of the cowering Dorothy. As the turmoil progressed to the other end of the landing, Rita popped her head round the cell door.

'You're a right bleedin' bother-causer you are,' she grinned. At that point Dorothy passed out.

Dorothy opened her eyes again. Susan was standing there, so was Jimmy, and two older people she'd never seen before. The last time she'd seen Susan there'd been a look of hatred on the girl's face, and for good reason.

'Where am I?' she asked, inevitably. The anaesthetic still dulling her senses.

'Told yer she'd say that,' grinned Jimmy, who'd apparently won a bet.

'You're in the prison hospital, Auntie Dorothy,' said Susan. 'Lucky to be alive apparently – which is more than can be said for the other poor lady.'

'Oh dear,' sighed Dorothy with genuine sadness. She'd quite liked Miss Netherton.

'We're just happy that you're okay,' said Susan, with a gentleness that told Dorothy all she wanted to know. The hatred had gone. She smiled up at her concerned niece.

'Are we friends again?'

Susan squeezed her hand and nodded. 'Friends,' she said. 'Mind you, there was no need to go to these lengths.'

Dorothy held out her other hand to Jimmy. 'Merry Christmas, Jimmy,' she said. 'It is still Christmas, isn't it?'

'Yes, it's still Christmas, Auntie,' Jimmy assured her. 'About half-past-five. We had a great dinner at Freddie's, turkey and everything, and we got some presents off the tree – yer should have seen their tree, it was massi . . .'

'Jimmy!' Susan stopped him there. 'Auntie Dorothy doesn't want to know about Freddie's Christmas tree!'

'Not at all,' smiled Dorothy, trying to clear her mind, 'I expect it was a beautiful tree. As a matter of fact, we were supposed to have turkey, but I expect I've missed it now.' She looked up at Freddie. 'I reckon you must be the famous Freddie Fiddler they're always going on about?'

'Pleased to meet you, Mrs Bairstow,' greeted Freddie, shaking

155

her hand lightly. 'I've heard a lot about you as well. Oh, this is my father.'

The Brigadier stepped forward and instead of shaking her hand, he gave her a smart salute. 'I gather you're a fighter, Mrs Bairstow. I salute that. Know a bit about you, like what I hear.' He stepped back, having said his piece.

A nurse bustled impatiently through and shooed them all away while she drew the curtains around Dorothy's bed. A few minutes later she opened the curtains and announced curtly to the waiting quartet, 'You can take her now,' then hurried away.

'What did she mean? "take her now"?' asked Dorothy.

The four of them grinned. Freddie took it upon himself to explain. 'Your niece here very neatly trapped the wicked Mr Simpson into confessing to your assault. With a policeman and his own ex-fiancée as witnesses.'

'And me,' added Jimmy.

'Sorry, Jimmy, you as well,' laughed Freddie.

'Anyway,' continued Freddie, 'my redoubtable parent here,' he inclined his head in the Brigadier's direction, 'being a magistrate of some standing, has been bullying people all afternoon into letting you out on bail – including the Chief Constable of Leeds, halfway through his Christmas pudding.'

'So, what are you saying?' asked an incredulous Dorothy.

'We're saying you're free to go home,' explained Freddie. 'Or rather you would have been if you could walk. Anyway, we're free to take you to a civilian hospital.'

'You're going to St Jimmy's for a few days, then it's back home. You'll be well looked after,' assured Susan. 'You've spent long enough looking after us, it's the least we can do.'

'Do you know,' said Dorothy tearfully, grimacing with pain as the anaesthetic began to wear off, 'this is one of the best Christmases I've ever had.'

The four of them stared at her in disbelief. Dorothy saw the funny side of what she'd said and burst out laughing, prompting them to join in. As they were lifting her onto a stretcher she looked at Susan and asked, 'Is there anything else I don't know about?'

Susan shook her head, 'I can't think of anything, can you, Jimmy?'

'We bought the house,' said Jimmy.

'Oh, yes,' remembered Susan. 'We bought our house off Simmo. Cheap as well.'

Dorothy lay back in the stretcher. She'd no right to believe such nonsense. But somehow she knew it would be true.

Chapter Seventeen

It was late February and Dorothy was faffing about, as she would call it, in the tiny scullery. There was no room for her wheelchair so she'd propped herself on a crutch, as she attempted, with her one good leg, to cook the children a hot meal for when they got in from school. The snow was quite heavy now and she knew they'd be glad of something warm inside them.

She was still trying to come to terms with their new-found wealth. Just as well really, because with her being out of work, things would have been desperate, despite the Brigadier's assurance that he'd do everything in his power to ensure that proper compensation would be awarded to make up for her recent troubles. She smiled to herself as she chopped the potatoes that Susan had peeled the night before. What a good man to have on your side.

The balance of Susan's money had been placed in what Susan insisted being called a 'family account'. To be administered by her and Dorothy. Dorothy had sold Jimmy's diamond ring to Blackstone's for two hundred and fifty pounds and the money placed into a separate account in his name, that he couldn't touch without Dorothy's signature.

Frank Sackfield had been round to congratulate her on her release and to tell her there was a job waiting for her as soon as she felt ready to start.

Freddie and the Brigadier had been round just once since she came out of hospital and stayed just long enough for it to become perfectly clear to Dorothy that Susan was besotted by Freddie.

'I know it's hard,' she explained to her tearful niece, who'd broken down under the gentlest of questioning by her aunt, 'but it's something you're going to have to accept.'

'Would you have accepted it?' challenged Susan, 'if Uncle Tommy had been going out with another girl when you met him?'

'No,' she admitted, 'probably not!' There was no *probably* about it, she'd fallen for Tommy the first time he'd winked at her from the bandstand of the Hippodrome.

'So, what do you think I should do?' agonised Susan.

'I honestly don't know what you can do, love. He's in Harrogate, you're in Leeds. He's a twenty-two-year-old, practically engaged man, you're a fifteen-year-old schoolgirl.'

'Sixteen soon!'

'If you call July soon,' said her aunt. 'But if you really want my advice you'll try and forget him. From a romantic point of view anyway. You're much better off with someone your own age. It's much safer in many respects.'

'Never,' declared Susan.

'Now why am I not surprised?' sighed Dorothy.

William was apparently in a children's home in Huddersfield. Dorothy, Susan, Jimmy, Freddie and the Brigadier had had a long discussion as to what to do about him and concluded that nothing could or should be done until Dorothy was completely in the clear. When they made their move to bring him back they wanted no unforeseen obstacles to add to young William's trauma. The prosecution had applied for a *sine die* adjournment pending the outcome of the case against Simpson.

'What does that mean?' she'd asked Alan Greenough, who came round to give her the news.

'In a nutshell, it means we have to nail him before you can apply for the charges against you to be dropped.'

'And how long's this likely to take?' she asked, mindful of not being able to get William back while the charge was still hanging over her.

'Could be a few months – even then we can't be certain of a prosecution. He's claiming you willingly had sex with him the week before,' explained Alan, 'and that he didn't try to rape you, it was just a lovers' tiff that got out of hand!'

'He's lying,' she retorted angrily. Despite there being a vague element of truth in Simpson's claim, no way was Dorothy about to admit to it.

159

'I know that and you know that, but if it gets to court, there'll be a lot of unpleasant things said about you that might well reach the papers.'

'I suppose you're right,' she admitted. 'You're trying to tell me something, aren't you?' She could see by his fidgety manner that there was something on his mind.

He nodded. 'It's just a suggestion, but if you drop the charges against him, I understand he'll do the same for you.'

'My word, that's good of him!'

'And it'll leave the way clear for you to get William back.'

This of course was the clincher.

'Where do I sign?' asked Dorothy.

Alan Greenough smiled, 'He didn't exactly get away with it though, did he, Mrs Bairstow?'

Dorothy laughed and looked round at the house her niece had almost conned Simpson out of.

'You don't know the half of it, constable,' she laughed.

With the charges against her withdrawn, they planned to make their move to get William the next week. Jimmy burst in first. He sniffed appreciatively. 'Ooh, that's smells great, Auntie. What're we having?'

'Sausage and mash, with bread and butter pudding to follow. Where's Susan?'

'Talking to her boyfriend. Just passed 'em on me way back.'

'Boyfriend? Who?' Dorothy asked suspiciously. Susan was turning into an exceptionally pretty young lady and she'd need to vet all prospective suitors. She didn't want her niece latching on to just anyone on the rebound from Freddie.

'Ray Donoghue.'

'Raymond? Ah yes, I quite like Raymond.' Dorothy was relieved that Susan had found an alternative to Freddie – a one-sided love affair if ever there was one.

'He's great at fighting,' enthused Jimmy. 'School boxing champion. Yer should've seen that fight he had with Boothie. I thought they were goin' ter kill each other. Boothie's in t' sixth form, two years older than Ray – but Ray knocked hell out of him.' Jimmy winced as the unintentioned expletive slipped out, but Dorothy didn't seem to notice.

'You shouldn't make heroes out of people, just because they fight,' she admonished. 'Look what happened to me?'

Jimmy failed to understand this. 'What do you think would have happened if you hadn't hit Simmo, Auntie?' he reasoned, innocently.

Dorothy narrowed her eyes. Trapped by his thirteen-year-old logic. 'What I meant to say was, you mustn't fight without good reason – and I had good reason, I doubt if Raymond had.'

Jimmy disagreed but let it go.

Susan held her breath as Ray walked up to the pay box. 'Two back stalls, please,' he asked commandingly.

The woman looked up momentarily, but long enough for Susan to wonder if they'd get in. They were at the Dominion Cinema to see Lana Turner and John Garfield in *The Postman Always Rings Twice*. It was an 'A' certificate and Susan was still well short of her sixteenth birthday, but eager to see what was described on the posters as M.G.M.'s 'raciest film ever'. Ray was just sixteen and therefore technically old enought to take Susan in as an accompanying adult. Providing they believed he was sixteen.

'Two and six, please,' sniffed the uninterested woman, sending a couple of tickets shooting out of the machine.

A gum-chewing usherette led them down the aisle, pointing out odd vacant seats in the otherwise full auditorium.

'Haven't you got two together?' asked a disappointed Ray.

'Can't see none, love.'

There was a shout from the back row, followed by a violent slap, as a woman stood up and pushed her way out past a dozen sets of reluctant knees, closely followed by a protesting gentleman friend, much to the amusement of the audience.

'Seems you're in luck,' grinned the usherette, pointing her torch at two recently vacated seats in the middle of the back row.

Ray and Susan settled down in the cramped and creaking seats to watch the Pathe News and learn that Al Capone had died and Crown Prince Gustaf of Sweden had been killed in a plane crash. Above them, the projector beam flickered down towards the screen, illuminating the constant clouds of cigarette smoke billowing through it, not to mention the occasional tab end, flicked by some playful youth in the hope that it might drop down someone's neck.

161

As the main feature came up, Ray slid a tentative arm around Susan. Maybe it wasn't as pleasant as she imagined Freddie's arm would be, but it was pleasant all the same. He gradually drew her to him until her head was resting on his shoulder. Perhaps she was better off with someone her own age. Ray was nice and uncomplicated. If she *had* to have a boyfriend, it might as well be him. He wasn't interested in the film, she knew that. Ray had other things on his mind. She knew that as well. What she didn't know were her own thoughts on the matter. She looked up at him and caught his attention. He nervously leaned across and gave her a tentative peck on the lips, before drawing away to test her reaction. Ray was as new to this as she was, but he wasn't going to tell her that.

'Is that it then?' she whispered. 'Is that all I'm going to get?' She was amazed at her own promiscuity, kissing a boy in the back row of the pictures. She'd heard about girls like that but she didn't realise how much fun it was.

They were still kissing when the national anthem came on at the end, urging them, reluctantly, to stand to patriotic attention.

As they moved to leave, a man on the row in front leaned over to them and commented drily, 'Good picture that. You want to come back tomorrow night and watch it!'

Susan and Ray grinned at his sarcasm as they walked out into the icy street, past a queue of people gradually moving forward to catch the second showing.

'Rubbish that, what do you think, Susan?' said Ray, loud enough for all the shuffling cinemagoers to hear.

'Worst picture I've seen for ages,' replied Susan, convincingly.

They trudged away, giggling to themselves, leaving in their wake a queue of people wondering at the wisdom of their choice of film that evening.

'What shall we do now? It's only ten-past-eight,' asked Susan.

'We could get some fish and chips and take them back to our house,' he suggested hopefully.

'You sure know how to spoil a lady,' laughed Susan, who was happier than she'd been for a long time.

'Well, me mam and dad have gone to the Empire with our Eileen. They won't be back till late. We'll have the house to ourselves'

'Oh.'

Susan found the unspoken implications of such privacy quite exciting. She'd enjoyed their flirtation on the back row and she rather fancied continuing it. The fact that it might lead to something else gave the whole affair an added frisson.

They ate their fish and chips in front of the roaring front room fire. Ray had thrown some more coal on to the smouldering embers that had greeted them; it has been damped down by Ray's father, pending their return from a rare visit to the Empire Variety Theatre.

'We've got some dandelion and burdock, if you'd like some,' offered Ray.

'Yes, please.'

Ray poured the red-brown liquid half way up a pint pot stamped, 'Melbourne Breweries' then poured himself some into a glass emblazoned, 'John Smith's Magnet Ales'.

'Me dad collects them,' he explained cheerfully. 'Brings one home every Saturday night – sort of a hobby.'

They finished their fish and chips and lay back on the settee, arms around one other. Comfortable in each other's company. Ray leaned over and kissed her. This time more passionately than in the pictures. Susan wasn't sure of this, she gently pushed him away.

'Phew! I couldn't breathe,' she said, by way of excuse.

'Sorry,' Ray blushed.

She'd never seen him blush before and felt slightly guilty. 'It's not your fault,' she consoled. 'Come here.'

She pulled him towards her and kissed him with the same passion as he'd been kissing her.

'You're a good kisser, Ray Donoghue,' she announced, breaking away for a moment. 'I bet you've kissed lots of girls.'

There was something in her voice that told him to answer carefully. If he told the truth, that she was his first girlfriend, it might jeopardise his prospects. Girls liked men with experience. But then again, if he lied, she might finish up asking all sorts of awkward questions. Ray was useless at lying.

He settled for, 'I realise now that I've never actually kissed any girl before.' The accent on the word 'any', designed to make Susan feel special. It appeared to work.

'I'll believe you, thousands wouldn't,' she pulled him back towards her, satisfied now that she was his first girlfriend.

They kissed with renewed vigour, Ray's rising passion getting the better of him as he pressed his hand against her breast, giving it a gentle squeeze.

She jerked away, whether with guilt or shock, she didn't know. Instinctively, she grabbed her half drunk glass of dandelion and burdock and threw it at him. Liberally dousing him and causing him to spring to his feet in acute embarrassment.

'Sorry, Susan, I didn't mean to, er – I just got carried away.' Ray cut a pathetic figure. His best shirt dripping wet, his face crimson, not knowing what to say or do.

Once again Susan felt guilty. She stood up and held him. 'No, it's me who should be sorry. You were only doing what it's natural for a boy to want to do.'

Raymond nodded his agreement through his discomfort, completely baffled by Susan's rapidly changing emotions. 'I think I'd better take me shirt off though,' he said. 'Blimey! you don't do things by halves, do you?'

He removed his shirt and placed it on the fireguard to dry.

'I'll wash it for you if you like,' offered Susan.

'No, it's okay. Me mam'll wash it in the morning.'

Raymond lay down on the floor in front of the fire and studied this complex girl smiling down at him. His pale-skinned body much better muscled than most sixteen-year-olds, mainly due to his love of sport. She knelt beside him and kissed him lightly on the lips, then said,

'I'm not ready for – you know what. It's nothing to do with you.'

'That's okay,' he accepted. 'I'm a bit scared myself. Certainly of going, well, all the way and all that.'

'All the way and all what?' she teased, gently running her fingers across the hard muscles of his stomach.

Ray closed his eyes to enjoy the tenderness of the moment as her fingers wandered over his body. His relaxed concave stomach leaving a small space beneath the waistband of his trousers, into which she allowed her hand to teasingly venture before withdrawing it, then gently caressing his stomach and his chest and his neck and his face. Unconsciously aroused by her little game, she allowed her hand to venture downwards time and time again, each time a little further. Ray was becoming quite disturbed and could feel himself rising up to meet her. He opened his eyes, but she wasn't looking at him, her eyes were fascinated by the daring of her own hand, her face was flushed with an excitement matched by his own.

Reaching under her dress, he placed a hand on the inside of her thigh. It felt glossy and warm and she froze momentarily, as though making a momentous but reluctant decision.

'Don't you dare, Raymond Donoghue!' she said eventually.

Ray retrieved his a hand, wondering whether to protest about the unfairness of it all, but decided against it. Their eyes met and Susan held him defiantly in her gaze as she ran her hand downwards once again, this time just touching him. Both hearts were thumping now as she stroked his stomach. Then, with a tantalising slowness, she allowed her fingers to move downwards once again, reaching down to hold him. There was a smooth, velvety feel to him that surprised and pleased her and she held him and caressed him with an exquisite gentleness he would probably never know again.

With her free hand, she undid his trousers, partly to release his erection and partly out of curiosity – she exposed him just as he exploded in a great moan of ecstasy, leaving her aroused and frustrated and knowing there was nothing left for her.

Susan hurried home that night engulfed in remorse and self-recrimination at her weakness. What must Raymond think of her? What would Freddie think if he knew? What if she'd gone all the way and lost her virginity? What would Freddie have thought of her then? She could still picture Raymond as she'd left him. Still lying there, eyes closed, a half smile on his face. His erection slowly subsiding in the light of the flickering fire.

Fancy a good Catholic girl like her being seduced by the sins of the flesh. And why did the memory still excite her? Did she really want to repeat it? Perhaps next time go a little further. Confession and absolution was the only answer. But who would she confess to? Certainly not Father O'Flaherty nor Father Proctor. They both knew her too well. They even called her Susan in the confessional where she was supposed to be anonymous. No, it had to be Father Helliwell in the school chapel, where confessions were heard every Friday. She rarely went there and anyway she could always disguise her voice a little. Her identity would remain secret.

*

165

'Good film?' asked Dorothy, looking up from a book as Susan came in and flopped down in a chair.

'Yes, thank you.'

'Where'd you go afterwards? Anywhere nice?' Dorothy wasn't trying to pry, but she was new at this parent business and felt she should keep herself informed of the whereabouts of her two charges.

Susan felt like telling Dorothy to mind her own business. Despite having told her aunt that she was forgiven for the William episode, she would probably hold it against her until the day they got their brother back, at least. However, she chose to be polite.

'Went back to Ray's house.'

'That's nice, meet his mam and dad, did you?'

She caught Susan blushing and instantly knew what she'd been up to. Smiling, she held Susan's hand. 'I was your age once, you know. They weren't in, were they?'

Susan said nothing. Dorothy knew she'd need to pick her words carefully – if she was to say anything at all.

'Look, Susan,' she said. 'I'm not a Catholic as you know, and I know it's difficult for a pretty young girl like you to, er – to resist her natural biological urges, if you get my meaning.' She was blushing now and Susan was squeezing her hand.

'It's alright, Auntie. It's not quite what you think – we didn't go all the way. In fact, we didn't even go half way.'

'Oh good, I, er— I was hoping you hadn't. Apart from anything else, you're under age.'

'It's just that . . .' started Susan.

'Just that what, love?'

'I'm going to have to go to confession.'

'Ah!' said Dorothy, wondering where the half way point was.

'I thought I'd go to the school chapel, Father Helliwell doesn't know me as well as the priests at church.'

'Sounds like a great plan to me. I know that's what I'd do – if I were a Catholic. You could disguise your voice as well, you're good at voices.'

'Hmm! Do you think God might object to that?'

'I think He'd regard it as a definite plus – making good use of your God-given talents and all that.'

'I'll do my Irish.'

'Oh, yes – that's your best one. Let me know how you go on, won't you?'

166

Susan laughed, 'I most certainly will not!'

Dorothy shrugged, disappointed. Susan stood up to go upstairs to bed. She turned back to her auntie.

'Auntie Dorothy,' she said.

'What, love?'

'Thanks.'

Dorothy went back to her book, happy at having been able to offer such useful parental advice.

'Bless me, Father, for oi have sinned. It is two weeks since me last confession Father . . .'

Susan had chosen to adopt the lilting County Mayo brogue of Sister Claire. Mimicry being a talent of Susan's. Especially her impersonation of the pretty young nun who taught geography and history to 5A.

'Father, oi've committed a sin of der flesh wid a young man!'

She heard the old priest catch his breath. 'Go on, my child,' he said quietly.

'Oi touched a part of his body dat's forbidden, causing him to,' she paused, wondering if she should use the word in such a holy place, '. . . to ejaculate, Father!'

She cringed, half expecting a bolt of lightning to come crashing down on her.

'Is that all, my child?' asked the priest gently, as though trying to coax more out of her.

She felt like saying, 'Isn't that enough?' – it was certainly her most productive confession to date.

'Yes, Father,' she replied truthfully, her accent still in place.

'Nothing else?'

'No, Father.'

There was a long silence before the priest said, 'For your penance I want you to say a Rosary each day for seven days. Now make a good Act of Contrition!'

Seven Rosaries! This was tantamount to capital punishment in confessional terms. Even Mary McAllister had never been given seven Rosaries and she'd definitely been 'all the way' with Kevin Murray from St Thomas's. Susan finished her Act of Contrition and stood up to leave.

'Thank you, Father Helliwell,' she said politely.

'Goodbye, Sister Claire,' sighed the shocked priest.

167

Chapter Eighteen

Dorothy read the letter twice. Assuming she'd misunderstood it the first time. But there was no mistake.

... *We are obliged to inform you that William Bairstow has been successfully placed for adoption. It is the express wish of his adoptive parents that their identity is not to be revealed and we are bound by their wishes in this respect* ...

She handed the letter to Susan who read it with increasing concern.

'They can't do this, can they, Auntie?' she gasped.

'I don't think so – but it appears they have.' She buried her head in her hands. The letter was from the Fairbank Home in Huddersfield, the last address they had for William. She'd written to formally request that William be returned to them immediately.

'I'll go and talk to them,' decided Dorothy.

'And how the devil are you going to get there?' snapped Susan resentfully. 'Hop there on one damn leg?'

'If I have to,' replied Dorothy softly. 'One way or another, William's coming back to live with us. It's just a question of time.'

Susan took some time to regain her composure, but she didn't apologise to her auntie for snapping at her. She read the letter again.

'I'll ring Freddie,' she said. 'His dad'll know what to do.'

'And I'll ring a solicitor, we need to find out what's going on as soon as possible – then I'll go talk to them, on one leg if need be!'

Her last remark was lost on Susan, who was already on her way out, leaving Dorothy hopping around frustratedly. 'I think the first thing we need in this house is a bloody telephone,' she cursed to herself as she finally got her coat on and hobbled off on her crutches to the phone box on Paradine Hill.

She was due to start her new job with Frank Sackfield in a few days. He'd been round and congratulated her on her release and told her the job was still on offer. 'It was pretty common knowledge you'd been badly done by. I knew if I hung fire for a while, the barmy buggers'd see sense. Didn't reckon on you coming home with a broken leg though!'

'I don't need a leg to do your book-keeping,' said Dorothy. 'The worst part is limping to work.'

Frank had offered to give her a lift until her leg was fully mended.

'You'll do no such thing, Mr Sackfield,' argued Dorothy. 'You've been good enough to give me a job. I'll do the rest – you'll not be disappointed in me.'

Susan was just emerging from the phone box as Dorothy arrived.

'The Brigadier asked why it had been so long since anybody had been to see our William,' she said, with uncharacteristic coldness. 'I didn't know what to say – I could hardly tell him we'd been told he was dead.'

Susan's words cut into Dorothy like a knife.

'I thought you'd told Freddie the truth,' she sighed.

'I did, but he didn't tell the Brigadier.'

'I'll tell him then. He needs to know the full story – the most important thing is to get William back. What he thinks of me is unimportant. I'll ring the solicitor first.'

She rang Mr Baldwin, the solicitor who'd represented her in court. Not that she'd been particularly impressed by him – just that he was the only lawyer she'd ever had anything to do with.

'Mr Baldwin,' she asked, after telling him the details over the phone. 'All I want to know is – can they do this?'

'I honestly don't know, Mrs Bairstow. You'd better come in and see me, oh, and while you're in here, there's the question of suing for compensation and injury for your stay in prison.'

'I'm not worried about that.'

'It's me that's worried, Mrs Bairstow – you'll need some money to pay me.'

'Oh!'

169

'Friday morning at ten okay?'

'That'll be fine, thank you.'

'I've been on to Fairbank Home,' began Victor Baldwin, 'and they seem to think everything's above board. They don't think they've done anything wrong.'

'But surely I should have been told.'

'It seems you weren't his legal guardian.'

'I'm his aunt, for God's sake.'

'Not a blood relative, and apparently . . .' he hesitated, trying to put this next bit as delicately as possible, 'no one went to visit him for a period of two years!'

Dorothy felt an intense dejection. Susan, sitting beside her, didn't trust herself to say anything.

'Look – it's maybe not as hopeless as it seems,' he added. 'Family matters are quite delicate things, and the feelings of William and his brother and sister may have to be taken into account. Also it could well be that the people who adopted him may want to give him up when they find out the true circumstances. I understand he's a bit of a handful.'

'How long's it all going to take?' asked Susan.

'If we have to go to court it could be months – but,' added Balwin, trying somehow to soften the blow, 'it may well be that we can deal with this outside court. The only thing I ask of you is, please – no matter how frustrated you feel – don't interfere. This is a very delicate matter. I'll keep you informed.'

'Every step of the way,' insisted Dorothy.

'Every step of the way,' agreed Baldwin.

Chapter Nineteen

This was the first time in the two weeks since she'd started working for Frank Sackfield that Dorothy had attempted the journey to work without crutches and she wasn't finding it easy. The journey had been somehow easier using crutches but now she walked with a stick, cursing regularly to herself, a legacy of her time in prison, eyes glued to the pavement in dread of slipping on some unseen crack in the pavement. She cursed her own stupidity at attempting to walk to work with a broken leg – and she cursed Victor Baldwin.

Baldwin's idea of keeping her informed 'every step of the way' had amounted to just the one letter she'd received that morning saying he'd now applied for a court hearing date and that there was no point him approaching the Fairbank Home as the matter was now *sub-judice*, whatever that meant.

To cap it all, this was the morning her dear old dad chose to stop and have a chat with her. It was almost as if he'd been waiting for her. She was just rounding the corner from the bottom of Paradine Hill on to Eccleston Road when his car swished to a halt beside her. She glanced to her left before carrying on. She'd planned on resting on the seat beside the tram stop but gave up that idea as it would mean talking to her father.

'Bugger off!' she snapped brusquely.

'Oh, I'm buggering off alright,' he sneered. 'I just hope you remember that promise I made a couple o' years back.'

Dorothy remembered Sid's threat only too well, but she wasn't about to give him that satisfaction. She jabbed the end of her walking stick viciously towards his open window, making him jerk his head away. His face turned ugly momentarily until

171

he realised this was the reaction she wanted. The sneer returned.

'Oh, and give my regards to Frank – tell him it's nothing personal, not between me and him anyway.'

He drove off, still sniggering to himself leaving Dorothy wondering what the hell he was up to.

Frank Sackfield walked into the office later that Monday morning, slamming the door behind him with a bad-tempered bang. A frown creased his usually cheerful face. He was a joiner by trade, although since returning to his business after being invalided out of the army with various 'hard to get at' bits of shrapnel still embedded in his body, he'd decided against going back on the tools and left the hard graft to fitter men than himself.

Dorothy was there to greet him, pouring boiling water into a chipped teapot. They shared the inner office which was mostly occupied by a huge desk with a chair at either side. On Frank's side was a telephone, four large pebbles weighting down a site plan, various scale rules, several cigarette packets, a pub ash tray, three cluttered wire trays, labelled, IN, OUT and SHAKE IT ALL ABOUT and a battered tin mug. Dorothy's side was well ordered; invoices ready to write up, a couple of ledgers, an antique Remington typewriter, a jam jar full of pencils, a bottle of Stephen's ink and a fountain pen.

'Problem, Frank?' asked Dorothy, who'd been working there long enough to spot a change in her boss's mood.

'You might say that,' replied Frank. 'You know that site on Moorcroft Road in Harrogate?'

Dorothy nodded. He was talking about a building site he'd just bought for a quality twenty-two house development. His most ambitious project to date.

'Well, someone's just bought the big field at the back and there seems to be a big problem with my drainage rights. If I can't drain through that field, I'm what's known in the trade as well and truly knackered!'

There was a fifteen-acre building plot at the back of Frank's site on which he had a verbal agreement with the owner to buy in small lots once he'd finished building on the first site.

'I thought you were buying that site, Frank?' asked Dorothy.

'Apparently not,' said Frank despairingly. 'Money talks in this business. Sid Allerdyce came right out of the blue and bought the whole lot. Doesn't make sense. He builds bread and butter houses, always has. This is choice land, he must have laid out a fortune for it. It'll take him three or four years to sell a site that size in this day and age. That's a hell of a lot of money to have standing around doing nothing. Unless he knows something that I don't!'

Dorothy's heart sank. So that was it! The lengths her father would go to just to get back at her. There must be more to this than pure revenge, there'd be something in it for Sid, that's for sure.

'Look, Frank,' she said. 'You know I said I'd had experience in the trade when you interviewed me?'

Frank nodded, 'You did – and you obviously weren't waffling. You know more than most of my men.'

'I learned all I know from my father – Sid Allerdyce.'

'What? You're Sid Allerdyce's daughter? That's good, isn't it? Why didn't you mention it before? Come to think of it, why are you working for me and not for him?'

Dorothy looked at Frank, waiting for him to answer his own question. 'Oh no! You don't get on with him, do you?' he moaned.

'That's putting it mildly, I'm afraid,' replied Dorothy. 'My father is an ignorant, arrogant pig of a man!'

'And those are just his good points,' grumbled Frank. 'So, there's no truth in this business of blood being thicker than water then?'

'None at all.'

'And we can't expect any favours from him on your account?'

'Quite the opposite, I'm afraid.'

'What? Surely you don't think he's doing this to have a go at you?'

Dorothy eyed Frank sadly. He was a nice-looking man, tall and strong with powerful arms developed by years of hammering and sawing. A thick head of hair going grey now, above a good-humoured, weathered face. His marriage, like so many others, had been a casualty of war. Elaine, his ever-loving wife, had ended up loving a visiting Yank and now lived in Ohio with Frank's beloved son and her new husband.

'I don't think, I know, Frank,' Dorothy said apologetically. 'It seems I'm a liability to you – if you want me to, I'll leave.'

'I think it might be too late now. Sid's got the smell of a quick

173

profit and I don't think you leaving's gonna make much difference now.'

'Sorry, Fra . . .'

Frank waved her apology away. 'Not your fault, shame though – I was beginning to look upon you as one of my biggest assets. Strikes me you can run the company as well as I can.'

'Well, maybe from a business point of view,' she agreed. 'You do tend to be a bit, well, slap-dash – but I know damn all about the practical side.'

'That's why we'd make such a great team. I'm useless at business, always have been. All I can do is build good houses.'

'What happens if my father refuses you drainage rights?'

'Apart from me going bankrupt, you mean?'

'That bad?'

'Bad enough,' said Frank miserably. 'It turns a twenty-two house development into a site for four pairs of semis, mind you everyone would have a back garden as big as a football pitch. Might just make enough to pay the bank back for the land. Assuming they give me building finance – which they won't.'

'So you'd have to sell it as a site for eight houses?'

'Correct,' said Frank. 'That's the new valuation the bank's going to put on it as soon as they find out what's happening.'

'And that's the price my father will get it for when the bank puts it up for sale,' concluded Dorothy. 'Doesn't make it such a bad deal for him then, does it? Seems to me there's method in his madness.'

She walked over to a wall on which was pinned a location plan of the site. 'Which is my father's field on this plan?'

Frank picked up a red pencil and outlined an area behind his site. 'All this lot,' he said dejectedly. 'Right up to Finnestone Lane.'

'And that's his access, is it? Finnestone Lane?'

'At the moment. He might well choose to use Moorcroft Road if he buys my site.'

Dorothy sat down, chewing the end of a pencil and staring back at the plan. Something wasn't right here. A germ of an idea was beginning to form in her sharp brain.

'What are you thinking?' asked her boss. 'There's something going on inside that brain of yours.'

Dorothy scratched her head with the point of the pencil. 'Has my father actually bought the land?'

'Bought and paid for, in full as far as I know,' replied Frank.

'No, he'd never do that if he could avoid it,' mused Dorothy, chewing the end of the pencil off, picking it daintily out of her mouth and dropping it in the ashtray. 'He could have offered the owner a similar deal to you, only on better terms. He's taking a gamble, is good old Sidney. He's like that. Something to show off about in front of his business pals.'

The telephone rang and Dorothy picked it up, still staring at the plan.

'Good morning, Sackfield Builders. I'll see if he's in, who shall I say is speaking? One moment, Mr Pomeroy.'

She covered up the earpiece with one hand, 'It's a Mr Pomeroy? Needs to speak to you urgently!'

'Bloody hell! How's he found out this quickly?'

'Not your bank manager?'

Frank nodded grimly and took the receiver from Dorothy. 'Hello, George, how are you? Good, the Moorcroft Road site? Yes, I'm expecting planning permission any day now. Pardon? You've heard what? No, there's probably some mistake. Tell you what, I'll check into it and ring you back as soon as I know anything – yes – tomorrow at the latest, bye, Mr Pomeroy.'

Frank sank back into his chair, pale with worry. 'He's found out. I didn't know myself till an hour ago. Who the hell's told him?'

Dorothy eyed him sadly. 'Do you really need to ask, Frank?'

She started on the end of another pencil. Sid was playing tricks. He was out to destroy Frank just because she worked for him, *and* make some money into the bargain. She knew it was a gamble her father was taking, and where there was a gamble there was a catch – and she'd a good idea what it was. She picked up the phone and dialled Freddie's number in Harrogate.

Dorothy looked around the table at her surrogate family. Susan's attitude to her over this past month had been lukewarm at best. Jimmy was the same old Jimmy, often bridging the rift between her and Susan and oblivious, it seemed, to any bad atmosphere in the house.

175

'Saw your dad today,' mentioned Jimmy in passing, as he excused himself from the table.

'My dad?' queried Dorothy, her dessert spoon hovering an inch from her open mouth, dripping custard onto the tablecloth. 'How do you know my dad?'

'From the time you asked him if he still farted like Flamborough foghorn,' grinned Jimmy.

'Would that be the time she asked him if he was still a big loud-mouthed toilet?' inquired Susan of her brother.

'Do you know, Susan, I do believe it was, only she didn't say toilet, she said sh—!'

'I know what I said!' interrupted Dorothy quickly. 'I just didn't realise you were listening!'

'The whole street was listening, Auntie Dorothy,' said Susan, getting up to leave the table. 'You certainly seem to have a way with your relatives!'

'If you knew him you'd realise why I . . .!' Dorothy started to explain, but Susan was gone. Dorothy looked at Jimmy, 'He's not a nice man,' she said.

'I know, Auntie Dorothy, so does our Susan. She's just bein' awkward.'

Dorothy nodded, maybe Susan had good reason to be awkward. 'Anyway,' she said, 'where did you see my father?'

'This morning on the way to school,' said Jimmy. 'He was just coming out of that bank on Priest Lane. He's put a lot of weight on.'

'You what? The Northern Bank? I wonder what he was doing in there, he's always banked at the Yorkshire Penny.'

Dorothy got up from her desk when she heard Frank arrive the following morning. She was standing at the outer door of his wooden office cum store room as he climbed out of his van.

'Are you in the mood for a gamble, Frank?' she called out to him.

'I'm actually in the mood for slitting my throat,' he called back, as he walked across the yard. 'What sort of a gamble?'

'One of the kids saw my father coming out of your bank yesterday morning.'

'That figures,' said Frank, following her back into the office. 'Pomeroy had to get the information from someone involved in the deal. It'd suit your dad to blow the whistle on me. Hurry things along a bit.' He sat down and lit up a cigarette, then remembered his manners and offered Dorothy one.

'That's what I thought,' agreed Dorothy, declining his offer with a wave of her hand. 'Then I thought, "Why didn't my father just ring Pomeroy up with the information? Why bother to go in and see him?" My father hates bank managers, he'd never go near one if he could help it. That was his accountant's job. My father's only ever happy when he's up to his knees in mud.'

'What're you getting at?' asked a mystified Frank, flicking through the morning post and putting it all down in disgust when he saw no cheques were there.

'I think Pomeroy and my father are cooking something up between them,' said Dorothy.

'Could be. Your dad's account's a pretty good one to have. I've known managers bend the rules to secure smaller accounts than that.'

'How much do you owe the bank?' asked Dorothy.

'Not a fortune, about a thousand, but if they call it in I'm out of business – and that'll cost me a lot more than a thousand quid.' He looked curiously at Dorothy, 'Anyway, what's this gamble you want me to take?'

Dorothy took a cigarette from Frank's packet, lit it up and blew a contemplative cloud of smoke over the top of her boss's head.

'Ring Pomeroy back and tell him you've found a way around the problem. If he asks how, just blind him with science – but make it sound convincing! Then when my father makes you an offer for your land, call his bluff, kick him out on his ear! Don't let him think you're in the least bit worried.'

Frank looked at her and nodded slowly. She had a quick, devious mind, much quicker than his. She was able to view the situation more dispassionately, see aspects that were clouded to his blinkered vision. All Frank could think about now was avoiding going broke, a damage limitation exercise. Sid Allerdyce knew Frank well and was relying on him reacting in a certain way; anything else and Sid would be worried. But Dorothy knew her father well and planned on playing him at his own game, albeit with Frank's money.

*

Frank was in the yard when Sid arrived later that morning. Sid arrogantly walked uninvited into the office and sat himself down in Frank's chair. A half smoked cigar protruding from his rubbery mouth dropped ash onto his suit. Frank left him there for ten minutes before he came in.

'Thought I'd try it out for size, Frank,' smirked Sid. jabbing his cigar out in Frank's ash tray among Frank's Senior Service stubs.

'You'll need a much bigger chair for your fat arse, Sid. Is there something you want, I'm a bit busy at the moment?' Frank retaliated with an air of impatience, elbowing Sid to one side as he took something he didn't need out of a drawer.

'I won't beat about the bush,' said Sid. 'That's not my style.'

'No, the only only thing you beat are small children!' cut in Dorothy hotly, sitting down opposite her father.

'Not often enough by the look of things,' sniggered Sid. He returned his attention to Frank, pushing back his chair to allow himself room to put his feet on the desk. 'Your bank's about to foreclose on your overdraft, Frank lad. They've found you've included in your list of assets a piece of land that's only worth a quarter of what they thought it was worth, you naughty lad!'

Frank returned Sid's belligerent gaze with a mildly bored expression, which had the desired effect of unsettling Sid, who continued. 'When they do, and your creditors find out, they'll all be down on you like a ton of bricks. Ever been bankrupt, Frank? Unpleasant experience so they tell me.'

The telephone rang, Dorothy picked it up and pressed a button to transfer it to the outer office. 'It's for me, Frank,' she explained, 'I'll take it through there.'

'I don't know,' sneered Sid. 'Allowing your staff to take private phone calls. No wonder your business is in the shit. Tell you what I'll do. I'll give you a grand for your bit of land. Pay off your overdraft, what do you say?'

'I paid three times that much for it!' snapped Frank, dropping his guard for a second. 'Anyway, how do you know how much my overdraft is, unless you're in league with Pomeroy?'

Sid held out his arms, and shrugged his shoulders, 'If you think I'm doing something illegal, Frank, sue me, phone the police. I'm a businessman, just looking for the best deal.'

Frank knew he had him there. He was doing nothing illegal,

Just unethical. A word alien to most businessmen. Sid took out his chequebook.

'Look, Frank lad, as an act of good faith I'll write you a cheque out now, just sign this contract to transfer the land to me and your bank's off your back just like that.'

He took a contract from his inside pocket and laid it on the desk in front of Frank, who made no move to pick it up. Sid looked up at him patronisingly. 'It's either this or let the bank foreclose. They'll have to sell to me. No one else is likely to show an interest and you'll finish up with, what? Nothing, after all the vultures have picked at what's left!'

Frank stared at the soles of Sid's shoes. Left to his own devices, this is when he would have capitulated. Accepted that he'd been done over by a craftier businessman. He then looked round at Dorothy as she spoke on the telephone in the outer office, she turned and winked at him and he felt a surge of relief that she was on his side.

'I see, and just how long have you been planning this, you fat-arsed bastard?' said Frank sarcastically, picking up the contract and tearing it down the middle. 'Get out before I kick you out! I'd sooner give the land away than sell it to you.'

'The bank won't let you do that, Frank,' retorted Sid, unsettled that Frank hadn't backed down as he expected. This wasn't the Frank he knew. 'The Northern's got first charge on it. Pomeroy won't be too pleased when I tell him you've turned down my offer!'

He stamped out of the office past Dorothy, who was just saying, 'Thanks, Freddie,' before putting the phone down. 'Bye, Sidney!' she called after Sid, who hated being called Sidney. Frank joined her at the door as Sid roared off in a cloud of dust.

'He offered me a grand for the land,' he said grimly. 'Trouble is, that's all it's worth without drainage rights onto his land.'

'Maybe not,' said Dorothy cheerfully, walking back inside. 'I've got some interesting news. That was a friend of mine on the phone. His father's on the Harrogate Planning Committee – and no way will my father be allowed access on to Finnestone Lane. It's apparently much too narrow to take all the additional traffic. The only viable access is through your site.'

'Do you think Allerdyce knows this?'

'Oh yes, I'm absolutely sure he does,' said Dorothy, 'He'll

have known before he applied – you see that's his big gamble. He needs both your bank and you to think he can get access to his site from Finnestone Lane, even though he knows he can't.'

'Christ! It's a hell of a gamble he's taking! So why don't we just tell the bank all this?'

'Because we're not supposed to know. It'll be at least a month before his application's officially rejected, during which time he'll have got your bank to force you out – and he'll be able to pick up your land for next to nothing!'

'The crafty old bugger!' There was a hint of admiration in Frank's voice.

Dorothy shrugged, not sharing Frank's grudging admiration of her father. 'That's how he's always done business. He won't see it as much of a gamble though, not with your bank manager in his pocket.' She eyed Frank seriously. 'You'll have to act quickly to stop the bank foreclosing. He'll sit on Pomeroy until he's got his hands on your land. Without your bit, his land isn't worth that!' She snapped her fingers.

Frank was shuffling through a sheaf of papers he'd just taken out of a drawer. He picked out one and studied it carefully.

'Seven days' notice,' he said dejectedly. 'They can give me seven days' notice then foreclose.'

'I think your call to the bank probably bought you a bit more time,' reasoned Dorothy. 'Pomeroy's not going to be too sure of anything now. He won't do anything until my father jumps on him and convinces him you're bluffing. I reckon we could have as much as a couple of weeks to raise the thousand pounds.'

The phone rang again. It was a man wanting his roof repairing, she handed it to Frank. 'In the meantime,' she smiled, 'we carry on as normal.'

Dorothy eyed her family as they finished their meal, wondering whether she was about to be fair to them.

'My boss is in trouble,' she announced. 'He needs money to stop my father taking over his business.'

'Your dad would kick you out if that happened, wouldn't he?' said Susan.

'Yes, he would. But that's not what I'm concerned about. If Mr Sackfield could find a thousand pounds now, it would be worth a lot more in a few months' time.'

180

Jimmy was about to leave the table; this conversation was of little interest to him, but Dorothy stopped him. 'Stay here, Jimmy, this concerns you as well.'

'I've been thinking about us giving him the thousand pounds, in exchange for a share in his business.'

'We haven't got a thousand pounds,' said Susan sharply.

'*I* certainly haven't,' agreed Dorothy. 'But you two have.' We'd have to take a mortgage out on the house, and give Frank the money from your two accounts.'

'How's this going to help us get William back?' asked Susan illogically.

'This has got nothing to do with William, as well you know,' sighed Dorothy patiently. She'd made a vow never to lose her temper with Susan, no matter how much she goaded her about William. Deep down she knew she deserved all she got. 'We're doing all we can to get William back. The solicitor's waiting for a court hearing date. I'm as frustrated as you are, believe me.'

'Then why bother with Frank Sackfield?' retorted Susan. 'Haven't we got enough to think about? And why risk our money on someone we hardly know?'

'If I thought it was a risk I wouldn't let you do it,' persisted Dorothy. 'Anyway, I'm not going to argue with you, it's your money and I've no right to ask.'

An embarrassed silence followed before Jimmy piped up, 'You can have my money, Auntie Dorothy.'

'Thanks, Jimmy, that's kind of you, but I'm afraid it's not enough. Let's just forget I ever mentioned it.'

Susan was shifting uncomfortably in her chair. All this talk of finance was way above her head. Freddie had organised the buying of the house for her and she knew she needed to be guided by Dorothy on many matters before she felt confident to face the world on her own. She knew she was being unreasonable, petulant even, but the anger she felt against her aunt for placing her baby brother in this awful position wouldn't go away.

Dorothy stood up to leave for work, taking her coat from the hook on the back of the scullery door and waving goodbye with her stick she went out of the door.

'I think you're rotten,' said Jimmy.

'I don't care what you think,' Susan answered sullenly. 'She shouldn't have done what she did!'

181

'She'd no need to look after us neither,' argued Jimmy. 'She could have sent me an' you to an 'ome.'

'Wish she had – at least we'd all have been together!'

'And she'd no need ter belt Simpson wiv a stool neither,' persisted Jimmy. 'She might have got hung fer that – and she only did it fer you. I think yer rotten!'

'Ohhh – go tell her we'll do it then!' snapped his sister. 'I'm getting ready for school.'

Jimmy didn't hear the last bit, he was already out of the door in pursuit of his aunt whom he seemed to understand better than most.

Frank was already there when Dorothy arrived, looking more relaxed than he'd been for a couple of days.

'I've found a commercial bank who'll lend me six hundred against the land,' he said. 'That leaves just four hundred to find.'

'Frank!' said Dorothy, trying to contain her exasperation. 'Under the circumstances, you need to own the land outright. You're just robbing Peter to pay Paul. We're heading for a stand-off with my father. We can't afford to have other interested parties.'

'Oh,' said Frank, gloomily. Dejected that his scheme was so easily shot down.

'Don't worry,' smiled Dorothy. 'I think I can raise the money. However, there is a catch.'

'There's always a catch,' moaned Frank, 'go on, what is it?'

'I want to buy into your company, or at least my family does. I'm offering you a thousand pounds for a fifty-per-cent share in Frank Sackfield Builders.'

'Fifty-per-cent? Blimey! you don't do things by halves do you?'

'Well, yes actually,' she laughed.

'Oh, right,' said Frank, realising what he'd said. 'You know there's a bit of your dad in you, don't you?'

'Don't start insulting me, Frank, or I'll withdraw my offer,' she said sharply. She didn't like being compared to her father, even jokingly.

'If you'd offered me twice that last week I'd have kicked you out on your ear,' grumbled Frank. He held out his hand, 'Forty-nine-per-cent and it's a deal. The extra one-per-cent means a lot to me.'

'It's a deal,' said Dorothy, taking his hand.

Frank looked at her as he shook her hand warmly and knew he was going to like being her partner.

As Dorothy forecast, the nervous Mr Pomeroy procrastinated almost a week before he put Frank on seven days' notice to clear his overdraft, giving Dorothy just enough time to raise a quick mortgage through the commercial bank Frank was going to use. On the seventh day they were sitting in the office as her father's car pulled into the yard.

Allerdyce, Pomeroy and a third man entered together. Sid was making no attempt to conceal his glee at what was about to happen. Pomeroy was long and thin with a cheap pin-stripe suit and the constipated expression of a man with something nasty under his nose. He pompously placed a piece of paper on the table.

'Mr Sackfield, this is a possession order for the land at Moorcroft Road, Harrogate. It comes into force at close of business tonight. I thought I'd present you with the opportunity to clear your debts now by selling on to Mr Allerdyce, thus avoiding bank and solicitor's charges, which can be quite prohibitive. I've brought my assistant, Mr Ellis, along to witness the signatures.'

'Could you all wait in the outer office, please, we're on our tea break,' said Frank impatiently.

'But . . .' protested Pomeroy.

'Out!' roared Frank.

Dorothy stood and ushered the three of them into the outer office, where they waited, not knowing what was happening. The outer office, as it was called, contained a kitchen table, a telephone, a sink, a worktop and gas ring, on which was balanced a battered kettle. The only place to sit was on pile of cement bags, left there for reasons best known to the yard man.

'Sorry about that,' apologised Dorothy with studied insincerity, 'but this is not a good time for Mr Sackfield,' she said.

'No, quite,' said Pomeroy.

'Bloody awful time, I hope,' growled Sid.

'It's his haemorrhoids, you see,' she explained. 'He's a martyr to his haemorrhoids. Oh, by the way, while you're here. I wonder if you could put this cheque in his account? Save my legs and all that.'

183

She casually handed Mr Ellis a banker's draft for a thousand pounds.

'And if you'd like to sign this receipt, just to say it's safely in your hands. We wouldn't want anything to happen to it, would we?'

Pomeroy went pale. Sid's mouth opened and shut with shock. Ellis, who had nothing to do with the subterfuge, happily signed the receipt, leaving Sid pacing up and down, clenching and unclenching his fists. Frank appeared at the door.

'Our solicitor will be in touch, Mr Pomeroy, instructing your bank to release us from the charge. Will there be anything else?' he asked innocently.

'Yes, there damn well is something else!' roared Sid. 'I need that bloody land and by hell I'm going to have it!'

'Tell me, Sidney dear,' sneered Dorothy. 'Did you plan all this just to have a go at me? Shame you had to drag Mr Pomeroy into it – you've probably cost him his job now.'

Pomeroy was now in a state of shock, with Mr Ellis looking accusingly at him. Sid was storming up and down kicking at anything in his way and shouting obscenities at Frank's yard man, who was quietly brewing himself a pot of tea in the corner.

Dorothy continued to bait her father. 'We all know you won't get permission to access your site on to Finnestone Lane! That application of yours is a cheap sham to fool the banks. Your only access is through Frank's site!'

She then turned to Pomeroy, whose jaw had fallen open with horror, at this piece of information. 'Surely not even you were fooled by that transparent little ruse, were you, Mr Pomeroy?' Dorothy put her hand to her mouth, as though shocked, 'Oh, dear!' she went on. 'I do believe you were!'

Pomeroy flopped down on the pile of cement bags.

'I wouldn't sit there, Mr Pomeroy,' warned Dorothy, 'that's how you get piles. You see, Mr Pomeroy, my dear daddy was banking on you kicking Frank off his land so he could buy it for next to nothing. What the silly man forgot to tell you, was that without Frank's land, his own land's worth, to use banking terminology, practically sod all! Will you still be wanting to take his account, Mr Pomeroy? I'm sure the Yorkshire Penny Bank will be only too delighted to hand it over!'

Frank was silently hoping that Dorothy would shut up at this point as Sid seemed to be taking things quite badly. Foolishly, however, she just couldn't resist one final taunt. Confronting her father, whose face was contorted with rage, she announced smugly:

'By the way, Daddy dear, as Frank's a member at that golf club that keeps turning you down he'll be able to tell all your friends there what a big brainless shit you really are!'

This proved too much for Sid. He punched Dorothy full in the mouth, then flung himself at Frank, who fell backwards into his office, punching wildly in self defence. Sid had gone berserk. With a strength born of madness, he had Frank on the floor with his hands around his throat, squeezing tighter and tighter until Frank's arms stopped flailing about.

A full milk bottle smashed over Sid's head causing him to release his grip and soaking his now unconscious body with Co-op Dairies sterilised milk. Mr Ellis, a youngish, broad-shouldered man, threw the broken bottle to one side, then heaved Frank over on to his stomach, frantically trying to pump air back into the builder's choking lungs.

Dorothy was just coming round, her face a mass of blood, when Frank coughed back to life. She staggered to the phone and dialled 999 asking for police and ambulance. The sight of her father lying unconscious and Mr Ellis tending to Frank, gave Dorothy a fair idea of what had happened.

'Thanks, Mr, er . . .?'

'Ellis, Peter Ellis, I'm afraid I had to hit your father with a bottle, to stop him choking Mr Sackfield – I was sort of trained to do this in the army.'

'What? Hit the Germans over the head with milk bottles?'

'Well, we were taught to improvise,' he explained.

'I'm sure the bank will be very grateful to both you and the army, Mr Ellis. I know Frank will be.'

Frank sat up and squinted at Dorothy through an eye that hadn't quite closed yet. 'He's a bad loser your dad, isn't he?' he croaked. 'Mind you, Dorothy, you did go on a bit!'

Dorothy was nodding painfully as the police and ambulance arrived. Mr Ellis advised the police to take away both Sid and Mr Pomeroy, as he suspected possible bank fraud. He then climbed into the ambulance taking Dorothy and Frank to hospital.

'You're probably wondering why I came along,' he ventured.

'There was no need for it,' assured Dorothy. 'You did enough for us back there.'

'I'm looking upon this as a damage limitation exercise,' he said. 'Under the circumstances I'm sure the Northern Bank will wish to review your account favourably and seek to help you in any way they can.'

'Providing we keep our mouths shut about your Mr Pomeroy?' grumbled Frank cynically.

'Well, I doubt if he'll be with us much longer, but yes, we would appreciate a certain amount of discretion,' admitted Mr Ellis.

Frank was about to tell him where the bank could stick their discretion, when Dorothy placed a gentle hand across his mouth.

'We'd like you to arrange us a meeting with Mr Pomeroy's replacement as soon as possible,' she said sweetly, but looking daggers at Frank. 'Wouldn't we, Mr Sackfield?'

Frank nodded, knowing his fifty-one-per-cent was never going to be enough to out-vote Dorothy.

Peter Ellis looked up and smiled at the group of people who'd just come into his office.

'Ah! So it's you, is it?' grinned Frank. 'They said there was a new manager. I suppose congratulations are in order.'

'Thank you,' smiled Peter. 'Oh, and thanks for pushing my promotion along. Anyway, how are you all?'

'Couldn't be better,' announced Dorothy. She was still walking with a stick and a large plaster covered her nose which, although swollen to twice its original size, was unbelievably not broken.

'Speak for yourself!' complained Frank who had two black eyes, bandages on his head and around his throat and a bandage around his wrist, which he'd sprained with the one good punch he'd managed to land on Sid.

'And how's Mr Pomeroy?' inquired Frank.

'Unemployed,' answered Peter with a satisfied grin.

'Right,' said Frank. 'I thought I'd bring my new business partners along to see you, with it being their half term holidays.'

He introduced Jimmy and Susan. Peter Ellis solemnly shook hands with them.

'Delighted to see Sackfield Builders pursuing a youth policy,' he approved.

186

'They own forty-nine-per-cent, which Dorothy administers on their behalf,'

'I think you've made a wise move, Frank,' said Peter. 'Your business expertise was always a worry to us. We only backed you because you're such a damn good builder.'

Dorothy sat down on one of the two chairs facing Peter. 'I'm glad you see it like that, because we need your help to squeeze my father off his land. Legally this time.'

Peter nodded, serious now. 'Depends on your proposal, what have you got in mind?'

'My father paid fifteen thousand pounds for his land. How much of that do you think his bank put up?'

'Off the record, we know they put up five and your father the other ten.'

'Knowing my father, that'll have stretched him to his limit and if his bank find out they've lent money on a piece of land that's worthless without Frank's bit they'll grab at any opportunity to get out, wouldn't you say?'

'With both hands,' confirmed Peter.

'In that case we'd like to make him an offer of five thousand, through his bank of course – but we'd need you to put up the lot.'

'You realise we never lend a hundred-per-cent on anything,' replied Peter.

'You'd be lending a just third of the land's value, of course you can lend us it,' countered Dorothy firmly.

Peter held her in his gaze. Underneath that plaster was a shrewd and beautiful woman. 'Okay, I think the bank could live with that,' he conceded. Then, 'You're a ruthless business woman, Mrs Bairstow.'

'Only where my father's concerned.'

'And how would you suggest we appraise his bank of their perilous situation?' he asked.

'I believe you people call it the "old boy network",' suggested Dorothy. 'As soon as you've "appraised" them, we'll make our offer. I imagine they'll be quite relieved.'

Peter smiled admiringly, 'Is there anything you haven't thought of?'

'I don't think so.'

'So, you're planning on screwing your own father out of ten

thousand pounds, that's my salary for twenty years. It could well ruin him. Don't you feel a twinge of guilt?'

'I feel my nose,' she replied, 'and I remember who caused it.'

'You can see where she gets it from,' said Frank.

'I've told you not to compare me to him,' snapped Dorothy.

'Leave it with me,' said Peter. 'If you can force your father to sell for five thousand, we'll put the money up. On one condition.'

'What's that?' asked Dorothy.

'That you sell the land immediately, to give yourself some proper working capital. You don't have the resources to develop a site that size. I want you to sell off to one of the big boys and buy something smaller.'

'You've been reading my mind,' laughed Dorothy. She turned and gave Frank a smug 'I told you so' look.

'We've been arguing about that all the way here,' grumbled Frank.

'Not any more you're not,' announced Peter. 'You've lost, and somehow, I don't think it's going to be the first time!'

'Does this mean we're rich, Auntie Dorothy?' asked Jimmy.

'No, it means for the time being we're skint, but at least we've got good prospects,' answered their auntie.

Good prospects mean very little to boys, whatever their age, and Jimmy decided against asking Mr Ellis if he should open an account for their thriving jam jar business.

Chapter Twenty

Dorothy jumped when the telephone rang for the first time. It had been installed over two weeks ago and this was their first incoming call. Altogether it had been used no more than half a dozen times, including a frustrated screaming match with the Fairbank Children's Home in Huddersfield when Dorothy had got to the end of her tether one day. It was Susan who'd taken the phone from her and stiffly reminded her of Baldwin's strict instructions about not interfering. Although secretly she was pleased that her auntie was becoming so passionate about getting her brother back as there was no questioning her auntie's tenacity. Frank Sackfield had confided in Susan one day that her auntie was the most 'bloody-minded female' he'd ever come across and he wouldn't like to get on the wrong side of her.

'Leeds three-oh-three-two-eight,' Dorothy recited her phone number for the first time.

'Mrs Bairstow?' It was a woman's voice, a timid, frightened voice.

'Yes.'

There was a silence for a while which Dorothy broke. 'Hello,' she said. 'Dorothy Bairstow here, who's speaking please?'

'Is it you what's trying ter find William Bairstow?'

'Yes, it is – do you know something?' Dorothy felt her heart pounding.

'He's not been adopted if that's what they're tellin' yer. They sent him away. They weren't supposed ter do it so they marked him down as adopted.'

'Where did they send him? Hello?'

The phone went dead and Dorothy looked it dumbly as she'd

seen people do on the pictures. She sat down for a while to collect her thoughts. Susan, who'd half overheard the conversation, came into the room.

'Was that about William?' she inquired hopefully. There'd been no mention of William on Dorothy's end of the conversation, but Susan had a fixation about her baby brother.

'It was a woman,' said her auntie. 'She said he wasn't adopted. She said he'd been sent away.' Dorothy was in a daze.

'Whereabouts? Did she say whereabouts?'

Dorothy repeated exactly what the woman had said, adding that she sounded frightened but genuine. Susan, for the first time in months, hugged her auntie. Jimmy walked in to find them both in tears, clinging on to one another.

'What's up?' he asked.

'We're going to get William back, that's what's up!' declared his auntie with tearful determination. 'I don't know how, but we're going to get him back!'

'Thanks for this, Frank,' said Dorothy as the car swung out of Broughton Terrace. Susan and Jimmy had wanted to come but there was too much uncertainty about what they were going to do and how long it was going to take, so the two children had already reluctantly left for school.

'We'll keep in touch,' she'd promised them, miming the making of a phone call.

She knew they'd be able to fend for themselves, even if she and Frank didn't get back that night. There was something about the mystery phone caller's voice that told her getting William back wasn't going to be easy.

Frank looked across at her and gave a big friendly grin. 'I think we can afford a day off after the deal you've just done,' he said.

'I've got something else in mind for that money as and when it comes in, so don't start getting big ideas,' warned Dorothy, settling back in her seat and pulling a pack of Craven A from her pocket. She took out two and lit them both at once, handing one to Frank, as she'd seen Paul Henreid do for Bette Davis in *Now Voyager*.

Had it not been for the job in hand, the journey would have been a pleasant one. Frank was an affable companion, easy-going and humorous. It was hard to understand why a wife would ever want

190

to leave such a man. Dorothy was secretly betting his ex-wife was already regretting it.

The cold spring sunshine brightened up the grey stone walls of Huddersfield. There was a grim solidity about the place that you couldn't get in the south. Perhaps in the soft south it wasn't needed. It was mid-morning and all the workers were already in their places. At their looms and lathes and tending their furnaces. The lucky ones had jobs that took them outdoors, where they could breathe the damp air gusting down from the bleak Pennines. Frank weaved his car through the narrow streets looking for a sign that would direct him towards Slaithwaite, which the natives had abbreviated to Slawit, just so that they could look pityingly on foreigners who pronounced it how it was spelt.

He was relieved to see the sign that saved him from stopping to ask. He'd lived in Yorkshire long enough to know they'd pretend not to know what he was talking about if he pronounced it wrong. Yorkshire people can be like that.

The Fairbank Home was a mile outside Huddersfield. Quite a pleasant-looking place, very much at odds with its immediate derelict surroundings. Frank drove up to the entrance and parked in a spot reserved for the H. Parkinson, Chief Warden.

'Chief Warden,' read Frank out loud.' That's a comforting title for homeless kids. I bet they feel right at home here.'

He and Dorothy knocked loudly on the door. There were no children about as it was a school day. The door was opened by an officious woman in a blue nurse's uniform.

She greeted them with a shocked 'Oh, dear, you've parked in the warden's spot. He won't like that.'

'Well, that's okay then,' breezed Frank cheerfully. 'I don't think I want him to like me!'

Dorothy wasn't sure if this was the right approach but had no option but to go along with it.

'Is the warden in?' she asked.

'No, but he'll be back shortly. I think you should move your car.'

'Oh, don't worry about that, there's a perfectly good spot right at the side of it,' Frank assured her. 'Where's his office?'

'Oh, dear. I suppose you'd better come in,' she said dismally. Turning and leading the way along a cream-coloured corridor and opening a door to a small office.

'This is Mr Parkinson's waiting room. I'll send him along as soon as he arrives.'

Frank and Dorothy sat down on the stiff, office-type chairs and surveyed their immediate surroundings. There was nothing homely about it. No pictures or flowers or evidence of the existence of children. More like a well-scrubbed office block. A vague smell of cooking pervaded the air.

'Not exactly "home from home", is it?' commented Frank.

Dorothy shook her head in agreement. She noticed the door to Mr Parkinson's inner office was slightly open.

'Keep an eye out, Frank,' she cautioned. 'I think I'll have a quick look in his desk before he comes.'

Frank grinned and needed no explanation. Nothing felt right about what had happened so far and he knew they'd have to fight like with like. He stood by the window and saw Parkinson's large black Humber arriving almost immediately.

'Get your skates on, Dorothy love, he's just parking up now! Florence Nightingale's dashed out to talk to him – he's on his way in!'

Dorothy was riffling through the desk drawers as neatly as she could. She tugged at a large drawer only to find it locked.

'Damn!' she cursed. 'I wouldn't mind a look in there.'

She pulled open the shallow central drawer, took out a small notebook and stuck it in in her cardigan pocket just as two sets of hurried footsteps clattered along the corridor.

Parkinson entered the outer office to find Frank and Dorothy sitting expectantly in their chairs. He was a tall man in late middle-age, who might have looked distinguished had his hair not been going bald in such a haphazard fashion. Neither Frank nor Dorothy stood up. Frank had already decided to adopt an unpleasant attitude from the start. He found it worked well when dealing with uncooperative workmen and he saw no reason to treat Parkinson differently.

The warden stood glaring down at them both; their attitude to his matron and the parking of their car did not endear them to him.

'Just who are you and what is your business?' he asked brusquely.

'This is Mrs Dorothy *Bairstow*,' announced Frank, emphasising her surname and searching Parkinson's face for any

192

reaction. There was none from him but the matron gave an involuntary nervous glance in her boss's direction.

'I see you recognise the name, madam,' pressed Frank, 'as well you might. 'A small boy of that name appears to have gone missing from the face of the Earth and we're here to find out why.'

Dorothy was impressed with Frank up to now. Pity he didn't use the same forcefulness in his own business dealings.

'I'm William Bairstow's aunt,' she explained in as cold a voice as she could muster.

'Ah, the one who never came to visit him. Shame that – cried his eyes out every visiting day, didn't he, matron?' observed Parkinson scathingly.

Matron gave a disapproving nod. Parkinson's words were like a stab through the heart for Dorothy. Frank came straight back at him.

'For reasons I wouldn't expect you to understand, Mrs Bairstow was unable to contact her nephew. We expected you to do the job you were paid to do and look after the boy until such time as a home could be provided for him.'

'And that's precisely what we did,' retorted Parkinson, with a smugness that had Dorothy clenching her fists. 'A suitable home was found for the boy and, as I told Mrs Bairstow over the telephone, I believe the boy is very happy there.'

'Happy where?' demanded Dorothy angrily.

'I'm sorry, madam. I cannot disclose that information for reasons I gave you over the telephone.'

Frank, who hadn't introduced himself, stood up and confronted Parkinson with a steely-eyed glare that forced the warden to take a step back.

'In view of reliable information we've received, I've been engaged by Mrs Bairstow to follow a report that William Bairstow has not been adopted by anyone and was in fact transferred to another home! I'll be checking this story with absolute thoroughness and if it's true, criminal charges will follow – against both of you!'

He shouted the last three words in the matron's face, causing her to blanch and look up at her boss with a startled expression on her face.

'Would you kindly leave now,' demanded Parkinson. If Frank had got him worried he certainly wasn't showing it.

'With pleasure,' said Frank. 'But I doubt if this is the last you'll be hearing of us.'

As the two of them left the office, Dorothy stopped beside the matron. 'I don't know what you're up to,' she said, looking the woman squarely in the eye. 'But surely it can't be worth it!'

The frightened look in the matron's eyes told her all she wanted to know. Dorothy looked back at Parkinson and asked sharply, 'I wonder what she's so worried about?'

'Well? What do you think?' asked Dorothy as they sat in the parked car, planning their next move.

'They're lying through their teeth,' replied Frank.

Dorothy took the stolen notebook from her pocket and flicked through it.

'Hmmm, this could be handy. It's an address book.' She read a few pages. 'Doesn't say exactly who everybody is, but there's certainly a lot of them.'

'It's something, I suppose,' conceded Frank, who didn't fancy spending the next few days knocking on the doors of strangers. 'If only we could get a friendly name – we could maybe match it up with an address.'

'The name of the woman who rang me, you mean?'

'She'd do for starters,' he agreed, pressing the starter button and reversing out of the warden's parking spot.

As they stopped at the end of the short driveway, about to turn into the road, Dorothy saw a group of youngsters approaching. She looked at her watch. 'Dinnertime,' she said. 'I bet they're from the home, coming back from school for their lunch. I could smell something cooking back there, couldn't you?'

Winding the window down, she signalled the group to approach. Her smile was all that was needed – especially for the boys.

'Hiya, kids,' she greeted them cheerily. 'Are you all from the prison camp here?'

Her gamble had paid off. All the children laughed, happy to hear an adult share their opinion of the place. They gathered round the car, perhaps wondering if any largesse might be coming their way. An icecream van pulled up at the opposite side of the road, the driver standing by the door and ringing a handbell to announce his arrival.

194

'Buy us an icecream missis!' demanded one short-trousered cheeky face, grinning through the window at Dorothy.

Dorothy laughed. 'Go on then, just for your cheek.'

Frank pulled the car into the road and stopped behind the icecream van. Dorothy got out and counted the heads.

'Six cornets? Right.'

'Seven, missis – Bernard Harrison's just comin'.'

'Seven then,'

'Can I have one, missis?' They were turning up in droves.

Frank joined her and went to the van window. 'Just keep on sending them till I say when,' he said to the icecream man.

The icecream man grinned back, happy to oblige. Dorothy leaned against the side of the van, licking the vanilla icecream from her cornet, surrounded by happy kids.

'Who's your favourite over there?' she asked casually.

The children jostled one another, eager to be the one to answer.

'Nobody, missis,' chirped the cheeky one who'd first demanded icecream. 'They're all arse'oles.'

'Mrs Atkin's not an arse'ole – she's alright is Mrs Atkins. She never hit yer or nowt,' argued a slightly older girl.

All the kids agreed that Mrs Atkins was the best of a bad bunch and definitely not an arse'ole. One young boy proudly displaying a livid bruise on his arm he'd received at the hands of one of the workers in the home. His display was greeted by a cry of derision from another youth.

'That's nowt that. I've got a better one than that!'

'Show us then,' challenged the first youth.

The second youth grinned and blushed slightly. 'Can't,' he admitted, 'it's on me arse!'

This revelation was greeted with howls of laughter. Then a teenage girl said something that had Frank and Dorothy looking at each other with excitement.

'She's not here no more isn't Mrs Atkins. She left t' other day. I reckon old Parky sacked her! She were alright were Mrs Atkins.'

'Oh dear,' commiserated Dorothy. 'I wonder if she's got another job – any idea where she's gone?'

'No idea. She didn't live in t' home. She lived in 'uddersfield somewhere.'

'Do you know if she was married or anything?' inquired Frank.

All the kids howled with laughter once again. 'Married? Mrs Atkins – blimey! Who'd marry her?'

Dorothy thought it time to ask the all important one. 'Did any of you know William Bairstow?'

They all shook their heads at first, then one shouted out. 'Hey! I bet she means Billy Bisto! His proper name were Bairstow – he told me once.'

'Oh aye, missis. Yer mean t' Bisto Kid – he were a little bugger were Bisto!'

'Anybody know where he is now?'

'Don't know, missis. They never tell us where no one's going. He went a few weeks ago.'

'Do you think he might have been adopted by someone?'

'Nah – no one ever gets adopted from here. Not unless yer a right little kid. Sometimes right little kids get adopted.'

The answers came from different children all eager to supply information. But none with anything helpful – apart from the interesting news about Mrs Atkins.

Frank and Dorothy watched the noisy mob stream through the gates of Fairbank Home.

'Funny, isn't it,' mused Frank, 'how kids always manage to adjust to whatever's going on around them.'

Laurence Parkinson watched through the window as Frank drove out through the gate.

'Shit! They're talking to the kids now!' He spat the words out with a vehemence that made the matron cringe.

'It'll be that bloody Atkins woman – she'll have been blabbing. She was in the office when that Bairstow bitch rang up!' He spun round on the matron. 'It's your bloody stupid fault for sacking her! She's trying to get her revenge. What's her address? I'll go round to shut her up.'

'But, you told me to sack her, you said she was too namby-pamby with the children.'

'I expect you to use your initiative, woman, and not create problems for me!' rasped Parkinson. He stormed into his office and began searching through his drawers for his address book.

'Have you taken an address book from this bloody drawer, you stupid bloody woman?'

'I haven't been near your drawers, Laurence. If you want her address I've got it in my office – and I'll thank you not to talk to me like that!'

Even the matron, who was unfortunately besotted by her boss, had a limit to just how much she'd take from him and was rapidly approaching that limit. Parkinson glared at her. He'd taken advantage of her in every way, for the seven years he'd been warden. No way would he ever marry the ridiculous woman, despite their having been engaged for three of those years.

'You don't think one of them took it, do you?' he asked at last, having regained his composure.

'How would they know where to look? They were only in there two minutes before you arrived.'

Parkinson nodded. She was probably right – anyway he was always losing things. She stood tentatively behind him and placed a hand on his shoulder. 'It will be alright, Laurence, won't it?'

Parkinson placed a reassuring hand on hers. 'Of course it will, matron – don't be such a worrier.' But he didn't sound too sure of himself.

Matron thought it was about time her fiancé started calling her by her Christian name.

Dorothy looked up at the house and then down to the address book. 'This is it. Seventy-six, Glenstone Terrace. Hilda Atkins.'

It was a long, neat street of small stone terraced houses. A street with no money and a lot of working class pride. Two small boys, too young for school, were having a peeing contest up a lavatory wall, both attempting to reach a chalked record set by a previous contestant called Razza.

'Could you beat that, Frank?' asked Dorothy playfully as they stopped opposite the peeing boys.

'I'll have you know I was Mill Street Junior School record holder for two years running. Mind you, I'm lucky if I can manage a horizontal stream nowadays. The water pressure drops as you get older.'

'Frank Sackfield, you smutty old man!'

'You started it!'

Dorothy's amusement turned to tension as they approached the door. This could be the last step before they located William. But the house looked lifeless. Not just that no one was in, it looked as though no one lived there. It was hard to tell why. There were still

197

curtains up at the windows and an empty milk bottle on the step which had been recently scoured – it just gave out the message that no one lives here any more.

'If yer lookin' for Hilda, she's done a moonlight!' The raucous information came from an upstairs window next door.

Frank and Dorothy stood back and peered up at the woman in the open window. Curlered hair and gigantic bosom. What Tommy would have called a Dead Heat in a Zeppelin Race.

'Do you know where she's gone?' shouted up Frank.

'Warra you? T' tally man or t' rent man?' she gave a loud toothless laugh. 'I shouldn't bother if I were thee, old lad. She hasn't a tanner ter scratch her arse wi hasn't Hilda! Buggered off last night – God knows where.'

'We're not after money,' called out Dorothy. 'Look, my name's Bairstow, Dorothy Bairstow from Leeds – she knows who I am and what I want. Tell her to give me a ring and I'll be able to help her out if she needs any money.'

'We all need brass, love. Yer can give some ter me – I'll give it to her when I see her.'

'So – you will be seeing her then?' persisted Dorothy hopefully.

The woman gave another toothless grin. 'Doubt it, love – I were just taking t' piss that's all.'

Without saying any more she slammed the window shut on Dorothy's hopes.

'Damn!' she said, with feeling. 'I could have sworn we were getting nearer.'

'Never mind,' consoled Frank. 'We've still got a book full of addresses to work on.'

Dorothy hopped over the low wall dividing the miniscule gardens and knocked on the toothless woman's door. The woman opened the door with a slightly annoyed look on her face which disappeared when Dorothy handed her a pound note.

'Here,' she said, 'this is for your help so far. I'm searching for my nephew who lived at the children's home Hilda worked at. He's left there now and I'm fairly sure Hilda knows where he is. You get her to ring and tell me, and there's twenty-five quid each in it for you.'

The woman looked suspiciously at Dorothy, then at Frank, then at the car. It was the car and Dorothy's accent that convinced her that she could afford to back up her words with cash. She nodded. Twenty-five quid was a lot of money – a month's wages for her old man, when he was working.

'Twenty-five quid *each*,' she clarified.

'*Each*,' confirmed Dorothy.

'I'll keep me eye out,' she said at last.

'Thanks,' smiled Dorothy. 'It's in a good cause. Here's my telephone number.' She handed the woman a scrap of paper on which she'd already written her number, then turned and let herself out of the low wooden gate.

'If it's owt ter do wi that bloody kids' 'ome yer mebbe right,' called out the woman as Dorothy got in the car.

'Would it be rude to ask where the fifty quid's coming from?' inquired Frank.

'Company funds,' explained Dorothy. 'Call it an investment. I'll work better when William's back.'

'Oh, right – you don't mind me asking, do you?'

'Not at all.'

They spent the rest of the afternoon calling at the addresses in the book. With exception of a window cleaner who'd seen one of the boys being severely beaten, no one was able to enlighten them. Frank suspected that many of the people they were calling on would be reporting their visit back to Parkinson. This didn't bother him as anything that unnerved Parkinson was a good thing, but as dusk fell there seemed to be a growing futility about the whole exercise. On a hunch he headed back to Glenstone Terrace and knocked once again on the toothless woman's door.

By now she had her teeth in and her hair combed out, ready for her weekly visit to the West Huddersfield Working Men's Club.

Frank instinctively doffed his trilby hat, a gesture she appeared to appreciate.

'Sorry to trouble you again,' he said. 'But would you mind telling me if anyone else has been round looking for Hilda?'

Flashing him a mouthful of ill-fitting teeth she nodded her head. 'Aye, mister. Big long streak of a feller, came in a big black motor. Ignorant bugger if yer ask me – wouldn't believe me when I said I didn't know where she'd gone.'

Frank doffed his hat again. 'Thanks, missis,' he said, 'that's all I want to know.'

He was turning to go when the woman shouted after him. 'He wanted to know if a man and a woman had been asking after her.'

Frank stopped in his tracks. 'What did you tell him?'

She cackled, 'I told him ter piss off. I didn't like his bleedin' manner.'

'You did the right thing,' Frank assured her. 'I hope to see you again.'

'Hilda's definitely the one we're looking for,' he announced as he got back in the car. 'Parkinson's been round looking for her, but your busty friend told him to piss off.'

'I think that quid might well have been one of my better investments,' replied Dorothy. 'Let's hope we have to fork out the fifty before much longer.'

Chapter Twenty-One

It was over a week since their trip to Huddersfield and each time the phone rang at home Dorothy, Susan or Jimmy had it off the hook before it finished its first ring.

'I'll give it one more week,' promised Dorothy, after the latest false alarm turned out to be a wrong number. 'Then we'll get on to the police. I'd prefer not to because I think Parkinson's somehow prepared for it – but if it's all we can do, then,' she shrugged and looked at Susan's disappointed face. 'Look, Susan – William's alive and kicking and out there somewhere and if you don't think I can get him back then you don't know me very well!'

Oddly enough she had great faith in herself; sadly, Susan didn't share that faith.

'We've got company!'

Dorothy had heard the car pull angrily into the yard and knew before she looked through the window just who it belonged to, and she was just in the mood for him.

'Who?' asked Frank.

'It's Sidney, and he doesn't look best pleased with himself.'

'Can't understand why,' grinned Frank.

Sid came through the door like petulant child. The telephone rang and Dorothy took the call with her back to her father.

'He's busy right now, can I take a message?' Dorothy said to the caller. She could feel her father quivering with emotion behind her as she wrote down the telephone message.

'Bastards!' he almost wept.

'Did someone come in?' asked Dorothy, putting down the

telephone and looking at Frank, who wished she didn't get so much pleasure out of baiting her father.

Frank stopped writing and regarded Sid coolly. 'Don't you ever knock, Allerdyce?' he said. 'This is a private office.'

'You can't do this ter me!' Sid lamented, flopping down in a corner chair. 'This could bankrupt me!'

'I think it's called "getting one's come uppance",' said Dorothy curtly, still not looking round at him.

'Look, you've got me all wrong,' her father whined. 'I were only taking the piss out of yer. I wouldn't have seen you go under. Come on, Frank lad, we're both builders, we help each other out in this business!'

'The only help you're gonna get from us is to help you through that door, you lying bastard!' snarled Frank. 'Now get out, Allerdyce, before I call the police!'

Dorothy swung round in her chair and looked at her father. For the first time in her life she felt pity for him. Sid had aged ten years in the last couple of weeks, the ebullience gone from his demeanour. He was broken and she was responsible – and it didn't feel quite as good as she thought it would.

'Why did you do it, Dad?' she asked at length.

It took Sid a while to collect sufficient thoughts to form an answer. 'Why did I do it?' he grunted. 'I'll tell yer why I did it. Because yer'd upset me, me girl, that's why I did it. Turning yer back on all I'd done for yer!'

'No – that's not what I was asking.' She looked at a bead of nervous sweat running down her father's face and knew she'd never had any love for this man, father or no father. 'I want to know why you treated me so badly when I was a child. You know, I can't remember you ever saying a single kind word to me!'

'Let's just say I had me reasons and leave at that, shall we?' Her questions were making him uncomfortable.

'No, I won't leave it at that,' persisted Dorothy, sensing he had an explanation for her. 'Even the most brutal of men have a soft spot for their daughters. Daughters are most men's Achilles Heel – but you never had a scrap of love for me. Why was that?'

'I said leave it!'

He got up to go, his discomfort was now turning to anger but Dorothy stood her ground. 'Alright,' she said coolly, 'I'll leave it – and I'll leave you as well, leave you out to dry. I was going to do a deal with you to help you out, but you can forget it now.'

'A deal? What sort o' deal?' It was as though a light had been switched on behind Sid's greedy eyes.

'A business deal – but first I want an answer to my question.'

Sid sat down again and rubbed the back of his neck with a beefy hand, ingrained with the dirt of years of hard graft.

'Yer not me daughter!' he rasped, his eyes looking away from her.

Despite this being one of the explanations Dorothy had considered, the reality of it still came as something of a shock to her.

'Oh,' was her immediate reaction. She wasn't disappointed. Finding out she was not Sid's daughter was more of a cause for celebration than regret. 'That's such a relief,' she added cruelly. 'Who is my father then?'

This was a much more crucial question than any she'd asked him before.

'I've no idea,' he said, looking her in the eye. 'And that's the God's honest truth, girl – I don't think yer mother ever knew neither. Yer can ask her if yer like, she can mebbe give yer a few names ter pick from – but mine won't be among 'em!'

'So, why did you marry her? She was obviously pregnant with me when you married her – I'd worked that one out myself.'

Sid's discomfort returned. His hand went back to rubbing his fat neck.

'If yer must know – it were money. It were her money what gave me a leg up in business. She married me cause it weren't respectable ter give birth ter bastards then any more than it is now. I was her only choice.'

Dorothy sat back, satisfied that his explanation was true. 'Right,' she said. 'I think we can do business now.'

Sid sat up in his chair. She had his full attention.

'Seems to me you've lost two things,' she began, smiling at the suspicious look on her father's face. 'A lot of money, but worst of all, your reputation as a businessman.'

Sid looked at the woman he had so despised for marrying a working man and saw in her a strength he couldn't match.

'If you like, we can give you back one of these, your reputation!' she offered suddenly.

Frank sat back. He knew enough not to contradict his junior

partner on matters of business. Whatever was in her mind it would be to his advantage.

Sid leaned forward expectantly. Was she throwing him a lifeline? No daughter of his would have done such a thing. He'd certainly never have thrown her one. He'd come to appeal to Frank's better nature, not hers.

'Don't get too excited, Sidney dear,' warned Dorothy, happy now at never having to call him Daddy again. 'It's a lousy deal we're offering – but it's the only one in town, as they say. Your land was worthless without ours, in fact,' she looked her watch, 'as of an hour ago we own your land. That means we'll have bought the whole shooting match, yours and ours, for eight thousand pounds, not a bad deal when you come to think of it.'

Sid was sitting up now. Despite everything, he could see a lot of himself in her, so could Frank, but Frank wasn't about to tell her that.

'Assuming you still have the connections to raise finance secured against prime building land, we'll sell the whole lot back to you for sixteen thousand.' She looked at Sid, who was doing a quick mental calculation. She was offering him three years' hard work at reduced profits, but he had no option. Anything was better than going under, he knew people who'd put the money up – at a price.

Sid laughed grimly, 'I'll say one thing for you, Dorothy lass. You're a chip off the old block, even if I'm not yer dad!'

'Don't say that, Sid,' warned Frank, 'or the deal might be off!'

Sid stood and reluctantly shook Frank's hand, then offered his hand to Dorothy who took it and eyed him squarely. 'I'm not doing this because you're my step-father or whatever you consider yourself to be,' she said coldly. 'I'm doing it because it's sound business. You've got a week to set the finance up!'

As Sid left the office, Frank turned to Dorothy with a hint of annoyance in his voice. 'I do think you ought to consult me before you make these deals, you sold him it for two thousand less than it was worth.'

'I'm sorry, Frank, but I needed to think on my feet. That telephone call was from the land surveyor about those trial holes you ordered to be dug. Apparently there's a lot of unstable ground on Sid's piece. It'll need piling, raft foundations, the lot. Sixteen thousand's not a bad price as it happens, it gives us eight thousand clear profit.'

'Dorothy, you're unbelievable!' gasped Frank. 'Well, I'd better get meself out there and tell 'em to fill them trial holes in before Sid thinks to dig any.'

'I think my father will have enough on his mind over the next few days to think of anything as sensible as that. He's not as meticulous as you in building matters.'

Frank walked round to her side of the desk and kissed Dorothy full on the lips.

'Mr Sackfield! What on earth was that for?'

'I just felt like it! So, what you going to do about it?' he asked with mock belligerence.

'Nothing, next time just give me some warning that's all.'

'Oh, so you reckon there's going to be a next time, do you?'

'I didn't mean it like that,' she laughed.

She watched Frank as he went back to his chair. He was a nice man. Too old for her of course, mid-forties at least. He caught her staring at him and grinned back at her. 'You're admiring my personal beauty, aren't you,' he joked. 'I get a lot of that.'

'No,' she said tartly. 'I was just trying to work out how much our forty-nine-per-cent was worth now.'

'We going to be bloody good partners me and you,' declared Frank.

Dorothy was wondering just how good. She'd quite enjoyed that kiss.

Chapter Twenty-Two

'Dorothy Bairstow?'

'Yes,' Dorothy's heart sank for the umpteenth time. This wasn't the woman who'd rung her the last time.

'Hang on, I'll just put another penny in then we'll not get cut off,' said the woman.

There was a clang of a coin dropping then the voice came again. 'Any road, I've found her,' it said.

Dorothy recognised the voice from somewhere, then a penny dropped in her brain just as it had in the coin box. It was the toothless woman, Hilda's next door neighbour.

'You've found Hilda?' asked an excited Dorothy.

'Aye. Have you got fifty quid?'

'Does Hilda know where William is?'

'Aye, but she'll not tell me. She'll not tell no one till she's got her twenty-five quid.'

'Right, that's no problem. Where can I meet you?'

'There's a big trannie café on t' Oldham Road. It's about a mile out of 'uddersfield on t' right hand side – yer can't miss it. Tomorrow mornin' at ten o'clock – alright?'

'That's fine, see you then.'

The last penny dropped and the pips went, signalling the end of the call. But Dorothy had heard enough, Susan and Jimmy were hovering over her shoulder.

'I think we're in business,' she announced. 'I'm meeting Hilda Atkins tomorrow in Huddersfield.'

'We're coming with you,' said Susan. The tone of her voice told Dorothy not to argue.

206

'Good,' she said. 'I'll ring Frank and tell him he's taking another day off.'

Dorothy remembered the cruel laughter of the children when she'd asked if Hilda was married and realised why they'd laughed. Hilda Atkins was a tiny sparrow of a woman who could have been anything between thirty-five and fifty-five. Her eyes darted up at Dorothy and Frank as they walked into the transport cafe. She was dwarfed by the monumental bosom of her friend who gave them a loose-toothed smile as they sat down at the table.

'What'll you have, ladies?' asked Frank.

'Eee! 'ark at 'im – callin' us ladies,' giggled Hilda's well-endowed friend.

'And why shouldn't I?' protested an indignant Frank. 'Yer as much of a lady as all them prancing about in their fancy dresses an' tiaras down in London.'

Hilda's friend gave him a playful slap on his arm, enough to make him wince. 'Two mugs o' tea and two sausage sandwiches,' she laughed. 'An' if my Walter finds out yer've been chatting me up he'll have yer by yer bollocks!'

She screamed with laughter at her own coarseness and Hilda joined with the shrillest laugh Dorothy had ever heard.

She joined the two women as Frank went off to get served. He looked back at them as he waited for his order to arrive. An incongruous a trio if ever there was one. The tiny wizened sparrow, the fat harridan and the alluring, self-assured beauty.

Dorothy saw no reason to beat about the bush. Jimmy and Susan were waiting in the car and all she wanted was the where-abouts of her nephew. She took two envelopes from her bag and placed them on the table.

'Twenty-five pounds in each envelope,' she said quietly, lest any other customers heard. In 1946, twenty-five pounds was not a sum to be sneezed at. Planting a well-turned elbow on either side of each envelope, she placed her hands together in a protective bridge over them, fingers linked as in prayer.

'Where's William?' she asked, firmly but quietly, her eyes boring into Hilda's.

Hilda's eyes darted round the bustling café, as if looking for eavesdroppers, then back at Dorothy.

'Go on! Tell her, yer barmpot – then we can have us brass!' urged her fat friend.

'He's in Oldham!' blurted out Hilda.

'Oldham?' queried Dorothy, as though Oldham was the last place on earth she'd expect them to send him.

'Ashton Lodge in Oldham,' Hilda went on. 'Quicker yer get him outa there the better!'

'It's a shit'ole,' explained the fat friend.

Frank arrived with the tea and sandwiches and sat beside Dorothy at the table.

'William's in Oldham,' Dorothy told him, with a note of triumph in her voice. Turning back to Hilda she asked. 'Why did they send him away?'

Hilda's eyes dropped. 'Yer wrote saying yer were comin' ter fetch him home. If yer'd seen t' state he were in yer'd have had the cops on Parkinson. They'd battered the poor little sod black and blue. So they sent him off ter Oldham an' told yer he'd been adopted – they never expected nobody ter come for him. He were cheeky were your Billy an' they wouldn't stand for it. There were five of us an' Parky an' every one were free wi their fists – even t' women.'

'You weren't,' said Dorothy.

'No, I never hit none of 'em. I reckon they'd enough ter put up with – poor little beggars.'

'Why did you ring me?'

'That snotty cow of a matron sacked me – she said I were being too soft. Reckoned I were letting t' little beggars have their own way too much. I knew yer'd rung – I were in t' office when yer gave old Parky a bollocking. Anyway when they sacked me I were waitin' in t' office for me cards an' I saw your number written down – so I rang yer. I had ter put t' phone quick 'cos Parky were comin'.'

Dorothy pushed the two envelopes across the table to be picked up by both women with undue haste. Hilda looked grateful but apologetic.

'Yer must think I'm rotten, takin' money off yer like this – but yer don't know how much this means ter me.'

Dorothy stood up to go, Frank had only brought food and drink for the two women. She smiled down at Hilda. 'You don't know how much this means to me, Hilda – you've got my number, give me a ring, I'd like to know how you're going on.'

Then she looked at the fat woman, counting her money, 'It's all there,' she chided. 'But thanks – I don't know how you managed to find Hilda, but I hope it wasn't too much trouble.'

Hilda gave her fat friend a quizzical look, then looked back at Dorothy, 'How d' you mean? Find me?' she asked. 'I'm lodging with her!'

The fat friend gave Dorothy and Frank a cherubic smile, 'When I said she'd done a moonlight,' she explained, 'what I should have mentioned was that she'd moved in with me!'

It took them under an hour to travel to Oldham from Huddersfield along bleak, winding roads. The windscreen wiper fighting a valiant battle against the driving rain as they made their way over 'the tops', as the Pennines were called locally.

'Right, this looks like Oldham,' announced Frank. 'All we need to do now is find Ashton Road.'

Dorothy, sitting beside him, looked at the road map on her knee. 'I imagine it's the road to Ashton-under-Lyne,' she deduced. 'Look, there's a sign, Ashton-under-Lyne five miles.'

Jimmy and Susan had actually found the journey quite exciting. Especially when a couple of sorry looking sheep had strayed onto the road and inexplicably refused to budge, eventually running into the mist as the four of them got out and shooed them away. After all, the alternative for them was a day at school. Frank pulled in to a petrol station. 'I'll get some juice and see if anyone knows where this place is,' he decided.

Looking through the car window they could see the petrol attendant shrugging his shoulders. He then disappeared into the office, followed by Frank, who came out looking cheerful, sticking a thumb up to the waiting trio.

'Bloke inside knows the home. Not got a brilliant reputation by the sound of it. Anyway it's only about five minutes away.'

Jimmy and Susan looked at each other. Both feeling the same surge of excitement. They were about to meet their long-lost brother. Dorothy blinked a way a tear as Frank looked momentarily across at her and smiled at this extraordinary lady he was growing so fond of.

Following the directions he'd been given, Frank turned up a grim-looking road. An empty tram clanked past them, its lights on despite it only being late morning. The rain was slanting down, hammering noisily against the car roof. They stared through the windows at the various buildings slowly passing them by. A row of shops with very few customers. People were either too broke or too cold to venture out and spend their money on such a day. There was a glum-looking Methodist Chapel, a bank, a dentist's and—

'There it is!' shouted Jimmy, who was first to spot the sign, to Susan's mild annoyance.

It stood beside a pair of huge iron gates and said in hard to read Gothic lettering.

ASHTON LODGE HOME FOR BOYS.
Warden. S. Wiggins

Lifting up the latch with her walking stick, Dorothy pushed open the gate and the four of them walked through. It was a large, forbidding place, probably the former home of some cotton mill owner. Built in soot-encrusted stone, it was three storeys high, completely square, completely symmetrical and, apart from a row of weathered gargoyles around the eaves, without a single redeeming architectural feature.

'Looks like a flippin' prison,' observed Jimmy.

'Scary,' said Susan

Dorothy frowned and said nothing as she led the way along the gravel drive leading to the large double doors and rapped on the peeling brown paint with her stick.

'There's a bell here,' noticed Jimmy, pressing a metal button beside the door.

A loud clanging inside told them the bell was working alright. After a while the door was opened by a small, emaciated, short-trousered boy who, stood and gawped at them as though they were from another planet.

'I'm off sick,' he blurted. 'I'm not supposed ter be at school!'

'Is Mr Wiggins about, son?' asked Frank.

Surprised at Frank's kindly manner, the boy asked nervously, 'Are you t' board man, mister?'

'He thinks you're from the school board, checking on truants,' explained Dorothy.

'No, son. I'm not the board man,' grinned Frank. 'Do you think you could show us Mr Wiggins' office?'

The boy stared at them for a moment, as though needing time for this request to sink in, then turned and walked away, his seg-studded boots clattering cheerfully on the worn parquet floor. A cheerfulness completely at odds with the general atmosphere of the place. No light was switched on to brighten up the dark winter afternoon. There was a stale smell of yesterday's food and no curtains at the grime-covered windows. A well-built young woman passed them, with a cigarette dangling from her mouth, carrying an empty bucket. She gave them a nod and paused momentarily, then shrugged and carried on.

'That were Mrs Abbotson. She's one o' them what looks after us,' explained the boy.

They followed, hoping he was taking them to Mr Wiggins. The boy stopped by a large, panelled door.

'He's in there,' he said in a low voice, before vanishing noisily up the gloomy corridor.

The door opened before Frank had a chance to knock. A surprised-looking man stood there, his face frozen for just a second then switching on the most insincere smile Dorothy had seen for a long time. There were heavy, dark red brocade curtains in this room, but there the colour ended. The walls were painted white, or had been many years ago. There were no pictures or photographs or ornaments of any kind to enliven the boredom. Just a large wooden desk on which stood a half drunk cup of something, a pub ashtray full of cigarette ends and a copy of *Tit-Bits* opened at the crossword page.

'Yes?' he said. 'Can I be of assistance?'

'I do hope so,' said Dorothy, accepting the man's unspoken invitation to accompany him into his office. Jimmy and Susan followed. 'You see, we're trying to track down a boy called William Bairstow and we understand from the last place he was at that he's one of your boys.'

'He's our brother,' explained Susan. 'We were told he was dead.' There was still a trace of bitterness here, 'But we've found out he's not and we've come to take him home.'

Mr Wiggins stroked his chin theatrically. A middle-aged, flabby man, with thinning hair and bad teeth. He had a floppy mouth and mean, piggy eyes, magnified several times through his bottle-bottom glasses.

'William Bairstow? Sorry, there's no boy of that name here.'

'Oh, no!' said Susan, her heart sinking.

211

'But the Fairbank Home in Huddersfield said they sent him here,' pursued Dorothy, hoping this might give him a jolt.

'I'm sorry, Mrs er . . .?'

'Bairstow, I'm the boy's aunt.'

'I'm sorry, Mrs Bairstow, but we've only got thirty-four boys here. I do know their names,' he said patronisingly.

Jimmy thought there was a sliminess about the man and he didn't trust him an inch. 'He's only six,' he blurted. 'How can he be missing?'

Wiggins fixed him with a cross between a smile and a sneer.

'If he's lost, sonny, it's not me what lost him. There's never been no William Bairstow at Ashton Lodge. Now if there's nothing else with which I can help you, I've got a lot of work to do.'

Frank glanced down at the half finished *Tit-Bits* crossword on Wiggins' desk and looked up at him. 'Yes, it looks like it,' he said scornfully. 'Thanks for all your help, Mr Wiggins.'

'Not at all,' smirked Wiggins, disregarding the sarcasm.

As they were about to leave the building, the short-trousered boy appeared as if from nowhere to open the outside door for them. 'You sure you're not a board man, mister?' he asked.

'Quite sure,' said Frank, who stuck his hand in his pocket and pulled out a shilling. He held it tantalisingly close to the boy as he asked. 'Do you know a boy called William Bairstow?'

The boy eagerly held his hand out to receive the money, then his face dropped as he realised he didn't have the required information. He pulled his hand away and took a disappointed step back, allowing them through the door.

'Nah, never heard of him,' he muttered.

'What school do the boys here go to?' asked Susan.

The boy's face lit up, a supplementary question, he knew the answer to this one. He held out his hand, into which Frank dropped the silver coin.

'Brewster Lane School, just round t' corner,' he answered triumphantly, taking his prize and clattering off joyously down the corridor.

'What made you ask that?' inquired Dorothy as they walked out through the gates.

'Don't know really,' answered Susan. 'There was something about that man I didn't like. Maybe we should check his story.'

'He was a slimy creep,' said Jimmy

'Well summed up, Jimmy,' praised Frank. 'I couldn't have put it better myself.'

'I see no harm in asking at the school,' decided Frank. 'Where did he say it was?'

'Brewster Lane,' answered Dorothy. Frank nodded and narrowed his eyes as he looked back at her. 'You do look pretty in that coat,' he said, then climbed quickly into the car for the short journey to Brewster Lane School. Dorothy dismissed his compliment, her mind on much more important things. Unlike Frank.

As the boy said, the school was just around the corner. It was 12 o' clock and the children were pouring out into the school yard for their lunch break. The rain had more or less stopped and a game of football got under way. Frank, Dorothy and Susan fought their way past the players as they made their way inside, Jimmy waited outside, sitting on a low brick wall.

'Who says you could sit on my wall, kid?'

The questioner was a belligerent youth, roughly Jimmy's age. He had a cast in his eye and Jimmy wasn't immediately sure he was talking to him.

'Sorry,' said Jimmy quickly, standing up. 'Didn't know it was your wall.'

'It's not,' smirked the youth, looking at the badge on Jimmy's blazer. 'Where're yer from?' he demanded.

'Leeds,' answered Jimmy, clenching his fists, in readiness for a surprise attack.

'Me uncle's been ter Leeds. He reckons it's a right mucky 'ole.'

'It is,' agreed Jimmy, deciding Leeds wasn't worth fighting about.

'Is it muckier than round 'ere?' asked the boy challengingly.

Jimmy wasn't sure how to answer this one.

'About the same,' he compromised.

This answer seemed to satisfy the boy, who then asked, matter of factly, 'D'yer wanna fight?'

'Can't. I've got me best clothes on.'

Another satisfactory answer. 'My name's Joe Conroy,' said the boy.

'My name's Jimmy Bairstow.'

'Watcha doin' round 'ere?'

'We've come ter look for our kid. We thought he was in an 'ome, but the feller there says he's not.'

'I live in an 'ome.'

'What? Ashton Lodge?'

'Yeah, it's rubbish – worst 'ome I've ever lived in. Have yer been ter see old Wanker Wiggins?'

'Yes,' laughed Jimmy. 'Why do yer call him Wanker?'

''Cos that's what he does. He's allus tossin' hisself off!'

'Yer what! Have yer seen him?'

The boy nodded and smirked. 'If yer do it for him he gives yer more pocket money. He gave me an extra tanner last week!'

Ignoring the disgust on Jimmy's face, the boy went on, 'All t'kids there are nutters. That's where they send 'em all.'

'You're not a nutter,' lied Jimmy.

'I am,' said the boy defensively. 'You ask anyone!' He called to a passing boy of similar age. 'Hey! Devlin, aren't I a nutter?'

'Biggest nutter in school!' confirmed Devlin.

'Told yer,' cackled Joe.

Jimmy nodded, he wasn't going to argue. 'They call our kid William Bairstow. Do you know him?'

'What? Bisto?' grinned the boy.

'No, Bairstow,' repeated Jimmy patiently.

'I've heard of the Bisto Kid,' chortled the youth. 'But he doesn't go to our school.' He laughed out loud at himself and ran off.

Jimmy breathed a sigh of relief at having come away from such a confrontation unharmed and looked up as Frank, Dorothy and Susan emerged from the school, looking disappointed.

'They've never heard of him,' said Dorothy. 'Sounds like old Wiggins was telling the truth.'

'I know,' confirmed Jimmy. 'I've just been talking to a kid who lives in Ashton Lodge. He's never heard of our William either. Tell yer what though. If all the kids there are like him, our William's better off living somewhere else. He was a right nutter!' He was too embarrassed to tell them about Wiggins' disgusting hobby.

Frank drummed his fingers on the steering wheel, uncertain what to do next. 'Look, Frank,' said Dorothy, 'we're not going back without him.'

'I know,' accepted Frank. 'Trouble is, where the devil is he?'

He looked at his watch. 'Look, it's half past twelve, we'd best get something to eat. We'll all think better on full stomachs.'

No one argued with this suggestion. A café lunch was a special treat for the Bairstow kids.

The café was emptying as they arrived and they were shown to a table for four by the window. 'Order what you like, kids,' said Frank, 'your Auntie Dorothy's paying.'

The two of them grinned at this. They liked Frank and his easy-going manner. Susan secretly thought her auntie could do a lot worse, and was slightly exasperated at Dorothy's romantic indifference to him – or to anybody for that matter. No one, it seemed, would ever be able to fill Uncle Tommy's shoes.

Frank was similarly aware of the gap Dorothy was keeping between them. His playful kiss apart, everything between them was strictly business. This was something of a disappointment to Frank as he was beginning to find this unusual woman more captivating by the day, but no way was he going to damage their tenuous relationship by pushing things along too fast.

Dorothy for her part had far too much to think about without complicating her life with such self indulgence. Romance was very much at the back of her mind when Frank's strong hand encased hers across the table.

'We'll not go back without him,' he promised, his solemn grey eyes resting gently on hers. 'No matter what it takes, we'll get him.'

'Thanks Frank,' she smiled. 'It means a lot to us to have you on our side.'

'I quite like being on your side, Dorothy love,' he replied earnestly. But if she caught any hidden meaning she didn't show it. Frank withdrew his hand and ordered steak pie and mash for four.

Dorothy sat for a while, still feeling the remnants of a pleasant tingle in her hand. No man had done that to her since since Tommy. Susan had seen it but Jimmy was too engrossed in a dog fight across the street.

'Tell you what,' said Dorothy. 'When we do get him back I don't think he'll want to be called William.'

'Why on earth not?' protested Susan. 'It's a lovely name is William.'

'I think he answers to Billy now,' explained Dorothy.

'*Billy* Bairstow,' repeated Susan. 'Is that that what they're calling him? Suppose we'd have started calling him that by now. Never thought of him as Billy.'

Frank laughed. 'Sounds an appropriate name to me. Apparently at Fairbank Home they called him the *Bisto Kid*.'

Jimmy laughed at first, then the laughter froze on his face. 'That kid at school said something about the Bisto Kid,' he blurted.

'What kid?' asked Frank.

'That kid I was telling you about. The nutter. He said something about the Bisto Kid!'

'What did he say?' demanded Susan. 'Come on, Jimmy. This could be important!'

'I know!' protested Jimmy. 'I'm trying ter think, leave me alone for a minute!'

The others sat there impatiently as Jimmy tried to collect his thoughts. 'I told him we were looking for our kid – and that his name was William Bairstow – and he said, "Bisto?" and I said, "No, Bairstow". I thought he was just being stupid, he was a real idiot, you know. Then he said something about he knows the *Bisto Kid*. How was I ter know he might have been talking about our William?'

'You weren't,' soothed Dorothy. 'Now, did he say anything else about this *Bisto Kid?*'

'I don't think so, oh yeah – he said something about, "But he doesn't go to our school".'

'It all fits!' cried Susan. 'That's why they didn't know him at Brewster Lane School!'

Frank turned to a young waitress, who had just arrived with a pot of tea, 'What other schools are there round here where the kids from Ashton House might go, apart from Brewster Lane?'

The waitress scratched her head, 'There's only St Theresa's Primary, but that's a Catholic school. They won't take non-Catholics there.'

'William's a Catholic!' shouted Jimmy. 'That's where he goes! He must do, stands ter reason!'

Frank held up his hands to calm them down. 'The great mystery is,' he mused, 'if this Bisto Kid *is* William, and if he *does* go to St Theresa's, then why did Wiggins say he'd never heard of him?'

Jimmy felt himself blushing now. There was something he

216

knew about Wiggins that they didn't. He wasn't sure what the connection with William was, but he knew he had to tell them.

He took a deep breath. 'That kid at Brewster Road had a nickname for Wiggins.' He paused, feeling four sets of eyes on him. Jimmy looked at the floor.

'They call him Wanker Wiggins!'

Susan was on the verge of chastising Jimmy for using such a word in front of the waitress, but Frank laid a restraining hand on her shoulder.

'Did he say why they call him that, Jimmy?' he asked.

Jimmy nodded, still looking at the floor. 'Because he's always doing it.'

'How do they know?' questioned Dorothy gently.

'They've watched him! Sometimes he gives 'em extra pocket money ter do it for him!'

The last words tumbled out, Jimmy looked up to see what effect they'd had. A devastating effect.

'I'd better ring the police,' said Frank.

'No,' warned Dorothy. 'There's something odd about all this. I think we need find out as much as we can before we start barging in anywhere.'

Susan nodded her agreement, she didn't want anything to jeopardise the situation now they were so close.

'Tell you what,' decided Dorothy. 'We'll have our lunch then I'll go back to Brewster Road school with Jimmy,' she looked at her watch. 'They should be having their afternoon break in about an hour. We'll have a word with this Joe Conroy and get the full story from him and you two go to St Theresa's and find out what you can.'

At two-thirty, the school doors opened to a galloping horde of children eager to enjoy every last second of their afternoon playtime. From their midst emerged Joe Conroy, heading for the gate at high speed and obviously intent on an early escape from the desperate boredom he'd already endured for too long that day.

Jimmy stood in front of him, arms outstretched, barring his way, but Joe didn't appear to see Jimmy and ran straight into him, both of them finishing in a heap on the pavement. Joe was wearing a corduroy windjammer which looked several sizes too small for him, a pair of patched grey flannel trousers tucked into Wellington boots and a balaclava with more holes than wool.

'Why didn't yer stop, yer barmy sod?' asked an irate Jimmy.

''Cos I'm a nutter,' explained Joe grinning up at an amazed Dorothy.

'Remember this morning, Joe?' inquired Jimmy, yanking Joe to his feet, 'when yer said yer knew the Bisto Kid?' Joe nodded dumbly as Jimmy continued, 'Where does he live, this Bisto Kid?'

'With us,' replied Joe, wondering what the mystery was.

'How old is he?' asked Jimmy, excited that the Bisto Kid was probably his brother.

'No idea. He's only a young 'un – he can be a cheeky little bastard though,' grinned the boy.

'Do you know where he is now, will he be at school?' asked Dorothy.

'Nah. I think he's still in t' roof room, been there a couple o' days. He gave Wanker some cheek – called him a mucky old bugger. Took Wanker ages ter catch him. We was all cheerin' Bisto on. Caught him in t' end though. Gave him a good hiding and locked in t' roof room. It's bloody freezin' up there. I were up there once. He asked me ter toss him off an' I didn't feel like it. I'd never done nowt like that before.'

'Is that why Bisto got locked up do you think?' inquired Dorothy, finding it hard to control her fury.

'Think so. That's why Bisto called him a mucky old bugger.'

'This roof room, where is it?' asked Jimmy.

'In t' roof, yer dozy bugger,' laughed Joe. 'Blimey yer a bigger nutter than me!'

He yelled his parting insult over his shoulder as he galloped off down the street to enjoy a couple of hours of freedom before returning to the grim place he had to call home.

They caught up with Frank and Susan in the headmistress's office at St Theresa's.

'It's definitely him!' said an excited Susan, turning to Dorothy and Jimmy. 'He goes to this school!'

'A boy of exceptional ability,' added the headmistress, Sister Frances, 'when he's in school that is. But he hasn't been for a couple of days.'

218

'We know,' said Jimmy angrily. 'Wanker Wiggins has got him locked up in t' roof room.'

Sister Frances, raised an eyebrow at Jimmy's language, until Dorothy explained.

'Sorry if he shocked you, sister, but I'm afraid the word described what this odious man does – and he apparently does it with the boys in his care! I think a phone call to the police might be in order.'

A shocked Sister Frances immediately picked up the telephone and was already talking to the police as the four of them left her office.

The iron gates were open when they arrived. Not yet closed after the lunchtime exodus of boys. Frank kicked open the door and led the angry quartet down the echoing corridor to Wiggins' office, out of which the short-trousered boy appeared, just as they arrived.

A half smile of recognition lit up his face, fading as he saw the fury on theirs. He wisely decided a retreat was in order and clattered off at high speed towards the front door.

Wiggins was sitting behind his desk, dabbing his forehead with a handkerchief as they arrived.

'No prizes for guessing what you've just been up to, you sick bastard,' roared Dorothy, swinging her walking stick in a long scything arc that hit Wiggins on the side of his head, knocking him clean out of his chair.

On his hands and knees, the man scrabbled across the floor, moaning with pain, clutching at a profusely bleeding ear and searching wildly for the glasses that Susan was callously crunching under her feet. Dorothy hooked her stick around Wiggins' neck, yanking him harshly to his feet; surprisingly strong for a woman, Frank thought admiringly.

'Where is he?' snarled Dorothy.

'I don't know who you mean,' wept Wiggins.

'William Bairstow! The boy you said doesn't live here!' roared Frank, grabbing Wiggins by the scruff of his neck.

'Oh, him? I had to punish him. He's . . .'

They were interrupted by the breathless return of the short-trousered boy, who viewed the scene at first with shock and then with satisfaction.

'If yer lookin' fer Bisto, he's up on t' roof. He says he's going ter jump off!'

Frank and Dorothy dashed outside, but Susan grabbed the boy and said fiercely, 'Show us how to get to this roof room – quick!'

The boy turned and charged up the stairs with Susan and Jimmy hard on his clattering heels.

Dorothy looked up at the roof and saw a small boy standing beside one of the stone gargoyles. He'd grown so much since she'd last seen him and her heart lurched at the sorrowful sight of this small, pathetic boy silhouetted against the bleak sky. There was fine, saturating rain in the air and the cold wind was tugging at his short trousers and torn shirt. Dorothy could see, even from that distance, that her nephew was crying, she felt sick with fear. The boy was lifting his arms forward, as though preparing to dive. Frank's mind raced. Must distract the boy, make him think about something other than jumping.

'Hello, William!' he shouted. 'I'm you're Uncle Frank and this is your Auntie Dorothy – we've come to take you home.'

The boy hesitated. This was good, thought Frank, anything to take his mind off jumping. 'Your sister Susan's here – and your brother Jimmy,' he continued desperately, looking round, wondering where they were.

'Please William,' pleaded Dorothy, her voice choking. 'We all love you, don't be a silly boy!'

The short-trousered boy had led Jimmy and Susan up to the second floor, then pointed at an iron spiral staircase leading up to the roof. They dashed up it and found themselves in a small dark room, lit only by a tiny window that was banging open in the wind. In front of the window a pile of books had been placed on top of one another. Susan stepped onto the top book and literally dived out of the window, landing in a puddle on the roof outside. Jimmy followed, almost falling on top of her. They could hear people shouting from below. Susan's eyes were drawn to a small figure standing at the edge of the roof. Her baby brother William, about to throw himself off. She could hear him sobbing as she gingerly crept towards him. She stopped.

'William,' she called softly. 'I said I was coming to get you, remember? Well here I am!'

The boy continued crying, Susan moved slowly towards him, frightened that he might slip over the edge.

'Leave me alone, yer rotten buggers,' sobbed the boy without turning round.

She took off her coat and held it out. 'I've brought you a coat, see. We're going home to Leeds in that car. Can you see it? The posh one – parked outside the gate.'

'The police are coming to get Wiggins, the mucky old bugger!' shouted Jimmy.

William liked these voices. These were nice voices. One of them sounded like the voice in his mind, the one who'd promised to come and get him. The other one somehow knew that Mr Wiggins was a mucky old bugger. He turned. Susan smiled and Jimmy grinned. William wiped his eyes and tried to smile back. He knew just by looking at them that these people were his big brother and sister. Then his foot slipped.

Above the wind, Dorothy thought she heard Susan's voice coming from behind the boy on the roof and willed him to take at least one step back from danger. She saw William half-turn round to see who was talking to him, then she saw him teetering over the edge.

'Please God, no!' gasped Frank.

The boy circled his arms frantically to regain his balance, but Dorothy knew he wasn't going to manage it, the boy was falling. Dorothy closed her eyes but the Frank's eyes remained transfixed.

An arm came out and grabbed one of the boy's legs, then another arm grabbed the other leg and the boy was pulled back to safety. Frank slapped Dorothy on the back.

'They've got him, he's alright!' he yelled ecstatically.

Dorothy opened her eyes in disbelief and looked up to see the three faces looking down at them.

'Do you know, Frank?' said Dorothy, after her heart had stopped racing. 'I haven't had a minute's flaming peace since they came to live with me!'

'I can well imagine it,' smiled Frank, placing a comforting arm around Dorothy. 'Trouble is, there's three of the buggers now!'

Dorothy was still alternately weeping and laughing as the police arrived to arrest Wiggins, who was still crawling blindly around, looking for his glasses, cruelly taunted by the short-trousered boy, who knew he had nothing more to fear from this evil man.

The journey back to Leeds was a silent journey. Billy, as he chose to be called, sat between Jimmy and Susan on the back seat. He cuddled up to Susan, his small arms gripping her tight as though frightened she might leave him. They'd all said comforting words to him, but everything seemed so inadequate. It was impossible to understand what was going through his six-year-old mind. Impossible to understand the mentality of the authorities who placed children like Billy in the hands of such foul men.

Susan had made a desperate grab for him as she saw him falling off the roof. She managed to get a grip on his ankle, but he was slipping away from her as Jimmy hurled himself forward and grabbed Billy's other leg. Between them they pulled their brother to safety.

Billy's face was still white with shock as the three of them looked down on the weeping face of their Auntie Dorothy being slapped on the back by Frank.

The police took a subdued Wiggins away, watched by Mrs Abbotson and various other members of staff who had appeared from the woodwork to witness their master's disgrace. Many of them had little to be proud of themselves; and their faces were shocked and sombre as they too were led away to various police cars. Frank spent some time explaining what had happened, making a particular point of mentioning the cruelty at the Fairfield Home in Huddersfield.

'For what damn good it'll do!' he said disparagingly to Dorothy, as they watched the convoy of police cars disappear.

Billy had insisted on bringing back with him just one treasured possession. A one-eyed rabbit he'd had with him all the time he'd been in care.

'Hey! That was mine,' cried Jimmy on seeing it. 'I often wondered where it had got to.'

'Well, yer not having it back, yer big bugger!' protested Billy.

'I think you'll need to tidy up his vocabulary,' suggested a grinning Frank.

As the car cruised through rain-swept hills on the bleak road back to Yorkshire, Susan hugged him and crooned to him as she'd heard their mam do. Billy fell fast asleep and didn't wake up until the car pulled in to Broughton Terrace.

'Coming in for a cup of tea, Frank?' asked Dorothy as they began to get out.

'No – I think I'll leave you all to it,' said Frank, 'I reckon

222

you've a lot to talk about and you don't want an outsider like me involved.'

'We don't think you're an outsider, Frank,' argued Susan stoutly. 'Not after today anyway.'

'From now on,' decided Jimmy, 'you're our Uncle Frank – isn't that right, our Billy?'

Billy was much too staggered by the dramatic turn round in his life to make any comment, he just shrugged.

Dorothy waved goodbye to Frank and turned the key in the lock. 'Right, William,' she smiled. 'We've got a brand new bed waiting for you.'

'Me name's Billy,' he said firmly.

'Sorry, Billy,' she laughed. 'You're sharing with Jimmy, is that okay?'

Although the question was rhetorical, due to there being nowhere else he could sleep, Dorothy thought it only fair to let him think he had a choice in the matter.

'Yes, thank you very much,' replied Billy, displaying the disciplined good manners of the institutionalised child.

'Good job yer said yes, or yer'd have sleeping in t' outside lavvie!' laughed Jimmy.

Billy laughed along with his new brother and followed him upstairs to see his new bed. Dorothy sat on the settee and patted the empty space beside her, inviting Susan to sit down.

'He's had a rough time, hasn't he? You couldn't begin to understand how guilty I feel.'

Susan shook her head. She still had ambivalent feelings towards Auntie Dorothy. It had taken an effort to forgive her for lying about Billy's death. The crime was partially absolved by Dorothy's willingness to sacrifice herself on Susan's behalf, when she laid into Simmo and finished up in jail. But this was different. Billy had almost made Dorothy's lie come true, driven to the brink of suicide by the people Dorothy had sent him to. She saw no reason to spare her auntie any feelings of guilt; after all, she'd been the architect of her brother's miserable existence.

'It's going to take him a long time to get over what's happened to him,' continued Dorothy sadly. 'Wouldn't surprise me if we didn't have to take him to some sort of psychiatrist. I wonder if he'll ever forgive me?'

'I don't suppose he even blames you,' said Susan

philosophically. 'He's just a kid. Kids never question what happens around them. They always think whoever's doing it knows best.'

Dorothy nodded sadly then stared hard at Susan. 'If it's any consolation,' she said, 'I'm not asking you to forgive me, that wouldn't be fair. I can't even forgive myself. What I did was the height of selfishness.'

Susan laid an arm around her auntie's shoulder. 'You're right, Auntie, it was; and maybe I can't forgive you. But I can't forget what you've done for us either, and I know what you've been through. So maybe it's quits.'

'Maybe' smiled Dorothy, but she wasn't convinced. Nor was Susan.

Billy bounced happily on his bed. 'Best bed I've ever had,' he yelled.

'It's better than my bed,' grumbled Jimmy. 'I've never had a new bed.'

'Hey! Yer not havin' my bed,' said Billy defensively.

'Don't get yer knickers in a twist,' grinned Jimmy. 'I don't want your flipping bed.'

'Good job,' warned his new brother, 'I won't have ter bray yer now.'

'Oh? Yer think yer can bray me do yer? Come on, Bisto, I'll take yer on with one arm behind me back.'

Jimmy wished he hadn't said that, for Billy gave a fierce war whoop and came windmilling into him, forcing Jimmy back on his bed, struggling to hold his six-year-old adversary.

'Bugger me! Billy,' he gasped. Holding his brother's arms tightly and as far away from him as he could. 'Yer a flippin' lunatic. Who taught yer how ter fight like that?'

'Joe Conroy, he were me best mate. Showed me how ter fight.'

'Yer best mate? I've met Joe Conroy – he's twice as old as you!'

'I know, but he's a bit thick. I used to help him with his homework.'

'You! Helping a thirteen-year-old kid with his homework? Pull the other one, it's got bells on!'

'I were teaching him how ter read,' continued Billy, ignoring

224

Jimmy's sarcasm. 'He were comin'on alright as well. Have you got any books?'

Jimmy was taken aback. 'I've got a Biggles and some Billy Bunter books in me cupboard, but I haven't got owt for a six-year-old.'

'I like Biggles. They had Biggles in t' school library. I've never read no Billy Bunter books, can I lend one off yer, please?'

Jimmy opened his bedside cupboard and brought out a book, which he handed to his brother. 'There yer go, our young 'un, give us it back when yer've finished with it.'

Billy took the book and looked across at Jimmy. 'Is that what yer gonna call me – 'our young 'un'?' he asked, seemingly proud of his new identity.

'Well, that who yer are, innit?'

'What shall I call you then?'

'Yer call me "our kid", wotcha think yer call me?' replied an exasperated Jimmy. 'Blimey, our young 'un, I hope yer can read better then yer can think!'

Billy grinned, delighted with his new brother. Jimmy studied him for a while, wondering if it was right to ask a six-year-old such a question, but quickly dismissed his misgivings.

'Yer know that mucky old bugger at Ashton House?' he asked, without a hint of tact. 'Why did he lock yer up in that roof room?'

Billy blushed – a Bairstow family weakness. 'Yer won't tell no one, will yer?'

'Scout's honour,' vowed Jimmy, who wasn't a scout so it didn't count.

'He got his willy out and asked me ter touch it!'

'Ugh! The mucky old sod. That's what Joe Conroy told me.'

'I know,' agreed Billy. 'He used to do it to all the kids, but I were t' youngest so he never did it ter me.'

'Till the other day yer mean?'

Billy nodded. 'He got me in his office and told me if I touched his willy he'd give me extra pocket money.'

'Hey! Is that what he called it, his willy?' giggled Jimmy. He himself having graduated to the dick, prick or nob stage.

'No,' grinned Billy. 'He called it his weasel! He asked me if I wanted ter stroke his weasel!'

'Stroke his weasel!' howled Jimmy, screaming with laughter, rolling back on his bed and waving his legs in the air. 'I've never heard it called that, stroking his weasel – that's a good 'un, that!'

Billy immediately saw the funny side of it and joined in his brother's convulsions. After they both calmed down, Jimmy asked, 'Wotcha do then?'

'I kicked him and called him a mucky old bugger. All t' kids were listening outside his office an' they started laughing. He didn't half get mad.'

'Where did you kick him?' asked Jimmy, dying for Billy to give the right answer.

'On his weasel!' he announced.

Jimmy fell back and howled once again, tears rolling down his face. This was the answer he wanted. 'Pop goes the weasel!' he sang. 'Hey! yer popped *his* weasel for him, our young 'un!'

There was more laughter coming from outside the bedroom door. Dorothy and Susan, on their way to see how the boys were getting along, had stopped to listen in on the conversation. They now clung to each other in sobbing hysterics

Billy wouldn't be needing any psychiatrist to release him from his trauma. He had Jimmy.

Chapter Twenty-Three

Jimmy and Susan came home from school together on the bus and decided to visit Mam and Dad's grave, and maybe have a look round to see if they could see a headstone that might be a suitable replacement for the stone they'd cracked.

The cemetery was in full bloom. The trees heavy with leaves and blossom, verges alive with summer flowers, graves freshly tended and decorated with sprays and wreaths and messages hopefully crossing across the great divide. Jimmy risked a glance across at where the armless angel looked sweetly down on the spot where the woman had been murdered, and was taken aback at the sight of Len Bateson, on his knees, talking to himself as if in prayer.

'Hiya, Len!' hailed Jimmy, much to Susan's consternation. But Len didn't seem to hear. His mouth was moving and Jimmy plucked up courage to walk over to him. There was a bunch of carnations on the very spot where the woman had fallen.

'It was her fault, she drove me to it,' Len seemed to be talking to the carnations. 'Anyway, like I say, I'm sorry. Not a day's gone by when I haven't regretted it. It should've been her not you!'

Jimmy froze in his tracks when he heard this. Susan who was following him out of some sort of sisterly protection, heard Len as well. She laid a cautioning hand on Jimmy's shoulder and pointed to the tree they'd hidden behind on that fateful night. With bated breath they edged behind the wide trunk, just as Len turned to leave, still muttering words of abject apology. As they heard him walk away they slowly moved around the tree, keeping it between them and the murderer at all times. For now they were as certain as they could be that it was Len who killed the woman.

*

227

'We'll tell P.C. Greenough,' decided Susan. 'He's alright is P.C. Greenough.'

Jimmy was unsure about it all.

'Can't yer just ring 'em anonywhatsit and tell 'em Len killed her?' he asked.

'Could do, I suppose,' she mused. 'No, it's better to do the job properly!'

Jimmy couldn't see why, but trudged disconsolately along with her all the same.

Engraved in the deep stone lintel above the door it said simply 'POLICE STATION' as it had for the seventy years it had stood there. The words always struck fear into Jimmy's heart. There were many other words written on the walls. Rude words of criticism by people who were not admirers of the police within. The odd times Jimmy been inside, mainly in the company of Jackie Crombie, had never been happy ones. He shuffled in behind his sister, who kept telling him he'd got nothing to worry about. The young policeman on the desk did a double take of this pretty schoolgirl walking through the door, with a scruffy young tyke skulking behind her.

'Yes, madam, what can I you for you?' he asked cheerfully.

'We'd like to see P.C. Greenough,' said Susan, 'on very important business.'

'Alan!' yelled the policeman through a door at the back of him. 'Customers for you!'

Jimmy's eyes were automatically drawn to a picture of the murdered woman on the wall, above a request for information leading to the apprehension of the killer. Alongside this was a poster advertising the Policemen's Summer Ball at the Leeds Town Hall, and a photograph of a grinning policeman above the words 'Have You Seen This Man?' All of which somehow detracted from the gravity of the murder they'd come to talk about.

Alan Greenough appeared with a half-eaten sandwich in his hand and his sleeves rolled up.

'Hello, you two,' he smiled, genuinely happy to see them.

'We've come to report a murder,' announced Jimmy solemnly. Susan kicked him because she'd always wanted to say that.

'The woman who was murdered in the cemetery last year,' she expanded. 'We know who did it!'

228

'Len Bateson,' blurted out Jimmy, who was determined to be the one with the news. Susan kicked him again, harder this time. He was a pest and she wished she'd come on her own.

'You'd better come in,' said Alan, with a mouthful of cheese and tomato, as he lifted up a hinged counter to allow them through.

He led them to a large office full of desks, mainly unattended apart from the unpleasant policewoman, to whom their Auntie Dorothy had taken exception, and with good reason.

'Sit yourselves down,' said Alan, 'and start from the beginning.'

Jimmy eyed the policewoman suspiciously as Susan began to speak. She was sitting at a nearby desk writing something, but kept looking up at Susan as the story unfolded, shaking her head sarcastically.

When Susan came to the second part of the story, how they'd seen him less than an hour ago, talking to a bunch of flowers, the policewoman threw down her pen and sat back laughing.

'They're the Bairstow kids, aren't they?' she called across to Alan.

'What of it?' replied Alan, who obviously had little time for the woman.

'And you believe all that rubbish?' she said pityingly.

'Is there some reason why I shouldn't?' he snapped angrily.

'No, none at all,' she said disparagingly. 'It's your career. 'If you want to waste your time believing every lying little toerag in the district, it's up to you!'

'You're dead right, Muscroft, it's up to me!'

Susan turned and looked at WPC Muscroft searchingly, before returning her attention to Alan.

'Is she the one Auntie Dorothy told us about?' she asked demurely, but loud enough for the WPC to hear. 'She said there was a fat, ugly one with a moustache, surely there can't be two like that!'

Alan, who had his back to Muscroft, winced in anticipation as Muscroft exploded across the room, grabbing Susan by her collar and dragging her to her feet. Alan intervened quickly.

'Do you mind, WPC Muscroft? You're intimidating witnesses to a major crime!'

Muscroft let go, shaking with anger.

'Thank you,' soothed Alan. 'Now sit down and mind your own

business and we'll say no more about it.' He turned to Jimmy and his shaking sister. 'Right, you two, I'm taking you to see Inspector Mansfield, let's see what he makes of your story.'

Jimmy for one was glad to get out of that room. Sometimes he wished Susan would keep her big mouth shut, he was a marked man now!

The following night Alan Greenough knocked on the Bairstows' door, taking off his helmet as he walked in. Jimmy and Susan stood before him expectantly, Dorothy offered him a welcoming cup of tea. She been forewarned about the visit, Susan having told her all about what had happened in the cemetery.

'Why didn't you tell me about it at the time?' asked a slightly put out Dorothy.

'We couldn't, you were in jail,' explained Susan.

'Oh, right,' said Dorothy. There were some answers you just couldn't argue with.

Alan Greenough faced his two star witnesses with a certain trepidation. 'I thought it only fair to let you know,' he said hesitantly, 'that we've had to let him go!'

'Oh, heck!' exclaimed Jimmy, who wasn't really sure what the implications of this were.

'Why?' inquired a shocked Susan. 'Don't you think he did it?'

'As a matter of fact we do,' admitted Alan, ruefully. 'But his wife's given him an alibi.'

'A what!' exclaimed Susan.

'It's when somebody says you were with them when you weren't really,' explained Jimmy.

'I know what an alibi is, thank you very much,' objected Susan scornfully.

'She swears he stayed in all that night,' went on the constable. 'So it would be their word against yours, and on the night you say you weren't dead sure it was him.'

'If they say it was him, then it was him!' declared Dorothy stoutly.

'Like I said,' continued Alan, 'it's the Batesons' certain word against their "not sure" word.' He turned to Jimmy and Susan, 'If you two are prepared to swear on oath that it was definitely him that night, then we'll pull him back in.' He looked at them. 'Well?'

Susan thought hard for a while, then shook her head, she didn't fancy swearing something like that on oath, Jimmy breathed a sigh of relief that he didn't have to go to court.

Alan took the cup of tea from Dorothy and took a sip. 'You make a nice cup of tea in this house,' he grinned.

Jimmy returned his grin, remembering who'd made the last cup of tea constable Greenough had drunk here.

'If it's any consolation,' said Alan. 'Bateson doesn't know it was you who saw him!'

'Thank heaven for that!' sighed a relieved Dorothy. 'We've had enough problems recently without having murderers breathing down our necks!'

Chapter Twenty-Four

Frank put down the phone looked across at Dorothy, who was juggling with a mass of figures on a piece of paper in front of her.

'That's it!' He rubbed his hands with glee. 'Allerdyce has completed. The money's in the bank – sixteen thousand lovely pounds. Leaves us eleven thousand in the black!'

'I know,' said Dorothy, not sharing Frank's jubilation. 'I'm just working out what best use to put it to. No point having it in the bank, we're in business to make money for ourselves not for the banks.'

'What have you got in mind now?' asked Frank guardedly. He'd never been so well off in terms of cash in the bank and just wanted to savour the moment.

'There's an eighteen-acre plot in Horsforth we could pick up for five thousand, the owner's desperate to sell.'

'Saw it last year, waste of time. There's room for over two hundred bread and butter houses. The planners'll pass it but the highways won't. They've got this daft idea about two out of three families owning a car within the next ten years. That site leads out onto a dangerous road junction, more houses means more cars using that junction – end of story. That's why it's so cheap. Once the council have improved the junction it'll be a different story.'

'And you're saying the council have no plans for improving it,' said Dorothy.

'Correct,' confirmed Frank.

'Wrong,' said Dorothy. 'The council drew up plans two years ago. What they don't have is money to do the work.'

'Nor are they likely to have in the near future,' argued Frank.

'Correct,' agreed Dorothy. 'Have you any idea how much it would cost to do that junction?'

'Haven't a clue,' admitted Frank, who also hadn't a clue where the conversation was leading.

'Ballpark figure,' said Dorothy. 'Three thousand, possibly less if put out to tender. I picked up a copy of the plans from a friend of mine in the Engineer's Department and dropped it into Gilchrist Brothers for a rough estimate.'

'Why are you telling me all this?'

'Because I want you to go to the council,' said Dorothy, 'and offer to do the junction for nothing in exchange for planning permission for two hundred houses. It's a perfectly legitimate request. They'd need a hell of a good reason to turn it down.'

'Why hasn't anyone else tried it then?' asked Frank, who thought there must be a catch here somewhere.

'Same reason as you didn't. They assume the council wouldn't entertain such an idea. But the council are obliged to look at it, and they'd need a damn good reason to turn it down. I think we should go to the council and confirm that the junction is still their only objection, then make our offer. Once we have their acceptance in writing, we go ahead and buy. Then you sub-contract the junction to the lowest bidder, payment on approval by the council and in three or four months' time we've got a piece of land for two hundred houses for what?'

'Eight thousand,' said Frank,

'And worth how much, would you say?'

'Twenty at least,' replied Frank, gazing fondly at this amazing woman chewing on a pencil at the other side of his desk.

'Dorothy.'

'What, Frank?'

'Do you think? I mean, would you like to, er – Oh, sod it! It's years since I asked a girl out on a date.'

Then realising that he'd done it, he looked at her expectantly. She'd looked back at him with a pretend coyness, teasing him with fluttering eyelashes.

'Oh, forget it,' he said, slightly embarrassed at the situation he'd just put himself in.

'I most certainly will not!' she replied indignantly. 'You can't just raise a girl's hopes just like that, then drop her flat without so much as a "by your leave". Where are we going?'

'Well,' said Frank, taken unawares. 'We could go dancing – do you like dancing?'

'Yes, I love dancing.'

'We could go to the Hippodrome on Saturday.'

'I'd like that, Frank,' she smiled. 'Oh, but, Frank,' she added, serious now.

'What?'

'No strings – I don't want to spoil what we have. We're friends and business partners – nothing else, never will be.'

'Fair enough,' accepted Frank, disappointed at the finality of her last three words.

Chapter Twenty-Five

'Morning, Jimmy, morning, Susan,' shouted Vera Bateson from across the street as they walked through the gate on their way to school. They felt uneasy. How could she be so cheerful knowing her husband was a murderer?

'Morning, Mrs Bateson,' they replied in polite unison.

'Vera, please. You're old enough to start calling me Vera surely?'

They both smiled nervously and went on their way.

Vera stood and watched them disappear round the corner, then looked up at her husband, staring blankly out of the bedroom window.

'Is Len not going to work this morning?' asked an inquisitive Mrs Byrne from next door, who'd never forgiven Vera for trying it on with her husband at the VE Day party.

'No, he's having a day off sick. It's all that burning rubbish – gets on his chest,' said Vera, who had little time for Mrs Byrne anyway.

Len was an odd job man at the destructor. It was all the work he could get despite having been an engineering draughtsman before the war. His nerves were shattered. He'd lost every decent job he'd been offered due to being completely unable to concentrate on his work. He'd gone from job to job, each one too much of a challenge, until eventually he'd found his niche at the destructor. He was happy in his work, he didn't have to think and he had no responsibilities. The worst part of his day was going home to Vera's constant nagging. She'd been an attractive woman, who'd married Len before the war as some sort of a status symbol. None of her friends had husbands with an office job – a job with real prospects. And now look at him – a labourer at the destructor, the lowest of the low. She knew her friends were laughing at her behind her back but she couldn't do anything about it. So she took it out on Len. He was barred from her bed. She was otherwise well catered for in that department. A couple of local husbands, whose wives weren't up to the job, called in at regular intervals, always leaving a ten bob note on the sideboard as they left.

She'd even got her rent free up to recently, until that idiot Simpson tried it on with Dorothy Bairstow. She wasn't all that sorry, he was repulsive – still fifteen bob a week wasn't to be sneezed at.

Vera had been quite happy thinking she was the widow of a war hero. Her lodger was making her happier still, he'd even proposed and she only just accepted, but the engagement was cut short when Len turned up alive and kicking and threw her fiancé out of the bedroom window.

She walked back into the house and went upstairs to where Len was lying on top of her bed, completely naked.

'Do you mind getting back in your own room!'

Len made no move, he just watched her.

'Is that little thing supposed to get me going?' she laughed scornfully. 'I'm not one of your whores, you know!'

'No! You're me wife. I shouldn't need to go with whores!'

'Well, there's evidently one less for you to go with now. What happened? Did she laugh at you? Did she find you pathetic? Because you are pathetic, just look at you! You're not a man, I don't know why I lied for you last night!'

Len sat up. 'Why did you lie for me?' he asked.

Vera poured more scorn on him. 'Don't you think it's bad enough having a loser like you for a husband without everybody knowing you're a murderer? I didn't lie for your benefit. Just put one foot wrong and I'll shop you just as soon as look at you!'

'You should have told the truth,' smiled Len. 'You should have got me locked up, got me hung – that's what I deserve. Trouble is I'm at your mercy now and I don't like that.'

Vera didn't like the way this conversation was going. She'd never seen Len like this before. He'd never frightened her before. She made for the door but Len anticipated this and moved to block her. A large kitchen knife appeared in his hand. He waved it menacingly in her face.

'Take your clothes off!' he said calmly.

'Stop acting stupid, Len!'

'Take your clothes off or I'll cut your throat!' He had a look in his eye that she'd never seen before and she didn't like it.

'Alright,' she said uncertainly, 'I'll play your stupid game, just this once!'

Without taking her eyes off the knife, she removed her clothes until she stood before him completely naked. He looked her up and down, shaking his head in disdain. She wasn't the woman he'd married. Her breasts were beginning to sag, her stomach was heavier and there were ripples of fat across her thighs.

'What happened to you?' he suddenly snarled, jabbing the knife towards her and forcing her to fall backwards to the floor.

'Please, Len,' she pleaded. 'You can have me if you like, I'm sorry for hurting you. Just put the knife down.'

She reached up between his legs and held him, moving up and down until he was erect. He stared wildly at her, the knife was now pointing at her throat. Vera felt more aroused than she'd ever been in her life before.

'Put it inside me, Len, now!' she almost begged, pulling him down towards her, ignoring the threat of the knife. If he was playing a game it sure as hell was working. If not, she'd worry about that once she'd had her fill of him.

She guided him inside her and he began thrusting insanely again and again with a strength she'd never known before, in him or any man. He went on and on, for what seemed like an age, then he was gasping for breath and she was shuddering to a climax with a molten surge that kept coming and coming as Len collapsed, spent and exhausted, on top of her.

She lay there for a while not quite knowing what to do. Was he still the madman she'd been so scared of just minutes ago?

'Len?' she said gently. 'Could I get up now, please?'

He slowly raised himself to his knees and looked down at her. That strange look still in his eyes. Vera suddenly felt sick with terror. She tried to scream but Len stifled it with his free hand. He raised the knife high above his head, her eyes were glued to it, hypnotised by this thing that was about to end her life.

Len gave a strangled, frustrated yell and brought the knife down viciously, stabbing time and time again at the threadbare rug beneath Vera's head. She was crying with shock, her breath coming in short gasps. Len pulled the knife out for the last time and got to his feet looking down at his wife who was now curled up in a foetal position, sobbing hysterically.

'Get up, Vera,' he said savagely.

She got to her knees and clung to him around his legs, but he kicked her away,

'I told you to get up!' He held the knife to her throat and followed her progress as she slowly raised herself up off the floor.

'Sit on that!' he commanded harshly, pointing to a high-backed chair at the bottom of the bed.

She sat down on the chair as he rummaged in a drawer and took out various scarves and belts with which he gagged her and expertly tied her to the chair and the chair to the iron bedpost.

'What are you going to do to me, Len?' she sobbed, still naked, still shaking with fear.

'I couldn't do it,' he said, shaking his head. 'But it's got to be done – and it's got to look like an accident!'

'I wouldn't tell anyone about you, Len! I'm your wife. I lied to the police, didn't I – you heard me lie to the police!'

'For your own benefit,' he said. 'That's what you told me. You only lied for your own benefit – shop me just as soon as look at me, that's what you said!' He bent down to kiss her. 'Goodbye, Vera,' he whispered, crying himself now.

Len dressed himself and went out to report late for work. A plan of sorts already forming in his head.

Dorothy took a last look at herself in the mirror, gave herself an appreciative nod and left her family their parting instructions.

'Don't be late to bed, any of you. I know it's Saturday tomorrow, but you all need your beauty sleep.'

'Susan does, we're beautiful enough, aren't we, Billy,' cracked Jimmy. He and Billy laughed, then ducked as Susan hurled a cushion in their direction.

'Billy, your bedtime's eight o'clock, not a minute later,' she added before kissing each of them goodbye.

Billy knew that there was no point thinking he'd get away with anything with Susan, she was stricter with him than Auntie Dorothy.

'Just get yourself off, and have good time,' laughed Susan. 'I'll make sure they behave themselves.'

Frank was already waiting for her in the car as she hurried out, stopping to wave again to the three of them as they came to the window to see her off.

'Do yer think owt'll come of it?' asked a curious Jimmy of his more worldly sister. 'This is the third time he's taken her out in two weeks!'

'No idea,' commented Susan, who thought it was rather nice that her auntie and Frank hit it off so well together.

'It'd be good if they got married,' said Jimmy. 'He's got a great house, has Frank. We could all go live there!'

'I like it here!' declared Billy, who, generally speaking, had never benefited from moves.

'It's not where you live, Billy,' said Susan sagely. 'It's who you live with. Oh, and while I'm at it – washed and pyjamas on, now!'

Billy slunk into the scullery and turned on the tap, before stripping off his shirt. There was no point him giving himself just a 'lick and a promise'. Susan would only make him start again, and he didn't want to miss Dick Barton on the wireless.

At eight o'clock on the dot he was on his way upstairs with his one-eyed rabbit and a glass of milk. He didn't mind though. Susan hadn't found out about his torch and his latest Biggles book, both on loan from Jimmy, who winked at him as he said goodnight.

He was fast asleep when the quiet knock came at the door. Susan looked at the clock and then at Jimmy.

'It's ten-past-ten, who on earth is that?'

Jimmy went with her as he always did when things weren't quite right. Susan turned the handle curiously and they both jumped back as the door was suddenly pushed open.

He stood there, holding the same kitchen knife he'd failed to stab his wife with earlier in the day. The same manic expression on his face and, like Vera, Susan and Jimmy went cold with terror. Neither could speak as he forced them backwards at the point of his knife.

'So, yer thought yer'd shop me to the law, did yer?' he snarled.

'We – we don't know w. . . . what your taking about, Mr B . . . Bateson!' stammered Susan.

'Don't lie ter me!' he yelled. 'She told me it were you, that fat copper. She doesn't like you two, does she?'

'We just said we saw you in the cemetery that's all, Mr Bateson.' Susan could see he was deranged and hadn't a clue how to deal with him.

'You saw me do it! That's what yer told the coppers. You were right an' all – I did do it. I killed that filthy whore – brayed her bleeding head in. Stopped her laughing at me, didn't it?' He started laughing himself now – then just as quickly stopped and his face grew ugly again. He indicated the door with his knife. 'Out!' he snarled. 'Now!'

The three of them walked slowly across the street to the Batesons' house, two hearts beating like hammer drills, the other scarcely beating at all.

The door was swinging open. Jimmy and Susan entered with a feeling of dread, wondering what he'd done with Mrs Bateson. She was nowhere to be seen, up to this point Jimmy hadn't spoken.

'I need to pee, Mr Bateson,' he said pathetically.

Len thought for a bit, then said harshly, 'Piss in yer pants!' but Jimmy had already beaten him to it.

He pushed them roughly to the floor, then bound and gagged them with the same efficiency as he'd tied up his wife, who was still trussed up in the room above them. They were tied together back to back on the floor. Jimmy had one leg tied to the cellar door handle, preventing them from moving across the room.

Len looked down with some satisfaction at his handiwork then turned out the light and left.

Dorothy looked at her watch and then at Frank. 'It's nearly the witching hour, boss, time for beddy byes.'

The Johnnie Goodman orchestra struck up the last waltz. 'Might as well eh?' asked Frank as he led her back on to the floor for the last time that evening.

'You're a wonderful dancer for a joiner,' complimented Dorothy.

'It comes from all the sawing,' he explained seriously. 'There's rhythm to it you see. Now bricklayers, they're a different kettle of fish altogether. If I was a bricklayer you'd be going home with sore feet!'

Dorothy laughed at this funny man. She'd enjoyed this evening. She felt comfortable with Frank. He wasn't as outrageous as

Tommy had been, but there again, even Tommy would have slowed down by the time he reached his forties. As the waltz whirled to a close, Frank bent over and kissed her gently on the lips. Sensing her respond he held her tightly and stopped dancing. Both of them were now alone in the centre of the dance floor locked in a passionate embrace.

Johnnie Goodman put down his clarinet and came to the microphone. 'Could someone bring a bucket of water to the dance floor, please, then we can all go home!'

Frank and Dorothy broke off their embrace to great laughter and tumultuous applause and hurried off the floor with red faces and embarrassed grins.

'Your place or mine,' asked Frank, holding the car door open for Dorothy. He laughed to himself. 'I've always wanted to say that. When I first went courting I didn't have a place. It was more a case of "your back alley or mine"?'

He walked round the car and climbed into the driver's seat. 'Well?' he asked.

'Well what?'

'Your place or mine?'

'Sorry, Frank, I didn't realise you were being serious. No, I must go back. I've left the kids on their own.'

'Are these the same kids who managed very well on their own for all those weeks you were in prison?'

'There's Billy there as well, he's only six.'

'And Susan's there as well. They don't come more capable than Susan,' argued Frank.

'Point taken, but if I don't go home they'll be worrying.'

'They'll be asleep! I'll have you back before they wake up, promise.'

'Do you make a habit of seducing young helpless virgins, Mr Sackfield?' Dorothy giggled; she'd had more to drink than she'd had for a long time.

'Everyone has to have a hobby!'

'Promise to get me back before they wake up?'

'Promise.'

There was a beguiling modesty about Frank which extended to his love-making. Like Dorothy, he'd had no one for a long time and

241

he didn't want to appear too pushy. He lived in a small detached house with an overgrown garden and a garage. So by nineteen-forties standards he was middle class.

He knocked on the bathroom door. She'd been in there a long time, not having had the luxury of a bathroom since she left her father.

'I er, I found a shirt you might like to wear,' he said hesitantly.

'Why would I want a shirt?' The drink was taking its toll on Dorothy, she was feeling daring.

'Oh, right. I'll get into bed then,' he called through the door. He climbed into bed, switching on the small light beside him.

Dorothy had been in the bathroom thinking about the last man who saw her strip naked. Why should this lovely man be deprived of something that the foul Neville Simpson had enjoyed? It was a logic tempered by drink, but Dorothy had recklessly convinced herself of its merit. She swung seductively round the bedroom doorway, smoking a cigarette in a long holder she'd found in the bathroom, dressed in bra, pants, stockings, suspenders – and a trilby hat she'd found in the hall. She hummed to herself as she moved, what she hoped, was gracefully around the room, followed by Frank's startled eyes. One by one the garments flew his way until she, quite brazenly, stood on the bed, looking sensuously down at him as she removed her panties and dropped them on his face.

'What do you think, Mr Sackfield?' she asked. 'Do I get the job?'

'I have to test you on the practical side of things before I make my final decision,' he said, finding it difficult to concentrate on the game she was playing. She threw the bedclothes back and expressed horror at his striped pyjamas.

'Mr Sackfield! You're out of uniform!'

He smiled and pulled her down to him, allowing her to make him as naked as she was. Frank had never seen anyone as beautiful as Dorothy, not even his ex-wife. She paled into insignificance beside this delightful woman, who was now squirming on top of him, easing herself onto him, her breasts swinging playfully against his chest. He closed his eyes and allowed her to carry him away to a pleasure he had never known before.

*

242

Billy was one of the few people in Broughton Terrace who hadn't had their sleep disturbed by the spasmodic hammering of a pneumatic drill coming from the destructor yard. But Billy had been used to spending his nights in dormitories full of disturbed boys, who often woke screaming and crying and shouting. It'd take more than a pneumatic drill to wake Billy up. He woke at seven o'clock as he always had. Jimmy wasn't in his bed. Now there was a surprise, especially since he now remembered it was Saturday morning and Jimmy never got up early on Saturday morning. It didn't even look as though Jimmy's bed had been slept in.

'Jimmy!' he shouted.

No answer.

He went to the bottom of the attic stairs.

'Susan!'

No answer.

He knocked on Dorothy's door, then opened it slightly, enough to see her bed hadn't been slept in. He dashed up to the attic and burst into tears at the sight of Susan's tidy bed.

'Rotten buggers!' he sobbed.

He ran back down stairs and out into the street, still in his pyjamas, tears streaming down his face. He knew it had been too good to be true.

'Rotten buggers,' he repeated, sitting down on the front step, totally dejected. They'd left him again. He knew they would of course. All the kids at all the homes he'd ever been in had warned him about this. They come and get you, but never for very long, they soon get fed up of you and back you come. But there was no way he was going back to that stinking home. No way. Still, it might be okay now that Wiggins had gone. I bet Joe Conroy's still there. He was alright was Joe. A bit thick but he'd never leave you – not like some people. What was he talking about? He'd left Joe, hadn't he? What would Joe think of him?

Dorothy and Frank drove back to Broughton Terrace in a contented silence. For both of them the evening and the ensuing lovemaking had given them something that had been missing from their lives for years. A slight hangover reminded Dorothy of the amount she'd drunk. She smiled to herself.

'I was a bit drunk last night, Mr Sackfield,' she said. 'I hope I didn't do anything naughty.'

243

'You behaved impeccably, Mrs Bairstow.'

'On a scale of one to ten – how impeccable?'

'Ten.'

'That's alright then – so long as it's understood,' she cautioned, 'that our relationship is purely platonic.'

'That's the word all the film stars use,' grumbled Frank.

'Then it's good enough for us.'

Frank gave a reluctant grin – it wasn't good enough for him. His face turned serious as he swung into Broughton Terrace.

'Isn't that your Billy sitting on the step?'

'Billy! What on earth are you doing out here in your pyjamas?'

He hadn't heard the car pull up, too full of self-pity for that. Auntie Dorothy got out and sat down beside him, hugging him to her. She could see he'd been crying. Frank looked out of the van, sharing Dorothy's guilt at somehow causing distress in such a small child.

'I thought yer'd left me again,' he said, drying his eyes and trying to smile up at his auntie.

'Oh, Billy, Billy – I'll never leave you, none of us will!'

'Jimmy and Susan have!'

'What are you talking about Billy?'

'They never slept here last night. I think they've buggered off!'

Dorothy started to correct Billy about his choice of verb but stopped when his statement had sunk in. 'How do you mean? Where are they?'

She was panicking now. Frank got out of the car and followed her inside as she dashed up the stairs and saw what Billy had told her was true. Neither bed had been slept in. They all came back down and realised that the back room light was on, so was the wireless – and the scullery door was wide open.

She started hammering on doors up and down the street. Beyond the destructor wall the pneumatic drill started again. People were coming to bedroom windows and shouting at Dorothy to 'be quiet, we've been awake all bloody night as it is'.

Still in her evening finery she jumped into Frank's car, shoved a bemused Billy, still in his pyjamas, in the back and the three of them drove the short distance to Paradine Hill Police Station. It was WPC Muscroft at the desk.

Dorothy didn't recognise her at first. 'I've come to report two missing children,' she said, unable to control the panic in her voice.

'Name?' said Muscroft, who knew very well what her name was.

'Shit!' groaned Dorothy, recognising Muscroft.

'And would that be your Christian name or your surname?' smirked Muscroft.

'What sort of a stupid question's that?' shouted Frank, who'd no idea who Muscroft was. 'There's two children missing and all you can do is make stupid jokes!'

A sergeant came through the door, 'Alright alright, calm down,' he said. 'What's all the noise about?'

'It's that Bairstow lot,' sniffed WPC Muscroft, as though the very name explained everything.

'My niece and nephew have gone missing, they didn't sleep in their beds last night!'

'Right, Mrs Bairstow,' said the sergeant, taking over the situation. 'When exactly did you notice they'd gone missing?'

'When I got back this morning and found young Billy sitting on the step crying his eyes out . . .'

The sergeant held up an interrupting hand. 'So, you're saying you weren't home last night? They were left to fend for themselves.' He was looking down his nose at Dorothy.

Frank sprang to her defence, 'Susan is sixteen – and they were left to fend for themselves for several weeks when you people arrested Mrs Bairstow for something she didn't do!'

'Yes, sir,' said the sergeant, suitably chastened. 'Now correct me if I'm wrong, but didn't they go off on their own once before, when they were less capable of fending for themselves?'

Muscroft was standing behind the sergeant's shoulder, a self-satisfied smirk on her face.

Dorothy looked back at the sergeant and said fiercely, 'Alright, alright, I get your message, let's hope nothing's happened to them then. We don't want to give the bearded lady here too much to laugh about, do we?'

Another constable appeared through the door with two cups of tea in his hand, one of which he gave to Muscroft, who was clearly angered by Dorothy's last remark.

'We'll keep an eye out for them, Mrs Bairstow, that's all we can do,' said the sergeant, taking the second cup.

As Dorothy turned to go, a frightening thought came into her head; she paused and looked back at the sergeant. 'You don't suppose it's got anything to do with Len Bateson, do you? My kids are convinced he's the murderer – and so are you lot by the sound of things.'

'There's no way Mr Bateson could know it was your children who informed us about him,' the sergeant reassured her. 'We certainly didn't tell him.'

Dorothy briefly held Muscroft in her gaze, causing the policewoman to lower her eyes, then she looked back at the sergeant. 'I do hope you're telling me the truth, sergeant. Up to now, you people haven't inspired much confidence.'

She turned to Frank and Billy, 'Right then, we'd better try and sort this out ourselves. The people who are paid to do it, have got cups of tea to drink!'

Dorothy hammered hard on the Batesons' door. The three occupants could clearly hear her, but could nothing about it. Jimmy tried to kick at the cellar door to make a noise she might hear, but Len had done his job too well, even making sure they had their backs to each other so they couldn't communicate. They'd been dozing on and off all night. Frightened, although not absolutely sure what they had to be frightened of. There was someone else upstairs, they both knew that. Every so often they could hear a thumping. Jimmy's legs were chapped where he'd wet himself the night before, Susan had somehow managed to control herself, although things were becoming urgent in that department.

'They're out, Dorothy love!' shouted Mrs Byrne from her next door bedroom window. 'Been out since yesterday morning. I heard 'em having a row, then he went off ter work, though he were supposed ter be off sick – and I think she must have cleared off as well.'

'Thanks, Mrs Byrne,' said Dorothy. She was not on first name terms with Mrs Byrne, who she thought was a busybody and a nuisance.

'That's alright, love. hey! Yer haven't got a cup of sugar I could borrow, have yer?' shouted Mrs Byrne, before slamming the window down in annoyance, because Dorothy was already gone. Her hand was firmly clutching Billy's as she and Frank drove round all the neighbouring streets in vain. Ray hadn't seen them, nor had any of Jimmy's pals. None of them seemed overly worried about their disappearance – such was Jimmy and Susan's reputation.

'Look, Dorothy,' Frank tried to reassure her. 'Knowing them two, they'll be okay. I've never come across two more resourceful kids than them. Why don't you wait at home? I've got to pop into work for half an hour, if they're not back by then, I'll have a good drive round.'

A game of cricket had started up in the street. The Gascoigne brothers had brought a team down from Bridge Street to challenge the depleted Broughton Terrace team. In the end, two mixed teams were picked in the time-honoured 'best gets picked first' method and the game started. Billy watched from his bedroom window, as Dorothy was too scared to let him out of her sight until Jimmy and Susan turned up.

A strange scenario ran through Billy's jumbled brain as he stared across at the Bateson house, which looked oddly quiet. Maybe Len Bateson was keeping them locked up and was torturing them this very minute. Maybe he'd already killed them!

He couldn't for the life of him understand why the police hadn't immediately rushed up there and shot their way in. If he knew Len Bateson had captured his brother and sister, why didn't anybody else? After all, everyone knew Len Bateson was a murderer. Grown-ups could be so stupid. Grown-ups could be so evil – Billy knew more than most about evil grown-ups.

He wished Jackie Crombie hadn't gone down with measles, between the two of them they could have easily rescued Jimmy and Susan. Ah well, he'd better tackle the job on his own. A ball flew high in the air, bouncing onto the Bairstow lavatory roof, then running back down into the rainwater gutter, where it lodged, safely out of the reach of the frustrated cricketers.

They saw Billy leaning out of the window, within easy reach of the ball.

'Nip out an' gerrus t' ball,' someone shouted.

Billy was out of the window and sliding along the slates in a flash. Throwing the ball down before lowering himself in to the hands of a helpful cricketer.

Deciding to make practical use of his unexpected freedom he made his way round to the front door of the Bateson house. Front streets were always quieter than back streets, but what front streets

247

had were coal grates leading into cellars. A small boy of Billy's size could just about squeeze through one of these and providing the householder hadn't locked the cellar door, entry to the house would be easy; and as such properties made poor targets for burglars, security was never much of a priority.

He lifted the grate and went in head first, sliding down the concrete shute and landing more or less unhurt in a pile of coal. The layout of the cellar being much the same as the one at home, Billy managed to find his way, without a light, to the steps, at the top of which would be the door to the Batesons' back room. He pushed at the door and managed to get his face round it to see what the obstruction was.

'Jimmy!' he gasped. 'Bugger me! What you doing here?'

As pleased as Jimmy and Susan were to see their younger brother, it was still exasperating to be asked such a question when they were trussed up like a couple of Christmas turkeys. They grunted at him to take their gags off, and both breathed sighs of relief when he did so.

Eventually freed of their bonds, the two of them stood up and stretched. They wanted to go home, to eat, to pee, but first they had another priority

'There's somebody upstairs,' Susan reminded Jimmy, he nodded. They'd heard scuffling sounds all night. 'You go up first,' she decided.

'Why me? You're the oldest!'

Susan sighed, she hated this constantly being used against her.

'Right, I'll go up first. Jimmy, you follow me. Billy, you wait here.'

As soon as Susan entered Vera's bedroom she spun round and blocked Jimmy's way.

'It's Mrs Bateson,' she whispered. 'She's tied up – she's got no clothes on!'

Jimmy now bitterly regretted not going first. 'Don't yer want me to help untie her?' he asked innocently, never having seen a naked woman.

'I think I can manage, thank you. Go downstairs and see what Billy's up to.'

A disgruntled Jimmy went back down the stairs, annoyed at his sister's attitude. It wouldn't have hurt her to let him have a quick look.

*

'How'd you figure out where we were?' asked Jimmy as they dodged across the cobbled cricket pitch, ignoring appeals from the fast bowler to, 'Gerrouta me sodding way!'

'Stands ter reason,' said Billy, who saw nothing but logic in his actions.

Dorothy had seen them through the scullery window and came dashing out to meet them. 'Thank God you're alright!' she pulled Jimmy to her, almost crushing him, forcing him to push her gently away so he could tell her what happened.

'Where's Susan?' asked Dorothy before Jimmy could say anything.

'She's untying Mrs Bateson!'

'She's what?'

'I'd have stopped to help, but Mrs Bateson hasn't got any clothes on – apparently!' he added the last word to emphasise that he actually hadn't seen their naked neigbour. 'Len Bateson tied her up,' he continued. 'He tied us up as well – we've been tied up all night. He's barmy is Len Bateson – and he did kill that woman – he told us he did!'

'Oh my God!' cried Dorothy, letting Jimmy go and dashing across the street to the Batesons' house.

Vera Bateson appeared at the door in a dressing gown, looking pale and shocked. Susan was supporting her.

'She's okay, Auntie Dorothy, we're both okay. Len said he was going to kill her. I think he must be coming back. We'd better get the police!'

Vera sat down on the step. 'Do you know what I'd like right now before we start bothering with the police?' she croaked hoarsely. 'A right nice cuppa tea.'

'You sit there, love, I'll make you one. Them coppers are a waste of time anyway!' comforted Dorothy, coughing as a gust of wind blew smoke over the destructor wall.

'Phew!' yelled one of the cricketers. 'What they burning today? Your old socks, Jimmy!'

Jimmy laughed and climbed up on to the back yard wall of the end house, then up on to the destructor wall to see where the smoke was coming from, pulling Billy up behind him. Billy sat beside his brother, a bit put out that he hadn't yet been accorded suitable thanks for his daring rescue. It wasn't every day that your little brother rescued you from a murderer, somebody should say 'thank you' surely.

They sat together, looking down at the smoke which was coming from a fire at the bottom of the chimney, trying to figure out what was going on. There was an odd crunching sound as the chimney seemed to shift slightly, then a man appeared out of the smoke and looked back at the fire, laughing loudly, but they couldn't see what was so funny.

'Isn't that him?' asked Billy.

'Who?'

'Len Bateson!'

Jimmy peered into the smoke. 'It flippin' is!' he gasped, as the crunching sound came again.

Jimmy grabbed his brother and lowered him down off the wall, making him drop at least six feet to the ground, before he himself jumped down on to the yard wall and then into the street. He looked back up at the chimney and then at the street full of children.

'Run!' he yelled. 'The chimney's falling down!'

Len Bateson laughed to himself as he cut out the bricks from the base of the chimney with the pneumatic drill. Nobody came to check on what he was doing, he was a law unto himself in the destructor yard. Everyone assumed he was carrying out someone else's instructions. But the fact that his was a menial job, didn't mean that he was stupid. He was brighter than the rest of them put together. None of them had been a Flight Engineer in Lancasters during the war – and they didn't let idiots do that job, it carried the rank of Flight Sergeant. He was the only survivor out of a crew of seven who'd taken off from RAF Mildenhall that March morning in 1944. They thought he was dead. 'No Survivors' was the verdict of the rest of the squadron who'd seen his aircraft explode in mid-air. He was the only one wearing a parachute, a wise precaution as it turned out. He remembered being blown out of the plane, then pulling the rip-cord, then nothing else. He must have been unconscious when he landed, because he woke up in a muddy German field surrounded by ugly women and old men armed with shovels. One of the women was a real Teutonic harridan, he thought she was going to lamp him one with her shovel, which was bigger than anyone else's. It took two of the men to stop her. What was it that woman had against him?

This pneumatic drill made his work easier, even so he reckoned the job would take him all night. It had to be done carefully. The base of the chimney was well over two feet thick, six layers of brick before he got through to the inner lining. He intended to leave that, better not cut through the lining whilst the chimney was in use. As he cut out a section of bricks, he replaced it with cut-down railway sleepers to prop up the chimney until he was ready. There was a pile in the yard he'd cut up into eighteen-inch lengths.

He'd been shunted from Stalag to Stalag. How was he to know his letters weren't getting through? The Germans were on the run and they were taking him with them for company. They'd more to think about than his letters home apparently. Then he'd finished up in Poland in the most God-forsaken hole. He'd never have survived it there. But the Russians came along and liberated him. Their idea of liberating was raping, pillaging and hanging people. They were wanting to hang him because they thought he was German, they'd already strung a few of the Polish prisoners up. Stupid bloody Russians, fancy not being able to tell the difference between a Kraut and a Leeds lad – anyway he didn't stop to argue, he did a runner.

Once he'd cut out two thirds of the way round the chimney, it would be effectively supported by the railway sleepers. He was breaking out the part of the chimney facing his house. His engineer's brain told him that as soon as the props became unstable the chimney would topple towards the street, straight on top of his house and his darling wife, she was the one he wanted dead. Her and them two meddling kids.

Had his engineer's brain been thinking straight he might have worked out that the chimney was in fact destined to miss his house completely and fall right in the middle of Broughton Terrace. There'd be people killed that day – but his darling Vera wouldn't be one of them.

He'd run and walked all the way across Europe. Spurred on by his love for Vera. Two months it had taken him, unsure of what was happening, of who was his friend. The place was full of displaced persons. None of them looked very friendly. Best to assume everyone was his enemy, couldn't go wrong then. He hid in empty houses and barns and woods until he was found asleep by a British Tommy, prodding him awake with his bayonet. They

251

made a fuss of him then alright. Couldn't believe it was possible to walk all that way, they said. Thought he was mad. But he wasn't mad, he did it because he had to – and because he wanted to get back to his beloved Vera.

They'd flown him home as a VIP. Rushed through his demob. First Class rail pass to Leeds, seventy-five quid demob money burning a hole in his pocket and every penny was going to be spent on Vera, his lovely Vera.

Once it was all cut out and propped, all he had to do was build a bonfire around the sleepers, douse the lot with paraffin, put a match to it and stand back. Once the fire burnt through the sleepers, down would come the chimney, bye bye, Vera and the meddling kids.

He still remembered the shock he felt when he found his Vera in bed with that man. He couldn't have timed it worse, both of them naked on top of the bed, he could hear them grunting as he crept upstairs but he didn't allow himself to think it might have been his wife screwing another man. Not his beloved Vera.

Where he got the strength from amazed him even today. He was emaciated from his time in the camps, not to mention his two-month hike. He'd dragged the man up by his hair and hurled him, still naked, through the bedroom window. With his world ruined, he refused to contest a charge of attempted murder, but when the judge heard his story he wouldn't accept his plea. He'd let him go with a ticking off. The poor bloody lodger was still in a wheelchair and serve him right.

When they heard Jimmy screaming with such urgency, the cricketers looked up at the wavering chimney and started to run. Jimmy was charging round like a maniac, pushing and kicking slow movers into action. Dorothy heard him shouting and without stopping to think, bustled Susan and Vera into the back door, through the house, out the front door and along the front street on to Paradine Hill.

She was choking with fear for the safety of Jimmy and Billy as, with a thunderous roar, the smoking edifice collapsed clean along the centre of Back Broughton Terrace. The main road was full of running children who'd only recently been playing cricket. She could just make out Billy, coughing as the dust cloud caught up with him, running beside a boy she took to be Jimmy. Her heart stopped momentarily as the masonry bounced around their heels then she breathed again as they managed to get clear. Children were running and stumbling and crying with fear. Choked by the dust and deafened by the noise. Many with cuts and bruises from flying masonry and nasty falls. Picking themselves up and charging blindly around, sometimes straight back towards danger.

Satisfied that he'd alerted everyone to the danger, Jimmy made his own bid to escape. He chanced a quick glance behind him as the rumbling grew louder. The chimney appeared to be collapsing from the bottom. Disappearing into the ground rather than toppling over. Then everything changed. It was falling straight down on him. The wall at the end of the street burst open and a moving mountain of rubble came bouncing towards him. One brick catching him on the back of his leg as he sprang after his pals, who were all several yards in front of him. Through the dust he could just see Billy galloping along at the back of them. The noise behind him was deafening. He was passing his own back yard when he realised he wasn't going to outrun the collapsing chimney so he flung himself sideways just as the huge tidal wave of rubble filled the area he'd just left. He took cover as best he could beside the lavatory wall then something hit him on the head and the world went black.

Alan Greenough was first on the scene. He was just about to walk into the station when he heard the roar. There was nothing he could do but watch with horror. He knew there'd be children playing in that street, there always were on a Saturday morning.

When the dust settled he was amazed to see it had settled on a great crowd of people of all sizes, some huddled together in the middle of Paradine Hill, some sitting on the Co-op wall. All of them covered in a thick layer of dust, but otherwise unharmed.

'Is that you Mrs Bairstow?' Alan was only a few feet away from Dorothy, but she was so filthy it was hard to distinguish even her handsome features.

'Yes,' she smiled, her white teeth dazzling out from within the grime. 'And we're okay thanks very much!'

The policeman went round checking on everyone, soon joined by his colleagues. Alan looked across at the gang of blackened cricketers sitting on the Co-op wall.

'Do you know if they all got clear?' he asked Dorothy.

'To be honest I don't know,' she replied grimly, 'But I think our Jimmy was at the back of them all and he got out alright.'

'Beats me how they managed it,' said the policeman.

'It were Jimmy mister, he shouted to us all to run, so we did, everybody in the street ran like mad!' The informant was Colin Gascoigne, acting as spokesman for his team, who all muttered their grimy agreement to his assessment.

Alan turned to Billy, who was now standing beside him. 'How did Jimmy know what was happening?'

'It were Len Bateson, he did it,' said Billy. 'Me an our Jimmy saw him. He lit a fire at the bottom of the chimney, we saw it moving so our kid yelled for 'em all ter run!'

'He tied me up all night,' added Vera, 'and Jimmy and Susan. He said he was going to kill us all! It was him what killed that woman . . .!'

Alan held up his hands. 'Look, I think you'd all better come down to the station. There's a lot needs clearing up here, and I don't just mean this mess,' he indicated the huge mound of smoking rubble piled all the way up the street. 'I wonder if there's still anybody under all that?'

Charlie Gascoigne took a hesitant step forward. 'There were an old woman sat on t' lavvie when t' chimney came down!'

'Are you sure?' asked Alan.

'I think so, mister. We were all laughing at her 'cos she'd left t' lavvie door open and – she were sat on t' pot with her umbrella up!'

'She allus did that, mister,' confirmed the fast bowler.

'What a way to go!' said Alan.

Dorothy and Susan felt themselves smiling and were suitably disgusted with themselves. As she, Susan, Vera and Alan Greenough left to go the police station Dorothy looked down at Billy. 'Go get Jimmy – tell him to come down to the police station.'

'And Billy,' added Alan Greenough with a twinkle in his eye, 'tell him he's not in any trouble.'

The three of them sat in the front office talking to Alan Greenough and Inspector Mansfield. Dorothy had already told them about her trip to the station earlier and how it had been left up to a six-year-old boy to do their job for them and rescue Jimmy, Susan and Mrs Bateson.

'Had it not been for our Billy and Jimmy,' added Susan, 'you'd have had a street full of dead kids' blood on your hands!'

'On *our* hands?' protested the inspector. 'I do hope you're not blaming the police for the chimney falling down, young lady!'

'You're to blame for letting Len Bateson go,' stormed Susan, angry now at being patronised. 'And he was the one who brought the chimney down – and you told him who informed on him!' she retorted. 'That's why he came for me and Jimmy.'

The inspector blanched, 'I'm sorry, but you're mistaken about that. There's no way we would have told him!'

'That's what he told us,' argued Susan, heatedly.

'He told me the same,' added Vera, who knew she was about to get in trouble for giving Len a false alibi, but the police seemed to have as many problems as her, so she wasn't too bothered. 'The fat one with the moustache, she told him!'

'I might have bloody known it!' shouted an enraged Dorothy leaping to her feet. 'Bring her in here! Let's see what she has to say!'

Without waiting for an answer she stormed out of the door into the main office, shouting as she went, 'Muscroft, you fat-arsed bastard! Come out here!'

The rest of them charged out after her, with Alan in the lead. He caught up with just her as WPC Muscroft emerged from an interview room, wondering what all the fuss was about. Dorothy made a desperate lunge for her, only to be pulled back by Alan.

'Trying to get yourself arrested, dear?' smirked Muscroft, unaware of how much trouble she was in.

'I want her arrested for telling a murderer that my children had informed on him!' roared Dorothy.

Muscroft's face dropped in horror as the magnitude of what had happened was gradually revealed to her by Alan Greenough, who saw no reason to gloss over her part in it all.

Another constable walked into the room with a white-faced Billy by his side. Billy opened his mouth to speak but the words wouldn't come.

'We can't find his brother,' said the constable grimly. 'He might not have got out of the street!'

Chapter Twenty-Six

Frank looked up at the sky, as you do when you think you hear thunder.

'Was that thunder?' he inquired of Alfie Featherstone, his yard man.

'Wouldn't have thought so,' replied Alfie. Looking up at the bright sky, broken by just the odd white cloud.

Frank shook his head and finished off checking his morning delivery of timber, before climbing into his car. It was mid-morning and he'd promised Dorothy he'd be back half an hour ago to look for the kids. He wasn't as worried about them as she was. They'd turn up in their own good time, after all, they were Bairstows.

A clanging ambulance passed him, followed by a string of fire engines, causing him to wonder what the hell was going on. The dust had just about settled when he arrived at the scene of devastation. His heart stopped. Flinging open the car door he rushed around trying to find out what had happened. Had anybody been hurt? Looking at the pile of rubble completely burying Back Broughton Terrace and blocking Paradine Hill, he'd be amazed if anyone had escaped alive.

'Has anyone seen Dorothy Bairstow?' he shouted. But everyone else was shouting as well and no one took any notice.

'Has anyone seen the Bairstow kids?'

Mothers were running up and down Paradine Hill. All they knew was that the destructor chimney had come down in Broughton Terrace, the street where their children were playing.

'Dorothy Bairstow!' he screamed. He didn't realise up until

then how much she meant to him. How much he loved her. Please God, don't take her away from me now!

Hysterical reunions were enacted as mothers found their dust-coated offspring wandering around, dazed and dirty. What traffic there was was either backed up the road or making diversions through the nearby streets. An enterprising icecream van had parked nearby. Its cheerful clanging bell mingling with the mayhem going on all around. It was doing a roaring trade as the inevitable spectators began to turn up in their dozens at first and then in their hundreds.

'She's gone to t' cop shop, mister,' squeaked a blackened urchin in eventual answer to Frank's desperate inquiries. The blackened child held out a hopeful hand in case his information was worth rewarding.

A tearful, relieved Frank took a ten shilling note from his pocket and pressed it into the boy's hand before pushing his way back through the crowd.

The amazed urchin thrust this huge reward into his trouser pocket before anyone could see it and went off in search of another desperate adult who might wish to reward him for information.

Billy yelled out to Frank and dashed up to him. 'Have yer seen our Jimmy?' he asked with a note of desperation in his voice.

Frank shook his head. 'I haven't, lad – isn't he with your Auntie Dorothy?'

'Me Auntie Dorothy told me ter fetch him down ter t'police station. I thought he were right behind me when we ran out of t' street.'

'And wasn't he?' Frank felt his heart sinking with dread. He caught a passing policeman by his sleeve. 'There's a young lad missing,' he said. 'This is his brother – I wonder if you could help.'

The policeman bent down to talk to Billy as Frank hurried off.

'Right, young 'un,' decided the constable, on hearing that the rest of Jimmy's family were at the police station. 'Me and you had better pop down to the station. You never know, your brother might have turned up there.'

In the meantime, Frank was dashing down the next street, to the Bairstows' front door. All was normal down this front street, apart from the dust drifting over the rooftops. Just a neat row of front doors and a three-legged dog attempting to pee up against the gas lamp. No hint at all of the mayhem round the back. Thankfully the front door wasn't locked.

Frank pulled open the scullery door and jumped back as the bricks piled against the outside of the door fell around his feet. The outside lavatory had completely collapsed into the yard and the scullery was threatening to do the same. He picked his way to the back gate and surveyed the scene, coughing and spitting as the dust swirled around his head. A fire had started across the street, probably a broken gas main. He could hear the hiss and saw a jet of water shooting high into the air from Mrs Harrison's house. People were beginning to venture down the street, scrambling over the rubble and calling out. A helmeted policeman appeared and told them not to be so stupid and to get out of the place so the firemen could get on with their bloody job.

Frank turned to go back the way he'd come. There was nothing he could do here, then he saw Jimmy's shoe poking out from under the rubble.

'Over here!' he shouted to anyone who might hear, but there were so many people shouting that no one seemed to take any notice.

Frantically, but methodically, he pulled away the broken bricks with his bare hands, toughened by years of hard graft on the sites, and soon uncovered an unconscious Jimmy. Huddled with his face to the ground, his head matted with blood.

Frank began clearing the bricks around the boy to allow him to lift him free.

'Over here!' he shouted again. 'I need help!'

This time his shouts were heard by a fireman who came hurrying and stumbling across the rubble towards the sound of Frank's voice. As he arrived he saw a movement in the scullery wall, below which he saw the crouched figure of Frank removing bricks from around a smaller figure beneath him.

'Watch out!' shouted the fireman. But it happened too quickly. Frank heard the shout and sensed the movement beside him. He instinctively threw himself across Jimmy, just as the scullery wall came down on top of him.

Chapter Twenty-Seven

Dorothy, Susan and Billy stood at the end of the street, watching as the police, firemen and ambulancemen struggled to release Frank and Jimmy.

Susan's lips moved in prayer, Dorothy's quivered in shock. What the hell was happening? Would this nightmare chain of events never come to an end? Frank was brought out first. His face was deathly pale but no one had taken the decision to cover it up which told Dorothy he was still alive. Susan gave him a cursory look. Not that she was unsympathetic, just that she was desperately concerned for her brother. The ambulancemen struggled back over the rubble with the now empty stretcher, cursing that one stretcher was all they'd been allocated.

Jimmy's face was also uncovered, so he must be alive. Congealed blood mixed with brick dust formed a sickly mask on his still face. Susan burst into tears as he was carried past. Dorothy gripped Billy tightly and followed the stretcher to the waiting ambulance.

The driver held up a hand as she and Billy tried to follow Susan into the ambulance. 'Sorry, missis,' he said apologetically, 'we can't carry any more.'

'I'll run you down,' offered Alan Greenough. 'There's a spare car down at the station.'

When they arrived, Susan was waiting and a stern-looking nurse marched towards them, forcing a rare smile to her lips. 'Mr Sackfield's regained consciousness,' she announced. 'He's quite poorly but he's in no danger – you can see him if you like.'

'What about our Jimmy?' asked Susan, ignoring the invitation to visit Frank.

259

'Jimmy?' The nurse hadn't realised they were waiting for news of two patients.

'James Bairstow,' said Dorothy. 'He and Mr Sackfield were brought in together.'

'I'll go and check.' The nurse spun round and clicked off round the corner, the sound of her feet dying away and being replaced by an approaching pair, heavier these, a man's feet.

The doctor, whose feet they were, made no attempt to smile. The message he had to deliver gave him nothing to smile about.

'Mrs Bairstow?'

'Yes.' Dorothy stood up to receive the news, Susan and Billy on either side of her, each with an arm around their auntie.

'James is on the danger list. We're having to operate to relieve a blood clot on his brain – I'm afraid he's very poorly but we're doing all we can.'

'Is he going to be alright, doctor?' The words were Dorothy's but she spoke for all three of them.

The doctor shook his head. 'There's just no way I can answer you truthfully,' he admitted. Then added, 'I believe he was saved from further injury by someone throwing themself over him. If James does come through, he can thank that person for his life.'

'Thank you, doctor,' murmured Dorothy.

The three of them sat down again as the stern nurse returned. Dorothy gave her a bleak smile.

'It's okay, nurse,' she said. 'The doctor's just been to tell us about Jimmy.'

The nurse nodded. 'Would you like to see Mr Sackfield now?'

Dorothy stood up, 'Yes thank you, nurse. I'll go.' She turned and looked questioningly at Susan and Billy. Susan looked up at the nurse.

'Is there a chapel in here?' she asked.

'Yes there is, dear. If you wait here a second I'll take you.'

The nurse took Dorothy and Billy to see Frank, leaving Susan alone with her thoughts. Her juvenile mind was flooded with a confusion of events and emotions. Of her mam and dad and Freddie and Ray and getting Billy back and their sudden change in fortunes. She remembered how quickly her mam and dad had been taken away from this world and Uncle Tommy and the woman in the cemetery with Len Bateson and she realised just how fragile life was. But, please God, enough's enough – don't let it happen to Jimmy.

The nurse returned and led her, with a comforting arm on her shoulder, to the chapel. A tiny inter-denominational room with a crucifix, a statue of Our Lady and half a dozen rows of pews. Susan turned to thank the nurse, then asked, 'What do you think his chances are, nurse?'

'If he's still with us in eight hours, I reckon he'll pull through,' answered the nurse decisively. 'As soon as there's any news, somebody will come and let you know.'

She clicked off up the corridor as Susan knelt down to begin her vigil.

Frank opened his eyes and attempted a smile, then grimaced at the pain he was causing himself.

'How's the boy?' he asked.

'Poorly,' Dorothy informed him.

'Is he . . .' He stopped not wanting to say the words.

'We don't know yet,' anticipated Dorothy. 'How're you feeling?'

'Like I've been ten rounds with Joe Louis.'

'They're saying you saved Jimmy's life.'

'So he is going to be alright then?' The look on Frank's face was desperately willing her to say yes. He was fonder of Jimmy than he realised – he was fond of the whole lot of them, especially Dorothy.

Dorothy looked down on him with a tenderness he could have mistaken for love if he didn't know better. 'We'll know more in a few hours,' she replied. 'Susan's in the chapel, praying.'

'I think I'll say a few myself if it'll help. Not that I'm much good at it, I'm a bit of a pagan really.'

'You've done more than anybody up to now.' She leaned over and kissed him softly. He held her in his eyes, unable to reciprocate, but it was surely more than just the kiss of a friend. The memories of the accident were quite blurred, but the memories of the previous night certainly weren't. Billy was standing beside her, otherwise he might have let her know what he felt about her. But this was neither the time nor the place for such things.

Presently he fell asleep and Dorothy and Billy were shown to a

261

relatives' waiting room. Mrs Veitch turned up and offered to take Billy home with her but Dorothy put an arm around her nephew and shook her head. She needed Billy by her side and by the look on Billy's face he wasn't going anywhere until this business was over.

'Thanks, Mrs Veitch, you're very kind, but Billy and I are alright here.'

Her neighbour stayed with her for a while in the warm corridor. A young lady sat opposite, her leg encased in plaster, almost obliterated by graffiti some of which bordered on the obscene. Billy was reading this with fascination, then looked away as the girl grinned at him.

'Oops!' she laughed. 'You shouldn't be reading this at your age, love. Me young man did most of it – he's a sailor.'

The two women absentmindedly nodded their understanding. Billy hadn't a clue what she was talking about. Further up the corridor a small boy with a bandaged arm was running a spoon up and down a radiator making a cacophonous noise, unchecked by his illegally smoking mother. Eventually, Mrs Veitch got to her feet and strode up towards them, grabbing the boy by his collar before confronting the mother.

'Are you going ter crack his flamin' ear'ole or would yer like me ter do it for yer?

Such was the menace in Mrs Veitch's voice that the boy dropped his spoon and flung himself into the protective arms of his shocked parent.

'An' yer can put that bleedin' fag out while yer at it,' added Mrs Veitch. 'We'd all of us like a fag, but some of us have got more bleedin' respect!'

The offending cigarette was immediately crushed underfoot. Thus satisfied that her hospital visit had not been in vain, Mrs Veitch returned to say her farewell to Dorothy.

Billy fell asleep, slumped against his aunt, and Dorothy held on to him. She'd developed a special bond with Billy, probably born from the guilt she still felt at what she'd put him through. An echoing voice summoned the girl opposite. She smiled her farewell as she hobbled off to have her plaster removed, touching Dorothy on the arm in passing.

'He's gonna be alright, love,' she promised.

Dorothy tried to return her reassuring smile and watched the girl limp away.

'God, I hope so,' she said to herself.

Billy's gentle snoring seduced his auntie into the same state. A piercing scream jolted her awake.

'It's okay, love,' a passing nurse assured her. 'Just a young lad having some stitches out.' Dorothy glanced up the corridor at the chairs recently vacated by the annoying boy and his mother. A clock ticked away the hours. Dorothy looked up expectantly at every passing doctor, nurse, porter or anyone who looked as though they might have news of Jimmy. Billy slept through it all, oblivious to his auntie's anxiety.

Susan had fallen fast asleep, slumped over a pew. She'd prayed continuously for several hours, her heart skipping a beat every time she heard footsteps in the corridor outside. The only news she could expect after such a short time would be bad news. She'd held her breath until the footsteps died away in the distance and resumed her fervent prayers.

And now she was dreaming jumbled dreams of her mam and dad. They were both in jail with Auntie Dorothy and the Brigadier was arguing with a prison warder and making them set Dorothy free but Mam and Dad were still locked up and that wasn't fair. And the chimney was falling, making the sky go black with a dusty choking fog and Freddie was running like mad trying to get away and there was Billy standing on the roof, jumping off now and never landing, but the chimney was landing right on top of Jimmy, smashing his head open.

'Jimmy!' she screamed.

And she heard a gentle voice calling her name.

'Susan!'

'Susan!' It was Dorothy.

Susan opened her eyes and looked around, suddenly realising where she was and that Dorothy was shaking her shoulder. She looked up questioningly at her aunt. Her question answered by Dorothy's reassuring smile.

'He's still with us,' she almost sobbed. 'I don't know who you've been talking to, but it seems they were listening. The doctor says he's over the worst. We can go in and see him if we like. Closest relatives first, that's you and Billy.'

263

Billy hurled himself into his Susan's arms as she looked up at her aunt with immense relief then said, with unbelievable calmness, 'It always works for me, Auntie. I did it once before when he was a baby, I only hope the little pest appreciates what I do for him!'

Chapter Twenty-Eight

As she rounded the corner into the broken limbs ward where her boss was lying with one plaster-encased leg up in the air, Dorothy was surprised to see him and Susan in deep conversation.

'What are you two plotting?' she asked suspiciously. 'If I'm getting the sack I need six months' notice – I wrote that one into my contract myself.'

'Just the opposite actually,' said Frank as Dorothy leaned over to kiss his cheek. If Susan hadn't been there he'd have turned his face round at the last second to trick her into kissing his lips. He'd done that a few times so far and Dorothy appeared to fall for it every time.

'What's the opposite of the sack?' mused Dorothy. 'More work? Short of laying the bricks, I'm doing most of the work already.'

'Frank's helping me to arrange splitting our forty-nine-per-cent four ways,' explained Susan. 'Me, Jimmy, Billy – and you.'

'That's a lot of money you're giving me – and thanks, but you know I can't accept it.'

'You don't have any option,' pressed Susan. 'You're having it whether you like it or not.'

'I am, am I?'

'Yes.'

'I wouldn't argue if I were you,' advised Frank. 'She's a right little madam is that one.'

Dorothy gave Susan a peck on her cheek. 'Okay, I accept. And just to show I'm worth it, I've got the council to agree to us doing that road junction in Horsforth. It'll be ratified at the next committee so we need to get our skates on and buy that land.'

Frank looked at Susan. 'I hope you realise what you've let me in for – she's only been a shareholder for two minutes and she's gone power mad!'

Susan smiled at the pair of them as she left to go. They were good for each other, not just in business either. Maybe one day her auntie would realise that, grown-ups could be so blind at times.

Susan read the invitation twice. The shock of it only sinking in after the second reading.

Mr and Mrs Roger Ibbotson cordially invite you to the
wedding of their daughter, Elizabeth Jane,
to Frederick Arthur Fforbes-Fiddler
at Ripon Cathedral on Saturday 17th August

R.S.V.P.

It was the Tuesday after the accident and Susan had called back to Broughton Terrace to see if there was any post. Whilst repairs were being carried out, Frank had insisted on her and Dorothy and Billy living in his house. A luxury not available to the other residents of the street who were having to make the best of things. Not that any of them begrudged the Bairstows, after all, Jimmy had saved many lives that day.

A shout from outside had her hurrying into the back street, now largely cleared of rubble. A crowd of workmen had gathered at the bottom of the street beyond the broken-down destructor wall. She pushed her way through and winced at the grisly sight of Len Bateson's broken body, recently uncovered beneath hundreds of tons of brick, a poetic end. He'd taken Mrs McGinty with him, but hers was perhaps a merciful release from a life of incontinence and senility.

'Best thing he could have done,' commented a burly constable, who stood and surveyed the scene with little compassion for the twisted war veteran. 'We'd have only had to hang the bugger – saves all that!'

The workmen muttered their agreement and stood back as a couple of ambulancemen arrived to hoist him unceremoniously onto a stretcher then curse in annoyance as one of them stumbled on the rubble, causing Len's bloodied carcass to fall off.

'Don't hurt him,' shouted one wag. 'He's been through enough already!'

There was a grisly ripple of laughter as Len was replaced on the stretcher and carried to the waiting ambulance. He collected a gob of spit as he passed what was left of Mrs McGinty's back yard. A farewell present from the dead woman's grieving son.

'Bastard!' was all he had to say.

Susan returned to the house and picked up the phone to offer her congratulations to Freddie, hoping the insincerity in her voice wasn't too obvious.

'Susan!' He sounded relieved to hear from her. 'I've just read about what happened to your street – are you okay? How's Jimmy, he was injured, wasn't he?'

'He's out of danger apparently.'

'Thank God for that! What a thing to happen. Hey! He was a bit of a hero, wasn't he? According to the *Evening Post* he ran around warning everybody!'

'He was a lot of a hero – nearly got himself killed. Would have been if Frank hadn't saved his life.'

'Good grief! Look, you must come over this Saturday, we're having an engagement party. Stay the night if you like – I expect you could use a bit of light relief after what's happened.'

Susan hesitated before replying, 'I'd love to come.'

'Brilliant, see you then. Give my love to everyone.'

The phone went dead, as did Susan's heart. Just the sound of his voice brought back a yearning for him. To Freddie she was just a schoolgirl and would always be so.

How she hated being young.

Dorothy gazed down on the sleeping face of her boss. She knew full well how deeply he felt about her, that's why she'd done her best to make light of their relationship. She just didn't know how she felt about him.

It was all Tommy's fault. Had he not been so out of the ordinary, perhaps his memory would be fading even now. But Tommy would always be there. He'd had her laughing from their first date, despite her misgivings at him and Fred bringing along a couple of ferrets. And it wasn't just the laughter, there'd been a magic between them. Something other people didn't seem to have

– maybe Fred and Lily – but there again, Fred was another Bairstow. She was only eighteen when she met Tommy – he'd been her first serious boyfriend. Maybe she was expecting too much at her advanced years. She was thirty-four now, practically middle-aged.

And let's face it, Tommy had been no angel. Nothing she could put her finger on, nothing she could prove – or would wish to. But he attracted girls like flies round a jam pot. Tommy had his share of weaknesses, not the least of which was succumbing to temptation. And there were plenty of girls trying to tempt her Tommy. But she was his girl and she knew it. No point trying to tie him down, waste of time anyway. She always felt secure with him – and he did love her. Of that there was no doubt.

Frank opened his eyes, blinked away the sleep then smiled quizzically up at her. A nurse bustled past her and leaned over him, sticking a thermometer in his mouth.

'Welcome back to the world, Mr Sackfield,' announced the nurse. 'The operation went fine.'

'What operation was that?' grunted Frank through the thermometer. His susceptibility to morphine had left him dopey.

'They reset your shoulder, Frank,' explained Dorothy. 'Put some metal in it.'

'Oh, right, sort of reinforcement-like.'

'Sort of,' agreed the nurse. 'How are you feeling?'

'Drunk,' said Frank, after considering his reply.

'Make the most of it,' grinned the nurse, retrieving the thermometer and looking at the reading. 'There'll be no alcohol for you for a while.'

'Thanks nurse,' moaned Frank. 'You're such a treasure.'

Susan had never drunk wine before and she wasn't quite sure if she'd ever get to like it. The party was in full swing. The Fiddler gramophone blasting out Glenn Miller's 'In The Mood' and the parlour was jumping with lively jitterbuggers. Tricky Dicky Dodsworth had been assigned by Freddie to look after her, and this eccentric young man undertook his assignment with an enthusiasm that kept Susan well amused. He was the only surviving son of Lord Sefton Dodsworth, a millionaire landowner. Dicky's two older brothers had been killed in the war and his mother in a riding accident.

He told endless tales of him and Freddie at school. Of pranks they'd got up to, of holidays spent together. All such information about her beloved Freddie was readily devoured by Susan with one eye on the storyteller and one eye on her Freddie. He was still her Freddie, despite Elizabeth. With the optimism of the very young she knew he'd succumb to her charms well before he married Elizabeth.

But no one had warned her of the maudlin effect a few glasses of wine would have, especially on the first-time drinker.

Dicky was in the middle of an hilarious story about how he and Freddie set fire to the chem lab, narrowly avoiding burning down the whole school, when it became obvious, even to him, that he didn't have her undivided attention.

'She doesn't love him, you know,' she suddenly blurted out. 'You've only got to look at them to see that!'

Susan's eyes were brimming with tears and she was staring at a spot somewhere behind him. Aware that his story, although riveting, was hardly likely to bring tears to a young girl's eyes, he followed her gaze to Freddie and Elizabeth, dancing very slowly to 'Moonlight Serenade'. Freddie had his back to them and Elizabeth was facing them, her head resting on his shoulders. She was running her fingers through his hair, an expression of mild boredom on her face.

'You're quite right there, old girl,' remarked Dicky. He turned back, perhaps to explain his observation to Susan, but she'd gone. Dicky shrugged and made his unsteady way to the bar.

The River Nidd slid quietly past the bottom of the Fiddler garden. Quite wide at this point as it meandered towards the Ouse and thence to the Humber. Years ago, the Brigadier had had a small jetty built and it was on this that Susan stood, gazing sorrowfully into the black waters.

Tonight was the end of a dream. She could never imagine loving anyone as much as she loved Freddie. The water looked so tempting. A swim would perhaps soothe her heartache. She loved swimming, although up to now she'd been restricted to ploughing up and down the chlorinated waters of Union Street Public Baths. A fresh water swim would be so nice. Any caution she would normally have felt at such a venture had been dispelled by the wine.

No one was there to see her strip naked and plunge in, leaving scarcely a ripple in her wake. A few strong strokes took her to the middle of the river, looking back at lights of the house, and wondering what Freddie was doing. Had he whisked Elizabeth off to some secluded room to make love to her? How could he love Elizabeth and not her? Surely he could see how she felt about him. There was something about Elizabeth that just didn't fit. Not once did she look at Freddie with the love in her eyes that Susan felt for him, nor did Freddie look at Elizabeth in such a manner. Susan felt some relief in this, although she was at a loss to know what to do about it. Perhaps she should let herself sink to the bottom of the river and end it all – but what would be the point? Freddie would never know why, and would therefore never suffer dreadful pangs of guilt he was entitled to. It would be nice to think he would be so devastated that he would want to follow her to her watery grave. She smiled sadly to herself, floating on her back and gazing up at the stars as, one by one, they winked out through the darkening sky. It was so peaceful. She wished Freddie could be here, swimming beside her. Perhaps they'd make love on the bank. Proper love, not the lusty fumblings she enjoyed with Ray. She'd been saving herself for Freddie – and now she'd never have him. She knew what people would say, 'You're only sixteen, you'll meet someone else.' But she wouldn't, there'll never be another Freddie. The river water diluted her tears as she kicked gently back towards the jetty, a bright new moon mocking her with its cheerfulness. So wrapped up was she in her own thoughts and self-pity that she didn't hear the splash.

'You're wishing he was with you, aren't you?'

Susan was shocked to hear Elizabeth's voice so close. She looked around, treading water, and saw Freddie's fiancée, bobbing up and down just a few yards away, as naked as she was, smiling at her.

'Saw how miserable you were,' Elizabeth said. 'Thought I'd join you. If it's any consolation,' she added teasingly, 'I've never done this with Freddie either!'

'I don't know what you mean!' protested Susan, swimming slowly back to the shore.

'Liar!' laughed Elizabeth. 'You're besotted with him. That's why you ran out of the room at Christmas!'

Susan felt herself colouring with anger. Elizabeth was playing a dangerous game. Susan could quite easily drown this gloating woman in seconds, nobody would be any the wiser – and Freddie would be hers.

She was shocked at harbouring such thoughts. Reaching the jetty she hoisted herself up the short ladder and sat on the wooden slats, legs dangling in the water, watching Elizabeth as she too climbed up the ladder, less agile than Susan, her breasts and hips slightly fuller, but no less beautiful. Her dark hair, limp with water now and clinging to her white, porcelain shoulders. Elizabeth sat down beside her, splashing her legs in the water. The two of them naked and lovely in the moonlight.

'Do you love him?' asked Susan. Slightly annoyed at herself for asking such a fatuous question, but somehow she needed to hear Elizabeth say it.

'Not in the same way as you do!' came Elizabeth's surprise answer.

'I don't understand. How many ways are there to love a man?'

'There's your way, and there's my way,' said Elizabeth mysteriously. She laid a hand on Susan's naked thigh and said suddenly.

'I was marrying him for his money!'

Susan absorbed this information with a mixture of anger and relief.

'How could you do such a thing? You'll ruin his life – he deserves someone who truly loves him!'

'Someone like you, you mean?' Elizabeth gave a short laugh. Then added, 'You didn't hear what I said, did you?'

Susan shook her head, not knowing what Elizabeth was getting at.

'I said, "I *was* marrying him for his money" – changed my mind tonight, can't go through with it. Struck me when I saw you run out of the room again. Besides, he fancies you a damn sight more than he fancies me – he's just too stupid to admit it. He's always talking about you – your family as well, but mainly you. It doesn't take a genius to figure him out. Men are like that you know. It's all a question of honour with him, he got engaged to me in a moment of drunken madness and he feels obliged to go through with it.'

Susan found all this too much to take. Elizabeth's hand tightened on her thigh and rubbed her gently, up as far as her damp pubic hair. Although naïve in such matters, it was enough of a

271

signal for Susan to understand. She turned and looked, shocked, at Elizabeth, who held up her hands and smiled apologetically.

'You can hardly blame me for finding you more attractive than men, I mean, look at you!'

Susan froze as Elizabeth leaned across and kissed her fully and sweetly on her mouth, one hand lingering on her breast. A kiss Susan would never know the like of again. Elizabeth pulled away as she sensed the tenseness in Susan's reluctant lips.

'Just thought I'd give it try,' she said cheekily, 'you never know!'

Susan stared into the water trying to make sense of this odd but beautiful woman splashing her feet in the water beside her.

'How long have you known – that you er, prefer women?' she asked curiously.

Elizabeth laughed at Susan's reluctance to say the word. 'Since I was seduced by my gym mistress at school,' she replied. 'I was fifteen and I enjoyed every minute. I've tried men but it's not the same. I find them all so incredibly unsavoury. Freddie was different, just about bearable. I can see how someone like you would fall in love with him.'

'Does he know?'

'What, that I'm a lesbian? Heavens, no!'

Susan had never heard anyone admit to such a thing before and she was filled with shock and admiration at Elizabeth's openness.

'But he's such a lovely man,' Elizabeth continued, 'I was prepared to make the supreme sacrifice in exchange for the Fiddler fortune. I know it sounds mercenary, but us queers are very much castigated by society. But the richer you are, the more you're accepted. So one has to make the best one can out of life. I'd have had private affairs that Freddie didn't know about, bless him, but I doubt if I'd have been able to do him justice between the sheets. No enthusiasm you see – sad isn't it? Lovely girl like me.'

Try as she might, Susan couldn't help but like this outrageous woman.

'You should try Tricky Dicky,' she said jokingly. 'You'd make a good pair and he is the heir to a fortune!'

'It's an option I'm keeping open,' said Elizabeth, mischievously. 'We'd make an interesting couple, don't you think?

Susan was grateful that Elizabeth had had the foresight to bring a couple of towels and was more or less dried off and amazingly refreshed in both body and soul as she followed Freddie's soon-to-be-ex-fiancée back into the house.

She watched with unbounded curiosity as Elizabeth took Freddie's hand and led him from the room to a chorus of misplaced ooohs. The party carried on as before, Tricky Dicky demonstrating an agile rubber-legged Charleston to an amazed crowd of modern young things who thought such dances had gone out with Lloyd George.

It was only a matter of minutes before Freddie reappeared: on his own, looking more confused than distressed. He turned off the gramophone.

'Just a short announcement,' he said, drily. 'Lizzie's gone home, the engagement's off.'

He switched the gramophone straight back on but the heart had gone out of the party – for the time being anyway. Susan made her tentative way towards him and took his hand.

'How're you feeling?' she asked.

'Numb!'

'I can imagine, it came as a bit of a shock to me as well.'

'Yes, I gather she told you,' he said, a half-smile playing on his lips. He looked round at the subdued room, then stood on a chair.

'I have another announcement,' he said loudly. 'Anyone not disgracefully plastered within an hour from now will be asked to leave this party!'

This was received with a loud, relieved cheer and the dancers took to the floor once again.

'Did Elizabeth say anything else about me?' inquired Susan, fortified by another large glass of wine.

'What would she say about you?'

'You know very well what.'

His eyes softened and he took her hand. 'Susan,' he said gently. 'I've tried my best to get you out of my mind over the last year or so – I know there's something between us – but I'm scared of ruining your life.'

'You could only ruin my life by not being part of it, Freddie Fiddler.'

Freddie took her in his arms and held her to him, kissing her lightly on her lips. 'You're sixteen,' he whispered, aware of the

273

curious eyes dancing around them. 'I've no intention of depriving you of your youth. It's much too precious – I know you don't realise it, but believe me I'm right.'

'The only thing I don't want to be deprived of is you,' she breathed, pulling him back towards her.

'I think I can promise not to do that.'

He put his hand in his pocket and brought out a ring she hadn't seen for two years.

'You found it! Freddie, it's the ring!'

'I know,' he grinned. 'Came to me where I'd hidden it in the middle of the blasted night. I'd stuck it under an old flagstone in the cellar of the cottage. Rang old Tricky up and we drove through the night to get it.' He held it affectionately between finger and thumb, reflected light playing on his face. 'I must say, it never felt right giving to Lizzie – came within a hair's breadth though!'

He took her left hand and folded it over the ring.

'There's only one person this ring was ever meant for,' he smiled. 'I'd like you to keep it as a token of our impending engagement. If you ever decide not to go ahead with it, I'll understand. Mind you,' he added, 'I'll want my ring back.'

'I think you can forget that,' gasped Susan, taken aback by this sudden turn of events. 'Does this mean we're enga . . .'

'Unofficially,' interrupted Freddie, placing a finger on her lips. 'For my part, I know full well there aren't two like you in the world, but I suspect we Freddie Fiddlers are a penny a dozen – I want you to give yourself time. Come and get me when you're ready – I'll be around – no fear of that!'

They kissed once again, this time it was the one she'd been dreaming of.

Frank watched the nurse stride away in that purposeful way nurses have and groaned to himself. Another week to ten days in this damn place. Had to give his shoulder a chance to knit together before they were prepared to let him out. His broken ribs were coming along okay and the lacerations were healing up – if only he hadn't broken his shoulder in three places, he'd be up and about now. Even Jimmy had been allowed home and he'd been at death's door only a week ago. He was still feeling sorry for himself when Dorothy turned up with a carrier bag full of goodies, including four bottles of pale ale, one of which he owed to the chap in the next bed.

'Business first,' she said. 'Sign here and here and here.'

Frank did as he was told, writing his name beside three pencilled crosses.

'What have I signed away?' he asked.

'Nothing, you've just signed a contract to buy the land at Horsforth, at least you have once I've witnessed it.' She wrote in her own name with a flourish.

'Right,' she said. 'Business concluded – what do you want to talk about?'

Frank was sitting up in his bed, propped by a mountain of pillows. He looked across at Dorothy, wondering if this was the right time to ask.

'What are you thinking, Mr Sackfield?' she asked curiously.

'I'm wondering how I'm going to take it.'

'Take what?'

'The feeling of rejection.'

'What are you talking about, Frank?'

'Dorothy – will you marry me?'

Dorothy tensed. She'd been dreading him asking her. She knew it was inevitable – but she just wasn't ready to give him an answer. Not even a maybe. It's even more of a rejection when a maybe turns into a definite 'no'. She looked at him for a long long time.

'I did tell you at the outset Frank that I didn't want to be anything but friends and business partners, so . . .'

'Don't say it!' interrupted Frank. 'I'd prefer not to hear it. Just forget I ever asked you.'

'Ever asked me what Frank?' she smiled sadly. Wishing she had it in her to say yes to this lovely man.

Frank gave her a resigned smile and settled back. 'What shall we do?' he asked. 'Stay as we are?'

'I'd suit me Frank. This way we can both leave our options open.'

'I don't think I like the sound of that.'

'Sorry.'

She stood up to leave, turning halfway down the ward to blow him a kiss.

'By 'eck! I wish my wife looked like that,' commented the

chap in the next bed as Frank secretly passed him a bottle of pale ale.

'So do I,' said Frank, closing his eyes, still drowsy with pain killers.

'Penny for them,' offered Susan as Dorothy gazed out of the scullery window, deep in thought.

'Frank's asked me to marry him,' she said absentmindedly. Her eyes fixed on a sparrow hopping round the dustbin lid, trying to find a way in.

'That's brilliant!' screamed Susan. 'Oh, Auntie Dorothy, I am pleased for you!'

'I turned him down,' went on Dorothy.

'Oh,' said a seriously disappointed Susan.

'I don't think I love him – certainly not like I loved your Uncle Tommy.'

Susan remained quiet. She had problems of her own and had been wondering whether to burden Dorothy with them. Perhaps now was a good time. A mutual unburdening of troubles.

'I don't know what to say,' commented Susan. 'Except that I think he's a great bloke and you seem to get on so well together.'

'Perhaps I'm asking for too much,' mused her auntie. 'Do you think I'm asking for too much?'

'Auntie Dorothy, I'm sixteen years old, what do I know?'

'Most sixteen-year-olds think they know everything.'

'Well, I'm not one of them – I've got problems of my own.'

This last remark roused Dorothy from her thoughts. 'Oh? What problems?'

'Freddie problems.'

'Oh dear.' Dorothy had told Susan on so many occasions that there was no future this.

'It's not quite as *oh dear* as it sounds,' retorted Susan. 'He never did get engaged to Elizabeth.'

'Didn't he now? Am I allowed to know why?'

Susan hesitated before replying. 'It turns out that Elizabeth's a lesbian.'

'Wow! I can see how this might put Freddie off – was he heart-broken?'

'More relieved than heartbroken – he found his diamond ring, you know.'

276

'No, I didn't know.'

'It's a beautiful ring,' said Susan. 'Would you like to see it – he was going to give it to Elizabeth, but obviously that fell through.'

'See it? What are you talking about? Where is it?'

Susan fumbled in her pocket and brought out the huge diamond solitaire. Dorothy gasped.

'Good grief! It's the most beautiful ring I've ever seen.'

'Hmm – I don't think you'd say that if you'd seen my blue diamond,' commented Susan matter-of-factly. 'Still, it is beautiful, isn't it?'

'*Fabulous* wouldn't be too strong a word. What are you doing with it?'

'Freddie gave it to me – sort of an unofficial engagement ring. I'm not to wear it of course – not until we're officially engaged.'

'Oh really? And when will that be, may I ask?' inquired Dorothy, who had learned long ago not to be surprised by anything Susan did.

'We haven't decided. He insisted I get on with my youth, whatever that means.'

'It's something amazingly sensible,' said Dorothy. 'Something that you'd never understand – not until you've finished getting on with your youth anyway.'

'That's what Freddie said. We'll see each other, of course – he's going to university to study medicine. He reckons he'll be waiting for me when I'm ready.'

'I'm absolutely sure he will.' Dorothy regarded her niece with some envy. Easily as beautiful as her auntie but with the glow of youth.

'Trouble is,' went on Susan, 'Ray's asked me out tonight and I don't know what to do.'

Dorothy smiled. 'I think going out with Ray's all part of getting on with your youth.'

Susan gave her a hug that said *I hoped you'd say that.*

'Just one word of warning,' cautioned Dorothy. 'I don't want you doing anything that might get poor Sister Claire into any more trouble – if you know what I mean.' She laughed as she had when Susan had confided in her what Father Helliwell had said. Her niece shook her head with the despair the young reserve for the old. Susan was saving herself for Freddie.

*

277

'Hello, Frank,' said the familiar voice. 'Long time no see.'

Frank peered at the face above him through slitted eyes, trying to bring it into focus.

'Oh my God! Elaine,' he gasped. 'How? What on earth are you doing here?'

'Well, I read about the accident and thought I'd pay you a visit.'

'What? You came all the way from America?'

'Not exactly – we came up from Berkshire. We've been living there for the last few weeks.'

'Who's "we' exactly?" asked Frank.

'Me and Kevin.'

'What about *Chuck*?' He said the name with the same sarcasm he'd used when he first heard about his American rival.

'He's still in the States – we're separated. Didn't work out.'

Frank stared at his ex-wife for a while. She'd hardly changed, still a beautiful woman. He'd really loved her once, but now? It had been over two years since he'd last seen her. Her Yank had been stationed here for a while then managed to get transferred back 'Stateside' as they called it. In his case he'd transferred himself, Elaine and their son Kevin. In the meantime Frank had been serving King and country, getting wounded into the bargain.

'Is Kevin with you?'

She nodded. 'I'll get him if you like.'

'I'd like that.'

Elaine went off to bring Kevin. His son would be five years old now. In the last two years he hadn't seen so much as a photograph of him. He'd ask her about that when she came back with the boy.

Kevin didn't appear to know who he was. Hardly surprising as he was only three the last time he'd seen his father.

'Kevin, this is your daddy.'

'No, he's not,' protested the boy with a distinct American accent that unaccountably depressed Frank.

'Don't be rude, Kevin, if I say he's your father he's your fa . . .'

'Leave it,' interrupted Frank. 'No sense confusing the boy.' He looked hard at his son. The boy glared back resentfully.

'I'd scarcely have recognised him. He's changed so much.'

'They do at that age.'

'I wrote and asked you for photographs – why didn't you send any?'

She lowered her eyes.

278

'Chuck said I mustn't.'

'Watching you twenty-four hours a day, was he?' Frank failed to keep the sarcasm out of his voice. He felt so indignant that this man had deprived him of the chance to see his son growing up. But he dropped the subject, having no strength for an argument. 'So?' he asked. 'Do you have a job?'

'Yes, I'm working as a shorthand typist at the Ministry of Pensions in Reading – and I'm doing a course in business administration at night school.'

Frank nodded his approval of this. 'And what about Kevin?' her asked, smiling at his son but getting no response.

'He just started at the local school,' she turned to their son. 'You like it there, don't you, Kevin?'

The boy remained mute. Elaine looked back at Frank, concern showing on her face. 'You don't look too good, Frank, are you okay?'

'Elaine, I'm in hospital. They don't let you stay in here if you're okay.'

'Oh, right . . . er, would you like me to visit you again?'

'What? All the way from Berkshire?'

'Actually, I'm staying at my mother's for a few days.'

Frank made no comment. He hated her mother. According to her, he'd never been good enough for Elaine. He had always suspected her mother of putting her up to running off with Chuck.

'I'll pop in tomorrow if you like,' she offered.

'Okay,' said Frank. Not entirely displeased with her offer. She leaned over and pecked his cheek as Kevin looked on gloomily. Frank looked past her at his son, his only child. It would be nice to get to know him.

He watched her walk away down the ward, idly pondering the pros and cons of a reconciliation. If he was reading her signals correctly, it was certainly on the cards. She was a good-looking woman and the mother of his son. And Dorothy had made it clear that she didn't want him. Not as a husband anyway.

Because of her rejection of his proposal, Dorothy thought it better to visit Frank with the frequency of a friend rather than a lover. Three visits during the course of the next week. Elaine had called in every day. Mostly without Kevin. The spark they'd had between them was gradually rekindling. Thanks to careful

279

nurturing by Elaine. Dorothy's visits were causing him more confusion than comfort. He'd thought of asking her to stop coming. Because of her he couldn't think with a clear mind, such was her effect on him. He'd made no mention of Elaine to her, their visits never coinciding, until the day Elaine made her play for him.

She was already there when Dorothy arrived. Apparently she'd been there for some time. Long enough for her to be holding Frank's hand as she spoke to him.

'I was young . . . not thinking straight. You'd gone away. I didn't even know when . . . or if . . . you were coming back.'

Dorothy could only hazard a guess as to who she was. The woman's voice reeked of insincerity, presumably Frank could spot that as well as she could. He was no idiot, wasn't Frank.

'Hello, Frank,' she greeted him cheerfully.

Frank's face creased into an uncertain smile. 'Hello, Dorothy . . . Dorothy, I'd like you to meet Elaine, my ex-wife.'

Dorothy gave her a pleasant smile. 'Pleased to meet you, Elaine . . . but I thought you lived in America.'

'She did,' explained Frank. 'Broke up with her husband. She's back in England now.'

'Didn't work out, eh?' said Dorothy with convincing sympathy. 'Sorry to hear that. Mind you, I imagine Frank's a hard act to follow.'

'Dorothy's my secretary,' explained Frank.

'And friend,' added Dorothy.

'And very good friend,' said Frank.

'Really?' Elaine sensed competition. 'And how good's "very good"?'

Frank gave a nervous laugh, and caught Dorothy's curious eye. 'Typical woman,' he admonished. 'Trying to read something that's not there.'

'Ooops!' laughed Elaine, with a certain amount of relief. 'It's just that you never mentioned Dorothy before.'

'Why should he mention me in particular?' asked Dorothy, lightly. 'Frank's got lots of friends, I don't suppose he mentioned them either.'

There was an impending friction here. Frank felt caught between the two of them. Elaine sensed his discomfort and decided on a strategic retreat. She looked at her watch.

'God! Is that the time? I must dash. I'll pop in and see you tomorrow evening, Frank. I'll bring our son with me. You and he can get to know each other properly.'

Dorothy watched her go, then looked back at Frank. 'What was all that about, Frank?'

'That's about me being confused. She hasn't actually said it yet, but I'm pretty sure she wants to get back with me.'

'And what do you want to do?'

He gave her a troubled smile. 'What I want is some time to think. I like the idea of bringing up my own son. Kevin's all I've got.'

Dorothy slid a bottle of pale ale under his bedclothes. 'I hope you know what you're doing, Frank. I'd hate to see you hurt.'

'Hurt?' he exclaimed. 'Look at me . . . I'm already hurt!'

'You know what I mean.'

'Dorothy, you and me have no future together . . . apparently. But me and Elaine used to have something. We were good together, maybe we'll get it back.'

It was Dorothy's turn to be confused now. Perhaps she had no right to pursue the matter. She changed the subject and told him about the land deal.

'Thanks very much, Mr Scanlon, that's just what I wanted to hear.'

Dorothy put the phone down and sat back in Frank's chair with a smile of triumph on her face. The council had formally approved her proposal to improve the road junction in exchange for planning permission for two hundred houses. The fact that Councillor Harry Scanlon had once employed both Bairstow brothers appeared to have had some bearing on the unusual swiftness of the decision.

She picked up the phone again and asked the operator to put her through to a London number.

'McDowd Construction?. . . Could I speak to Mr James McDowd please? Dorothy Bairstow . . . yes, he knows what it's about.' She drummed her fingers on the desk, holding the receiver between her shoulder and her cheek as she'd once seen Humphrey Bogart do. Then she lit a cigarette as she waited. 'Hello, Mr McDowd – fine thank you, he'll be out in a couple of days hopefully, I'll tell him you were asking after him. Right – we're all set. The council approved our proposals this morning, and we're ready to sell to the highest bidder – or to you if you meet our price.' She smiled as the man at the other end grumbled good naturedly at the slick way she'd handled the deal. 'I know, Mr McDowd, it's a tough old world, I don't suppose the previous owner will be too pleased when he finds out. We completed the purchase last night – I got our solicitor to rush it through with what you might call unseemly haste. Yes, I was holding my breath a bit.'

She looked up in surprise as Elaine walked in and sat herself down on the chair opposite. Nodding her a quizzical greeting, Dorothy concluded the conversation.

'That's right, twenty-two,' she would have added the word 'thousand' but for Elaine's unexpected presence. 'Oh, and, Mr McDowd – I believe it's customary for the purchaser to pay all legal fees.' She laughed at the outburst from the other end. 'Goodbye, Mr McDowd, I'll tell our solicitor to get on with it shall I? Wonderful, pleasure doing business with you, Mr McDowd.' She laughed again at some farewell comment from the other end before replacing the receiver.

Elaine looked at her quizzically. 'So, you're running Frank's business while he's away, are you?'

'Sort of, why do you ask?'

'It's just that . . .' Elaine stopped, choosing her words carefully. 'Oh, hell! I might as well tell you. It's just that Frank and I are getting back together again.'

'Really?' Dorothy didn't want to hear this.

'Oh, yes. We had a long chat last night and decided to put everything behind us and start afresh. There were faults on both sides of course. There always are when a marriage breaks down.'

Dorothy was wondering how much Frank was to blame for his wife running off with a Yank, but she didn't voice her thoughts.

'He's a good man is Frank when you get to know him,' said Elaine, giving Dorothy an annoying smile. 'I don't suppose I need to tell you this though. With you working for him.'

'What exactly did Frank say about me working with him?'

Elaine shrugged. Not quite sure why Dorothy was asking such a question. 'Nothing much,' she replied. 'We didn't talk about work much. I gather he's doing okay though.' She looked at Dorothy, as though seeking her confirmation of this. Dorothy's face remained expressionless as Elaine went on. 'I seem to remember him mentioning some sort of land deal?'

I bet you do, thought Dorothy.

'A bit above my head really,' continued Elaine. 'Still, I am doing a night school course in business administration. It should come in handy for a business such as this.' She smiled the same patronising smile once again. Blissfully unaware of how dangerous an enemy she was making. 'No offence, Dorothy, but there are some up-to-date methods of running a business that my Frank doesn't know about. It was always his weak point . . . but you know that.'

'Do I really?'

There was more than a hint of sarcasm in Dorothy's voice that Elaine didn't pick up on. Dorothy didn't trust this woman. Much as she wanted to see Frank settled down and happy, she didn't like the idea of this grasping bitch getting her claws into him. The very thought of her and Frank together made her stomach lurch.

'Tell you what, Elaine,' she suggested. 'Frank comes out of hospital on Monday. Why don't we all meet round here? I've got to bring Frank up to date on a few things and it'll be a good opportunity for you to get to know his business if you're to become involved in it.'

Elaine's eyes lit up at this suggestion, although she wasn't sure whether Dorothy had authority to call such a meeting. 'Well, I'm not sure whether Frank will be up to it, but I'll put it to him,' she replied, somewhat loftily.

'You do that,' said Dorothy.

Chapter Twenty-Nine

Dorothy pottered round in her bedroom at Broughton Terrace. She'd hardly been back since the accident and the whole house was covered in a thick layer of dust. Most of which had drifted in through the broken windows before the council managed to board them up. Jimmy was outside re-acquainting himself with old friends and neigbours and modestly accepting their admiration of his heroism. Billy was in the front street with Susan, watching a Salvation Army Band gather itself into a circle before playing a stirring 'Abide with Me', making sure no one was still asleep that Sunday morning

The hymn came to an end and was followed by the customary tuning up noises that Sally Army Bands always made between numbers. A solo cornet struck up above the mild cacophony, forcing them into silence. It was the unseasonable tune that brought Dorothy to the window. A Christmas carol in the middle of summer. And not just any Christmas carol – and not just any instrument.

A huge smile lit up her face as she looked down on the puffing cheeks of Rita Doidge belting out 'Hark! The Herald Angels Sing'. Within seconds Dorothy was in the street, hugging her old friend, both of them awash with tears.

'When did you escape?' asked Dorothy.

The Sally Army captain gave her a stern look.

'I broke out last week,' rejoined Rita, winking at the captain. 'Got nine months – less good behaviour.'

'Good behaviour, you?'

'Read about you and your lot in the papers,' said Rita. 'So I asked the band to pop round and serenade you – hoped you might be in.'

284

Susan and Billy stepped forward, curious to meet this unusual Salvation Army lady.

'This is Susan,' introduced Dorothy, 'and this is Billy – Jimmy's in the next street signing autographs, I shouldn't wonder – this is my good friend Rita.'

Rita laughed as she took the hand of each of the children. 'Bit of a hero, young Jimmy – I gather.'

'They're all heroes, Rita, one way or another.' She looked at Billy and Susan with immense affection. 'My cobblestone heroes. God knows what I'd have done without them.'

'Uncle Frank's a hero as well,' Billy reminded her.

'Uncle Frank? who's he?' inquired Rita nosily, sensing interesting romantic involvement.

'He's my boss, if you must know, nothing more,' declared Dorothy. 'And he saved Jimmy's life.'

'Bugger me! Dolly – yer surrounded by bleedin' heroes!'

'Rita! You promised!' Rita cringed as the Salvation Army captain admonished her for such language.

'Sorry, Henry!'

Rita gave Dorothy a rueful smile. 'I promised ter watch me language, an' I'm tellin' you – it's not bleedin' easy.'

Billy howled with delight at this latest slip and sat on the step as his auntie and her friend exchanged stories and made plans for a future reunion. Dear old Delma had gone off to spend the rest of her natural life in a secure nuthouse, to use Rita's terminology. The band played a couple of numbers as they chatted, then the captain, with a look of mild exasperation on his face, strode across to them.

'Excuse me, madam,' he doffed his cap politely to Dorothy. 'But we need Rita for "Jerusalem," she's our soloist.'

Rita stood up and planted a kiss on the reddening cheek of the captain.

'Dorothy,' she announced, 'meet my fiancé Henry Evans. Takes his job of saving people very seriously, does my Henry.'

'Above and beyond the call of duty,' said an amazed Dorothy. 'Pleased to meet you, Henry.'

Henry doffed his cap once again, then led Rita away to rejoin the band. Dorothy, Susan and Billy waved their goodbyes as they marched off, out of step, down the street to the uplifting Sunday sound of 'Jerusalem'.

*

Dorothy deliberately positioned herself beside Frank, with Elaine sitting opposite them. Frank's arm was in a sling and Elaine had gone overboard, Dorothy thought, with her twitterings of concern for him. Pity she didn't show the same concern when she cleared off to America with her Yank.

'I'm still not sure you're ready for this, Frank darling,' Elaine cooed. 'Straight from hospital to here, I really think it's too soon.'

'Tough old bird, our Frank,' grinned Dorothy, patting him on the back and making him wince slightly.

'Oh, dear,' sympathised Elaine. 'I bet that hurt.'

'Not really,' said Frank, slightly embarrassed at being fussed over so much. 'Right, Dorothy – what have you got for us?'

'Well,' began Dorothy. 'It was something Elaine said the other day that prompted me to call this meeting so quickly.'

Frank frowned.

'You see,' she continued. 'I understand that you and Elaine are getting back together – and I'm very happy for you. I also understand that Elaine would like you to benefit from her knowledge of business administration, which I believe she is studying at night school.'

Frank's frown remained in place. 'What are you getting at, Dorothy?' His tone was slightly impatient and drew a small smile of approval from Elaine.

'Now from my knowledge of business administration, that I learnt at work, it's obvious that there's only room for one secretary – so I'm pulling out.'

Her last remark broadened Elaine's smile and staggered Frank. Before he could say anything, Dorothy opened a desk drawer, pulled out a sheet of paper and pushed it across to Elaine.

'This is our partnership agreement if you'd like to cast a business eye over it.'

'Partnership? You didn't say anything about a partnership, Frank?' Elaine picked up the agreement with marked reluctance.

'Should I have?' asked Frank, puzzled as to where this was all leading. He knew Dorothy had something up her sleeve, but somehow he didn't think it would be to his advantage this time.

'I just thought . . .' began Elaine, looking at the agreement.

'If you look at it carefully, Elaine,' explained Dorothy, 'you'll see that I and my family own forty-nine-per-cent of the business – but what's more important is Clause Twelve, right at the bottom.'

Frank's frown had become a permanent fixture. He looked at Dorothy but her attitude to him seemed to have changed. This was the businesslike Dorothy, detached from all emotion. The one who'd fleeced Sid Allerdyce out of several thousand pounds.

'In a nutshell,' explained Dorothy, 'it says that in the event of our partnership being dissolved within the first twelve months, Frank's financial position will revert to the status quo as at the time of signing. In other words, whatever the company was worth at that time is exactly what Frank gets out of it. No more, no less.'

'And how much will that be?' asked Elaine. Her concern for Frank's physical welfare now replaced by a greater concern for his financial well being.

'Well, Frank doesn't actually know this, but I had a valuation done on his business before we put our investment in. It wouldn't be an exaggeration to say that Sackfield Builders was in a perilous position. Not to put too fine a point on it, he was facing bankruptcy.'

'You never mentioned a valuation,' protested Frank. 'You didn't show me this blasted Clause Twelve either – or I never would have signed it. I though it was a standard partnership agreement.'

'Sorry, Frank,' said Dorothy coldly. 'But I had to protect my family's interests.'

'How much was the valuation?' he asked resignedly.

'Two thousand pounds,' answered Dorothy.

'Two thousand pounds? Is that all?' Elaine's face was a mask of disappointment.

'Less legal costs and disbursements,' added Dorothy. 'Frank should end up with eighteen-fifty – give or take a few quid.'

Frank sat back, his face paler than it ever had been during his stay in hospital. Elaine looked at him with contempt.

'How could you let her trick you into this?' she said scathingly.

'I don't know, I didn't realise,' said Frank weakly, taking the agreement from her and looking at the last clause with dismay. Elaine couldn't contain her disgust.

'You bloody idiot, Frank! Eighteen hundred and fifty pounds – and how much does she get?'

'About twenty-two thousand – after this latest deal goes through,' said Dorothy.

'Twenty-two thou . . . Jesus Christ!'

Elaine stood up and stormed to the door. 'Just forget me and you getting back together, Frank! You haven't got the brains you were born with!'

Frank watched her go, 'Apparently not,' he said dispassionately.

Elaine left behind her an awkward silence. Each one of them not wanting to speak before they'd marshalled their thoughts properly.

'That's buggered that then!' said Frank at last.

'Well and truly,' agreed Dorothy. 'Still – everyone has their price and hers was a bit more than eighteen-fifty.'

'So it seems.' said Frank, looking accusingly at Dorothy. 'You did it on purpose, didn't you?'

'No! Well – yes actually,' admitted Dorothy, 'sorry!'

'You thought she was just after my money, didn't you?'

'She was.'

'And I suppose you think you're a cut above her, do you?' Frank's voice had an edge to it she never heard before, not when he'd been talking to her anyway.

'How do you mean, Frank?'

'You know very well what I mean – I mean Clause bloody Twelve and your valuation.'

'Oh, that.' She picked up the agreement and looked at it admiringly. 'It's a fake, Frank – I only had it printed this morning – good, isn't it?'

Frank snatched it off her. 'You rotten sod! What did you want to go and do that for?'

'To save you from a conniving gold-digger, Frank. She's not interested in you, only in your money. There was no valuation either,' she added guiltily.

Frank's face dropped, he knew she was right. 'It's all your fault!' he said. 'You should never have turned me down.'

'Turned you down? When did I do that?' Dorothy asked innocently.

'When I asked you to – oh never mind – you know very well when!'

'I know nothing of the sort.'

'I asked you to marry me and you said "no".'

'I did not!'

288

'Yes you di ... how do you mean you didn't?' Frank was confused now.

'Think back – I didn't say no.' she said adamantly.

Frank didn't trust this cunning, devious woman who made his heart lurch just looking at her.

'Why don't you ask me again?' she challenged.

Twisting painfully round in his chair, he looked directly into her eyes. Gone was the detached, businesslike expression. There was genuine affection in these eyes.

'Will you marry me?' he asked.

'Yes.'

'What? Why?'

'Because I love you, why do you think?' said Dorothy.

'I suppose I'd better kiss you or something,' said Frank, desperately fighting back tears of emotion.

'I wish you would!' replied Dorothy, who'd already lost that fight.

Dorothy took him in her arms, Frank reciprocating with his one workable arm and they kissed. This time with the love of two lost souls who'd at last found what had been under their noses all the time.

It was a while before a tooth-grating rubbing of dirt from the window alerted Frank to the Peeping Toms outside. Three of them, grinning like Cheshire cats and blowing mute kisses through the grimy glass. Frank grinned and winked at his future step-children over Dorothy's shoulder, then once again kissed their unsuspecting aunt, passionately and unashamedly.

'Soppy buggers!' said Billy happily.

ZOO
STATION
DAVID DOWNING

In memory of

Martha Pappenheim (1900-2001)
who escaped from Germany in 1939
and went on to help the children of
those who did not, and

Yvonne Pappenheim (1912-2005)
who married Martha's brother Fritz,
and spent a lifetime fighting injustice

Author's Note

This is a work of fiction, but every attempt has been made to keep within the bounds of historical possibility. References to the Nazis' planned murder of the mentally handicapped are mostly taken from Michael Burleigh's exhaustive history *Death and Deliverance*, and even the more ludicrous of the news stories mentioned in passing are depressingly authentic.

Into the blue

There were two hours left of 1938. In Danzig it had been snowing on and off all day, and a gang of children were enjoying a snowball fight in front of the grain warehouses which lined the old waterfront. John Russell paused to watch them for a few moments, then walked on up the cobbled street towards the blue and yellow lights.

The Sweden Bar was far from crowded, and those few faces that turned his way weren't exactly brimming over with festive spirit. In fact, most of them looked like they'd rather be somewhere else.

It was an easy thing to want. The Christmas decorations hadn't been removed, just allowed to drop, and now formed part of the flooring, along with patches of melting slush, floating cigarette ends and the odd broken bottle. The Bar was famous for the savagery of its international brawls, but on this particular night the various groups of Swedes, Finns and Letts seemed devoid of the energy needed to get one started. Usually a table or two of German naval ratings could be relied upon to provide the necessary spark, but the only Germans present were a couple of ageing prostitutes, and they were getting ready to leave.

Russell took a stool at the bar, bought himself a *Goldwasser* and glanced through the month-old copy of the *New York Herald Tribune* which, for some inexplicable reason, was lying there. One of his own articles was in it, a piece on German attitudes to their pets. It was accompanied by a cute-looking photograph of a Schnauser.

Seeing him reading, a solitary Swede two stools down asked

him, in perfect English, if he spoke that language. Russell admitted that he did.

'You are English!' the Swede exclaimed, and shifted his considerable bulk to the stool adjoining Russell's.

Their conversation went from friendly to sentimental, and sentimental to maudlin, at what seemed like breakneck pace. Three *Goldwassers* later, the Swede was telling him that he, Lars, was not the true father of his children. Vibeke had never admitted it, but he knew it to be true.

Russell gave him an encouraging pat on the shoulder, and Lars sunk forward, his head making a dull clunk as it made contact with the polished surface of the bar. 'Happy New Year,' Russell murmured. He shifted the Swede's head slightly to ease his breathing, and got up to leave.

Outside, the sky was beginning to clear, the air almost cold enough to sober him up. An organ was playing in the Protestant Seaman's church, nothing hymnal, just a slow lament, as if the organist was saying a personal farewell to the year gone by. It was a quarter to midnight.

Russell walked back across the city, conscious of the moisture seeping in through the holes in his shoes. The Langermarkt was full of couples, laughing and squealing as they clutched each other for balance on the slippery sidewalks.

He cut over the Breite Gasse and reached the Holzmarkt just as the bells began pealing in the New Year. The square was full of celebrating people, and an insistent hand pulled him into a circle of revellers dancing and singing in the snow. When the song ended and the circle broke up, the Polish girl on his left reached up and brushed her lips against his, eyes shining with happiness. It was, he thought, a better than expected opening to 1939.

• • •

His hotel's reception area was deserted, and the sounds of celebration emanating from the kitchen at the back suggested the night staff were enjoying their own private party. Russell thought about making himself a hot chocolate and drying his shoes in one of the ovens, but decided against. He took his key, clambered up the stairs to the third floor, and trundled down the corridor to his room. Closing the door behind him, he became painfully aware that the occupants of the neighbouring rooms were still welcoming in the new year, a singsong on one side, floor-shaking sex on the other. He took off his sodden shoes and socks, dried his wet feet with a towel and sank back onto the vibrating bed.

There was a discreet, barely audible tap on his door.

Cursing, he levered himself off the bed and prised the door open. A man in a crumpled suit and open shirt stared back at him.

'Mr John Russell,' the man said in English, as if he was introducing Russell to himself. The Russian accent was slight, but unmistakable. 'Could I talk with you for a few minutes?'

'It's a bit late...' Russell began. The man's face was vaguely familiar. 'But why not?' he continued, as the singers next door reached for a new and louder chorus. 'A journalist should never turn down a conversation,' he murmured, mostly to himself, as he let the man in. 'Take the chair,' he suggested.

His visitor sat back and crossed one leg over the other, hitching up his trouser leg as he did so. 'We have met before,' he said. 'A long time ago. My name is Shchepkin. Yevgeny Grigorovich Shchepkin. We...'

'Yes,' Russell interrupted, as the memory clicked into place. 'The discussion group on journalism at the fifth Congress. The summer of '24.'

Shchepkin nodded his acknowledgement. 'I remember your contributions,' he said. 'Full of passion,' he added, his eyes circling the room and resting, for a few seconds, on his host's dilapidated shoes.

Russell perched himself on the edge of the bed. 'As you said – a long time ago.' He and Ilse had met at that conference, and set in motion their ten-year cycle of marriage, parenthood, separation and divorce. Shchepkin's hair had been black and wavy in 1924; now it was a close-cropped grey. They were both a little older than the century, Russell guessed, and Shchepkin was wearing pretty well, considering what he'd probably been through the last fifteen years. He had a handsome face of indeterminate nationality, with deep brown eyes above prominent slanting cheekbones, an aquiline nose and lips just the full side of perfect. He could have passed for a citizen of most European countries, and probably had.

The Russian completed his survey of the room. 'This is a dreadful hotel,' he said.

Russell laughed. 'Is that what you wanted to talk about?'

'No. Of course not.'

'So what are you here for?'

'Ah.' Shchepkin hitched his trouser leg again. 'I am here to offer you work.'

Russell raised an eyebrow. 'You? Who exactly do you represent?'

The Russian shrugged. 'My country. The Writers' Union. It doesn't matter. You will be working for us. You know who we are.'

'No,' Russell said. 'I mean, no I'm not interested. I…'

'Don't be so hasty,' Shchepkin said. 'Hear me out. We aren't asking you to do anything which your German hosts could object to.' The Russian allowed himself a smile. 'Let me tell you exactly what we have in mind. We want a series of articles about positive aspects of the Nazi regime.' He paused for a few seconds, waiting in vain for Russell to demand an explanation. 'You are not German but you live in Berlin,' he went on. 'You once had a reputation as a journalist of the left, and though that reputation has, shall we say, faded, no one could accuse you of being an apologist for the Nazis…'

'But you want me to be just that.'

'No, no. We want positive aspects, not a positive picture overall. That would not be believable.'

Russell was curious in spite of himself. Or because of the *Goldwassers*. 'Do you just need my name on these articles?' he asked. 'Or do you want me to write them as well?'

'Oh, we want you to write them. We like your style – all that irony.'

Russell shook his head – Stalin and irony didn't seem like much of a match.

Shchepkin misread the gesture. 'Look,' he said, 'let me put all my cards on the table.'

Russell grinned.

Shchepkin offered a wry smile in return. 'Well, most of them anyway. Look, we are aware of your situation. You have a German son and a German lady-friend, and you want to stay in Germany if you possibly can. Of course if a war breaks out you will have to leave, or else they will intern you. But until that moment comes – and maybe it won't – miracles do happen – until it does you want to earn your living as a journalist without upsetting your hosts. What better way than this? You write nice things about the Nazis – not too nice, of course, the articles have to be credible… but you stress their good side.'

'Does shit have a good side?' Russell wondered out loud.

'Come, come,' Shchepkin insisted, 'you know better than that. Unemployment eliminated, a renewed sense of community, healthy children, cruises for workers, cars for the people…'

'You should work for Joe Goebbels.'

Shchepkin gave him a mock-reproachful look.

'Okay,' Russell said, 'I take your point. Let me ask you a question. There's only one reason you'd want that sort of article – you're softening up your own people for some sort of deal with the devil. Right?'

Shchepkin flexed his shoulders in an eloquent shrug.

'Why?'

The Russian grunted. 'Why deal with the devil? I don't know what the leadership is thinking. But I could make an educated guess, and so could you.'

Russell could. 'The western powers are trying to push Hitler east, so Stalin has to push him west? Are we talking about a non-aggression pact, or something more?'

Shchepkin looked almost affronted. 'What more could there be? Any deal with that man can only be temporary. We know what he is.'

Russell nodded. It made sense. He closed his eyes, as if it were possible to blank out the approaching calamity. On the other side of the opposite wall, his musical neighbours were intoning one of those Polish river songs which could reduce a statue to tears. Through the wall behind him silence had fallen, but his bed was still quivering like a tuning fork.

'We'd also like some information,' Shchepkin was saying, almost apologetically. 'Nothing military,' he added quickly, seeing the look on Russell's face. 'No armament statistics or those naval plans that Sherlock Holmes is always being asked to recover. Nothing of that sort. We just want a better idea of what ordinary Germans are thinking. How they are taking the changes in working conditions, how they are likely to react if war comes – that sort of thing. We don't want any secrets, just your opinions. And nothing on paper. You can deliver them in person, on a monthly basis.'

Russell looked sceptical.

Shchepkin ploughed on. 'You will be well paid – very well. In any currency, any bank, any country, that you choose. You can move into a better rooming house…'

'I like my rooming house.'

'You can buy things for your son, your girlfriend. You can have your shoes mended.'

'I don't…'

'The money is only an extra. You were with us once…'

'A long long time ago.'

'Yes, I know. But you cared about your fellow human beings.

I heard you talk. That doesn't change. And if we go under there will be nothing left.'

'A cynic might say there's not much to choose between you.'

'The cynic would be wrong,' Shchepkin replied, exasperated and perhaps a little angry. 'We have spilt blood, yes. But reluctantly, and in faith of a better future. *They* enjoy it. Their idea of progress is a European slave-state.'

'I know.'

'One more thing. If money and politics don't persuade you, think of this. We will be grateful, and we have influence almost everywhere. And a man like you, in a situation like yours, is going to need influential friends.'

'No doubt about that.'

Shchepkin was on his feet. 'Think about it, Mr Russell,' he said, drawing an envelope from the inside pocket of his jacket and placing it on the nightstand. 'All the details are in here – how many words, delivery dates, fees, and so on. If you decide to do the articles, write to our press attaché in Berlin, telling him who you are, and that you've had the idea for them yourself. He will ask you to send him one in the post. The Gestapo will read it, and pass it on. You will then receive your first fee and suggestions for future stories. The last-but-one letters of the opening sentence will spell out the name of a city outside Germany which you can reach fairly easily. Prague, perhaps, or Cracow. You will spend the last weekend of the month in that city. And be sure to make your hotel reservation at least a week in advance. Once you are there, someone will contact you.'

'I'll think about it,' Russell said, mostly to avoid further argument. He wanted to spend his weekends with his son Paul and his girlfriend Effi, not the Shchepkins of this world.

The Russian nodded and let himself out. As if on cue, the Polish choir lapsed into silence.

Russell was woken by the scream of a locomotive whistle. Or at least, that was his first impression. Lying there awake all he could hear was a gathering swell of high-pitched voices. It sounded like a school playground full of terrified children.

He threw on some clothes and made his way downstairs. It was still dark, the street deserted, the tramlines hidden beneath a virginal sheet of snow. In the Hauptbahnhof booking hall a couple of would-be travellers were hunched in their seats, eyes averted, praying that they hadn't strayed into dangerous territory. Russell strode through the unmanned ticket barrier. There were trucks in the goods yard beyond the far platform, and a train which stretched out beyond the station throat. People were gathered under the yellow lights, mostly families by the look of them, because there were lots of children. And there were men in uniform. Brownshirts.

A sudden shrill whistle from the distant locomotive produced an eerie echo from the milling crowd, as if all the children had shrieked at once.

Russell took the subway steps two at a time, half-expecting to find that the tunnel had been blocked off. It hadn't. On the far side, he emerged into a milling crowd of shouting, screaming people. He had already guessed what was happening – this was a *kindertransport*, one of the trains hired to transport the ten thousand Jewish children that Britain had agreed to accept after *Kristallnacht*. The shriek had risen at the moment the guards started separating the children from their parents, and the two groups were now being shoved apart by snarling Brownshirts. Parents were backing away, tears running down their cheeks, as their children were herded onto the train, some waving frantically, some almost reluctantly, as if they feared to recognise the separation.

Further up the platform a violent dispute was underway between an SA Truppführer and a woman with a red cross on her sleeve. Both were screaming at the other, he in German, she in northern-accented English. The woman was beside herself with anger, almost spitting in the Brownshirt's eye, and it was obviously taking all the control he had not to smash his fist in her face. A few feet away one of the mothers was being helped to her feet by another woman. Blood was streaming from her nose.

Russell strode up to them and flashed his Foreign Ministry press accreditation, which at least gave the man a new outlet for his anger.

'What the fuck are you doing here?' the Truppführer shouted. He had a depressingly porcine face, and the bulk to go with it.

'Trying to help,' Russell said calmly. 'I speak English.'

'Well then tell this English bitch to get back on the train with the kike brats where she belongs.'

Russell turned to the woman, a petite brunette who couldn't have been much more than twenty-five. 'He's not worth screaming at,' he told her in English. 'And it won't do you any good. In fact, you'll only make matters worse.'

'I …' She seemed lost for words.

'I know,' Russell said. 'You can't believe people could behave like this. But this lot do. All the time.'

As if to emphasise the point, the Truppführer man started shouting again. When she shouted back he seized her arm, and she kicked him in the shin. He backhanded her across the face with what seemed enormous force, spinning her round and dumping her face-first on the snowy platform. She groaned and shook her head.

Russell put himself between them. 'Look,' he said to the man, 'this will get you court-martialled if you're not careful. The Führer doesn't want you giving the English this sort of a propaganda victory. I know they're only kikes, and I'm sure you feel like I do – that we should put all the adults on the damn train with them, and get rid of the vermin once and for all – but that's for the Führer to decide, not us.'

The British woman was groggily raising herself onto all fours. The storm trooper took one last look at his victim, made a 'pah!' noise that any pantomime villain would have been proud of and strode away down the platform.

Russell helped her to her feet.

'What did you say to him?' she asked, gingerly feeling an already swelling cheek.

'I appealed to his better nature.'

'There must be someone…' she began.

'There isn't,' he assured her. 'The laws don't apply to Jews, or anyone who acts on their behalf. Just look after the children. They look like they need it.'

'I don't need you to tell me…'

'I know you don't. I'm just trying…'

She was looking past his shoulder. 'He's coming back.'

The Truppführer had a Sturmführer with him, a smaller man

with round glasses and a chubby face. Out of uniform – assuming they ever took them off – he put them down as a shopkeeper and minor civil servant. Danzig's finest.

'Your papers,' the Sturmführer demanded.

'They're in my hotel room.'

'What is your name?'

'John Russell.'

'You are English?'

'I'm an English journalist. I live in the Reich, and I have full accreditation from the Ministry of Propaganda in Berlin.'

'We shall check that.'

'Of course.'

'And what are you doing here?'

'I came to see what was happening. As journalists do. I intervened in the argument between your colleague and this Red Cross worker because I thought his behaviour was damaging the reputation of the Reich.'

The Sturmführer paused for thought, then turned to his subordinate. 'I'm sure my colleague regrets any misunderstanding,' he said meaningfully.

The Truppführer looked at the woman. 'I apologise,' he said woodenly.

'He apologises,' Russell told her.

'Tell him to go to hell,' she said.

'She accepts your apology,' Russell told the two Brownshirts.

'Good. Now she must get back on the train, and you must come with us.'

Russell sighed. 'You should get on the train,' he told her. 'You won't get anywhere by protesting.'

She took a deep breath. 'All right,' she said, as if it was anything but. 'Thank you,' she added, offering her hand.

Russell took it. 'Tell the press when you get back to civilization,' he said. 'And good luck.'

He watched her mount the steps and disappear into the train. The children were all aboard now; most had their faces pressed against the windows, and were frantically wiping their breath from the glass to get a last clear look at their parents. A few had managed to force back the sliding ventilators and wedge their faces in the narrow. Some were shouting, some pleading. Most were crying.

Russell tore his gaze from the windows just in time to see a small girl leap nimbly down from the train and race across the platform. The storm trooper by the door spun to catch her, but slipped in the slush as he did so, and fell face-first onto the platform. As he struggled to his feet a boy of around ten rushed past him.

The little girl's arms were tightly wrapped around her kneeling mother's neck. 'Esther, we have to get on the train,' the boy said angrily, but daughter and mother were both crying too hard to notice him. The father's anguished appeals to reason – 'Ruth, we have to let her go; Esther, you must go with your brother' – fell on equally deaf ears.

The storm trooper, red-faced with anger, took a fistful of the girl's long black hair and yanked. The shock tore her arms from her mother's neck, and he started dragging the girl across the slush-strewn platform to the train. The mother shrieked and went after them. The man let go of the girl and crashed his rubber cosh across one side of the mother's face. She sank back, a rivulet of blood running onto her coat collar. As the storm trooper went to hit the woman again, her husband grabbed for the cosh, but two other Brownshirts wrestled him to the ground, and started raining down blows on his head. The boy picked up his whimpering sister and shepherded her back onto the train.

More storm troopers came racing up, but they needn't have

bothered. Like Russell, the watching parents were too stunned to protest, let alone intervene.

'I don't want to go,' a small voice said behind him.

He turned to find its owner. She was standing on a seatback in the train, her face twisted sideways in an open ventilator window, brown eyes brimming with tears. She couldn't have been more than five.

'Please, can you tell the policemen that I don't want to go? My name is Fraulein Gisela Kluger.'

Russell walked across to the train, wondering what on earth he could say. 'I'm afraid you have to make this trip,' he said. 'Your mother and father think you'll be safer in England.'

'But I don't want to,' she said, a large tear sliding down either cheek.

'I know, but…' Another whistle shrilled down the platform; a spasm of steam escaped from the locomotive. 'I'm sorry,' he said helplessly.

The train jerked into motion. A momentary panic flitted across her face, followed by a look that Russell would long remember – one that blended accusation, incomprehension and the sort of grief that no five year-old should have to bear.

As the train pulled away a tiny hand poked out through the window and waved.

'I'm sorry,' Russell murmured.

A hand grasped his arm. The Truppführer's. 'You, English. Come with us.'

He was ushered down the platform in the Sturmführer's wake. Most of the mothers and fathers were still focussed on the disappearing train, their eyes clinging to the red tail-light, the last flicker of family. They had sent their children away. To save their lives, they had turned them into orphans.

One woman, her eyes closed, was kneeling in the snow, a low keening noise rising up from inside her. The sound stayed with Russell as he was led out of the station. The sound of a heart caving in.

In the goods yard the Truppführer pushed him towards a car. 'My hotel's just across the road,' Russell protested.

'We will collect your papers,' the Sturmführer said.

As they bundled him into the car, it occurred to Russell that Shchepkin's envelope was still sitting on his nightstand.

Danzig was waking up as they drove back towards the city centre, shopkeepers clearing the night's snow off their patches of sidewalk. Russell kept his eyes on where they were going, hoping to God it wasn't some SA barracks out of humanity's hearing range. As they pulled up outside an official police station on Hundegasse he managed to suppress a sigh of relief.

The Truppführer pulled him out of the car and pushed him violently towards the entrance doors. Russell slipped in the snow, and fell onto the steps, catching a shin on one of the hard edges. He had no time to check the wound, though – the Truppführer was already propelling him forward.

Inside, a uniformed police officer was cradling a steaming cup of coffee. He looked up without much interest, sighed, and reached for the duty book. 'Name?'

Russell told him. 'I'm English,' he added.

The man was not impressed. 'We all have to come from somewhere. Now empty your pockets.'

Russell did as he was told. 'Who's in charge here?' he asked.

'The police or the SA?'

The policeman gave him a contemptuous look. 'Take a guess,' he suggested.

Russell felt a sinking sensation in his stomach. 'I want to speak to the British Consulate,' he said.

'No need for that,' the Truppführer said behind him. 'What's your hotel name and room number?' Armed with this information, he went back out through the doors. Russell had a glimpse of grey light in the eastern sky.

He tried pleading with the duty officer, and received a shrug for his pains. A younger policeman was summoned to take him downstairs, where two rows of cells lay either side of a dimly-lit corridor. They had tiled floors and brick walls, black up to waist level, white above. It only needed a splash of blood to exhaust the Nazi palette.

Russell slumped to the floor, his back against the far wall. No need to feel frightened, he told himself. They wouldn't do any permanent damage to a foreign journalist.

They would if they thought he was a spy. What had Shchepkin put in the damn envelope? If Russell's past experience of Stalin's NKVD security police was anything to go by, there was an institutional reluctance to spell anything out which verged on paranoia. And they wouldn't want to leave him with anything he might conceivably use against them.

All of which was good news.

But what language was the damn letter written in? If it was in Russian, or if roubles were mentioned, that would be enough for goons like the Truppführer.

He told himself to calm down. He had talked himself out of worse situations than this.

His shin was oozing blood, but didn't look too bad. His stomach felt queasy, though whether from hunger or fear was hard to tell. Both, probably.

It felt like more than an hour had passed when he heard feet on the stairs. Booted feet, and several of them.

The sliding panel on his door clanged open and clanged shut again. The boots moved on. Another clang, but this time a door swung open. A voice protested – a voice Russell thought he recognised – the Jew who'd tried to protect his wife. The voice rose, and was cut off, leaving echoes inside Russell's head. What had cut it off? A fist? A knee? A cosh? A door slammed shut.

Silence reasserted itself, a heavy silence which offered no reassurance. Eventually a door scraped open, a remark drew laughter, and the boots were back in the corridor. Russell felt his breath catch as they headed his way, but they clattered on past and up the stairs, leaving him staring at his shaking hands. Pressing his ear to the door he could hear no groans of pain, only the stillness of unconsciousness or death.

Time went by. He'd rushed out of the hotel without his watch, and when a tray of food was eventually shoved through his hatch he wondered if it was lunch or supper. The boots never came back, and with each hour that passed he found himself feeling a little more optimistic. When the door finally opened, his stomach lurched, but it was only the policeman who'd brought him down.

'This way, Herr Russell,' the man said, nodding him towards the stairs.

They beat people up in the cells, Russell told himself. Upstairs had to be better.

Two corridors and two flights of stairs later, he was ushered through a door labelled Kriminalinspektor Tesmer. The man himself had greased black hair, blue eyes, thin lips, and a bad case of five o'clock shadow. 'Please sit,' he told Russell.

He took one last look at the Englishman's passport, and then passed it across the desk along with the journalist's accreditation. There was no sign of Shchepkin's envelope.

'Everything is satisfactory,' Tesmer said with a sudden,

unconvincing smile. 'And I'm sorry this has taken so long.'

Russell reached for his documents. 'I can go?' he asked, trying not to sound too relieved.

'Just one question.'

'Yes?' There was no life behind the eyes, Russell thought. This was a man to be careful with.

'Why did you come to Danzig, Herr Russell? To write a story about the Jewish children?'

'No. I had no idea a *kindertransport* was leaving from here. I'm staying at the hotel opposite the station, and the noise woke me up. I just walked across to see what was going on.'

'Then why did you come?'

Why indeed? Because he'd felt drawn to the place, the way a good journalist was always drawn to a story that mattered. A city in thrall to thugs and fools, and doomed for precisely that reason. Danzig was Europe writ small. It was a story for everyone.

Almost everyone.

'Stamps,' he said, suddenly remembering a conversation he'd overhead in the Café Weitzke. The city's German and Polish post offices were both putting out stamps to commemorate centuries-old victories over each other. 'I do occasional pieces for philately journals, and the two Post Offices here are bringing out some interesting new issues. I'm hoping to interview the postmasters tomorrow.'

Tesmer looked disappointed, like a fisherman realising that this catch was too small to eat. 'Enjoy your stay,' he said curtly.

Once outside, Russell discovered it was almost ten o'clock. A bar supplied him with a sandwich and a much-needed drink, and he trudged back to his hotel through mostly empty streets. Shchepkin's envelope was still lying where he'd left it.

It had been opened, though. Russell took out the single sheet and read it. They wanted four articles of between 1,200 and 1,500 words, delivered at fortnightly intervals, beginning in mid-January. The money was more generous than he'd expected – as much as an ordinary Soviet worker earned over a Five Year Plan. The thought crossed his mind that a car would transform his Saturdays with his son Paul.

The letter was in German, the promised fee in Reichsmarks. There was nothing to say where the offer came from or what the articles would be about. 'God bless the NKVD,' Russell murmured to himself.

He woke around ten. Thick snow was cascading past his window, almost obscuring the station opposite. He used the lobby phone to call the two Post Offices, and was granted audiences with their Postmasters late that afternoon. When he emerged from the Café Weitzke on Langgasse, replete with scrambled eggs, Kashubian mushrooms and a mocha, it was still only midday. He had five hours to kill.

It had almost stopped snowing, but the sky was still heavy with cloud. As he stood there wondering what to do, there was a sudden swell of music from the loudspeakers which peppered the city. Hitler's New Year speech to the nation, Russell remembered. Danzig wasn't yet part of the German Reich, but try telling the Nazis that.

Russell sometimes enjoyed listening to Hitler. The man's sheer effrontery was entertaining, and knowing that millions were being taken in by his ludicrous bloodlust gave the whole experience a deplorably thrilling edge. If the Führer told them that gravity was a Jewish trick then millions of Germans would be practising levitation before the sun set.

Russell wasn't in the mood. A couple of hours by the sea, he thought. There wouldn't be any loudspeakers on the beach.

Hitler was just being introduced when a tram with a Brosen destination board burrowed out of the Langgasse Gate. Russell took a seat on the right and watched through the window as the tram skirted the Holzmarkt, swung right into Elisabethwall, and passed his hotel at the bottom of the Stadtgraben.

It was about six kilometres to Brosen. Russell had taken the same ride back in 1935, during his last visit to Danzig. He'd been doing a series of articles on Germans at play, and it had been the middle of summer. The resort had been awash with holiday-makers, and he had gone for a paddle.

Not today. It was as dark as it had been all morning, and the sparks from the overhead wires lit up the housefronts on either side of the street as the tram clanged and squealed its way out of the city. The loudspeakers were still audible, though. As they passed through the outlying suburbs of Langfuhr and Saspe, Russell caught snatches of the familiar voice, and one short passage in which the Führer offered the German people his fulsome congratulations for their 'wonderful behaviour' in 1938. He was probably talking about *Kristallnacht*.

By the time the tram reached Brosen the sky had visibly lightened. Russell got off outside the closed casino, where a single loudspeaker was doing its manful best to distort the Führer's message. Russell listened to the crackle for a few seconds, struck by the notion that he and Hitler were sharing a private moment together. The latter was promising help with the 'general pacification of the world'. Russell wondered how much irony one nation could eat.

He walked down past the boarded-up refreshment stands and padlocked beach huts to the snow-strewn beach. The previous season's final water temperature was still legible on the lifeguard hut blackboard, alongside a poster explaining the mysteries of artificial respiration. The men in the poster all wore striped bathing suits and moustaches, like a posse of cartoon Führers.

The sea was gunmetal grey, the sky almost as dark, slate grey with a yellowish tinge. There was no one in sight.

A couple of kilometres to the east, two beacon lights marked the end of Danzig's channel to the sea, and Russell started walking towards them. Out to the left the lighthouse at the end of the dredged channel flickered into life with each revolution. To the north, a darker line marked the outflung arm of the Hela peninsular. Between the two a smudge of a freighter was inching out across the bay.

The stamp story was made for him, he thought. A story that amused, and didn't condemn. A story of stupidity, and rather lovable stupidity at that. He could implant a few ironies just beneath the skin of the text for those who wanted to pick at it, leave enough clues to the real situation for those who already understood it. They would congratulate themselves on reading between the lines, and him for writing between them. And he could sit on his necessary fence for a few more months, until Hitler drove something through it.

Too many metaphors, he told himself. And not nearly enough satisfaction.

He thought about the real Danzig story. Ten years ago he'd have written it, and written it well. But not now. Step out of line that far, and the toadies at the Propaganda Ministry would have him deported before he could say 'Heil Hitler'. He'd be saying goodbye to his son, probably for the duration of a war. And probably to Effi as well. She'd told him often enough that she'd go to England, or better still America, with him, but he had his doubts whether she meant it, whether she'd ever willingly leave her sister, parents, agent and vast array of friends for life in a new country where no one knew who she was.

He left the path and walked down to the edge of the water, searching for pebbles to skim. He wanted to take Shchepkin's offer, he realised, but he wasn't sure why. He only half-bought the argument that by helping the Soviets he'd be hurting the Nazis. If he really wanted to take Hitler on there were more effective ways, most of them depressingly self-sacrificial. The money would be nice, but the risks would be high. The Nazis still beheaded spies.

He skimmed a flat pebble between two waves. Could he trust Shchepkin? Of course he couldn't. The Soviets might want what they said they wanted – no more, no less – but even if they did, that wouldn't be the end of it. You didn't do a few articles for Stalin, bank the cheques and move on. You would be on a list, one of their people, someone to call up when something else was needed. And once you were on the list, they took refusals badly.

And then there was the attitude of his own country to worry about. He didn't need England now, but the way things were going he soon might, and writing for Stalin would hardly endear him to the Foreign Office. He could end up *persona non grata* with just about everyone. Why was he even thinking about it?

He knew why. A couple of weeks before Christmas Paul had told him about an exercise that new recruits into the *Jungvolk* were forced to undergo. They were taken out into the countryside without maps and invited to find their way back home the best they could. It was called a *Fahrt ins Blau*, a journey into the blue.

The idea had appealed to Paul, as it probably did to most boys of eleven. It appealed to Russell too. If he took this journey into the blue he might, conceivably, find his way home again.

He skimmed his last stone, a large one that took a single bounce and sunk. The sparse daylight was receding. The freighter and the

Hela peninsula had both been sucked into the surrounding grey, and the beam from the lighthouse was sending shivers of reflection back off the darkening sea. He was in the middle of nowhere, lost in space. With ice for feet.

The two postmasters were both short-sighted men in sober suits with small moustaches. The Polish one could hardly wait for the honour of distributing his new stamps. A minion was sent for samples, and came back with King Jagiello and Queen Hedwig. The Polish queen, the postmaster explained, had spurned a German prince in favour of marrying the Lithuanian Jagiello. Their joint kingdom had forced the Prussians to accept the first Polish Corridor and bi-national status for Danzig. Admittedly this had all happened in the early fifteenth century but – and here the postmaster leaned back in his chair with a self-satisfied smile – the contemporary relevance should be obvious. Even to a German.

The German postmaster had his own sample. His stamp featured a beautiful miniature of stout Danzigers routing the Polish forces of King Stephan Batory in 1577. 'A German city defended by German arms,' he announced smugly. Russell repeated the question he had put to the Polish postmaster – weren't these stamps a little provocative? Shouldn't the civil authorities be trying to reduce the tension between their two countries, rather than using their stamps to stoke up old quarrels?

The German postmaster gave the same reply as his Polish opposite number. How, he asked, could anyone take postage stamps that seriously?

Russell's train left the Hauptbahnhof at ten o'clock. After paying for a sleeping berth he could barely afford, he sat in the restaurant car for the better part of two hours, nursing a single gold-flecked schnapps, feeling restless and uncertain. The Polish customs checked his visa just before Dirschau and the German authorities examined his passport at Flatow, on the far side of the Polish Corridor. He had no trouble with the latter – if the Danzig SA were submitting a report on his visit they were probably still struggling with their spelling.

He thought about the *kindertransport*, and wondered where it was at that moment. Still chugging west across Germany, most likely. The Englishwoman's cheek would be purple by now – he hoped she would go to the press when she got back and make a real stink. Not that it would do any good. It had taken her five minutes to learn what Nazism was all about, but there was no substitute for first-hand experience. If you told people they didn't believe you. No one, their eyes always said, could be as bad as that.

He walked back down the train to his sleeping compartment. The two lower berths were empty, one of the upper pair occupied by a gently snoring German youth. Russell sat on the berth beneath him, pulled back the edge of the curtain, and stared out at the frozen fields of Pomerania.

He lay back and shut his eyes. Fraulein Gisela Kluger looked back at him.

He would write Shchepkin's articles. See where the journey took him. Into the blue. Or into the black.

Ha! Ho! He!

Russell's train steamed across the bridge over Friedrichstrasse and into the station of the same name just before eight in the morning. An eastbound Stadtbahn train was disgorging its morning load on the other side of the island platform, and he stood behind the stairwell waiting for the crowd to clear. On the other side of the tracks an angry local was shaking a burnt almond machine in the vain hope that his coin would be returned.

A railway official intervened and the two men stood there shouting at each other.

Welcome to Berlin, Russell thought.

He took the steps down to the underground concourse, bought a newspaper at the waiting room kiosk, and found himself a seat in the station buffet. The sight of his neighbour, a stout man in an Orpo uniform, cramming his mouth with large slices of blood sausage did nothing for Russell's appetite, and he settled for a buttered roll and four-fruit jam with his large milky coffee.

His newspaper shielded him from the blood sausage eater, but not from Nazi reality. He dutifully read Goebbels' latest speech on the vibrancy of modern German culture, but there was nothing new in it. More anti-Jewish laws had come into force on January 1: driving automobiles, working in retail and making craft goods had all been added to the *verboten* list. What was left, Russell wondered. Emigration, he supposed. So why make it so hard for the poor bastards to leave?

He skimmed through the rest. More villages *judenfrei*, more kilometres of autobahn, more indignation about Polish behaviour in the Corridor. A new U-boat epic at the cinema, children collecting old tin cans for Winter Relief, a new recipe for the monthly one-pot-stew. A Reich that will last a thousand years. Six down, nine hundred and ninety-four to go.

He thought about taking the U-bahn but decided he needed some exercise. Emerging onto Friedrichstrasse he found the remains of the last snowfall dribbling into the gutters. A ribbon of pale sunlight lit the upper walls on the eastern side of the street, but the street itself was still sunk in shadows. Little knots of people were gathered at the doors of about-to-open shops, many of them talking in that loud, insistent manner which non-Berliners found so annoying.

It was a three-kilometre walk to his rooms near Hallesches Tor. He crossed Unter den Linden by the Café Bauer, and strode south through the financial district, towards the bridge which carried the elevated U-bahn over Mohrenstrasse. Berlin was not a beautiful city, but the rows of grey stone had a solidity, a dependability, about them.

On one corner of Leipzigerstrasse a frankfurter stall was gushing steam into the air, on another the astrologer whom Effi sometimes consulted was busy erecting his canvas booth. The man claimed he'd prepared a chart for Hitler in pre-Führer days, but refused to divulge what was in it. Nothing good, Russell suspected.

Another kilometre and he was turning off Friedrichstrasse, cutting through the side streets to Neuenburgerstrasse and his apartment block. Walking south from Leipzigstrasse was like walking down a ladder of social class, and the area in which he lived was still hoping for a visit from the twentieth century. Most of the apartment blocks were five storeys high, and each pair boasted a high brick archway leading into a dark well of a courtyard. A bedraggled birch tree stood in his, still clinging to its mantle of snow.

The concierge's door was open, light spilling into the dark lobby. Russell knocked, and Frau Heidegger emerged almost instantly, her frown turning to a smile when she saw who it was. 'Herr Russell! You said you would be back yesterday. We were beginning to worry.'

'I tried to telephone,' he lied, 'but…'

'Ah, the Poles,' Frau Heidegger said resignedly, as if nothing better could be expected from her neighbours to the east. She wiped her hands on her apron and ushered him in. 'Come, you must have a coffee.'

Accepting was easier than refusing. He took the proffered seat in her living room and gazed about him as she re-heated – for the last of heaven knows how many times – her eternal pot of coffee. Her Advent wreath was still hanging from the light fixture along with its four gutted candles. On the walnut chest of drawers two packs of cards stood beside her precious People's Radio. It was Tuesday, Russell realised, the day Frau Heidegger and three of her opposite numbers in the nearby blocks played skat.

She came back with the coffee and a small pile of post: a postcard from Paul, a probable Christmas card from his mother in the US, a letter from his American agent and a business letter with a Berlin postmark.

'You had two telephone messages,' the concierge said, looking down through her pince-nez at a small piece of paper. 'Your fiancée' – Frau Heidegger always referred to Effi in that way, despite the fact that no prospective marriage had ever been mentioned – 'says she will be back extremely late on Thursday night and will meet you at the Café Uhlandeck at noon on Friday. Does that sound right?'

'Yes.'

'And a Herr Conway – yes? – he would like you to call him as soon as possible.'

'I'll call him after I've had my coffee,' Russell said, taking a first exploratory sip. It was burnt, but so strong and sweet that you hardly noticed.

Frau Heidegger was telling him how she'd recently caught one of the tenants – the Sudeten German on the first floor who Russell hardly knew – opening a window. This was strictly forbidden when the heating was on, and the tenant had only been forgiven on the grounds that he came 'from the mountains' and could hardly be expected to know any better. He didn't know how lucky he was, Russell thought; his own rooms on the fourth floor sometimes resembled neighbouring ovens. During one warm week in December he had regularly set his alarm for 3 a.m., when the concierge was fairly certain to be asleep and he could throw open his windows for a life-saving blast of cool air.

He took another sip of coffee, idly wondering whether the War Ministry would be interested in developing it as a weapon. 'Thank you, Frau Heidegger,' he said, carefully replacing the half-full cup in its saucer and getting to his feet. 'I've had two cups already this morning,' he added by way of an excuse.

'It's good to have you back,' she said, following him to the door. She didn't close it though, presumably because she might miss something.

He walked over to the telephone at the foot of the stairs. It had been a source of great pride to Frau Heidegger when it was installed a couple of years earlier – her block was the first on Neuenburger-strasse to be connected. But it had soon turned into something of a mixed blessing. A popular propensity for ringing at all times of the day and night had necessitated the introduction of a curfew, and the phone was now off the hook from ten at night till eight in the morning. It could still be used for outgoing calls during that time, but heaven help anyone who forgot to take it off again. He unhooked the earpiece and dialled the British Embassy's number. Doug Conway worked in the commercial department, or so he claimed. Russell had met him at the Blau-Weiss Club, where English-speaking expatriates played tennis, talked about how beastly their German hosts were, and lamented the lack of reliable domestic help. Russell hated the place, but time spent there was often good for business. As a journalist he had made a lot of useful contacts; as a part-time English tutor he had been pointed in the direction of several clients. He hoped Doug Conway had found him another.

'I'm rushed off my feet today,' Conway told him. 'But I can squeeze in an early lunch. Wertheim at 12.30?'

'Fine,' Russell agreed, and replaced the receiver. He started up the four flights of stairs which led to his rooms. At the top he paused for breath before unlocking the door, and wondered for the umpteenth time about moving to a block with a lift. His rooms were stuffy and hot, so he left the front door ajar and risked opening a window by a few millimetres.

Stretched out on the threadbare sofa, he went through his mail. Paul's postcard began 'Dear Dad', but seemed mostly concerned with the Christmas presents he'd received from his stepfather. The boy did say he was looking forward to the football on Saturday, though, and Russell took another look out of the window to convince himself that the weather was warming up and that the game would be played.

The American envelope did contain a Christmas card from his mother. Above the picture of a snowbound Times Square she had written one cryptic line: 'This might be a good year to visit me.' She was probably referring to the situation in Europe, although for all Russell knew she might have contracted an incurable disease. She certainly wouldn't tell him if she had.

He opened the business letters. The one from America contained a cheque for fifty-three dollars and twenty-seven cents, payment for an article on 'Strength Through Joy' cruises which a dozen US papers had taken. That was the good news. The Berlin letter was a final, rather abusively written demand for payment on a typewriter repair bill, which would account for more than half the dollar inflow.

Looking round the room at the all-too-familiar furniture and yellowing white walls, at the poster from Effi's first film, the tired collage of photographs and the dusty overloaded bookshelves, he felt a wave of depression wash over him.

The city's largest Wertheim occupied a site twice the size of the late-lamented Reichstag, and a frontage running to 330 metres. Inside, it boasted 83 lifts, 100,000 light bulbs and 1,000 telephone extensions. Russell knew all this because he had written an article on the store a year or so earlier. More to the point, the restaurant offered good food and service at a very reasonable rate, and it was only a five minute walk from the British Embassy on Wilhelmstrasse.

Doug Conway had already secured a table, and was halfway through a gin and tonic. A tall man of around thirty-five with sleek blond hair and bright blue eyes, he looked custom-made for Nazi Berlin, but was in fact a fairly decent representative of the human race. State-educated and lowly-born by Embassy standards – his father had been a parks superintendent in Leeds – he had arrived in Berlin just as the Nazis seized power. His pretty young wife Phyllis was probably brighter than he was, and had once jokingly told Russell that she intended to torch the Blau-Weiss Club before she left Berlin.

Conway's taste in food had not travelled far from his roots.

He looked pained when Russell ordered the pig's knuckle and sauerkraut, and plumped for the pot roast and mash for himself.

'I've got some teaching work for you if you want it,' he told Russell while they waited. 'It's a Jewish family called Wiesner. The father is – was – a doctor. His wife is ill most of the time, though I don't know what with – worry, most likely. Their son was taken off to Sachsenhausen after *Kristallnacht* and they haven't seen him since, though they have heard that he's still alive. And there are two daughters, Ruth and Marthe, who are both in their teens – thirteen and fifteen, or something like that. It's them you'd be teaching.'

Russell must have looked doubtful.

'You'd be doing me a real favour if you took them on,' Conway persisted. 'Dr Wiesner probably saved Phyllis's life – this was back in 1934 – there were complications with our daughter's birth and we couldn't have had a better doctor. He wasn't just efficient, he went out of his way to be helpful. And now he can't practise, of course. I don't know what he intends to do – I don't know what any of them can do – but he's obviously hoping to get his daughters to England or the States, and he probably thinks they'll have a better chance if they speak English. I have no idea what his money situation is, I'm afraid. If he can't earn, and with all the new taxes to pay... well... But if he can't pay your normal rate, then I'll top up whatever he can afford. Just don't tell him I'm doing it.'

'He might like the idea that somebody cares,' Russell said.

'I don't know about...'

'I'll go and see him.'

Conway smiled. 'I hoped you'd say that.' He pulled a folded piece of paper out of his inside pocket and passed it across the table. 'Here's his address.'

It was in Friedrichshain, hardly a normal stomping ground for high class Jewish doctors.

'He used to live in Lützow,' Conway explained. 'Now, of course, they're all hunkering down together in the poorest areas. Like medieval ghettos.'

The food arrived and they ate in silence for a couple of minutes, before exchanging news of their children and the German schools they were attending. Conway and his wife had also seen Effi's musical, and clearly wished they hadn't, though Conway was much too diplomatic to actually say so.

Over coffee Russell asked how the Embassy saw the next few months.

'Off the record?'

'Off the record.'

'We're on a knife-edge. If our moustachioed chum is happy with what he's got, then fine. The appeasers will say, "I told you so – he may be a nasty little shit, but he can be managed." But if he goes after more – Danzig or the Corridor or the rest of Czechoslovakia – then Churchill and his pals will be the ones saying, "I told you so." And there'll be a war.'

'Doug, how do you persuade the British people that the Czechs weren't worth fighting for, but the Poles are? The Czechs have a functioning democracy of sorts. The Poles would be just like this lot if they had any talent for organisation.'

Conway grimaced. 'That'll be up to the politicians. But I'll tell you what London's really worried about. If Hitler does behave for a few years, and if he keeps building tanks, U-boats and bombers at the current rate, then by '41 or '42 he'll be unstoppable. That's the real nightmare. As far as we're concerned – from a purely military point of view – the sooner the better.'

There was no telephone at the Wiesners' so Russell couldn't check on the convenience of his visit. But, as Conway had noted, the doctor didn't have much to go out for. No U-bahn had been built out into the working-class wastes of Friedrichshain, so Russell took a 13 tram from the Brandenburg Gate to Spittelmarkt and a 60 from there to Alexanderplatz and up Neue Konigstrasse. The city deteriorated with each passing kilometre, and by the time he reached his destination most of it seemed to be for sale. The sidewalk was lined with makeshift tables, all piled high with belongings that would-be Jewish emigrants were trying to shift. The complete works of Dickens in German were on sale for a few Reichsmarks, a fine-looking violin for only a little more.

The Wiesners' block made his own seem middle class. The street was cobbled, the walls plastered with advertisements for auctions and lists of items for sale. On the pavement a group of painfully-thin young girls were hopping their way through a game of Heaven and Earth on a chalk-marked grid. In the courtyard of the Wiesners' building the far wall still bore the faintest outline of a large hammer and sickle and the much-faded slogan ERST ESSEN, DANN MIET – first food, then rent.

The Wiesners shared two over-crowded rooms on the second floor. Contrary to Conway's expectation, the doctor was out. He was only attending to a neighbour, however, and the older of the two daughters was sent to fetch him, leaving Russell to exchange small talk with his wife and their younger daughter Ruth. Frau Wiesner, a small woman with tied-back blonde hair and tired grey eyes, looked anything but Jewish, while Ruth bore a striking resemblance to Effi, both physically and, Russell judged, temperamentally. Effi had often been mistaken for a Jew, and various employers had insisted she always carry the *fragebogen* which testified to her aryan descent. She, of course, liked nothing better than shoving the mistake back in people's faces.

Dr Wiesner appeared after a few minutes looking decidedly

harassed. His wife and two daughters abruptly withdrew to the next room and closed the door behind them.

He was about fifty, Russell guessed, and ageing fast. He ran a hand through his thinning hair, and got straight down to business – as Conway had said, he hoped to send his daughters away to relations in England. He was working on getting them visas and exit permits, and in the meantime he wanted them to learn English.

'I speak a little,' he said in that language, 'and I will try and help them, but they need a proper teacher.'

'I've taught around twenty German children,' Russell said.

Wiesner grunted. 'German children,' he repeated. 'I'm afraid my children are no longer considered German.'

Russell said nothing.

'You are wondering why we stayed,' Wiesner said. 'I ask myself the same thing every day and I have many answers, but none of them is worth anything. My wife is not Jewish,' he added, 'so my children are only half-Jewish, or *mischlings* as the Nazis call them, and perhaps I thought... Well, I was a fool.' He reached behind himself and plucked a piece of paper from a shelf-full of music. It was, of all things, a page of *Der Stürmer*. 'Listen to this,' the doctor said, adjusting his glasses on his nose and holding the page almost at arm's length. '"Even if a Jew slept with an Aryan woman once, the membranes of her vagina would be so impregnated with alien semen that the woman would never again be able to bear pure-blooded Aryans".' He lowered the paper and looked at Russell. 'Who could believe such pre-scientific nonsense? It doesn't even make sense on their own illiterate terms – surely the master race would have the all-powerful blood, not the people they despise.' He saw something in Russell's face. 'I'm sorry. I don't know why I am telling you all this. It's just so hard to accept.'

'I understand,' Russell said.

'So why do you, an Englishman, stay in Germany?' Wiesner asked him.

Russell gave a short account of his situation.

'That is difficult,' the doctor agreed. 'But good news for my daughters if you agree to teach them.'

'How many lessons do you have in mind?'

'As many as you can manage. And as often.'

'Three times a week? Monday, Wednesday, Friday? It'll have to vary a bit, though. I can't do Friday this week, but I could do Thursday.'

'Whatever you say. Now for the difficult part. I have some money, but not very much. And – here I must trust you – I have some valuable stamps. I can show you the valuation in the current catalogue and add another ten per cent. It was a generous offer, but Russell couldn't accept it. 'The catalogue value will suit me fine.'

It was almost dark when he emerged from the Wiesners' block, and the tram rides home through the evening rush hour seemed endless. By the time he reached Hallesches Tor he was ready for supper, and his favourite beerhouse beneath the elevated U-bahn provided the necessary meatballs and potato pancakes. Over a second beer he decided not to sell any of Wiesner's stamps unless he really needed to. He would give them to Paul, whose collection could do with some rarities.

Always assuming his son would accept them. Paul was forever worrying about his father's financial state – an anxiety which Russell occasionally, and without much conviction, tried to blame on his ex-wife Ilse.

He looked at his watch. He needed to get home to ring Paul before his bedtime. A U-bahn rattled into the station above as he emerged from the beerhouse, and a stream of people were soon pouring down the iron staircase, exhaling puffs of yellow gas in the cold evening air. It was one of those Berlin days when the weather seemed uncertain what to do, one minute veering towards a western warmth, the next favouring an eastern chill.

As he turned into his street Russell noticed what looked like an empty car parked across from his apartment block. This was unusual – very few people in the area could afford one. He thought about crossing the street to take a look inside, and decided he was being paranoid. He hadn't done anything to upset the authorities. Not yet, anyway.

A blast of hot air greeted him as he opened the outside doors of the apartment block. Frau Heidegger's skat evening was in full swing, the volume of laughter suggesting a large consignment of empty bottles for the morning collection. Russell dialled the number of the house in Grünewald, then put the earpiece to one ear and a finger in the other. As he half-expected, Ilse picked up. They asked each other the usual questions, gave each other the usual answers, all with that faint awkwardness which they never seemed able to shake. The family had just got back from Hanover, and when Paul came on he was full of the wonders of the autobahn and his stepfather's new Horch. As far as Saturday was concerned, his usual school lessons had been replaced by *Jungvolk* meetings, and these ran on until one o'clock. 'Muti says you can pick me up then.'

'Right.' Effi would be pleased, Russell thought. He wouldn't have to leave while she was still fast asleep.

'And we're still going to the Viktoria match?'

'Of course. I expect Uncle Thomas and Joachim will come as well.'

They chatted for another couple of minutes, before Ilse's voice in the background decreed that time was up. Feeling the usual mixture of elation and frustration, Russell started up the stairs.

He was waylaid on the third floor landing by the other resident journalist, a young American named Tyler McKinley. 'I thought I heard your weary tread,' the American said in English. 'Come in for a minute. I want to ask you something.'

It seemed simpler to say yes than no. McKinley's room wasn't particularly hot – like the other residents he took advantage of skat night to freshen the air – but it was full of pipe-smoke from the atrocious Balkan mixture he had adopted during a weekend trip to Trieste.

'How was Danzig?' his host asked, though Russell could see he was bursting with stuff of his own. There was something lovable about McKinley, but also something profoundly irritating. Russell hoped that this wasn't just because McKinley, with his quasi-religious belief in crusading journalism, reminded him of himself in long gone days. That was the trouble with the young – their stupidities brought back one's own.

'Interesting,' he answered, though it had been anything but in the way that McKinley meant. He considered telling him about the stamp wars, but could imagine the look of incomprehension and vague derision which that would elicit.

The younger man was already back in Berlin. 'I'm chasing a really interesting story,' he said. 'I don't want to say anything yet,' he added quickly, 'but... do you know anything about the KdF, the *Kanzlei des Führers*.'

'It's the great man's private chancellery.'

'Is it a government office?'

'No, it's a Party office, but an independent one. There's no connection to Bormann's bunch in Munich.'

McKinley was visibly excited. 'So who is it connected to?'

Russell shrugged. 'Nobody. It reports directly to Hitler as far as I know.'

'So if he wanted to do something on the quiet, it would be the ideal instrument.'

'Uh-huh.'

McKinley beamed, as if he'd just awarded himself a gold star.

'You want to tell me what you're talking about?' Russell asked, interested in spite of himself.

'Not yet,' the American said, but he couldn't resist one more question. 'Does the name Knauer mean anything to you?'

'A full back with Tennis Borussia a few years back?'

'What? Oh, a soccer player. No, I don't think so.' He reached for a lighter to re-start his pipe. 'But thanks for your help.'

'You're welcome,' Russell said, opening the door to leave. His room at the top of the building was sweltering, but mercifully smoke-free. Guessing that the skat game still had a couple of hours to run, he threw one window wide open and gazed out across the rooftops. In the far distance the red light atop the Funkturm winked above the roofscape.

He sat down at the typewriter, inserted a sheet of paper, and reminded himself that the letter he was about to write was – as far as the Soviets were concerned – just a long-winded way of saying yes. His real audience was the Gestapo.

Play the innocent, he thought. The Gestapo would think he was trying to fool the Soviets, and assume he was just being cynical.

He began by asserting the happy coincidence that National Socialism and the Union of Soviet Socialist Republics had one crucial word in common – socialism. That should give them both a laugh, he thought. They might seem like enemies, he continued, but clearly they had something important in common – socialism's determination to serve all the people. What could serve the people better than peace? And what served peace better than mutual understanding? If the Soviet people were offered, in a series of articles, a clearer idea of how much National Socialism had achieved for ordinary German people, then the chances of peace were bound to be enhanced. As an Englishman with a long experience of Germany, he was ideally placed to explain it to foreigners. And he had a strong personal reason for desiring peace – if war came, he added pathetically, he and his German-born son might be separated for years and years. 'Here I am,' he murmured to himself, 'a propaganda tool for the taking.' The Gestapo would lap it up.

He copied the address from Shchepkin's note onto an envelope, unearthed a stamp from the table drawer, and perched the completed missive on his typewriter. Hearing the sounds of departing concierges floating up from the courtyard he made a dive for the window and pulled it shut.

Bed, he thought. The bathroom on the floor below which he shared with McKinley and two other men – a stationery rep from Hamburg and a waiter from the Harz Mountains – was empty for once, though the lingering odour of McKinley's pipe smoke suggested a lengthy occupation earlier that evening. There was still a crack of light under the American's door, and Russell could hear the soft clicking of his typewriter – the newer machines were much quieter than his own antique.

In bed, he re-read Paul's postcard and resumed reading the detective novel he had forgotten to take to Danzig. Unable to remember who anyone was, he turned out the light and listened to the muffled hum of the traffic on nearby Lindenstrasse. The Führer was probably allowed to sleep with his windows open.

The next day was Wednesday, and he made the long trek out to Friedrichshain for his first session with the Wiesner girls. The elder daughter Marthe was a bit shy at first, but Ruth's enthusiasm proved infectious enough to bring her out. The two of them knew very little English, but they were a joy to teach, eager to learn and markedly more intelligent than the spoilt daughters of suburban Grünewald and Wilmersdorf whom Russell had taught in the past.

On Thursday, though, both girls looked as though they'd seen a ghost, and Russell wondered whether they'd had bad news about their brother in Sachsenhausen. When he asked if they were all right, he thought Marthe was going to cry, but she took a visible grip on herself and explained that her brother had come home the previous evening.

'But that's wonderful…' Russell began.

'He doesn't seem like Albert,' Ruth broke in, looking over her shoulder at the door through to the other rooms. 'He has no hair, and he doesn't say anything,' she whispered.

'He will,' Marthe told her sister, putting an arm round her. 'He's just seen some terrible things, but he hasn't been hurt, not really. Now come on, we have to learn English. For everyone's sake.'

And they did, faster than any pupils Russell could remember. Neither mother nor brother emerged from the other rooms, and Doctor Wiesner was out on both days. On the Thursday he left Russell three stamps in an envelope on top of the latest Stanley Gibbons catalogue from England. Russell didn't bother to check the listings.

When he got back to Neuenburgerstrasse a telegram had arrived from his London agent, pointing out the need for exclusive photographs with his projected piece on Hitler's new Chancellery. After a quick lunch Russell dragged himself out to a photographic studio in the wilds of Neukölln, only to discover that the photographer in question, a Silesian named Zembski whom he'd used in the past, had just lost his official accreditation after starting a brawl at one of Goering's hunting parties. Zembski weighed over two hundred pounds, and could hardly be smuggled into the Führer's new insult to architecture, but he did prove willing to rent out one of his better cameras. After a short instruction course Russell carried the Leica back to Hallesches Tor.

Frau Heidegger was waiting for him – or anyone – in the lobby. Her husband had been killed in the last war – 'You might have been the one who shot him,' as she frequently told Russell – and his brother had just been round to see her, full of frightening information about the next one. She had assumed it would take place at some distance from her door, but this illusion had just been cruelly shattered. 'Cities will be bombed flat,' her brother-in-law had told her. 'Flat as ironing boards.'

Russell told her that, yes, English or French or Russian bombers could now reach Berlin, but that most of them would be shot down if they tried, because air defences were improving all the time. She didn't look convinced, but then neither was he. How many Europeans, he wondered, had any idea what kind of war they were headed for?

Friday morning was sunny and cold. After a late breakfast of rolls and coffee at a local café, Russell walked west along the Landwehrkanal. He wasn't due to meet Effi for a couple of hours, so he took his time, stopping to read his morning paper on a bench near the double-decker bridges which carried the U-bahn and Reichsbahn lines over the torpid brown water. Coal-laden barges chugged by, leaving thin trails of oil in their wake.

He walked along the footpath for another kilometre or so, leaving the canal where it passed under Potsdamerstrasse. Almost exactly twenty years earlier, the bodies of Rosa Luxemburg and Karl Liebknecht had been fished out of the waters close to this spot, and the empty site on the other side of the road had been home to a synagogue until the previous November. Rosa, of course, had been everything the Nazis despised – a Jew, a communist, a woman who refused to stay home and rear children. Russell was surprised that no official celebration had been decreed for the anniversary of her death.

Cutting through side streets, he eventually reached the domed U-bahn station at Nollerndorfplatz, and started walking up Kleist-strasse towards the distant spires of the Kaiser Memorial church.

As the U-bahn tracks beside him slid slowly underground, the shops grew progressively larger and richer, the awnings of the pavement cafés more decorative. Despite the cold, most of the outside seats were occupied; men and women sat in their overcoats, or tightly wrapped in large blankets, chewing their cream cakes and sipping at their steaming coffees.

Both sidewalks and road were crowded now. Shoppers streamed in and out of the Ka-De-We department store on Wittenbergplatz; cars and trams ran bumper to bumper along the narrower Tauenzienstrasse, jostling each other round the neo-Gothic pile of the Memorial Church, with its distressingly secular mosaics celebrating the highly dubious glories of past German emperors. Walking past it, and thinking about his conversation with Frau Heidegger, Russell had a sudden vision of jagged spires looming out of a broken roof, a future Berlin pre-figured in his memories of northern France.

He started up the busy Kurfürstendamm, or the Ku'damm, as everyone called it. The Uhlandeck Café, where he was due to meet Effi, was a ten minute stroll away, and he still had half an hour to spare. An African parrot in a pet shop caught his attention – it was the sort of birthday present Effi would love, but he doubted her ability to look after it properly. For one thing she was away too often; for another, she was Effi.

A woman in a fur coat emerged from the shop with two pedigree schnausers in tow. Both had enamel swastikas fastened to their collars, and Russell wondered whether they had pictures of the Führer pinned up inside their kennels. Would that be considered a sign of respect, or the lack of it? Political etiquette in the Third Reich was something of a minefield.

He passed the 'aryanised' Grunfeld factory, and the site of another destroyed synagogue. A photographic album of such sites could, he thought, be a best-seller in Nazi Germany. *Judenfrei: the photographic record.* Page after page of burnt synagogues, followed by 'then and now' pictures of aryanised firms. A foreword by the Führer, which would probably turn out to be longer than the book. The lucky author would probably get invitations to Goering's hunting weekends and Streicher's whipping orgies.

Russell stopped and watched a tram cross the intersection, bell clanging. Why was he feeling so angry this morning? Was it the *kindertransport* and the Wiesner girls? Or just six years of accumulated disgust? Whatever it was it served no purpose.

Reaching the Café Uhlandeck he sat at one of the outside tables and stared back down the Ku'damm in search of Effi's familiar silhouette. He had met her a few days before Christmas 1933, while researching a piece on Leni Riefenstahl for a Hollywood gossip magazine. At a studio party someone had pointed out a slim, black-haired woman in her late twenties, told Russell that her name was Effi Koenen, and that she had appeared alongside Riefenstahl before the actress had turned director.

Effi's part in that film, as she'd been only too happy to inform him, had consisted of 'five lines, two smiles, one pout and a dignified exit.' She had thought Riefenstahl a good actress, but had hated Triumph of the Will for its humourlessness. Russell had asked her out to dinner, and rather to his astonishment she had accepted. They had got on wonderfully – in the restaurant, on the half-drunken walk home to her flat, in her large soft bed. Five years later, they still did.

Effi's flat was a couple of blocks north of the Ku'damm, a three room affair which her wealthy parents had bought in the early 1920s from a victim of the Great Inflation, and given to her as a twenty-fifth birthday present. Her acting career had been moderately successful – a film here, a play there, a musical if nothing else was on offer – without making her rich or particularly famous. She was occasionally recognised on the street when Russell was with her, and almost always for the part she had played in a 1934 film, the wife of a stormtrooper beaten to death by communists. That had been a 'seventeen line, one smile, one scream, dignified-at-funeral' part.

She was currently appearing in *Barbarossa*, a musical biography of the twelfth century Holy Roman Emperor, Frederick I. As one of his generals' wives, she sang part of the joyous send-off when they left for the Crusades, and part of the lament for those who failed to come home. Like most of the cast, she wasn't much of a singer, but no one had bothered to include musical ability, a decent script or memorable songs in the production. It was, as one of the early Berlin reviews put it, 'a hymn to national consciousness.'

Much to Effi's disgust it had pulled in large audiences, both in Berlin during the weeks leading up to Christmas and across the Reich during the holiday season itself. A second season in Berlin was beginning that night and Effi expected the seats to be full again – 'All those who couldn't believe how bad it was the first time will be coming back to make sure.'

Russell hadn't seen her for almost a fortnight, which seemed a long time. They generally spent as much of the weekend together as their – mostly her – work allowed, along with at least one

- 43 -

night in midweek and an unpredictable number of lunches and afternoons. She was fond of saying that her three-year marriage to a now-famous actor had left her with a love of living alone, and had never suggested that Russell move in with her. He told himself and everyone else that he was happy, more than happy, with their days and nights together, and happy to spend the other days and nights without her. And most of the time he believed it. Just occasionally he found himself thinking that love was a full-time occupation, and that loving someone was resenting each hour apart. He did love Effi, from her long raven hair to her small brown toes. He loved everything about her, he thought, looking at his watch, except for her complete inability to arrive anywhere on time.

It was 12.25 when she finally appeared. She was wearing the black overcoat that almost reached her ankles, a new crimson scarf wrapped around her neck, chin and mouth, and the Russian fur hat she had bought in Moscow ten years before. Yet even trussed up like a mummy she turned the heads of male passers-by. 'I've got a cold,' was the first thing she said once they'd embraced. 'I need soup.'

Russell suggested going inside, but she refused. 'Fresh air's the best thing for colds,' she insisted.

He bought them bowls of soup and watched as she gulped hers down. 'We got in at four in the morning,' she said between spoonfuls, 'and we've got to be in early this evening to discuss some changes the musical director has in mind.'

'A new score?' Russell asked.

'If only. It'll be nothing. He just has to justify the fact that he's still being paid.' She started tearing up a roll and dropping it in the soup. 'You'll pick me up after the show?'

'Of course. I'll come and watch the last half hour if they'll let me in. Is it the same man on the door?'

'I don't know. But I'll make sure they know you're coming.' She spooned a chunk of sodden bread into her mouth. 'This is good. I feel better already. How have you been? How's Paul?'

'Haven't seen him yet. But he sounds all right.'

'Danzig?'

'Suitably gloomy,' he said. He told her about the stamp wars, which made her laugh, and the Soviet request for articles, which drew a raised eyebrow. 'It's just work,' he said. There didn't seem any point in mentioning the oral reports, or in spoiling their reunion with an account of the *kindertransport* and his day in jail.

She stole the last of his roll to soak up the last of her soup. 'I feel much better,' she said again. 'And I've still got three hours before I have to be at the theatre,' she said, reaching out a slender hand for his. 'Shall we go back to the flat?'

Later that evening, Russell arrived backstage in time to hear the lament for the fallen heroes. It seemed more Wagnerian than ever, and he realised that the musical director had decided to apply the Third Reich's guiding principle – never speak when you can shout. The military widows now had an entire choir of breast-swelling Valkyries to augment their lamentations. The front rows of the audience looked suitably stunned.

After the show, Russell talked football with the stage-door-keeper while he waited for Effi. She emerged after half an hour or so, still snuffling, but full of post-performance energy. It was clear and cold outside, the sidewalks crowded with people. They walked arm in arm past the entrance to the Aquarium, and along the southern side of the Zoo towards the glowing glasshouse which straddled the elevated lines at Zoo Station. The station buffet was packed, but they managed to find a couple of free stools and order a nightcap. This was the last place in Berlin where Jews could still buy a coffee, but there were no obvious Jewish faces. The city by night was an aryan preserve.

As they left the buffet an international express steamed out across Hardenbergstrasse, rumbling the girders of the bridge and pumping bursts of white smoke towards the stars. Russell found himself wishing, if only for a moment, that he and Effi were two of the silhouettes in the necklace of illuminated windows, headed for another life in Amsterdam or Paris or New York, anywhere, in fact, beyond Hitler's rancid realm.

It was almost one when they got back to the flat. Their lovemaking that afternoon had been almost frenzied, but now they took it slowly, luxuriously, taking each other to the brink again and again before finally, joyously, tumbling over it together. Wrapped in his arms, Effi went to sleep almost immediately, but Russell's brain refused to let him be. He had not been angry with the Nazis that morning, he realised. He had been angry with himself. Angry at his own helplessness. Angry that all he could manage were fantasies of escape.

It suddenly occurred to him that his imaginary book of photographs might make a real impact abroad. Especially in America, where the Jewish organisations had some political clout. He could get pictures of old Jewish businesses and synagogues from press libraries and shoot the ruins himself with Zembski's camera. Getting it out of the country would be a problem, but he'd worry about that – and ensuring his own anonymity – when the time came. And if anyone noticed him taking pictures of burnt-out synagogues he could say he was compiling the record of anti-Semitic triumphs he had originally envisaged. He smiled to himself in the dark.

Next morning they walked to their usual café in the Tiergarten for milky coffee and rolls. The winter sun was already high in the south-eastern sky, and as they strolled back along the northern bank of the Landwehrkanal it seemed as if most of Berlin had had the same idea. Effi had arranged to meet her older sister Zarah for lunch, something she often did when Russell was seeing his son. He had never really liked Zarah, who had none of Effi's fitful ability to look beyond herself, and had married an ambitious Nazi civil servant. Soon after Russell met Effi, she had asked for his help in arranging an abortion for Zarah in England. Zarah had travelled to London, decided at the last moment she couldn't go through with it, and had eventually given birth to a boy. Much to everyone's surprise, she had doted on the child from day one. Much to Russell's annoyance, she blamed him for the fact that she had nearly had an abortion.

After he and Effi parted, Russell caught a 76 tram outside the Zoo for Grünewald, and watched the houses grow bigger as it worked its way past Halensee and into Berlin's prosperous south-western suburbs. Paul's school was a five minute walk from the tram terminus, and just down the road from the large tree-shrouded villa which his stepfather Matthias Gehrts had inherited from his father. Both school and villa backed onto one of the small lakes which dotted the area, and sitting on the low wall beside the school gates Russell had occasional glimpses of sailboats between buildings.

A couple of women arrived on foot to pick up their sons, but his fellow dads all arrived in cars, and stood around discussing the reliability of their mechanics.

The *Jungvolk* appeared soon after one, buttoning their overcoats over their uniforms as they walked to the gate. Paul half-ran to greet him, a big smile on his face.

'So where shall we go today?' Russell asked.

'The Funkturm.'

'Again?' They had visited Berlin's radio tower at least half a dozen times in 1938.

'I like it there.'

'Okay. Let's get a tram then. Do you want me to carry that?' he asked, indicating the large book his son was holding.

'We'll take turns,' Paul decided.

'What is it?' Russell asked.

'It's the Yearbook,' Paul said, holding it out.

The Hitler Youth Yearbook, Russell realised, as he skimmed through the pages. There were five hundred of them. 'So what did you do today?'

'The same as usual to begin with. Roll-call and gymnastics and then the history lesson – that was all about Germania and the Romans and how most history people get it wrong about them. They think the Romans were civilised and the Germans were barbarians, but in fact it was the other way round – the Romans got mixed up with other races and got soft and lazy and forgot how to fight but the Germans stayed German and that made them strong.' They reached the tram stop just as a tram squealed to a halt. 'And after the history lesson,' Paul went on, once they were in their seats, 'we did some work on the map wall – remember? – we're doing a whole wall of maps of Germany from the beginning to now. It's beginning to look really good.' He looked out of the window. 'There's a shop down here that sells model soldiers, and they've got the new set of dead ones. Someone at school brought them in. They're really real.'

They would be, Russell thought. Death and toys, the German specialities.

'If they'd come out before Christmas, I'd have them now,' Paul said wistfully.

They reached Halensee Station and climbed down the steps

to the Ringbahn platform. 'And then we had a talk from this old man,' Paul said, as they watched an electric train pull away from the opposite platform and accelerate down the cutting. 'Quite old, anyway – he was much more than forty. He came to talk about the last war and what it was like. He said there weren't many aeroplanes or tanks, and there was lots of hand–to–hand fighting – is that true?'

'There was some. Depends what he meant by lots.'

'I think he meant it was happening all the time.' Paul looked up at Russell. 'I didn't believe a lot of the things he said. I mean, he said that the best thing a soldier could do was to die for his country. And one of the boys in the back asked him if he was sorry that he hadn't died, and the man didn't reply. The boy was told to report to the leader's room after the talk, and he looked pretty sick when he came out.'

'Did they give him a whacking?'

'No, I think they just shouted at him. He wasn't trying to be clever – he's just a bit stupid.'

Their train pulled in, and Paul spent the single stop ride staring out of the window at the skeletal Funkturm rising out of the tangle of railways. Erected in 1926, it looked like a smaller version of the Eiffel Tower, which probably galled the Nazis no end. 'The lift's going up,' Paul said, and they watched it climb towards the viewing platform 126 metres above the ground.

Fifteen minutes later they were waiting at the bottom for their own ride. One lift carried them to the restaurant level, 55 metres up, another to the circular walkway with its panoramic view of the city. The viewing platform was crowded, children queuing to use the coin-operated binoculars. Russell and his son worked their way slowly round, gazing out beyond the borders of the city at the forests and lakes in the south-west, the plains in the north and east.

The Olympic Stadium loomed close by to the west, and Berlin's two other high buildings – the office tower of the Borsig locomotive works and the futuristic Shellhaus – both seemed closer than usual in the clear air. As tradition demanded, once Paul got his hands on the binoculars he turned them towards the northern suburb of Gesundbrunnen, where Hertha's flag was fluttering above the roof of the Plumpe's solitary grandstand. 'Ha! Ho! He! Hertha BSC!' he chanted underneath his breath.

In the restaurant below they both ordered macaroni, ham and cheese, washed down, in Paul's case, with a bottle of Coca Cola.

'Would you like to see New York?' Russell asked, following a thread of thought that had begun on the viewing platform.

'Oh yes!' Paul exclaimed. 'It must be fantastic. The Empire State Building is more than three times as high as this, and it has a viewing platform right near the top.'

'We could stay with your grandmother.'

'When?'

'Not for a few years yet. When you finish school, maybe.'

Paul's face fell. 'There'll be a war before then.'

'Who says so?'

Paul looked at him with disbelief. 'Everybody does.'

'Sometimes everybody's wrong.'

'Yes, but...' He blew into his straw, making the Coke bubble and fizz. 'Dad,' he began again, then stopped.

'What?'

'When you were in the war, did you want to die for England?'

'No, I didn't.' Russell was suddenly conscious of the people at the tables nearby. This was not a conversation to have in public.

'Did you want to fight at all?'

'Let's go back up top,' Russell suggested.

'Okay,' Paul agreed, but only after he'd given Russell one of those looks which suggested he should try harder at being a normal father.

They took the lift once more, and found an empty stretch of railing on the less popular side, facing away from the city. Down to their left an S-bahn train was pulling out of the Olympic Stadium station.

'I didn't want to fight,' Russell began, after pausing to marshal his thoughts. 'I didn't volunteer – I was conscripted. I could have refused, and probably gone to prison instead, but I wasn't certain enough about my feelings to do that. I thought maybe I was just afraid, and that I was hiding behind my opinions. But once I got to the trenches it was different. There were a few idiots who still believed in death and glory, but most of us knew that we'd been conned. All the governments were telling their soldiers that they had God and right on their side, and that dying for their country was the least they could do, but – well, think about it – what does it mean, dying for your country? What exactly is your country? The buildings and the grass and the trees? The people? The way of life? People say you should love your country, and be proud of it, and there are usually things to love and be proud of. But there are usually things to dislike as well, and every country has things to be ashamed of. So what does dying for your country achieve? Nothing, as far as I could see. Living for your country, you get the chance to make it better.' He looked at his son, whose expression was almost fierce.

'Our leader says that people who don't want to fight are cowards.'

'I expect some of them are. But… you remember the Boer War in South Africa, between the English and the Boers? Well, the Indian nationalist leader Gandhi, he was a leader of the Indians in South Africa then, and he refused to fight. Instead he organised medical teams which helped the wounded on the battlefield. He and his people were always in the thick of the action, and lots of them were killed. They wouldn't fight, but they were about as far from cowards as you can get.'

Paul looked thoughtful.

'But I shouldn't say anything like that at a *Jungvolk* meeting,' Russell went on, suddenly conscious of the Yearbook he was carrying. 'You'd just get yourself in trouble. Think about things, and decide what you think is right, but keep it to yourself, or the family at least. These are dangerous times we're living in, and a lot of people are frightened of people who don't think like they do. And frightened people tend to lash out.'

'But if you know something's wrong, isn't it cowardly to just keep quiet?'

This was what Russell was afraid of. How could you protect children from the general idiocy without putting them at risk? 'It can be,' he said carefully, 'but there's not much point picking a fight if you know you're bound to lose. Better to wait until you have some chance of winning. The important thing is not to lose sight of what is right and what is wrong. You may not be able to do anything about it at the time, but nothing lasts for ever. You'll get a chance eventually.'

Paul gave him a grown-up look, as if he knew full well that his father was talking as much about himself as his son.

After taking Paul home, Russell took the long tram ride back down Ku'damm, spent a couple of hours over dinner in a bar, and then went in search of a movie to watch. The new U-boat drama was showing at the Alhambra, a Zara Leander weepie at the Ufa Palast, and an American Western at the Universum. He chose the last, and reached his seat just as the weekly newsreel was getting started. A rather beautiful piece on Christmas markets in the Rhineland was followed by lots of thunderous marching and a German volleyball triumph in Romania. Suitably lifted, the audience noisily enjoyed the Western, which almost made up in spectacle what it lacked in every other department.

Effi's audience had gone home by the time he reached the theatre on Nurnbergstrasse, and he only had to wait a few minutes for her to emerge from the dressing rooms. She had forgotten to eat anything between the matinee and evening shows, and was starving. They walked to a new bar on the Ku'damm which one of the new Valkyries had told her served the most incredible omelettes.

They were indeed, but the male clientele, most of whom seemed to be in uniform, left a lot to be desired. Four SS men took a neighbouring table soon after their food arrived, and grew increasingly vocal with each round of schnapps. Russell could almost feel their need for a target take shape.

Effi was telling him about her sister Zarah's latest neurosis – she was increasingly worried that her infant son was a slow learner – when the first comments were directed at their table. One of the SS men had noticed Effi's Jewish looks, and loudly remarked on the fact to his companions. He was only about twenty, Russell thought, and when he succeeded in catching the young man's eye, had the brief satisfaction of seeing a hint of shame in the way he quickly looked away.

By this time Effi was rifling through her purse. Finding what she was looking for, she stood up, advanced on the SS table and held the *fragebogen* up to them, rather in the manner of a schoolteacher lecturing a bunch of particularly obtuse children. 'See this, you morons,' she said, loud enough for the whole bar to hear. 'Aryan descent, all the way back to Luther's time. Satisfied?'

The manager was already at her shoulder. 'Fraulein, please…' he began.

'I want these drunken pigs thrown out,' she told him.

The oldest of the SS men was also on his feet. 'I would advise you to be careful, Fraulein,' he said. 'You may not be a Jew, but that does not give you the right to insult members of the Führer's bodyguard.'

Effi ignored him. 'Are you going to throw these pigs out?' she asked the manager.

He looked mortified. 'I…'

'Very well. You won't get any more business from me. Or any of my friends. I hope,' she concluded with one last contemptuous glance at the SS, 'that you can make a living selling swill to these pigs.'

She headed for the door, as Russell, half-amused and half-fearful, counted out a few marks for their meal and listened to the SS men argue about whether to arrest her. When one of them took a step towards the door he blocked the way. 'You did call her a Jew,' he said mildly, looking straight at the oldest man. 'Surely you can understand how upsetting that might be. She meant no disrespect.'

The man gave him a slight bow of the head. 'She would do well to control her anger a little better,' he said coldly.

'She would,' Russell agreed. 'Have a good evening,' he added, and turned towards the door.

Outside he found Effi shaking with laughter, though whether from humour or hysteria he wasn't quite sure. He put an arm around her shoulder and waited for the shaking to stop. 'Let's go home.'

'Let's,' she agreed.

They crossed the busy avenue and headed up one of the side streets.

'Sometimes I wish I was a Jew,' she said. 'If the Nazis hate them that much, they must be real human beings.'

Russell grunted his agreement. 'I heard a joke the other day,' he said. 'Hitler goes rowing on the Wannsee, but he's not very good at it, and manages to overturn the boat. A boy in a passing boat manages to haul him out and save him from drowning. Hitler, as you can imagine, is overcome with gratitude and promises the boy whatever he wants. The boy thinks for a moment, and asks for a state funeral. Hitler says, "You're a bit young for that, aren't you?" The boy says, "Oh, mein Führer, when I tell my dad I've saved you from drowning he's going to kill me!".'

Effi started laughing again, and he did too. For what seemed like minutes they stood on the sidewalk, embracing like lovers, shaking with mirth.

Next afternoon Thomas and Joachim were waiting in the usual place, sitting on a low wall with cartons of half-consumed frankfurters and *kartoffelsalat* between them. Russell bought the same for himself and Paul.

Once inside the Plumpe they headed for their usual spot, opposite the edge of the penalty area, halfway up the terrace on the western side. As their two sons read each other's magazines, Russell and Thomas sat themselves down on the concrete step and chatted. 'How's business?' Russell asked.

'It's good,' Thomas said, unbuttoning his overcoat. He'd been running the family paper business since his and Ilse's father died a few years earlier. 'It's getting harder to find experienced staff, but other than that...' He shrugged. 'There's no lack of orders. How about you?'

'Not too bad. I've got the opening of the new Chancellery tomorrow, and there should be a decent piece in that – the Americans like that sort of thing.'

'Well that's good. How about Danzig? Did you get anything there?'

'Not really.' Russell explained about the stamp wars.

Thomas rolled his eyes in frustration. 'Like children,' he muttered. 'Speaking of which, Joachim's been called up for his *arbeitsdienst*.'

'When?'

'The beginning of March.'

Russell looked up at Joachim, engrossed in his magazine. 'Ah,' he said, glad that Paul was still six years away from the year of drilling, draining swamps and digging roads which the Nazis imposed on all seventeen-year-old boys. 'How does he feel about it?'

'Oh, he can't wait,' Thomas said, glancing affectionately up at his son. 'I suppose it can't do him any harm. Unlike what'll probably follow.'

Russell knew what he meant. When they'd first become friends almost ten years ago, he and Thomas had talked a lot about their experiences in the war. Both had friends who'd survived the war in body, yet never recovered their peace of mind. And both knew that they themselves had been changed in ways that they would never fully understand. And that they had been the lucky ones.

'Happy days,' Russell murmured, and then laughed. 'We had a run-in with the SS last night,' he said, and told Thomas the story.

He wasn't as amused as Russell had expected. 'She'll go too far one of these days. The *fragebogen*'s just a piece of paper, after all. One day they'll take her in, tear it up, and the next thing you know her parents will be getting a bill for her burial.' He shook his head. 'Being right doesn't count anymore.'

'I know,' Russell said. 'She knows. But she does it so well.'

A chorus of catcalls erupted around them – Viktoria Berlin were on their way out. As the two men got to their feet, Hertha emerged to a more affectionate welcome. Casting his eyes over the towering grandstand and the high crowded terraces behind each goal, Russell felt the usual surge of excitement. Glancing to his left, he saw Paul's eyes mirror his own.

The first half was all Hertha, but Viktoria scored the only goal in a breakaway just before the interval. Joachim seethed with indignation, while Paul yo-yoed between hope and anxiety. Thomas smoked two cigarettes.

The second half followed the same pattern, and there were only ten minutes left when Hertha's inside-left was tripped in the penalty area. He took the penalty himself. The ball hit both posts before going in, leaving the crowd in hysterics. Then, a minute from time, with evening falling and the light swiftly fading, Hertha's centre-forward raced onto a long bouncing ball and volleyed it home from almost thirty yards. The Viktoria goalkeeper hadn't moved. As the stadium exploded with joy he just stood there, making angry gestures at his team-mates, the referee, the rest of the world.

Paul was ecstatic. Eyes shining, he joined in the chant now echoing round the ground – 'Ha! Ho! He! Hertha BSC! Ha! Ho! He! Hertha BSC!'

For an eleven-year-old, Russell thought fondly, this was as good as it gets.

It was dark by the time he dropped Paul off. He took a 76 back into town, ate supper at a beer restaurant just off the Potsdamerplatz, and walked the last kilometre home. Reaching his street, he noticed what looked like the same empty car parked across from his apartment block. He was on his way to investigate it when he heard the scream.

It was no ordinary scream. It was loud, lingering, and somehow managed to encompass surprise, terror and appalling pain. For a brief instant, Russell was back in the trenches, listening to someone who'd just lost a limb to a shell.

It came from further down the street.

He hesitated, but only long enough for his brain to register his hesitation as an essential corollary of living in Nazi Germany. All too often, screams meant officialdom, and experience suggested that officialdom was best avoided at such moments.

Still, investigating a scream of agony seemed legitimate behaviour, even in Nazi Germany. Not all crimes were committed by the state or its supporters. Russell walked resolutely on past the courtyard which his block shared with its neighbour, telling himself that valour was the better part of discretion.

The source of the disturbance was the further of the two blocks off the next courtyard. A couple of men were hovering in the entrance, obviously uncertain what to do. They eyed Russell nervously, and just looked at each other when he asked them what was going on. Both were in their forties, and an obvious facial similarity suggested brothers.

In the courtyard beyond, an open-backed lorry was parked with its engine running, and a single man in an SA uniform was walking towards them.

'Keep moving,' he told them, without any real conviction. His breath stank of beer.

'But we live here,' one of the two men said.

'Just wait there then,' the storm trooper said, looking up at the illuminated windows on the third floor. 'You might get some free entertainment,' he added over his shoulder as he walked back towards the lorry.

Seconds later, another blood-curdling scream reverberated round the courtyard.

'What in God's name...' Russell began. 'Who lives up there?' he asked the two men.

'Two actors,' the older of the two replied.

'*Warmer brüder*,' the other added, using the current slang for homosexuals. 'They've been brazen as hell. Someone must have denounced them.' He didn't sound too upset about it.

No other lights were showing in either block, but Russell could almost feel the silent audience watching from behind the tiers of darkened windows. He thought about calling the police, but knew there was no point.

One of the illuminated windows was suddenly flung open, and a man was silhouetted against the opening, looking out and down. A crying, whimpering sound was now audible, and just as the man disappeared another scream split the night, even more piercing than the last. There was a flurry of movement inside the lighted room, and suddenly a naked body was flying out through the window, dropping, screaming, hitting the floor of the courtyard with a sickening, silencing thud. The body twitched once and lay still, as desperate, sobbing pleas of 'no,please,no' leaked out of the open window. Another flurry, another naked body, this one twisting in flight like an Olympic diver who'd mistaken concrete for water. here was no twitch this time, no last-second adjustment to death.

The two bodies lay a couple of feet apart, in the thin pool of light thrown by the block's entrance lamp. One man was face down, the other face up, with only a glistening mess where his genitals had been.

With a shock, Russell recognised the man's face. He'd seen him – talked to him even – at one of Effi's theatrical gatherings. He had no memory of the man's name, but he'd been nice enough. With a passion for Hollywood movies, Russell remembered. Katherine Hepburn in particular.

'Show's over,' the SA man was saying loudly. 'You saw it. They must have cut each other's pricks off before they jumped.' He laughed. 'You can go in now,' he added.

Russell's two companions looked to be in shock. One started to say something, but no sound emerged, and the other just gave him a gentle push on the shoulder. They walked towards their door, drawing a wide circle around the two corpses.

'And you?,' the SA man shouted at Russell.

'I was just passing,' he said automatically.

'Then keep moving,' the SA man ordered.

Russell obediently turned and walked away, his eyes still full of the mutilated bodies. The bile in his stomach wouldn't stay down. Supporting himself against a lamp post he retched his supper into the gutter, then leaned against a wall, brain swirling with the usual useless rage. Another crime that would never be punished, another story that begged to be told.

And would he risk losing his son to tell it? No, he wouldn't.

And was he ashamed of his silence? Yes, he was.

He levered himself off the wall and walked slowly on towards his own courtyard and block. As he reached the entrance he remembered the empty car. It was gone.

As usual, Frau Heidegger seemed to be waiting for him. 'What was all that noise about?' she asked, then noticved his face. 'Herr Russell, you look like you've seen a ghost!'

'The SA came for a couple of homosexuals in the next block,' he said. There seemed no point in giving her the gory details.

'Oh,' she said, shaking her head in involuntary denial. 'I know the men you mean. They… well… it's not our business, is it?' She ducked back inside her door and re-emerged with two envelopes, only one of which was stamped. 'These came for you this morning,' she said. 'A policeman delivered the one in the plain envelope.'

He opened the stamped one first. It was a reply from the Soviet press attaché, reiterating the terms of Shchepkin's original offer.

He opened the other, conscious of Frau Heidegger's interest. The Gestapo wanted to see him. Within three days.

'They just want a chat,' he reassured her. 'Something to do with my accreditation, I expect.'

'Ah,' she said, sounding less than completely convinced.

Russell shared her misgivings. As he climbed the stairs, he told himself there was nothing to worry about. They'd read his letter to the Soviets, and just wanted to clarify his intentions. If it was anything else, they wouldn't be delivering invitations and letting him pick the day – they'd be throwing him out of the window.

A frisson of fear shot across his chest, and his legs felt strangely unsteady. Suddenly the photographic book seemed like a very bad idea.

'Ha ho bloody he,' he muttered to himself.

The Knauer boy

The Gestapo's invitation to dance was still on Russell's desk when he got up the following morning. One Sturmbann-führer Kleist was expecting to see John Russell in Room 48, 102 Wilhelmstrasse within the next seventy-two hours. No explanation was offered.

It wasn't actually the Gestapo – 102 Wilhelmstrasse was the headquarters of the Party intelligence organization, the *Sicherheits-dienst*. Though both were run by Reinhard Heydrich with a cheery disregard for legal niceties, the SD had a reputation for more sophisticated thuggery – same pain, cleaner floors.

He read the letter through again, looking for a more sinister message between the lines, and decided there was none. Shchepkin had said they'd want to talk to him, and they did. It was as simple as that. A friendly warning was waiting in Room 48, and nothing more. Sturmbannführer Kleist would turn out to be a Hertha supporter, and they would chat about what had gone wrong this season.

Still, Russell thought as he shaved, there was no reason to hurry down there. He couldn't afford to miss the new Chancellery opening at noon, and there was no telling how long the various ceremonies would take. Tomorrow would do. Or even Wednesday.

Back in his room, he picked up the Leica and took a few imaginary photos. It had no flash, but Zembski had said the lens was good enough for indoor shooting as long as he held the camera steady and used the right film. And he could always ask the Führer for the loan of a shoulder.

Cheered by this thought – feeling, in fact, unreasonably buoyant for someone with an appointment at 102 Wilhelmstrasse – he headed downstairs and out into the grey January morning. As if in response to his mood, a tram glided to a halt at the stop on Friedrichstrasse just as he reached it. Ten minutes later he was ensconced in a Café Kranzler window seat, enjoying a first sip of his breakfast coffee as he examined the morning papers.

Foreign Minister Ribbentrop had been talking to the visiting Polish leader, Colonel Beck – now there were two men who deserved each other. The new battleship *Scharnhorst* had been commissioned at Wilhelmshaven, complete with nine eleven-inch guns, two catapults and four planes. The captain's main claim to fame was his shelling of a Spanish seaside town in 1937, while commanding the pocket battleship *Admiral Scheer*. On the home front, Pastor Martin Niemoller's brother Wilhelm had delivered a sermon attacking government policy towards the churches. He had read a list from the pulpit of all those churchmen – including his brother – currently enjoying the state's hospitality. The newspaper was not sure whether this constituted a crime: 'It has recently been established in certain cases,' the editor wrote, 'that to read the names of persons in custody may itself be an offence.'

On a more positive note, the French were demonstrating their usual sound sense of priorities. Parisian cinemas had been closed for a week in protest against a new tax on receipts, but a compromise had now been agreed: the taxes would remain in force, but would not be collected.

Russell smiled and looked out of the window, just in time to see two young women walk by, their faces shining with pleasure over some shared secret. The sun was struggling to emerge. Hitler had probably ordered it for noon; a few shafts of light would show up the medieval perfection of his new castle. Russell wondered how far Speer and his mentor had gone. Would it be the usual Graeco-Roman monstrosity, or something more ambitious? A Parthenon decked out in runes, perhaps.

Another coffee brought the time to 11.45. He walked to the top of Wilhelmstrasse, and headed down past the Hotel Adlon and serried government buildings to the new Chancellery. After showing his journalist's pass and invitation to a security guard, Russell took a photo of the crowd already gathering behind the cordon. The security guard glared at him, but did nothing else.

Russell joined the knot of privileged journalists and photographers already gathered around the entrance, almost all of whom he recognised. Somewhat to his surprise, Tyler McKinley was among them. 'My editor was keen,' the young American said resentfully, as if nothing else could have persuaded him to bless Hitler's new building with his presence. Russell gave him an 'Oh yeah?' look and walked over to Jack Slaney, one of the longer-serving American correspondents. Russell had been in Slaney's office when the latter's invitation had arrived, complete with an unsolicited – and presumably accidental – extra. Slaney had been good enough to pass it on – he had been a freelance himself in the dim distant past, and knew what this sort of exclusive could be worth.

'A one-man band,' he muttered, looking at Russell's camera.

'I prefer to think of myself as Renaissance Man,' Russell told him, just as the doors swung open.

The fifty or so journalists surged into the lobby, where a shiny-looking toady from the Propaganda Ministry was waiting for them. There would be a short tour of the new building, he announced, during which photographs could be taken. The ceremonial opening would take place in the Great Hall at precisely 1 pm, and would be followed by a worker's lunch for the thousands of people who had worked on the project.

'There might be some meat, then,' one American journalist muttered.

The toady led them back outside, and around the corner into Vosstrasse. Huge square columns framed the double-gated main entrance, which led into a spacious vestibule. Russell hung back to take a couple of photos before following his colleagues up a flight of steps to the reception hall. From there, bronze eagles clutching swastikas guarded fifteen foot doors to a bigger hall clad in grey and gold tiles. The Führer was unavailable, so Russell used Slaney's shoulder to steady the Leica.

More steps led to a circular chamber, another door into a gallery lined with crimson marble pillars. This, their guide told them, was, at 146 metres, twice as long as the Hall of Mirrors in Versailles. 'And my mother told me size didn't matter,' one journalist lamented in English. 'I expect your father had a whopper,' another said, provoking an outburst of laughter. The ministry toady stamped his foot on the marble floor, and then took a quick look down to make sure he hadn't damaged it.

The next hall was big enough to build aircraft in. Several hundred people were already waiting for the official opening, but the space still seemed relatively empty, as if mere people were incapable of filling it. Though released by their Ministry minder, the group of journalists stuck together in one corner, chatting among themselves as they waited for Hitler's entrance.

'We used to have arms races,' Slaney observed. 'Now we have hall races. Hitler had this built because he was so impressed by the size of Mussolini's office. And the moment Benito sees this he'll have to have one in Rome that's even bigger. And they'll both keep outbidding each other until the world runs out of marble.'

'I have a feeling they're building arms too,' Dick Normanton said wryly, his Yorkshire accent sounding almost surreal in this setting. He was one of the veteran English correspondents, much pampered by the Propaganda Ministry. This was hardly his fault: Normanton had an acute understanding of where Nazi Germany was headed, and often said as much in his reporting. Unfortunately for him, his London proprietor admired Hitler, and made sure that his editor edited accordingly.

'If you're interested in a horror show,' he told Russell, 'try the University on Wednesday. Streicher's inaugurating a new Chair of Anti-Jewish Propaganda and giving a speech. There should be some good Mad Hatter material.'

'Sounds suitably gruesome,' Russell agreed.

'What does?' McKinley asked, joining them

Normanton explained reluctantly – McKinley was not noted for his love of irony.

'Why would anyone want to listen to Streicher?' the American asked after Normanton had drifted away. 'It's not as if he's going to say anything interesting, is it?'

'I guess not,' Russell agreed diplomatically, and changed the subject. 'What do you make of the building?' he asked.

McKinley sighed. 'It's gross. In every meaning of the word,' he added, looking round.

Russell found this hard to disagree with – the new Chancellery was indeed gross. But it was also impressive, in a disturbing sort of way. It might be a monument to Hitler's lack of aesthetic imagination, but it was also proof of intention. This was not the sort of building you could ignore. It meant business.

It was Russell's turn to sigh. 'How was your weekend?' he asked McKinley.

'Oh, fine. I caught up on some work, saw a movie. And I went dancing at one of those halls off the Alexanderplatz. With one of the secretaries at the Embassy.' He smiled in reminiscence, and looked about sixteen years old. 'And I saw a couple of people for that story I told you about,' he added quickly, as if he'd caught himself slacking.

'You didn't actually tell me anything about it.'

'Ah. I will. In time. In fact I may need your help with...'

He was drowned out by an eruption of applause. Right arms shot towards the ceiling, as if some celestial puppeteer had suddenly flicked a finger. His Nibs had arrived.

Russell dutifully lined up the Leica and squeezed off a couple of shots. The Führer was not in uniform, and looked, as usual, like an unlikely candidate for leadership of a master race. One arm was stuck at half-mast to acknowledge the welcome, the mouth set in a self-satisfied smirk. The eyes slowly worked their way round the room, placid as a lizard's. This man will kill us all, Russell thought.

A builder's mate in the traditional top hat of the German artisan – his name, the toady had told them, was Max Hoffman – presented Hitler with the keys to his new home. Flashbulbs popped, hands clapped. The Führer volunteered a few words. He was, he said, the same person he had always been, and wished to be nothing more. 'Which means he's learnt absolutely nothing,' Slaney whispered in Russell's ear.

And that was that. Moving like a formation dancing team, Hitler and his ring of bodyguards began mingling with the guests in the privileged section of the hall, the ring working like a choosy Venus Fly-trap, admitting chosen ones to the Presence and spitting them out again. Much to the interest of the watching journalists, the Soviet Ambassador was given by far the longest audience.

'Fancy a drink?' Slaney asked Russell. Two of the other Americans, Bill Peyton and Hal Manning, were standing behind him. 'We're headed over to that bar on Behrenstrasse.'

'Suits me,' Russell agreed. He looked round for McKinley, but the youngster had disappeared.

The sun was still shining, but the temperature had dropped. The bar was dark, warm and blessed with several empty tables. A huge bear's head, half-hidden in the dense layer of smoke which hung from the ceiling, loomed over the one they chose. Slaney went off to buy the first round.

'It's hard to believe that Hitler got started in places like this,' Manning said, lighting a cigarette and offering the pack around. He was a tall, thin man with greying hair and a cadaverous face, and like Slaney a veteran foreign correspondent, in his case having worked his way up through Asian capitals and more obscure European postings to the eminence of 1939 Berlin. Peyton was younger – somewhere in his mid-thirties, Russell guessed – with clipped blonde hair and a boyish face. He worked full-time for a national weekly and sold stuff to the business monthlies on the side.

Russell found Peyton irritatingly sure of himself, but he had soft spots for both Manning and Slaney. If Americans remained ignorant about Nazi Germany, it wouldn't be their fault.

'So how do we tell this one, boys?' Slaney asked once the beers had been passed round. 'Just another grand building? Or megalomania run riot?'

'New Lair For Monster,' Manning suggested.

'I like it,' Slaney said, wiping froth off his nose. 'Adolf was getting chummy with Astakhov, wasn't he?'

Manning agreed. 'And Astakhov was lapping it up. Looks as if Stalin's given up on the Brits and the French.'

Russell remembered what Shchepkin had said on the subject. 'You can hardly blame him after Munich.'

'True, but you can hardly blame Chamberlain and Daladier for not trusting Stalin,' Peyton said.

'Bastards all,' Slaney summed up. 'I see Chamberlain's on his way to see the Duce' – he pronounced it 'Dootch' – 'in Rome. On some train called the Silver Bullet.'

Russell laughed. 'It's the Golden Arrow.'

'Whatever. A week with Mussolini. I hope he likes parades.'

'Why's he going?' Peyton asked.

'God knows. You'd think that by now someone in London would have noticed that the Duce is a man of moods. If he's feeling good he'll promise the world, set their Limey minds at rest. If he isn't, he'll try and scare the pants off 'em. Whichever he does, he'll be doing the opposite before the week's out.'

'Pity his German chum isn't a bit more mercurial,' Manning said. 'Once he gets his teeth into something, it stays bitten.'

'Or swallowed, in the Jew's case,' Russell added. 'Why the hell isn't Roosevelt doing more to help the Jews here?'

'He's building up the air force,' Peyton said. 'There was another announcement over the weekend.'

'Yes, but that won't help the Jews.'

'He can't,' Slaney said. 'Too much domestic opposition.'

Russell wasn't convinced. 'The British are doing something. Nothing like enough, I know. But something.'

'Two reasons,' Manning said. 'One, and most important – they just don't get it back in Washington. Or out in the Boonies. When Americans think about German Jews having a hard time, the first thing they think about is what American Jews have to put up with – restricted golf clubs, stuff like that. When they realise that Hitler doesn't play golf, they still find it hard to imagine anything worse than the way we treat our negroes. Sure, the negroes are condemned to segregation and poverty, but lynchings are pretty rare these days, and the vast majority get a life that's just about livable. Americans assume it's the same for the German Jews.'

'But what about the concentration camps?' Russell asked.

'They just think of them as German prisons. A bit harsh, maybe, but lots of Americans think our prisons should be harsher.' He shrugged and took a gulp of beer.

'And the second reason,' Russell prompted.

'That's easy. A lot of Americans just don't like Jews. They think they're getting their comeuppance. If they had any idea just how harsh that comeuppance is, some of them might – *might* – have second thoughts, but they don't.'

'I guess that's down to us.'

'Us and our editors,' Slaney said. 'We've told the story often enough. People just don't want to hear it. And if you keep on and on about it they just turn off.'

'Europe's far away,' Manning said.

'And getting farther,' Slaney said. 'Jesus, let's think about something pleasant for a change.' He turned to Russell. 'John, I'm organizing a poker night for next Tuesday. How about it?'

The foursome emerged into the daylight soon after three, and went their separate ways – Peyton to his mistress, Slaney and Manning to write their copy for the morning editions. Walking south down Wilhelmstrasse, Russell decided on impulse to drop in on Sturmbannführer Kleist. A small voice in his head protested that the *Sicherheitsdienst* was best encountered stone-cold sober, but was promptly drowned out by a louder one insisting that there was nothing to be afraid of. The meeting was just a formality. So why not get it over with?

The fresh-faced blonde receptionist seemed pleased enough to see him, gesturing him through to an ante-room with the sort of friendly smile that could soften up any man. Sunk into one of the leather chairs, Russell found himself staring at the latest creation of the Propaganda Ministry's poster artists, Hitler complete with visionary stare and catchy slogan – 'ein volk, ein Reich, ein Führer'. On the opposite wall a more colourful poster showed apple-cheeked youth frolicking in the Alps. That was the thing about these people, he thought: they never surprised you.

The minutes dragged by; the later pints of beer pressed ever more urgently for release. He went back out to the receptionist, who pointed him in the direction of a toilet with the same sunny smile. The toilet was spotless and smelt as if it had just been hosed down with Alpine flowers. One of the cubicles was occupied, and Russell imagined Heydrich sitting with his breeches round his ankles, reading something Jewish.

Back in the ante-room he found company. A man in his sixties, smartly-dressed, probably German. They exchanged nods, but nothing more. The man shifted nervously in his seat, causing the leather to squeak. Hitler stared at them both.

After about twenty minutes the sound of clicking heels seeped out of the silence, and another young blonde appeared in the doorway. 'Herr John Russell?' she enquired. 'Follow me, please.'

They went down one long corridor, up some steps, down another corridor. All Russell could hear was the rhythmic click of the blonde's shoes – no sounds escaped through the numerous doors they passed, no talk, no laughter, no typewriters. There was no sense that the building was empty, though, more a feeling of intense concentration, as if everyone was thinking fit to burst. Which, Russell realised, was absurd. Maybe the SD had a half-term break, like British schools.

Through the window on a second flight of stairs he caught a glimpse of a large lawn and the huge swastika flying over Hitler's new home. At the end of the next corridor the heels swung right through an open doorway.

Room 48 was not so much a room as a suite. The secretary led him through her high-ceilinged ante-room, opened the inner door and ushered him in.

Sturmbannführer Gottfried Kleist – as the nameboard on the desk announced – looked up, gestured him to the leather-bound seat on the near side of his leather-bound desk, and carried on writing. He was a stout man in denial, his black uniform just a little too tight for what it had to contain. He had a florid face, thinning hair and rather prominent red lips. He did have blue eyes, though, and his handwriting was exquisite. Russell watched the fountain pen scrape across the page, forming elegant whorls and loops from the dark green ink.

After what seemed like several minutes, Kleist carefully replaced the pen in its holder, almost daintily blotted his work and, after one last admiring look, moved it to the right hand side of his desk. From the left he picked up a folder, opened it, and raised his eyes to Russell's. 'John Russell,' he said. It wasn't a question.

'You asked to see me,' Russell said, with as much bonhomie as he could muster.

The Sturmbannführer ran a hand through his hair, straightening a few rebellious wisps with his fingers. 'You are an English national.'

'With resident status in the Reich.'

'Yes, yes. I know. And a current journalistic accreditation.'

'Yes.

'Could I see it please?'

Russell removed it from his inside jacket pocket and passed it over.

Kleist noticed the invitation card. 'Ah, the opening,' he said. 'A success, I assume. Were you impressed?'

'Very much so. The building is a credit to the Fuhrer.'

Kleist looked sharply at Russell, as if doubtful of his sincerity.

'So much modern architecture seems insubstantial,' Russell added.

'Indeed,' Kleist agreed, handing back the press pass. Apparently satisfied, he sat back in his seat, both hands grasping the edge of his desk. 'Now, it has come to our attention that the Soviet newspaper *Pravda* has commissioned you to write a series of articles about the Fatherland.' He paused for a moment, as if daring Russell to ask how it had come to their attention. 'This was at your suggestion, I believe.'

'It was.'

'Why did you suggest these articles, Mr Russell?'

Russell shrugged. 'Several reasons. All freelance journalists are always looking to place stories with whoever will buy them. And it occurred to me that the Soviets might be interested in a fresh look at National Socialist Germany, one that concentrates on what the two societies have in common, rather than what divides them. What I...'

Kleist stopped him with a raised hand. 'Why did you think this would interest the Soviets?'

Russell took his time. 'Soviet propaganda has generally been very hostile towards the Reich,' he began. 'And by taking this course, they have backed themselves into a corner. There's no doubt that Germany is the rising power in Europe, and the Soviets – like everyone else – will sooner or later have to deal with that reality. But as things stand at the moment, their own people would not understand a more... a more accommodating attitude towards the Reich. The articles I propose would prepare the ground, so to speak. They would help restore the Soviet government's freedom of movement, allow them to act in concert with the Reich if and when the two states' interests coincide.'

Kleist looked thoughtful.

'And I see such articles as a contribution to peace,' Russell went on, hoping he wasn't over-egging the pudding. 'I fought in the last war, and I have no desire to see another. If nations and governments understand each other, there's less chance we'll all blunder into one.'

Kleist smiled. 'I don't think there's much chance of the Führer blundering into anything,' he said. 'But I take your point. And we have no objection to your articles, subject to certain conditions. These are sensitive subjects – I'm sure you'd agree. And while you are English, you are also living in the Reich under our protection. Your views would not be seen as official views, but they would be seen as views we are prepared to tolerate. You understand me? Whatever you write could be construed as having our blessing.'

Russell felt anxious for the first time. 'Yes…' he said hesitantly.

'So, you see, it follows that we cannot permit you to write anything that we violently disagree with. Your articles will have to be pre-submitted for our approval. I am sure,' he added, 'that this will only be a formality.'

Russell thought quickly. Should he at least recognize the implied dismissal of his journalistic integrity, or just play the cynic? He opted for the practical approach. 'This is unusual, but I see your point,' he said. 'And I have no objection, provided that your office can approve – or disapprove – the articles quickly. The first one is due in a couple of weeks, and at fortnightly intervals after that – so, a couple of days…'

'That will not be a problem. Nothing gathers dust here.'

Kleist looked pleased, and Russell had the sudden realisation that the SD were as eager to see these articles as Shchepkin and his people. He decided to go for broke. 'Sturmbannführer, could I make a request? In order to write these articles I shall need to travel a great deal around the Reich, and talk to a lot of people. I shall be asking them questions which they may find suspicious, coming, as they will, from a foreigner. A letter from this office confirming my credentials, and stating that I have permission to ask such questions, would be very useful. It would save a lot of time talking to local officials, and might help me avoid all sorts of time-consuming difficulties.'

Kleist looked momentarily off-balance – this was not in his script – but he soon recovered. He scratched his cheek and rearranged his hair again before answering. 'That seems a reasonable request,' he said, 'but I'll have to consult with my superiors before issuing such a letter.' He looked down at his pen, as if imagining the pleasure of writing it out.

'Is there anything else?' Russell asked.

'Just one thing. Your business with the Soviets – you are conducting it by post, I presume?'

'So far,' Russell agreed, hoping to God that Kleist knew nothing of his meeting with Shchepkin. 'Though of course I may have to use the phone or the wire service at some point.'

'Mm. Let me be frank with you, Mr Russell. If, in the course of your dealings with the Soviets, you learn anything of their intentions, their capabilities, we would expect you to pass such information on.'

'You're asking me to spy for you?'

'No, not as such. Mr Russell, you've lived in Germany for many years…'

'Almost fourteen.'

'Exactly. Your son is a German boy, a proud member of the Hitler Youth, I believe.'

'He is.'

'So presumably you feel a certain loyalty to the Reich.'

'I feel affection, and gratitude. I am not a great believer in loyalty to countries or governments.'

'Ah, you were a communist once, I believe.'

'Yes, but so was Mussolini. A lot of people were in the early 1920s. Like Mussolini, I got over it. As for my loyalty or lack of it… Sturmbannführer, what would you think of a German who, after a decade spent in England, proclaimed his loyalty to the English King? I suspect you would consider him a traitor to the Fatherland.'

'I…'

'I have a German son,' Russell ploughed on. 'I have an American mother, and I had an English father. I was brought up in England. Insofar as I am able, I am loyal to all three countries.'

'But not to the Soviets?'

'No.'

'So if a Soviet contact told you of a threat to the Reich, you would not keep it to yourself.'

'I would not.'

'Very well. Then I think our business is concluded.' Kleist stood up and offered his hand across the desk. 'If you get the articles to me, either by hand or post, I will guarantee to return them within twenty-four hours. Will that suffice?'

'It will.'

'Then good day to you. Fraulein Lange will see you back to the entrance.'

She did. Russell followed the clicking heels once more, picked up his coat from the smiling receptionist, and found himself out on the Wilhelmstrasse pavement. It was dark. In more ways than one.

Tuesday was clear and cold. Walking down to the U-bahn at Hallesches Tor, Russell was more conscious of the icy wind from the east than any theoretical warmth from the sun. At the studio in Neukölln he waited while Zembski shouted at someone down the phone, and then persuaded the Silesian to develop his film that day. Back at the U-bahn station he bought the *Tageblatt* and *Allgemeine Zeitung* at a kiosk and skimmed through their accounts of the Chancellery opening as he waited for a train. As far as he could tell, he'd seen all there was to see.

The only other items of interest were the imminent departure of Reichsbank President Schacht, the Danzig stamp row – which had finally reached the German nationals – and the unsurprising news that US government spokesmen were less than impressed by the Nazis' latest idea of sending all the Jews to either Manchuria or Alaska.

Back at Neuenburgerstrasse Russell settled down to work. If you had a green light from the SD, he noted cynically, it probably paid to get moving. First off, he needed a list of topics for *Pravda*. What was so great about Nazi Germany if you didn't like flags and blood in the gutter? Full employment, for one. A national sense of well-being. Worker's benefits, up to a point. Cheap organized leisure activities – sport, culture, travel. All these came at a cost, and only, needless to say, to aryans, but there was something there. As an English advertising man had once told him, there had to be *something* in the product that was worth having.

What else? Health care was pretty good for the curable. And transport – the rocket trains, the autobahns and the people's car, the new flying-boats and aeroplanes. The Nazis loved modernity when it speeded things up or made them simpler, hated it when it complicated things, or made it harder for them to live in their medieval mind-set. Einstein being Jewish was most convenient.

He could write something perceptive about Nazi Germany if he had the mind to, Russell thought. Unfortunately…

He could write these articles in his sleep. Or almost. The Soviets liked lots of statistics – something they shared with the Nazis – and that would involve a little work. But not much. Shchepkin's oral reports on the other hand…

He'd been trying not to think about them. Kleist's question about other contacts had also been intended as a warning – he was sure of that. And the Soviets expected him to meet one of their agents outside Germany once a month. Which would no doubt make things safer for the agent, but how was he supposed to explain this new and oddly regular penchant for foreign travel? Could he refuse this part of the Soviet job? He suspected not. He wasn't sure how the Soviets would make any hard feelings felt, but he was sure they'd manage it somehow.

Nor did he feel that happy about wandering round Germany asking questions, even if Kleist did come up with some sort of protective letter. He supposed he could invent any number of imaginary responses – how, after all, could the Soviets check up on him? Then again, who knew what was left of the communist network in Germany? And in any case, part of him liked the idea of finding out what ordinary Germans were feeling in Year Six of Hitler's thousand.

That was it, he thought. 'Ordinary Germans.' The British and American tabloids liked series: the *Daily Mail* was currently running one on 'European Troublespots' – he'd read No.4 ('Memel – Europe's Nagging Tooth') the previous week. He could do something similar about ordinary Germans. The Worker. The Housewife. The Sailor, the Doctor, the Schoolboy. Whatever, as Slaney would say. Interviewing them would provide the ideal cover for gathering the information Shchepkin wanted.

And the trips abroad? It was obvious – 'Germany's Neighbours'. Another series, this one looking at how people in the neighbouring countries viewed Germany. He could travel all he wanted, talk to all the foreigners he wanted, without arousing suspicion. In Poland, Denmark, Holland, France, what was left of Czechoslovakia. He could take Effi to Paris, visit his cousin Rainer in Budapest. He leaned back in his chair feeling pleased with himself. These two series would make him safer and richer. Things were looking up.

The feeling of well-being lasted until the next day. After posting off his text and photos of the Chancellery opening he travelled across town to the University, where Julius Streicher was inaugurating the new chair. It wasn't, as Normanton had mischievously claimed, actually called the Chair of Anti-Jewish Propaganda, but it might have been. There was no sign of Streicher's famous bullwhip, but his veins bulged just the way Russell remembered. The Nazi angrily denied the claim that National Socialism had put fetters on science or research. Restrictions, he insisted, had only been placed on the unruly. In fact decency and sincerity had only obtained their freedom under National Socialism.

He had been ranting for an hour and a half when Russell left, and looked set for many hours more. Coming away, Russell knew what Normanton had meant about Mad Hatter material but, for once in his life, he felt more emotionally in tune with McKinley's simple disgust. Perhaps it was the fact that his next port of call was the Wiesners.

He picked up a *Daily Mail* while changing trams in Alexanderplatz and went through it with the two girls. They pored over the fashion pictures and ads, puzzled over the headline which read MAN WHO SLAPPED WOMAN MAYOR SAYS 'I'M ASTOUNDED', and objected to the one which claimed ALL WOMEN ARE MAGPIES. A photograph of the King of Egypt out duck-shooting reduced Ruth to such a fit of giggles that her mother came out to see what was happening.

After the lesson she brought out the best coffee and cake Russell had tasted for months, and insisted on thanking him profusely for all he was doing. Her husband was well, she said, but her face clouded over when he asked about Albert. He was 'finding things difficult,' she said. He had the feeling she thought about saying more, but decided against it.

He'd planned a few more hours of work before picking up Effi from the theatre, but after Streicher and the Wiesners he felt more like punching someone. He found another Western on the Ku'damm and sank into a world of huge skies, lofty canyons and simple justice. Chewing gum for the heart.

Effi was tired and seemed as subdued as he felt. They walked slowly back to her flat, went to bed, and lay quietly in each other's arms until she went to sleep. Her face grew younger in sleep, and she looked even more like Ruth Wiesner.

Wednesday evening, Russell was listening to dance band music on the BBC when McKinley knocked on his door and suggested a drink. While he collected his shoes from the bedroom the young American scanned his bookshelves. 'Half of these are banned,' he said admiringly, when Russell returned.

'I haven't got round to burning them yet,' he said, reaching for his coat.

Outside it was warmer than it had been, but there were specks of rain in the air. As they turned the corner into Lindenstrasse McKinley took a sudden look over his shoulder, as if he'd heard something.

'What?' Russell asked, seeing nothing.

McKinley shook his head. 'Nothing,' he said.

They walked under the elevated U-bahn tracks at Hallesches Tor, and across Blücherplatz to the bar they used for their infrequent drinks together. It was almost empty, the barman yawning on his stool, two old men in the corner staring morosely at each other. McKinley bought them beers – dark for Russell, light for himself – while Russell commandeered the only bowl with any nuts and carried it across to the table with the fewest standing pools. As he lowered himself into the seat it groaned alarmingly but held together. 'We have to find a new bar,' he murmured.

McKinley tried his beer and smiled in satisfaction. 'Okay,' he said. 'Now tell me about Schacht.'

'He's dead in the water.'

'Okay, but why? I never understood economics.'

'Schacht does. That's why.'

'What do you mean?'

Russell thought about it. 'Schacht wants to see the economy run according to the laws of economics. He did when he was finance Minister, and as long as he's in charge of the Reichsbank he'll keep beating the same drum. The trade deficit is soaring, the Reichsbank's holdings of foreign exchange are dwindling, and there's a real possibility of another runaway inflation. The economy's running out of control. Schacht would like to raise taxes and switch production from armaments to something that can be sold abroad. Some hope, eh? If Hitler and Goering have to choose between their armament programme and the laws of economics, which do you think they'll choose?'

'But if the economy is in real trouble?'

'Nothing a war won't fix.'

'Ah.'

'Ah, indeed. Schacht, shall we say, has the narrow view. He's assuming several years of peace, at the very least. Hitler, on the other hand, sees a choice. He can either do what Schacht wants – rein back the war machine, raise taxes and get the real economy moving again – or he can go for broke, and use the army to put things right. He sees all that wealth beyond his borders, just begging to be collected. That's why Schacht has to go. Hitler's not going to risk higher taxes in Germany when he can steal the same money from conquered foreigners.'

McKinley looked at him. 'I never know how serious you are. If this is such a big story – Schacht going, I mean – then why isn't it on the front pages back home? If war's so absolutely certain, how come you're the only one who knows it?'

Russell smiled. 'Just gifted, I guess. Another beer?' When he got back from the bar, McKinley was making notes in his little black book. 'Was your dance night a one-off, or are you going out with that girl from the embassy?' Russell asked him.

McKinley blushed. 'We've only been out twice. Merle, her name is – you know, like Merle Oberon. Her father's just a storekeeper in Philadelphia but she's determined to really see life. She wants to see Europe while she's working here, and then the rest of the world if she can.'

'Good for her.'

'You've travelled a lot, haven't you?'

'Once upon a time.'

'Have you been to Russia?'

'Yes. I met my wife there – my ex-wife, I should say. At a Comintern youth conference in 1924. Lenin had just died and Trotsky hadn't noticed that the rug was gone from under his feet. It was a strange time, a sort of revolutionary cusp – not the moment it all went wrong, but the moment a lot of Party people realised that it already had. Does that make sense?'

'I suppose. I'm hoping to go in March. The nineteenth Congress is being held in Moscow and I'm trying to persuade the paper to send me.'

'That'll be interesting,' Russell said, though he doubted it would be.

Neither of them wanted another drink, and the nuts were all gone. It was raining outside, and they stood for a moment in the doorway, watching the neon shimmers in the puddles. As they passed under the elevated tracks a Warschauer Brucke train rumbled across, its sides streaming with water.

At the bottom of Lindenstrasse McKinley took a look back across the Belle Alliance Platz. 'I think I'm being followed,' he said, almost guiltily, in response to Russell's enquiring look.

'I can't see anyone,' Russell said, staring into the rain.

'No, neither can I,' McKinley said, as they started up Linden-strasse. 'It's more of a feeling… I don't know. If they are following me, they're really good.'

Too many *Thin Man* movies, Russell thought. 'Who's they?' he asked.

'Oh, the Gestapo, I suppose.'

'Moving like wraiths isn't exactly the Gestapo style.'

'No, I suppose not.'

'Why would they be following you?'

McKinley grunted. 'That story I told you about. That story I was going to tell you about,' he corrected himself.

'I'm not sure I want to know anymore,' Russell said. 'I don't want them following me.'

It was meant as a joke, but McKinley didn't take it that way. 'Well, okay…'

Russell was thinking about the car he'd seen outside their block. He couldn't imagine the Gestapo being that patient, but there were other sharks in the Nazi sea. 'Look, Tyler. Whatever it is, if you really are being stalked by the authorities I should just drop it. No story's worth that sort of grief.'

McKinley bristled. 'Would you have said that ten years ago?'

'I don't know. Ten years ago I didn't have the responsibilitiesI have now.'

'Maybe you should ask yourself whether you can still be an honest journalist with those sort of responsibilities.'

That made Russell angry. 'You haven't cornered the market in honest journalism, for God's sake.'

'Of course not. But I know what matters. That once mattered to you.'

'Truth has a habit of seeping out.' Russell wasn't even convincing himself, which made him angrier still. 'Look, there's seventy-five million people out there keeping their heads down. I'm just one of them.'

'Fine. If you want to keep your head down, wait until it all blows over – fine. But I can't do that.'

'Okay.'

They walked the rest of the way in silence.

The conversation with McKinley – or, more precisely, the sense of letting himself down that it engendered – lurked with annoying persistence at the back of Russell's mind over the next few days. He finished his first article for *Pravda* – a paean to organized leisure activities – and delivered it himself to the smiling blonde at 102 Wilhelmstrasse. He received a wire from his US agent bubbling with enthusiasm for the two series. And, by special delivery, he received the letter he had asked Sturmbannführer Kleist for. It was typed rather than written, which was something of a disappointment, but the content left little to be desired – John Russell, it seemed, had full authority from the Propaganda Ministry and Ministry of the Interior to ask such questions 'as would widen the foreign understanding of National Socialism and its achievements'. Those shown the letter were 'asked and expected to offer him all the assistance they could'. All of which would have felt much better if he hadn't seen the disappointment in McKinley's eyes.

The weekend gave him a welcome break from worrying about his journalistic integrity. On Saturday afternoon he and Paul went to the Zoo. They had been so many times that they had a routine – first the parrot house, then the elephant walk and the snakes, a break for ice cream, the big cats and, finally, the *pièce de résistance*, the gorilla who spat, with often devastating accuracy, at passers-by. After the Zoo, they strolled back down the Ku'damm, looking in shop windows and eventually stopping for cake. Russell still found his son's Hitler Youth uniform slightly off-putting, but he was gradually getting used to it.

Sunday, a rare treat – an outing to the fair at the end of Potsdamerstrasse with both Paul and Effi. Getting them together was always harder than the actual experience of their being together – both worried overmuch that they'd be in the other's way. It was obvious that Paul liked Effi, and equally obvious why. She was willing to try anything at least once, was able to act any age she thought appropriate, and assumed that he could too. She was in fact, most of the things his mother wasn't, and had never been.

After two hours of circling, sliding, dropping and whirling they took a cab to Effi's theatre, where she showed Paul round the stage and back-stage areas. He was particularly impressed by the lift and trapdoor in mid-stage which brought the Valkyries up to heaven each evening. When Russell suggested that they should build one for Goebbels at the Sportspalast, Effi gave him a warning look, but Paul, he noticed delightedly, was unable to suppress his amusement.

The only sad note of the weekend was Paul's news that he would be away for the next weekend at a Hitler Youth adventure camp in the Harz Mountains. He was sorry not to be seeing his Dad, and to be missing the next Hertha home game, but Russell could see he was looking forward to the camp. It was particularly annoying because he would be away himself the following weekend, delivering his first oral report to Shchepkin. And on that weekend he would also be missing Effi's end-of-run party – *Barbarossa* had apparently raised all the national consciousness it was going to raise.

Early on Monday morning, he took the train to Dresden for a one-night stay. It was only a two-hour journey, and he had several contacts there: a couple of journalists on the city paper; an old friend of Thomas's, also in the paper business; an old friend of his and Ilse's, once a union activist, now a teacher. Ordinary Germans, if such people existed.

He saw them all over the two days, and talked to several others they recommended. He also spent a few hours in cafés and bars, joining or instigating conversations when he could, just listening when that seemed more appropriate. As his train rattled northwards on Tuesday evening he sat in the buffet car with a schnapps and tried to make sense of what he had heard. Nothing surprising. 'Ordinary Germans' felt utterly powerless, and were resigned to feeling so for the foreseeable future. The government would doubtless translate that resignation as passive support, and to some extent they were right. There was certainly no sense that anyone had a practical alternative to offer.

When it came to Germany's relations with the rest of the world, most people seemed pleasantly surprised that they still had any. The Rhineland, the Anschluss, the Sudetenland – it was as if Hitler had deliberately driven his train across a series of broken points, but

– thanks be to God – the train was still on the track. Surely, soon, he would pull the damn thing to a halt. Once Memel and Danzig were back in the fold, once the Poles had given Germany an extra-territorial corridor across their own corridor, then that would be that. Hitler, having expanded the Reich to fit the Volk, would rest on his laurels, a German hero for centuries to come.

They all said it, and some of them even believed it.

Their own daily lives were getting harder. Not dramatically, but relentlessly. The economic squeeze was on. Most people were working longer hours for the same pay; many ordinary goods were growing slightly harder to find. The relief which had followed the return of full employment had dissipated.

Children seemed to be looming ever-larger in their parent's minds; the demands in time and loyalty of the Hitler Youth, the year-long exile of the *arbeitsdienst*, the prospect of seeing them marched off to war. If Ordinary Germans wanted anything, it was peace. Years of the stuff, years in which they could drive their people's cars down their new autobahns.

Only one man mentioned the Jews, and then only in a dismissive preamble – 'Now that the Jewish question is nearing solution.' What did he mean? Russell asked. 'Well,' the man replied, 'they'll all be gone soon, won't they? I have nothing against them personally, but a lot of people have, and they'll be happier elsewhere – that's obvious.'

The Wiesners would have agreed with him. The girls seemed subdued when he saw them on Wednesday morning, polite and willing as ever, but less perky, as if more bad news had just descended on the household. One reason became clear when Frau Wiesner asked for a word with him after the lesson.

She wanted to ask him a favour, she said. She didn't want her husband to know, but could he, Russell, have a word with Albert? He was behaving recklessly, just saying whatever came into his mind, associating with... well, she didn't know who, but... he wouldn't listen to his father, she knew that, and he wouldn't listen to her, but Russell, well, he was outside it all – he wasn't a Jew, wasn't a Nazi, wasn't even a German. He knew what was happening, how dangerous things were. They were working on getting visas, but it took so long. Albert said they were dreaming, they'd never get them, but he didn't know that, and he was putting the girls' future at risk as well as his own...

She ran out of words, and just looked at him helplessly.

Russell's heart sank at the prospect, but he agreed to try.

'I'll make sure he's here on Friday, after the lesson,' she said.

That evening, he was getting his Dresden notes in order when Tyler McKinley knocked on his door. 'I've come to apologise,' the American said.

'What for?' Russell said.

'You know. The other night.'

'Oh that. Forget it.'

'Okay. How about a drink?'

Russell rubbed his eyes. 'Why not?'

They went to their usual bar, sat at the same table. Russell thought he recognised the stains from the previous week. His companion seemed relieved that he wasn't holding a grudge, and he was drinking dark beer for a change. The bar was more crowded than usual, with a population reaching towards double figures.

McKinley got out his pipe and tin of Balkan mixture.

'What got you started in journalism?' Russell asked.

'Oh, I always wanted to be one. Long as I can remember.' The American smiled reminiscently. 'When I was a kid I used to spend the summer with my mother's folks in Nugget City – you probably never heard of it – it's a small town in California. Grew up in the Gold Rush days, been shrinking ever since. My granddad ran the local paper in his spare time. Just a weekly. Two pages. Four if something had actually happened. I used to help him with stuff. On print day we'd both come home covered in ink. I loved it.' He picked up the tobacco tin, and put it down again. 'Granddad and grandma both died when I was twelve, so all that stopped. I tried offering my services to the San Francisco papers, but they didn't want kids hanging around in their print rooms. Not surprising really. Anyway, I got involved with my high school paper, and then the college paper, and eventually got a job at the *Examiner*. Three years in sports, three on the city desk, and I finally got myself sent to Europe.' He grinned. 'I still love it.'

'What did your family think?' Russell asked. He meant about coming to Europe, but McKinley, busying loading his pipe, answered a different question.

'My father was furious. He has his own law firm, and I was supposed to sign up, start at the bottom and eventually take over. He thinks journalists are grubby little hacks, you know, like *The Front Page*.' His eyes lit up. 'Did you know they're re-making that, with a woman reporter? Rosalind Russell, I think. And Cary Grant's her editor. I read about it in one of Merle's Hollywood magazines.'

'Your Dad still furious?'

'Not so much. I mean, they're happy enough to see me when I come home.' He sounded like he was trying to convince himself. 'It's funny,' he added, 'my sister seems angrier than my father.'

'What does she do?'

'Nothing much, as far as I can tell. She'd make a much better lawyer than I would, but... well, you know... Dad would never take a woman into the firm.' He struck a match, applied it to the bowl, and sucked in. The bowl glowed, and a noxious plume of smoke escaped from his lips.

'That's enough to make anyone resentful,' Russell said. 'Not being offered something you want is bad enough; someone else turning it down just adds salt to the wound.'

McKinley looked at him as if he was a magician. 'You know, that never occurred to me.'

'When did you last go home?' Russell asked.

'Oh, the Thanksgiving before last. But I write quite often.'

Russell thought about his own family. His mother in America, his half-brother in Leeds. Bernard was well over fifty now, the single offspring of his father's brief liaison with the army nurse who treated him – in more ways than one – after the Gordon campaign in Sudan. Russell hadn't seen him in years, and had no particular desire to. There were a couple of uncles in England, one aunt in America, cousins dotted here and there. He hadn't seen any of them either. It was time he took Paul on a visit to England, he thought.

He looked at McKinley, happily puffing away at his pipe. 'Do you never get homesick?' he asked.

'Sure, sometimes. Days like today I miss the sunshine. I know everyone thinks San Francisco is always shrouded in fog, but it isn't. It's still the loveliest city I've seen.' He smiled. 'But this is where the story is.'

'Unfortunately.'

'Well, yes. I was wondering… I'm arranging this interview next week – I don't know which evening yet – and I wondered if you'd be willing to come along. My German is pretty good, but yours is obviously a lot better, and the only time I met this woman I could hardly understand anything she said. And I really can't afford to misunderstand anything she tells me.'

'Who is she?'

McKinley hesitated. 'She used to work for the Health Ministry.'

'This is the big story?'

McKinley grinned briefly. 'You could say that. You remember that story I did on asylums last year?'

Russell did. It hadn't been at all bad. The American had managed to raise quite a few awkward questions, and it was hardly his fault that no one else had demanded any answers. 'I remember,' he said.

'Well, this woman was one of the people I interviewed. She told me a pack of lies, as far as I could tell. And then last week she contacted me out of the blue, said she was willing to give me some information about some of the other stuff I've heard.'

'About the asylums?'

'Yes and no. Look,' he said, looking round. 'I don't want to talk about it here. Let's go back to the house.'

'Okay,' Russell agreed. He was beginning to feel intrigued, despite himself.

As they walked back to Neuenburgerstrasse he kept an eye open for possible shadows, and noticed that McKinley was doing the same. None crept into view, and the street outside their block was empty of cars.

'The Knauer boy,' McKinley said, once they were ensconced in Russell's two armchairs. 'I don't think his parents gave him a Christian name. He was blind, had only one arm, and part of one leg was missing. He was also, supposedly, an idiot. A medical idiot, I mean. Mentally-retarded. Anyway, his father wrote to Hitler asking that the boy should be killed. Hitler got one of the doctors employed by the KdF to confirm the facts, which they did. He then gave the child's own doctors permission to carry out a mercy-killing. The boy was put to sleep.' He paused to re-stoke his pipe.

'That's a sad story,' Russell said cautiously.

'There's two things,' McKinley said. 'Hitler has never made any secret of his plan to purify the race by sterilizing the mentally-handicapped and all the other so-called incurables. And the Nazis are always going on about how much it costs to keep all these people in asylums. They actually use it as an example in one of their school text-books – you know, how many people's cars you could build with what it costs to feed and clothe ten incurables for a year. Put the two things together, and you get one easy answer – kill them. It purifies the race and saves money.'

'Yes, but…'

'I know. But if the Knauer boy is expendable, why not the others? About 100,000 of them, according to the latest figures. Tell the parents they're doing it to cut short the child's suffering, give them an excuse not to have the problem anymore. In fact, don't even tell the parents. Spare their suffering by saying that the child died of natural causes.'

'100,000 of them?'

'Perhaps not, but…'

'Okay, it sounds feasible. It sounds like the Nazis, for Christ's sake. But are they actually doing it? And if they are, do you have any proof that they're doing it?'

'There are all sorts of indications…'

'Not good enough.'

'Plans then.'

'On paper?'

'Not exactly. Look, will you come and see this woman with me?'

Russell knew what the sensible answer was, but McKinley had

him hooked. 'Okay,' he said, checking his watch and realising that he'd be late for Effi.

Once out on Lindenstrasse he decided to spend some of his anticipated earnings on a cab. As it swung around the Belle Alliance Platz and headed up Königgrätzerstrasse towards Potsdamer Bahnhofplatz, he watched the people on the sidewalks and wondered how many of them would protest the mercy killing of 100,000 children. Would that be one step too far, or just another milestone in the shedding of a nation's scruples?

Russell didn't expect to find many similarities between Tyler McKinley and Albert Wiesner. On the one hand, a boy from a rich family and country with a rewarding job and instant access to a ticket out of Nazi Germany. On the other, a boy without work or prospects of any kind, whose next forwarding address was likely to be a concentration camp. Russell, however, soon realised he'd been wrong. The characters and personalities of both young men had been formed in successful families and, it seemed, in reaction to powerful fathers. And both seemed blessed with enough youthful naivety to render them both irritating and likable in turn.

Frau Wiesner produced her son at the end of Friday's lesson. For his mother's and sisters' sake the boy made a token effort to mask his sullen resentment at this unnecessary intrusion on his time, but once out of the door he swiftly abandoned any pretence of amiability.

'Let's get some coffee,' Russell said.

'No cafés will serve us,' was Albert's reply.

'Well, then, let's go for a walk in the park.'

Albert said nothing, but kept pace at Russell's side as they strolled down Greifswaldstrasse towards the northern entrance of the Friedrichshain, the park which gave the whole district its name.

Once inside the main gates Russell led them past the Märchen-Brunnen, a series of artificial waterfalls surrounded by sculptured characters from fairytales. He had brought Paul to see it several years ago, when Hansel and Gretel – the figures in the foreground – could still conjure up night-time terrors of wicked witches. As Ilse had bitterly complained on the following day.

Albert had a more topical agenda in mind. 'The witch must have been Jewish,' he said.

'If she wasn't then, she will be now,' Russell agreed.

They walked on into the park, down a wide path through the leafless trees. Albert seemed unconcerned by the silence between them, and made a point of catching the eyes of those walking in the opposite direction.

Russell had mentally rehearsed a few lines of adult wisdom on the U-bahn, but they'd all sounded ridiculous. 'Your mother wanted me to talk to you,' he said at last. 'But I have no idea what to say. You and your family are in a terrible situation. And, well, I guess she's frightened that you'll just make things worse for yourself.'

'And them.'

'Yes, and them.'

'I do realise that.'

'Yes…' This is a waste of time, Russell thought. They were approaching one of the park's outdoor cafés. 'Let's have a coffee here,' he said.

'They won't serve me.'

'Just take a seat. I'll get them.' He walked up to the kiosk window and looked at the cakes. They had *mohrenkopfen*, balls of sponge with custard centres, chocolate coats, and whipped cream hats. 'Two of them and two coffees,' he told the middle-aged man behind the counter.

The man was staring at Albert. 'He's a Jew,' he said finally, as if reaching the end of an exhaustive mental process. 'We don't serve Jews.'

'He's English,' Russell said. 'As am I.' He showed the man his Ministry of Propaganda accreditation.

'He looks Jewish,' the man said, still staring at Albert, who was now staring back. Why don't you just take out your circumcised prick and wave it at him, Russell thought sourly. 'He may be Jewish for all I know,' Russell told the man, 'but there's no law against serving English Jews.'

'There isn't?'

'No, there isn't.'

The man just stared at him.

'Do you need to hear it from a policeman?'

'Not if you say so.' He gave Albert one final glare and concentrated on pouring out the coffee.

God help us, Russell thought. He could understand Albert's reaction, no matter how counter-productive it was. But this man – what was he so outraged about? There were no SS men lounging at his tables, no ordinary citizens on the brink of racial apoplexy. Why did he care so much that a Jew was sitting at one of his rusty tables? Did he really think Jewish germs would rub off on his cups and saucers?

The coffee was slurped in the saucers, but it didn't seem worth complaining. He carried them back to the table, where Albert was now slouched in his chair, legs splayed out in defiance. Russell resisted the temptation to say 'sit up in your chair' and handed him a *mohrenkopf*. His eyes lit up.

They concentrated on eating for a few minutes.

'Do you really think there's any chance we'll get visas?' Albert asked eventually, allowing the merest hint of hope to mar his cynicism.

'Yes,' Russell said, more convincingly than he felt. 'It may take a while, but why not? The Nazis don't want you, so why shouldn't they let you go?'

'Because they're even more interested in hurting us?'

Russell considered that. It had, unfortunately, the ring of truth. 'The way I see it,' he said, 'you don't have many options. You can fight back and most likely end up in a camp. Or dead. Or you can try and work their system.'

Albert gave him a pitying look. 'There are half a million of us,' he said. 'At the current rate it'll take seven years for us all to get visas.'

Russell had no answer.

'And how long before we're at war?' Albert persisted.

'Who knows…'

'A year at most. And that'll put a stop to emigration. What do you think they'll do with us then? They won't let us work for a living now, and that won't change. They'll either leave us to starve or put us in work camps – slave labour. Some of my friends think they'll just kill us. And they may be right. Who's going to stop them?'

He could add Albert to the list of people he'd under-estimated, Russell thought.

'My father's Iron Cross was First Class,' Albert said. 'Unlike our beloved Führer's.'

Russell stared out at the winter trees, and the roof of the old hospital rising above them to the south. 'If you're right – if your friends are right – then all the more reason not to jeopardise your chances – your family's chances – of getting out.'

'I know that,' Albert said. 'But what about the others? One family's success is another family's failure.'

Russell had no answer to that either.

'But thanks for the coffee and cake,' Albert said.

• • •

Lying in bed unable to sleep, Russell thought about Papa Wiesner's Iron Cross First Class. It wasn't a medal given to many – he must have done something pretty special. He supposed he should have realised that a Jew of Wiesner's age would have fought in the war, but it hadn't occurred to him. Goebbels' propaganda was obviously working.

He wondered which front Wiesner had served on. He wondered, as he often did with Germans of his own age, whether they'd been facing him across those hundred yards of churned-up meadow near Merville. He sometimes wondered whether Frau Heidegger's repeated accusation that he might have shot her husband was simply her way of warding off the possibility that he really had.

He had once thought that he was over the war, that time and circumstance had turned the horror into anger, the anger into politics and the politics into cynicism, leaving only the abiding belief that people in authority tended, by and large, to be incompetent, uncaring liars. The war, by this accounting, had been the latest demonstration of a depressingly eternal truth. Nothing more.

He'd been fooling himself. All those who'd been in that particular place at that particular time had been indelibly marked by the experience, and he was no exception. You never shook it off completely – whatever it was it had left you with, whether nerves in tatters, an endless rage or a joy-sapping cynicism. And the memories never seemed to fade. That sudden waft of decomposing flesh, the rats' eyes reflected in the shell-burst, the sight of one's own rotting feet. The unnerving beauty of a flare cracking the night sky open. Splashed with someone else's brain. Slapped in the face by death.

Jimmy Sewell his name was. After helping carry what was left of him back to the medical station, Russell had somehow ended up with the letter he had just written to his girlfriend. Things were looking up, Sewell had told her, now that the Yanks were arriving in force. It had been late June or early July, 1918. One of a string of sunny days in northern France.

He and Razor Wilkinson had hitched a ride to Hazebrouck that evening, and got pissed out of their minds in a dingy back street bar. The more he drank, the more his brain-spattered face seemed to itch, and he had ended up wading into the River Lys and frantically trying to wash himself clean. Razor had stood on the bank laughing at him, until he realised that Russell was crying, and then he'd started crying too.

Twenty-one years ago, but Russell could still feel the current tugging at his legs. He levered himself out of bed and went to the window. Berlin was sleeping, but he could imagine Albert Wiesner lying in bed on his back, hands clenched around the blankets, staring angrily at the ceiling.

With Paul off on his *Jungvolk* adventure weekend, Russell and Effi spent most of Saturday morning in bed. Russell slipped on some clothes to bring back pastries and coffee from the shop around the corner, and slipped them off again when making love seemed more urgent than eating. Half an hour later Effi re-warmed the coffee on her tiny stove, and brought it back to the bedroom.

'Tell me about the film part,' Russell said, once they were propped up against the headboard. Effi had told him about the offer the night before, but had been too tired to go into details.

'They start shooting on the thirteenth,' she said. 'Two weeks on Monday. Marianne Immel had the part, but she's sick – pregnant, probably, though no one's said so. They want me to audition on Tuesday morning, but I'll have to be pretty bad to miss out – they won't have time to find anyone else.'

'What's it called?'

'*Mother*. And that's me. It's a big part.'

'Can I see the script?'

'Of course, but let me tell you the story first.' She licked a pastry crumb from her upper lip and pushed her hair back behind her ears. 'I am Gerta,' she said. 'I have a job in a factory, an important administrative job. I almost run the place for the owner. I like my work and I'm good at it.'

'But only a woman,' Russell murmured.

'Indeed. My husband Hans has a good job on the railways. And needless to say he's active in the SA, very active in fact. Hans earns more than enough money to support the family – we have two children by the way, a sixteen year-old girl and eleven year-old boy – and he rather thinks that I should give up work and look after them. But he's too kind-hearted to insist, and I keep on working.'

'I sense tragedy in the offing.'

'Ah, I should add that my boss fancies me no end. I don't fancy him – he looks decidedly Jewish by the way – but Hans is always away on Party business – you know, organizing parades, running youth camps and generally saving the nation – and the boss is kind enough and smooth enough to be good company, so I flirt with him a little and let him buy me pastries. Like you, in fact,' she added, looking at Russell.

'Do you flaunt your beautiful breasts at him?' Russell asked.

'Certainly not,' she said, pulling her nightdress closed. 'Now concentrate.'

'I'll try.'

'One day she and the boss go to visit a factory he's thinking of buying, and on the way back they decide to stop off at a guesthouse with a famous view. On the way down the mountain his car gets a puncture, and she's late home. Meanwhile, son and daughter have arrived home from school, and can't get in. They wait for a while, but it's raining – buckets of the stuff – and son already has a cold.

Daughter notices that one of the upstairs windows is ajar, and decides to climb up and in.'

'Only she doesn't make it.'

'How did you guess?'

'Dead or just paralysed?'

'Oh, dead. Though I suppose having her in a wheelchair would provide a constant reminder of my guilt. Which is, of course, enormous. I give up my job, despite the pleas of my boss. But the guilt is still too much, so I try and kill myself. And guess who saves me?'

'Son?'

'Exactly. He comes home with a couple of *Jungvolk* buddies to find me head down on the kitchen table with a empty bottle of pills. They rush me to the hospital on the cart they've been using to collect old clothes for Winter Relief.'

'And when you come round you realize that you can only atone for daughter's death by becoming the perfect stay-at-home mother.'

'Hans comes to collect me, takes me home, and tells me he can't bear me being so unhappy and that I can go back to work if I want to. Whereupon I give the speech of my life, castigating him for letting me have my own way in the past, and saying that all I really want to be is a wife and mother. He weeps with joy. In fact we both do. The end.'

'It does bring a tear to the eye,' Russell said. 'Is it going to make you famous?'

'Shouldn't think so. But the money's good, and it will involve some acting.'

'But no breast-flaunting.'

'I only do that for you,' she said, pulling the nightdress open.

• • •

After he'd walked Effi to the theatre for the *Barbarossa* matinee, Russell ate a snack lunch at the Zoo Station buffet, climbed up to the elevated platforms and sat watching the trains for a while. It was something he and Paul did on occasion, marvelling at the long lines of carriages snaking in across the bridge from Cologne or Paris or the wonderfully-named Hook of Holland. Today, though, he waited in vain for a continental express. There were only the neat little electric trains of the Stadtbahn, fussing in and out of the local platforms.

He walked round the northern wall of the Zoo and, for want of something better to do, headed home along the Landwehrkanal. It was a long time since he'd spent a Saturday afternoon in Berlin alone, and he felt unexpectedly disoriented by the experience. To make matters worse it was the sort of winter day he hated: grey, damp and almost insultingly warm, so that the canal smelled even worse than usual.

When he reached home Frau Heidegger was lying in wait. Schacht's long-expected dismissal as President of the Reichsbank had been all over the front pages that morning, and she was worried about how this might affect share prices. 'My Jurgen's family gave me some Farben shares after the war,' she explained, after press-ganging him in for coffee. 'Just a few, you understand, but I always thought they might come in handy in my old age.'

Russell reassured her that Schacht's dismissal was unlikely to have any lasting affect. Unlike the coming war, he added to himself. Or her coffee.

'The Führer's angry with the Czechs,' she said from the kitchen, as if following his thoughts.

'What about?' Russell asked.

'Does it matter?' she asked, coming in with the familiar pot.

'No,' he agreed. He was often surprised by Frau Heidegger's perceptiveness, and surprised he could still be surprised.

'I told my brother-in-law what you said about air defences,' she went on. 'He said he hoped you were right.'

'So do I,' Russell agreed.

After climbing the stairs to his apartment he wished he hadn't: the combination of muggy weather and full throttle heating had turned it into a Turkish bath. He tried opening a window, but there was no welcome hint of cooler air. He tried reading, but nothing seemed to stick.

He went back out again. It was just after four – he had about six hours to kill. He walked south down Belle-Alliance Strasse to Viktoria Park, climbed to the brow of the Kreuzberg and found an empty bench with a view across the city. There was even a slight breeze.

The sky darkened, and his mood seemed to darken with it.

He thought about Effi and the film. They'd had fun that morning, but it was a pretty disgusting piece of work. Did she have any qualms about doing it? She hadn't said so. He couldn't believe she needed the money, and he'd heard her views on the Nazi attitude to women often enough. So why was she doing it? Should he ask her? Was it possible to ask someone a question like that without making it an accusation?

He decided it wasn't, but later that night, halfway down an empty street on their way home from the theatre, he asked it anyway.

'To make a living?' she answered sarcastically.

'But you don't…' he said, and stopped himself. But not soon enough.

'Lots of people think that because my family is rich, I'm rich,' she said coldly. 'I took the flat when they offered it. Ten years ago. And I haven't taken anything since.'

'I know.'

'Then what.'

He sighed. 'It's just so sordid. I hate the idea of you playing in something… of you playing a part that goes against everything you believe.'

'That just makes it more of a challenge.'

'Yes, but the better you do it, the more convincing you are, the more women will think they have to accept all this nonsense.'

She stopped in her tracks. 'Are we talking about my work or yours?' she asked. 'How about your paean to Strength Through Joy cruises? Or your "car for every German worker" piece. You've hardly been cutting the ground from under their feet.'

He bit back the surge of anger. She was right.

They both were.

Next afternoon, he went to the Plumpe. Paul had asked him for a programme, and with Effi visiting her family that seemed a good enough reason for going. He had Thomas and Joachim for company, but he missed Paul, and the game itself was dire – a dull 1-1 draw with Berliner SV. Thomas was subdued – like Frau Heidegger and seventy-five million other Germans he'd noticed the tell-tale flurry of government antagonism towards the Czechs. Sandwiched between SV supporters on the southbound U-bahn they arranged to have lunch on the following Thursday.

Back at the apartment he found a courier delivery waiting for him: a copy of the previous day's *Pravda*, complete with his first article. His Russian wasn't up to much, but as far as he could tell they hadn't altered anything. 'Approved by the SD, approved by the NKVD,' he thought out loud. 'I should have been a diplomat.' More gratifying still was the accompanying bank draft in Reichsmarks.

There was also the promised list of suggestions for future articles. The last-but-one letters of the opening sentence – who thought up this stuff? – spelled Cracow. Russell groaned. Two sixteen-hour train journeys, just for a chat with Shchepkin. At least, he hoped it was just for a chat.

Zygmunt's Chapel

'This is it,' McKinley said, with the sort of enthusiasm others reserved for stumbling across El Dorado. The object of his excitement was a short cul-de-sac of decaying tenement blocks wedged between railway arches, small industrial workshops and the Neuköllner-Schiffahrtkanal. One forlorn streetlight threw a faint yellow glow over glistening brickwork and rusty iron. It looked, Russell thought, like the sort of place a particularly sentimental German communist would come to die.

They had been looking for it for almost an hour, ever since playing hide-and-seek with their probably imaginary Gestapo tail in Neukölln's famous Karstadt department store. The object of their quest had, according to McKinley, told them to make sure they were not followed, and he had done his best to oblige, leading Russell into the store by the main entrance and out through the kitchens, pursued only by the shouts of an enraged chef. They had then headed east on foot, turning this way and that down a succession of rapidly darkening and profoundly unwelcoming streets. Russell had expected streams of workers returning home, but they had only come across a few, and McKinley's requests for navigational assistance had been met with either guarded suspicion or outright hostility. There were lights behind the curtains of the residential streets, but they felt far away.

Schönlankerstrasse was no exception. The block they were looking for was the last, pushed up against the elevated tracks of what was probably a freight line. As they reached the entrance another source of light came into view – the red glow of a signal hanging in the darkness.

The limp swastika over the entrance looked like it hadn't been washed since 1933. Entering the dimly-lit hall, they found the concierge's door. McKinley tried two taps with the door-knocker – too softly, Russell thought, but the door swung open almost immediately. A middle-aged woman with a rather striking face ushered them inside and quickly closed the door behind them.

'Who is this?' she asked McKinley with an angry gesture towards Russell. She had a thick Rhenish accent, which explained why the American had so much trouble understanding her.

'He's a friend. He speaks better German than I do,' McKinley explained, rather in the manner of someone reassuring a foolish child.

She gave Russell another look, thought for a moment, then shrugged. 'Come through,' she said shortly.

The living room was clean but almost bare. There were no comfortable chairs, only a couple of upright chairs beside a small table and what looked like homemade cushions on the floor. A tattered but once-expensive rug occupied the centre of the wooden floor. A girl of around five or six was sitting on it, leaning forward over a drawing she was doing. She didn't look up when they entered.

'That's Marietta,' the woman said. 'She gets very absorbed in what she's doing,' she added, as if she needed to explain the child's lack of reaction.

Her name, as McKinley had already told Russell, was Theresa Jürissen. She was younger than he'd first thought – around thirty-five, probably – but she looked both exhausted and malnourished. Only the eyes, a penetrating grey, seemed full of energy.

'Please take the chairs,' she said, but McKinley insisted that she took one. He remained standing, his lanky bulk seeming somewhat incongruous in the centre of the room. Apparently realising as much, he retreated to a wall.

'Have you brought the money?' Frau Jürissen asked, almost apologetically. This was not a woman who was used to poverty, Russell thought. 'This is the only work I can do and look after her all day,' she added, as if more explanation was needed.

McKinley produced his wallet, and counted what looked like several hundred Reichsmarks into her hand. She gazed at the pile for a moment, and then abruptly folded the notes over, and placed them in the pocket of her housecoat. 'So, where shall I begin?' she asked.

McKinley wasted no time. 'You said in your letter that you could not keep silent when children's lives were at stake,' he said, pronouncing each word with the utmost care. 'What made you think they were?'

She placed her hands on the table, one covering the other. 'I couldn't believe it at first,' she said, then paused to get her thoughts in order. 'I worked for the Brandenburg Health Ministry for over ten years. In the Medical Supplies department. I visited hospitals and asylums on a regular basis, checking inventories, anticipating demands – you understand?'

McKinley nodded.

'After the Nazi take-over most of the women in my department were encouraged to resign, but my husband was killed in an accident a few weeks after I had Marietta, and they knew I was the only bread-winner in the family. They wanted me to find another husband of course, but until that happened… well, I was good at my job, so they had no real excuse to fire me.' She looked up. 'I'm sorry. You don't need to know all this.' She looked across at her daughter, who had still shown no sign of recognition that anyone else was in the room. 'I suppose I knew from the start that she wasn't, well, ordinary, but I told myself she was just very shy, very self-absorbed… I mean, some adults are like that – they hardly notice that anyone else exists.' She sighed. 'But I got to the point where I knew I had to do something, take her to see someone. I knew that might mean she'd be sterilized, but… well, if she stayed the way she is now, she'd never notice whether she had any children or not. Anyway, I took her to a clinic in Potsdam, and they examined her and tested her and said they needed to keep her under observation for a few weeks. I didn't want to leave her there, but they told me not to be selfish, that Marietta needed professional care if she was ever to come out of her shell.'

'Did they threaten you?' McKinley asked.

'No, not really. They were just impatient with me. Shocked that I didn't immediately accept that they knew best.'

'Like most doctors,' Russell murmured.

'Perhaps. And maybe they were completely genuine. Maybe Marietta does need whatever it is they have to offer.'

'So you took her away?' McKinley asked.

'I had to. Just two days after I left her in the clinic I was at the Falkenheide asylum – you know it? – it's just outside Fürstenwalde. I was in the staff canteen, checking through their orders over a cup of coffee, when I became aware of the conversation at the next table. I tried to ignore it, but I couldn't. And they were speaking quite normally – there was nothing clandestine about it. In a way that was what was most shocking about it – they assumed that their topic of conversation was common knowledge. As far as the asylum staff were concerned, that is.' She paused, and glanced across at Marietta. 'What they were talking about was a letter which had been sent out by the Ministry of Justice to all Directors of asylums. That letter wanted the Directors' opinions on how they should change the system to allow the killing of incurable children. Should they announce a new law, or should they issue administrative decrees and keep the public in ignorance? This is what the people at the next table were debating, even joking about. Three of them were doctors I recognised, and the woman looked like a senior nurse.'

'This was all spelt out?' Russell asked incredulously. He instinctively trusted her – could see no reason for her to lie – but her scene in the canteen sounded like one of those stage conversations written to update the audience.

'No,' she said, giving Russell an indignant look. 'They were talking more about how the parents would react, whether they would prefer to hear that their child had simply died of whatever illness they had. It was only when I read the letter that it all made sense.'

'How? Where?' McKinley asked excitedly.

'Like I said, I was in that job a long time. I was on good terms with people in all the asylums. I knew I had to see the letter for myself, and I waited for a chance. A few days later a Director was called out early, and I pretended I had to work late. I found the letter in his office.'

'I wish you'd kept it,' McKinley said, more to himself than her.

'I did,' she said simply.

'You did!' McKinley almost shouted, levering himself off the wall he'd been leaning against. 'Where is it? Can we see it?'

'Not now. I don't have it here.'

'How much do you need?' Russell asked.

'Another five hundred Reichsmarks?' The question mark was infinitesimal.

'That's...' McKinley began.

'Good business sense,' Russell completed for him. 'She needs the money,' he added in English.

'Yes, of course,' McKinley agreed. 'I just don't know how... But

I'll get it. Shall I come back here?' he asked her.

'No,' she said. 'It's too risky for me. Send the money to the Post Restante on Heiligegeiststrasse. When I get it, I'll send you the letter.'

'It'll be there by tomorrow evening,' McKinley said, as he wrote out the Neuenburgerstrasse address.

Russell stood up. 'Did you have any trouble getting Marietta back?' he asked Theresa Jürissen.

'Yes,' she said. 'They wouldn't let me take her. I had to steal my own child. That's why we're here in this place.'

They both looked down at Marietta. Her drawing looked like a forest after a hurricane had hit it. 'I wish you luck,' Russell said.

He and McKinley reached the street as a coal train thundered across the arches, and set about retracing their steps. It was raining now, the streets even emptier, a rare neighbourhood bar offering a faint splash of light and noise. They didn't speak until they reached the tram stop on Berlinerstrasse.

'If you get this story out, it'll be your last one from Germany,' Russell said.

McKinley grinned at him. 'Worth it though, don't you think?'

Russell saw the excitement in the young American's eyes, like an echo of his own younger self. He felt a pang of envy. 'Yes, I do,' he agreed.

Russell's first port of call on the following morning was about ten kilometres, and several worlds, away from the dingy Schönlankerstrasse. The villa, just around the corner from the State Archive in the wealthy suburb of Dahlem, was surrounded by trees full of singing birds, most of whom were probably warbling their gratitude to the Führer. In Schönlankerstrasse it was probably still raining in the dark, but here the sun shone down out of a clear blue sky. The coffee had not been as good since the Jewish cook was 'allowed to leave,' but everyone had to make sacrifices.

His pupil Greta was a sixteen-year-old with no interest in learning English. She did, however, like practising her flirting techniques on him. Today it was a new wide-eyed expression which she seemed to think was appealing. She was, he had to admit, a lesson in the nature of beauty. When he'd first set eyes on her, he'd been struck by how gorgeous she was. But after eighteen months of getting to know her, he found her only marginally more attractive than Herman Goering. Her grasp of English had hardly improved at all in that time, but that didn't seem to worry anybody. Her father, a doctor of similar age to Wiesner, had not been cursed with the same tainted blood.

An hour later, richer in Reichsmarks but poorer in spirit, Russell retraced his steps down the sunny avenues to the Dahlem Dorf U-bahn station. Changing at Wittenbergplatz, he bought a paper at a platform kiosk and glanced through it on the ride to Alexanderplatz. The Swiss were the latest target – as neutrals, a lead writer announced, they should refrain from expressing opinions about other countries and refuse to take in refugees. The Germans, on the other hand, should get their colonies back. Three reasons were given. The first was 'inalienable right,' whatever that was. The second was 'economic need,' which presumably came under the inalienable right to loot. The third, which made Russell laugh out loud, was Germany's 'right to share in the education of backward peoples'. 'Thanks to her racial principles,' the writer announced confidently, 'the Third Reich stands in the front rank of Powers in this respect.' Russell thought about this for a while, and decided it could only mean that Germany was well-placed to educate the backward peoples in how deserving their backwardness was.

At Alexanderplatz he picked up the previous Saturday's *Daily*

Mail for the girls, and discovered that rain was likely to affect the weekend's English cup-ties. Several columns were given over to Schacht's dismissal, though, and he found three other articles on German matters. This, as McKinley had said, was where the story was.

Most interesting to Russell, though, was the picture on the back page of the streamlined steam locomotive *Coronation*, hanging between ship and quay en route to America for some celebration or other. He would keep that for Paul.

He thought about his son as the tram ground its way north-west towards Friedrichshain. On the telephone two nights earlier Paul had used all the right words to describe a thrilling weekend with the *Jungvolk*, but there had been a different story in the tone of his voice. Or had there? Maybe it was just that adolescent reticence which psychiatrists were so full of these days. He needed a proper talk with the boy, which made this weekend's summons to Cracow all the more annoying. And to make matters worse, Hertha were at home two Sundays running. Paul could always go with Thomas, but... An away game, he thought suddenly. He could take Paul to an away game the following Sunday. A real trip. He could see no reason why Ilse would object.

And Cracow would be interesting, if nothing else. He had already booked his sleeper tickets and hotel room, and was looking forward to seeing the city for the first time. Both his agents had loved the 'Germany's Neighbours' idea, so there should be some money in it too.

He reached the Wiesners' stop, walked the short distance to their block, and climbed the stairs. Dr Wiesner, who he hadn't seen for a couple of weeks, opened the door. He looked noticeably more careworn, but managed a smile of welcome. 'I wanted to thank you for talking to Albert,' he said without preamble. 'And I'd like to ask you another favour. I feel awkward doing this – and please say no if it's too difficult – but, well, I am just doing what I must. You understand?'

Russell nodded. What now? he wondered.

Wiesner hesitated. He also seemed more unsure of himself, Russell noticed. And who could blame him?

'Is there any way you could check on the rules for taking things out of the country? For Jews, I mean. It's just that they keep changing the rules, and if I ask what they are then they'll just assume I'm trying to get round them.'

'Of course,' Russell said. 'I'll let you know on Friday.'

Wiesner nodded. 'One person I know asked about a miniature which had been in his family for a hundred years, and they simply confiscated it,' he went on, as if Russell still needed convincing.

'I'll let you know,' Russell said again.

'Yes, thank you. I'm told there's a good chance that the girls will be allowed to go, and I'd like to…well, provide for them in England. You understand?'

Russell nodded.

'Very well. Thank you again. I mustn't take up any more learning time.' He stepped to the adjoining door and opened it. 'Girls, come.' He said it gruffly, but the smile he bestowed on them as they trooped in was almost too full of love. Russell remembered the faces on the Danzig station platform, the sound the woman had made.

The two girls fell on the *Daily Mail*.

'You can keep it apart from the back page,' he told them, and explained that he wanted the picture for his son.

'Tell us about your son,' Marthe said. 'In English, of course,' she added.

He spent the next twenty minutes talking and answering questions about Paul. The girls were sympathetic to the philatelist, indulgent towards the football fan and lover of modern transport, dismissive of the toy soldier collector. They were particularly impressed by the tale of how, around the age of five, he had almost died of whooping cough. Telling the story, Russell felt almost anxious, as if he wasn't sure how it was going to end.

He turned the tables for the second half of the lesson, inviting them to talk about their own histories. He regretted this almost instantly, thinking that, given their situation, this was likely to prove upsetting for them. They didn't see it that way. It wasn't that they thought the family's current difficulties were temporary; it was more a matter of their knowing, even with all their problems, that they had more love in their lives than most other people.

It was one of the nicest hours he had ever spent, and walking back to the tram stop on Neue Konigstrasse he reminded himself to thank Doug Conway for the introduction the next time he saw him. The opportunity soon presented itself. Back at the apartment, he found a message from Conway, asking him to call. He did so.

Conway didn't sound like his usual self. 'One of our people would like a word,' he said.

'What about?' Russell asked warily.

'I don't know. I'm just the messenger.'

'Ah.'

'Could you come in, say, tomorrow morning, around 11?'

'I suppose so.'

'I'd like to see you too. We're leaving, by the way. I've been posted to Washington.'

'When? And why haven't you told me?'

'I'm telling you now. I only heard a couple of days ago. And we're going in a couple of weeks.'

'Well I'm sorry to hear that. From a purely selfish point of view, of course. Is it a promotion?'

'Sort of. Touch of the up, touch of the sideways. Anyway, we're having a dinner for a few people on the third – that's next Friday – and I hoped you and your lady friend could come.'

'Oh, Effi will be…' Working, he was going to say. But of course she wouldn't – *Barbarossa* would be over, and *Mother* didn't start shooting until the thirteenth. 'I'll ask her,' he said. 'Should be okay, though.'

The Café Kranzler was full of SS officers the next morning, their boots polished to such perfection that any leg movement sent flashes of reflected light from the chandeliers dancing round the walls. Russell hurried his coffee and, with half an hour to burn, ambled down Unter den Linden to the Schloss. The Kaiser's old home was still empty, but the papers that morning were full of his upcoming eightieth birthday party in Holland. 'Come back, all is forgiven,' Russell murmured to himself.

After the Unter den Linden the British Embassy seemed an oasis of languor. The staff drifted to and fro, as if worried they might be caught speeding. Was this the new British plan, Russell wondered. Slow the drift to war by slowing diplomats.

Doug Conway eventually appeared. 'One of our intelligence people wants to talk to you,' he said quietly. 'Nothing formal, just a chat about things.' Russell grunted his disbelief, and Conway had the grace to look embarrassed. 'Not my idea – I'm just the messenger.'

'You said that yesterday.'

'Well, I am. Look, I'll take you up. He's a nice enough chap. His name's Trelawney-Smythe.'

It would be, Russell thought. He had a pretty good idea what was coming.

The office was a small room high at the back of the building, with a compensating view of the Brandenburg Gate. Conway introduced Russell and withdrew. Trelawney-Smythe, a tall dark-haired man in his thirties with a worried-looking face, ushered him to a seat.

'Good of you to come,' he began, rifling through papers on his over-crowded desk. Russell wondered if Sturmbannführer Kleist gave private lessons in desk arrangement. 'Ah,' Trelawney-Smythe said triumphantly, extracting a copy of *Pravda* from the mess. A hand-written sheet was attached with a paper clip.

'My latest masterpiece,' Russell murmured. Why was it, he wondered, that British officialdom always brought out the schoolboy in him? After reading one of the *Saint* stories Paul had asked him why the Saint was so fond of prodding Chief Inspector Teal in the stomach. He had been unable to offer a coherent explanation, but deep down he knew exactly why. He already wanted to prod Trelawney-Smythe in his.

The other man had unclipped the handwritten sheet from the newspaper, and carefully stowed the paper clip away in its rightful place. 'This is a translation of your article,' he said.

'May I see it?' Russell asked, holding out a hand.

Somewhat taken aback, Trelawney-Smythe handed it over.

Russell glanced through it. They had printed it more or less verbatim. He handed it back.

'Mr Russell, I'm going to be completely frank with you,' Trelawney-Smythe said, unconsciously echoing Sturmbannführer Kleist.

Don't strain yourself, Russell thought.

'You used to be a member of the British Communist Party, correct?'

'Yes.' He wondered if Trelawney-Smythe and Kleist had ever met.

'Then you know how the communists operate?'

'You think they all operate the same way?'

'I think the Soviets have certain well-practised methods, yes.'

'You're probably right.'

'Well, then. We don't think this will be the end of it. We think they'll ask for more and more.'

'More and more articles? And who is we?'

Trelawney-Smythe smiled. 'Don't play the innocent. You know who "we" are. And you know I'm not talking about your articles, amusing as they are. We think they'll be asking you for other information. The usual method is to keep upping the ante, until you're no longer in a position to refuse. Because they'll shop you to the Germans if you do.'

'As you said, I know how they operate. And it's my lookout, isn't it?'

'Not completely. Do you see this?' Trelawney-Smythe asked, indicating the words at the foot of the article, which identified the name, nationality and credentials of the author.

'Yes.'

'An Englishman currently living in Germany,' Trelawney-Smythe read out, just to be sure.

'That's me.'

Trelawney-Smythe tapped on the paper with an index finger. 'You are English, and your behaviour will reflect on the rest of us. Particularly at a time like this.'

'A "don't-rock-the-boat-for-God's-sake" sort of time?'

'Something like that. Relations between us and the Soviets are, shall we say, difficult at the moment. They don't trust us and we don't trust them. Everybody's looking for signals of intent. The smallest thing – like *Pravda* inviting you to write these articles – could mean something. Or nothing. They could be planning to use you as a channel to us or the Germans, for passing on information or disinformation. We don't know. I assume you don't know.'

'I'm just doing my job.'

'All right. But how would you feel about providing us with advance copies of your articles. Just so we know what's coming.'

Russell laughed. 'You too?' He explained about his arrangement with the SD. 'Why not?' he said. 'I might as well run off a few carbons for Mussolini and Daladier while I'm at it.' He put his hands on the chair-arms, prior to lifting himself up. 'Anything else?'

'We would appreciate being told if this goes beyond a mere commercial arrangement. And obviously we'd be interested in anything you learn which might be of use to your country.'

'I've already learned one thing. The Soviets think the British and French are trying to cut them out. Look how long Hitler gave the Ambassador at the opening last week. Look at the new trade deal talks. If you don't start treating the Soviets as potential allies, they'll do a deal with Hitler.'

'I think London's aware of that.'

'You could have fooled me. But what do I know?' He looked at his watch. 'I have a lunch date.' He extended his hand across the desk. 'I'll bear what you've said in mind.'

'Enjoy your lunch.'

Russell dropped in on Conway on his way out.

'Still talking to me?' the diplomat asked.

'You, yes; the Empire, no.'

'He's just doing his job.'

'I know. Look, thanks for the dinner invitation. I'll let you know soon as I can.' He paused at the door. 'And I'll be sorry to see you go,' he added.

• • •

It was a fast five minute walk to the Russischer Hof on Georgenstrasse, where he and Thomas usually met for lunch. As he hurried east on Unter den Linden Russell replayed the conversation with Trelawney-Smythe over in his mind. Rather to his surprise it had been refreshingly free of threats. If British intelligence wanted to, he imagined that they could make his life a lot more difficult. They could take away his passport, or just make renewal harder. They could probably make it harder for him to sell his work in England, his prime market. A word to a few knighthood-hungry editors – in fact, a mere appeal to their patriotism – and his London agent would be collecting rejections on his behalf. On the plus side it was beginning to look as if every intelligence service in Europe was interested in employing him.

It was a raw day, the wind whipping in from the east, and Russell turned up his collar against it. A tram slid under the railway bridge, bell frantically ringing, as he turned off Friedrichstrasse and into Georgenstrasse. The Russischer Hof was a nineteenth century establishment once favoured by Bismarck, and sometimes Russell wondered if they were still recycling the same food. The elaborate décor created a nice atmosphere though, and the usual paucity of uniformed clientele was a definite bonus.

Russell's ex-brother-in-law was seated at a window table, glass of Riesling in hand, looking dourly out at the street. The dark grey suit added to the sober impression, but that was Thomas. When they'd first met in the mid-twenties Russell had thought him the epitome of the humourless German. However, once he got to know him, he had realised that Thomas was anything but. Ilse's brother had a sly, rather anarchic sense of humour, completely lacking in the cruelty which marked much popular German humour. If anything he was the epitome of the decent German, an endangered species if ever there was one.

The pot roast with cream sauce, red cabbage and mashed potatoes seemed an ideal riposte to the weather, which was now blowing snow flurries past their window. 'How's the business?' Russell asked, as Thomas poured him a glass of wine.

'Good. We've got a lot of work, and exports are looking up. The new printers have made a huge difference. And you know the World's Fair in New York this April? It looked for a moment as if we might have a stand there.'

'What happened?'

'It seems the organizers have decided to include a pavilion celebrating pre-Nazi German Art. And émigré art. If they do, the government will boycott the Fair.'

'That's a shame.'

Thomas gave him a wintry smile. 'Given the context, it's hard to be that upset. And there's always the chance that the Ministry would have refused to let us go. Because of our employment policies.'

Only one firm in Berlin employed more Jews than Schade Printing Works.

'You don't have room for one more, I suppose,' Russell asked, thinking of Albert Wiesner.

'Not really. Who do you have in mind?'

Russell explained the Wiesners' situation.

Thomas looked pained. 'I have a waiting list of around two hundred already,' he said. 'Most of them are relatives of people who already work there.'

Russell thought of pressing him but decided not to. He could hear Albert in his head – 'One family's success is another family's failure.' 'I understand,' he said, and was about to change the subject when the waiter arrived with their meals.

Both men noticed that the portions seemed smaller than usual. 'Sign of the times,' Thomas observed.

'Any chance of things getting better?' Russell asked. Thomas had no more inside information than Russell's other friends in Berlin – and considerably less than many – but he'd always had a knack of knowing which way the wind was blowing.

'I don't know,' was his answer. 'Ribbentrop's off to Warsaw again. They seem to be trying.' He shrugged. 'We'll probably find out more on Monday.'

That was the day of Hitler's annual speech to the Reichstag commemorating his own accession to the Chancellorship. 'I'd forgotten about that,' Russell admitted.

'You're probably the only person in Europe who has. I think the whole continent's hanging on it. Will he keep the pressure up, demand more? Or will he take the pressure off? That would be the intelligent move. Act as if he's satisfied, even if he's only pausing for breath. But in the long run it's hard to see him stopping. He's like a spinning coin. Once he stops spinning, he'll fall flat.'

Russell grunted. 'Nice.'

They asked after each other's better halves, both current and former.

'You're asking me?' Thomas said when Russell enquired after Ilse. 'I haven't see her for weeks. Last time we went over there, well…' He didn't continue.

'You didn't have a row?'

'Oh no, nothing like that,' Thomas said, as if rows were something that happened to other people. Which, in his case, they usually were. 'I just find Matthias so…oh, I don't know…complacent? Is that the right word for people who say they fear the worst but live their lives as if there's bound to be a happy ending?'

'It might be,' Russell agreed. He realized he hadn't told Thomas about his trip to Cracow, or asked him to take Paul to the match on Sunday, and did so now.

Thomas was happy to take Paul, but bemused by Russell's choice of Cracow for the 'Germany's Neighbours' series. 'Wouldn't a day trip to Posen have been good enough?' he wanted to know.

Russell had a sudden desire to tell Thomas about Shchepkin – if something went wrong, there would be someone to offer some sort of explanation to Paul and Effi – but he held himself back. He would be compromising Thomas, and to what real end? What could go wrong?

Waiting behind another customer for his Friday morning paper, Russell caught sight of the headline – BARCELONA FALLS. On impulse, he turned away. That was one story he didn't want to read. The Spanish Civil War was over. The good guys had lost. What else was there to say?

As it had gone down so well on his last visit, he bought another ancient *Daily Mail* at the Alexanderplatz kiosk. This had an article on young English girls collecting stamps, which he knew would interest Ruth and Marthe, and a big piece on the recent loss of the Empire Flying Boat *Cavalier*, complete with map and diagram, which Paul would love. He saved the best, however, for the very end of the girls' lesson – a report of a tongue-twisting competition on the BBC. Trying to say 'should such a shapeless sash such shabby stitches show' soon had Ruth giggling so hard she really was in stitches, and Marthe fared little better with 'the flesh of freshly fried flying fish.'

The doctor was not at home, so Russell handed the copy of the latest rules governing Jewish emigration to Frau Wiesner. He had collected them the previous day from the British Passport Control Office. 'But they ignore their own rules half the time,' the young official had told him bitterly. 'You can count on getting a change of clothes past them, but anything else is as likely to be confiscated as not. If your friends have any other way of getting stuff out, they should use it.'

Russell passed on the advice, and watched her heart sink.

'If you need help, ask me,' he said, surprising himself. 'I don't think I'd have any trouble shipping stuff to my family in England.'

Her eyes glowed. 'Thank you,' she said, and reached up to kiss him on the cheek.

He journeyed home to pack, stopping off in Alexanderplatz for a late lunch. At least he was pleasing some people. He hadn't seen Effi since Sunday and the round of mutual accusations which he had so stupidly instigated. They hadn't had a row – they had even managed two reasonably friendly conversations on the telephone – but he knew she was angry with him, and his non-availability for the *Barbarossa* send-off had made things worse.

Paul didn't seem that much happier with him, despite the promise of a trip the following Sunday to see the cup-tie in Dresden. There was something going on, but Paul wasn't prepared to talk about it, or at least not on the telephone.

Frau Heidegger was glad to see him, and sorry his imminent train prevented him from joining her for coffee. Up in his apartment, he threw a few spare clothes into a suitcase, checked he had his notes for the next article, and headed back down. On the next landing he ran into a smiling McKinley.

'Everything okay?' Russell asked in passing.

'Uh-huh. I'm just waiting for our friend's letter and… bingo!'

Russell laughed and clattered on down the stairs.

He arrived at the Schlesinger Bahnhof with twenty minutes to spare. The train was already sheltering under the wrought iron canopy, and he walked down the platform in search of his carriage and seat. As he leaned out of the window to watch a train steam in from the east a paper boy thrust an afternoon edition under his nose. The word 'Barcelona' was again prominent, but this time he handed over the pfennigs. As his train gathered speed through Berlin's industrial suburbs he read the article from start to finish, in all its sad and predictable detail.

Three years of sacrifice, all for nothing. Three years of towns won, towns lost. Russell had registered the names, but resisted further knowledge. It was too painful. Thousands of young men and women had gone to fight fascism in Spain, just as thousands had gone to fight for communism in Russia twenty years earlier. According to Marx, history repeated itself first as tragedy and then as farce. But no one was laughing. Except perhaps Stalin.

Russell supposed he should be glad that Spain would soon be at peace, but even that was beyond him. He stared out of the window at the neat fields of the Spree valley, basking in the orange glow of the setting sun, and felt as though he was being lied to. Seconds later, as if in confirmation, the train thundered through a small town station, its fluttering swastika deep blood-red in that self-same glow, a crowd of small boys in uniform milling on the opposite platform.

The food in the restaurant car proved surprisingly good. The menu had a distinctly Polish flavour, although as far as Russell could see there were few Poles on the train. Most of his fellow-passengers were German males – mainly commercial travellers or soldiers on leave. There was only a sprinkling of couples, though the pair at the next table had enough sexual energy for ten. They could hardly keep their hands off each other while eating, and the young man kept checking his watch, as if willing the train on to Breslau, where the sleeping coaches would be attached.

The couple soon disappeared, probably in search of an empty

bathroom. The romance of trains, Russell thought, staring at his own reflection in the window. He remembered the overnight journey to Leningrad with Ilse in 1924, just after they'd met. People had slept in the bathrooms on that train, and anywhere else they could find a space. He and Ilse had had to wait.

Fifteen years. The Soviet Union had come a long way since then, one way or another. Some people came back from visits singing its praises. There was still much to do, but it was the future in embryo, a potential paradise. Other returnees shook their heads in sadness. A dream warped beyond recognition, they said. A nightmare.

Russell guessed the latter was nearer the truth, but sometimes wondered whether that was just his natural pessimism. It had to be a bit of both, but where the balance lay he didn't know.

More to the point, what did Moscow want with him? What they said they wanted? Or something else? Or both? Trelawney-Smythe had been certain they would ask for more, and Kleist had hinted as much. He didn't even know who he was dealing with. Was Shchepkin NKVD or GRU? Or some other acronym he hadn't even heard of? A French correspondent in Berlin had told him that the NKVD was now split between a Georgian faction and the rest, and for all Russell knew the GRU was eaten up by factional rivalry over how much salt they put in the canteen borsht.

And why was he assuming it would be Shchepkin again? The revolution was burning its human fuel at quite a rate these days, and Shchepkin, with his obvious intelligence, seemed highly combustible.

He would have to deal with whoever presented himself. Or herself. But what would he or she want? What could they want? Information about German military strengths and weaknesses? About particular weapons programmes? Political intentions?

Military plans? He had no information – no access to information – about any of that. Thank God.

What did he have that they valued? Freedom to move around Germany. Freedom to ask questions without arousing suspicion. Even more so now, with Kleist's letter in his possession. Maybe one of their agents had gone missing, and they would ask Russell to find out what had happened to him. Or they might want to use him as a courier, carrying stuff to or from their agents. That would explain the meetings outside Germany.

Or they could use him as a conduit. The Soviets knew the Germans would check up on him, and assumed he would be asked for reports on his meetings And the British too. They would have counted on the British calling him in. They could use him as a human post-box, with Kleist and Trelawney-Smythe as the sorters.

They might be just making it up as they went along. His unusual situation made him potentially useful, and they were still looking for a way to realise that potential. That would explain the articles and oral reports – a sort of halfway house to prepare him for a truly clandestine life. There was no way of knowing. Russell leant back in his chair, remembering the remark of a Middlesex Regiment officer he'd met in 1918. 'Intelligence services,' the man had said, 'were prone to looking up their own arses and wondering why it was dark.'

Soon after ten the train reached Breslau, the destination of most passengers. As they filtered out through the dimly-lit exit, many of the remaining passengers took the chance to stretch their legs on the snow-strewn platform. Russell walked to the back of the train and watched a busy little shunter detach four saloons and replace them with three sleepers. It was really cold now, and the orange glow from the engine's firebox made it seem more so.

He walked back up the platform, arms clasped tightly across his chest. 'Cold, eh,' a young soldier said, stamping his feet and taking a deep drag on his cigarette. He was only about eighteen, and seemed to be wearing a summer uniform.

As Russell nodded his agreement a whistle sounded the all aboard.

Walking up the train, he reclaimed his seat in an almost empty carriage. The sleeping car attendants would be rushed off their feet for the next quarter of an hour, and he wasn't ready for sleep in any case. As the train pulled out of the station the ceiling lights were extinguished, allowing him a view through the window of flat meadows stretching north towards a distant line of yellow lights. The Oder river, likely as not.

Hoping for some conversation he revisited the restaurant car, but the only customers were a middle-aged German couple deep in the throes of an argument. The barman sold him a *Goldwasser*, but made it abundantly clear he was through talking for the day. Around eleven-thirty Russell reluctantly worked his way back down the train to the sleeping cars. The attendant showed him to his berth, and generously pointed out that the one above was unoccupied. He could take his pick.

Russell tossed his bag on the upper bunk, used the bathroom, and climbed half-dressed into the lower bunk. He would have a bath when he reached his hotel, he thought. It was an expensive one, so there shouldn't be any problem with hot water.

As usual he had trouble getting to sleep. He lay there, feeling the sway of the train, listening to the click of the wheels on the rail joints, thinking about Effi. She was younger than him – eight years younger. Maybe people's expectations shifted after a certain age, which he'd reached and she hadn't. Was that why they were still living apart? Why had neither of them ever mentioned marriage?

Was he afraid of something? He didn't think so. But then what was the point of turning their lives upside-down when the Führer was about to do it for them?

Shortly after eight in the morning he was standing, yawning, on one of Cracow Plaszów Station's snow-covered platforms. After eventually getting to sleep, he had twice been roused for border inspections, and could hardly have felt worse if he'd been awake all night.

He started towards the exit, and almost went over on a patch of ice. Further up the platform a line of young railway employees were working their way towards him, breath pumping, shovelling snow and noisily digging at the ice beneath with their spades. The sky above them seemed heavy with future snowfalls.

His hotel was on the other side of Cracow's old town, some three miles away. He found a taxi outside the station, and a taxi-driver who wanted to practise his English. He had a cousin in Chicago, he said, but he wanted to go to Texas and work in the oil industry. That was where the future was.

As they drove north through the Jewish quarter Russell noticed the Marx Brothers adorning a cinema on Starowislna Street. The name of the film was in Polish, but his driver's English failed him. He asked again at the Hotel Francuski reception, and received a confident answer from a young man in a very shiny suit. The film, which had only just opened, was called 'Broth of the Bird.'

His room was on the third floor, looking out on Pijakska Street. This was full of well-insulated, purposeful walkers, presumably on their way to work. A church stood just across the way, the beauty of its rococo façade still visible beneath the clinging snow.

The room itself was large, high-ceilinged and well-furnished. The bed gave without sagging, the two-person sofa was almost luxurious. The small table and upright chair by the window were custom-made for the visiting journalist. There was a spacious wardrobe for hanging his clothes. The lights all worked, both here and in the adjoining bathroom, which seemed almost as big. The water ran hot in the big four-legged bath, and Russell lay soaking until he realised he was falling asleep.

After a shave and change of clothes he ventured out again. As expected it was snowing, large flakes of the stuff floating down in dense profusion. Following the receptionist's directions, Russell turned right outside the door, and right again opposite the church, into Sw Jana Street. Following this south across two intersections he reached the Rynek Główny, Europe's largest market square. The centre of the huge expanse was occupied by a Gothic hall, but Russell's eyes were instantly drawn to his left, and the loveliest church he had ever seen. Two asymmetrical towers soared skyward through the curtain of snow, one climaxing in a flurry of spires, the other, slightly less high, in a small renaissance dome. Both were stacked with windows, like a medieval skyscraper.

For several minutes he stood there entranced, until the cold in his feet and a hunger for coffee drove him into one of the cafés that lined the square. Two cups and a roll packed with thick slices of bacon later he felt ready to face a day of work. The café might be half-empty, but all the customers were 'Germany's Neighbours'. He introduced himself to one young Polish couple and took it from there. For the next few hours he worked his way round the cafés and bars of the old town, asking questions.

Most of those he approached spoke some English or some German, and he didn't get many refusals. His own Englishness usually got him off to a favourable start, since many of his interviewees chose to believe that he had a personal line to Neville Chamberlain. Would England fight for Poland? they all asked. And when Russell expressed a sliver of doubt as to whether she would, they couldn't believe it. 'But you fought for Belgium!' several of them said indignantly.

There was virtual unanimity about Poland's situation. Germany was a menace, the Soviets were a menace – it was like choosing between cholera and the Black Death. What did they think about the German request for an extra-territorial road across the corridor? They could whistle. Would they fight for German Danzig? Every last stone. Would they win? He must be joking.

He couldn't be certain of course, but the few people who refused him all looked Jewish. A shadow dropped over their eyes when he introduced himself, a hunted look on their faces as they backed away, pleading lack of time or some other excuse. As if he was an advance guard for the Nazis, his very presence in Cracow a harbinger of disaster.

The snow kept falling. He ate an omelette for lunch in one of the Rynek Główny cafés, and then trudged up and down the main shopping streets in search of a present for Effi. He half-expected Shchepkin to suddenly appear at his shoulder, but there was no sign of him or anyone else. As far as Russell could tell, no one was tracking his footsteps in the snow.

After slipping on some icy cobbles and being almost run over by a tram he decided a rest was in order, and retreated to his hotel for a nap. It was seven by the time he woke, and he felt hungry again. A new receptionist recommended a restaurant on Starowislna Street, which turned out to be only a few doors from the cinema showing the Marx Brothers movie. It was too good an opportunity to miss. After partaking of a wonderful *wienerschnitzel* – at least Cracow had something to thank the Hapsburg Empire for – he joined the shivering queue for the evening showing.

Inside the cinema it was hot, noisy and packed. Surveying the audience before the lights went down, Russell guessed that at least half of it was Jewish. He felt cheered by the fact that this could still seem normal, even in a country as prone to anti-Semitism as Poland. He wished Ruth and Marthe were there with him. And Albert. He couldn't remember ever seeing Albert laugh.

The newsreel was in Polish, but Russell got the gist. The first item featured a visit to Warsaw by the Hungarian Foreign Minister, and no doubt claimed that he and Colonel Beck had discussed matters of mutual importance, without spelling out what everyone knew these were – choosing their cuts of Czechoslovakia once the Germans had delivered the carcass. The second item concerned Danzig, with much piling of sandbags round the Polish Post Office. The third, more entertainingly, featured a man in New York walking a tightrope between skyscrapers.

The movie proved a surreal experience in more ways than one. Since it was subtitled in Polish, the audience felt little need to keep quiet, and Russell had some trouble catching all the wisecracks. And as the subtitling ran a few seconds behind the visuals, he often found himself laughing ahead of everyone else, like some eccentric cackler.

None of it mattered, though. He'd loved the Marx Brothers since seeing *Animal Crackers* during the last days of the Weimar Republic, before Jewish humour followed Jewish music and Jewish physics into exile. By the time 'Broth of the Bird' was half an hour old he was literally aching with laughter. The film's subject-matter – the approach of an utterly ridiculous war between two Ruritanian countries – was fraught with contemporary relevance, but any dark undertone was utterly overwhelmed by the swirling tide of joyous anarchy. If you wanted something real to worry about, there were cracker crumbs in the bed with a woman expected. The only sane response to rampant patriotism was: 'Take a card!' As the audience streamed out of the cinema, at least half the faces were streaked with tears of laughter.

It had stopped snowing. In fact, the sky seemed to be clearing. As he walked back towards the city centre, Russell had glimpses of the Wawel Castle and Cathedral silhouetted against a starry slice of sky. Following the tram-lines through a gap in the old medieval walls he eventually reached the Rynek Główny, where the cafés and restaurants were humming with conversation and all sorts of music. Standing in mid-square beside the Cloth Hall he could hear pianos playing Mendelssohn, Chopin and American blues.

People were having fun. They did that in Berlin too, but there was something different in the air. In Berlin there was always an edge of caution: looks over the shoulder, a rein on the tongue. Maybe there was one here too – heaven knew, the regime in Warsaw was illiberal enough – but he couldn't feel it. If the Poles were facing the most threatening year of their recent existence, they weren't letting on.

He thought about having a nightcap, but decided not to make things any more difficult for Shchepkin than he needed to. He was only spending one night at the hotel.

There was no sign of him in the lobby, or of anyone else, suspicious or not. There was no message at reception when he collected his key. After ascending in the delightful glass and wrought iron cage, he found his corridor silent, his door locked. The room was empty. Laughing at himself, he checked the wardrobe. No Shchepkin. No Harpo Marx.

It was almost midnight. He stretched out on the sofa with the John Kling detective stories which Paul had loaned him weeks before, one ear cocked for footsteps in the corridor, but all he heard was an occasional drunken shout from the street below. At 12.45 he gave up and went to bed, laughing in the dark about cracker crumbs.

He was woken by church bells. It was just after eight, a thin line of grey light separating the curtains on the near window. Russell clambered out of bed and pulled them back. The tip of the church spire opposite was lit by an invisible sun, the sky clear. It looked bitterly cold.

He had mixed feelings about Shchepkin's non-appearance. He couldn't help feeling annoyed that he might have come all this way, missing a weekend with Effi and Paul, only to be stood up. On the other hand, he could hardly say the weekend had been wasted – he liked Cracow, had loved *Duck Soup*, and had the makings of a 'Germany's Neighbours' article. If the Soviets were already tired of him he supposed he should feel relieved, but he couldn't help feeling a poignant sense of anti-climax.

Whatever, he told himself. If nothing else, the projected Soviet series had inspired him to generate others. And Shchepkin – he looked at his watch – still had seven hours to make contact before his train left.

He was damned if he was going to stay cooped up in his room, even if the hotel would let him. He decided to pack and take his bag to the left luggage at the main station, which was only five minutes walk away. He could get a taxi from there to the Plaszów station when the time came.

An hour later, he was enjoying coffee and rolls in an almost empty station buffet. There were no English or German papers for sale, and – it being Sunday morning – little activity to observe. One small shunting engine chugged its way through in apparent search of work, but that was it. Russell was about to leave when a dark-haired young man loomed over his table. 'Have you a pencil I could use?' he asked in German.

Russell handed his over.

The man sat down, wrote out what appeared to be train times on the corner of his newspaper, and handed the pencil back. 'Zygmunt's Chapel,' he said pleasantly as he got to his feet. 'Two o'clock.'

Russell reached the foot of the ramp leading up to the Wawel with time to spare. On the slopes of the hill several bunches of children were throwing snowballs at each other and squealing with delight, while their parents stood and chatted, plumes of breath coalescing in the air between them. Away to the left, the yellow walls and red tile roof of the Royal Palace stood stark against the clear blue sky.

The ramp ended in a gate through the old fortifications, close by the southern end of the Cathedral. This – in contrast to the church on the Rynek Główny – was an elegant mess featuring spires and domes in a bewildering variety of styles and sizes, as if the whole thing had been arranged by a playful child.

The Zygmunt Chapel was off the nave to the right. The tombs of two men – kings, Russell assumed – were vertically stacked amidst a feast of renaissance carving. The accompanying writing was in Polish, but he recognised the name Jagiello from the Danzig stamp wars.

'Beautiful, yes?' said a familiar voice at his shoulder.

'It is,' Russell agreed. Shchepkin was wearing the same crumpled suit, and quite possibly the same shirt, but on this occasion a dark green tie was hanging, somewhat loosely, beneath the collar. A fur hat covered his hair.

'Have you visited Cracow before?' the Russian asked.

'No, never.'

'It's one of my favourite cities.'

'Oh.'

'Have you seen the Holy Cross Chapel?' Shchepkin asked.

'No...'

'You must. Come.' He led the way back towards the entrance, and the chapel to its left. Russell followed, somewhat amused at being shown the wonders of Christendom by a communist agent.

The chapel was extraordinary. There was another Jagiellonian tomb, carved in marble in the year Columbus stumbled across America, and a series of slightly older Byzantine frescoes. As they emerged, Shchepkin stood looking down the nave, then turned his eyes upwards toward the soaring roof.

'My father was a priest,' he said in reaction to Russell's look. 'One thing more,' he added, gesturing toward the shrine in the centre of the nave. It held a silver coffin of staggering workmanship. 'It was made in Danzig,' Shchepkin pointed out, as if their relationship needed geographical continuity. 'Enough,' he added, seeing Russell's expression, 'we'll save the crypts for another time. Let's go outside.'

Between the cathedral and the walls overlooking the Vistula there was a large open space. Russell and Shchepkin joined the scattering of couples and small groups who were following the freshly-cleared circular path, almost blinded for a while by the brightness of sun on snow.

'The article was perfect,' Shchepkin said eventually. 'Just what was required.' He produced an envelope from his pocket and slipped it into Russell's. 'For your research work,' he said.

Russell stole a quick look at it. It was a banker's draft in Reichsmarks. Lots of them.

'What's the next article about,' Shchepkin asked.

'Transport.'

'Excellent. So what are you telling me today?'

Russell went through the results of his visit to Dresden, his impressions and analysis. It all seemed pretty obvious to him, but

Shchepkin seemed satisfied enough, nodding and interjecting the occasional question or comment. Russell had the feeling he could have listed the stations on the Ringbahn.

After one circuit they started another. They were not alone in this, but one man in particular, limping along fifty yards behind them, struck Russell as suspicious. But when he glanced over his shoulder for the third time Shchepkin told him not to worry. 'One of mine,' he said almost affectionately. 'Local help,' he added, rubbing his hands together. 'What did the SD have to say?' he asked.

Russell recounted his meeting with Kleist, and the demand for previews of each article. He also told Shchepkin about the letter Kleist had written for him, and regretted doing so almost instantly – he wanted the Russian worried for his safety, not encouraged to risk it. 'And the British want previews too,' he added quickly, hoping to divert his listener with an unwelcome shock.

Shchepkin, though, just laughed. 'And how are you explaining these trips?' he asked.

Russell explained about 'Germany's Neighbours' and 'Ordinary Germans'.

'Not bad,' Shchepkin said. 'We will make an intelligence officer of you yet.'

'No thanks.'

Shchepkin gave him one of those looks, amused but disappointed. 'Are you planning to take sides in the coming war?' he asked.

'Not if I can help it,' was Russell's instinctive response.

'Have you heard of the poet Yeats?' Shchepkin asked out of the blue.

'Of course.'

Shchepkin grunted. 'One never knows with the English. So many of you look down on anything Irish.'

'Yeats is a wonderful poet.'

'He died yesterday,' Shchepkin said.

'I didn't know.'

'You know that poem – "The Stolen Child"? I always loved that line – "For the world's world more full of weeping than you can understand."'

Russell said nothing.

Shchepkin shook his head, as if to clear it. 'We'll meet in Posen next month. Or Poznan as the Poles call it now. And we'd like you to talk to armament workers,' he said. 'In Berlin, the Ruhr – you know where the big factories are. We need to know if there are problems there, if the workers are ready for political action.'

'That'll be difficult,' Russell said.

'Ordinary German workers, caught between their natural desire for peace and patriotic concern for the Fatherland,' Shchepkin suggested. 'I'm sure you can manage it.'

'I'll try,' Russell agreed.

'You must,' Shchepkin said. 'And you really should wear a hat.'

Idiots to spare

Berlin was grey and overcast. As his train drew into Friedrich-strasse Station, Russell thought about taking the Stadtbahn another couple of stops and surprising Effi in bed, but decided against. She was rarely at her best this early in the morning.

Having breakfasted on the train, he skipped coffee in the buffet and headed straight for his bank on Behrenstrasse, where he deposited Shchepkin's banker's draft. As he headed for Französischestrasse in search of a tram home Russell felt an almost dizzying sense of solvency. Presents for everybody, he thought. Including himself.

The sense of well-being evaporated the moment he saw Frau Heidegger's face. 'Oh Herr Russell,' she said, grabbing his left arm with both hands. 'Thank God you're back. I…'

'What's happened?'

'Herr McKinley – he's dead. He committed suicide – can you believe it? The poor boy… And he seemed so happy these last few weeks. I can't…'

'How?' Russell asked. He felt cold all over, and slightly nauseous. 'How did he kill himself?' He couldn't believe it. He didn't believe it.

Frau Heidegger mopped up a tear. 'He threw himself in front of a train. At Zoo Station. There were lots of witnesses.'

'When?'

'Late on Saturday. The police came just before midnight and locked his room. Then they came back yesterday. They were up there for hours.'

'The Kripo?'

She looked bewildered for a second. 'Yes, yes, I think so. There were so many of them. They must have been looking for a suicide note, I think. Or something to tell them why he did it.'

Or a letter, Russell thought.

'But I don't think they found anything,' Frau Heidegger went on. 'They seemed very frustrated when they went. I suppose they're worried that the Americans won't believe he killed himself.'

'Perhaps,' Russell said. He still felt stunned.

'They left the room very tidy,' Frau Heidegger said inconsequentially. 'And they want to talk to you,' she added. '"As soon as he gets back" they said. And they put a note under your door saying the same thing. I have the telephone number.' She disappeared back into her apartment for a few seconds and re-emerged with what looked like a torn-off page from a police notebook. There was a number and a name – Kriminalinspektor Oehm.

'I'll ring him now,' Russell said.

'Yes, please,' Frau Heidegger said, as if it would take a huge weight off her mind.

The underling who answered knew who Russell was. 'The Kriminalinspektor would like to see you immediately,' he said, with the stress on the last word. 'At the Alex. Room 456.'

'I'm on my way,' Russell said. It seemed the politic thing to do.

'I'll look after your bag,' Frau Heidegger said, picking it up and moving towards her door. 'You can collect it when you get back.'

He started walking towards the U-bahn, thinking it would be quicker, but changed his mind once he reached Lindenstrasse. Why was he hurrying? A tram ride would give him time to think.

He climbed aboard the first Alexanderplatz-bound tram and stared blankly out of the window. If there was one thing he knew, it was that McKinley hadn't killed himself. In fact, he could hardly think of anyone less likely to do so. He supposed it could have been an accident – the platforms got pretty crowded at Zoo Station after theatre-closing time – but if so, why the rush to a suicide verdict? Frau Heidegger had mentioned witnesses – lots of them. An apparent suicide, Russell realized, offered stronger grounds for a police investigation than a simple accident. They'd spent most of yesterday in McKinley's room, and they must have been looking for something. Theresa Jürissen's letter was an obvious candidate, but who knew what other pieces of paper McKinley had collected in support of his story. And it looked as though they hadn't found what they were looking for. Russell wasn't sure how reliable a judge of Kripo moods Frau Heidegger was, but the urgency of his summons certainly suggested they were missing something.

If they hadn't found the letter, then where the hell was it? Six days had passed since he and McKinley visited Theresa Jürissen, and McKinley had been in a hurry – it didn't seem likely that he'd taken his time sending her the money. Unless, of course, he'd had trouble raising it. And she might have had trouble getting down to the Poste Restante to pick the money up. The letter could still be in the post. Or in her possession. He'd have to warn her, for his own sake as well as hers. If she was arrested, his own involvement would come out, and even if the Kripo accepted that he'd only been along as an interpreter, he'd still failed to report a possible crime against the state. At the very least, grounds for deportation. At worst... it didn't bear thinking about.

If McKinley had received the letter and they hadn't found it, then what had he done with it? He might have risked posting it off to the States, but Russell didn't think so. If they'd been watching him – and it seemed likely that they had – then any outgoing mail would have been intercepted. Russell remembered McKinley's reluctant admission that he thought he was being followed, and his own scarcely-concealed derision. 'Sorry, Tyler,' he murmured out loud, drawing a stare from a woman opposite.

Of course, McKinley's suspicions would have made him doubly careful. Which meant there was a good chance he had hidden the letter. But where? If he hadn't stashed it in his room, where could he have hidden it? Just about anywhere in Berlin, Russell thought, looking out at the Konigstrasse. McKinley had probably stolen an idea from one of the endless detective novels he read.

He got off outside the Alexanderplatz branch of Wertheim and walked under the railway bridge and into the square itself. The station and another department store, Tietz, occupied the northern side, the huge drab mass of the police praesidium – the 'Alex' as all Berliners called it – the southern side. Russell walked past entrances 4, 3 and 2 – the latter housing the morgue where McKinley's body was presumably residing – and in through the doors of 1, the all-purpose entrance.

The whole Berlin detective force, around 1,800 strong, worked out of this building, and Russell imagined some of them were still waiting for their offices to be discovered. He was gestured towards one of several staircases, and then spent about ten minutes pacing down a succession of identical-looking corridors in search of Room 456. The windows overlooking the inner courtyard were all barred, suggesting a guests' penchant for self-defenestration which Russell found less than comforting. Eventually he was intercepted by a surprisingly helpful detective, who took him down the right flight of stairs and turned him into the right corridor.

Kriminalinspektor Oehm's office looked like a work in progress. There were files everywhere – piled on the desk, floor, windowsill and filing cabinets. Oehm, a chubby man with florid face, abundant fair hair and sharp-looking blue eyes, seemed unconcerned by the chaos, but his companion, a redhead with unusually pale skin, kept looking round in apparent disbelief. He was not introduced, but even without the tell-tale leather coat Russell would have assumed Gestapo.

Oehm invited him to sit down. 'We've been trying to contact you since yesterday morning,' he said.

'I've been out of town,' Russell said.

'So your fiancée told us.'

Russell said nothing. He hoped Effi had behaved herself.

'Where exactly were you?' the Gestapo man asked.

'Poland. Cracow to be precise. I'm working on a series of articles on Germany's neighbours.'

'You know why we wish to talk to you?' Oehm said.

'I assume it's about Tyler McKinley.'

'Correct. You were surprised by the news?'

'That he committed suicide. Yes, I was.'

Oehm shrugged. 'He must have had his reasons.'

'Perhaps. Are you certain he killed himself?'

'Absolutely. There is no doubt. We have several witnesses. Reliable witnesses. A police officer, for one.'

'Then he must have,' Russell agreed. He still couldn't see why they – whoever, exactly, they were – had needed to kill McKinley, and he didn't suppose he would ever find out. It didn't much matter, really. His knowing certainly wouldn't help McKinley.

'There is one possible reason for his action,' Oehm said. 'I do not wish to speak ill of the dead, but…well, we have good reason to believe that your friend had become involved with political elements hostile to the state, that he may have become part of a plot against the state involving forged official documents – documents, that is to say, which have been fabricated to create a misleading and slanderous impression of activities inside the Reich.'

'What sort of activities?' Russell asked innocently.

'That is not your concern,' the Gestapo man said.

'And he wasn't my friend,' Russell added. 'I liked him, but we hardly ever saw each other for more than a chat on the stairs.

A drink every month or so, perhaps. Nothing more.'

'Ah…'

'And if he was involved in this plot, why would that lead him to kill himself?' Russell asked.

'Perhaps it all got too much for him, and he couldn't think of any other way out,' Oehm suggested.

'He didn't give you anything to keep for him?' the Gestapo man asked.

'No, he didn't.'

'You are sure about that.'

'One hundred per cent.'

The Gestapo man looked sceptical, but said nothing.

'One more thing,' Oehm said. 'Herr McKinley's sister will be arriving in Berlin on Wednesday. To take the body home…'

'How's she getting here so quickly?' Russell asked.

'She is apparently flying across the Atlantic. The Americans have these new flying-boats – Clippers I believe they're called – and though they're not yet in public service, there are frequent trials. Proving flights, they call them…'

'Yes, yes,' the Gestapo man murmured, but Oehm ignored him.

'I am a flyer myself,' he told Russell. 'Weekends only, of course.'

'We all need hobbies,' Russell agreed. 'But how has McKinley's sister wangled a flight on one these…'

'Clippers. I imagine Senator McKinley used his influence to get his niece a place on one of them.'

'*Senator* McKinley?'

'Tyler McKinley's uncle.' Oehm noticed the surprise in Russell's face. 'You did not know his uncle was a US Senator?'

'Like I said, we weren't exactly friends.' He could understand why McKinley had kept quiet about it – the boy would have hated anyone thinking he owed anything to family connections. But he was amazed that none of his fellow American journalists had spilled the beans. They must have assumed Russell knew.

'As I was saying,' Oehm continued. 'His sister will arrange for the body to be sent home and collect her brother's effects. I was hoping you could be here when we talk to her, as an interpreter and someone who knew her brother.'

'I can do that.'

'Her plane from Lisbon arrives around eleven. So, if you could be here at one?'

'I will be. Is that all?'

'Yes, Herr Russell that is all.' Oehm smiled up at him. The Gestapo man gave him the merest of nods.

Russell retraced his steps to the main entrance. As he emerged into the open air he took a deep breath in and blew it out again. One thing was certain – they hadn't found the letter.

He crossed the square and walked into a café underneath the Stadtbahn tracks which he occasionally frequented. After ordering a couple of frankfurters and a *kartoffelsalat* he perched on a stool by the window, cleared a hole in the condensation, and looked out. No one had followed him in, but was anyone loitering outside? He couldn't see anyone obvious, but that didn't mean much. He would have to make sure in Tietz, pull a variation of the same trick he and McKinley had pulled in the Neukölln Karstadt department store. But it would have to look like an accident. He didn't want them thinking he'd lost them on purpose.

The food tasted bad, which was unusual. It was the taste in his mouth, Russell thought. Fear.

He crossed the road and walked into Tietz, heading for the rank of telephone booths that he remembered outside the store's ground floor tea room. Ensconced in the first booth, he looked back along the aisle he had just walked. No one looked furtive. He dialled Effi's number.

She answered on the second ring. 'You're back. I had the police…'

'I know. I've just spent twenty minutes in the Alex. I'm sorry you got…'

'Oh, it was no problem. They didn't break anything. I was just worried about you. Are you really upset? You didn't know him that well, did you?'

'No, I didn't. I feel sad, though. He was a nice enough man.'

'Are you coming over?'

'Yes, but it'll be a few hours. Say around six. I have to see someone.'

'Okay.'

'I'll see you then.'

'I love you.'

'I love you too.'

He replaced the receiver and scanned the aisle again. Still nothing. A taxi, he decided. From this side of the station, where there were often only two or three waiting.

He was in luck – there was only one. 'Friedrichstrasse Station,' he told the driver, and watched through the rear window as they swung round beneath the railway and headed down Kaiser Wilhelmstrasse. There was no sign of pursuit. At Friedrichstrasse he hurried down the steps to the U-bahn platform, reaching it as a Grenzallee train pulled in. He stepped aboard, standing beside the doors until they closed, but no one else emerged through the platform gates.

The train pulled out and he sank into the nearest seat. Should he be waiting for darkness, he wondered. Or would that be even riskier? He had no real idea, and felt shaken by how important such a decision could be.

It took twenty minutes to reach Hermannplatz. Russell climbed up to the street, where the loudspeakers were broadcasting Hitler's long-awaited speech to the Reichstag. A small crowd had gathered around the one outside Karstadt, their faces as overcast as the sky. The Fuhrer's tone was calm and reasonable, which suggested he was still warming up.

Russell walked on, following a trail of street-names familiar from the week before. It was a good thing he recognised these, because the area seemed utterly different by daylight, its workshops and factories bursting with noisy activity, its cobbled streets full of rumbling lorries. Most of the workplaces were broadcasting the speech to their employees, and Hitler's words seeped out through doors and over walls, a promise here, a threat there, a piece of self-congratulation sandwiched in between. Stopping for a moment on a bridge across the Neukollner-Schiffahrtkanal Russell heard fragments of the speech tossed around on the breeze, like the puffs of wind-strewn smoke belching from the myriad chimneys.

Schönlankerstrasse was empty, the block door wide open. He walked in and knocked on Theresa Jürissen's door. There was no answer. He knocked again with the same result, and was wondering what to do when footsteps sounded on the stairs. It was her.

Her face registered alarm, and then anger. Without speaking, she opened her door and gestured him in. Marietta was sitting exactly where she had been on his last visit, still drawing, still oblivious.

'What do you want?' Theresa asked, the moment the door was closed behind her.

'I'm sorry,' he said. 'I know this is dangerous for you, but not coming might have been more dangerous.'

He told her about McKinley's death.

'Could the police connect you?' he asked. 'Did you ever write to him?'

'No,' she said. 'Never.'

'What about the document you told us about?'

'I sent it, but that's all. I gave no name or address.'

Russell sighed in relief. 'When did you send it?'

'Last week. Thursday afternoon.'

McKinley had received it. He must have. Russell explained why he had asked. 'They haven't found it,' he told her. 'He must have hidden it somewhere.'

'There's nothing to connect me,' she said. 'Except you,' she added, the look of alarm back on her face.

'They won't hear about you from me,' Russell promised her, hoping he could live up to such an assurance.

'Thank you,' she said doubtfully, as if she wasn't that sure either. 'And their secret will stay secret,' she added, as much to herself as to him.

'Looks like it.'

She nodded, her view of the world confirmed.

'I'll be going,' he said.

'Let me make sure there's no one about,' she cautioned him. A few moments later she returned. 'It's all clear.'

Russell smiled goodbye to a closing door and began the long walk back to the centre of Neukölln. The Führer was well into his stride now, each torrent of words reinforced by the sound of his fist hammering at the lectern. By the time he reached Karstadt the listening crowd had spilled into the street, all eyes raised to the crackling loudspeaker, as if Hitler would emerge genie-like from the mesh, a head spouting venom on a shimmering tail.

It was dark by the time he reached Effi's flat. She was wearing a dress he hadn't seen before, deep red with a black lace collar. And she wanted to eat out, at a Chinese restaurant which had opened a few weeks earlier at the Halensee end of the Ku'damm.

'I've been learning my lines,' she announced as they walked downstairs. 'Would you hear me later?'

It was a peace offering, Russell realised. 'Love to,' he told her.

They walked through to the Ku'damm and took a westbound tram. The wide pavements were crowded with homegoing workers, the restaurants and cinemas gearing up for the evening as the shops closed down. Alighting at Lehninerplatz they found the Chinese restaurant already filling up. 'Goering eats here,' Effi said, as if in explanation.

'He eats everywhere,' Russell said. 'And this is on me,' he added.

Effi gave him a look.

'I've sold a lot of work lately,' he explained.

They were shown to their table, which stood beneath a huge scroll of dragons. Russell picked up the menu, hoping it was in German, but needn't have bothered.

'Let me order,' Effi said.

'Include beer,' Russell insisted. He was still feeling tense, he realised. And maybe still a little in shock. Sitting there, half-listening as Effi questioned the waiter, he found himself imagining McKinley's death – the moment of falling, of realisation. Of terror. 'How was your weekend?' he asked.

'Miserable. You know I hate going to parties on my own. All

the women I know were queuing up to ask if you'd left me – none of them asked whether I'd left you – and all the men were trying to work out how available I was, without actually asking. Every conversation was fraught with significance. Every dance was a means to an end. I couldn't just *be* for a single moment. When I go to something like that with you, I can just enjoy myself.' She sighed. 'Anyway, the party went on to about six, so I got to bed about seven, and the Kripo started hammering on the door at about nine. So I wasn't in a good mood. And I was upset for you too. I know you liked him, even if he was a bit Rin Tin Tin-like. And I could just see it too. Zoo Station gets so crowded on a Saturday evening.' She watched a tray of food go by, and sniffed at the passing aroma. 'And my dear sister Zarah's such a misery as well. She's convinced there's something wrong with Lothar. I tell her she's jumping to conclusions, that he's probably just a slow learner. She was herself, according to Muti. But she's convinced there's something wrong. She's made an appointment with a specialist.'

'When for?' Russell asked.

'Oh, I don't know. Next week sometime. I think she said Monday. Why?'

'Just wondered.' The arrival of their drinks gave Russell a few seconds to think. He couldn't say anything, he realised. And probably didn't need to. Zarah's husband Jens was a Party official, and Russell couldn't believe the Nazis would start killing their own children. And if he did say anything to Effi, and she said something to Zarah, then he might end up in a Gestapo cellar trying to explain where he'd got his information from.

'You look worried,' Effi said.

'I've heard a few rumours, that's all. Just journalist talk probably. The word is that the government's thinking of tightening up the

Law on the Prevention of Hereditary Diseases. Sanctioning mercy killing when the parents agree.'

She gave him an angry look. 'There's nothing wrong with Lothar,' she said. 'And even if there was, Zarah would never agree to… I can't believe you think…'

'I don't. But Jens is a Nazi, after all. He believes in all this purification of the race nonsense.'

Effi snorted. 'Maybe he does. But if he tried to take Lothar away from Zarah she'd never forgive him. And he knows it.'

'Okay.'

'And there's nothing wrong with Lothar,' she insisted once more.

He read the Fuhrer's speech next morning on his way home for a change of clothes. The editorials were calling it 'a major contribution to world peace', and the speech certainly seemed accommodating by Hitler's standards. There were friendly references to Poland and the non-aggression pact between the two countries. There was a marked absence of attacks on the Soviet Union. But one passage chilled Russell to the bone, and that concerned the Jews, who were only likely to start a war in Hitler's frenzied imagination. If they did, 'the result would not be the Bolshevisation of the earth and victory for the Jews but the annihilation of the Jewish race in Europe.' Russell wondered how the Wiesners felt reading that, even if Hitler was not speaking about physical annihilation. At least he hoped he wasn't. He remembered Albert's words in the Friedrichshain park: 'They'll just kill us. Who's going to stop them?'

Frau Heidegger had listened to the speech and found only grounds for optimism. 'There'll be an agreement with the Poles,' she said. 'Like the one with the Czechs at Munich. And then they'll be nothing more to fight over.'

Russell said he hoped she was right.

'The police were back yesterday,' she went on. 'Herr McKinley's sister will be here on Wednesday or Thursday to collect his things.'

'I know,' Russell told her. 'They want me to interpret for them.'

'That's nice,' Frau Heidegger said.

Once upstairs, Russell bathed, changed and worked for a couple of hours planning his transport piece for *Pravda*. Autobahns and the people's car, streamlined trains and new U-bahn lines, the latest Dornier flying-boats. Perhaps a hint of regret for the passing of the Zeppelins, he thought, but absolutely no mention of the *Hindenburg*.

He fried up a potato omelette for lunch, found a dusty bottle of beer to accompany it, and reluctantly considered the prospect of interviewing Hitler's armament workers for Stalin. It could be done, he supposed, but he'd have to be damn careful. Start off by talking to the Party people in the factory, the managers and Labour Front officials. Only move out onto the metaphorical lake if the ice feels really solid. Don't do a McKinley.

He thought about the missing letter. If he was going to take a look around the American's room it had to be today.

He walked down to the ground floor, and tapped on Frau Heidegger's open door. 'Have you still got a spare key for Tyler's room?' he asked. 'I loaned him some books, and it would be awkward searching for them when his sister's here, so I thought I could slip in and get them today. You don't need to come up,' he added quickly, hoping that Frau Heidegger's bad knees would triumph over her curiosity.

They did. 'Make sure you bring it back,' she told him.

McKinley's room was still suffused with the faint odour of his Balkan tobacco. As Frau Heidegger had intimated, the room was almost preternaturally tidy, and now he knew why the Kripo had refrained from leaving their usual mess. A Senator's nephew! No wonder they were on their best behaviour.

The clothes were neatly put away – shirts, jacket and suit in the wardrobe, socks and underwear in drawers. There was a thin pile of papers on the desk – left for show, Russell guessed – he remembered two great towers of paper on his last visit. The desk, too, had been mostly emptied. One drawer contained a single eraser, another, three pencils. It was as if the Kripo had decided to spread things out.

There was no obvious reduction in the number of books, but the lines on the shelves seemed anything but neat. Each had been taken out and checked for insertions, Russell assumed. Well at least that meant he didn't have to.

The same applied to the floorboards. The Kripo weren't amateurs. Far from it.

He sat on McKinley's bed, wondering why he'd imagined he could find something which they couldn't. The shelf above the headboard was full of crime novels, all in English. More than fifty, Russell guessed: Dashiell Hammett, Edgar Wallace, Dorothy L. Sayers, several authors he hadn't heard of. There were around a dozen Agatha Christies, and a similar number of 'Saint' books. Russell's earlier notion that McKinley had stolen an idea from one of these stories still seemed a good one, but the only way of finding out for certain was to go through them all, and that would take forever.

And what would he do with the letter if he found it? He had no proof of its authenticity, and without such proof there was little chance of anonymously arranging its publication outside Germany. He would have to guarantee it with what was left of his own reputation, either risking arrest by doing so inside Germany or forfeiting his residence by doing so from the safety of England. Neither course appealed. 'And their secret will stay secret,' he murmured to himself. He took one last look round the room and took the key back to Frau Heidegger.

Early that evening he telephoned Paul. The conversation seemed oddly awkward at first – his son seemed happy to talk, but there was something in his voice that worried Russell, some faint edge of resentment which was quite possibly unconscious. His *Jungvolk* group had spent much of Saturday making model gliders out of balsa wood and glue, something which Paul had obviously enjoyed, and on the coming Saturday they were visiting an airfield to examine the real thing. At school a new music teacher had given them a talk on the different types of music, and how some of them – jazz for example – were fatally tainted by their racial origins. He had even played several pieces on the school gramophone, pointing out what he called 'animal rhythms'. 'I suppose he's right,' Paul said. 'I mean, jazz was invented by negroes, wasn't it? But most of my friends thought the records he played were really good,' he admitted.

Russell looked in vain for an adequate response.

'What are you doing?' Paul asked, somewhat unusually.

'This and that,' Russell said. Paul was probably too old to have nightmares about falling under trains, but it wasn't worth the risk. 'Actually I'm looking for something that someone hid,' he said. 'If the Saint wants to hide something, how does he do it?' he asked, not really expecting an answer.

'What sort of thing?'

'Oh, money, a letter…'

'That's easy. He sends it to himself. At a – what do you call it?'

'Poste restante.'

'That's it. He sends diamonds to himself in *Getaway* and *The High*

Fence. And he does it in another story, I think. I can't remember which, though…'

Russell was no longer listening. Of course. If McKinley had forgotten the Saint's trick, then Theresa's use of the poste restante would have reminded him. He sighed inwardly. There was no way of collecting anything from a poste restante without identification. McKinley's sister could probably get access, but only by asking permission from the police.

'Dad, are you listening?'

'Yes, sorry – I think you've solved it for me.'

'Oh.'

'And I'm reading the book you loaned me,' he added, eager to please his son.

'Isn't it great?'

'It's pretty good,' Russell agreed, though he'd only read thirty pages. 'I haven't got far,' he admitted, hoping to ward off a cross-examination. 'I'll talk to you about it on Saturday.'

'Okay. On Sunday are we getting the train from Anhalter Bahnhof?'

'I expect so. I'll let you know.' Actually, a different means of transport was suggesting itself.

The first day of February was as grey as nature intended. His Wednesday morning lesson with Ruth and Marthe was enjoyable as ever, but there was no sign of their brother or parents. Arriving back at Alexanderplatz with twenty minutes to spare he stopped for a coffee in Wertheim and ran into Doug Conway. They chatted for a few minutes, until Russell realised he was late for his appointment. The search for Oehm's office made him even later, and McKinley's sister was looking none too happy when he finally arrived.

'We were talking about Fraulein McKinley's flying boat,' Oehm said, which further explained her look of irritation.

She was almost as tall as her brother – about five foot eleven, he guessed – and even thinner. Severely-cut brunette hair framed a face that might have been pretty if the already-thin lips had not been half-pursed in disapproval, but Russell sensed that her current expression was the one she most usually presented to the world. She was wearing a cream blouse and smart, deep blue suit. There was no hint of black and no obvious sign of grief in her face. He told himself that she'd had several days to take it all in.

He introduced himself and offered his condolences.

'Eleanor McKinley,' she responded. 'Tyler never mentioned you.'

'We weren't close friends – just neighbours. I'm here because the police thought an interpreter would make things easier for everyone. Have they told you what happened?'

'Oh, we got all the details from the German Embassy in Washington. A man came out to the house and explained everything.'

Russell wondered what to say next. He found it hard to credit that the family believed Tyler had committed suicide. But it was hardly his place to question it, particularly with Oehm trying to follow their conversation.

The German interrupted. 'There are papers to sign.' He passed them to Russell. 'If you could...'

Russell looked through them, and then explained the gist to Eleanor McKinley. 'There's two things here. One is an account of the investigation, complete with witness statements and the police conclusion that Tyler committed suicide. They need your signature to sign off on the case. The other form waives your family's right to an inquest. This is because you're taking him home with you.'

'I understand,' she said.

'I'll read it through then.'

'No, no, don't bother,' she said, extracting a pack of Chesterfields from her handbag. 'You won't mind if I smoke?' she asked Oehm, holding up a cigarette in explanation.

Russell felt taken aback. 'You understand that you're accepting their version of events, that this exempts them from any further investigation?' he asked.

'Are there any other versions?' she asked.

'No. I just wanted to be sure you knew that this puts an end to any…'

'Good,' she interrupted. She made a writing mime at Oehm, who handed her his pen.

'Here and here,' Russell said, placing the papers in front of her. She signed both, writing Eleanor V. Tyler in a large looping hand.

'Is that it?' she asked.

'That's it.'

'What about Tyler's… what about the body?'

Russell asked Oehm. It was still in the morgue, he thought, but phoned to check.

It was. 'They need her for a formal identification before they can release it,' Oehm told Russell in German. 'But not now – they're still trying to repair his face. If she comes at eleven in the morning they'll have plenty of time to seal it for transport and get it across to Lehrter.'

Russell relayed the salient points.

'Can't we do it now?' she asked.

'No, I'm afraid not.'

She made a face, but didn't press the issue. 'All right. Well, let's get out of this dreadful place.' She offered Oehm her hand and the briefest of smiles, and headed for the door. 'I suppose I can get Tyler's apartment over with instead,' she said as they walked back to the entrance. 'You'll come with me,' she added. It was more of an assumption than a question.

They took a taxi. She said nothing as they drove through the old city, just stared out of the window. As they swung through Spittelmarkt towards Dönhoffplatz and the bottom of Lindenstrasse she murmured something to herself, then turned to Russell and said: 'I've never seen such a grey city.'

'The weather doesn't help,' he said.

She was even less impressed with Neuenburgerstrasse. Frau Heidegger climbed the stairs to let them in, and insisted that Russell pass on her deepest condolences. 'And tell Fraulein McKinley how much I liked her brother,' she added. 'How much we all did.'

Russell did as he was bid, and McKinley's sister flashed another of her brief smiles in Frau Heidegger's direction. 'Tell her we'd like to be alone,' she said in English.

Russell passed on the message. Frau Heidegger looked slightly hurt, but disappeared down the stairs.

Eleanor sat down on the bed looking, for the first time, as if her brother's death meant something to her.

Now was the moment, Russell thought. He had to say something. 'I find it hard to believe that your brother killed himself,' he said tentatively.

She sighed. 'Well, he did. One way or another.'

'I'm sorry...'

She got up and walked to the window. 'I don't know how much you knew about Tyler's work...'

'I knew he was working on something important.'

'Exposing some terrible Nazi plot?' she asked.

'Maybe.' She was angry, he realised. Furious.

'Well, that was a pretty effective way of committing suicide, wouldn't you say?'

Russell bit back an answer. He'd said much the same thing to McKinley himself.

'Look at this,' she said, surveying the room. 'The life he chose,' she said bitterly.

That you couldn't, Russell thought. He reluctantly abandoned the idea of asking for her help in checking out the poste restante.

She picked up McKinley's pipe, looked round, and took one of his socks to wrap it in. 'I'll take this,' she said. 'Can you get rid of the rest?'

'Yes, but…'

'I can't imagine it would be much use to anyone else.'

'Okay.'

He accompanied her downstairs and out to the waiting taxi.

'Thank you for your help,' she said. 'I don't suppose you're free tomorrow morning? I could use some help at the morgue. My train leaves at three and I can't afford any hold-ups. And some moral support would be nice,' she added, as if it had just occurred to her that identifying her brother might involve an emotional toll. 'I'll buy you lunch.'

Russell felt like refusing, but he had no other appointments. Be generous, he told himself. 'It's a deal,' he said.

'Pick me up at the Adlon,' she told him. 'Around ten-thirty.'

He watched the cab turn the corner into Lindenstrasse and disappear. He felt sorry for McKinley, and perhaps even sorrier for his sister.

He arrived at the Adlon just before ten, and found Jack Slaney sitting behind a newspaper in the tea room. 'I've got something for you,' Russell said, sitting down and counting out the ninety Reichsmarks he owed from the last poker game.

'A sudden inheritance?' Slaney asked.

'Something like that.'

'What are you doing here?' the American said, as he gestured the waiter over to order coffees.

Russell told him.

'He was a nice kid,' Slaney said. 'Shame about his family.'

'The uncle's not one of your favourite Senators?'

Slaney laughed. 'He's a big friend of the Nazis, anti-Semitic through and through. The usual broken record – on the one hand, we should be leaving Europe well alone, on the other, we should be realising that Britain and France are on their last legs and Germany's a progressive powerhouse, our natural ally. Bottom line – it's just business as usual. The Senator's brother – McKinley's Dad – has a lot of money invested here. One plant in Dusseldorf, another in Stuttgart. They'll do well out of a war, as long as we stay out of it.'

'The daughter's not exactly soft and cuddly,' Russell admitted.

'I know. Hey!' Slaney interrupted himself. 'Have you heardthe latest? Over the weekend some Swedish Member of Parliament nominated Hitler for the Nobel Peace Prize. Wrote a letter of recommendation and everything.' Slaney flipped back the pages on his notebook. 'He praised "Hitler's glowing love of peace, heretofore best documented in his famous book *Mein Kampf.*"'

'A spoof, right?'

'Of course. But at least one German paper missed that bit. They printed the whole thing as if it was completely kosher.' He threw back his head and laughed out loud, drawing stares from across the room.

At ten-thirty Russell asked the receptionist to let Eleanor know he was in the lobby. She appeared a couple of minutes later. The suit was a deep crimson this time, the silk scarf a shimmering gold. The heels were higher, the seams of her stockings straight as arrows. The fur coat looked expensive. 'It doesn't look like they're getting ready for a war,' she said, as their cab motored down Unter Den Linden.'

The morgue was ready for them. McKinley's body was laid out on a trolley in the middle of the spacious cold store. She marched confidently forward, heels clicking on the polished floor, then suddenly faltered and looked back at Russell. He came forward, took her arm, and together they advanced on the trolley.

A white sheet concealed whatever injuries her brother had suffered below the neck. The familiar shock of dark hair had been burnt away at the front, and the entire left side of his face looked blackened beneath the mortician's make-up. The eyes looked as though they'd been re-inserted in their sockets; one was not quite closed, and presumably never would be again. The bottom lip had been sewn back on, probably after McKinley had bitten clean through it. An angry red-brown wound extended round the American's neck above the uppermost edge of sheet, causing Russell to wonder whether he had been decapitated.

'It's him,' Eleanor said in a voice quivering with control. She signed the necessary documentation on the small table by the door and left the room without a backward glance. During the first part of their ride back to the Adlon she sat in silence, staring out of the window, an angry expression on her face. As they crossed over Friedrichstrasse she asked Russell how long he'd lived in Berlin, but hardly listened to his answer.

'Come up,' she said when they reached the lobby, and gave him a quick glance to make sure he hadn't read anything into the invitation.

Her suite was modest, but a suite just the same. An open suitcase sat on the bed, half-filled with clothes, surrounded by bits and pieces. 'I'll only be a minute,' she said, and disappeared into the bathroom.

An item on the bed had already caught Russell's eye – one of the small grey canvas bags that the Kripo used for storing personal effects.

There was no sound from the bathroom. Now or never, he told himself.

He took one stride to the bed, loosened the string, and looked inside the bag. It was almost empty. He poured the contents onto the bed and sorted through them with his fingers. A reporter's notebook – almost empty. German notes – almost 300 Reichsmarks' worth. McKinley's press accreditation. His passport.

The toilet flushed in the bathroom.

Russell slipped the passport into his pocket, rammed the rest back into the bag, tightened the string and stepped hastily away from the bed.

She came out of the bathroom, looked at the mess on the bed, staring, or so it seemed to Russell, straight at the bag. She reached down, picked it up… and placed it in the suitcase. 'I thought we'd eat here,' she said.

Five minutes later, they were being seated in the hotel restaurant. Having locked her brother away in some sort of emotional box, she chatted happily about America, her dog, the casting of Vivien Leigh as Scarlett O'Hara in the new film of *Gone with the Wind*. It was all very brittle, but brittle was what she was.

After they had eaten he watched her look round the room, and tried to see it through her eyes – a crowd of smart people, most of the women fashionably dressed, many of the men in perfectly-tailored uniforms. Eating good food, drinking fine wines. Just like home.

'Do you think there'll be a war?' she asked abruptly.

'Probably,' he said.

'But what could they gain from one?' she asked, genuinely puzzled. 'I mean, you can see how prosperous the country is, how content. Why risk all that?'

Russell had no wish to talk politics with her. He shrugged agreement with her bewilderment and asked how the flight across the Atlantic had been.

'Awful,' she said. 'So noisy, though I got used to that after a while. But it's a horrible feeling, being over the middle of the ocean and knowing that there's no help for thousands of miles.'

'Are you going back the same way?'

'Oh no. It was Daddy who insisted I came that way. He thought it was important that I got here quickly, though I can't imagine why. No, I'm going back by ship. From Hamburg. My train leaves at three,' she added, checking her watch. 'Will you take me to the station?'

'Of course.'

Upstairs he watched her cram her remaining possessions into the suitcase, and breathed a silent sigh of relief when she asked him to close it for her. A taxi took them to the Lehrter Bahnhof, where the D-Zug express was already waiting in its platform, car attendants hovering at each door.

'Thank you for your help,' she said, holding out a hand.

'I'm sorry about the circumstances,' Russell said.

'Yes,' she agreed, but more in exasperation than sadness. As he turned away she was reaching for her cigarettes.

Near the front of the train three porters were manhandling a coffin into the baggage car. Russell paused in his stride, and watched as they set it down with a thump by the far wall. Show some respect, he felt like saying, but what was the point? He walked on, climbing the steps to the Stadtbahn platforms which hung above the mainline station's throat. A train rattled in almost instantly, and three minutes later he was burrowing down to the U-bahn platforms at Friedrichstrasse. He read an abandoned *Volkischer Beobachter* on the journey to Neukölln, but the only item of interest concerned the Party student leader in Heidelberg. He had forbidden his students to dance the Lambeth Walk, on the grounds that it was foreign to the German way of life, and incompatible with National Socialist behaviour.

How many Germans, Russell wondered, were itching to dance the Lambeth Walk?

Not the family in Zembski's studio, that was certain. They were there to have their portrait taken, the father in SA uniform, the wife in her church best, the three blonde daughters all in pigtails, wearing freshly-ironed BDM uniforms. Nazi heaven.

Russell watched as the big Silesian lumbered around, checking the lighting and the arrangement of the fake living room setting. Finally he was satisfied. 'Smile,' he said, and clicked the shutter. 'One more,' he said, 'and smile this time.' The wife did, the girls tried, but the father was committed to looking stern.

Russell wondered what was going through Zembski's mind at moments like this. He had only known the Silesian for a few years, but he'd heard of him long before that. In the German communist circles which he and Ilse had once frequented, Zembski had been known as a reliable source for all sorts of photographic services, and strongly rumoured to be a key member of the Pass-Apparat, the Berlin-based Comintern factory for forged passports and other documents. Russell had never revealed his knowledge of Zembski's past. But it was one of the reasons for his using him for his photographic needs. That and the fact that he liked the man. And his low prices.

He watched as Zembski ushered the family out into the street with promises of prints by the weekend. Closing the door behind them he rolled his eyes toward the ceiling. 'Is smiling so hard?' he asked rhetorically. 'But of course he'll love it. I only hope the wife doesn't get beaten to a pulp for looking happy.' He walked across to the arc-lights and turned them off. 'And what can I do for you, Mister Russell?'

Russell nodded towards the small office which adjoined the studio.

Zembski looked at him, shrugged, and gestured him in. Two chairs were squeezed in either side of a desk. 'I hope it's pornography rather than politics,' he said once they were inside. 'Though these days it's hard to tell the difference.'

Russell showed him McKinley's passport. 'I need my photograph in this. I was hoping you'd either do it for me, or teach me how to do it myself.'

Zembski looked less than happy. 'What makes you think I'd know?'

'I was in the Party myself once.'

Zembski's eyebrows shot up. 'Ah. A lot's changed since then, my friend.'

'Yes, but they're probably still using the same glue on passports. And you probably remember which remover to use.'

Zembski nodded. 'Not the sort of thing you forget.' He studied McKinley's passport. 'Who is he?'

'Was. He's the American journalist who jumped in front of a train at Zoo Station last weekend. Allegedly jumped.'

'Better and better,' the Silesian said dryly. He opened a drawer, pulled out a magnifying glass, and studied the photograph. 'Looks simple enough.'

'You'll do it?'

Zembski leaned back in his chair, causing it to squeak with apprehension. 'Why not?'

'How much?'

'Ah. That depends. What's it for? I don't want details,' he added hurriedly, 'just some assurance that it won't end up on a Gestapo desk.'

'I need it to recover some papers. For a story.'

'Not a Führer-friendly story?'

'No.'

'Then I'll give you a discount for meaning well. But it'll still cost you a hundred Reichsmarks.'

'Fair enough.'

'Cash.'

'Right.'

'I'll take the picture now then,' Zembski said, manoeuvring his bulk out of the confined space and through the door into the studio. 'A plain background,' he muttered out loud as he studied the original photograph. 'This'll do,' he said, pushing a screen against a wall and placing a stool in front of it.

Russell sat on it.

Zembski lifted his camera, tripod and all, and placed it in position. After feeding in a new film, he squinted through the lens. 'Try and look like an American,' he ordered.

'How the hell do I do that?' Russell asked.

'Look optimistic.'

'I'll try.'

'I said optimistic, not doe-eyed.'

Russell grinned, and the shutter clicked.

'Let's try a serious one,' Zembski ordered.

Russell pursed his lips.

The shutter clicked again. And again. And several more times. 'That'll do,' the Silesian said at last. 'I'll have it for you on Monday.'

'Thanks.' Russell stood up. 'One other thing. You don't by any chance know of a good place to pick up a second-hand car?'

Zembski did – a cousin in Wedding owned a garage which often had cars to sell on. 'Tell him I sent you,' he said, after giving Russell directions, 'and you may get another discount. We Silesians are all heart,' he added, chins wobbling with merriment.

Russell walked the short distance back to the U-bahn, then changed his mind and took a seat in the shelter by the tram stop. Gazing back down the brightly-lit Berlinerstrasse towards Zembski's studio, he wondered whether he'd just crossed a very dangerous line. No, he reassured himself, all he'd done was commission a false passport. He would cross the line when he made use of it.

After teaching the Wiesner girls next morning, Russell headed across town in search of Zembski's cousin. He found the garage on one of Wedding's back streets, sandwiched between a brewery and the back wall of a locomotive depot, about half a kilometre from the Lehrter Station. Zembski's cousin Hunder was also a large man, but looked a lot fitter than Zembski. He seemed to have half a dozen young men working for him, most of them barely beyond school age.

The cars for sale were lined round the back. There were four of them: a Hanomag, an Opel, a Hansa-Lloyd, another Opel. 'Any colour you want as long as it's black,' Russell murmured.

'We can re-spray,' Hunder told him.

'No, black's good,' Russell said. The more anonymous the better, he thought. 'How much are they?' he asked.

Hunder listed the prices. 'Plus a ten per cent discount for a friend of my cousin,' he added. 'And a full tank. And a month's guarantee.'

The larger Hansa-Lloyd looked elegant, but was way out of Russell's monetary reach. And he had never liked the look of Opels.

'Can I take the Hanomag out for a drive?' he asked.

'You do know how?' Hunder enquired.

'Yes.' He had driven lorries in the War, and much later he and Ilse had actually owned a car, an early Ford, which had died ignominiously on the road to Potsdam soon after their marriage had gone the same way.

He climbed into the driving-seat, waved the nervous-looking Hunder a cheerful goodbye, and turned out of the garage yard. It felt strange after all those years, but straightforward enough. He drove up past the sprawling Lehrter goods yards, back through the centre of Moabit and up Invalidenstrasse. The car was a bit shabby inside, but it handled well, and the engine sounded smooth enough.

He stopped by the side of the Humboldt canal basin and wormed his way under the chassis. There was a bit of rust, but not too much. No sign of leakages, and nothing seemed about to fall off. Brushing himself down, he walked round the vehicle. The engine compartment looked efficient enough. The tyres would need replacing, but not immediately. The lights worked. It wasn't exactly an Austro-Daimler, but it would have to do.

He drove back to the garage and told Hunder he'd take it. As he wrote out the cheque, he reminded himself how much he'd be saving on tram and train tickets.

It was still early afternoon as he drove home, and the streets, with the exception of Potsdamerplatz, were relatively quiet. He parked in the courtyard, and borrowed a bucket, sponge and brush from an excited Frau Heidegger. She watched from the step as he washed the outside and cleaned the inside, her face full of anticipation.

'A quick drive?' he offered, and she needed no second bidding. He took them through Hallesches Tor and up to Viktoria Park, listening carefully for any sign that the engine was bothered by the gradient. There was none. 'I haven't been up here for years!' Frau Heidegger exclaimed, peering through the windscreen at the Berlin panorama as they coasted back down the hill.

Effi was just as excited a couple of hours later. Her anger at his late arrival evaporated the moment she saw the car. 'Teach me to drive,' she insisted.

Russell knew that both her father and ex-husband had refused to teach her, the first because he feared for his car, the second because he feared for his social reputation. Women were not encouraged to drive in the new Germany. 'Okay,' he agreed, 'but not tonight,' he added, as she made for the driver's seat.

It was a ten minute drive to the Conways' modern apartment block in Wilmersdorf, and the Hanomag looked somewhat overawed by the other cars parked outside. 'Don't worry,' Effi said, patting its bonnet. 'We need a name,' she told Russell. 'Something old and reliable. How about Hindenburg?'

'He's dead,' Russell objected.

'I suppose so. How about Mother?'

'Mine isn't reliable.'

'Oh all right. I'll think about it.'

They were the last to arrive. Phyllis Conway was still putting the children to bed, leaving Doug to dispense the drinks. He introduced Russell and Effi to the other three couples, two of whom – the Neumaiers and the Auers – were German. Hans Neumaier worked in banking, and his wife looked after their children. Rolf and Freya Auer owned an art gallery. The third couple was Conway's replacement Martin Unsworth and his wife Fay. Everyone present, Russell reckoned, was either approaching, enjoying or had recently departed, their thirties. Hans Neumaier was probably the oldest, Fay Unsworth the youngest.

Effi disappeared to read the children a bedtime story, leaving Russell and Doug Conway alone by the drinks table. 'I asked the Wiesners,' Conway told him. 'I went out to see them.' He shook his head. 'They were pleased to be asked, I think, but they wouldn't come. Don't want to risk drawing attention to themselves while they're waiting for their visas, I suppose. They talk highly of you, by the way.'

'Is there nothing you can do to speed up their visas?'

'Nothing. I've tried, believe me. I'm beginning to think that someone in the system doesn't like them.'

'Why, for God's sake?'

'I don't know. I'll keep trying, but...' He let the word hang. 'Oh,' he said, reaching into his jacket pocket and pulling out two tickets. 'I was given these today. Brahms and something else, at the Philharmonie, tomorrow evening. Would you like them? We can't go.'

'Thanks. Effi'll be pleased.'

'What's she doing now? *Barbarossa* has finished, hasn't it.'

'Yes. But you'd better ask her about the next project.'

Conway grinned. 'I will. Come on, we'd better join the others.'

The evening went well. The conversation flowed through dinner and beyond, almost wholly in German, the Conways taking turns at providing translation for Fay Unsworth. The two German men were of a type: scions of upper-middle-class families who still prospered under the Nazis but who, in foreign company especially, were eager to demonstrate how embarrassed they were by their government. They and Freya Auer lapped up Effi's account of the *Mother* story-line, bursting into ironic applause when she described the hospital bed denouement. Only Ute Neumaier looked uncomfortable.

Among her fellow-housewives in Grünewald she would probably give the story a very different slant.

Rolf Auer was encouraged to recount some news he'd heard that afternoon. Five of Germany's most famous radio comedians – Werner Finck, Peter Sachse, and the Three Rulands – had been expelled from the Reich Cultural Chamber by Goebbels. They wouldn't be able to work in Germany again.

'When was this announced?' Russell asked.

'It hasn't been yet. Goebbels has a big piece in the *Beobachter* tomorrow morning. It's in there.'

'Last time I saw Finck at the Kabarett,' Russell said, 'he announced that the old German fairytale section had been removed from the programme, but that there'd be a political lecture later.'

Everyone laughed.

'It'll be hard for any of them to get work elsewhere,' Effi said. 'Their sort of comedy's all about language.'

'They'll have to go into hibernation until it's all over,' Phyllis said.

'Like so much else,' her husband agreed.

'Where has all the art gone?' Effi asked the Auers. 'Six years ago there must have been thousands of modern paintings in Germany – the Blau Reiter group, the Expressionists before them, the Cubists. Where are they all?'

'A lot of them are boxed up in cellars,' Rolf Auer admitted. 'A lot were taken abroad in the first year or so, but since then… A lot were owned by Jews, and most of those have been sold, usually at knock-down prices. Bought mostly by people who think they'll make a good profit one day, sometimes by people who really care about them as art, and want to preserve them for the future.'

It sounded as if the Auers had a few in their cellar. 'I've heard Hermann's building up his collection,' Russell said.

'He has good taste,' Auer replied, with only the faintest hint of sarcasm.

The conversation moved on to architecture, and Speer's plans for the new Berlin. Russell watched and listened. It was a civilised conversation, he thought. But the civilisation concerned was treading water. There was an implied acceptance that things had slipped out of joint, that some sort of correction was needed, and that until that correction came along, and normal service was resumed, they were stuck in a state of suspended animation. The Conways, he saw, were only too glad to be out of it – America would be a paradise after this. The Unsworths hadn't got a clue what they were getting into and, unless they were much more perceptive than they seemed, would draw all the wrong conclusions from gatherings like this one. But the three German couples – he included himself and Effi – were just waiting for the world to move on, waiting at the Führer's pleasure.

'What'll happen to you if there's a war?' Unsworth was asking him.

'I'll be on the same train as you, I expect,' Russell told him. Across the table, Effi made a face.

'That'll be hard, after living here for so long.'

'It will. I have a son here too.' Russell shrugged. 'But it'll be that or internment.'

On the way home, sitting in a line of traffic at the eastern end of the Ku'damm, Effi suddenly turned to him and said: 'I don't want to lose you.'

'I don't want to lose you either.'

She slipped an arm through his. 'How long do you think a war will last?'

'I've no idea. Years, at least.'

'Maybe we should think about leaving. I know,' she added

quickly, 'that you don't want to leave Paul. But if there's a war and they lock you up you'll be leaving him anyway. And we… Oh I don't know. It's all so ridiculous.'

Russell moved the car forward a few metres. 'It's something to think about.' And it was. She was right – he'd lose Paul anyway. And he couldn't spend the rest of his life clinging to the boy. It wasn't fair on her. It probably wasn't fair on Paul.

'I don't want to go either, but…'

'I know. I think we've got a few months at least.' He leaned over and kissed her, which drew an angry blow of the horn from the car behind them. 'And I can't let Paul run my whole life,' he said, testing the thought out loud as he released the clutch.

'Not for ever, anyway. Has he seen the car yet?'

'No. Tomorrow.'

There was sunshine on Saturday, the first for a week. He arrived at the Gehrts' house soon after two, and felt somewhat deflated by the sight of Matthias's almost new Horch. How had he expected Paul to get excited by a 1928 Hanomag?

He needn't have worried. His son, happily changed out of his *Jungvolk* uniform, was thrilled by the car, and thrilled by their exhilarating 100kph dash down the new Avus Speedway, which took them from the eastern end of the Ku'damm to the first completed stretch of the Berlin orbital outside Potsdam. On their way back they stopped for ice cream at a café overlooking the Wannsee, and Russell allowed his son to work the petrol pump at the adjoining garage. 'Father – I mean Matthias – wouldn't let me do this,' Paul said, anxiously scanning Russell's face for signs of hurt or anger at his slip.

'It's okay. You can call him Father,' Russell said. 'Short for stepfather.'

'All right,' Paul agreed.

During their four hours together, his son showed none of the reticence he'd displayed on the phone. Just a passing something, Russell hoped. He had a wonderful afternoon.

The evening wasn't bad either. Effi looked stunning in another new dress – *Mother* was certainly paying well – and three members of the Philharmonie audience came up and asked for her autograph, which pleased her no end. Unlike Russell, she had been brought up on a diet of classical music, and sat in rapt attention while his wandered. Looking round the auditorium, it occurred to him that this was one of the places where nothing much had changed. The music was *judenfrei*, of course, and Hitler's picture dominated the lobby, but the same stiff-necked, over-dressed people were filling the seats, wafting their fans and rustling their programmes. It could have been 1928. Or even 1908. All across Germany there were people living in time bubbles like this one. That was the way it was, and would be, until Hitler marched across one border too many and burst them all.

Russell couldn't complain about the effect the music had on Effi – she insisted on their going straight home to make love. Afterwards, lying in an exhausted heap among the tangled sheets, they laughed at the trail of clothes disappearing into the living room. 'Like our first time, remember?' Effi said.

Russell couldn't remember a better day, and hated to spoil it. 'I've got something to tell you,' he said, propping himself up against the headboard. 'You know I said I'd heard rumours that they were planning to change the Law on the Prevention of Hereditary Diseases?'

'Yes.' She sat up too.

'I didn't.'

'Then why…'

'Tyler McKinley was working on a story about it. He got me to go with him when he interviewed this woman in Neukölln.' Russell told her about Theresa Jürissen, about Marietta, about the KdF letter to clinic heads and what she had claimed was in it.

'Why didn't you tell me?' Effi asked, more surprised than angry.

'Because you'd have to tell Zarah, and Zarah would have to tell Jens, and I'd have to explain where I got the information from.' He looked her in the face. 'McKinley's dead, Effi. And he didn't commit suicide. He was murdered.'

She took that in, looking, Russell thought, extraordinarily beautiful.

'So why are you telling me now?' she asked calmly.

He sighed. 'Because I hate keeping things from you. Because I owe it to Zarah. I don't know. Could you swear Zarah to secrecy, do you think?'

'Maybe. But in any case I don't think Jens would turn you in. Zarah would certainly kill him if he did. For my sake, of course, not yours.'

'Of course.'

'But – and I hate to say this – given how Zarah feels about you, she'll want more than your word. So will he. They'll want some sort of proof.'

'I don't blame them. When's that appointment you mentioned?'

'Monday.'

'She should put it off.'

'How will that help?'

He explained his hunch about the poste restante, about McKinley's passport and Zembski's commission. 'On Tuesday, if I've guessed correctly, I can pick up the letter and whatever else McKinley had.'

'You're going to claim it using a bogus passport? Isn't that risky? What if they remember McKinley from when he handed it in?'

'He won't have handed it in – he'll have posted it. It'll be okay.'

'Are you sure?'

He laughed. 'No, of course not.'

Sunday was another cold bright day. Russell picked his son up in Grünewald soon after ten, and headed for Potsdam on the Avus Speedway. From there they took the Leipzig road, driving south-west through Treuenbrietzen and over the hills to Wittenberg, stopping for an early lunch by the bridge across the Elbe. They reached Leipzig ninety minutes ahead of kick-off, and did a quick spin round the town centre. Paul, though, was eager to reach the ground, and seemed somewhat lacking in faith that his father would find it in time.

He found it with twenty minutes to spare. They followed another father-son couple wearing Hertha favours through the turnstiles, and worked their way round to where the hundred or so others who'd made the trip from Berlin were standing, behind one of the goals. The stadium was bigger than the Plumpe, and seemed almost full for this cup-tie. Standing there waiting for the teams to come out, watching the flicker of matches being struck in the shadowed grandstand, Russell felt a sudden surge of sadness. Another time bubble, he thought.

The home crowd greeted their team with a hearty roar, but that was almost the last thing they had to cheer. The home team had one of those afternoons, doing everything but score on numerous occasions, before making one fatal mistake at the back. Paul was ecstatic, and quite unwilling to admit there was anything undeserved in Hertha's victory. 'It's about goals, Dad,' he said trenchantly, before Russell could suggest anything to the contrary. On the way out, Paul scanned the ground for a discarded programme and finally found one. 'For Joachim,' he said triumphantly.

Russell had thought about inviting Thomas and Joachim to join them, but had decided he wanted the time alone with his son. If Paul wanted to get something off his chest, he wouldn't do it with Thomas and Joachim in the car.

The decision bore fruit, though hardly in the way Russell had expected. It was dark by the time they left Leipzig, the road lit only by their own lights and the occasional passage of a vehicle in the opposite direction. On either side the darkness was relieved only by the dim lights of an occasional farm.

They had been driving about ten minutes when Paul broke the silence. 'Dad, I think you should move to England,' he blurted out, as if he couldn't hold the thought in any longer.

'Why?' Russell asked, though he could guess the answer.

'Well, you can't help being English, can you?'

'No, I can't.'

'But that won't help. I mean it doesn't help the Jews, does it?'

'No,' Russell agreed. 'What made you think about this?' he asked. 'Has something happened? Has someone said something?' He half expected to find that Paul had overheard a conversation between his mother and stepfather.

'Not exactly,' Paul replied. 'At the *Jungvolk*... no one has actually said anything, but they know I'm half-English, and when they look at me it's like they're not sure whose side I'm on. I'm not saying it's bad being half-English – it's not like being half-Jewish or half-Polish or anything like that – and if there's a war with England I can tell everyone I'm loyal to the Führer, but you won't be able to do that. I don't think you'll be safe in Germany. You'll be much safer in England.'

'Maybe,' Russell said, for want of something better.

'Wouldn't Effi go with you?'

'She might.'

'I really like her, you know.'

'I know you do. And I'm glad.'

'I don't want you to go. I just…'

'What?'

'I just don't want you to stay for my sake. I mean, I'm twelve next month. It's not like I'll be a child for much longer.'

'I think you have a few more years yet.'

'Okay, but…'

'I understand what you're saying. And I appreciate it. But I don't want you to worry about this. If a war comes I'll probably have to leave – there won't be any choice. But until then, well, I can't leave while we're still in the Cup, can I?'

After dropping Paul off, Russell found a bar off Hochmeisterplatz and sat for almost an hour nursing an expensive double whisky. His life seemed to be breaking up in slow-motion, with no clear indication of where any of the pieces might land. Moving to England might seem like a sensible move, but it was sensible moves that had landed him in his current predicament. The peculiarity of his situation, he thought, might be a double-edged sword. It could be the death of him, or at least the death of those relationships which had made his life worth living these last few years. There was no doubt about that. But was there also a chance that he could exploit that situation to save himself, and those relationships? Shchepkin, Kleist and Trelawney-Smythe had no compunction about making use of him, and he felt none about making use of them. But could he pull it off? Was he still quick enough on his feet? And was he brave enough to find out?

Driving east along the Ku'damm towards Effi's, he realised he didn't know. But that, he told himself, the Wiesners uppermost in his mind, was another sign of the times. When the time bubbles burst, you got to find out all sorts of things about yourself that you probably didn't want to know. And maybe, if you were lucky, a few that you did.

Arriving at Effi's flat, he was almost bundled into the kitchen by Effi herself. 'Zarah's here,' she whispered. 'I've told her about the letter to the asylum directors, but nothing about you knowing where it is now. Or the passport. Okay?'

'Okay,' Russell agreed.

Lothar was there too, sitting with his mother and a picture book on the sofa.

'You remember Uncle John?' Effi asked him.

'No,' he said authoritatively, looking up briefly and deciding that Russell was less interesting than his book. If there was anything wrong with him, it wasn't the same thing as afflicted Marietta.

Russell leant down to kiss Zarah's upturned cheek. Effi's older sister was an attractive woman of thirty-five, taller and bigger-boned than Effi, with larger breasts and wider hips. Her wavy chestnut hair, which usually fell to her shoulders, was constrained in a tight bun, and there were dark circles of either tiredness or sadness around her brown eyes. Russell had never actually disliked Zarah, but he had never felt any real connection either. She had none of her younger sister's fearless appetite for life: Zarah was the careful, responsible one, the one who had always sought safety in conventionality, whether of ideas or husbands. Her positive feature, as far as Russell was concerned, was her obvious devotion to Effi.

'Effi told me what you told her,' she said, 'but I want to hear it from you.'

Russell retold the story of his and McKinley's visit to Theresa Jürissen, omitting her name.

'She stole this letter?' Zarah asked, as if she couldn't believe people did things like that.

'She was desperate.'

'That I can understand,' Zarah said, glancing sideways at the happily-engaged Lothar. 'But are you sure she was telling the truth?'

'As sure as I can be.'

'But you don't know any of the details of this new law those doctors were talking about? What it will say? Who it will affect?'

'No. But whatever it says, the first thing they'll need is a register of all those suffering from the various conditions. All the institutions and doctors will be asked to submit lists, so that they know exactly what they're dealing with. And any child on that list will be subject to the new law, whatever it is. That's why I think you should cancel your appointment. Wait until I can tell you more.'

'But when will that be?'

'Soon, I hope.'

'But what if it isn't?' She was, Russell realised, on the edge of tears. 'I have to talk to someone about him.'

Russell had an idea. 'How about abroad? Go to Holland or France. Or England even. See a specialist there. No one here will know.'

He watched her eyes harden as she remembered the aborted abortion, then soften again as the idea impressed itself. 'I could, couldn't I?' she said, half to herself, half to Effi. 'Thank you, John,' she said to him.

'Will Jens agree to that?' Effi asked.

'Yes, I think so.'

'You do understand how dangerous this will be for John if anyone finds out he knows about this law?' Effi insisted.

'Oh yes.'

'And you'll make sure Jens understands it too.'

'Yes, yes. I know you disagree about politics,' she told Russell, 'but Jens is as crazy about Lothar as I am. Believe me, even the Führer comes a long way second. Jens will do anything for his son.'

Russell hoped she was right. After driving Zarah and Lothar home to Grunewald he watched Jens in the lighted doorway, picking up his son with every sign of fatherly devotion, and felt somewhat reassured. In the seat next to him, Effi sighed. 'Did you see anything wrong with Lothar?' she asked.

'No,' Russell said, 'but Zarah sees more of him than anyone else.'

'I hope she's wrong.'

'Of course.'

'How was your day with Paul?'

'Good. He's away again next weekend.'

'Then let's go away,' Effi said. 'I start filming on the Monday after, and I'll hardly see you for two weeks after that. Let's go somewhere.'

'How about Rügen Island?'

'That'd be lovely.'

'We can drive up on Friday afternoon, come back Sunday. I'll teach you to drive.'

Russell woke early, with an empty feeling in his stomach which toast and coffee did nothing to dispel. 'Are you going to get the passport today?' Effi asked, brushing hair out of her eyes before sipping the coffee he'd brought her in bed.

'I hope so.'

'Do you want me to come with you? As cover or something?'

'No thanks. You'd make me even more anxious.' He kissed her, promised to ring the moment he had something to tell, and walked out to the car. There was no sign of the weekend sunshine – a thick blanket of almost motionless cloud hung over the city, low enough to brush the spires of the Memorial Church. As he drove on down Tauenzienstrasse, Russell decided to leave the car at home – the U-bahn seemed more anonymous. On arrival, he steeled himself to refuse a coffee from Frau Heidegger, but for once she wasn't at home. He put on fresh clothes and was soon on the train to Neukölln.

Zembski had the passport waiting in a desk drawer. 'A nice job, if I say so myself,' he muttered, using a photographer's black cotton bag to pick it up and hand it over. 'You should keep your own fingerprints off it,' he advised. 'And please – burn it the moment you're finished with it. I've already burned the negatives.'

'I will,' Russell said, examining the photograph inside. It looked as though it had always been there.

He walked back to the U-bahn station, hyper-conscious of the passport in his pocket. Pretending to be McKinley might get him through a spot check, but anything more rigorous and he'd be in real, real trouble. The passport was far too big to eat, though he supposed he could just tear the picture out and eat that. Explaining why he'd done so might prove difficult, though.

He reminded himself that he was only guessing about the poste restante, but it didn't feel like guessing – he knew it was there. Once on a train, he decided on another change of plan. The U-bahn might be anonymous, but he would be needing somewhere to read whatever it was McKinley had accumulated. He couldn't take it to his own flat or Effi's, and he had no desire to sit in a park or on a train with a pile of stolen documents on his knee. In the car, on the other hand, he could drive himself somewhere secluded and take his time. This seemed like such a good idea that he wondered why it hadn't occurred to him earlier. How many other obvious possibilities had he failed to notice?

Frau Heidegger was still out. He backed the Hanomag out of the courtyard, accelerated down Neuenburgerstrasse, and almost broad-sided a tram turning into Lindenstrasse. Calm down, he told himself.

On the way to the old town his head raced with ideas for foiling discovery and capture. If he checked who was on normal duty in the poste restante, and then waited till whoever it was went to lunch, he'd probably be seen by someone less liable to go over the passport with a magnifying glass. Or would the lunchtime stand-in, being less used to the work, be more careful? A crowded post-office would give more people the chance of remembering him, an empty one would make him stand out.

He parked the car on Heiligegeiststrasse, a hundred metres north of the block which housed the huge Post Office, and walked down to the main entrance. The poste restante section was on the second floor, a large high-ceilinged room with high windows. A line of upright chairs for waiting customers faced the two service windows. One of these was occupied, the other not.

Heart thumping, Russell walked up to the available clerk and placed McKinley's passport on the counter. 'Anything for McKinley?' he asked, in a voice which seemed to belong to someone else.

The clerk took the briefest of looks at the passport and disappeared without a word. Would he come back with a sheaf of papers or a squad of Gestapo? Russell wondered. He stole a look at the other customer, a woman in her thirties who was just signing for a parcel. The clerk serving her was now looking at Russell. He looked away, and wondered whether to put the passport back in his pocket. He could feel the man still looking at him. Don't do anything memorable, he told himself.

His own clerk returned, quicker than Russell had dared hope, with a thick manila envelope. Letting this drop onto the counter with a thump, he reached underneath for a form. A couple of indecipherable squiggles later he pushed the form across for signing. Russell searched in vain for his pen, accepted the one offered with a superior smirk, and almost signed his own name. A cold sweat seemed to wash across his chest and down his legs as he scrawled an approximation of McKinley's signature, accepted his copy of the receipt and picked up the proffered envelope. The five yards to the door seemed endless, the stairs an echo chamber of Wagnerian proportions.

On the street outside a tram disgorging passengers was holding up traffic. Fighting the ludicrous temptation to run, Russell walked back towards his car, scanning the pavement opposite for possible watchers. As he waited to cross Kaiser Wilhelmstrasse he snuck a look back. There was no one there. If there had been, he told himself, they'd have seen the envelope and arrested him by now. He'd got away with it. For the moment, anyway.

Much to his relief the car started straightaway. He turned onto Konigstrasse by the Post Office and headed up towards the railway bridge, chafing at the slowness of the tram in front of him. As he rounded Alexanderplatz he decided, at the last moment, that Landsbergerstrasse offered the quickest route out of the city, and almost collided with another car. Away to his right the grey bulk of the Alex leered down at him.

He slowed the Hanomag and concentrated on driving the three kilometres to the city's ragged edge without getting arrested. As he swung round Büschingplatz he thought for one dreadful moment that a traffic cop was flagging him down, and the beads of sweat were still clinging to his brow as he drove past the huge state hospital on the southern edge of the Friedrichshain. Another kilometre and he could smell the vast complex of cattle markets and slaughter houses that sprawled alongside the Ringbahn. As he reached the top of the bridge that carried the road over the railway by Landsbergerallee Station he had a brief panoramic view of the countryside to the east: the two small hills rising, almost apologetically, from the vast expanse of the Prussian plains.

Mentally searching, earlier that day, for a safe place to study McKinley's material, he had recalled a picnic with Thomas' family on one of those hills. As he remembered it, a road ran south from Marzahn between them, and a winding access road led up to a picnic area on the hill nearest the city.

His memory was correct. The road wound up through dark, dripping trees to the bald brow of the hill, where picnic tables had been arranged to take advantage of the view across the city. There was no one there. Russell parked in the allotted space behind the tables and gazed out through the windscreen at the distant city. The nearest clump of large buildings, which Thomas had pointed out on their previous visit, made up Berlin's principal home for the mentally ill, the Herzberge Asylum. Which was highly apt, given the probable content of the reading matter on the seat beside him.

He reached for the envelope and carefully prised it open. There were about fifty sheets of paper in all, a few in McKinley's writing, most of them typed or printed. Russell skipped through them in search of Theresa Jürissen's letter. He found it at the bottom of the pile, with a date – the date it had been written – scrawled in pencil across the right-hand corner. Going back through the other papers, Russell found other dates: McKinley had arranged his story in chronological order.

The first document was a 1934 article from the *Münchner Zeitung*, a journalist's eye-witness report of life in an asylum entitled 'Alive Yet Dead.' McKinley had underlined two sentences – 'They vegetate in twilight throughout the day and night. What do time and space mean to them?' – and added in the margin: 'Or life and death?' The second document was a story from the SS journal *Das Schwarze Korps*, about a farmer who had shot his mentally-handicapped son and the 'sensitive' judges who had all but let him off. A reader's letter from the same magazine begged the authorities to find a legal and humane way of killing 'defective' infants.

Russell skipped through several other letters in the same vein and numerous pages of unattributed statistics which demonstrated a marked decline in the space and resources devoted to each mental patient since 1933. So far, so predictable, Russell thought.

The next item was an article by Karl Knab in the *Psychiatrisch-Neurologische Wochenschrift* journal. Again, McKinley had underlined one passage: 'We have before us in these asylums, spiritual ruins, whose number is not insignificant, notwithstanding all our therapeutic endeavours, in addition to idiots on the lowest level, patient material which, as simply cost-occasioning ballast, should be eradicated by being killed in a painless fashion, which is justifiable in terms of the self-preservatory finance policy of a nation fighting for its existence, without shaking the cultural foundations of its cultural values.' This was chilling enough, Russell thought, but who was Knab? He was obviously far from a lone voice in the wilderness, but that didn't make him a spokesman for government.

There was a lot of stuff on the Knauer boy, but most of it was in McKinley's writing – guesses, suppositions, holes to be filled.

It was the last few sheets of paper which really caught Russell's attention. Most were from a memorandum by Doctor Theodore Morell, best known to the foreign press community as Hitler's Quack. He had been given the task of gathering together everything written in favour of euthanasia over the last fifty years, with a view to formulating a draft law on 'The Destruction of Life Unworthy of Life'. Those eligible included anyone suffering from mental or physical 'malformation', anyone requiring long-term care, anyone arousing 'horror' in other people or anyone situated on 'the lowest animal level'. The Nazis qualified on at least two counts, Russell thought.

As Theresa Jürissen had said, the main area of controversy among those who favoured such a law was the openness or otherwise of its administration. In this memorandum Morell concluded that secrecy was best, that parents would be much happier thinking that their child had simply succumbed to some illness or other. He hadn't yet decided whether doctors should be involved in the actual killing of their patients, but he insisted on their compulsory registration of all congenitally ill patients.

The final item was the letter, and Russell now realised why McKinley had been so excited by it. Theodore Morell might be Hitler's doctor, but he was a private citizen, entitled to his own ideas, no matter how psychopathic they might be. The letter, though, was something else. It confirmed the gist of Morell's memorandum under the imprint of the KdF, the Kanzlei des Führers. It tied Hitler to child-killing.

Russell shook the papers together and stuffed them back into the envelope. After sliding the whole package under the passenger seat, he got out of the car and walked across the damp grass to the lip of the slope. A small convoy of military trucks was driving east down Landsbergerallee, a solitary car headed in the opposite direction. A dense layer of cloud still hung over the city.

McKinley had had his story, Russell thought. The sort of story that young journalists dreamt of – one that saved lives *and* made you famous.

But what was *he*, John Russell, going to do with it? Get rid of it, was the obvious answer. Along with the passport.

He watched a distant Ringbahn train slide slowly out of sight near the slaughter houses. It might be the obvious answer, but something more courageous was required. He owed it to McKinley, and probably to himself. He owed it to all those thousands of children – tens of thousands, for all he knew – that a creep like Morell found 'unworthy of life'.

McKinley had probably thought his story would save them all. Russell had rather less faith in the power of the press, but having everything out in the open would at least make it more difficult for the bastards.

How could he get the stuff to McKinley's paper? Not by post, that was for sure. He'd have to carry it out himself, and that would be no fun whatever.

How had McKinley planned to file the story? Or had he been just as stuck as he now was? That would explain why he'd put it in the poste restante.

Which had been a good idea. And still was, Russell decided. Under his own name this time. The passport would have to go.

But how could he get rid of it? Burning it made sense, but flames tended to be conspicuous, particularly on a day as dark as this one, and in any case he had no means of creating any. He could burn the damn thing in his apartment, but he felt reluctant to carry it a moment longer than he had to, and particularly reluctant to bring it home, where the Gestapo might be waiting on his sofa. Somewhere on the open road, he thought, with a good view in either direction. Back in the car, he slid it under his seat. Driving back down the hill he felt a strange urge to sing. Hysteria, he told himself.

At the post office in Marzahn he bought a book of matches and – since it seemed less suspicious – a packet of cigarettes to go with them. He also purchased a large envelope which he addressed to himself, care of the poste restante in Potsdam – he had no desire to revisit the counter at Heiligegeiststrasse under a different name. He then used the public telephone to call Effi.

'Is everything all right?' she asked anxiously.

'Too wonderful to talk about,' he said pointedly. 'What are you doing?'

'Trying to memorise my part.'

'Can you meet me in the Zoo Station buffet?' he asked. 'At four o'clock,' he added, checking his watch.

'I'll be there.'

Once back on the Landsberg road Russell started looking for a suitable place to burn the passport. A mile or so short of the Ringbahn bridge he found a wide entrance-way to a farm track and pulled over. Retrieving the passport from under his seat he ripped it into separate pages and set light to the first one, holding it down between his knees until it was too hot to hold, then shifting it to and fro with his feet until all that remained were black flakes. With his other hand he wafted the resulting smoke out through the open windows.

In the time it took him to burn the remaining five sheets only two lorries went by, and their drivers showed no interest in Russell's slightly smoking car. He gathered the blackened remains in his handkerchief, which he knotted and placed in his pocket before resuming his journey. Twenty minutes later he consigned both handkerchief and contents to a lonely stretch of the scum-covered Luisenstrassekanal. The final remains of Zembski's handiwork disappeared with a dull plop, leaving Russell with several burnt fingers to remember them by.

It was almost three-fifteen. He got back in the Hanomag, and drove west towards Potsdamerplatz. The traffic round the southern edge of the Tiergarten was busy for the time of day, but he reached his destination – a street halfway between Effi's flat and Zoo Station

– with five minutes to spare. He parked facing the direction she would come from, assuming she hadn't picked this day of all days to change her usual route.

Ten minutes later she came into view, walking quickly in her high heels, a few wisps of dark hair floating free of the scarf and hat.

She didn't see him, and jumped with surprise when he told her to get in. 'You said Zoo Station,' she said angrily, as he moved the car down the road. As far as he could see no one had been following her.

'That was for the benefit of anyone listening. I've got something to show you. In private.'

'Why didn't you just come to the flat then?'

'Because,' he explained, 'anyone caught with this lot in their flat is likely to end up like McKinley.'

'Oh.' She was taken aback, but only for a second. 'So where are we going?'

'Along the canal, I thought, opposite the Zoo restaurant. There's always people parked there.'

'Mostly kissing and cuddling.'

'We can always pretend.'

Once they were there, Russell reached down for the manila envelope under Effi's seat. Even with the assistance of the nearby streetlamp, reading was difficult, but he didn't dare turn on the car's internal light. 'Look,' he said, 'you don't need to read all of this. These last few pages – he handed her Morell's memo and Theresa's letter – should be enough to convince Zarah.'

'You want me to show them to her?'

'God, no. I want you to tell her what they are and what's in them. She'll believe you. If you tell her, she won't need to see them.'

'Okay.' Effi started to read, her face increasingly frozen in an expression of utter disgust. Russell stared out of the window, watching the last of the daylight fade. A coal barge puttered by on the canal, the owner's dog howling his response to an unknown animal's cry emanating from deep within the zoo. 'My country,' Effi murmured, as she moved on to the next sheet.

She read the whole memorandum, and then the KdF letter. 'You were right,' she said. 'If she'd kept that appointment, Lothar would be on a list by now.'

'And it won't be an easy list to get off,' Russell said.

They sat there in silence as another barge went by. In the Zoo restaurant across the water someone was stacking dishes.

'What can we do?' Effi wanted to know.

'I don't know. But you can tell Zarah you're convinced. And tell her I'm destroying the papers.'

'You're not going to?'

'I don't know. Not yet, anyway. I'm going to put them somewhere safe for a while.'

She gave him a searching look, as if she wanted to reassure herself of who he was. 'All those children,' she said.

'Achievements of the Third Reich'

After the excitement of the previous day, Russell spent Tuesday trying to work. The third article for *Pravda* was due by the end of the week, and one of the Fleet Street heavies wanted a second 'Ordinary Germans' piece before committing themselves to a series. It was write-by-numbers stuff, but he kept finding his mind drifting away from the subjects at hand, usually in the direction of potential threats to his liberty.

If the SD had the same bright idea about the poste restante that he had had, and checked through the records, they'd discover that McKinley had collected something nine days after his death. Everyone knew that Himmler was prone to strange flights of dark fantasy – rumour had it that SS agents were searching for the elixir of eternal life in Tibet – but he'd probably draw the line at mail-collecting ghosts. A light bulb would go on over his head, complete with the word-bubble: 'It must have been someone else!' And who would he and his minions think of first.

There'd be no point in denying it – they'd just drag him down to Heiligegeist and have him identified. He'd have to blame Eleanor McKinley, who was now beyond their reach. She'd given him the passport, he'd say. Asked him to pick up the papers, and he'd sent them on to her. Simple as that. What was in the envelope? He hadn't opened it. A different photograph in the passport? The clerk must have imagined it. The passport? He'd sent that on as well.

It was about as convincing as one of Goering's economic forecasts. And if some bright spark of Heydrich's decided to find out if there was anything under his name in any German poste restante, he'd be left without a prayer. He'd just have to hope that no one in the SD had read *Getaway* or *The High Fence*, which was at least possible – The Saint seemed far too irreverent an hero for Nazis.

Such hopes notwithstanding, every sound of a car in the street, every ring of footsteps in the courtyard below, produced a momentary sinking of the stomach, and later that evening, over at Effi's, a sharp rat-a-tat on the door almost sent it through the floor. When Effi ushered a man in uniform through the door, it took him several seconds to realize it was only Zarah's husband.

Jens Biesinger worked for some Government Inspectorate or other – Russell had never bothered to find out exactly which – and was on his way home. He accepted Effi's offer of coffee, shook Russell's hand, and took a seat, boots and belt creaking as he leaned back with a tired sigh. 'How is your work?' he asked Russell politely.

Russell made appropriate noises, his mind working furiously on what the man could want. His only real conversation with Jens, almost three years earlier, had escalated into a serious argument almost immediately, and Effi of all people had been forced to adopt the role of peacemaker. They had rarely been in the same room since, and on those occasions had treated each other with the sort of icy politeness reserved for loathed relations.

Jens waited until Effi was with them before he stated the object of his visit. 'John,' he began, 'I have a large favour I would like to ask you. Zarah wishes to take Lothar to England, for reasons that you are aware of. I cannot go with her, for reasons that I'm sure you will understand. And Effi starts work on her film on Monday. Zarah doesn't want to wait, so… would you escort them? Someone has to, and as an English-speaker – and, of course, someone who is almost part of the family – you would be the ideal person. Naturally, I would pay all the expenses – the flights, the hotel, whatever else is necessary.'

Recovering from his surprise, Russell considered the idea. And had another.

'I'd feel happier if you went with them, John,' Effi interjected.

'When are you thinking of?' Russell asked Jens. 'We're going away this weekend, and I'll be in Hamburg on Monday and Tuesday – the *Bismarck* launch. So it couldn't be until the middle of next week – Thursday perhaps?'

'That sounds reasonable.'

Russell brought up his other idea. 'I'd like to take my son too. I'll pay for him, naturally, but if you could arrange the trip for four… I'll need his mother's agreement, of course,' he added.

Jens smiled. 'An excellent plan – it will look more… natural. I'll arrange things for four. If your son can't go we can always amend the reservations.' He placed the cup of coffee on the side table and got up, looking pleased with himself. 'Zarah will be relieved,' he said. 'She was not looking forward to making such a journey alone.'

'I'm sure she'd have managed,' Effi said with a slight edge, 'but this will be better.'

'This is my number at the Ministry,' Jens said, handing Russell a card.

'This is mine at home,' Russell replied, tearing a sheet from his notebook and pencilling out the Neuenburgerstrasse number. England with Paul, he thought, and he was still revelling in the notion when Effi returned from seeing Jens out. 'You're not to fall in love with my sister,' she told him.

He phoned Ilse from Effi's flat early next morning and arranged to have coffee at a café in Halensee which they knew from their earlier life together. Russell wanted to ask her in person rather than over the phone, and she sounded more than willing – eager, in fact – to get out of the house for a couple of hours.

The café looked more run-down than Russell remembered, a

consequence, perhaps, of the fact that a large proportion of its former clientele had been Jewish. Ilse was already there, looking less severe than usual. Her shoulder-length blonde hair, which over the last few years had invariably been tied back in a knot, hung loose, softening the stretched lines of her face. She still seemed painfully thin to Russell, and her blue eyes never seemed to soften as they had once, but she seemed genuinely pleased to see him.

He told her what he wanted, at worst expecting a flat refusal, at best a painful argument.

'I think it's a wonderful idea,' she said. 'We'll have to inform the school of course, and his *Jungvolk* leader, but I don't see how either of them could object. It'll be an educational experience, won't it?'

'I hope so. Matthias won't object?'

'Why should he?'

'No reason at all. Well, that's good. I expected more of an argument,' he admitted.

'Why, for heaven's sake? When have I ever tried to come between you and Paul?'

He smiled. 'You haven't.'

She smiled back. 'You must be getting lots of work,' she said. 'Paul's very impressed with the car.'

They talked about Paul, his interests and anxieties, for more than half an hour. Afterwards, driving back across the city for his Wednesday appointment at the Wiesners, Russell found it hard to remember a warmer conversation with his ex-wife. He was still bathing in its glow when he rapped on the door of the apartment in Friedrichshain.

There was no answer for several moments, then an anxious voice called out, 'Who is it?'

'It's John Russell,' he shouted back.

The door opened to reveal a haggard-looking Frau Wiesner.

'I'm sorry,' she said, looking down the stairs behind him. 'Come in, please.'

There was no sign of the girls.

'I'm afraid there will be no lesson today,' she said. 'And perhaps no more lessons for a while. My husband has been arrested. They have taken him to a camp. Sachsenhausen, we think. A friend of a friend saw him there.'

'When? When was he arrested? What was he arrested for?'

'They came here on Monday. The middle of the night, so it was really Tuesday.' She sat down abruptly, as if she needed all her strength to tell the story. 'They kept hitting him,' she almost whispered, a solitary tear running down her right cheek. 'He wasn't resisting. He kept saying, "I'm coming with you – why are you hitting me?" They just laughed, called him names. Called the children names. I only thank God that Albert wasn't here when they came.'

Russell sat down on the settee beside her and put an arm round her shoulder. 'Frau…' he started to say. 'I should know your name by now.'

'Eva.'

'Did they give a reason for his arrest?'

'Not to me. Our friends are trying to find out whether there was a reason… not a real reason, of course… but surely they have to say something, write something down in their record books.' She looked at him almost imploringly, as if their having a reason would make a difference.

'Where are the girls?' he asked. 'And where's Albert?'

'The girls are with friends down the road. They love your lessons, but today… they couldn't…'

'Of course not.'

'And Albert… He came back on Tuesday morning, heard what

had happened, and ran straight out again. I haven't seen him since.'

'The Gestapo haven't been back?'

'No. If they came back, I could ask them about Felix. I don't know what to do. Some friends say kick up a fuss, or you'll never be told anything. Others say that if you do it makes matters worse, and that Felix will be released eventually, like Albert was. And I wouldn't know where to go if I wanted to make a fuss. The Alex? If I go there and demand to know where Felix is and why they've arrested him they might arrest me, and then who'll look after Albert and the girls?'

'That wouldn't be a good idea,' Russell agreed. He wondered what would be.

'Have the Conways gone?' she asked.

'I'm afraid they have.' They'd been at sea for at least thirty-six hours. 'But I can try talking to someone at the Embassy. I doubt whether they'll be able to do anything, but it's worth a try.'

'They're not allowed visitors in Sachsenhausen,' she said. 'We found that out when Albert was there. Not family or friends that is. But perhaps they'd let you visit him. You could say he owed you money for the girls' lessons, and you need his signature for something – a cheque on a foreign bank account or something like that.'

'You don't have a foreign bank account?'

'No, of course not, but they think we have – they think we all have them.'

Russell winced. What could he do? The embassy certainly, but how much would a Jewish doctor's kindness to a now-departed colleague count for in the grand scheme of things? Not much. He could go to the Alex – or, more worryingly, the Gestapo HQ on Prinz Albrechtstrasse – and make some polite enquiries. Not as a journalist, of course. In fact, Eva Wiesner's suggestion was a good one. He could say that Wiesner owed him for the girls' lessons, and that the Jewish swine wasn't going to get out of it by running away to a Kz. That should give the bastards a good laugh.

And then there was Jens, who now owed him a favour. A last resort, Russell decided. That was one favour he wanted to keep in reserve.

'I'll make some enquiries,' he told her. 'Tactfully. I won't stir up any resentment. I'll try and find out where he is and why he's been arrested. And if there's any chance of arranging a visit.'

She gave him a despairing look. 'Why is it that you can see how wrong this is, and so many people can't?'

'I like to think most people can,' he said. 'And that they're just too afraid to speak up. But lately…' He spread his hands. 'If I find out anything definite, I'll be back to let you know. Otherwise I'll come on Friday at the usual time.'

'Thank you, Mr Russell. You are a real friend.' Another solitary tear crawled down her cheek, as if her body was conserving its supply for future contingencies.

As he walked back to the car, Russell found himself hoping he was the friend she thought he was. He had considered giving her his address, but there was no way he could keep one or more of the Wiesners in his apartment. If Frau Heidegger didn't report it, one of his neighbours would.

Driving down Neue Konigstrasse he decided on visiting the Gestapo first. Another voluntary encounter with the Nazi authorities, he told himself, would weaken any suspicions they might hold with regard to McKinley's missing papers. He knew, deep down, that was wishful thinking, but the idea helped to strengthen his nerve.

He parked behind a shiny, swastika-embossed limousine on

Prinz Albrecht Strasse, and approached the impressive portals of the State Police HQ. Taking a deep breath, he walked up the steps and in through the revolving door. As usual, the Führer was up there in his frame, beady eyes tracking you round the room like some scary inversion of the Mona Lisa – you *knew* what *he* was thinking.

Russell explained his plight to the receptionist: the Jew, the debt, the joke about Wiesner running away to a Kz. She laughed, and directed him to the appropriate office for Ongoing Cases. Another receptionist, another laugh, and he was on his way to Completed Cases, which sounded bad for Felix Wiesner.

The officer in charge was in a good mood. It took him less than a minute to find the file for Dr Wiesner, and less than that to read it. 'You're out of luck,' he said. 'The kike's in Sachsenhausen, and he won't be back. Your money's gone.'

'What did the bastard do?' Russell asked.

'Gave a German girl an abortion. That's twenty-five years, if he lasts that long.'

Russell felt his heart sink, but managed not to show it. 'Win some, lose some,' he said. 'Thanks for your help.'

He made his way back to the entrance, half-expecting to hear muffled screams from the rumoured torture chambers in the basement, but, as in the SD HQ round the corner, there was only the whisper of typewriters to break the silence.

He left the car where it was, walked up Wilhelmstrasse to the British Embassy and sat beneath the latest King's picture – the third in two years – while he waited for Martin Unsworth to see him. It proved a waste of time. Unsworth had heard about the Wiesners from Doug Conway, but felt no dramatic compulsion to risk his career on their behalf. He pointed out, reasonably enough, that a British Embassy could hardly involve itself in the domestic criminal matters of a host nation. He added, just as reasonably, that the host nation would, at best, ignore any request in such a matter and, at worst, make use of it for propaganda purposes. Russell hid his fury, elicited a promise from Unsworth to investigate the Wiesners' visa applications, and then thumped the wooden banister so hard on his way down that he feared for a moment he'd broken his hand. Walking back down Wilhelmstrasse, surrounded by billowing swastikas, he simmered with useless rage.

Back at Effi's – he seemed to be living there at the moment – he told her what had happened. She advised him to ring Jens – 'There's a human being in there somewhere,' she said. 'Though you have to dig a bit.'

Why not, he told himself. Cash in the favour owed while it was still fresh in the memory.

After talking his way past two secretaries, Russell was finally put through to Jens. 'I haven't managed to arrange anything yet,' Zarah's husband said, trying and failing to conceal his irritation.

'This is about something else,' Russell told him. 'I need a favour from you this time.'

Something between a groan and a grunt greeted this statement.

Russell ploughed on. 'Someone I know has been arrested and taken to a camp. A Jew.'

'I...'

'Please, hear me out. This is nothing to do with politics – it's a matter of honour. This man's a doctor and back in 1933, before the Jews were forbidden to practice, he saved the life of my friend's child.' He went on to explain who Conway was, how he'd involved Russell in teaching Wiesner's daughters, and his current unreachability in mid-Atlantic. 'This is not about helping the Jews, it's about repaying a debt.'

'I understand what you...' Jens began, his tone now mixing sympathy with the reluctance.

'I don't want you to do anything,' Russell insisted, somewhat disingenuously. 'I just need to know the details of why he's been arrested, and what the chances of a visit are. A visit from me, I mean – I know there's no chance of a family visit. At the moment, his wife and children are in limbo – they can't do anything but wait. I think the wife needs his blessing to do what's best for the children.'

There was a moment's silence at the other end. 'I'll find out what I can,' Jens said eventually.

'Thank you,' Russell said. He put down the phone. 'I'll drive over to the Wiesners and tell them,' he told Effi.

She went with him. Frau Wiesner seemed calmer, or perhaps just more resigned. When Russell reported the Gestapo claim about an abortion she seemed torn between derision and despair. 'Felix would never – never – do anything so foolish,' she said.

At first, she looked somewhat askance at Russell's glamorous-looking companion, but Effi's obvious empathy quickly won her over. The girls were there, and both insisted on getting the visiting film star's autograph. Marthe produced her movie scrapbook and the three of them took over the sofa. Watching their dark heads together, poring over the neatly-arranged photographs of German and Hollywood stars, Russell found he was fighting back tears.

He spent Thursday immersed in work, his apartment door open to catch the sound of the ground floor telephone. It was late afternoon when Frau Heidegger shouted up the stairs that the call was for him.

'I have the tickets and reservations,' Jens told him. 'We were lucky – there were four seats left on next Thursday's London flight.

It leaves at two, but you should be there half an hour earlier. The return flight is on Sunday, at eleven. I have booked two rooms at the Savoy Hotel – have you heard of it? – on a road called Strand. And a car to take you from the airport in Croydon to the hotel and back again. And of course the appointment. I hope that covers everything.'

Russell almost asked where the appointment was, but presumed Jens was being cagey for a reason. 'It sounds perfect,' he said. The Savoy! he thought.

'Good. Now, this other business.' He paused for a moment and Russell could imagine him checking that his office door was shut. 'Your friend's Jewish doctor has been arrested for conducting an abortion on a girl of seventeen. Her name is Erna Marohn, from a good German family. Her father is an officer in the Kriegsmarine.'

'Who made the complaint?'

'The mother. The father is away at sea. There is no doubt the girl had an abortion – she was examined by a police doctor. And there is little doubt that Wiesner carried it out – she was seen entering the clinic he runs in Friedrichshain for other Jews.'

'That sounds bad.'

'It is. A German doctor caught performing an abortion can expect a lengthy term of imprisonment. A Jewish doctor caught performing one on a German girl, well…'

'Yes.'

'But there is some good news. I have managed to arrange a pass for you to visit him in Sachsenhausen. Next Wednesday, the day before you go to England. A courier will bring the pass to your house. You should be at the camp by 11 a.m. But you will not be able to take anything in or out. And you must not report anything you see or hear. They are letting you in as a favour to me, but not as a journalist. You do understand that?'

'Absolutely.'

'If anything appears in print, in England or anywhere else, describing the conditions there, they will assume that you have broken your word, and, at the very least, you will lose your journalistic accreditation. I was asked to tell you this.'

'I understand. And thank you, Jens.'

'You are welcome.'

Friday was clear and cold. Russell packed a bag for the weekend, and headed towards Friedrichshain, stopping for a newspaper and coffee at Alexanderplatz Station. The only interesting piece of news concerned a train: in Westphalia a thirty-seven ton excavating machine had run amok on a night freight. Whatever it was that pinioned the steel arms in an upright position had come undone, dropping them into their working position over one side of the wagon. A mile's worth of telegraph poles, signals and huts had been demolished, and a station reduced to rubble when the canopy supports were swept away. The train had only been stopped when a witness phoned ahead to a signal box. The guard hadn't noticed anything was amiss. Hitler's Germany in microcosm – flailing away in the darkness, ruins piling up behind.

At the apartment in Friedrichshain he told Frau Wiesner what Jens had told him. 'I don't believe it,' she said. 'Felix will tell you what really happened.' He gave the two girls an English lesson, and promised to come by on the following Tuesday when he returned from Hamburg. Driving back across town to pick up Effi, he wondered how to dispel the sense of gloom that seemed to be enveloping him.

He needn't have worried. It was about two hundred kilometres to Stralsund, and by the time they reached it Effi's defiant mood of romantic adventure had taken him over. After crossing the narrow sound on the steam ferry, they drove the last forty kilometres to Sassnitz in gathering darkness, their headlights catching nothing on the road except two deer hurrying each other across.

As Russell had expected, the small resort was virtually empty, and they had their pick of those hotels not closed for the winter break. They chose the Am Meer, right on the promenade, and were given a room with views across the darkened Baltic. With the dining room closed for refurbishing, dinner was served in the lounge, in front of a dancing fire, by a girl of about fourteen. Happy and full, they walked out across the promenade and listened to the comforting caress of the tide. Above the sea the sky was bursting with stars, and over the hills behind them a thin crescent moon was rising. As they clung together for warmth, and kissed on the stony beach, it crossed Russell's mind that this was as perfect as life ever got.

Back in their room they discovered, much to Effi's amusement, that the bed squeaked and creaked at their slightest movement, and midway through making love she got the giggles so badly that they had to take a break before resuming.

The good weather continued, sunlight advancing across their bed the following morning. After wrapping up warmly they set out for the famous Stubbenkammer cliffs, a ten kilometre drive through the Stubnitz beech woods. After gingerly looking over the 140 metre precipice, Russell gave Effi her first driving lesson on the large expanse of tarmac laid out for the summer charabancs. Clanking the gears atrociously, she jerked her way through several circuits before pronouncing: 'This is easy!'

They had lunch in a restaurant they had noticed on the drive up, a sprawling wooden building with intricately-carved facades which nestled among the beeches, and then spent a couple of hours walking along the well-tended paths of the sun-dappled forest. The only other humans were several fragments of a Hitler Youth group on a weekend trip from Rostock: groups of two or three boys, their eyes flickering from compass to path and back again. Their leaders, who brought up the rear, claimed to have seen a bear, but the beer on their breath suggested otherwise.

It got dark too early, but there was always the creaking bed. Afterwards, they drank, ate and sat in front of the same fire, hardly speaking, and not needing to. The bed was uncomfortable as well as noisy, but Russell slept better than he had for weeks.

On their final morning he drove them north-west towards the long sandspit that connected the Jasmund and Wittow peninsulas. Seeing that the road along the spit was empty he gave the wheel to Effi, and she drove the next twenty kilometres, far too fast, with a huge smile lighting up her face. At the end of the spit they walked on the sandy beach, a kilometre or more and back again, watching the wind raising whitecaps on the water, and the clouds scudding eastwards across the blue-grey Baltic. No cars went by, no walkers. No ships appeared on the horizon. The earth was theirs.

But not for long. Effi's train back to Berlin left Stralsund at three, and as they made their way back across the island the sunshine became increasingly intermittent, finally disappearing beneath a wall of cloud. The short ferry ride was choppy, the railway carriages clanking ominously in their chains, and rain was falling by the time they reached the Hauptbahnhof.

'This is really sad,' Effi said. 'You'll only be back for a day or so, and you'll be gone to London again. And I've no idea what the filming schedule's going to be.'

'It's only a couple of weeks,' he told her.

'Of course,' she smiled, but he knew he'd said the wrong thing.

'Let's do this again,' he said. 'Soon.'

'Please.' A whistle sounded, and she leaned out of the window to kiss him. 'Are you sure we have this the right way round?' she asked.

'You should be on a train to Hamburg and I should be driving back to Berlin.'

'Sometimes other people want to use the road,' he told her as the train jerked into motion.

She made a face, and blew him a kiss. He stood there watching the train's red tail light recede into the distance, then strode back down the platform and out of the station. The car seemed colder without her.

The road across the damp northern heathland was mostly empty, the rain persistent and occasionally heavy. He drove west at a steady fifty kilometres an hour, half-hypnotised by the steady slap of the windscreen wiper as his eyes struggled to pierce the gloom ahead. Darkness had fallen by the time he left Lubeck, and on the last stretch across southern Holstein a stream of lorries did their best to blind him with their headlights. The dimly-lit suburbs of eastern Hamburg came as a blessed relief.

He had already booked himself a room with bath at the Kronprinz Hotel on Kirchen-Allee. This was one of the Hamburg establishments favoured by journalists on an expense account. It was expensive, but not that expensive – the journalists concerned could always produce proof that other hotels were more so. The receptionist confirmed what he already expected, that he was a day ahead of the crowd. With the launch set for lunchtime Tuesday, most of the press would be arriving late on Monday.

After examining his room and eating dinner in the hotel restaurant he went out. The Kronprinz was just across from the main station, which lay at the eastern end of the old town. Russell walked through the station and down Monckebergestrasse towards the looming tower of the Rathaus, turning right before he reached it, and headed for the Alster-Bassin, the large square of water which lay at the city's heart. He had visited Hamburg many times over the last fifteen years, and walking the mile-long, tree-lined perimeter of the Alster-Bassin had become almost a ritual.

Despite the damp cold, many others were doing the same. On summer days the water was usually busy with rowing, sailing and steam-boats, but on this winter evening the seagulls had it to themselves. Russell stopped for a beer at a café on one of the quays, and thought about Effi. She was wonderful with children, but he couldn't remember her ever saying she wanted them. Did he want another one, with her? Despite the fact that the world was about to collapse around them, he rather thought he did. Far across the water a seagull squawked in derision.

He slept well, ate a large breakfast, and drove across the city to St Pauli, the suburb between Hamburg and Altona which housed a high proportion of the city's seafaring population. His British agent had particularly liked the idea of including sailors among his 'Ordinary Germans', and this was an obvious place to find them. Interviewing men past active service seemed like a good way of deflecting any suspicion that he was collecting intelligence rather than human interest news, and his first port of call was one of several homes for retired seamen close to the waterfront.

Over the next couple of hours he talked to several delightful pensioners, all eager to share the sources of alcohol concealed on their persons. They had all fought in the war: one was a rare survivor from the Battle of the Falklands; two others had been participants in the Battle of Jutland. Both of the latter offered broad hints that they'd taken part in the High Seas Mutiny of 1918, but they clearly hadn't suffered for it, either then or under the Nazis. Their retirement home seemed comfortable, efficient and friendly.

All the residents he talked to admired the new ships, but none were impressed by the current standards of gunnery. Not, they admitted, that this mattered that much. Ships like the new *Bismarck* looked good – and were good – but the money and labour would be better spent on U-Boats. That, unfortunately, was where future naval wars would be won or lost.

Russell had less success with working sailors. Trawling the waterfront bars he found some amiable seamen, but rather more who treated his questions with suspicion verging on hostility. Some were clearly supporters of the regime: one young officer, pacified by a brief perusal of Sturmbannführer Kleist's letter, was particularly optimistic about Germany's naval prospects: he saw the *Bismarck*, in particular, as symbolic of a burgeoning renaissance. 'In five years' time,' he promised, 'we'll have the British hiding in their harbours.' Others, Russell guessed, would once have been open opponents of the regime – Hamburg, after all, had been a KPD stronghold, and a key centre of the Comintern's maritime organization. As far as these men were concerned he was, at best, a naïve English journalist, at worst, an agent provocateur.

That afternoon Russell spent a few marks on the circular tour of Hamburg harbour, an hour and a half of channels, shipyards, quays and towering cranes. Coloured bunting was going up everywhere, and the Blohm and Voss slipway which housed the future *Bismarck* was a ferocious hive of activity, as last-minute preparations were made for the launching ceremony. The ship itself was disappointing. Still lacking a superstructure, it looked more like a gigantic canoe than the future of naval warfare. The overall impression Russell carried back to the hotel, however, was of power and energy, of a nation with a long and lengthening reach.

He ate dinner at a small restaurant on the Jungfernstieg which he'd been to before – the oysters were as good as he remembered – and made his way back across town to the Klosterburg, the beer restaurant near his hotel where journalists usually gathered. Hal

Manning and Jack Slaney were sitting at the bar, staring across the room at a boisterous table of SA men. One man, beer slopping from a raised glass, was outlining what he'd do to Marlene Dietrich if she ever dared set foot in Germany again. His proposal made up in violence what it lacked in imagination.

Russell hoisted himself onto the vacant stool next to Slaney's and bought a round of drinks.

'She's making a film with Jimmy Stewart at the moment,' Slaney said. 'And her character's called Frenchie. I guess that shows which side she's on.' He carried on staring at the SA table, whisky chaser poised in his hand. 'We should think up a new collective noun for these people – you know, like a gaggle of geese. A crassness of stormtroopers. No, that's much too kind.' He threw his head back and tipped in the chaser.

'A void,' Manning suggested.

'Too intellectual.'

'A deposit,' Russell said.

'Mmm, not bad. A passing, perhaps.' He reached for his beer. 'If only they would,' he added sourly.

At eleven the next morning, two buses sent by the Ministry of Propaganda arrived at the forecourt of the Reichshof, just up the road from the Kronprinz, to collect the assembled foreign press corps. 'We'll be hanging around for hours,' Slaney complained, as their bus headed south towards a bridge across the Norder Elbe, but he had reckoned without the traffic. There was only one road through the docks to the Blohm and Voss shipyard, and forward movement was soon reduced to a crawl.

'Adolf won't like sitting in a jam,' Russell said.

'He's coming by yacht,' Manning told him. 'The *Grille*. A little journalistic detail for you.'

'Thanks, Dad.'

They reached Slipway 9 at quarter past twelve, and were dragooned, rather like schoolboys, into an enclosed area behind, and slightly to the right, of the ship's towering bow. From here a flight of steps led up to a platform around ten metres square, and from that a smaller flight of steps to the actual launching platform, right up against the bow.

It wasn't 'Hitler weather', but at least it was dry, with a few desultory streaks of blue amidst the grey. Several thousand people were present, lining the sides of the slipway and the area behind the platforms. Some shipyard workers were leaning over the ship's rail, others perched precariously on the vast scaffolding of girders which rose above the ship. The larger platform was full of city and state officials, naval brass and party hacks.

The first of several loud booms silenced the crowd.

'Naval salutes,' Slaney murmured. 'Unless they're firing on Hitler's yacht.'

'No such luck,' Russell said, indicating the man in question, who had just appeared at the bottom of the steps leading to the first platform. Bismarck's elderly grand-daughter was climbing the steps ahead of him, and Hitler was visibly chafing at the delay, casting frequent glances at her progress as he talked to the portly Goering.

Once the Führer, Dorothea von Bismarck and the three service chiefs were all gathered on the higher platform, the former gave, by his own standards, a remarkably brief speech extolling the virtues of Germany's last navy – scuttled to spite the British in 1919 – and of the Iron Chancellor himself, 'a true knight without fear or reproach.' Bismarck's grand-daughter then named the ship – her quavering voice barely audible above the raucous shouts of the seagulls – and broke the traditional bottle of champagne on the bow.

There was a sound of blocks being knocked away, and then... nothing. The ship failed to move. Hitler continued staring at the bow, like a cat facing a door which refused to open. One of the service chiefs looked round, as if he was asking himself, 'What do we do now?' A couple of seagulls hovered above the upper platform, as though intent on mischief.

'If this goes on much longer,' Slaney said, watching them, 'the Limeys will be running a book on who gets crapped on first.'

There were more knocking noises from below, but still no sign of movement. Russell looked at his watch – two minutes and counting. Hitler was still staring rigidly ahead, but what else could he do? It was hardly the place for a major tantrum.

One of the service chiefs leaned over to say something, and stiffened as if he'd been slapped. And then a cheer burst forth from those lining the slipway – at last the ship was inching forward. The figures on the platform visibly relaxed, and as the stern slid into the river, Hitler, turning slightly to one side, smiled and brought a clenched fist sharply down on the railing.

'They must have sent Goering down to give it a push,' Slaney said. 'Anyway,' he added, 'the good news is that it won't be ready for sea until 1941.'

Slaney's train wasn't until nine that evening, and he jumped at the offer of a lift back to Berlin in the car. There was little conversation – Slaney slept for most of the journey, despite snorting himself awake on several occasions – and Russell was left to brood on his visit to Sachsenhausen the following day. At least he'd have no trouble getting there. Come to think of it, that was what made car ownership in Germany special – the concentration camps became so accessible.

After dropping Slaney off in the city centre he drove up Neue Konigstrasse to see if the Wiesners had any news, or any last-minute instructions for his visit. There was none of the former, but Frau Wiesner had written a short letter to her husband.

'They won't allow...' Russell started to say, but then relented. 'I'll try,' he promised.

'Please read it,' she said, 'and if they take it then you can tell him what's in it.'

'Tell Daddy we love him,' Ruth said, her head suddenly appearing round the door to the other room. The voice was brittle, the smile almost unbearable.

'I will.'

He motored back down Neue Konigstrasse, and stopped at the Alexanderplatz station to call Effi. The phone just rang, so he drove home to Neuenburgerstrasse. Frau Heidegger's skat evening was in boisterous swing, but she'd pinned a message for him beside the phone: 'Herr Russell! Your fiancée is working late tonight and early tomorrow morning. She finishes work at six tomorrow evening!'

Russell went upstairs and ran a bath. The water was almost scalding, the pain of immersion almost pleasurable.

Wednesday was a nice day for any drive but this one. Berlin looked its best under a pale sun: the Spree sparkled, the windows glittered, the brightly-coloured trams shone in the grey stone streets. While walkers huddled against the brisk cold wind, mouths and ears swathed in wool, the Hanomag proved remarkably draught-proof for a ten year-old car. As he drove up Brunnenstrasse towards Gesundbrunnen he murmured a prayer of thanks for the Zembski cousins. More than a thousand kilometres in twelve days, and no sign of a problem.

As he drove over the Ringbahn bridge he could see the Hertha flag flying from the Plumpe grandstand. This was the way he and Effi had come on the previous Friday, but the feeling on that day was one of leaving Hitler's world behind. Today he was journeying into its heart, or the space where a heart might have been.

Sachsenhausen was only an hour's drive from Berlin, a reasonable commute for the Gestapo interrogators who had previously plied their trade in the modern dungeons of Columbia Haus. According to Slaney, the new camp was a lot bigger, but neither he nor any other member of the foreign press corps had ever visited it. They had been shown round a sanitised Dachau in the early days, but that was that.

Ten kilometres short of his destination, Russell pulled into a small town garage for petrol and used the stop to read Eva Wiesner's letter to her husband. It was simple, touching, to the point. Heartbreaking.

Back on the Stralsund road, a neat sign announced the turn-off to Sachsenhausen Concentration Camp and Re-Educational Facility. Two or three kilometres of newly-laid road led through a flat land of pastures and small woods to the gates of the camp. Parallel wire fences ran off to both left and right, one of which was clearly electrified. The gates themselves were flanked by a concrete watchtower and gatehouse.

Russell pulled up beside the latter, as a man in *Totenkopfverbände* uniform emerged with palm raised and a sub-machine gun cradled in his other arm. Russell wound down the window and handed over his documents. The guard read through them twice, told him to wait, and walked back inside the gatehouse. Russell heard him talking, presumably on the telephone, and a few moments later he re-emerged with another guard. 'Get out,' he said.

Russell obliged.

'Raise your arms.'

He did as he was told. As one guard checked his clothes and body for weapons, the other went over the car.

'What is this?' the first guard asked, taking the letter from Russell's coat pocket.

'It's a letter for the man I've come to see. From his wife.'

'Not permitted,' the guard said, without apparent emotion. He crumpled the letter in his fist.

Russell opened his mouth to protest but thought better of it.

'The car's clean,' the other guard reported.

'Turn left inside the gate, and report to the *Kommandantura*,' the first guard said. 'It's the second building on the left.' He handed back the documents and gestured to the guard who had now appeared inside the gates to open them. Russell thanked him with a smile – which was not returned – and drove carefully through the opened gates, conscious that they would soon be closing behind him. Turning left, he could see, in a wide space some distance ahead, several hundred prisoners standing in formation. Most had bare arms and heads, and must have been freezing in the cold wind. Two *Totenkopfverbände* officers were ambling along the front rank, shouting something indecipherable. One had a muzzled Alsatian on a lead.

He stopped outside the two-storey concrete building which bore the label *Kommandantura*, took one last look at the apparent roll-call, and headed for the door. On either side of the entrance two large pots held the withered remains of what might have been geraniums.

Inside, a middle-aged Gestapo officer looked up from his desk, wordlessly extended a hand for Russell's documentation, and gestured him to a chair. As he examined the pass and accompanying letter he repeatedly ran his right hand through his thinning hair, as if intent on wearing out what little remained. Picking up the phone with that hand, he switched to using the other on his head. 'You are needed here,' he told someone, and hung up.

A minute later the someone – a younger man with a remarkably unintelligent face – arrived. 'Hauptscharführer Gründel will take you to your meeting,' the adjutant announced.

Russell stood up. 'This way,' the Hauptscharführer barked, leading him through a door, down a short corridor and out through another door into the open air. A short walk down a gravel path brought them to another, larger two-storey building, and a small windowless room on the ground floor. Several chairs and a table were arranged round the walls, leaving the centre of the room empty. The floor had a thin covering of sawdust.

'Why are you so interested in this Jew?' the Hauptscharführer asked, sounding almost bewildered beneath the bluster.

'He helped a friend of mine – years ago,' Russell said shortly.

The Hauptscharführer thought about that, and shook his head. 'Wait here,' he said.

Russell waited, pacing too and fro across the room. There was a dark residue in the centre of the floor which could have been dried blood. He squatted on his haunches for a better look, but admitted to himself that he didn't really know what dried blood in quantity looked like. It was the sort of thing you needed to know in Hitler's realm, he thought. If the Eskimos had fifty words for snow, the Nazis probably had fifty for dried blood.

The minutes stretched out. At one point a frenzied burst of barking erupted in the distance, and died out with equal abruptness. Almost twenty minutes had gone by when the door opened and Felix Wiesner was pushed inside, the Hauptscharführer close behind him. Russell had expected cuts and bruises, and there were lots of them – one of Wiesner's eyes was swollen shut, there were dark bruises on his neck, throat and cheeks, and blood in his hair. But that was just the superficial damage. His right hand was encased in a bloody bandage, concealing God knew what injuries, and the doctor was hunched over, apparently unable to walk upright. He looked, Russell thought, like a man who'd just been kicked in the genitals. Many, many times.

He was obviously surprised to see someone he knew. 'Come,' Russell said, helping Wiesner into a chair and feeling the pain it cost him.

The Hauptscharführer, who had taken a chair by the door, watched with contempt.

'Can we speak in private?' Russell asked, knowing what the answer would be.

'No. This bastard has forfeited any right to privacy. You have ten minutes,' he added, looking at his watch.

Russell turned to Wiesner. 'Your wife wrote you a letter, but they confiscated it. She told me to read it in case that happened. She wrote that she and the children love you and are dreaming of the day when you come home.'

Wiesner sighed, then made a visible effort to gather himself. 'Thank you,' he said quietly, moving his mouth with obvious difficulty. 'Why are you here?' he asked, as if there had to be more.

'To help, if I can,' Russell said. 'You know what they accuse you of?'

'Yes.'

'Did you see this girl?'

Wiesner shifted his body in a vain search for comfort. 'She came to the clinic. Wanted an abortion. Abused me when I said no.'

'You don't know who gave her the abortion?'

'No. But look,' he said, speaking slowly, making sure the words came out right, 'that doesn't matter. That's over. We are all guilty here.' He reached out his good hand and laid it on Russell's arm. 'You must tell my wife to go if she can. To save the girls. And

Albert if he's willing to be saved. And herself. She mustn't count on my getting out of here. In fact, she must act as if I were already dead. Do you understand? Can you tell her that? Can you make her believe it?'

'I can tell her.'

'She knows where my stamp collection' – he used the English words – 'is. It would be worth a lot to Stanley Gibbons. And I would be greatly in your debt.'

'No you wouldn't,' Russell said, glancing across at the Hauptscharführer, who was looking at his watch.

'I am ashamed to say it,' Wiesner continued, still struggling with every word, 'but I thought Albert was exaggerating about this place – that he had been less than a *mensch*. Tell him I am sorry, that now I know.'

'One minute,' the Hauptscharführer said.

'Don't tell my wife how bad it is,' Wiesner said. 'Tell her I'm all right. There's nothing she can do.'

Russell looked at him. 'I feel like I want to apologise,' he said.

'Why – you have done nothing.'

Russell grimaced. 'Maybe that's why. I don't know if there's anything I can do to help you, but I'll move heaven and earth to get your family out. I promise you that.'

Wiesner nodded, as if that were a deal worth having. 'Thank you,' he whispered as the Hauptscharführer got to his feet.

'Time,' the man shouted with evident satisfaction. 'You wait here,' he told Russell, shoving Wiesner in the direction of the door. Russell watched the doctor shuffle painfully out, arms folded against the wind, the Hauptscharführer demanding greater speed. The door slammed shut behind them.

Russell sat and waited, staring numbly into space, until the Hauptscharführer returned. Back at the *Kommandantura* he insisted on asking the Gestapo officer whether the doctor's account of events had been checked out. The man hesitated, as if wondering whether the offer of an answer could be justified, and decided it could. 'Our interrogations are not yet complete,' he said dismissively.

'You mean he's not dead yet,' Russell said.

The Gestapo man gave him a thin smile. 'What happens here is no concern of foreigners,' he said.

Several retorts sprang to mind, but silence seemed wiser. 'I can leave?' he asked.

'You can leave.'

Russell walked outside to the car. The prisoners were still lined up in the distance, the icy wind still blowing. He reversed the car, drove back to the gates, and waited for them to be opened. As he motored out past the gatehouse he saw the crumpled ball of Eva Wiesner's letter lying where the wind had blown it, up against the concrete wall. A kilometre or so down the access road he pulled to a stop, slumped forward with his head against the wheel, and let the waves of rage wash over him.

A little over an hour later he was pulling up outside the Wiesners' apartment block in Friedrichshain. He sat in the car for a while, reluctant to go up, as if bringing the bad news would make it real. Many of the people walking by looked Jewish, and most of them looked as if they'd seen better times. Did the faces look haunted, or was he just thinking that they should? Could they see the fist coming? The coshes, the belts, the whips?

Russell wearily climbed the stairs and knocked on the familiar door. It opened immediately, as if Frau Wiesner had been waiting behind it. 'He's all right,' Russell said, the lie sour on his tongue.

The girls' faces filled with hope, but Frau Wiesner searched his face, and saw a different truth. 'They are not treating him badly?' she asked, almost incredulously.

'Not too badly,' Russell said, glancing pointedly at the girls.

Her face sank with the knowledge that he needed to talk to her alone, but she managed a smile as she shooed the girls back into the other room. 'Tell me how bad it is,' she asked, once the door had closed behind them.

'He's been beaten. But not too badly,' Russell lied. 'He has cuts and bruises. What you'd expect from those animals.'

'God save us,' she said, her legs buckling.

Russell helped her into a seat, and steeled himself to pass on her husband's words. 'He gave me a message for you,' he began. 'You must leave the country if you can, you and the children. He hopes he will be released eventually, but for the moment – for the moment,' he emphasised – 'he says you must act as if he were dead.'

He expected tears, but she gave him a look full of defiance. 'The children, yes,' she said. 'But I will not go.'

'The children will need you,' Russell said. And your husband will not be coming back, he thought.

'They will be all right,' she said firmly, as if trying to convince herself. 'In a decent country, they will be all right. Albert is old enough to look after the girls.'

'Where is Albert?'

'Out somewhere. But I will make sure that he looks after the girls.'

'Your husband sent him a message too,' Russell said. 'He says he understands now what Albert must have been through in the camp. He wants Albert to know he's sorry for doubting him.'

'Oh, God,' she said, burying her face in her hands.

Russell pulled her to him, feeling her silent, racking sobs through his shoulder. 'One other thing,' he said when she was finally still. 'I am going to England tomorrow. For a few days, taking Effi's sister to see an English doctor. Your husband asked if I could get his stamps out of Germany, and this seems like an ideal opportunity. If you agree, I can put them in a safety deposit box in London, and leave the key with my agent. He's trustworthy.'

'You are sure?'

'That he's trustworthy? Yes. That I can get them past customs? Not completely, but I'm travelling with the wife of a Nazi and two children. It seems like the best chance we're likely to get.'

She got up and disappeared into the other room, returning a few moments later with a large, soft-covered book called *Achievements of the Third Reich: The First Five Years*. 'Collect all fifty full-colour stickers!' a splash in the corner announced, and Felix Wiesner obviously had. Stickers displaying busy factories, the People's car, Strength through Joy cruise ships and forty-seven other bounties of Hitler's reign were neatly affixed to their appropriate squares.

'The pictures are only stuck around the edges,' she explained. 'There's a stamp behind each one.'

Effi seemed happy enough to see him, but was, in her mind, it seemed to him, still on the film-set. Russell could have shocked her out of her absorption with an account of his visit to Sachsenhausen, but there didn't seem any point. He gave her a sanitised version of the visit, more sanitised indeed than the one he'd given Frau Wiesner. They made love that night in a friendly, somewhat desultory fashion, rather in the way, Russell imagined, that 'Mother' made love to her over-sensitive SA husband.

The dawn was only breaking over the mist-shrouded Havelsee location when he dropped her off, and he arrived outside the British Embassy almost an hour before it opened. The queue of

Jews seeking visas was already stretching round the corner into Pariserplatz.

Coffee and hot rolls in the Café Kranzler restored his body, but the morning's *Beobachter* further sank his spirits. An editorial congratulated the British on their obvious willingness to give up their empire – sarcasm was the *highest* form of wit in Goebbelsland – before condemning that same willingness as a clear sign of weakness and decadence. The British had succumbed to *humanitäts-duselei*, humanitarian nonsense. This was not something the Reich would ever countenance.

The queue of people eager to escape Hitler's paradise was receding round another corner when Russell got back to the Embassy. Martin Unsworth was in a meeting, and had nothing good to tell him when he eventually came out of it. Someone had stuck a 'to be refused' note on Frau Wiesner's file, but he didn't know when or why. He was still working on it but, as Russell could see, they were pretty busy. Russell's graphic account of his visit to Sachsenhausen elicited sympathy but little else. He had telegraphed the Washington Embassy with a message for Conway, Unsworth said, but had not had a reply. For all he knew, Conway was taking a few days' holiday in New York. And in any case, he didn't see what Conway or anyone else could do about one Jew in a concentration camp, no matter how innocent he was, or how badly he was being treated.

More resigned than raging, Russell left without hitting the banister and drove home to Neuenburgerstrasse. Frau Heidegger's door was open, his Sudeten neighbour sitting helplessly in the chair she reserved for the sacrificial coffee-drinker. Russell flashed him a sympathetic smile and ran upstairs to pack the larger of his two worn-out suitcases with three changes of clothes, a toothbrush and several books. The latter included *Achievements of the Third Reich* and the 1937 Coronation edition of the A1 Guide and Atlas of

London, which he'd discovered the previous year in a secondhand bookshop on the Ku'damm. Miniatures of their majesties sat side by side over a scrolled 'Long May They Reign'.

The aerodrome at Tempelhof field was on the other side of the Kreuzberg, about three kilometres away. As they lived fairly close together, Jens had agreed to pick up Paul for a noon arrival at the aerodrome, and Russell arrived with some twenty minutes to spare. The car park was small, but the quality of cars – his Hanomag excepted – made up for the lack of quantity. Flying was not for the poor.

The others arrived five minutes later, Paul with a *Jungvolk* rucksack on his back, his face a study in repressed excitement. The fur-coated Zarah looked anxious, Lothar like a normal four year-old. Jens ushered them into the one-storey terminal building, clearly intent on smoothing their path. As Zarah disappeared in the direction of the ladies room, he took Russell aside.

'It went well yesterday?' he asked.

Russell nodded.

'And you understand that you must not talk or write about your visit?'

Russell nodded again.

'For everyone's sake,' Jens added pointedly.

'Look!' Paul called out from a window. 'It's our aeroplane.'

Russell joined him.

'It's a Ju-52/3m,' Paul said knowledgeably, pointing at the plane being fuelled out on the tarmac. 'It has a cruising ceiling of 5,000 metres. It can go 264 kilometres an hour.'

Russell looked up. The sky was clearer than it had been. 'We should see a lot,' he said.

'We'll be over the Reich for two hours,' Paul said, as if nothing else was worth seeing.

Zarah had returned. 'Time to go through customs,' Russell told his son, feeling a flutter of nerves run down his spine.

Jens led the way, chatting and laughing with the officials as if they were old friends. Zarah's large suitcase was waved through unopened, as was Paul's rucksack. Russell's suitcase, however, they wanted to inspect.

He opened it up and watched, heart in mouth, while the customs official ran his hands through the clothes and came to the books. He looked at these one by one, ignoring those in English and settling on *Achievements of the Third Reich*. He skipped through a few pages, and gave its owner a quizzical look.

'It's for a nephew in England,' Russell explained, suddenly conscious that Paul was looking at the book with some surprise. Don't say anything, he silently pleaded, and Paul, catching his eye, seemed to understand.

The man put it back with the others and closed the suitcase. 'Enjoy your journey,' he said.

Once Jens and Zarah had said their goodbyes, the four of them walked out across the tarmac to the silver aeroplane. It had a stubby nose, three engines – one at the front, one on either wing – and windows like rectangular portholes. LUFTHANSA was stencilled on the side, a large swastika painted on the tailfin. A short flight of steps took them up to the door, and into a vestibule behind the passenger cabin, where their cases were stowed. In the cabin itself there were ten leather-covered seats, five on each side of the carpeted aisle, each with a high head-rest. Theirs were the four at the rear, Russell sitting behind Paul, Zarah behind Lothar.

The other passengers came aboard: a youngish English couple whom Russell had never seen before and four single men, all of whom looked like wealthy businessmen of one sort or another.

Judging from their clothes one of these was English, the rest German.

A mail lorry drew up beside the aeroplane. The driver jumped down, opened the rear door and dragged three sacks marked *Deutschespost* to the bottom of the steps. A man in a Lufthansa uniform carried them aboard.

'We used these against the communists in Spain,' Paul said, leaning across the gangway to make himself heard above the rising roar of the engines. 'They were one of the reasons we won.'

Russell nodded. A discussion with his son about the Spanish Civil War seemed overdue, but this was hardly the place. He wondered if Paul had forgotten that his parents had both been communists, or just assumed that they'd seen the errors of their ways.

The pilot and co-pilot appeared, introducing themselves with bows and handshakes as they walked down the aisle to their cabin. The stewardess followed in their tracks, making sure that everyone had fastened their leather safety belts. She was a tall, handsome-looking blonde of about nineteen with a marked Bavarian accent. A predictable ambassador for Hitler's Germany.

Out on the tarmac a man began waving the plane forward, and the pilot set them in motion, bumping across the concrete surface towards the end of the runway. There was no pause when they reached it, just a surge of the engines and a swift acceleration. Through the gap between seat and wall, Russell could see Paul's ecstatic face pressed to the window. On the other side of the aisle, Zarah's eyes were closed in fright.

Seconds later, Berlin was spreading out below them – the tangle of lines leading south from Anhalter and Potsdamer stations, the suburbs of Schonefeld, Wilmersdorf, Grunewald. 'There's my school!' Paul almost shouted. 'And there's the Funkturm, and the Olympic Stadium!'

Soon the wide sheet of the Havelsee was receding behind them, the villages, fields and forests of the northern plain laid out below. They were about a mile up, Russell reckoned, high enough to make anything look beautiful. From this sort of height a *Judenfrei* village looked much like one that wasn't.

They flew west, over the wide traffic-filled Elbe and the sprawling city of Hannover, crossing into Dutch air space soon after three o'clock. Rotterdam appeared beneath the starboard wing, the channels of the sea-bound Rhine – or whatever the Dutch called it – beneath the other. As they crossed the North Sea coast the plane was rocked by turbulence, causing Zarah to clutch the handrests and Paul to give his father a worried look. Russell gave him a reassuring smile. Lothar, he noticed, seemed unconcerned.

The turbulence lasted through most of the sea crossing, and the serene sea below them seemed almost an insult. Looking down at one Hook of Holland-bound steamer Russell felt a hint of regret that they'd travelled by air – not for the lack of comfort, but the lack of romance. He remembered his first peacetime trip to Europe – the first few had been on troopships during the war – the train journey through Kent's greenery, the Ostend ferry with its bright red funnels, the strange train waiting in the foreign station, the sense of striking out into the unknown. He hadn't been on a plane for the better part of ten years, and he hadn't missed them.

But Paul was having the time of his life. 'Can you see England yet?' he asked his father.

'Yes,' Russell realised. The Thanet coast was below him. A large town. Margate probably, or Ramsgate. Places he'd never been. And within minutes, or so it seemed, the south-eastern suburbs of London were stretching beneath them in the afternoon sun, mile upon mile of neat little houses in a random mesh of roads and railways.

The pilot brought the plane down on the Croydon runway with only the slightest of jolts. The entry formalities were just that, and the car Jens had ordered was waiting at the terminal doors. They drove up the Brighton Road, slowed by the busy late-afternoon traffic. Paul marvelled at the double-decker buses, but was more astonished by the paucity of buildings reaching above two storeys. It was only after Brixton that third, fourth and fifth floors were grudgingly added.

Russell asked the driver to take them across Westminster Bridge, and was rewarded by the singular sight of Big Ben and the Houses of Parliament aglow in the light of the setting sun. As they drove up Whitehall he pointed out Downing Street and the Horseguards; as they swung round Trafalgar Square, Nelson on his lonely column. The Strand seemed choked with buses, but they finally arrived at the Savoy to find that their fifth floor rooms overlooked the Thames.

They must have cost a fortune, Russell thought. He and Paul looked out of the window at the barges on the tide-swollen river, the electric trains of the Southern Railway moving in and out of Charing Cross Station. Away to their left the piles of the new Waterloo Bridge stuck out of the water like temple remains. 'This is good,' Paul said, with the air of someone truly satisfied.

Russell got an outside line and phoned his London agent Solly Bernstein, hoping to catch him before he went home. 'I'm just on my way out of the door,' Bernstein told him. 'What the hell are you doing in London?'

'Hoping to see you. Can you squeeze me in tomorrow afternoon?'

'Well, all right. Just this once. Four o'clock?'

'Fine.'

Russell hung up and explained the call to Paul. 'I'm hungry,' was the response.

They ate with Zarah and Lothar in the hotel restaurant. The food was excellent, but Zarah, clearly anxious about the next morning, just picked at it. When she and Lothar wished them goodnight and retired to their room, Russell and his son took a stroll down to the river, and along the Embankment towards the Houses of Parliament. Opposite County Hall they stopped and leant against the parapet, the high tide slurping against the wall below. Pedestrians and buses were still crowding Westminster Bridge, and long chains of lighted carriages rumbled out of Charing Cross. A line of laden coal barges headed downstream, dark silhouettes against the glittering water. Some lines of Eliot slipped across his brain:

The barges wash
Drifting logs
Down Greenwich reach
Past the Isle of Dogs

He had hated 'The Wasteland' when it came out – its elegant despair had felt like defeatism. But the words had stuck. Or some of them at least.

'It's been a long day,' he told Paul. 'Time for bed.'

Zarah looked exhausted over breakfast next morning, as if she'd hardly slept. Lothar, by contrast, seemed more animated than usual. Paul, asked by his father for an opinion of Zarah's son, had shrugged and said, 'He's just a bit quiet, that's all.'

Reception suggested a bank on the Strand which offered currency exchange and probably a safety deposit service, and Russell left Paul examining the huge model of the *Queen Mary* in the hotel lobby while he swapped his and Zarah's Reichsmarks for pounds. Safety deposit boxes were available, the cashier informed him proudly. The bank was open until three.

Their appointment in Harley Street was at eleven, and Zarah had booked a taxi for ten. Trafalgar Square was busy, but the cab then raced round Piccadilly Circus and up Regent Street, delivering them to the doctor's door with forty-five minutes to spare. A stern-looking receptionist showed them into the waiting room, which was full of highly-polished wooden chairs. Paul found a few children's comics among the society magazines, and went through one with Lothar, pointing out what was happening in the various pictures.

'How did you find this doctor?' Russell asked.

'A friend of Jens' at the Embassy here,' she replied. 'He said this man was highly thought of. And he speaks a little German.'

'Little', as they eventually discovered, was the operative word, and Russell had to function as a full-time interpreter. Doctor Gordon McAllister was a tall ginger-haired man in his forties, with a rather gaunt face, a slight Scottish accent and an almost apologetic smile. He seemed a nice man, and one who clearly liked children. Effi always claimed that doctors who specialised in women's problems were usually women-haters, but apparently the same logic did not apply to paediatricians.

His office was a bright, spacious room with windows over-looking the street. In addition to his desk, there were several comfortable chairs and a large wooden box full of children's toys and books. 'So tell me about Lothar,' he asked Zarah through Russell.

She started off nervously but grew more confident as she went on, thanks in large part to the doctor's obvious involvement. She said that Lothar sometimes seemed uninterested in everything, that he didn't respond when people talked to him, that at other times he would suddenly seem to lose interest in whatever it was he was doing, and just stop. 'He'll be in the middle of eating,' she said, 'and just leave the table and go and do something else. And he doesn't always seem to understand what I'm telling him to do,' she added.

'He's four, yes?' the doctor asked.

'And three months.'

'Can he recognise different animals?' He walked over to the box and took out a tiger and a rabbit. 'Lothar, what's this?' he asked holding out the tiger.

'A tiger.'

'And this?'

'A rabbit.'

'No problems there, then. How about colours? Can he recognise then?'

He could. A red balloon, a blue sky, a yellow canary. Having done so, without warning he walked across to the window and looked out.

The doctor asked Zarah about the birth, about Lothar's eating habits, whether there was any history of problems in her or her husband's family. She answered each question, and, in a halting voice, volunteered the information that she had considered aborting Lothar before he was born. 'I can't help thinking there's a connection,' she said, clearly close to tears.

'You're completely wrong about that,' the doctor insisted, the moment Russell had translated her words. 'There is no possible connection.'

'Then what is it?' she asked, wiping a tear away.

'Does he get tired easily? Does he seem weak – physically weak, I mean? Can he lift things?'

She thought about that. 'Jens – my husband – he sometimes says that Lothar lacks strength in his fingers. He doesn't like carrying things. And yes, he does get tired.'

The doctor leaned forward on his desk, fingers intertwined beneath his chin. 'I don't think there is anything seriously wrong with Lothar,' he said. 'Or at least, nothing that cannot be corrected. There is no name for this, but it isn't uncommon. Essentially, he has a weaker link with the rest of the world than most people do, but everyone is different in this respect – he's just a bit more different than the norm. And his link can be strengthened. What Lothar needs,' – he ticked them off on his fingers – 'is fresh air and exercise, really good, nutrient-rich, food – fresh eggs, fresh fruit, fresh everything – and physical stimulation. Regular massage would help. Give and take games – the sort that involve instant physical reactions. And music. All these things stimulate the body, make it more responsive.'

'But there's nothing seriously wrong?' Zarah asked.

'Not in my judgement. No.'

'And he doesn't need any tests?'

'No.'

She took a deep breath. 'Thank you, doctor.' She reached inside her handbag for the neat package of pound notes.

'You pay the receptionist,' he said with a smile.

But not usually with cash, Russell thought, as they waited for the taxi which the receptionist had ordered. Zarah, who looked as if a huge weight had been lifted off her shoulders, was eager to get back to the Savoy, where she could telephone Jens. 'It's wonderful news,' Russell told her, and received the warmest of smiles in return.

Once back at the hotel, they agreed to meet for lunch in an hour. Leaving Paul exploring the lobby, Russell retrieved *Achievements of the Third Reich* from their room, and came back down.

'Here's the room key,' he told Paul. 'I'll be back in half an hour or so.'

Paul was looking at the book. 'Where are you taking that?' he wanted to know. 'I didn't know you had a nephew in England,' he added suspiciously.

'I don't,' Russell admitted. 'I'll explain it all this afternoon.'

He walked down to the Continental Bank, paid a year's rent in cash for the safety deposit box, and was shown into a small room with a single upright chair and table. A clerk brought him a rectangular metal box and two keys, and told him to press the buzzer when he was finished. 'I already am,' Russell said, placing *Achievements of the Third Reich* inside and locking the box shut. If the clerk was surprised by the nature of the deposit he didn't show it.

'There's more to the Nazis than meets the eye,' Russell said.

'I don't doubt it,' the clerk replied gloomily.

Lunch was an altogether more cheerful affair than breakfast or the previous night's dinner, but twenty-four largely sleepless hours had taken their toll on Zarah. 'I'm going to take a nap,' she said. 'We'll see you this evening.'

Asked if there was anything he wanted to do, Paul suggested a walk down to Big Ben. 'I didn't see it properly in the dark,' he explained.

They set off down the Strand, stopping in at Charing Cross to see the Southern trains and admire the cross itself. After circling the Trafalgar Square ponds and climbing on a lion they marched down the Mall towards Buckingham Palace. 'The King's out,' Russell said, pointing out the lowered flag. 'Kings are out-dated,' Paul told him.

They cut through to Parliament Square and walked out onto Westminster Bridge, stopping in the middle to turn and admire Big Ben. 'You were going to tell me about that book,' Paul said rather hesitantly, as if unsure how much he wanted to know.

A small voice in Russell's head reminded him how many children had already denounced their parents to the authorities in Germany, and a whole host of other voices laughed out loud. And if he was so wrong about his own son, he told himself, then he probably deserved to be denounced.

He told Paul about the Wiesners. The family's need to emigrate, the father's arrest, the certain confiscation of their savings – the savings they would need to start a new life somewhere else.

'The savings are in that book?' Paul asked incredulously.

'Valuable stamps,' Russell told him. 'Hidden behind the stickers.'

Paul looked surprised, impressed, and finally dubious. 'They collected the stamps? Like ordinary Germans?'

'They *are* ordinary Germans, Paul. Or they were. How else do you imagine they would get hold of them?'

Paul opened his mouth, then obviously thought better of whatever it was he was going to say. 'They paid you to bring them?' he asked, as if he couldn't quite believe it.

'No. I did it because I like them. They're nice people.'

'I see,' Paul said, though clearly he didn't.

It was almost 3.30. Back in Parliament Square they joined the queue for a 24 bus, and managed to find seats upstairs for the short ride up Whitehall and Charing Cross Road. Solly Bernstein's office was two storeys above a steam laundry in Shaftesbury Avenue and its owner was accustomed, as he frequently observed, to hot air. A bulky, middle-aged man with gold-rimmed glasses, a notable nose and longish black hair, Russell's agent seemed unchanged by the last three years.

'This is my son, Solly,' Russell said.

'My, he's bigger than I imagined. Welcome to England, young man.'

'Thank you,' Paul said in English.

'Ah, a linguist. I have just the book for him.' He searched through the piles on the floor and extracted a large picture book of world aeroplanes. 'Have a look at that and tell me what you think,' he said, handing it over. 'Throw those books on the floor,' he added, indicating a loaded seat in the corner.

He turned back to Russell's grinning face. 'It's good to see you in the flesh. Three years, isn't it? A long time in today's world.'

'Something like that,' Russell agreed, taking a seat.

'You haven't come to tell me you've found a better agent?'

'Good God, no.'

'Well then, I can tell you we've sold the "Germany's Neighbours" series in both Canada and Australia. And here' – he rummaged in a drawer – 'is a cheque to prove it.'

Russell took it, and passed a sheaf of papers in the opposite direction. 'One for each series,' he said. 'I thought I'd save the postage.'

'An expensive way to do it. You came by train, I take it?'

'Nope. We flew.'

Bernstein's eyebrows rose. 'Even more expensive. My percentage is obviously too low.'

'I came for another reason. Two, actually. And one was to ask you a favour.' Russell outlined the Wiesners' circumstances, his hope that at least some members of the family would be given exit visas before a war broke out. Paul, he noticed, was listening with great interest to his recital. 'I've just put the family wealth in a safety deposit box,' he told the unusually sober Bernstein. 'There are two keys, and I was hoping you'd hang on to one of them. They'll have the other, but there's a good chance it would be confiscated at the border.'

'Why, in heaven's name?'

'Simple spite. If Jews are caught carrying a key out, the Nazis will guess it's for something like this.'

'I'd be happy to keep one of them.'

'Thanks,' Russell said, handing the key over. 'That's a weight off my mind.' He stole a glance at Paul, who looked more confused than anything else.

'How long are you here for?' Bernstein asked.

'Oh, only till Sunday. I came with my girlfriend's sister – that was the other reason – she wanted to have her son examined by an English doctor. A long story. But if there's a war, well, I guess I'll be back for the duration.'

'Without him?' Bernstein said, nodding in Paul's direction.

'Without him.'

Bernstein made a sympathetic face. 'Anyway, at least you've got a lot of work at the moment. No other ideas you want to talk about?'

'Not at the moment,' He looked at his watch. 'We'd better go. Paul?'

His son closed the book and brought it over. 'You can keep it,' Bernstein said. 'Practise your English on the captions.'

'Thank you,' Paul said. 'Very much,' he added carefully.

'It's working already.' He smiled and offered Paul his hand, then did the same to Russell.

'He was a nice man,' Paul said, as they made their way down the steamy stairwell.

'He is,' Russell agreed, as they reached the pavement. 'And he's Jewish,' he added, hoping that Paul was not going to wipe the handshake off on his coat.

He didn't, but he did look upset.

'They're wrong about the Jews,' Russell said firmly. 'They may be right about many things, but they're wrong about the Jews.'

'But everyone says…'

'Not everyone. I don't. Your mother doesn't. Your Uncle Thomas doesn't. Effi doesn't.'

'But the government says…'

'Governments can be wrong. They're just people. Like you and me. Look what foreign governments did to Germany in 1918. They were wrong. It happens, Paul. They get things wrong.'

Paul looked torn between anger and tears.

'Look. Let's not spoil the trip arguing about politics. We're in London – let's enjoy it.' They were walking down Charing Cross Road by this time. 'I know where we can get a cup of tea and a cake,' he said, steering Paul off to the left. A few minutes later they were on the edge of Covent Garden market, dodging lorries piled high with crates of fruit and vegetables. Russell led Paul into one of the cafés.

It was full of men sawing at rashers of bacon and dribbling egg down their chins. Fried grease in its gaseous, liquid and solid forms filled the air, lay congealing on the tables and covered the walls. England, Russell thought. He had a sudden memory of a similar café just outside Victoria Station, where he'd eaten his last meal before service in France. Twenty-one years ago.

Russell bought two large cups of tea and two aptly-named rock cakes. Paul nibbled at the edges of his, rightfully fearing for his teeth, but liked the tea once he'd added four teaspoons of sugar. 'The cake is terrible,' he told his father in German, causing several sets of less-than-friendly eyes to swivel their way.

'Do you know anything about football?' Russell asked the nearest man in English.

'Maybe.'

'Are there any games on in London tomorrow?'

'Arsenal are playing Chelsea,' another man volunteered.

'At Highbury?'

'Of course.'

'And the games still kick off at three? I've been working abroad for a while,' he added in explanation.

'So we see,' the first man said with a leer. 'Yeah, they still kick off at three.'

'Thanks. Would you like to see a game tomorrow?' he asked Paul. 'Arsenal are playing Chelsea.'

His son's eyes lit up. 'Arsenal are the best!'

'Well I'm sure Zarah and Lothar can look after themselves.'

They finished their teas, abandoned the half-excavated rock cakes, and picked their way through the vegetable market, taking particular care outside the skin-strewn frontage of a banana wholesalers. It was getting dark now, and Russell wasn't sure where he was. Looking for a street sign they found one for Bow Street.

'Bow Street,' Paul echoed. 'This is where Chief Inspector Teal brings the men he's arrested.'

Away to their left a blue light was shining. They walked up the street and stood across from the forbidding-looking police station, half-expecting the fictional inspector to emerge through the double doors, busily chewing on a wodge of Wrigley's as he adjusted his bowler hat.

Back on the Strand they found the Stanley Gibbons stamp shop was still open, and Paul spent a happy twenty minutes deciding which packets of cheap assorted he most wanted. Russell looked in the catalogue for the ones Wiesner had given him in payment and was surprised to find how valuable they were. He wondered how many pounds-worth were nestling behind the stickers in their safety deposit box.

Zarah was more talkative at dinner than he ever remembered, and seemed newly determined to encourage the idea of his marrying her sister. She and Lothar accompanied them on their after-dinner walk this time, and Lothar, like Paul, seemed enthralled by the huge glittering river and its never-ending procession of barges and other boats. Russell and Zarah agreed their plans for Saturday: shopping in the morning, football for him and Paul in the afternoon, dinner with Jens' embassy friend for her and Lothar in the evening. When they said goodnight outside her and Lothar's room, she thanked him warmly for his help. They'd almost become friends, Russell thought. Effi would be amazed.

Paul was yawning, but Russell felt far too restless for sleep. 'Bedtime for you,' he told his son. 'I'm going back downstairs for a drink. I won't be long.'

'You're just going downstairs?'

'Yes. No stamp-smuggling tonight. Just a drink.'

Paul grinned. 'All right.'

For a Friday night, the cocktail lounge seemed unusually empty. Russell bought a pint of bitter, parked himself on a stool at the end of the bar, and played with a beer mat. The taste of the English beer made him feel nostalgic. He had thought about taking Paul out to Guildford, to show him the house where he'd spent most of his own boyhood, but there wouldn't be time. The next trip perhaps, if there was one.

He pictured the house, the large garden, the steeply-sloping street he'd walked to school each day. He couldn't say he'd had a happy childhood, but it hadn't been particularly unhappy either. He hadn't really appreciated it at the time, but his mother had never really settled in England, despite almost thirty years of trying. His father's inability or unwillingness to recognise that fact had undermined everything else. There had been a lot of silence in that house. He should write to her, he thought.

A quick trip to reception provided him with a few sheets of beautifully-embossed Savoy writing paper, and he ordered another pint. But after telling her where he was and why, and sketching out the plot of Effi's new film, he could think of nothing else to say.

She hadn't seen Paul since he was four, and it would need a book to explain his son and their relationship.

He comforted himself with the knowledge that her letters to him were equally inadequate. On those rare occasions when, as adults, they'd been together, they had both enjoyed the experience – he was sure of that – but even then they'd hardly said anything to each other. His mother wasn't much of a talker or a thinker, which was why she had never liked Ilse. She and Effi, on the other hand, would probably become bosom friends. They were both do-ers.

A shadow crossed the paper as a man slid onto the stool next to his. He had short dark, brilliantined hair, a sharpish face with a small moustache and skin that looked unusually pink. He looked about twenty, but was probably older.

'John Russell?' he asked.

Oh God, Russell thought. Here we go again. 'I think you're mistaking me for someone else,' he said. 'I'm Douglas Fairbanks Jr.'

'Very good,' the man said admiringly. 'Can I get you another drink?'

'No thanks.'

'Well, I think I'll have one,' he said, raising a finger to the distant barman.

'Are you old enough?' Russell asked.

His new companion looked hurt. 'Look, there's no need to be offensive. I'm just…' He paused to order a Manhattan. 'Look, I think you know Trelawney-Smythe in Berlin.'

'We've met.'

'Well, he passed your name onto us, and…'

'Who might you be?'

'War Office. A department of the War Office. My name's Simpson. Arnold Simpson.'

'Right,' Russell said.

Simpson took an appreciative sip of his Manhattan. 'We checked up on you – we have to do that, you understand – and it looks as if Trelawney-Smythe was right. You are a perfect fit. You speak German like a native, you have family and friends there, you even have Nazi connections. You're ideally placed to work for us.'

Russell smiled. 'You may be right about means and opportunity, but where's the motive? Why would I want to work for you?'

Simpson looked taken aback. 'How about patriotism?' he asked.

'I'm as patriotic as the next businessman,' Russell said wryly.

'Ah. Very good. But seriously.'

'I *was* being serious.'

Simpson took a larger sip of the Manhattan. 'Mr Russell, we know your political history. We know you've been badgering the Berlin Embassy about a Jewish family. Whatever you write for the Soviets, we know you don't like the Nazis. And there's a war coming, for God's sake. Don't you want to do your bit to defeat them?'

'Mr Simpson, can't you people take no for an answer?'

Now the young man looked affronted. 'Of course,' he said. 'But…'

'Goodnight, Mr Simpson.'

They spent the first part of Saturday morning following Zarah in and out of clothes stores on Bond Street, the second scouring Hamleys for the stimulating toys which Dr McAllister had recommended. They found nothing which Zarah considered suitable in either. 'German toys are much better,' she announced with a satisfied air on the Regent Street pavement, and Paul agreed with her. There had been no dead soldiers, and those still breathing had been markedly inferior to the ones back home.

They parted at midday, Russell and Paul cutting through the streets beyond Oxford Street to the trolleybus terminus at Howland Street. The 627 took them up the Hampstead, Camden and Seven Sisters Roads to Finsbury Park, where the pubs were already overflowing with men en route to the match. It was a cold afternoon, the would-be spectators exhaling clouds of breath and clapping their gloved hands together as they threaded their way down the back streets to the ground. A rosette seller offered red and white for Arsenal, blue and white for Chelsea, and Paul wanted both. 'Covering the field, eh?' the man asked with a grin. He had a red and white scarf wrapped around his head, and a flat cap rammed on top of it.

The match itself was a disappointment – another point in Germany's column as far as Paul was concerned. It was hard to argue with him – if this was the best football in the world, then the world of football was in trouble. There was none of the magic England had shown in Berlin nine months earlier. In fact, both teams seemed markedly less endowed with basic skills than poor old Hertha.

What Paul did find fascinating was the crowd. He had no way of appreciating the wit, but he revelled in the sheer volume of noise, and the swirling currents of emotion which rose and fell all around him. 'It's so…' he began, as they crunched their way out across the carpet of roasted peanut shells, but an end to the sentence eluded him.

At the Arsenal station they shared a seemingly endless tunnel to the platform with several thousand others, and their Piccadilly Line train was full to bursting until it reached King's Cross. After the relative spaciousness of the U-bahn, the train itself seemed ancient, airless and claustrophobic – another point in the German column.

They walked back to the Strand through Covent Garden Market, and ate another delicious dinner in the Savoy restaurant. Paul was quiet, as if busy absorbing his impressions of the last two days. He seemed, Russell thought, more German somehow. But that, he supposed, was only to be expected in England. He hadn't anticipated it though.

On the way to breakfast next morning he stopped off at reception to consult the hotel's ABC Railway Guide, and after they'd eaten he told Paul there was something he wanted to show him. They took a bus up Kingsway and Southampton Row to Euston, and walked through the giant archway to the platforms. The object of their visit was already sitting in Platform 12 – the blue and silver Coronation Scot. They bought platform tickets and walked up to where a dozen youngsters were paying court to the gleaming, hissing, streamlined 'Princess Alice'.

'It's beautiful,' Paul said, and Russell felt a ridiculous surge of pride in his native country. Paul was right. The German stream-liners reeked of speed and power, but this train had a grace they lacked. One mark at least for England.

Back at the Savoy they packed, took a last look at the Thames, and joined Zarah and Lothar in the lobby. The car was on time, the Sunday roads empty, and they arrived at Croydon airfield almost two hours early. While Paul stood transfixed by the planes outside the window, Russell scanned the *News of the World* for a clue to British concerns. He discovered that a vicar had been assaulted by a young woman in a village street, and that now was the time to protect your crocuses from sparrows. A half-page ad for constipation relief featured a wonderful photograph – somehow, the man really did look constipated. And much to Russell's relief, the game they'd seen the previous afternoon got a highly critical write-up – so at least it wasn't the norm.

It was the same aeroplane and crew that had brought them over. This time though, the clouds were lower, the flight rockier, the view more restricted. Jens, waiting for them at Tempelhof, hugged Zarah and Lothar as if they'd been away for weeks and thanked Russell profusely. He also offered to take Paul home, but Russell demurred, unwilling to sacrifice half an hour of his son's company.

As it was, Paul sat mostly in silence, as they drove west, gazing out of the window at his home city. 'It seems… well, strange,' he said, as they turned into his road. 'After being there, the idea of a war against England seems… it seems silly.'

'It is,' Russell agreed. But coming nevertheless. And, in one way, the sooner the better. Say it lasted four years, like the last one. Assuming they stuck to the current call-up at eighteen, Paul would be drafted in March 1945. For the war to be over by then, it had to get started early in 1941.

No need to worry, Russell told himself. Hitler wouldn't be able to wait that long.

Blue scarf

After spending the night with Effi he drove her out to the studio for an early start. She was pleased but not surprised by Dr McAllister's diagnosis – 'I said there was nothing wrong with him!' – but despondent about *Mother*. The director was a mechanic; her co-stars all thought, wrongly, that they were God's gift to acting; the on-set adviser from the Propaganda Ministry kept trying to clarify the film's 'social role' by inserting lines that even a baboon would have trouble misunderstanding. 'I suppose I should be grateful,' she said, as they drove in through the studio gates. 'I'll probably go down in history as one of Germany's great *comédiennes*.'

Russell drove back to Zoo Station, where he bought breakfast and a paper. Nothing unusual seemed to have happened during his time in England. The widening of the Kiel Canal had been decreed – it obviously wasn't big enough for the *Bismarck*. Hitler had opened the International Motor Show just down the road, and unveiled a model of the new People's Car. For 950 marks – about 50 British pounds – the average German would get a small five-seater, with deliveries to begin in about fifteen months' time. Having been in at this birth, the Führer had proceeded to the funeral of some obscure Carinthian Gauleiter – the man had probably held his hand when the bullets started flying in 1923. He'd certainly been given all the Nazi trimmings – swastikas everywhere, black banners with runic emblems, lines of flaming pylons to light his way across the Hesperus.

Back at Neuenburgerstrasse, Frau Heidegger was waiting to ply him with coffee. She was elated by his impression of British unreadiness for war, which she thought, rather perceptively, both lessened the chance of war and increased the chance of German success if there was one. Before retiring upstairs to work, Russell phoned Unsworth at the British Embassy. He was told that Conway had been in touch, and that representations were being made in the appropriate quarters. Russell thought about visiting the Wiesners but decided against. He had nothing really to tell them, and instinctively felt that it was safer to limit his visits to the scheduled lessons.

He spent most of the next forty-eight hours working in his room, writing the fourth *Pravda* article, which he hoped to deliver in Posen that weekend, and sketching out a piece on artists and entertainers for the 'Ordinary Germans' series. His only trip out was to the Greiner Works in Wedding, one of the Reich's major production centres for military vehicles. Expecting suspicion and probable refusals, he went straight to the Labour Front office, and was almost laughably surprised by the warm welcome he received. Yes, of course the German worker was torn between his love of peace and his desire to arm the Fatherland against its foes. What human being would not be? And of course Herr Russell could talk to the workers about their feelings. The rest of the world should be given every chance to understand both the German hunger for peace and the nation's determination to defend its rights and its people.

After this, talking to several groups of workers in the canteen proved something of an anti-climax. Most were understandably reticent, and those prepared to speak their minds had nothing surprising to say. It was a job, that was all. As usual, the pay was bad, the hours too long, management more of a hindrance than a help. The Labour Front at least listened, if only to ward off potential trouble. Open discussions were infinitely preferable to either non-cooperation – slow working, mostly – or the sort of covert resistance that could lead to sabotage. Reading between the lines and facial expressions of the men he spoke to, Russell decided that the level of non-cooperation was probably significant without seriously affecting production levels or quality, and that the amount of real resistance was negligible. And when war came, he guessed, both would decrease.

Wednesday morning, he called in at the Embassy on his way to the Wiesners. The moment he saw Unsworth's face he knew what had happened. 'He's dead, isn't he?'

'The official line is that he hanged himself,' Unsworth said. 'I'm sorry.'

Russell sat down. A wave of sadness – of utterly useless sadness – seemed to flow through him. 'When?' he asked. 'Has the family been told?'

Unsworth shrugged. 'We received this note from the Foreign Ministry this morning.' He passed it over. 'A reply to our representations on Friday.'

The message comprised one sentence: 'In response to your enquiries of 18 February, we regret to inform you that the prisoner Wiesner has taken his own life, presumably out of guilt for his crime.'

Wiesner had been dead within two days of his visit, Russell thought. Beaten to death, most probably. A blessed release, perhaps. But not for his family.

'We assume the family has been informed,' Unsworth was saying.

'Why?' Russell asked, handing back the note. 'Because it's the decent thing to do?'

Unsworth nodded, as if taking the point.

'What about the visa situation?' Russell wanted to know. 'There's nothing to keep them here now. And surely…'

'I'm told the decisions on the next batch are being taken tomorrow afternoon. If you come back Friday morning I hope I'll have some good news for you.'

Russell walked down the stairs and out past the line of visa-seekers on Unter den Linden. Once behind the Hanomag's driving wheel, he just sat there, staring down towards the Brandenburg Gate and the distant trees of the Tiergarten.

Eventually, almost somnambulantly, he put the car into gear and moved off, circling Pariserplatz and heading back up Unter den Linden towards Alexanderplatz and Neue Konigstrasse. What did you say to someone whose husband or father has just been murdered for the sin of being born into a particular race? What could you say? All around him the people of Berlin were going about their usual business, walking and driving and shopping and talking, laughing at jokes and smiling in friendship. If they'd heard of Sachsenhausen, they no doubt imagined neat rows of barracks, and some well-merited hard labour for the criminals and perverts residing there at the state's pleasure. They hadn't seen a man they knew and liked twisted and torn out of human shape for the pleasure of others.

He couldn't even tell the story, not without Jens suffering for it. And even if he could, he had no evidence to back up his suppositions. The Nazis would claim that a crime like Wiesner's was bound to provoke an angry reaction from his aryan guards, and that the wretched Jew had simply taken the easy way out when he received a few well-deserved bruises. What, they would say, was the problem? Everyone had behaved in a racially appropriate manner, and the world had one less Jew to worry about.

On the Wiesners' street he sat in the car, putting off the moment of truth. There was another car parked on the other side of the road, its windows open, with two bored-looking men smoking in the front seat. They looked like Kripo, Russell thought, and they were probably on loan to the Gestapo, which was notorious for believing itself above the more mundane aspects of police work.

Well, there was no law against teaching Jewish children English. He got out, walked up the familiar steps, rapped on the familiar door. An unfamiliar face appeared in the opening. A rather attractive woman, with a mass of curly brown hair and suspicious eyes. In her late thirties, Russell guessed.

He introduced himself, and her face changed. 'Come in,' she said. 'You've heard?' she added.

'About Dr Wiesner's death? Yes. Half an hour ago, at the British Embassy.'

As he spoke, Marthe Wiesner emerged from the other room, closing the door behind her. 'Herr Russell…' she began.

'I can't tell you how sorry I am to hear about your father,' he said. There were two broken table lamps on the wooden chest, he noticed, and the curtain rail was hanging at an awkward angle.

'Thank you,' she said stiffly. She seemed calm – almost overly so – but for the moment at least the light in her eyes had gone out. 'This is Sarah Grostein,' she said, introducing the other woman. 'She's an old friend of the family. Mother is… well, you can imagine. The shock was terrible. For all of us, of course. Mother and Ruth are sleeping at the moment.'

'Please give her my condolences,' Russell said, the hollow words tripping off his tongue. He wondered whether to leave the safety deposit box key with Marthe, especially in the presence of a stranger. He decided against. 'I need to talk to your mother,' he said. 'Not now, of course,' he added quickly. 'I'll come at the usual time on Friday.'

Marthe nodded, just as the sound of wailing erupted in the other room. A few seconds later Eva Wiesner called her elder daughter's name. 'I must go,' she said.

'Of course.' He waited till the door had closed before asking Sarah Grostein when the family had heard of Felix Wiesner's death.

'Saturday evening,' she said. 'I wasn't here of course, but the police behaved abominably. I can understand why Albert lost his head.'

Russell's heart sank. 'What did he do?'

'Oh, don't you know? He attacked the Gestapo bastard, hit him with one of these table lamps. The man's in hospital. They said he might die, but Marthe says it didn't look that bad. I think they were just trying to scare Eva.'

'Where have they taken Albert?' he asked. The wailing was quieter, but just as insistent.

She gave a bitter laugh. 'They haven't. He got away. Pushed the other bastard over the sofa and ran for it. He got out the back – there's a maze of alleys out there – and the conscious one knew better than to follow him. He wouldn't have found Albert, and he knew damn well he might not come out again.'

'Where's Albert now?'

'No one knows,' she said, leaving Russell with the distinct impression that she was lying. 'They came back yesterday,' she went on. 'Shouted at Eva to tell them where he was, which she couldn't have told them if she'd wanted to. But they didn't arrest her. Maybe they realised that there was no one else to look after the girls, that they'd be up to their eyes in paperwork if they tried to send them away somewhere.'

'Maybe,' Russell agreed. He thought it more likely that the British expression of interest in Wiesner's fate had kept the Gestapo in check. 'Can you pass on a message to Frau Wiesner? Tell her…' He paused. 'I was going to say that it looks like the children will get

British visas in the next week or so, but it doesn't seem as though Albert will have any use for his. If he goes to the Germans for an exit visa, they'll just arrest him. Still, the girls should be able to go. And maybe their mother too.'

'She won't leave Albert.'

'Perhaps he can persuade her.'

'Perhaps. But the Gestapo are parked outside, which makes arranging meetings rather difficult.'

He looked at her, standing there with arms crossed and anger simmering behind her eyes. 'Are you trying to get out?' he asked.

'Not at present,' she said, in a tone that didn't invite questioning.

'I'll get going,' he said. 'I'll be back on Friday morning.'

She nodded, opened the door, and closed it behind him. He walked out to the car, ignoring the watching police, and drove it slowly down Neue Konigstrasse towards the city centre. He knew there was nothing more he could do, but that knowledge did nothing to diminish the sense of anger and helplessness that dogged him through the rest of that day and the next. By the time he entered the British Embassy on Friday morning he felt ready to explode, but was equally certain that murdering anyone other than Hitler would only make matters worse.

British entry visas for the three Wiesner children were waiting on Unsworth's desk, but Unsworth had the decency not to be too pleased with himself. 'I've found out why the mother's been refused,' he told Russell. 'Our intelligence people have quite a dossier on her. She was a Spartacist – you know what they were? Of course you do. Apparently they grade communists out of ten, and anyone scoring over seven is refused immigration. Eva Wiesner's an eight.'

Russell was astonished. 'How recent is this information?'

'It isn't. The dossier has nothing later than 1919, so she probably gave up politics when she got married. But that won't help her. An eight's an eight – that's what their man told me…'

'Trelawney-Smythe?'

'You've met him? No exceptions, he said.'

Russell didn't know whether to laugh or cry. 'I don't suppose it matters,' he said, before explaining about Albert.

Half an hour later he was back in Friedrichshain. This time Frau Wiesner opened the door, and managed a slight smile as she let him in. After brushing aside his condolences, she sat him down and made them both coffee. 'He was a wonderful man,' she said. 'And nothing can take that away from him, or from me.'

He gave her the British entry visas for the three children, and explained why she was being refused.

She smiled sadly at that. 'I thought that must be the reason,' she said, 'but it doesn't matter now. Take this back,' she added, handing over Albert's visa – 'Someone else can take his place.'

He also gave her the safety deposit box key, and a piece of paper containing two names and addresses. 'This is the bank where the box is, and this is my agent in London, Solly Bernstein. Get the girls to memorize it all, and then burn it,' he said. 'And I think it would probably be safer for you to keep the key yourself. Solly has another one, and they can use that when they get to London.'

She stared at the writing, as if it was in a foreign language.

'Have you seen Albert?' he asked.

She shook her head. 'But he's all right.'

After leaving Effi at the studio early the next morning, he took the car back to her street and walked to Zoo Station. With an hour to wait for the Warsaw train, he had breakfast in the buffet before climbing up to the eastbound platforms. It was the first time, he realised, that he'd been up there since McKinley's death. He had no idea where the American had gone under his train, and a morbid search for tell-tale signs came up empty. If there was one thing the Germans were good at, it was cleaning up after themselves.

He put five pfennigs in a burnt almond machine, and walked down the platform feeding from his cupped hand. It was a misty morning, the trees in the Tiergarten fading by stages into nothing. Some geese flew across the glass dome of the station, squawking noisily, heading God-knew-where considering it was late February. There were few finer sights, Russell thought, as their V-formation curled and furled like a banner in the wind. He remembered the seagulls at the *Bismarck* launching, and laughed out loud.

The Warsaw train arrived, empty save for the few who had boarded at Charlottenburg. Russell found his seat by the time it reached Friedrichstrasse, and dropped off to sleep as the last of the south-eastern suburbs slid past his window. Dimly aware of the stop at Frankfurt-am-Oder, he was roused by officialdom for the customs stops on either side of the Polish border, and spent the rest of the journey staring out of the restaurant car window. A wintry sun had finally burnt off the mists, and the rye and potato fields of Prussia's lost province stretched away into the distance, interrupted only by the occasional dirt-track or farm, the odd meandering stream.

The train rolled into Posen – or Poznan, as the plethora of signs proclaimed – a few minutes early. Russell took a taxi from the forecourt to the Bazar Hotel, where he'd booked a room. 'Just the one night?' the receptionist asked incredulously, as if the charms of Posen required weeks to appreciate. 'Just the one,' Russell agreed, and was shown rather begrudgingly to an adequate first floor room. There were only a few hours of light remaining, so he went straight back out again, pausing only to examine the display in the lobby, which documented the hotel's pre-war role as a hotbed of Polish nationalism.

The town, though pleasant enough, suffered by comparison to Cracow. Its churches were not quite as beautiful, its streets not quite as charming, its square – the Stary Rynek – not quite as grand. As he wandered somewhat aimlessly around the city centre he noticed several faded German names on streets and buildings, but the German language was still audible on those same streets, along with Polish and Yiddish. It would take another war, Russell thought, before the winners could take it all.

He dined in the hotel restaurant. The veal escalopes – *zrazikis* – were excellent, the wine surprisingly good, but neither could dispel his deepening depression. It wasn't just McKinley and Wiesner – he had hardly spent two waking hours with Effi since Rügen Island, and his contact with Paul since returning from England had consisted of two friendly, but brief, telephone conversations. And here he was in the gloom of Posen, waiting for Shchepkin to go through one of his cloak-and-dagger mating rituals.

He went back to his room, hoping against hope for a simple knock on the door. An hour or so later he got one, but it wasn't Shchepkin. A short woman in a long skirt and blouse brushed past him and into the room before he could say anything.

'Close the door, Mr Russell,' she said. The language was definitely German, but not a sort that Russell had ever heard before.

The woman had roughly-parted blonde hair which just failed to reach her shoulders, blue-eyes, thin lips and heavily-accented cheekbones. In another life she might have been attractive, Russell thought, but in this one she wasn't really trying. She wore no make-up, and her cream-coloured blouse badly needed a wash. He now remembered seeing her on the other side of the dining-room, arguing with one of the waiters.

'John Russell,' she said, as much to herself as him. 'I am your new contact.'

'Contact with whom?' he asked. It was hard to imagine her as a Gestapo agent provocateur, but how would he know?

'My name is Irina Borskaya,' she said patiently. 'I am here in place of Comrade Shchepkin,' she added, glancing round the room and finding a chair.

'Has something happened to Comrade Shchepkin?' Russell asked.

'He has been re-assigned. Now, please sit down Mr Russell. And let us get down to business.'

Russell did as he was told, feeling a pang of sorrow for Shchepkin. He could see him on the Cracow citadel – 'You really should wear a hat!' But why assume the worst? Perhaps he really had been re-assigned. Stalin couldn't kill everyone who'd ever worked for him.

He pulled the latest article out of his briefcase and handed it over. She took a cursory glance at the first page and placed it in her lap. 'You were asked to talk to armament workers.'

He recounted his visit to the Greiner Works, the conversations he had had with Labour Front officials and ordinary workers. She listened intently but took no notes. 'Is that all?' she said when he was finished.

'For the moment,' Russell said. 'Where is your accent from?' he asked, partly out of curiosity, partly to take her mind off his skimpy research.

'I was born in Saratov,' she said. 'In the Volga region. Now, we have another job for you…'

Here it comes, Russell thought – the point of the whole exercise.

'We need you to collect some papers from one of our people and bring them out of Germany.'

Not a chance, Russell thought. But refuse nicely, he told himself. 'What sort of papers?' he asked.

'That doesn't concern you.'

'It does if you expect me to bring them out.'

'They are naval plans,' she said grudgingly.

Russell burst out laughing.

'What is so amusing?' she asked angrily.

He told her about Shchepkin's comment in Danzig – 'None of those naval plans Sherlock Holmes is always having to recover.'

She wasn't amused. 'This is not a Sherlock Holmes story – the comrade in Kiel has risked his life to get a copy of the German fleet dispositions for the Baltic.'

'Then why not risk it again to bring them out?' Russell argued.

'His life is worth something,' she said tartly, and quickly realized that she had gone too far. 'He is too valuable to risk,' she amended, as if he might have mistaken her meaning.

'Then why not send someone else in to get them?'

'Because we have you,' she said. 'And we have already established that you can come and go without arousing suspicion. Were you searched on your way here, or on your way to Cracow?'

'No, but I wasn't carrying anything.'

She put the article on the carpet beside her chair, crossed her legs and smoothed out the skirt on her thigh with her left hand. 'Mr Russell, are you refusing to help us with this?'

'I'm a journalist, Comrade Borskaya. Not a secret agent.'

She gave him an exasperated look, delved into her skirt pocket and brought out a rather crumpled black and white photograph. It was of him and Shchepkin, emerging from the Wawel Cathedral.

Russell looked at it and laughed.

'You are easily amused,' she said.

'So they tell me. If you send that to the Gestapo I might get thrown out of Germany. If I get caught with your naval plans it'll be the axe. Which do you think worries me more?'

'If we send this to the Gestapo you are certain to be deported, certain to lose your son and your beautiful bourgeois girlfriend. If you do this job for us, the chances of your being caught are almost non-existent. You will be well-paid, and you will have the satisfaction of supporting world socialism in its struggle against fascism. According to Comrade Shchepkin, that was once important to you.'

'Once.' The clumsiness of the approach angered him more than the blackmail itself. He got up off the bed and walked across to the window, telling himself to calm down. As he did so, an idea came to him. An idea that seemed both crazy and compelling.

He turned to her. 'Let me sleep on this,' he said. 'Think about it overnight,' he explained, in response to her blank expression.

She nodded. 'Two p.m. in the Stary Rynek,' she said, as if she'd had the time and place in reserve.

'It's a big square,' Russell said.

'I'll find you.'

Sunday was overcast but dry. Russell had coffee in one of the many Stary Rynek cafés, walked up past the Garbary Station to the Citadel, and found a bench overlooking the city. For several minutes he just sat there enjoying the view: the multiplicity of spires, the Warta River and its receding bridges, the smoke rising from several thousand chimneys. 'See how much peace the earth can give,' he murmured to himself. A comforting thought, provided you ignored the source. It was a line from Mayakovsky's suicide note.

Was his own plan a roundabout way of committing suicide?

Paul and Effi would miss him. In fact, he liked to think they'd both be heartbroken, at least for a while. But he was neither indispensable nor irreplaceable. Paul had other people who loved him, and so did Effi.

All of which would only matter if he got caught. The odds, he thought, were probably on his side. The Soviets would have no compunction about risking him, but their precious naval plans were another matter – they wouldn't risk those on a no-hope adventure. They had to believe it would work.

But what did he know? There could be ruses within ruses; this could be some ludicrously Machiavellian plot the NKVD had thought up on some drunken weekend and set in motion before they sobered up. Or everyone concerned could be an incompetent. Or just having a bad day.

'Shit,' he muttered to himself. He liked the idea of the Soviets having the German fleet dispositions for the Baltic. He liked the idea of doing something, no matter how small, to put a spoke in the bastards' wheels. And he really wanted the favours he intended asking in return.

But was he fooling himself? Falling for all the usual nonsense, playing boys' games with real ammunition. When did self-sacrifice become a warped form of selfishness?

There were no answers to any of this, he realized. It was like jumping through an open window with a fuzzy memory of which floor you were on. If it turned out to be the ground floor, you bounced to your feet with an heroic grin. The fifth, and you were jam on the pavement. Or, more likely, a Gestapo courtyard.

A life concerned only with survival was a thin life. He needed to jump. For all sorts of reasons, he needed to jump.

He took a long last look at the view and started back down the slope, imagining the details of his plan as he did so. A restaurant close to the Stary Rynek provided him with a plate of meat turnovers, a large glass of Silesian beer, and ample time to imagine the worst. By two o'clock he was slowly circling the large and well-populated square, and manfully repressing the periodic impulse to simply disappear into one of the adjoining streets.

She appeared at his shoulder halfway through his second circuit, her ankle-length coat unbuttoned to reveal the same skirt and blouse. This time, he thought, there was worry in the eyes.

She managed to leave the question unspoken for about thirty metres, and then asked it with almost angry abruptness – 'So, will you do this job for us?'

'With one condition,' Russell told her. 'I have a friend, a Jewish friend, in Berlin. The police are looking for him, and he needs to get out of the country. You get him across the border, and I will do the job for you.'

'And how are we supposed to get him across the border?' she asked, suspicion in her tone.

'The same way you always have,' Russell said. 'I was in the Party myself once – remember? I knew people in the Pass-Apparat,' he added, stretching the truth somewhat. 'Everyone knew about the escape routes into Belgium and Czechoslovakia.'

'That was many years ago.'

'Not according to my information,' Russell bluffed.

She was silent for about fifty metres. 'There are a few such routes,' she admitted. 'But they are not safe. If they were, we would not be asking you to bring out these papers. Maybe one person in three gets caught.'

'In Berlin it's more like three out of three.'

She sighed. 'I can't give you an answer now.'

'I understand that. Someone will have to contact me in Berlin to make the arrangements for my friend's journey, and to give me the details of the job you want me to do. Tell your bosses that the moment my friend calls me from outside the Reich, I will collect your papers from wherever they are and bring them out.'

'Very well,' she said after a moment's thought. 'You had better choose a point of contact in Berlin.'

'The buffet at Zoo Station. I shall be there every morning this week. Between nine and ten.'

She nodded approvingly. 'And a mark of identification. A book works well.'

'*Storms of Steel*? No, half the customers could be reading that. Something English.' He mentally pictured his bookshelves at Neuenburgerstrasse. 'Dickens. *Martin Chuzzlewit*.'

'A good choice,' she agreed, though whether for literary or other reasons she didn't say. 'Your contact will say that he's been meaning to read it, and will ask you if it's any good.'

'He?' Russell asked.

'Or she,' she conceded.

Nine o'clock on Monday morning found him in the Zoo Station buffet, his dog-eared copy of *Martin Chuzzlewit* prominently displayed on the counter beside his cup of mocha. He wasn't expecting the Soviets to respond that quickly, and he wasn't disappointed – ten o'clock came and went with no sign of any contact. He collected the car from outside the Zoo and drove across town to the Wiesners. There was no obvious police presence outside, which probably meant that they'd recruited some local busybody for their observation chores. A curtain twitched as he walked up the outside steps, but that could have been coincidence.

The sense of raw pain had gone from the Wiesners' flat – replaced by a grim busyness, a determination to do whatever needed doing. There was grief to spare, the faces seemed to say – no need to spend it all at once.

And there was good news, Frau Wiesner told him. They had old friends in England, she said, in Manchester. The Doctor had written to them several weeks ago, and a reply had finally arrived, offering a temporary home for the girls. They had tickets to travel a week from Thursday.

'I may have more good news,' Russell told her. 'I have friends who may be willing to smuggle Albert across the border.'

Mother and daughters all stared at him in amazement. 'What friends?' Frau Wiesner asked.

'The comrades,' he said simply. The comrades they had both abandoned, he thought.

'But I had no idea you were…'

'Like you, I left a long time ago. And I can't go into details about the arrangements. But if I can fix things, can you get in touch with Albert at short notice?'

'Yes.' The hope in her eyes was painful to see.

'And will he trust me, do you think?

She smiled at that. 'Yes, he likes you.'

'And if we can get him out, there is nothing to keep you here?'

'The lack of a visa. Nothing else.'

'I'm still working on that.'

He tried to write that afternoon, but the words refused to matter. As evening fell he took himself off to the Alhambra and sat through an overblown Hollywood musical, murmuring sour asides to himself in the dark. The film had been made on the sort of budget which would feed a small country, but was mercifully devoid of consciousness-raising pretensions. The consciousness-lowering effect was presumably accidental.

As he emerged the Ku'damm was gearing up for the night, thick with human and motorised traffic. He walked slowly westwards with no real destination in mind, looking in windows, studying faces, wondering if the Soviets would agree to his terms. People queued outside the theatres and cinemas, streamed in and out of the restaurants, most of them laughing or happily talking, living the moment as best they could. A police car careened up the centre of the wide road, its siren parting the traffic like waves, but the visible signs of a police state were thin on the ground. In fact, Russell thought, it was the absence of violence which told the real story. The blood and the broken glass, the groups of men on corners, clutching their razors and itching for a brawl – they were all gone. The only violent law-breakers left on the streets of Berlin were the authorities.

He walked back down the opposite pavement, picked up the car and drove home.

Tuesday offered more of the same: waiting in vain at the buffet counter, working with words like a juggler in mittens. Frau Heidegger seemed irritating rather than quirky, Paul almost provokingly gung-ho in his description of the previous Saturday's *Jungvolk* outing. Even the weather was bad: a cold rain fell throughout the day and into the evening, creating lake-size puddles in many of the streets. The Hanomag, as Russell discovered on his way to collect Effi, had a less than waterproof floor.

At least her film was finished. 'I have seen the error of my ways, and a good wife is all I want to be!' she exclaimed as they left the studio. 'But only,' she added as they reached the car, 'after I've slept for at least a week. In the meantime you may wait on me hand and foot.'

Later, he was still working up to telling her about his weekend in Posen when he realised she'd fallen asleep. Which was all for the best, he decided. There'd be time enough for explanations if and when the Soviets said yes. As he looked down at her sleeping face, the familiar lips ever-so-slightly curled in a sleeper's smile, the whole business seemed utterly absurd.

• • •

Contact was made on Thursday. The buffet clock was reaching towards ten when a man loomed over Russell's shoulder and almost whispered the pre-arranged sentence. 'Let's walk,' he added, before Russell had time to declaim on the virtues or otherwise of *Martin Chuzzlewit*.

The man made for the door with what seemed unnecessary haste, leaving Russell floundering in his wake. He seemed very young, Russell thought, but he looked anonymous enough: average height and build, tidy hair and a typical German face. His suit was wearing at the elbows, his shoes at the heels.

At the station exit he turned towards the nearest Tiergarten entrance, pausing for a nervous look back as they reached it. Russell glanced back himself – the street was empty. Ahead of them, a few solitary walkers were visible among the leafless trees.

'It's not a bad day,' the young man said, looking up at the mostly grey sky. 'We will walk to Bellevue Station, like friends enjoying a morning stroll in the park.'

They set off through the trees.

'I am Gert,' the young man said. 'And it is agreed. We will take your friend across the Czech border, and you will bring the papers to us in Prague.' He fell silent, as a steady stream of walkers passed them in the opposite direction – a middle-aged couple and their poodles, a younger couple arm in arm, an older man with a muzzled Doberman – and paused to offer Russell a cigarette on the Lichtenstein Bridge across the Landwehrkanal. The young man's hand, Russell noticed reluctantly, was shaking slightly.

The paths around the Neuersee were mostly deserted, just a couple of women with small children happily feeding the ducks. 'You must memorise the arrangements,' Gert said, with the air of someone reading from a script. 'Your friend must be in the station buffet at Görlitz at five o'clock on Monday afternoon.

He must wear workingmen's clothes, with a blue scarf around his neck. He must not have a suitcase or bag of any kind. When a man asks him if he knows where the left luggage is he should say, "Yes, but it's easier to show you than explain," and walk out with that man. Understood?'

'Yes.'

'Then repeat what I've just told you.'

Russell did so.

'Good. Now for your part. Your contact is in Kiel. Or in Gaarden, to be precise. You must be in the Germania Bar – it's on the tram route to Wellingdorf, just outside the main entrance to the Deutsche Werke shipyards – at 8 p.m. on Friday the 10th. With your *Martin Chuzzlewit*.'

'I made it clear to the comrade in Posen that I wouldn't collect your papers until I knew my friend was safe.'

Gert gave an exasperated sigh. 'He will be in Czechoslovakia by Tuesday morning, Prague by the afternoon. You should hear from him that day. Either that, or some of our people have been captured or killed with him. And if that happens, we hope you will honour their memory by honouring the bargain.'

Russell gave him a look. 'Let's hope it doesn't come to that.'

'Of course. Now, you will bring the papers back to Berlin, and then take them on to Prague as quickly as possible…'

'I have to be in Berlin on that Sunday,' Russell said.

'It would better if you travelled before that. The border guards tend to be less vigilant on a Saturday night.'

'Sorry, it'll have to be Monday,' Russell said. The Sunday was Paul's birthday.

Gert controlled himself with a visible effort. 'Very well,' he agreed, as if he'd made a huge concession.

'And how do you suggest I carry them?'

This was clearly in the script. 'We do not know how many papers there are. If it is a matter of a few sheets, they can be sewn into a lining, of your coat or your jacket. If there are a lot, then that will not be possible. If they search you and your luggage, they will probably find them. The best thing is not to be searched.'

'And how do I manage that?'

'You probably won't have to. They only search about one in ten, and foreigners very rarely. As long as you don't draw attention to yourself, everything should be fine. Now, once you reach Prague, you must check in to the Grand Hotel on Wenceslas Square. You will be contacted there. Is that clear? Now please repeat the details of your *treff* in Kiel.'

Russell repeated them. 'What if no one approaches me on that day?' he asked.

'Then you return to Berlin. Any other questions?' Gert's hands seemed to be writhing in his coat pockets.

He had none, or none that could be answered. At Bellevue Station they went their separate ways, Gert bounding up the stairs to the eastbound Stadtbahn platform, Russell ambling along the bank of the Spree to the kiosk beneath the Bellevue Schloss. He bought a cup of hot chocolate, took it to a riverside table, and watched a long train rumbling across the bridge to his left. 'Everything should be fine,' he told himself in Gert's Bavarian accent. It was the 'should' which worried him.

His next stop was the British Embassy. Rather than return for the car, he walked down the river to Kurfürstenplatz, and then along Zellen Allee to the Brandenburg Gate and the western end of Unter den Linden. The queue outside the Embassy seemed longer than ever, the atmosphere inside the usual mix of irritation and self-righteousness. He asked to see Unsworth, and was shown up to his office. Once there, he admitted it was Trelawney-Smythe that he really wanted to see. 'But I didn't want to announce that in reception,' he explained to Unsworth. 'I wouldn't put it past the Nazis to include an informer or two among the Jews.'

Unsworth looked slightly shocked at the thought, but agreed to escort Russell to the MI6 man's door. Trelawney-Smythe looked startled to see him, and somewhat put out. 'I know why you're here, and the answer is no. We cannot make exceptions.'

Russell sat himself down. 'I take it this room's secure,' he said.

'We went over the whole building with a fine toothcomb a few months ago,' Trelawney-Smythe said proudly.

Russell looked up, half expecting to see a microphone hanging from the ceiling. 'How interested would the Admiralty be in the German Navy's Baltic Fleet dispositions?' he asked.

To his credit, Trelawney-Smythe didn't jump out of his seat. Instead, he reached for his pipe. 'Very, I should imagine. After all, if a ship's in the Baltic it won't be in the North Sea.'

'That's the conclusion I came to,' Russell said. He smiled at the other man. 'Don't ask me how, but at some point in the next two weeks I should have my hands on those dispositions. Not to keep, mind you, and not for long. But long enough to copy them out.'

Trelawney-Smythe lit his pipe, puffing vigorously out of the corner of his mouth.

A technique learned in spy school, Russell thought.

'You would be doing a tremendous service to your country,' the other man said in an almost torpid tone.

'But not only for my country. There's a price.'

'Ah.' Trelawney-Smythe's eyes narrowed. 'You want money,' he said, with the air of a disappointed vicar.

'I want you to make an exception, and come up with a visa for Eva Wiesner. And while you're at it, I'd like an American passport.'

That surprised the MI6 man. 'How on earth do you expect us to get you one of those?'

'I'm sure you'll have no trouble if you set your mind to it. I do have an American mother, you know, so it's hardly a huge stretch.'

'Why do you want one?'

'I'd have thought that was obvious. If there's a war in Europe, anyone with a British passport will be sent home. With an American passport I can stay.'

Trelawney-Smythe puffed at his pipe, digesting the idea, and Russell watched the slight widening of the eyes as he appreciated the possibilities – MI6 would have a man in Germany once the war started!

Not that Russell had any intention of doing anything more for them, but they weren't to know that.

'In the next two weeks, you said.'

'Yes. But I want the visa for Eva Wiesner by Monday. That should give her time to arrange her exit visa, and she can travel with her daughters on Thursday. There's no hurry about the passport,' he added. 'So long as I have it before a war breaks out.'

'You must like this family,' Trelawney-Smythe said, sounding almost human.

'I do. The girls have only just lost their father, and there's no good reason why they should lose their mother as well. She left the communists twenty years ago, for God's sake. She's not going to start a revolution in Golders Green.'

'I hope not,' Trelawney-Smythe said wryly. 'All right. I can get her a visa by Monday. The passport... I can't promise anything – the Yanks dig their heels in about the silliest things – but we'll do our best. You weren't born in America, were you?'

'I was born in mid-Atlantic, if that helps. But on a British ship.'

'Probably not, then.' He was sounding almost chummy now.

'I'll see you then,' Russell said, resisting the temptation to be churlish. On his way out he noticed that the reading room was empty, and took time to consult the Embassy atlas. Görlitz was about two hundred kilometres south-east of Berlin, and about twenty from the Czech border. There were direct trains from Berlin, but they took most of the day and were probably checked as they neared the border area. If Albert got safely through the ticket barrier at this end he'd probably be picked up at the other. Russell was going to have to take him in the car.

There were two obvious routes: he could stick to the old road or take the Silesian autobahn to just south of Kottbus, and join it there. He liked the idea of escaping Hitler's Germany by autobahn, but the old road, for reasons he couldn't explain, felt safer.

So, two hundred kilometres – say, three hours. Stick in an extra half-hour in case he had a puncture. If the car broke down they were sunk, but spending more than a few minutes in Görlitz, with Albert eye-wrestling anyone in uniform, seemed like an excellent way of committing suicide. When it came down to it, the car seemed worthier of trust than Albert's temperament.

Russell walked out to Unter den Linden, climbed into the Hanomag and headed east. If only Albert didn't look so damned Jewish! The boy could hardly wear a mask, though the lifelike Goebbels mask which one of the American correspondents had made for last year's Halloween party would have been entertaining. How could he hide the boy's face? A cap over the eyes, perhaps. Collar turned up and the required blue scarf. A pair of glasses? None of it would help if Albert insisted on visibly seething with rage.

And where was he going to pick him up? Not at the flat, that was for sure. Somewhere crowded? Only if it was somewhere a Jew didn't stick out like a sore thumb, and places like that were thin on the ground. And the police would be looking for him – a Jew who knocked down a Gestapo officer with a table lamp was going to be high on their wanted list. They'd probably taken his picture in Sachsenhausen, and now all the Orpo stations would have copies hanging on their walls.

He parked the car in the Wiesners' street and went up. The girls were out – starting to say their 'goodbyes' – and their mother seemed exhausted by grief and worry. Russell told her about Albert's Monday appointment in Görlitz, and his own role as chauffeur. 'Tell him to join the visa queue outside the British Embassy between twelve and one – as one Jew among several hundred he should be invisible. I'll walk by and collect him soon after one. He should be wearing workingmen's clothes, nothing too smart. But a decent coat on top of them for the queue. People try to look their best for the Embassy.'

'I will tell him.'

'He must be there,' Russell insisted. 'If he's not, that's it. We won't be given a second chance.'

'He'll be there.'

'And I think I've got you a visa. You should be able to go with the girls next Thursday.'

She looked as though she was having trouble believing it all. 'We'll know by then? About Albert?'

'We should,' he said. One way or the other.

Russell's weekend followed the familiar pattern, but thoughts of the week ahead kept spinning around his head, sending his stomach into momentary freefall. It wasn't every week he delivered a fugitive from the Gestapo to the communist underground, went looking for military secrets in a dockside bar, and played some lethal form of hunt the parcel with the border police. In fact, it wasn't any week, and he was scared. The only time he could remember feeling like this was in the trenches, on those few occasions when he'd been ordered over the top. What had he let himself in for?

Paul was too distracted himself to notice his father's distraction. On Saturday they did the rounds of Berlin's best toy-shops, so that Paul could provide Russell with some useful hints on which birthday presents to surprise him with. On Sunday they went to another away game, at Viktoria Berlin's stadium in Steglitz, and came away delighted with a fortunate draw. Paul was still full of the trip to London, and eager to know when they could visit his grandmother in New York. 'Maybe this summer,' Russell said, surprising himself. But why not? The money was there.

Effi did notice. On Saturday evening they went to a Comedy Theatre revue involving friends of hers, and he twice needed prodding to join in the applause. An hour's dancing in one of the halls off Alexanderplatz took his mind off everything else, but on the drive home he almost drove through a red light at Potsdamerplatz.

'What's eating you?' she asked.

As they drove along the southern edge of the Tiergarten he gave her the whole story of his dealings with Shchepkin and Borskaya, ending with the request to take out the documents, and his realisation that he could use the situation to help the Wiesners. 'Seduced by my own cleverness,' he admitted. 'And now I feel like digging myself a very deep hole and hiding in it.'

'Like a fox?'

'More like a rabbit.'

She took his right hand and squeezed it.

Glancing to his right, he could see the worry in her face. 'I can't back out now,' he said.

'Of course not. Why don't we stop here?' she added.

He pulled up under the trees, and turned to face her.

'You couldn't go on the way you were,' she said.

'What do you mean?'

She took his hand again. 'You know what I mean,' she insisted. And he did.

Monday was a rush. Effi insisted on coming to the Embassy with him – 'Everyone says I look Jewish, so they'll think I'm his sister' – and then displayed her usual inability to be ready on time. Once Russell had finally got her to the car, he suddenly remembered, with another downward lurch of his stomach, that he'd forgotten to tell Eva Wiesner about the blue scarf. A ten-minute search for something suitable in the KaDeWe on Wittenbergerplatz made them five minutes late, a derailed tram in Potsdamerplatz five minutes more. Russell had a mental picture of a Gestapo officer walking along beside the queue, then suddenly stopping and pointing at Albert.

They left the car on Dorotheenstrasse and walked the single block to the Unter de Linden. Across the wide, now *lindenfrei* avenue, they could see the queue stretching up Wilhelmstrasse past the side of the Adlon. There were no uniforms in sight, no pointing finger, no scuffle in progress.

They crossed Unter den Linden and walked towards the end of the queue. Albert was about ten from the back, standing close to the stone building on his right, but making no effort to conceal himself. When he saw Russell he simply walked out of the queue. 'This is hopeless,' he said to no one in particular. 'I'll come back tomorrow.'

'We were looking for you,' Russell said. 'The car's this way,' he added, thinking that he'd seen pantomimes with more convincing scripts. Several facial expressions in the queue offered unwelcome confirmation of this opinion.

But there was no sign of the audience that mattered. The three of them walked back to Dorotheenstrasse.

'In the back,' Russell told Albert, indicating the tight space behind the seats. He drove three blocks down Dorotheenstrasse, turned right onto the much busier Friedrichstrasse and headed south towards Hallesches Tor. He dropped Effi off by the elevated station.

'Be careful,' she said, as she kissed him goodbye through the driver's window. 'I'll see you tonight.'

I hope so, Russell thought. He glanced across at Albert, who was now sitting beside him. The boy looked about sixteen.

'How old are you?' he asked.

'I was eighteen last month.'

The age I was when I went to war, Russell thought. A tram swung in front of him, causing him to brake sharply. Concentrate, he told himself. An accident now really would be fatal.

They drove past Tempelhof as a small plane took off, then under the Ringbahn and on towards Mariendorf, the city growing thinner with each mile. A police car went past in the opposite direction, two plainclothes Kripo men chatting in the front seats, but that was all. Twenty minutes after leaving Dorotheenstrasse they were out on the lake-strewn Mittelmark, passing under a completed section of the orbital autobahn.

So far, so good, Russell thought.

'My mother gave me the message from my father,' Albert said, breaking the silence. 'What exactly did he say?'

Russell repeated what he remembered.

'They beat him badly, didn't they?' Albert asked.

'Yes, they did.'

Albert fell silent again. They passed through Zossen, where a surfeit of signs pointed would-be visitors in the direction of

General Staff HQ. The complex of buildings came into view, and Russell found himself wondering which maps the planners had on the tables that day. Poland, most likely, and all points east.

He wondered if the Soviets would put up a fight. Their German operation was hardly impressive – a boy with shaky hands and a man in Kiel they couldn't risk. Where had all the communists gone? Seven years ago they'd been slugging it out with the Nazis – millions of them. Some would still be lying in wait for the right moment, but most, he suspected, had simply turned their backs on politics. He hoped that whoever was waiting in Görlitz knew what the hell he was doing.

'Where have you been staying?' he asked Albert, once they were back in open country.

'It's better you don't know,' the boy said.

'It probably is,' Russell agreed.

Silence descended again. Albert seemed calm enough, Russell thought. Calmer, in fact, than he felt himself. At least the car was behaving, its engine purring smoothly as they cruised along the mostly deserted road at 65 kph. Everyone else had chosen the autobahn.

The sky to the south seemed clearer, which suggested a cold, clear night. Did that augur well or badly for an illicit border crossing? Visibility would be better for everyone – pursuers and pursued. He tried to remember what phase the moon was in, and couldn't.

Albert had rescued the *Beobachter* from the floor between them. 'Why do you read this rubbish?' he asked, scanning the front page.

'To know what they're doing,' Russell said.

Albert grunted disapproval.

'Which reminds me,' Russell went on. 'There's a piece in there about the crisis in Ruthenia...'

'Ruthenia? Where's that?'

'It's part of Czechoslovakia. Look, you need to know this stuff. Czechoslovakia is more than Czechs and Slovaks. There's Moravians and Hungarians and God knows who else. And Ruthenians. The Germans are encouraging all these groups to rebel against the Czechoslovak government, in the hope that they'll provoke a major crackdown. Once that happens, they'll march in themselves, saying that they're the only ones who can restore order and protect these poor victimised minorities.'

'All right.'

'And the Czech government has started taking action against the Ruthenians. Read the piece. See how pleased the Germans are. "This is not the sort of behaviour that any government could tolerate in a neighbouring state, etc" – you can practically see them rubbing their hands with glee. They're preparing the ground. So keep an eye on the news. Don't hang around in Prague any longer than you have to, or you'll find Hitler's caught up with you.'

'I have the names of people in Prague,' Albert insisted. 'They will tell me.'

'Good. But remember *Kristallnacht* – and what a surprise that was, even after five years of persecution. If I were you, I'd head for Hungary as soon as I could. Once you're there you can work out the best way to England.'

'I don't think I will be going to England. My plan is to go to Palestine.'

'Oh,' Russell said, taken by surprise. 'Does your mother know?'

'Of course. I am a man now. I must do what is best for the whole family. When I get work and somewhere to live, I can send for them.'

'Immigration is restricted.'

'I know that. But we will find a way.'

'If there's a war, they'll stop it altogether.'

'Then we will wait.'

They were entering Kottbus now, and Russell concentrated on not drawing attention to his driving. But the market town seemed caught in its afternoon nap, and they were soon back in open country. A few kilometres more, and they passed under the Silesian autobahn. Their road grew suddenly busier, and a sign announced that they were 93 kilometres from Görlitz.

It was not yet three o'clock. At this rate they would arrive far too early. They needed one of those stopping places with a view which the Germans loved so much.

The Germans, Russell repeated to himself. After fifteen years of living there, of feeling a little more German each year, the process seemed to have slipped into reverse. Lately, he seemed to be feeling a little less German each day. But not more English. So what did that make him?

'Why are you doing this?' Albert asked him.

Russell just shrugged. 'Who knows?'

'The reason I ask – a year ago, before *Kristallnacht*, I used to wonder how people could be so cruel, but I never questioned why someone was kind. Now it's the opposite. I can see all sorts of reasons why people are cruel, but kindness is becoming a mystery.'

He was six years older than Paul, Russell thought. Just six years. He tried to think of an adequate answer to Albert's question.

'Whatever the reason, I thank you anyway,' Albert said. 'My family thanks you.'

'I think there are many reasons,' Russell said. 'Some good, some not so good. Some I don't understand myself. I like your family. Maybe it's as simple as that.' And maybe, he thought, any half-decent family in the Wiesners' situation would have been enough to push him off his fence.

The phrase 'I used to be a good journalist,' passed through his mind, leaving him wondering where it had come from. This had nothing to do with journalism. He thought about McKinley's papers, uselessly hidden in the poste restante, and came, with a sudden lift of the heart, to a realisation so obvious that he couldn't believe he had missed it. If he was going to risk his life and liberty for a few military secrets, then why not take out McKinley's papers as well? He had only one head to cut off.

The road was climbing now, and the sky was almost cloudless. Around ten kilometres from Görlitz Russell found the stopping place he had been looking for, a wide gravelled ledge overlooking a pretty river. Eager to stretch, they both got out, and Russell ran through the arranged script for the Görlitz buffet. 'Once you are in Prague, the first thing you must do – the first thing – is to telephone me. Your mother won't leave Germany until she knows you're safe.'

'You haven't given me the number,' Albert said sensibly.

Russell made him repeat it several times, wondering as he did so how long the boy would resist a Gestapo interrogation.

Albert seemed to know what he was thinking. 'I won't give you up,' he said simply.

'None of us know what we'll do in a situation like that.'

'I won't get into a situation like that,' Albert said, pulling a grubby-looking Luger from his coat pocket.

Oh shit, Russell thought, glancing left and right in search of approaching traffic and barking: 'Put it away!' The road was blissfully empty. 'That's…' he started to say, and stopped himself. What right did he have to give the boy advice? Albert had been in Sachsenhausen once, and his father had died there. It wasn't hard to see why going out in a blaze of gunfire seemed preferable to going back.

He breathed out slowly. 'You have to leave the coat with me,' he said. 'Won't the gun be obvious in your jacket pocket?'

'I'll put it in my belt,' Albert said, and did so. He then took the coat off and offered Russell a 360° turn, like a model at a fashion show. The gun didn't show.

Back in the car, Albert pulled a workingmen's cap from a pocket of the discarded coat, and Russell reached into the KaDeWe bag for the blue scarf. 'The recognition signal,' he explained, and Albert wrapped it around his neck, reminding Russell of Paul on a skating trip.

They drove on, the sky a deepening blue as dusk approached, the mountains slowly creeping above the southern horizon. As they reached the outskirts of Görlitz it occurred to Russell that anyone with a brain would have studied a plan of the town – the last thing he wanted to do was ask directions to the station. Go to the town centre and look for signs, he told himself. The Germans were good at signs.

He picked up some tram tracks and followed them in what seemed the obvious direction. After passing several large industrial concerns, the road narrowed through a handsome arch and arrived in a wide street full of old buildings. There were theatres, statues, a large water fountain – in any other circumstances, Görlitz would be worth an afternoon stroll.

'There!' Albert said, indicating a sign to the station.

They drove down a long straight street, towards what looked like a station. It was. The station building was about a hundred metres long, the entrance to the booking hall right in the centre. There were lighted windows to the left of this entrance, and steam billowing out of two large vents.

Russell pulled the car to a halt behind a Reichsbahn parcels lorry. 'The buffet,' he said, pointing it out. 'There'll be an entrance from the booking hall.'

It was ten to five.

Albert just sat there for a few seconds, then turned to shake

Russell's hand. The boy looked nervous now, Russell thought. 'Safe journey,' he said.

Albert climbed out and, without a backward look, headed towards the entrance. There was nothing furtive about his stride – if anything it was too upright. He leapt up the two steps and in through the doorway.

Start driving, Russell told himself, but he didn't. He sat there watching as the minutes passed. Two men in SA uniform emerged, laughing at something. A man ran in, presumably late for a train. Only seconds later a spasm of chuffs settled into the accelerating rhythm of a departing engine.

He imagined Albert sitting there, and wondered whether he'd tried to buy a coffee. If he had, he might have been refused; if he hadn't, some power-mad waiter might have tried to move him on. He imagined a challenge, the gun pulled out, the sound of shots and a frantic Albert flying out through the doorway. Russell wondered what would he do. Pick him up? Race out of Görlitz with the police in hot pursuit? What else could he do? His mouth seemed suddenly dry.

And then Albert did come out. There was another man with him, a shortish man in his forties with greying hair and a very red nose, who shifted his head from side to side like an animal sniffing for danger. The two of them walked across to the small open lorry with a timber load which Russell had already noticed, and swung themselves up into their respective cab seats. The engine burst into life and the lorry set off down the street, leaving a bright tail of exhaust hanging in the cold evening air.

Left luggage

After leaving Görlitz, Russell took the next available chance to telephone Effi. A brass band was practising in the first bar he tried, but with receiver and hand clamped tight against his ears he could just about hear the relief in her voice. 'I'll be waiting,' she said.

He chose the autobahn north from Kottbus, hoping to speed the journey, but an overturned vehicle in a military convoy had the opposite effect. By the time he reached Friedrichshain it was almost nine o'clock. Frau Wiesner could hardly have opened the door any faster if she'd been waiting with her hand on the knob.

'He was collected,' Russell said, and her lips formed a defiant little smile.

'Sit down, sit down,' she said, eyes shining. 'I must just tell the girls.'

Russell did as he was told, noticing the bags of clothing piled against one wall. To be given away, he supposed – there was no way they would be allowed to take that much with them. He wondered if the Wiesners had any more valuables to take out, or whether the bulk of the family assets had been concealed behind the stickers in *Achievements of the Third Reich*. It occurred to him that Germany's Jews had several years' experience in the art of slipping things across the German border.

'And my visa has arrived,' Frau Wiesner said, coming back into the room. 'By special courier from the British Embassy this afternoon. You must have some influential friends.'

'I think you do,' Russell told her. 'I'm sure Doug Conway had a hand in it,' he explained, somewhat untruthfully. There seemed no reason for her to know about his deals with Irina Borskaya and Trelawney-Smythe. 'But there is something you might be able to do for me,' he added, and told her what he wanted. She said she would ask around.

He left her with a promise of driving over the moment Albert phoned, and a plea not to worry if the wait lasted more than a day. If they still hadn't heard anything by Thursday he knew she'd be reluctant to leave, even though they both knew that in this context no news was almost certain to be bad news.

On the other side of the city, Effi welcomed him with an intense embrace, and insisted on hearing every detail. Later, as they were going to bed, Russell noticed a new film script on the dressing table and asked her about it. It was a comedy, she told him. 'Twenty three lines, four come-on smiles, and no jokes. The men got those.' But at least it was pointless, a quality which *Mother* had taught her to admire.

Next morning, Russell left her propped up in bed happily declaiming her lines to an empty room, and drove home to Neuenburgerstrasse. There was no sign of Frau Heidegger, and no messages on the board, from either Albert or the Gestapo. He went up to his room and read the newspaper, his door propped open in case the phone rang. The paper revealed that Jews had been forbidden to use either sleeping or restaurant cars on the Reichsbahn, on the grounds, no doubt, that they would appreciate their hunger more if they were kept awake.

He heard Frau Heidegger come in, and the clink of bottles as she set them beside her door. It was Tuesday, Russell realised – skat night. With Effi not working, and his own weekends given over to espionage, he was beginning to lose track of the days. He went down to warn her about his expected call, and paid the price in coffee.

Back upstairs, the hours ticked by with agonising slowness, and the only calls were for Dagmar, the plump little waitress from Pomerania who had taken McKinley's room. She, not unusually, was out. According to Frau Heidegger she sometimes came in at three in the morning with beer on her breath.

Russell nipped out to buy some eggs while Frau Heidegger kept guard, and cooked himself an omelette for dinner. Most of the other tenants returned home from work, and the concierges arrived, one by one, bottles in hand, to play skat. The waves of merriment reached higher up the stairs as the evening went on, but the telephone refused to ring, and Russell felt his anxiety grow. Where was Albert? Sitting in some border lock-up waiting to be picked by the Gestapo? Or lying dead in some frozen mountain meadow? If so, he hoped the boy had managed to take some of the bastards with him.

The skat party broke up soon after ten-thirty, and once the other concierges had passed noisily into the street Frau Heidegger took the phone off the hook. Russell went to bed and started reading the John Kling novel which Paul had leant him. Next thing he knew, it was morning. He walked briskly down to Hallesches Tor for a paper, skipping through it on the way back for news of spies or criminals apprehended on the border. As he replaced the phone a red-eyed Frau Heidegger emerged with an invitation to coffee, and they both listened to the morning news on her People's Radio. The Führer had recovered from the slight illness which had caused the cancellation of several school visits on the previous day, but no young Jews named Albert had been picked up trying to cross into Czechoslovakia.

The morning passed at a snail's pace, bringing two more calls for Dagmar and one from Effi, wanting to know what was happening. Russell had no sooner put the phone down on her than it rung again. 'Forgot something?' he asked, but it was Albert's voice, indistinct but unmistakably triumphant, which came over the line. 'I'm in Prague,' it said, as if the Czech capital was as close to heaven as its owner had ever been.

'Thank God,' Russell shouted back. 'What took you so long?'

'We only came across last night. You'll tell my mother?'

'I'm on my way. And they'll be on the train tomorrow.'

'Thank you.'

'You're welcome. And good luck.'

Russell hung up the phone and stood beside it, blissfully conscious of the relief spreading out through his limbs. One down, three to go. He called Effi back with the good news and then set off for the Wiesners.

Frau Wiesner looked as if she hadn't slept since he left her on Monday, and when Russell told her Albert was in Prague she burst into tears. The two girls rushed to embrace her and started crying too.

After a minute or so she wiped her eyes and embraced Russell. 'A last coffee in Berlin,' she said, and sent the two girls out to buy cakes at a small shop on a nearby street which still sold to Jews. Once they were out of the door, she told Russell she had one last favour to ask. Disappearing into the other room, she re-emerged with a large framed photograph of her husband and a small suitcase. 'Would you keep this for me?' she asked, handing him the photograph. 'It is the best one I have, and I'm afraid they will take it away from me at the border. Next time you come to England…'

'Of course. Where is he, your husband? Did they bury him at Sachsenhausen?'

'I do not know,' she said. 'I did not tell you this, but on Monday, after the visa came, I gathered my courage, and I went to the Gestapo building on Prinz Albrechtstrasse. I asked if his body could be returned to me, or if they could just tell me where he is buried. A man was called for, and he came down to see me. He said that my son could claim my husband's body, but I could not. He said that was the legal position, but I knew he was lying. They were using my husband's body as bait to catch my son.'

Sometimes the Nazis could still take your breath away.

'And this,' she continued, picking up the suitcase, 'is what you asked for on Monday.' She put it on the table, clicked it open, and clicked again, revealing the false bottom. 'Before the Nazis, the man who made this was a famous leather craftsman in Wilmersdorf, and he has made over a hundred of these since coming to Friedrichshain.'

'And none have been detected?'

'He doesn't know. Once Jews have left they don't come back. A few have written to say that everything went well, but if it hadn't…'

'They would be in no position to write.'

'Exactly.'

Russell sighed. 'Well, thank you anyway,' he said, just as the girls came back with a box of assorted cream cakes. They insisted on Russell having the first pick, then sat round the table happily licking the excess cream from their lips. When he suggested driving them to the station the next day, he could see how relieved Frau Wiesner was, and cursed himself for not putting her mind at rest sooner. How else could they have got there? Jews were not allowed to drive, and most cab-drivers wouldn't carry them. Which left public transport, and a fair likelihood of public abuse from their fellow passengers. Not the nicest way to say goodbye.

The train, she said, was at eleven, so he was back the next morning at nine-thirty. The girls squeezed into the back with their small bags, Frau Wiesner in the front with a suitcase on her lap, and as they drove down Neue Konigstrasse towards the city centre

Russell watched the three of them craning their necks and filling their memories with the sights of their disappearing home.

Effi was waiting at the Zoo Station entrance, and all five of them walked up to the westbound express platform. A pale sun was shining, and they stood in a little knot waiting for the train to arrive.

'You didn't tell me Albert was going to Palestine,' Russell said to Eva Wiesner.

'I should have,' she admitted. 'Distrust becomes a habit, I'm afraid.'

'And you?' he asked.

'I don't know. The girls prefer England. The clothes are better. And the movie stars.'

'You come see us in England?' Marthe asked him in English.

'I certainly will.'

'And you as well,' Marthe told Effi in German.

'I'd love to.'

The Hook of Holland train steamed in, hissing and squealing its way to a stop on the crowded platform. Russell carried Eva Wiesner's suitcase onto the train, and found their assigned seats. Much to his relief, there were no Stars of David scrawled on the girls' seatbacks. Once the three of them were settled he went in search of the car attendant, and found him in the vestibule. 'Look after those three,' he said, pointing them out and wedging a five hundred Reichsmark note in the man's outside pocket.

The attendant looked at the Wiesners again, probably to reassure himself that they weren't Jews. Fortunately, Eva Wiesner looked as aryan as anyone on the train.

Russell rejoined Effi on the platform. The signals were off, the train almost ready to go. A piercing shriek from the locomotive's whistle brought an answering scream from an animal in the adjoining Zoo, and the train jerked into motion. The girls waved,

Eva Wiesner smiled, and they were gone. Russell and Effi stood arm in arm, watching the long train as it rumbled across the iron bridge and leant into the long curve beyond. Remember this moment, Russell told himself. This was what it was for.

After a quick lunch with Effi in the Uhlandeck Café he set off for Kiel. The Berlin-Hamburg autobahn was still under construction, which left him with the old road through Schwerin and Lübeck, around 350 kilometres of two-lane highway across the gently undulating landscape of the North German plain. After three hours of this he began to wonder whether the train would have been better. The car had seemed a safer bet, but only, he realised, because he had fallen for the juvenile notion that it made escape seem more feasible. In reality, he had about as much chance of outrunning the Gestapo in the Hanomag as an aryan sprinter had of outrunning Jesse Owens.

He arrived in Kiel soon after dark, stopped at the railway station to buy a town guide at one of the kiosks, and studied it over a beer in the station buffet. Kiel itself stretched north along the western shore of a widening bay which eventually opened into the Baltic. Gaarden was on the other side of the bay, accessible by steam ferry or a tram ride around its southern end.

Russell decided on a hotel near the station – nothing too posh, nothing too seedy, and full of single businessmen leading relatively innocent lives. The Europaischer Hof, on the road which ran alongside the station, met the first two requirements, and on a busy day might have met the third. As it was, several lines of hopeful keys suggested the hotel was half empty, and when Russell asked for a room the receptionist seemed almost bemused by the scope for choice. They settled on a second floor room at the front, which looked out across the glass roof of the station, and the seagull colony which had been founded on it.

The hotel restaurant showed no signs of opening, so Russell walked north down the impressive Holstenstrasse and found an establishment with a decent selection of seafood. After eating he walked east in the general direction of the harbour, and found himself at the embarkation point for the Gaarden ferry. The ferry itself had left a few seconds earlier and was churning across the dark waters towards the line of lights on the far side, some half a kilometre away. Looking left, up the rapidly widening bay, Russell saw what looked like a large warship anchored in midstream.

He stood there for several minutes enjoying the view, until the icy wind became too much for his coat to cope with. Back at the hotel he had a nightcap in an otherwise deserted bar, went to bed, and fell asleep with surprising ease.

He woke early, though, and found that the Europaischer Hof considered breakfast an unnecessary luxury. There were, however, plenty of workingmen's cafés selling hot rolls and coffee around the station. By eight he was driving through the town centre, heading for the northern suburb of Wik, where the main harbour for merchant ships was situated. He had already finished his article on German sailors, but the Gestapo weren't to know that, and he needed an honest reason for being in Kiel. Over the next couple of hours he talked to sailors in the cafés on the Wik waterfront, before moving on to the eastern end of the Kiel Canal, which lay just beyond. There he watched a Swedish freighter pass through the double locks which protected the canal from tidal changes, chatting all the while with an old man who used to work there, and who still came to watch. Driving back along the western shore of the haven Russell got a better view of the warship he'd seen the night before. It was the recently commissioned *Scharnhorst*, and its guns were lowered towards the deck, as if apologising for their existence. Two U-boats were tied up alongside.

He wasn't hungry but had lunch anyway, along with a couple of beers to calm his nerves, before following the tracks of the Wellingdorf tram through Gaarden. The Germania Bar wasn't hard to spot – as Gert had said, it was almost opposite the main gate of the Deutsch Werke shipyard – and there was no shortage of places to leave the car. The bar itself was on the ground floor of a four-storey building, and seemed remarkably quiet for a lunch hour. He drove another few hundred metres towards Wellingdorf before turning and retracing the route back to Kiel.

With Paul's birthday in mind, he spent the rest of the afternoon looking round the shops in the town centre. The two toy emporiums he found were uninspiring, and he'd almost given up when he came across a small nautical shop in one of the narrower side streets. Pride of place in the window display had been given to a model of the *Preussen* which, as Paul had once told him, was the only sailing ship ever built with square sails on five masts. The price made him wince, but the model, on closer inspection, looked even better than it had in the window. Paul would love it.

Russell carefully carried the glass case back to the car, did his best to immobilise it in the back, and covered it with the small rug he'd bought for Effi's use on Rugen Island. He checked his watch – another five hours until his appointment at the Germania Bar – and went back to the Europaischer Hof, hoping to wile the time away with a nap. Despite the unexpected bonus of a hot bath, he found sleep impossible, and just lay on the bed watching the room grow darker. Around five o'clock he turned on the lights and expanded the notes he'd made that morning.

At seven he walked across to the station for something to eat and another beer, eschewing a second with some difficulty. The concourse was full of boisterous sailors in *Scharnhorst* caps, presumably going on leave.

Back at the hotel, he collected his suitcase, handed in his key, and walked out to the Hanomag. As he headed for Gaarden the road seemed empty, but Gaarden itself was getting ready for Friday night, the open doorways of numerous bars and restaurants spilling light across the cobbled streets and tramlines. There were a lot of sailors in evidence, a lot of women awaiting their pleasure, but no sign of the police.

He parked up against the shipyard wall and sat for a minute, examining the Germania Bar. Conversation and laughter drifted out through the open door, along with a smell of fried onions. Light edged the closed curtains in all but one of the upstairs windows; in the darkened exception a man could be seen leaning out, a cigarette bobbing between his lips. It was a brothel, Russell realised. And it was three minutes to eight.

He could feel his heart beating as he climbed out of the Hanomag, checked it was locked, and waited for a tram to pass before crossing the road. The bar was bigger inside than the outside suggested, with two walls of booths, a few tables and a small area for dancing should anyone feel the need. It was plusher than he'd expected, and cleaner. The booths were bound in leather, the bar itself highly polished. There were several young sailors to be seen, but most of the men, like Russell, were either entering or enjoying middle age inside their respectable overcoats. He took his off, seated himself in one of the two remaining empty booths, and laid *Martin Chuzzlewit* face up on the table.

'Good book?' the waitress asked him. 'Chuzzlewit,' she said with a laugh, 'what sort of name is that?'

'English,' he told her.

'That explains it. What would you like?'

He ordered a *Goldwasser*, and looked round the room. A few faces had looked his way when he entered, but no one had shown any obvious interest since. One of the sailors stood up, playfully pulled his female companion to her feet, and headed for a door in the back wall. As it opened, the bottom of a staircase came into view.

The *Goldwasser* arrived, and a female companion shortly thereafter. She was about his age, thin verging on scrawny, with dark-circled eyes and a tired smile. 'Buy me a drink, Herr Russell,' she suggested in a low voice, before he could say he was waiting for someone else. She leaned across the table, put a hand over his, and whispered: 'After we've had a drink we'll go upstairs, and you'll get what you came for.'

He ordered her drink, a sweet martini.

'I am Geli,' she said, stroking his hand with an absent-minded air. 'And what are you doing in Kiel?'

'I'm a journalist,' he said, joining the charade. 'I'm writing a story about the widening of the Kiel Canal.'

'Extra width is always good,' she said wryly. 'Let's go up. I can see you're impatient.'

He followed her up two flights of stairs, watching the hem of her red dress swish against her black-stockinged calves. There were four rooms on the second floor, and pleasure was being noisily taken in at least one of them. Through the open door of a bathroom he caught sight of a plump blonde wearing only black stockings and a suspender belt, drying herself with a towel.

'In here,' Geli said, opening a door and gesturing him in. 'I'll be back in a few minutes,' she added, closing it behind him.

There was a window that overlooked an alley, and a threadbare carpet that covered half the wooden floor. A bare light bulb illuminated a large unmade bed which was supported in one corner by a pile of books. On the bed's wooden headboard someone had written 'Goebbels was here,' and someone else had added 'So that's how I got this disease.' Enough to put anyone off, Russell thought.

The door opened and a man came in, closely followed by Geli. He was younger than her, but not by much. He had fair hair, blue eyes and skin which had seen too much sun and wind. He was wearing a sailor's greatcoat.

He shook Russell's hand, and sat down heavily on the bed, causing it to creak alarmingly. Geli stood with her back to the window, half-sitting on the sill, watching the man unpick the seam of his coat lining with a penknife. It only took a few seconds. Reaching inside he pulled out a small sheaf of papers and handed them over to Russell.

It looked like a small sheaf, but there were more than thirty sheets of text and diagrams, all copied out onto the thinnest available paper. 'These are not the originals,' Russell thought out loud.

'If they were, the Navy would know they were gone,' the man said wearily, as if he was explaining matters to a particularly obtuse child.

'Are there other copies?' Russell asked.

'One. For your successor, should you fail.'

'And then you'll need another one for his successor.'

The man offered him a grudging smile. 'Something like that.'

'Can I ask you a question?'

'Go ahead.'

'Why not send this out by radio?

The man nodded at the papers. 'Look at it. By the time we got that lot out every direction-finding squad in Germany would be banging on our door. And you can't convey maps by radio, not with any ease.' He offered a fleeting smile. 'We used to post stuff to the Soviet Embassy in Berlin, but they got wise. They open everything now. Everything.'

Russell folded the papers in two and stuffed them into his inside pocket. 'I have a better hiding place in my car,' he explained.

'Thank God for that. Look, I must go before…'

There was a sudden roar from below. 'The stormtroopers have arrived,' Geli said. 'Don't worry,' she told Russell, 'they're not here for you.'

'They fuck our women, fuck our country, and soon they'll be fucking Europe,' the man said. 'But we'll have them in the end.' He shook Russell's hand again and wished him good luck. 'I'll see you later,' he told Geli, and slipped out of the door.

'Just wait a few minutes,' she told Russell, 'and I'll take you down.'

They were long minutes, but they eventually passed. As they went down, a storm trooper was coming up, almost dragging a girl in his wake. 'Slow down, Klaus,' Geli pleaded with him – 'she'll be no use to you unconscious.' He grinned at her, as if consciousness was neither here nor there.

The noise from the bar had grown deafening. 'The back door might be better,' Geli said, and led him out through a bright but empty kitchen. 'Just right and right again,' she said, and closed the door behind him, removing most of the light. Russell felt his way along the back wall to the building's corner, from where he could make out the dimly lit road. As he started down the side of the building a silhouette loomed in the mouth of the alley, a man in high boots, with a cap on his head.

Russell froze, heart thumping in his chest. The man was moving towards him, reaching for something with his hand…

His trouser buttons. A couple of metres into the alley he turned, pulled out his penis and, with a loud exhalation, arced a fierce stream of dull golden piss against the wall. Russell stood there, petrified of making any movement, wondering whether it would ever end. A ship in the bay sounded a long and mournful blow on its horn, but still the piss streamed out, forcing the man to shift his feet away from the spreading lake.

The arc finally collapsed. The stormtrooper gave a few pumps for luck, stuffed himself into his trousers and headed for the alley entrance. And then he was gone.

Russell hurried forward, hoping to escape before someone else had the same idea. He almost stepped in the prodigious puddle, but reached the entrance without mishap. His car was sitting across the road, hopelessly sandwiched between the two open lorries which had brought the storm troopers.

He hurried across, climbed in and started the engine. Five or six manoeuvres later, he was still only halfway out. The temptation to ram the lorries was almost overwhelming, but he doubted whether the Hanomag had the weight to move them if he did. Fighting back desperation, he shifted the car, inch by inch, further into the road. He was almost there when several storm troopers emerged from the door across the road and started shouting at him. He was about to try a final, metal-scraping, lunge for freedom when he realised they were killing themselves with laughter. They had hemmed him in as a practical joke.

He opened the window and made a wry face, acknowledging their brilliant sense of humour. Three more manoeuvres and he was free, U-turning the Hanomag in front of them with a triumphant raise of the hand. As he headed south towards the centre of Gaarden he could see them happily waving goodbye in his rear-view mirror.

His hotel bed was waiting for him, but it didn't seem far enough away. He wanted, he realised, to get out of Kiel, and as quickly as possible. It was still only nine – time enough to find a small guesthouse in a small town, somewhere between here and Lübeck.

He took the more northerly of the Lübeck roads, and once in open country found a wide verge on which to pull over. With ears alert for approaching traffic he turned on the car light, opened up the false bottom of the suitcase, and placed the papers inside. He had planned to copy them for the British that night, but he'd need a whole weekend to copy this lot. He would have to be selective. They'd be none the wiser.

About ten kilometres further on, he found the town and guesthouse he was looking for. It wasn't much more than a village bar, but the woman who ran it was happy to provide him with a room. 'It was my son's,' she said, without explaining where he'd gone. The sundry toys and books suggested he was expected back.

Once locked in, Russell retrieved the papers from the false bottom and skip-read through them. They were what Irina Borskaya had claimed they were – a detailed rundown of the German Navy's current and contingency disposition in the Baltic. Most of the key information seemed to be included in the three maps which accompanied the text, and Russell set out to copy these. The British, he thought, should be thankful for whatever he could give them.

The maps were highly detailed, and it took him almost four hours to finish his work. He felt as if he had only just got to sleep when the landlady knocked on his door suggesting breakfast, and it was indeed only seven o'clock. Still, breakfast was good, and the sun was already above the horizon. Her son, it transpired, had joined the Navy.

Russell set out for Berlin soon after nine, papers and copies hidden in the false bottom, the suitcase itself wedged under the eye-catching model of the *Preussen*. There was no need, of course – no roadblock, no spot-checks, no officious small-town policemen eager to find fault with a car bearing a Berlin licence plate. Soon after one, he parked the Hanomag outside Zoo Station, pulled out the suitcase and nervously carried it in to the left luggage.

'Nice day,' the clerk said, taking the case and handing over a numbered ticket.

'So far,' Russell agreed. He rang Effi from the telephone stand along the hall and told her things had gone to plan. She sounded as relieved as he felt. 'I'm going home to collect some clean clothes, and do a bit more shopping for Paul,' he told her. 'I'll see you about six.'

She told him they had tickets for a revue at one of the smaller theatres near Alexanderplatz, and he tried, in vain, to sound enthusiastic. 'I'm just tired,' he explained. 'I'll be fine by then.'

He certainly felt safer with the suitcase squirreled away in Zoo Station's cavernous left luggage. There was always the ticket of course, but if the worst came to the worst that was small enough to eat. Back at the car, he examined the model ship for the first time in daylight, and congratulated himself on his choice – it really was beautiful.

Frau Heidegger thought so too, and conjured up a bright red ribbon which she'd been saving for such an eventuality. There were messages from both his agents: Jake Brandon had sent a sarcastic wire from New York demanding copy, and Solly Bernstein had phoned to tell Russell that 'his friends' had arrived in London. He was still smiling when he reached his third floor room.

After a much-needed bath and change of clothes, he piled several more changes into his usual suitcase and carried it out to the car. Lunch at Wertheim was followed by a leisurely stroll round the toy department, and the acquisition of two other gifts which Paul had expressed an interest in. A book shop further down Leipzigstrasse supplied a third. He was probably spending too much, but he might never get another chance.

He managed to stay awake through the revue, but was unable to conceal his dismay when Effi suggested dancing. She took pity on him. 'I know what'll wake you up,' she said as they climbed the stairs to her flat, and she was right. Afterwards, she showed him what she had bought for Paul – the gorgeous encyclopaedia of animals which he had admired on their last visit to the zoo shop.

Next morning they joined several hundred other Berliners on the sidewalk of the Ku'damm, well-wrapped against the cold at their outside table, rustling newspapers, sipping coffee and nibbling cake. This was how it used to be, Russell thought – ordinary Germans doing ordinary things, enjoying their simple civilised pleasures.

His newspaper, though, told a different story. While he'd been slinking round Kiel, the Czechs had lost patience with the German-backed Slovaks, sacking their provincial government and arresting their prime minister. The *Beobachter* was apoplectic – what nation could countenance such a level of disturbance just beyond its borders? Some sort of German intervention seemed inevitable, but then it always had. If the separatists won then Czechoslovakia would disintegrate; if denied, their campaign would simply continue. Either set of circumstances would generate enough turmoil for Hitler's purposes.

Looking up from his paper, the sidewalk café-dwellers no longer seemed content in their simple pleasures. They looked tense, weary, anxious. They looked as though a war was hanging over their heads.

After lunch with Effi he drove over to Grunewald, dropped off his presents, collected his son and gave him a birthday hug. Twenty minutes later they were picking up Thomas in Lutzow and heading for the Plumpe. Thomas's son Joachim had started his *arbeitsdienst* the previous week, and was repairing roads in the Moselle valley.

The weather was fine, but the team proved incapable of providing Paul with a birthday present. They lost 2-0, and were lucky not to lose by more. Paul's despondency didn't last long – by the time they were halfway to his home he was full of the party in prospect, and forgetful of Hertha's dark betrayal.

Effi was already there when they arrived, talking happily to Thomas's fourteen-year-old daughter Lotte. Over the next hour around a dozen of Paul's friends – all of them male – were delivered by their parents, some in their Sunday best, some, for reasons best known to their parents, in their *Jungvolk* uniforms. The games they played seem surprisingly violent, but that, Russell supposed, was part of the same depressing mind-set. At least they hadn't replaced 'pin the tail on the donkey' with 'pin the nose on the Jew.' Yet. He would write a piece on children for the 'Ordinary Germans' series, he decided. When he got back from Prague.

Still, Paul seemed happy and popular, which was something to celebrate. The adults – Ilse and Matthias, Thomas and his wife Hanna, Russell and Effi – sat together in the huge kitchen, drinking Matthias's excellent wine. They smiled and laughed and toasted each other, but the talk was of happier times in the past, of how things used to be. At one point, watching Ilse as she listened to somebody else, Russell had a mental picture of her in Moscow fifteen years earlier, eyes alive with hopes of a better world. Now all of them were backing into the future, frightened to look ahead. They had their own bubble, but for how long?

The evening ended, bringing tomorrow that much closer. After congratulating each other on how well their presents had been received, both he and Effi lapsed into silence for most of the journey home. They were turning into her street when she suddenly suggested accompanying him to Prague.

'No,' he said. 'There's no point in us both taking the risk.' He switched off the car. 'And you're a German – they'd try you for treason. They'd have more options with me.'

'Like what?'

'Oh, I don't know. Swapping me for one of their spies, maybe.'

'Or just shooting you.'

'I doubt it. But I think having you there would make me more nervous. And more likely to give myself away.'

She searched his face, and seemed satisfied with what she found. 'All right,' she said. 'It's no fun just waiting by the phone, you know.'

'I know.'

Upstairs, he noticed the script on her dressing table and had an idea. 'Can you get another copy for yourself?' he asked.

'I don't see why not. I could say I burnt the first one in a fit of despair. But why?'

'I thought I'd take it with me in the suitcase. Camouflage. And one of your publicity shots would be good.'

She went and got one, a head and shoulders shot taken a couple of years earlier.

'Your face would distract anyone,' he said.

It was still dark when Russell woke and he lay there for a while, listening to Effi's breathing and enjoying the warmth of her body. At seven-thirty he forced himself out of bed, washed and dressed in the bathroom, and finally woke her to say goodbye as she had insisted he must. She enfolded him in a sleepy embrace, then swung her legs out of bed and arched her back in a huge stretch. As he descended the stairs she stood in her nightdress by the half-open door, blowing him a farewell kiss.

Berlin was already waking to another working week. The Avus Speedway was busy, but only in the other direction, and he reached

Potsdam well before nine. After parking the Hanomag near the main post office in Wilhelmplatz, he lingered over breakfast in the coffee shop next door. The newspapers, as expected, were revelling in the misery of the Czechs.

At ten past nine he presented himself at the poste restante desk, and signed for the familiar envelope. Walking back to the Hanomag, he felt like a man who'd just been handed a ticking bomb. Not to worry, he thought – he'd soon have two.

The drive back was slower, and it was gone ten when he turned off the Ku'damm and saw the glass roof of Zoo Station framed by the buildings on either side of Joachimsthaler-strasse. He parked the Hanomag near the Tiergarten gate which he and Gert had used, inserted the folded envelope in his inside coat pocket, picked up the suitcase, and walked back to the nearest station entrance.

There was a queue for the left luggage, but no sign of the police, or of anyone loitering suspiciously. When his turn came Russell handed over his ticket, watched the clerk disappear, and waited for a thousand sirens to go off. A child in the queue behind him suddenly screeched, making him jump. A train rumbled overhead, but the roof didn't fall. The clerk returned with the suitcase, took Russell's money, and handed it over.

Next stop was the men's toilet. The cubicles were small, and entering one with two suitcases required a level of planning which was almost beyond him. He clattered his way in, locked the door behind him, and sat on the seat for a few moments to recover what fragments of equanimity he still retained. The walls didn't reach to the ceiling, but the adjoining cubicles were both empty, at least for the moment.

He stood up, put the smaller suitcase on the toilet seat, and opened it up. After unclicking the false bottom, he removed the three maps he had copied, replaced them with McKinley's papers, and closed the false bottom again. A brief struggle then ensued, as he fought to open the other suitcase in what little remaining space the cubicle had to offer. Half its contents ended up on the floor, but all were eventually transferred to the smaller suitcase, which was now satisfyingly full. After checking that the three maps were in his coat pocket, he closed both suitcases, pulled the chain, and fought his way out of the cubicle.

The man at the left luggage looked surprised to see him again, but accepted the empty suitcase without comment, and handed him a new ticket. On the platform above he waited for a westbound Stadtbahn, thinking that this was where McKinley had died and where the Wiesners had left Hitler behind. On the far platform a man was angrily shaking a burnt almond machine, just as another man had been doing at Friedrichstrasse on the morning he returned from Danzig.

His train arrived and set off again, skirting the northern edge of the Tiergarten, crossing and re-crossing the Spree on its three-stop journey to Friedrichstrasse. Russell went out through the less frequented car park entrance and walked briskly towards the embassy. His steps on the pavements sounded unusually loud, and every car that didn't stop seemed like a gift from God. Halfway across the Unter den Linden he decided that if anyone challenged him now, he would sprint through the Embassy doors and never come out again.

But no one did. As before, he asked the receptionist for Unsworth and Unsworth for Trelawney-Smythe. The latter looked at the three maps as if he couldn't believe his luck. 'Where did you get them?' he demanded.

'A comrade in Kiel,' was all Russell would tell him. 'A one-off,' he added. 'There won't be any more.'

'But how do I know these are genuine?'

'I guess you don't. But they are. And your people must have ways of confirming at least some of it.'

'Perhaps.'

Russell took a meaningful look at his watch. 'I have a train to catch.'

'And where are you off to this time?' Trelawney-Smythe asked, sounding almost friendly.

'Prague.'

'Ah, joining Adolf's reception committee.'

'I hope not.'

Dropping in on Unsworth to say goodbye, he was told much the same. 'And the British guarantee of Czechoslovakia?' Russell asked sarcastically.

'Without Slovakia there is no Czechoslovakia,' Unsworth said. 'And therefore no guarantee.'

'Neat,' Russell said.

'Very,' Unsworth agreed.

Out on the street, Russell hailed a passing taxi. 'Anhalter Bahnhof,' he told the driver. It seemed that he and Hitler were heading in the same direction.

The train to Prague left at noon, and was scheduled to arrive in the Czech capital shortly before seven. Russell boarded it with a sinking sensation in his stomach, and an alcohol-rich lunch in the dining car did nothing to improve matters.

The lunchtime editions carried the news that the Slovak premier Monsignor Tiso had been 'invited' to Berlin. He had, over the past couple of days, seemed surprisingly reluctant to tip over the Czech applecart, and the Führer was doubtless anxious to offer him some kindly advice. Their trains would cross at some point, Russell guessed. He would watch the passing windows for a prelate with a death wish.

Speaking of which… he reminded himself that the Wiesners were in London, that foreigners were hardly ever searched, that the next life was bound to be better than this one. He fought off a momentary impulse to quit the train at Dresden, the only stop before the frontier. If he did, the Soviets would probably come looking for him with murder in mind. And he could hardly blame them – a deal was a deal.

As the train wound its way up the upper Elbe valley towards the frontier he compiled a compendium of possible explanations for the material in his false-bottomed suitcase that a reefer-smoking Neville Chamberlain would have found impossible to believe. As Gert had said, the important thing was not to be searched.

As the train slowed for the border inspection his heart speeded up. They came to a halt in a wide ravine, shared by double tracks and the loud, foaming river. The snow-speckled walls of the valley rose steeply on either side, and the long, low building which housed the emigration and customs services was partly suspended over the rushing waters. The river ruled out escape in one direction, and the tall electrified fence beyond the tracks precluded any hope of flight in the other. Like rats in a maze, Russell thought – only one way to go.

The loudspeakers suspended from the searchlight pylons crackled into life. All passengers were requested to leave the train and form a queue on the narrow strip of tarmac alongside the tracks.

There were about two hundred people in the queue, Russell reckoned, and they were filing into the building at a gratifying rate. Just a quick look at documents, he thought, and on we go. Beside him the train lurched forward, ready to pick up its passengers on the other side. Without its comforting presence Russell felt suddenly vulnerable.

Finally, he could see through the doorway. Uniformed officers sat behind two desks, while others hovered in the background, sizing up potential prey. Further on, two pairs of officers stood behind tables, searching through bags and suitcases. The first hurdle presented itself. The officer looked at his passport, and then at his face. 'Your name?' he asked, and for a split second Russell's mind was a terrifying blank.

'John Russell,' he said, as if he hadn't been concentrating.

'Birth date?'

That was easier. '8 August 1899.'

'Thank you,' the official said, and handed him back his passport. Russell moved on, carefully avoiding all eye contact. Ignore me, he silently pleaded with the customs officials behind the tables.

In vain. 'You,' the nearest said. 'Open your case, please.'

Russell placed it on the table, willing his hands not to shake as he clicked the case open. The man and his blond partner stared for a second at the top layer of clothes, and the partner started digging around with his hands. 'What's this?' he asked, pulling out Effi's script. 'A Girl from the Mountains?'

'It's a film script,' Russell said. 'My girlfriend's an actress,' he added. 'Her photograph's inside.'

The partner extracted it and both men took a good look. 'I've seen her in something,' the first man said.

His partner rubbed his chin with forefinger and thumb. 'I have too.'

'I remember,' the first man said. 'She was the wife of that guy who got killed by the Reds…'

'*The Necessary Sacrifice*,' Russell suggested helpfully.

'That's the one. And she's your girlfriend?'

'Uh-huh.'

'You're a lucky man,' the partner said, replacing the photograph and closing the suitcase.

Russell had never heard a more beautiful click. 'I know it,' he said with a grateful smile. Suitcase in hand, he walked out through the open doorway, repressing the urge to skip and dance.

The train pulled into Prague's Masaryk Station at twenty past seven. On the streets it felt more like midnight – they were dark and mostly deserted, as if the city's people were all at home, hunched over their radio sets. He had never seen Wenceslas Square so empty, even at four in the morning.

The Grand was fully operational though, its multi-lingual staff and art nouveau fittings a match for any barbarian invasion. Russell had stayed there twice before, once in the late twenties and once, the previous September, when Chamberlain and Daladier were licking Hitler's boots in Munich. He asked the receptionist if anything crucial had happened in the last seven hours, and was told that it hadn't. Monsignor Tiso, he supposed, was still *en route* to Berlin.

Russell's room was on the first floor, at the back. Apart from the lack of a view it seemed thoroughly adequate. But then, after those few moments at the frontier, a pigsty would have seemed adequate, provided it was in Czechoslovakia. He dumped the unopened suitcase on the bed and went back down in search of dinner.

The hotel restaurant also seemed a lot emptier than usual, but the baked carp, fruit dumplings and South Moravian white wine were all delicious. A walk seemed in order, but he reluctantly decided against one – his train left at 11.40 on the following morning and he was anxious for the Soviets to collect their papers. The thought of having to dump them in the Vltava was more than he could bear.

He didn't have long to wait. Shortly before ten he answered a familiar-sounding tap on his door, and found Irina Borskaya anxiously glancing up the corridor. 'Come in,' he said superfluously – she had already dodged under his arm. She was wearing the same long, charcoal grey skirt, but a different blouse. Her hair seemed a shade lighter, and this time there was a hint of bright red lipstick on her thin lips.

'The papers,' she said, sitting down on the upright chair.

'It's nice to see you too,' Russell said, opening the suitcase. After dumping his possessions onto the bed, he clicked the false bottom open, removed the sheaf of papers he'd picked up in Gaarden, and handed it over.

'What are those?' she asked, as he placed the envelope containing McKinley's papers on the bedside table.

'A story I'm working on.'

She gave him a disbelieving look, but said nothing. After flicking through the naval dispositions, she reached inside her blouse and brought out a money clip containing Swiss Franc notes. High denomination Swiss Franc notes. 'We promised to pay you well,' she said, as if reprimanding him for any possible doubts he might have had on that score.

'Thank you,' he said. 'It's been a pleasure doing business with you.'

'There is no need for the pleasure to end,' she said. 'We have other work…'

'No,' Russell said firmly. 'We had a simple deal – you helped my friend out of Germany, I brought your papers to Prague. We're quits. I wish the Soviet Union well, but not well enough to die for it.'

'Very well,' she said, rising from the chair and cradling the papers in one arm. The fact that she had no obvious place to conceal them led Russell to the conclusion that her room was close to his own. 'If that is how you feel,' she told him, 'then we understand. And we thank you for what you have done.'

Somewhat astonished by the ease with which his resignation had been accepted, Russell opened the door for her.

'When are you leaving?' she asked.

'Tomorrow morning.'

'Then have a good journey.' She put her head out, glanced to left and right, and walked off down the corridor in the direction of the stairs. The whole encounter had taken less than five minutes.

Before going downstairs next morning Russell wrote a short covering letter to McKinley's editor in San Francisco, explaining how he had come by the papers and offering his own brief summary of their significance. After breakfast in the hotel restaurant he walked around the corner to the main post office on Jindrisská, bought and addressed a large envelope, and asked for the quickest possible delivery. 'It'll be gone before he gets here,' the clerk observed, reading Russell's mind. 'On the afternoon plane to Paris,' he added in explanation.

Satisfied, Russell walked back to the Grand, collected his suitcase and checked out. He was early for the train but he liked Masaryk Station, and he liked the idea of being closer to home.

As it turned out, it didn't matter, because he no longer had a seat or even standing room on the train. Two carriages, including his own, had been commandeered by President Hacha and his swollen entourage. The Czech President, Russell gathered from discussions with sundry railway officials, had also been 'invited' to Berlin, and a heart condition prohibited him from flying. Russell was assured that two extra carriages would be added to the night train, but no one seemed capable of explaining why they couldn't be added to this one.

Oh well, Russell thought, there were many worse places to spend a day than Prague. As President Hacha and his dicey heart were about to find out.

He left the suitcase in the left luggage, took a tram back to the town centre, and spent the next couple of hours ambling down the east bank of the river. The Czech flag was still flying from the ramparts of the famous castle, but for how long? A few days at most, Russell thought, and the city's residents seemed to agree with him. As he walked back through the old town in search of a late lunch, he noticed rapidly lengthening queues at one baker after another. News of Hacha's trip had obviously spread.

This was it, Russell thought – the end of any lingering hopes for peace. There was no way of presenting this as part of some grand scheme to bring Germans home to the Reich. Hitler had thrown off the cloak. It was no longer if, but when.

The sight of an orthodox Jew on Národní Street reminded him of Albert. Long gone, he hoped, but what of Czechoslovakia's 100,000 Jews? What were they doing this afternoon? Crowding the stations, loading their cars – or just sitting tight and hoping for the best, as so many German Jews had done? This orthodox Jew had a bagful of groceries, and seemed in no hurry to go anywhere.

He thought about what Albert had said during the drive to Görlitz, that kindness had become more worthy of note, and more interesting to fathom, than cruelty. It was certainly harder to find.

With darkness falling he sought out a bar, and sampled several different Bohemian beers. Each tasted better than the last. He raised a toast to McKinley's papers, now hopefully resting in some Parisian sorting-office, and another to McKinley himself. From time to time, over the last six weeks, he had found himself wondering why they had killed the young American. It was the wrong question to ask, he realised. It was like asking why they had killed Felix

Wiesner. They might have had, or thought they had, particular motives, but the real reason was much simpler – they were killers. It was what they were. It was, in truth, all that they were.

The cold air streaming through his cab's broken window kept him awake on his way back to the station, but once ensconced in the overheated train he soon found himself falling asleep. The jerk of departure woke him for long enough to recline his seat, and the last thing he remembered was that he should have phoned Effi.

The next thing he knew he was waking with a sudden feeling of panic. He looked at his watch. Almost three hours had passed – they had to be nearing the frontier. But that didn't matter any more, he told himself. His subconscious was obviously stuck on the outward journey.

And then it occurred to him. He had never closed the false bottom. After Borskaya had gone he had just shifted the suitcase onto the floor, and this morning he had simply shovelled all the clothes back in.

The thought of another wrestle with a suitcase in a toilet made him groan, but it had to be done. He took it down from the overhead rack, and carried it out to the vestibule at the end of the car. Shading his eyes with his hands, and sticking his face up against the window, he could just make out the river running beside the tracks.

Inside the toilet he opened the suitcase, threw all the clothes on the floor, and went to close the false bottom.

It was already closed.

He stood there for a few moments, thinking back. When had he done it?

He hadn't.

Clicking it open, he found several sheets of paper hidden inside.

Holding the first one up to the dim light of the cubicle, he found that it contained a list of names and addresses – six under Ruhr, three under Hamburg. The other sheets – there were nine of them – followed a similar pattern. There were almost a hundred people listed, from all the different parts of Germany.

Who were they? No indication was given, none at all. But one thing was certain – the Soviets meant them to be discovered. That was why Borskaya had asked him when he was leaving, Russell thought – they had been inserted while he was downstairs at breakfast or out posting McKinley's papers. That was why she'd accepted his resignation so easily. And the money – that worked both ways. Such generosity might keep him working for them, but if it didn't, it could be turned into a threat – possession of so much foreign currency would be hard to explain.

The names, he realised, had to be German communists – real or imaginary. Were these men and women whom Stalin wanted culled, but who were beyond his reach? Or was the list a work of fiction, something to keep the Gestapo busy while the real communists got on with their work? A bit of both, Russell guessed. A few real communists to keep the Gestapo believing, and then the wild goose chase.

He shivered at the nearness of his escape, and realised that the train was slowing down. He shoved the suitcase to the floor, yanked up the lid of the toilet, and started tearing the sheets of paper into smaller and smaller pieces. Once these were all in the bowl he reached for the lever, filled with the sudden dread that it wouldn't work.

It didn't. As beads of cold sweat multiplied on his forehead, Russell worked the lever again. It coughed up some water, but nowhere near enough.

There was a heavy knock on the door. 'We are approaching the frontier,' a German voice said.

'Right,' Russell shouted back. What should he do? Try and swallow all the bits of paper, along with whatever international germs the toilet bowl had been saving for him? Anything but that.

The train was still decelerating. He looked for some access to the toilet's workings, but everything was screwed down. He tried the lever one more time, more out of habit than hope, and for reasons known only to God it flushed. He stood there, revelling in the sight of empty water, until sweet relief gave way to a nightmare vision of Gestapo officers combing the tracks for all the pieces and painstakingly gluing them back together.

'Get a grip,' he murmured to himself. He picked up the suitcase, clicked the false bottom shut, and covered it with clothing retrieved from the floor. As he left the toilet he caught a glimpse of his face in the mirror, and wished he hadn't. He looked deranged.

The train was still moving, the lighted platform of the Czech border point unrolling past the window. It was snowing now, thick flakes drifting down through the cones of light. 'We are not stopping at the Czech crossing point tonight,' the German railway official was saying to a female passenger. No Czechoslovakia, no border, Russell thought. Did that mean they were not stopping at the German border either?

No such luck.

The passengers climbed down onto the platform, a long strip of spotlit tarmac in a sea of darkness. As Russell joined the queue, a new and highly unwelcome thought occurred to him. If the sheets were meant to be found, there had to have been a tip-off. The false bottom might be empty, but it was still a false bottom.

One explanation seemed workable, but only if the officials on duty were different from the ones he had encountered the day before. As the queue sucked him out of the snow and into the building, he anxiously examined the faces, but there were none he recognised.

The immigration official took one look at his passport and gestured to a man in plain clothes behind him. Gestapo. 'This way, Herr Russell,' the man said, without looking at his passport. He walked across to a large table, where another man in plain clothes was waiting.

'Put your suitcase on the table,' the first man said. He had long hair for the Gestapo, and an almost likable face. As he opened the suitcase, Russell noticed that his fingernails badly needed trimming.

'Could I have your name and rank?' Russell asked.

'Ascherl, *Kriminalassistent*,' he said without looking up.

He carefully took out the clothes, and piled them on the other end of the table. Effi's script was placed on the top. Then he ran his hands round the inside of the suitcase, obviously looking for a way of accessing the false bottom. Borskaya had been behind him when he opened it in the hotel room, Russell remembered.

'How do you open it,' Ascherl asked him.

Russell looked perplexed. 'It's open.'

'The hidden compartment,' the Gestapo officer said patiently.

Russell tried to look even more perplexed. 'What are you talking about?'

Ascherl turned to his subordinate. 'Your knife, Schneider.'

Schneider pulled out a large pocket-knife. Ascherl looked at the suitcase for a moment, ran his hand along inside it, then abruptly turned it upside down, pressed in the knife, and patiently sawed from one side of the bottom to the other. 'This hidden compartment,' he said, reaching in a hand.

His look of triumph faded as his scrabbling hand failed to find anything in it. Two more cuts and he was able to wrench back a section of the reinforced leather bottom and shine a torch inside.

'Where is it?' he asked patiently.

'Where is what?' Russell replied, trying to sound bewildered. Most of the others in the room were watching them now, eager to see how the situation played out.

'Let me put it another way,' the Gestapo officer said. 'What reason do you have for carrying a suitcase with a hidden compartment?'

'That's simple. I didn't know it had one. I only bought it yesterday, from a Jew in Prague.' He smiled, as if the answer had just occurred to him. 'The bastard probably used it to smuggle valuables out of the Reich.'

'Undoubtedly,' Ascherl said.

Russell was still thanking heaven for his inspiration when he noticed a new face in the room – one of the customs officials from the day before. The man was looking straight at him, with an expression on his face that seemed part indignation, part amusement.

'But you are from Berlin,' Ascherl continued. 'Did you travel to Prague without a suitcase?'

'It fell apart when I was there. I needed a new one.' Russell braced himself for an intervention by the customs official, but there was none.

'And this Jew just happened along?'

'No, there's a market, like the ones they used to have in Berlin.' The customs official was still looking at him, still saying nothing. Was it possible that he didn't remember this suitcase from the day before?

'You wallet, please,' the Gestapo officer said.

Russell handed it over, and watched him remove the currency – a few Czech notes, some Reichsmarks, the clip of Swiss Francs.

'Where did these come from?' Ascherl asked.

'I wrote an article for a Soviet paper, and they paid me in Swiss Francs. Several months ago now. I thought they might be useful in

Prague. The SD knows all about this,' he added. 'Look,' he said, indicating the wallet, 'can I show you something?'

Ascherl handed it back, and Russell pulled out the folded sheet of Sturmbannfuhrer Kleist's letter.

As the Gestapo man read it, Russell watched his face. If the list had been found in the hidden compartment then the letter could have been ignored. As it was, all Ascherl had was a story full of holes that he couldn't fill in. Would he keep on trying, and risk falling foul of the big boys on Wilhelmstrasse?

'I see,' he said finally, and looked up at Russell. 'It seems we are all victims of the same plot. We received information... well, I won't go into that. It looks as though the Reds have tried to set you up.'

'The suitcase was suspiciously cheap,' Russell admitted. Across the room the customs official was still watching, still doing his Mona Lisa impersonation.

'It's not worth much now,' Ascherl said, surveying his knife-work.

Russell smiled. 'You were doing your duty, as any friend of the Reich would wish.'

Ascherl smiled back. 'We have others. Confiscated from Jews. Perhaps we can find you another one with a hidden compartment. Schneider?'

Ascherl's assistant disappeared into an adjoining room and re-emerged almost immediately with two suitcases. Russell chose the smaller of the two, and packed it with his clothes and Effi's script. The customs official had disappeared.

But not for long. As Russell came out of the building the man fell into step beside him. 'Nice suitcase,' he said.

Russell stopped.

'I'm getting married next month,' the man said, carefully

positioning himself between Russell and any watchers in the building they had just left.

Russell took out his wallet, removed the clip of Swiss francs, and handed it over. 'A wedding present?'

The man smiled, gave him an ironic click of the heels, and strode away.

Russell walked on towards the train. The snow was heavier now, tumbling down through the pools of light, flakes clinging to the glistening wire. He could feel the sweat on his body slowly turning to ice.

The train, it seemed, was waiting only for him – the whistle shrilled as he stepped aboard. He made his way forward through the swaying cars, slumped into the reclining seat, and listened to the rhythmic clatter of the wheels, rolling him into the Reich.